PEOPLE OF THE DEAD

A MAGE NOVEL

E. RENEE SOBIEN

Author's Note

While you don't have to read the first Mage Novel, *Woman of Fire,* before reading this standalone book, please be advised that the two stories intersect, and *People of the Dead* does contain spoilers for *Woman of Fire.*

People of the Dead deals with intense subject matter. The below content warnings contain possible spoilers. If you do not have the need for trigger warnings, you may wish to skip the following list.

Content warnings: Sexual abuse, self-harm, bullying, pet death, suicide, murder, gun use, kidnapping, abortion, pregnancy, pregnancy loss, war, graphic and supernatural violence, drug use, incest, child abuse.

Prologue: The Prophecy

The old prophet, Luther, stood watching the clouds. The wind whipped his white hair and the whiskers on his face as his robe billowed around his body.

The thick, dark early-evening clouds held a strong warning for Luther as they converged into grim gray thunderheads. As the first hints of thunder began to rumble far off in the rolling hills on the horizon, the wind picked up and the clouds blended into an image that only Luther, with his foresight, could see.

The message sent a warning about people with a set of abilities different from Luther's own. The necromancers. The church sometimes called them the Children of Samael, also known as the angel of death. This clan could harness the power of the earth, and power over life and death—and thus, carried the fears of the other clans.

The clouds told a harrowing story of the future. Grotesque beasts leapt from rooftop to rooftop, street to street, grabbing bystanders in their fangs and tearing them to shreds. Undead forms shuffled along mindlessly on streets lined with strange shiny machines that had wheels and somehow no horses attached. Fires and pestilence ran rampant.

Luther doubled over, gasping and retching. The people of the dead had to be stopped before this vision came to fruition. Every last one of them.

Trembling, the elderly prophet turned down the dirt path, heading to the hall of magic where his fellow gifted ones gathered. Some were there today. With Luther being the most senior, well-respected prophet in the circle, they paid rapt attention when he told them to all listen carefully to what he was about to say.

It was not long before they all became panicked at the gravity of Luther's visions. "We must do something at once!" they agreed.

"We will begin anon!" Luther promised. "We will find somehow, some way, to rid the earth of the Children of Samael."

As rain fell outside that evening, a few of the prophets remained at the hall, still mulling over Luther's vision. One of them, Adler, who had water powers, was stricken by a strong buzz inside his head. He took a prick of blood from his finger, squeezed the droplet into a bowl of water, and crumbled a dried bay leaf into the bowl, swirling the mixture together.

"Warring against the people of the dead is not the answer," Adler spoke up.

Quite a murmur rippled through his companions.

"You heard me earlier, correct?" Luther argued back. "We cannot just sit and allow them to destroy humanity!"

"This message that just came to me—there is one who can change it."

"Who?"

"I don't know, but it's none of us. And neither is anyone who would go slaying all of the people of the dead."

"Do you have any idea of who it is?"

"The one who decides. My visions of him aren't clear yet; it will take time as... ah, wait!" Adler peered back down into his murky bowl, the water glinting in the light from a nearby candle on the wooden table. "The one who decides is not born yet. It could be a long, long time, as he will live during the time your vision comes to fruition, Luther."

"Who is he, and what will he decide?" Luther began to laugh at Adler.

"Even if I cannot tell you when he will walk this earth, I can tell you that he shall be a man of great magic and great courage. And while he will be very strong, he will also live in a mortal body for a time, and we must protect him."

"Adler, I am older and have practiced magic and received prophecies for a much greater deal of time. I am the most well-respected mage in this hall, while your powers are in their infancy. Unless you have something more useful to tell me, we will seek out and destroy the people of the dead at once."

For the rest of the prophet Adler's time on earth, almost no one listened to him. Meanwhile, Luther's message of fear spread like wildfire to the other magical people of the world.

Adler's fellow prophet Armand, who possessed air powers like Luther's, was the only one who took Adler seriously. Armand received messages from plumes of herb-infused smoke, dictating that he must be the keeper of the one who decides, even if he had died by then and would need to observe quietly from the spirit world.

Adler got stricken with a fever and passed away three days after his last vision. Armand joined him in death ten years later. The two spirits found each other in the afterlife, more vibrant than most ghosts yet still mostly trapped behind the silent barrier that kept them apart from the living. As the years sped past, the two dead men waited for signs of the much-awaited birth of their hopeful hero.

Nearly two hundred years after Luther's vision, a day of victory came for his people, the air people. After suspected witches were burned at the stake in increasing numbers, magical people had hidden their powers and lived in secrecy. But word of the air people's accomplishment quickly spread among other underground circles. They were certain that they'd rid the world of the last necromancers. Those who would someday destroy the world if they were allowed to live.

In the centuries since Luther's prophecy, magical people had banded together across the world to seek and kill the people of the dead. Sometimes, they hid their mission within other, larger wars.

A group of mages, two of them direct descendants of Luther himself, gathered to concentrate their powers together and exterminate the last known holdouts near the coast of northern Scotland. This community was an especially miserable one, guarding the houses of their misty little village with smelly, undead things dug up from the nearest graveyard. Decayed corpses stood at attention by the gates, awaiting commands from their masters as chunks of flesh fell away to expose the glinting bone beneath. Something even worse than the zombies paced in a heavy cage, snarling and crashing against the thick iron bars. Within their dank wooden houses, the necromancers kept shelves lined with herbs, potions, skulls, and ancient spells.

Those in the closest village gave the settlement a very wide berth. The villagers' children suffered nightmares about the necromancers. They were simply called witches, and it was common knowledge that anyone who dared to cross a witch would regret it. Mothers told bedtime stories about the witches or their zombies preying on naughty children to scare their young ones into behaving.

The air people also kept their distance that momentous day, working their deadly magic from atop a cliff to lay waste to the compound. Lightning boomed powerfully from the sky, looking to most people like a bad but spectacular storm, nothing more. The lightning smashed the necromancer village to the ground, burning the undead guards to almost nothing and killing the inhabitants before they even knew what had hit them.

Once it was over, the triumphant group of air people hiked down the mossy cliffside and examined the scorched remains of the compound. Not a single living person was found. The Children of Samael were now completely extinct, their hideous guards gone as well. No longer did they pose any threat to the good citizens of the earth. The air people could not contain their joy as they danced, laughed, and cried. For the magical people, that day in 1755 would go down in history. Luther's grim prophecy would not come to pass after all.

When word went around the nearby villages about the lightning strike, the locals also praised God that the witches were gone after a seemingly divine intervention, no longer befouling the countryside.

Never did the group of lightning warriors learn that they had failed to wipe out all of the necromancers. Shortly before the storm began, five adults and a babe in arms had escaped unseen into a nearby thicket of trees.

The baby's mother, Mary Fraser, was a prophet, the destruction haunting her in a vision the day before. A man in a hooded cloak, calling himself Armand, told her to save herself and her family before it was too late. As soon as the premonition released its hold on Mary, she ran around the village, warning anyone she found. Not everyone had listened to this nervous woman with wild red-gold hair, since she had a reputation as eccentric and unbalanced. Even her husband had tuned her out, and now she was a widow.

Those few who heeded Mary's word accompanied her as she balanced her infant son on her hip, racing through the trees as the storm began to rumble in the clouds. Mary's friend Malvina took a green crystal, passed down through the generations, from her grandfather's house and tucked it into a secret pocket. In the trees, they joined hands, Mary gripping the crystal between her fingers and Malvina's as she chanted and focused and balanced her baby with her other hand. The air shimmered and glittered around them, and they vanished.

After they reappeared, the small group hid in another cluster of trees, sleeping huddled together in a warm ball for three damp, bone-chilling nights. Three days later, they arrived at the shore. Just south of them, a ship was at the waterfront, preparing to depart. They ran toward it.

Mary perceived a lot, but she did not know this ship's destination. Still in shock from losing the only home they had ever known, she and her companions didn't care where it was going. With Mary's baby tucked protectively in her dress, they sneaked on board, blending into the middle of a group of legitimate passengers. They crept below the wooden deck and hid among luggage, stowing away.

During the rocky journey across the Atlantic to the colonies of North America, the group occasionally pretended to blend in with the other passengers in order to get food, as no one else on the ship possessed magic or the ability to see what they really were. Most of the passengers were moving away to make a new life and some hoped to earn a tobacco fortune. The necromancers knew that they could never return to the place of their birth, though they had no idea if they would be any safer from harm in these colonies, a place they knew little about. They grieved the deaths of the rest of their clan, ate bites of stolen food, and wasted away until their ribs showed under their tattered clothing. Mary's baby became ill halfway through the voyage and nearly died, and in her hungry state she no longer made quite enough milk to feed him. The whole group summoned their powers and cast a healing spell on him, chasing the sickness from his fevered little body one night. Mary joined hands with her companions below deck while the wind whipped fiercely above and the ship creaked around them. She tipped a canteen of water to his lips to keep him from dehydrating. The baby held on.

The ship arrived at a large bay in the colony of Maryland. The passengers selected plots on the grassy flatlands near the water to create farms and homes. As the few necromancers left on earth looked for a place to settle, they did not see any other magical people, much to their relief. This allowed them to stay under cover. The group built a homestead and grew crops, taking advantage of their naturally superior farming skills.

One of the men wanted to search a small nearby cemetery and dig up something to guard their new farm, but the rest of the group insisted that he must not do anything that could make them stand out. Certainly not that. The women covertly made a little money healing minor illnesses and telling fortunes with their potions and herbs, but the group did not dare to openly practice their witchery tactics in front of their deeply religious new neighbors. Quickly, they learned not to tell authentic fortunes, giving people the feedback they wanted to hear to avoid nasty accusations.

Years went by. Necromancers took comfort in staying in one place, to be near their dead ancestors. This clan had lived in their former small village since the age when they were healers and warriors dressed in furs and bones, and now that they were established here, they did not stray far from where they landed.

After Mary's son grew up, he fought against the British in the American Revolution. Whispers went around that a few of the redcoats went still in their tracks, their eyes glazing over, before he killed them. After the war, he married and had quite a few children. One of his sons married Malvina's granddaughter. Marriages continued to happen, some of them branching out but some overlapping as they had back when the original colony lived an isolated life across the ocean. The group never grew back to its former size. With the influence of church and desires to fit in with friends who had no powers, the generations lost much of their knowledge of chants, spells, and herbs. But they carefully hung on to the green crystal, never forgetting the story of their narrow escape from death.

One winter in the 1850s, a trio of merchants, a father and his two sons, stumbled upon the necromancers. These men had fire powers, and reacted with great hostility to the discovery that necromancers, believed to be dead, still existed after all. They attempted to burn their cluster of wood and brick homes to the ground. In the middle of their attack, the three men went still, and then walked into the freezing water nearby until it engulfed their heads. They were not seen again until their bodies bobbed above the water. Among magical people, rumor had it that necromancers could summon the devil to steal the souls of their victims. To anyone else, these looked like simple drownings.

Mary's great-grandson, Edward Frazier, was conscripted into the Confederate army during the Civil War. Edward had the powers, spelling potential disaster if another magical person spotted him. After a bloody battle in Virginia that left many dead, Edward, uninjured but devastated, held his best friend who had just been killed. Despite a lifetime of being taught to conceal his powers, Edward brought movement back to the muscles of his fallen friend. As soon as he realized what he'd done, Edward cut up and burned the corpse. Afterward, Edward shot himself in the head with a revolver. He was survived by a wife and two small children.

After the war ended, the small family unit steadily survived in Edward's absence. As they bred more with the ordinary people around them, fewer magical children were born.

Still, the line persisted.

A Beginning

Lou woke up with an eerie feeling running cold over his body. The air was thicker. Different. And too chilly for the middle of summer. It was the Fourth of July. With his nursery business shuttered for the holiday, Lou treated himself to sleeping in a bit, as rest would be in short supply when the new baby arrived in the next week or so. What was he thinking, a fifty-year-old man having another kid? Did he really have the energy to ride out the sleep-deprived newborn period and then chase after a rambunctious toddler all over again?

Lou got up, changing into a button-down shirt and jeans and putting on his wire-rimmed glasses. Vanessa still slept in the bed they'd only started sharing when her room down the hall was converted into the nursery, brown hair tossed over her pale, thin face. She'd stayed in bed a lot lately, and last night she'd complained of back cramps. At nine months pregnant, aches and pains were hardly any surprise.

Lou brushed his teeth and combed his gray-streaked reddish-blond hair. He froze as he stepped out of the bathroom. A figure in a tattered, hooded brown cloak stood to face him. Semi-transparent, with glowing eyes in a decayed, shadowed face.

Lou saw ghosts in this house with some frequency, including his mother who had died in childbirth, her gleaming, long red hair flowing behind her. This man had also appeared to him a couple of times, once as a young boy, once in his twenties. After living in this house his entire life, born in the same bedroom where he now slept, Lou had learned long ago to shove his fear aside and ignore the ghosts, even savoring the occasional sightings of the mother he never knew. The spirits wouldn't hurt him or his family, nor did they even see the living, still existing in their own times.

But today, this apparition was different. More purposeful, more present, directly meeting Lou's eyes.

Lou had never spoken to a ghost before. But this time, he talked out loud, voice low so as not to wake Vanessa. "Hello? Who are you?"

The man dissolved.

Trying to shake off the unusual sighting, Lou went downstairs and found his seven-year-old daughter Evelyn already awake, dressed in the special shirt and shorts she'd picked for today, covered in stars and stripes. A star-splashed headband held back her long, dark red hair. Lou and his nephew Denny planned to take Evelyn out to watch a fireworks show tonight, and she couldn't wait. Vanessa wanted to stay home. People might bring picnic baskets of fragrant food or smoke cigarettes, and the smells would spur her nausea. For this same reason, Lou hadn't grilled up bacon or sausage for breakfast in months, and served Evelyn a couple of odorless toaster pastries and some fruit.

The past months had been hell for Vanessa, so unexpected after her easy pregnancy with Evelyn. And an easy birth, after everyone in the family had worried that her small-boned stature would make it difficult. This time, Vanessa became violently ill with morning sickness that never went away, vomiting until she lost weight from her already skinny body and a blood vessel burst in her eye, turning the white a demonic red. More than once, she was hospitalized and put on an IV. Denny and his wife often stepped in to help with Evelyn or around the house. The doctor prescribed a bland diet that she could keep down, and those around her were forced to make accommodations. No smelly foods, no perfumes or incense, no smokes. Lou had to quit cigarettes, even though he'd always smoked them outside. If any wisps of tobacco lingered on his clothes, Vanessa threw up.

Though on the fence about a second baby, Lou and Vanessa had faced pressure to not allow Evelyn to grow up an only child. She had asked her parents, "Can you go to the store and buy me a little brother?" It was hard not to chuckle at that request, though they discouraged Evelyn, telling her that a new baby was a lot of work, not all fun and games. There'd be sleepless nights, less attention from Mom and Dad, and she might get jealous.

But Evelyn still wanted a sibling. Something shifted in Lou's head, a force he couldn't explain urging him to produce another child.

A few months ago, Evelyn watched the ultrasound where they discovered she would have a sister, not the brother she wanted. Disappointment had crossed her face for a brief moment until she pictured a cute little girl to dress up and hold tea parties with. Evelyn bragged that she'd be the world's best big sister. She would teach the baby to walk and talk and was even in a hurry to change diapers.

After her parents explained the process, Evelyn insisted on watching her baby sister's birth and cutting the umbilical cord. Lou tried to talk her out of it, warning that it might be too gross of a sight for young eyes, that her mother might make scary noises, and that there would be blood. But Evelyn was bulldog-stubborn. Nothing changed her mind.

The outcome Lou was afraid of happened before his eyes as the pregnancy progressed toward the end.

Like him, the new baby would be a necromancer.

The telltale colors, the green aura that no camera or ultrasound could capture, came through Vanessa's belly stronger every day. It came as a relief when Evelyn was born without those dangerous powers. Like any child born to a magical parent, she had mage blood, but she would never need to even know. She would enjoy a perfectly ordinary childhood.

Vanessa and Evelyn would not know the truth. They could not. Raising the second child to keep her rare perceptions and the powers that would later develop private from her own mother, of all people, would present a challenge. The code of secrecy included family members. Though he'd known he was risking such a child the minute he decided to procreate with Vanessa, Lou did not feel ready for a type of parenting most people could not imagine. Vanessa was due on the tenth. There was no going back now.

After eating breakfast, Evelyn went out back to play with sparklers. Vanessa, shuffling slowly and groggily, joined Lou on the porch to watch as she nibbled on toast.

"I'm not having any more kids, but if I did, it wouldn't be in the summer," Vanessa grumbled in her high-pitched, childlike voice. "It was so much easier having a baby in October. This heat and humidity is killing me."

"The due date's just six days away."

"Remember, Evelyn went six days past her due date. I think due dates are just some number. Is it just me, or does something feel kinda creepy this morning?"

"How so?"

"For the past few days, I feel like I'm being watched. I mean, I don't believe in haunted houses or anything, but I was uneasy this morning."

"I think everything is fine. The house is not haunted." Lou was confident that Vanessa had not seen the ghosts. She had never complained of them before. A plain-spoken woman, she was less likely than most people to keep quiet about things out of embarrassment. Not being a mage, she was unlikely to spot any but the most powerful apparitions.

But even she had felt something.

Who was that man in the hall?

After neighbors started up their barbecue grills, the family went inside to shield Vanessa from the scents. Instead of burgers or hot dogs, lunch was the same bland, non-smelly fare they'd eaten for months: mashed potatoes and simple sandwiches.

Vanessa took a bite of her sandwich and then put it down, looking at her stretchy jeans, wet between the legs. "I think my water broke."

Evelyn's eyes shot wide open in excitement as she bounced in her chair. "Is the baby getting here today? I still get to go, right?"

"We don't know how long it might be," said Lou, getting up to fetch a towel just as Vanessa put her hands on her belly, gripped with a contraction. After the pains ramped up in much quicker succession than they had the last time seven and a half years ago, Lou grabbed the hospital bag waiting by the door. Evelyn wasn't even disappointed that she might miss tonight's fireworks show.

After their admission at the quiet, nearly-empty wing at the hospital, the on-call doctor rushed into the room with salt-and-pepper hair plastered wet to his head. "The nurse said we're progressing really fast. Sorry I'm a couple minutes late; I just took a quick shower. I've been grilling up burgers and ribs, and I didn't want to make you sick with barbecue smells."

"You smell like shampoo. Appreciate the shower," Vanessa said with a small, grateful smile. Lou had a pang of guilt for interrupting the doctor's feast, but babies did not wait for a convenient time.

The birth happened within an hour of the doctor's arrival, quick and simple enough that Vanessa did not think to ask for pain medication. After these months of stomach-turning illness, Lou was frightened to see an emaciated, too-small baby, but she looked healthy, bigger than Evelyn was, pink and screaming with a full head of pumpkin-orange hair as she was laid on Vanessa's chest. Lou had hoped that he was imagining things over the past several months and that this baby would come out not a mage, just half of one like her sister, not needing to know that necromancers walked the earth. But the powerful aura did not lie. His prediction had been right. And it scared him to death.

"She looks like a Halloween candy corn!" Vanessa squealed. "My stomach feels better already!"

Evelyn proudly cut the cord, beaming the whole time and not getting faint with disgust at all. After the baby sister was weighed and wrapped up, it was hard to pry her out of Evelyn's arms to return her to her mother for the first feeding.

From the phone on a nearby table, Lou made calls to some of his nearest and dearest, including his nephew Denny. Ravenously hungry, Vanessa demanded the kind of fast food she had not been able to eat for quite a while. Denny brought a grease-spotted bag with a burger and fries. His tinted shooting glasses were pushed up on his head of buzzed brown hair.

Denny held the baby as Vanessa ate. He exchanged a knowing look with Lou, eyebrows raised. Like Lou, Denny could see what the rest in the room could not. They shared the powers.

"Hell of a day to have a baby, huh?" Denny said, skirting around the topic he and his uncle actually wanted to discuss, but couldn't with Vanessa, Evelyn, and a nurse nearby. "What are you gonna name this kid? How about Independence?"

"Well, I'd told you we were wanting to name her Lillian."

"Oh, after your aunt, right? What's the middle name gonna be?"

"Margaret. After my mother."

"Oh, Jesus, you're going to do that to the poor kid? That name sounds like somebody's grandmother! Cut her a break and name her Independence."

"Such an unusual name might get her teased at school."

"And that old granny name won't?"

Since there was still plenty of time left in the day, Denny and Lou decided to watch fireworks later and take Evelyn, giving her mother a chance to rest. Lingering at the hospital and waiting for the sun to go down, Lou gave in to temptation when Denny offered a cigarette. He hoped to quit eventually for the sake of his girls, not wanting them to cry over the memory of their deceased father at their high school graduations, but today would not be that day. Vanessa kept down her burger and fries and now she talked about ordering a pizza the minute she got home tomorrow; it was a good bet she could tolerate a faint whiff of smoke. The two men walked down the dead-quiet hall toward the exit.

The fluorescent lights flickered. A chill washed over Lou, similar to the ones he'd felt at home. He turned to peer over his shoulder.

There it stood, the ghost in the ratty robe, the hood around the indistinct face, green marble eyes staring straight at him. Ghosts usually stayed in one place. How had this man followed him to the hospital? It was only a few miles from the house, but still, this spirit had quite a range of movement.

"Denny, look behind you. What is that?"

Denny turned. "What's behind us? I thought I felt something weird, but there's nothing."

The ghost was gone.

As they stood outside and smoked, Lou described today's sightings.

"That sounds similar to a ghost my mom claimed she saw," Denny revealed. He did not bring up his mother, Lou's sister Sarah, often. After her suicide when her son was eleven years old, she remained a sensitive subject.

Like Lou and Denny, Sarah had been a necromancer.

"I don't believe you told me that before," said Lou.

"Mom saw lots of stuff in her dreams. I don't remember all of it, but as the years go by, more and more of it comes true. When I was little, she said something about a nuclear power plant blowing up, then that Chernobyl thing happened a few years back. Same with that space shuttle explosion."

"She had those dreams of future disasters since we were children. She even predicted the assassination of John F. Kennedy, when none of us had even heard of him yet. But she could never tell us *when* these things would happen. And some of them haven't happened... I'm not sure when or if they will. What did she say about the ghost?"

"He spoke to her, which is weird for a ghost. Talked to her in a dream or something. It was about some guy who might not have been born yet. It didn't make a lot of sense. I didn't always listen to Mom, since I thought she'd lost her marbles. Now I wish I'd listened, especially after Chernobyl happened."

"Her stories did sound pretty wild and unbelievable at the time. What did this ghost say about this man?"

"That she had to take care of him. I still don't know who the guy was. Maybe the ghost was talking about me." Denny sighed, dropping his cigarette and grinding it out with the heel of his boot. "And she didn't stick around for very long to take care of me."

Excerpt from The Autobiography of Gerald Frazier: Architect of a New World

I come from a remarkable family. My ancestors were said to go back to the time of the Druids. The history is murky, but tells us that they were well-respected shamans. Later on, they formed a clan of mages and kept to themselves, as most necromancers tend to do. They came from three families, and after the rest of the necromancers across the world were killed off by other mages, they became the last on earth. I'm not sure what their numbers were when the lightning people of Europe started their attack on my ancestors, but it may have been in the hundreds.

Somehow, they were caught by surprise and only a few escaped from the Scottish Highlands with their lives. They stowed away on a ship. Our few remaining heroes settled on the eastern bank of the Chesapeake Bay, back in the colonial days.

For generations, they mostly lived in obscurity, even though I carry the distinction of being a son of the Confederacy and a son of the American Revolution. According to my genealogical research, the Frasers, later corrupted to the current spelling, intermarried quite a bit with the Mackenzies. There was a bit of inbreeding. But even if the family tree more closely resembled a trunk at times, it was well worth it, because it kept the necromancer blood strong in the family line at least for a while.

My father, John Robert Frazier, was an only child. At the time of his birth, he and his father were literally the last two necromancers on earth, bringing us dangerously close to extinction.

We were born and raised in a small town called Easton, Maryland, which is located on the rural Eastern Shore. A lot of water and a lot of pine trees composed the landscape of my boyhood. It was quite a lovely place to grow up, and I had an unforgettable childhood filled with outdoor adventures, unlike today's children who pass the time staring at televisions and telephone screens.

My father was reserved, stern, and strict. His deeply religious parents instilled shame within him and implied that he was a witch. I suspect he was not the first generation in our family taught to loathe themselves for their inborn talents. And that is just a shame. We should not hate ourselves for having these wonderful gifts. We should embrace them!

In 1927, my father married my mother, nineteen-year-old Margaret Ellen Lindsey. My Momma had some relations to the Mackenzies and carried their magical blood, not knowing it. I could tell by the intensity of the auras surrounding my mother and aunts that they had the trait.

Momma and her two blond-haired sisters, Rosemary and Lillian, were all pretty women. But my mother, in particular, was a knockout. She was tall and shapely, with bright green eyes, a little ski-slope nose, and hair as red as a fire engine. Yet she married a more average-looking man. Few photos of Momma remain, though I saw her ghost as a boy, pacing through the halls of my home. From the memories I've read in people's minds, she was a gentle, caring mother, though also vain and shallow. She spent quite a bit of time combing that long red hair of hers and admiring herself in the mirror. Though short hair was a fad in the 1920s, Momma never cut hers. She only lived for thirty years, so she never grew old or unattractive.

My father was a blond-haired fisherman. Or a waterman, as they call it in the Chesapeake region. His arms bulged with muscles from hauling in crabs and oysters to support the family through the Great Depression.

My oldest sister, Violet Ellen, was born in the summer of 1928. She was a half-breed like our mother, lacking the powers yet carrying the trait.

Even though my parents didn't specifically set out to make necromancers, it happened with their genetic makeup. Sarah Rose, the first necromancer child, was born in 1933. She emerged in the caul, or the unbroken amniotic sac. Some cultures have a superstition that children born in the caul are blessed with good luck or "second sight," able to see future events. I'm not sure about good luck, but the other myth came true!

I was the third baby born into the family. Momma had difficult pregnancies with both me and Sarah. Had I been the girl Momma thought she'd have, she would have called me Geraldine Anne. Instead, I was the first boy, Gerald Robert. I made my debut on the cold, clear morning of February 4, 1936. My siblings and I were all born at home in our parents' bedroom. Our family physician, Dr. James Lowhorn, had the honor of being the first to spank my chubby baby bottom. The tall pinch-faced doctor had no idea just what a legacy he was holding in his hands! I was born with bright orange hair. Then that hair fell out and Momma's shade of apple-colored red hair grew in.

No mage baby is born with superpowers. These do not develop until later childhood and puberty. This must be nature's way of protecting the world from destruction during a toddler temper tantrum! But I believe that those few of us blessed with mind reading have it from birth. I started talking earlier than most babies. My elder sisters delighted in teaching me new words. Papa figured out I was a mind reader before I was two years old. I wasn't much older than that when he started having to hush me to keep me from giving my talent away.

It took me less than two years to start using the toilet. I could see that my parents and sisters did not want to spend the rest of their lives crapping in diapers, nor did they want me to. I can vaguely remember how the whole family clapped when I successfully made it to the little white pot!

It would be far from the last time mind-reading served me well.

I do not have many firsthand memories of my mother, and sometimes the lines blur between my own memories and those of other people. In one of the memories that I'm sure is mine, though I was only two years old, I'm in her lap, listening to her heartbeat, and connected to her thoughts and the thoughts of my new sibling on the way. Though there is nothing to see in a mother's womb, an unborn child close to birth can hear your voice, and they're already trying to figure out what you're saying. When Momma spoke to me, the baby kicked her insides to let her know it was listening.

On November 30, 1938, our family's life as we knew it fell apart. That morning, Momma went into labor and our aunt Rosemary took me and Sarah to her house. Ten-year-old Violet stayed home to help boil water and such. I don't remember that day, but the recollections of Dr. Lowhorn, Papa, and Violet are still burned into my mind. That evening became a horror show. Shortly after my brother Loudon John was born, the doctor had trouble delivering the afterbirth. It did not come loose like it should have, and when the doctor gave the cord a good yank, Momma hemorrhaged to death. It happened too quickly to get her to the hospital.

The doctor felt guilty for attempting to fix the problem on his own, rather than sending Momma to the hospital where they might have safely removed the afterbirth. Papa dealt with a lot of regret as well. He later believed he could have somehow used his powers to save Momma while she lay dying on their blood-drenched bed. But he followed the code of mages to the letter. He swore to never use the powers in front of non-mages, not even to save his beautiful wife as her life poured out between her legs. I understand that us mages have minor healing powers. Maybe she bled out too quickly, beyond saving, but my father could have at least tried. Never could I be weak like him! The tragedy that upended our lives when I was just a toddler strengthened my convictions and made me who I am today.

Dr. Lowhorn prescribed my father some downers to help him through his grief. My father wanted more and more tranquilizers and sedatives as the months went by, "for his nerves." Dr. Lowhorn gave in to Papa's whims, coming over with needles full of drugs to put in his arms.

Our aunts took up much of the childcare now that we were motherless. Aunt Lillian, who'd just had a baby herself, took in Loudon for the first year of his life. We all called him Lou. My aunt nursed my baby brother on one breast and our cousin Alicia on the other. Both babies slept in the same crib.

Fifty years later, when our aunt Lillian was dead, Lou, who happens to still live in the same house where we were born, had a late-in-life child and named her after this aunt who had cared for him. She does not look like her namesake, but she is a dead ringer for my mother. About that daughter of his... I'll get there.

Childhood

For Lou, January 23, 1993, was just another Saturday. He busied himself in the kitchen, getting food ready for lunch, wrapping potatoes in foil. Eleven-year-old Evelyn was absorbed in a shopping-mall-themed board game with two friends. Kids hung out at the house frequently. With such a popular daughter, Lou had to buy extra potatoes, pizzas, and chicken nuggets to keep all these visitors fed.

Three-year-old Lillian sat in the living room, stacking big plastic blocks to make a castle as her apple-red ponytail cascaded down the back of her pink overalls. Barney the purple dinosaur frolicked with his friends on the television.

Lou had just popped the potatoes into the oven when Lillian's small dimpled hands grabbed at the leg of his blue jeans. "Daddy, I just went with Mommy."

"Went where, sweetheart? Your mommy isn't here."

Vanessa had moved out last year. A couple of weekends ago, she'd caught a ride and visited with an armful of gifts, but the children hadn't seen their non-custodial mother since. As far Lou knew, right now she'd be in the upscale Washington, D.C. apartment she shared with her boyfriend, Karl.

"We went. She's not coming back." Lillian's face transformed into a pout. Her lower lip quivered, and then out came a shriek. "*Gone!*"

"What? What does that mean?"

Lillian ran from the room, crying. Distracted from their board game, Evelyn and her friends turned to stare.

"I'm sure everything's fine. It's just a tantrum of some kind," Lou assured the kids.

"Mom's okay, right?" Evelyn asked over the sound of the sobs.

"Of course she is, sweetheart. Why wouldn't she be?"

That afternoon, nothing seemed to soothe Lillian. Not lying down in bed, not food, not hugs, not a Popsicle. She kept crying, yet denied she was in pain.

Just to make sure that Vanessa was all right, Lou called her apartment, only to get her and Karl's answering machine. Though he left a message, no one returned his call. The longer he waited for the phone to ring, the more an unsettled feeling tugged at him.

Lillian did not have the appetite to eat dinner that night, and after her friends rode their bikes home, Evelyn grew quiet, chewing her lip in anxiety.

The phone rang at the tail end of dinner. Finally! Lou went to the kitchen to answer it, waiting to announce to both girls that Vanessa was fine and they had nothing to worry about.

Instead, it was an unfamiliar voice. "Hello, is this Loudon Frazier?"

"Speaking."

"My name's Dan Stevens, and I'm with the Washington, D.C. Metro Police. I'm calling regarding Vanessa Christensen."

"Is she okay?" Lou's heart dropped.

"Mr. Frazier, I'm very sorry to have to inform you that this afternoon, she passed away."

"What?"

"Unfortunately, Vanessa has died from a gunshot wound. It's still under investigation, but we believe it's foul play, and we have a suspect in custody."

The phone dropped from Lou's fingers and clattered to the floor.

"Mom's okay, right?" Evelyn pleaded, tugging at Lou's shirt. "She's okay! Right?"

"I'm afraid not. I'm so sorry."

Evelyn screamed at the top of her lungs.

The pale blue sky filtered through a humid atmosphere, punctuated by light fluffy clouds. Lillian crouched down next to Lou on their screened back porch. They looked over their summer garden. Huge squash, zucchini, and shiny eggplants peeked out from under canopies of fuzzy leaves.

Lillian sat hugging her knees, anxious about the upcoming start of kindergarten. She didn't want to go to that noisy place full of strangers.

"Lillian, you may find this very hard to understand at first," her father began. "But you do know that you can see things most people cannot, right? We've talked about the colors."

Oh, yes, those. As soon as Lillian grew old enough to understand basic rules, her father and cousin established that she could not talk about auras with anyone else, not even her sister who could not see them. Auras were the coronas of color around every living thing, even slightly visible in the air around the trees, weeds, and backyard garden.

The auras belonging to Lillian's father, her older cousin Denny, and a few other relatives, like her uncle Gerald, were far more magnificent than most people's. They extended in snakelike rays of green, with other colors, sometimes green and sometimes not, underneath. Lillian puzzled at the reasons behind these auras when she could not even see her own.

"Right now," said Lou, "I am going to tell you what it all means. You promise to keep it secret? Are you listening to me?"

"Yeah, I promise."

"The word some of us use is 'mage' or 'magical people.' It means we can do things that some folks might call magic."

"Really?!" Lillian said excitedly, envisioning hats spitting out a hundred rabbits, or people levitating in the air at the flick of a sleek black wand in a gloved hand.

"Sweetheart, before you get ahead of yourself, you need to know how dangerous the magic is. It could get you in trouble."

"Aww!"

"We can't have people finding out. You are not to tell anyone at school. And even though most children your age have not grown into magic yet, you must not try it under any circumstances."

This demand brought Lillian to the verge of tears, and would leave her terrified to so much as learn a card trick for years. "Why not? Why can't I?"

"When you get older, you will be able to move things without even going near them. I've been able to do that since early on, but most children can't do it until well into their school years. But, that's not all. We can do something that other magical people cannot. There are three other kinds of magical people. Fire, water, and air. We are much rarer than them, and we have to stay away from them, because they don't like us."

"Why? Are we in trouble?"

"A long time ago, they decided that we were out to get everybody else, even though we weren't. They don't like some of our powers."

"What are the powers they don't like?"

"You're too young to know the rest. It could frighten you."

"I wanna know!" Lillian pouted, tears leaking from her eyes.

"I'm concerned it would give you nightmares."

"Come on, I wanna *know!*"

"I'll tell you when you're older."

"How old?"

"Maybe eight."

Three years sounded like an eternity for a child whose curiosity had been baited, but who followed the rules no matter what. Three years was more than half a lifetime. "It's not fair," Lillian whimpered.

After her father spent some time comforting her, they went inside to set the table, readying it for the pot roast simmering in the Crock-Pot. Evelyn came home on her bicycle from a friend's house. She was lean and pale, with pink-framed glasses and a red-brown ponytail dangling from a scrunchy. To Lillian's eyes, Evelyn had a more pronounced aura than most people, but not the green extensions their father had.

As they ate, Evelyn began to gripe, furrowing her brow in her stress. "I did better than Jamie Sayers at clarinet practice. I know I did. But Miss Lavine liked Jamie's performance better!"

"Oh, Evelyn. You're wonderful at playing the clarinet. I'm sure she was just as impressed with you," their father tried to reassure her.

"I tried my hardest and she hardly said anything to me!"

Lou sighed, not liking how much pressure Evelyn put on herself to be the best, feeling like she was not good enough for her absent mother. Evelyn quickly ate before deciding to skip dessert to practice her clarinet. She rushed upstairs to her bedroom.

Left alone with bowls of ice cream between them, Lou lowered his voice and reminded Lillian to keep quiet about their previous conversation.

"Dad," Lillian asked, "can Evelyn do magic?"

"No. Like most of the people around us, she was born without it."

"Could Mommy do magic?"

"No. She was like Evelyn. But I believe it's because of your powers that you knew the moment your mother passed away."

Vanessa's boyfriend, Karl Thiessen, had recently been sentenced to life in prison for shooting her dead in their apartment. Though all evidence pointed to him, he claimed that he had no intent to kill her, and no memory of committing the crime.

Lillian's father distracted her from thoughts of her mother; he didn't like his girls dwelling too much on the tragedy. He gave her a final reminder to carefully guard their secret trait. The topic changed as Lou put Lillian's things together in her new plastic backpack to prepare her for school. The sun went down, and bedtime came. Lou read Lillian a story about a wizard, and then she knelt at her bedside in her pajamas to say her nighttime prayers. After her father tucked her underneath her quilt, her mind refused to shut off, active with the mysteries of the magic she wasn't allowed to use.

Evelyn's little sister, now six years old, loved to play tag and hide-and-go-seek. When Lillian was two or three, it was easy enough for Evelyn and her friends to play pretend that they were teachers in a classroom with her as the student. Now, bigger and a ball of energy, Lillian wanted to play exhausting games all day long.

Evelyn knew all of the best hiding spots: in the back of the shed behind the lawn mower; deep in the coat closet; under Dad's bed concealed from view by his rows of shoes; and—the best hiding spot of all—a trunk in the attic, nestled beneath old, stale-smelling dresses. Every time Evelyn hid in that trunk, her friends were never able to find her and eventually gave up the search. Even though it was hard to breathe in that trunk, with the air filtered through the musty clothes, Evelyn was always willing to endure that discomfort if it meant winning the game.

Evelyn was thirteen and going through a growth spurt, yet still small and sleek enough to fit into most of her old hideouts. She did not want to make things too hard for Lillian, who wasn't great at hiding. All it took to find her, usually, was a peek in a cardboard box, behind a door, or under a blanket with an obvious lump in it. But no matter where Evelyn hid, be it crouched in the kitchen cabinet or curled up in the backyard shed, Lillian was always quick to find her. "Gotcha!" she would say, pouncing triumphantly on Evelyn.

Evelyn started to increase the challenge by tucking herself in the back of the coat closet wrapped in dark coats, or sliding under Dad's bed. Still, she was discovered every time.

After growing increasingly irritated at her sister's nonstop success in ferreting her out, Evelyn climbed into the hiding spot that never failed her in the past: the trunk in the attic, underneath those smelly, ancient clothes. Little footsteps climbed up the narrow stairs.

The trunk lid opened, and then the clothes were flung aside. "Gotcha!" Lillian said triumphantly, poking Evelyn in the side and laughing.

That evening, Evelyn confessed to her father that it seemed to take Lillian almost no effort to find her during these games. "I don't know how she does it!"

A short while later, Lou took Lillian out to the porch. As Evelyn did her homework in the kitchen, they spoke in low voices. These private little talks made Evelyn wonder bitterly if Lillian was their father's favorite. She felt inadequate.

After that night, Lillian stopped asking Evelyn to play hide-and-go-seek, instead requesting occasional board games or rounds of checkers. Evelyn was glad to leave behind most of the child's play as she experimented with makeup, began dating, read teen magazines, got her hair permed, and gave her boxed-up toys to her little sister. As Evelyn left childish things in the past, she never forgot how Lillian found her every time during hide-and-go-seek. How did her kid sister pull it off?

One evening, Evelyn spotted a spirit board in the games closet during a sleepover at her friend's house. An idea popped into Evelyn's head. Maybe not all hope was lost that she'd speak with her mother again. Evelyn asked to borrow the board and hid it in the bottom of her duffel bag, knowing that her father would not approve.

During a summer afternoon, their father left Evelyn to watch Lillian while he ran errands. Evelyn took the spirit board out, figuring that it would not be hard to talk Lillian into helping her. Lillian had reading skills advanced for her age, but might not fully understand what was going on. When Evelyn set up the board on the wood floor in her bedroom, drew the window curtain shut, and lit a few candles, she warned Lillian to keep this quiet from Dad.

"Why are we going to do this?" Lillian wanted to know. "Who are we going to talk to?"

"We're going to talk to our mom."

"But she's dead."

"That's the point. This is for talking to dead people."

"How do you know you're gonna get Mommy to talk to us? There's dead people everywhere."

"I just want to try, okay? I just miss Mom. You miss her too, don't you? This will just be between us. Okay?"

"Okay."

The two sisters knelt in front of the board and placed their hands on the planchette. After a few basic questions, which got the simple response of "Yes," Evelyn asked for their mother. "Mom, are you here with us?"

The planchette again slid to the word "Yes."

"This is Vanessa, right?"

The planchette moved away and then came back to the word. "Yes."

Tears of joy filled Evelyn's eyes. This was not the same as a warm hug from their mother when she was still alive, or hearing her voice on the phone, but this was the hello she longed for.

Lillian looked up and straight ahead. "Stop," she said sharply.

"Sssh!"

"We have to stop."

"Why?"

"This thing isn't Mommy."

"How do you know? It said it is her!"

"It's just pretending it's her."

"How do you know?"

"Because I see it."

Hands still on the planchette, Evelyn looked up and around the dim, candle-lit room, empty except for them. "I don't see anything. What does it look like?"

"A black cloud thing!"

Evelyn's skin crawled, even though she was sure Lillian's imagination was just running wild yet again. "But... it's our hands that are moving. There's nothing else moving... is there?"

"*It* is moving our hands."

Evelyn's hands got increasingly cold, as if pierced by an icicle. In that moment, she became convinced that something outside of herself was indeed manipulating their movements.

"We have to stop now!" Lillian yelled.

Evelyn took her hands off the board, quickly like it was on fire.

"It went away," Lillian assured her. "If you do the board again, it might come back. I don't think we can talk to Mommy like this."

After Dad got home, Lillian told on Evelyn, confiding in their father about the spirit board in her fear after seeing the black, amorphous, cloud-like entity that was invisible to her sister. Dad was not happy. He could understand missing their mother, but he ordered the girls to never allow one of those boards in the house again, and for Evelyn to give it back to her friend immediately.

"You could attract some very bad creatures into the house," he warned. "Even your cousin Denny will not play with these, and you know how he messes around with tarot cards."

Lillian had asked persistently for a puppy since she was three. A single father with his hands full, Lou wanted to wait. Unlike a child, he understood that a dog wasn't just fun, like a stuffed animal. It meant a years-long commitment.

One late-summer day, right after school started, seven-year-old Lillian got her wish at last. Now a freshman in high school, Evelyn could be a reliable helper with care and feeding. An elderly woman who lived two houses down was in a hurry to give away a litter of freshly weaned puppies born to her beagle. Lillian picked out one fuzzy brown mixed-breed puppy and named him Buster.

Two days after bringing the puppy home, keeping him confined to the kitchen with baby gates while they tried to house-train him, little Buster lost his appetite. No longer the energetic, squirming little furball they'd picked out from the litter, Buster became lethargic, splaying out on the kitchen linoleum like a starfish. The puppy's aura flickered and grew a bit dull. Concerned, Lou called a veterinarian, who was able to squeeze in an appointment for the next afternoon. Lou fed Buster extra water, in the hopes that the puppy was simply dehydrated and that a night of rest would bring him back around.

When Lou and Evelyn awoke early the next morning, they came downstairs to an acrid, horrendous smell. Almost the smell of death, yet somehow even worse.

Lillian was up too, earlier than usual. "Dad, it stinks!" she complained. "Something is wrong with Buster!"

"Both of you, wait there. I'll check on him." Lou headed to the barricaded kitchen. Lillian followed him despite his order to stay put and headed straight to her new puppy. She stopped at the baby gate and screamed. The kitchen floor was stained with pools of blood.

"It'll be all right," Lou reassured his hysterically crying daughter as he grabbed a towel and wrapped up Buster, weak and breathing fast. "He's just sick. The vet will make him all better. Both of you, get dressed and get in the car. Hurry."

Lou knew exactly what this was. He'd never seen it up close before, though he'd heard enough stories about dogs losing their lives to it.

Parvo.

Her expression steely and grave, Evelyn sat in the backseat and kept the towel wrapped around the ailing puppy, while Lillian buckled herself into the front seat. Right now, the only goal was to get Buster to the veterinary emergency room. If they even made it in time. Lou was ready to max out his credit card if that was what it took to save Buster's life.

As Lou pushed the speed limit, Lillian went still next to him, quieting her sobs and sniffles. A shimmer went through the air, hitting him like a faint earthquake. A brief flash of light filled his vision, threatening to distract him from the road.

"Dad," Lillian said, staring straight forward. "Buster's all right. He's running and wagging his tail!"

"He's still back here with me," Evelyn announced from behind. "He's not wagging his tail. He's too sick."

"But he's all right! Can't you see us? We're in this building. This big, green building. It's beautiful. There's bones."

She can't possibly be seeing that, Lou thought to himself. *She needs the crystal to see that. She's far too little. This makes no sense.*

"Huh, where's Buster?" Lillian blinked, turning her head around, as if she'd just woken up from a trance.

"In the back with me, like I just said!" Evelyn snapped.

"But... we were just running, and then there was light..."

"You're scared and confused," Evelyn sighed. "We've been in the car this whole time. You and Buster weren't running anywhere. He's too sick."

Lou squealed into the parking lot of the vet clinic just as Lillian cried out, "He's dead! He's gone!"

"No, he isn't, sweetheart," Lou promised, his words ringing hollow. "They'll help him. But we have to hurry!"

"I'm sorry, I think she's right." Evelyn's voice went somber.

Lou and Lillian hopped out of his car and threw open the back doors. Buster was still and silent in the towel, his aura gone. They hadn't made it in time.

"No!" Lillian screamed, gathering up the puppy in her arms and rocking him like a baby. "No! You can't die! Wake up! Wake up! Please, come back! Wake up! Move! Come back!"

I hope to God she's too young to bring a corpse back.

"I'm going to take Buster now," Lou said, attempting to pry the bundle from his younger daughter's arms.

"No!" Lillian screamed. "He has to live! I have to help him!"

"I'm sorry, sweetheart, but you can't help him."

"Noooo!"

"I have to take him now!"

"No!"

It was a struggle to get the puppy away from Lillian. She let go only when she was exhausted from her sobs.

Later that week, Lou confronted the neighbor who gave them the puppy. She admitted that she didn't believe in taking her dogs to the vet or ever getting them vaccinated. By then, she had lost most of her dogs.

Lillian was extremely disappointed on top of her grief. She still dreamed of having a puppy to play fetch with, and Lou resented that she was robbed of that happy memory. All he wanted was for his girls to enjoy growing up while they still could, to not have to witness anything so gruesome before their young minds could handle it.

But sometimes the world's cruelty could not be avoided.

Excited, Lillian got up earlier than usual on the morning of her eighth birthday, bouncing down the stairs in her pajamas with her large eyeglasses on and her hair in two messy braids. Even though her father was no early bird either, he'd learned that nothing stopped kids from waking early on Christmas or their birthdays, so he'd gotten everything prepared. The cake, not to be eaten until one of Lillian's few friends from school and her cousin Denny came over for that evening's small party, was covered in foil and set out on the dining room table. Once the red, white, and blue cake was eaten, the whole family would go out and watch fireworks.

Lou sipped his black coffee in the dim dawn light streaming through the window. He opened it to let in the dewy morning air, filled with the pithy green smell of summer and cut grass. Lillian felt the shiny wrapped presents on the table, guessing which were books and which were video games.

"Dad, remember what we talked about?" she asked her father after joining him in the kitchen.

"What? When?"

"The magic."

"What about it?"

"You said you'd tell me when I was eight. And now I'm eight."

Lou shook his head. "When did I say that?"

"When I was five."

He chuckled. "You have a memory like an elephant, kid. You want to get right to it, don't you? You aren't going to turn eight until a little after two in the afternoon."

"But it's my birthday! Doesn't the whole day count? Why the afternoon?"

"It's the time you were born. But since Evelyn's still in bed, we can talk about it now as long as we keep our voices down. Come on out to the porch."

They sat down on two chairs behind the porch screen.

"You said you'd tell me what kind of magic I can do," said Lillian. "Except moving things around. You already told me about that, and I've never done it."

"Your cousin Denny wants to teach you about moving things once you're older. But you must swear you'll only do it when he says so, is that clear?"

"Yeah."

"Have you noticed that, for instance, I never take you to the cemetery?"

"Yes." Lillian would have questioned this more if her mother were buried in town, but instead, she was laid to rest in Cincinnati, her hometown. Though Lillian had never placed a rose on the headstones of the local deceased relatives, either.

"There's a reason for that. You would get certain urges around dead people."

"Like what?"

"Urges to make them move. You need to learn to control those impulses."

"What? Making dead people move? That sounds scary!" After thinking about this in bewilderment, Lillian made the connection. When she stumbled upon a gnarled bird or squirrel on the ground, or when Denny took the girls on his hunting trips—a practice her father was not thrilled about—and packed away his kills, she hovered over the dead things, filled with visceral longings.

When Lillian held her puppy's still-warm body last year, she was transfixed, overcome with the sense that if she focused, if she willed him back to life hard enough, his body might wiggle and his little tail might wag.

"Do you know why we get these urges, sweetheart?" Lillian's father explained. "Because we can bring them back. In a way."

"Really?!"

"Not to what they used to be. They cannot think for themselves. We control what they do. But once they're brought back, the danger's closer than you might think."

"So we turn them into zombies? That's scary! I'm *never* doing that!"

"That's good. After that transition, they may be changed into something else. Something worse."

"What? What do you turn them into?" What could possibly be more disturbing than zombies?

"Ssh, not so loud. I'd rather not describe it; you are better off not knowing. I have never made or even seen one of those creatures. I don't want you trying any of that. You promise?"

"I promise. But I want to know!"

"Maybe I'll tell you someday. I don't want you to think too much about these things. Now let's come in and have breakfast."

Excerpt from The Autobiography of Gerald Frazier: Architect of a New World

Violet, the eldest of us four children, was also the meanest. Violet resented having to do a large share of the cooking and cleaning. She ordered me, Sarah, and Lou around, sometimes punching and kicking us as she walked by. While she took her grief and anger about Momma's death out on us, she had no idea how easily her younger siblings could have destroyed her when we came into our powers... the powers she did not have.

When she got a bit older and wiser, Violet apologized for the way she'd treated us. We appreciated her change in attitude, though none of us grew close to her.

Sarah, the second-born, looked nothing like Violet, who was blonde and skinny as a rail. A chubby, freckled girl with pale red hair, Sarah also had an opposite personality. Painfully shy, she bent to the will of the people around her. For a necromancer, this was not a good thing! Since Sarah and I both shared the necromancer abilities, we confided in each other. We stuck close together and it was often just the two of us in the sandbox. By the age of four or five, I was in charge of most of the games. I could read Sarah's mind along with everyone else's, but she could only barely read mine. I liked to keep things unpredictable and stay ahead in our Cowboys and Indians wars.

Like much of our generation, we did not have a television and instead gathered around the radio for our entertainment. I remember one early childhood day when little Lou was maybe two or three years old, sitting with me and Sarah. Lou kept reaching for the knobs. Anxious to keep listening to the show that had our attention, we pulled his little hands away. Sarah and I finally got him to stay put. And then the station got fuzzy and changed. I looked up to find the knob turning slightly. Sarah and I yelled over to Papa in his easy chair. "Did you do that?"

"Do what?" Papa asked, coming over to investigate. That day, he wasn't too far gone on his tranquilizers. We told him what we saw, whispering so Violet would not hear from the kitchen while she made dinner. Papa was puzzled, knowing he did not turn that knob. My father was so repressed from his religious upbringing that he never used his powers, not once in his life. And it couldn't have been me or Sarah, since we had not developed our telekinesis yet. Sarah thought she saw a ray of power coming from our little brother. Even more impossible, because he was so young. But Papa thought it must be him!

"Unheard of," Papa warned us. "The boy must be very special. We must be very careful with him."

Since Lou didn't yet fully understand the code of the mages, which demands secrecy, Papa had another thorny situation to deal with. For the next year or so, he tried to wean off his downers and laudanum so that he could watch my little brother like a hawk.

The Summer with Julius

The summer between seventh and eighth grade, Lillian's father did something out of character. Normally intent on keeping her close and protected, save for the small nearby summer camp Lillian went to for a few weeks last year, he sent her into the hands of a cherished, trusted relative: his nephew Julius, Uncle Gerald's son who lived in Ohio and ran a luxury car dealership. Like his father, the CEO of a medical supply company, Julius was well off.

Julius complained that his hired help was too unreliable. So he made an offer, promising that if Lillian stayed at his home to help with his gardens for a month and a half, he would pay generously for the labor. And it would be a good learning experience. Lillian wanted to buy herself a guitar and a PlayStation 2. Her father wished to pad her college fund. This would be a good deal for everyone involved.

Evelyn, attending college in Georgia, stayed home for the summer. Evelyn was invited too, but her severe cat allergy kept her from taking Julius up on the offer. Julius owned enough cats that the dander would make Evelyn's throat swell shut.

Twelve going on thirteen, Lillian wore large, plastic-framed glasses that made her self-conscious. Her much-regretted sixth-grade pixie cut was growing out, falling straight and fine to her shoulders. Lillian had cut it short after years of stressful, unwanted attention. Adults out in public and a few classmates had treated her like a petting zoo exhibit, stroking and grabbing her long locks without permission and gushing over the vivid red color, saying that she must have one hell of a temper with that hair and expressing pity for her father. The stereotype of the explosive redhead, untrue in Lillian's case, got just as tiring as the people who couldn't keep their hands to themselves.

While it came as a temporary relief when her hair was too short for strangers to grab a handful, Lillian hated the pixie cut and now it could not grow out fast enough.

Julius purchased a plane ticket for Lillian to travel to Columbus. This would be her first flight, and she'd take it alone. All part of the learning experience, according to Julius, a good preparation for her approaching adulthood.

On the morning of the departure, Evelyn drove Lillian across the long bridge traversing the Chesapeake Bay to the busier, more built-up western shore. As Lillian watched the sailboats out on the water, Evelyn played her pop music that Lillian didn't like and reminded her that she needed to be extra-nice to their cousin for doing her such a favor.

After they reached the airport, Evelyn stayed with the increasingly nervous Lillian as she checked in, right up until the point where the security screening forced them apart. According to Evelyn, flying had gotten weird since the terrorist attacks last September.

After landing in Columbus, Lillian grew even more confused among the crowds and loudspeakers. She sat down near the baggage carousel. Julius knelt in front of her with a smile that reassured her immediately. Though he occasionally visited her father, this would be her first time seeing Julius' own house. And she'd heard it was a nice place.

Julius had nearly translucent reddish-orange hair, a pinkish complexion, and a fairly slender form in a gray business suit. His eyes were a pale, watery shade of blue, not the green that Lillian, her father, and her sister had. His cologne and aftershave washed over Lillian, the scent overpowering. A gold watch glittered just underneath the cuff of his sleeve.

Julius was so different from Denny, Lillian's local cousin, an unpretentious, rough-and-ready type who hated wearing anything but a T-shirt and jeans and his signature shooting glasses. While Julius seemed to want to show off his means.

Julius and Denny had something in common, however. Julius was surrounded by the aura that defined a necromancer. Green, shining protrusions left his body, invisible even to the strangers who walked right through them. Green and dark gray, very nearly black, caressed his form beneath the outer green coating. Red buzzed occasionally near his head.

They walked to the parking garage, where his black two-doored BMW gleamed with a fresh coat of wax. He tossed Lillian's bags in the trunk as she sat in the leather front passenger's seat that still carried a hint of the delicious new-car smell.

"You look like your dad," Julius said during the ride. "Not the hair color so much. Before he went gray, your dad was strawberry blonde. But you two have the same eyes, same nose. What grade are you going into in the fall?"

"Eighth."

"You really turned out beautiful. You know that?"

Embarrassed, Lillian did not reply. Julius had lavished a bit of similar praise in the letters he wrote, but hearing it from his lips was more awkward. Lillian felt ugly and self-conscious about her hips and thighs. She was already taller than her size-zero adult sister, outweighed her, and wore a larger size. Lillian believed she was a pear-shaped giant next to Evelyn, even though few people could ever fit into her sister's clothes.

"Do you have a boyfriend? Lots of friends?" Julius asked.

"No." Lillian kept her massive crush on her friend Adam, one of the only two friends she had, a secret to take to her grave.

"I do wish you had never cut your hair. You had the most beautiful long hair. Are you trying to grow it out again?"

"Yes." Uncomfortable with how much people focused on her hair, Lillian changed the subject the way she often did: with a cool fact. Right now, the focus of her fascination was whales, a subject her father and sister had gotten sick of. "Guess what? Did you know that when a whale sleeps, only one eye closes and only half of its brain is asleep at a time?"

"Huh, interesting," Julius nodded.

"Yeah, isn't that neat? It's so the whale can keep swimming."

"My friend in Michigan has sent her little sister, Mandy, to help me out this summer. Mandy has never cut her hair. It's quite nice. How is your sister Evelyn doing? I heard that she's going to Georgia Tech?"

"Yes."

"Wasn't she the valedictorian of her high school class?"

"No, she came in second. The salutatorian, I think it's called. Boy, was she mad she wasn't valedictorian."

"That girl always did have one hell of a competitive streak. How's college going for her?"

"Great. She's made a lot of friends. She got a full-ride scholarship because she's a lacrosse champion and won all those science fairs. She's good at everything."

"Your father is damn proud of her, but Lillian, no one is good at everything. Even Evelyn has weaknesses. What are her flaws? I'm sure you can name a few."

"Hmm... she gets in these grouchy moods sometimes. And I don't care for her taste in music."

"I remember checking out your father's record collection and feeling bad for you kids, having to grow up on that elevator music. Perhaps it's rubbed off on Evelyn."

"I just wear my headphones to block it out."

"Smart girl. There are bigger shortcomings than being a little temperamental and listening to bad music. There is something that Evelyn is sorely lacking. What is it?"

"I don't know... the powers?"

"You hit the nail on the head. Always remember, we're good at things most people can't even fathom, including the sister who seems close to perfect. The next time you think of her talents, look at yourself and what you're capable of."

"Um, thanks." This was not an ego boost. Evelyn had always been known for stellar grades and athletic prowess. But the thing that made Lillian special was a closely guarded secret. In a sense, her father had taught her to live in a closet of shame.

"You can't read minds, can you?" Julius asked.

"Nope."

"Neither can I. I have always been jealous of my father. He can read the mind of the devil."

The world went past, a moist green blur outside of the car window. The suburban houses spread out into a slightly more rural setting. Lillian could not imagine how Julius could stand this long commute to work.

Lillian thought about her father's over-protectiveness, how he worried about her traveling the world someday in case rival mages targeted her, how she had to beg and beg for him to bring her and her sister to Disney World. They eventually did take a road trip down to Orlando, bravely exposing themselves to the masses of tourists without incident. Lillian also had to plead to join a recent class trip to New York City. Convincing her father to sign the permission slip to board the bus was like pulling teeth. And now Dad let her stay in another state without him?

Julius had lived here for most of his life and remained unscathed to this day. Maybe mages of all kinds were especially rare here, and that kept Julius safe. Who knew? Julius was one of her father's favorite people, not to mention the childhood best friend of her deceased mother, and that was why Dad trusted him to host her. But Lillian was still surprised that she didn't even have to ask to come here.

"You'll see that I'm a man of culture," Julius explained. "I have an English room, where we can sit with cups of tea and enjoy clotted cream. In my French room, we can nibble on pastries and quiches. I've got an Italian room and, well, you get the idea. You'll feel like you've stepped into Tuscany."

Even for a bachelor living alone, that sounded like a lot of extra rooms.

Lillian had one of her flashes just then, scattered symbols streaking across her mind's eye that she never could be sure how to interpret. Vines grew visibly fast, their tendrils snapping out, roots pushing and crunching through damp soil. Something was sinister about them. Like the roots were too hungry.

Lillian's father had a couple of theories about these flashes. They could be a symbolic form of mind reading, very hard to interpret. Or they could be little snippets of the future.

As Julius pulled up to a red-brick wall, he punched a combination into a keypad. The iron gate creaked open for the car, and closed behind it. High walls surrounded the property, wrapped in clinging, flowering vines. Julius pulled into a carport under a trellis of wood, twined with vines that eerily resembled Lillian's vision.

They walked down a cobblestone path and past some neatly trimmed rosebushes bearing creamy yellow petals. Honeysuckle added pops of color to the sides of the brick house. Lillian's father grew vegetables and herbs year after year, but Julius was all about flowers, it appeared. Lillian had a lot of labor ahead of her, caring for these plants.

A skinny teenage girl with long brown hair and thundercloud-gray eyes opened the door. Her nose was a sharp point. Lillian could tell from the lower strength of her lavender aura that like most people, this girl had no powers. But the genes ran in her blood, like they did in Evelyn's. Interesting coincidence.

"Hello, Mandy," Julius said. "Have you done all your watering?"

"Yes."

"Very good. This is my cousin Lillian. Mandy, do me a favor. Go straighten the English room. I think we'll have a little tea party."

Obediently, Mandy scurried off. Julius led Lillian into the house. Cats slept peacefully here and there, and the faint scent of cat urine stung Lillian's nose. Either there were too many cats for Julius to keep up with scooping their litter, or they held pissing contests inside the house.

Upstairs, they reached the English room, brightly lit from the afternoon sun streaming in the window. Curio cases of fine china and expensive hand-painted teacups lined the walls. Framed, reproduced portraits of British royalty hung between the cases. Julius directed Mandy to go down to the kitchen to heat a tea kettle.

Once Mandy was out of earshot, Julius lowered his voice. "I want you to understand Mandy has a difficult family situation. She's the youngest child. Her parents lost custody of her because they're drug addicts. Her oldest sister, Jana, is raising her. Jana's a real estate agent. Lately, sales have been dragging and money is a bit tight for them. I'm paying

Mandy and Jana for the help, just like I'm paying you and your father. Figured it was the least I could do."

After a dinner of hot tea and lukewarm, bland soup, Julius showed Lillian the bedroom where she would spend part of her summer, next to his own. A quilt was thrown over the bed. Framed photographs covered the walls, displaying rocky cliffs in Spain, boats on the blue Mediterranean Sea, and vine-covered passageways in France.

"I've got a closet of clothes that I think will fit you," Julius pointed out. "I have a clean toothbrush set up for you in the bathroom across the hall."

"Can I watch *Star Trek*?"

"Sure, but that's the only TV time you'll have during the week. And before you ask, since your father says you like your Nintendo: no, I don't have video games. You'll be kept quite busy, I'm afraid."

Lillian already regretted agreeing to come here. This place did not seem fun. She wished she could be back at home, cozied up on her bean bag in the living room, getting lost in her favorite game, *The Legend of Zelda: Ocarina of Time*.

Lillian and Mandy were both sent to bed much earlier than they would have liked. After crawling into the lumpy, unfamiliar bed, Lillian embraced her blue-nosed long-tongued Stimpy plush, who had spent every night with her since she was little. Lillian's cousin Denny had given her Stimpy for Christmas, even though her father disapproved of that cartoon with its gross-out bathroom humor.

After finally drifting off, Lillian tumbled into a dream that happened every year or two, taking place in a flower-dotted meadow ringed by evergreens. A red fox hid among the pines at the edge, peeking toward her with glowing orange eyes. When she tried to chase the animal, it retreated into the shadows, slyly peeking back out at her. After it stopped hiding so much, the gleaming red creature grew tall, walking on two back legs and reaching out with a human hand to take Lillian's. As she walked through the sunny meadow with her hand in the fox's, she felt safe, warm, and loved, even though she could not see its face.

Early in the morning, a hand jabbed roughly at Lillian's shoulder. Julius hovered over her in a yellow polo shirt and pajama bottoms. He said something about how late in the morning it was—even though the sky was still lavender outside the window, the sun just barely up—and that he'd need to place an alarm clock in this room. Julius urged Lillian to check the closet instead of her suitcase for something to wear.

Lillian had never liked dresses, especially not the flowery ones her dad made her wear on Easter. However, all of the outfits hanging in her closet were dresses. Some of them kitschy and vintage, some of them flat-out hideous.

"Why do I have to wear these?" Lillian asked. "Why can't I just wear my own clothes?"

"Please, humor me and try them on. I need to know that they fit."

Wanting to be polite, as her family had always stressed, Lillian chose at random a red polka-dotted dress with boxy shoulder pads. After changing and brushing her hair and teeth, she followed Julius down the stairs, hungry for breakfast.

The humid green backyard was quite large. Foliage arched over every path. Lillian trailed Julius down one of his cobblestone paths, under hummingbird feeders full of liquid red sugar. In a vision that could be just a flash or simply her imagination, skeletal gray hands slithered out of the dirt to encircle her ankles and drag her down a tunnel of soil. If she ever went to a cemetery or funeral home and broke her father-enforced, code-enforced rules just for fun, would it be like that, slimy like in the B-rated horror movies?

Why was she thinking of this? Was it the cats who'd passed on, buried in the soil beneath her feet in various stages of decomposition? Lillian didn't have to ask to know they were there. Along with something strange, a powerful coldness radiating from some distant corner of the property.

Julius' greenhouse was almost as big as those at the nursery Lillian's father owned. As they looked over the long tables of flowers and vegetables, Julius explained that his automatic drip system was not completely up and running just yet, so he needed Lillian to water these plants.

They started back toward the house, passing by Mandy, already working and digging. Julius set out bowls of fishy-smelling wet food for his cats.

"Heeeere kittykittykitty!" Julius trilled. His voice, otherwise somewhat deep, sounded hilariously annoying when it went up to that high register. Cats came out from the open back door and the bushes to lick at their meal. Fine, itchy cat hairs clung to Lillian as she went inside and sat at the kitchen island. Julius fed her an omelet, protein to carry her through the day.

Lillian looked over the metal refrigerator and freezer doors as she ate. The photos and papers that people pinned up with their magnets always gave interesting hints at their lives.

Julius had put up a brochure for a nearby Episcopalian church, the same denomination her father belonged to. "Do you go to church?" she asked between bites, wondering if Julius was like Dad, going almost every Sunday like clockwork.

"It's been too long since I went. I've just been so swamped, especially after the people I hired for my gardens walked out on me. My cleaning lady stopped coming by, as well. It's an odd thing when the people you are paying don't care to do the job. Once you girls help me to catch up, maybe I'll get back in the habit."

Nearby, held up with a frog magnet, was a snapshot of a bone-thin teenager with carroty red hair, pointy features, and sad-looking eyes ringed heavily with eyeliner. She sat on a narrow pink bed, leaning against a wood-paneled wall.

"Who is that?" Lillian asked, not recognizing the bedroom or the girl.

"Ah... that's my niece Katrina. My sister's daughter. Has anyone told you about her?"

"My dad has mentioned her a couple times, but I don't know much about her." Lillian had also heard vaguely about Theresa, Julius' sister, a drug addict whom Uncle Gerald had practically disowned.

"I find that sad. Katrina is almost seventeen. She is like us, blessed with powers. I highly encourage you to bond with her. You'll be meeting this summer."

Still studying the mixed canvas of the refrigerator, Lillian's eyes landed on a black-and-white picture. A small boy, pale hair in a buzz cut, posed in a striped suit with an older, slightly taller girl with dark hair in ribbon-tied pigtails. The date was printed on the margin: SEP 1966.

"And who's that? Is that..." Lillian figured it out just then. The mother she'd been cheated out of growing up with.

"You guessed it, that's your mother. And that's me when I was five years old. We were best friends as kids. And, just between you and me, she was my first crush. We lived in different cities and had a bit of an age difference, but my father was kind enough to arrange regular playdates. That's what brought our families together, and enabled your parents to eventually meet. Even though Vanessa's mother was, pardon my French, a bit of a controlling bitch. I don't believe you knew that grandmother of yours. When Vanessa was about fourteen and I was about ten or eleven, her mother demanded that we stop seeing each other, as she didn't like her teenage daughter hanging out with a younger boy who had it bad for her. Vanessa and I kept in touch anyway. I asked her out when I was in high school. She rejected me, ended up choosing your father instead. Her death hit me hard."

That evening, Julius provided his two young guests with bratwurst. He was not the fabulous chef he boasted about being, overcooking Lillian's sausage and undercooking Mandy's. The girls put on a polite smile as they forced themselves to chew. Grownups had taught Lillian that playing a pretend game to please others, convincingly donning false expressions and saying phony words, was one of the most important things in life. But why?

Julius set up an alarm clock in Lillian's room to wake her at six, an hour when she didn't care to get up. The days that followed were rigidly scheduled. Before his morning commute, Julius printed complex schedules and left them on the refrigerator for his young helpers, telling them where to water and how much, which plants to stake.

Before starting their days of gardening, Mandy and Lillian put on sunscreen and wide-brimmed, grandmotherly hats. Lillian took her daily printouts in her hand and spent mornings watering in the greenhouse and refilling empty hummingbird feeders. After a quick break to eat sandwiches, she and Mandy tended to their own assigned squares of the outdoor gardens, marked with stakes and a few garden gnomes. Their noses ran and itched from hay fever as honeybees and hummingbirds orbited around their heads. Lillian attempted to befriend Mandy, asking if she'd read any of Isaac Asimov's books. Mandy had never heard of the science fiction author.

Julius let Lillian call home a few times a week. But talking to her father or sister was not the same as being with them. Lillian missed them. She wished she could complain to her father about the ugly dresses Julius insisted she wear, but Julius always hung around within earshot of his kitchen phone, making her scared to get in trouble.

One evening a couple of weeks into Lillian's stay, they had guests for dinner: Julius' sister, Theresa, and niece, Katrina, the girl in the photo on the refrigerator.

When they showed up, Katrina looked just as she did in the picture, clear gray eyes surrounded in dark raccoon makeup, her stringy light red hair held back in hair clips shaped like small butterflies. And Julius was right—she was a necromancer. Katrina's mother, Theresa, was not; just a person with a stronger-than-average aura. This quiet, baggy-eyed cousin smelled of cigarette smoke. Her brown hair, streaked with a few gray threads, hung from a disheveled, tangled ponytail.

They all ate together in an awkward near-silence, with another mediocre home-cooked meal. The usual pleasure of eating was absent. Mandy shuddered and gagged, trying to get her food down. Lillian was not at all a picky eater, sometimes joking that she had the appetite of a garbage disposal, that she'd eat just about anything as long as someone didn't poop on a plate. But Julius' bland, tough-textured meat was a bit much even for her.

After Julius served a dessert of strawberry shortcake, Katrina invited Lillian on a one-on-one walk through the garden as the sun began to set behind orange clouds.

Once they were shrouded in sufficient privacy, Katrina pointed out, "So, we're, like, the same. That's so cool."

"You mean..."

"We're both necromancers."

"Where did you get it from? Your mom's not a necromancer."

"Yeah, I don't think it was from my mom."

"Maybe you got it from your dad. But would that mean there's other necromancers out there?"

"I don't even know who my father is. My mom and grandpa won't tell me, I can't read minds like my grandpa can, and there's no dad on my birth certificate. Maybe my parents were both half-breeds."

"Half-breeds?"

"Yeah, people like my mom and that girl Mandy. You can see it. Weird coincidence that Mandy's not even related to us and she's a half-breed too. Hey, do you ever feel proud of yourself?"

"Umm... not really."

"You should. You've got some serious powers, Lillian. And so do I. It just sucks that we have to hide them. That we have to hide from all the normal people around us, when they should be the ones serving us. We should start to, you know, write to each other. Write letters and emails and stuff after you go back home."

"Okay," Lillian meekly agreed, intimidated by this girl. Something about Katrina put her ill at ease; she didn't know what.

Close to bedtime, after Katrina left with her mother and Mandy retreated to her room downstairs, Julius lingered in Lillian's room to say goodnight. He asked a question seemingly out of nowhere. "I'm assuming you menstruate?"

Words did not come in response to this completely unexpected question.

"I'm only asking because I need to know if I ought to keep supplies around for you."

"Yeah," Lillian finally, shyly nodded.

"How old were you when you had your first time?"

"Umm... eleven." Lillian remembered that winter day in sixth grade. A year later came the worst humiliation of her life, bleeding through her jeans in seventh-grade history class. Until school let out for the summer, Lillian was teased, as if the same thing couldn't just as easily happen to the girls who threw tampons at her and taped maxi pads to her locker while she wished to just sink into the ground and disappear.

"You must have reached your full potential with your powers by now. Just so I know what to buy at the store, do you prefer pads or tampons?"

"Tampons, I guess." Lillian had packed plenty in her luggage. After that mortifying moment at school, she made sure never to be caught unprepared again.

"So you can get them in at your young age. Are you a virgin?"

Red heat came over Lillian's face at the personal turn this already uncomfortable line of questioning was taking. Lillian had never dated, had never been kissed or so much as held hands with a boy, and felt too shy and embarrassed to confess to her friend Adam that she daydreamed about their wedding day.

"Yes," she mumbled.

"I'm sorry if I am weirding you out, but this is something that most people worry about too much and don't talk about enough. I'll bring some stuff home from the store tomorrow. Sleep tight; don't let the bedbugs bite."

After he shut off the light, Lillian put her arms around Stimpy in bed, unable to sleep. She was caught off guard that Julius needed to know so much about her menstrual cycle, when it was a topic that men often avoided, especially with twelve-year-olds. If her father brought it up, he simply asked if he needed to pick up supplies at the store. As a single father, he went to the ex-wife he'd been married to long ago for advice on puberty and bra shopping. And he never, ever asked his kids if they were virgins.

The following week, Julius took Lillian on a road trip to see her mother's grave in Cincinnati, where she was born and raised. Mandy stayed behind to do the chores.

"There was no funeral service," Julius explained during the drive. "Your grandmother wasn't up to planning anything, since losing your child to a murderer is one of the most devastating losses, and she was tight on money. Funerals are expensive. I offered to help pay for a service, as Vanessa meant so much to me, but her mother declined."

At the cemetery, a cast-iron gate opened to soft velvet grass shaded under leafy trees. A few gothic-looking headstones towered over the rest, with most of the more recent headstones barely visible, recessed into the grass with little cups to hold flowers. Faint whitish wraiths and transparent human forms hovered here and there. Ghosts.

"You might feel strange urges," Julius warned as they walked among the graves. "It is best that you ignore them as much as you can. Keep your focus on honoring your mother. However much you might want a mother in your life, don't bring her back. After being gone for almost ten years, she's just bones. Not something you need to see, even if those bones could dig their way out of the coffin."

"I won't. I've never brought anyone... anything... back." Lillian saw no point in resurrecting zombies from six feet under, reuniting with a skeleton, though there had been times of temptation, like those hunting and fishing trips with her other cousin Denny and the day her new puppy passed and her seven-year-old heart shattered.

Julius and Lillian searched up and down a few rows as twinges of surreal feelings arose in Lillian's gut, tempting her toward burial sites. The fresher the bodies, the stronger the emotions got, like an itch. Lillian tried to brush them away.

They found it, one of those little engraved squares sunken and half-hidden, like her mother was not worth noticing. *Vanessa Michelle Christensen. Beloved daughter and mother. November 2, 1957 – January 23, 1993.* Buried beside her, with similar small headstones, were her parents. Lillian's grandfather, George, gone for over forty years, and her grandmother Irina, who had followed her daughter to the grave in 1994 after cardiac complications. Dead from a broken heart, the family believed.

Their cups looked like they had been empty for some time, caked with a bit of dirt and dried-up sand. Julius filled them all with bouquets he'd clipped from his garden.

"I never met Vanessa's father," he said. "He died from a stroke when she was very small. I'll still give him some flowers to make sure he's not forgotten. I bet you don't remember Vanessa. You were quite young when she was taken from us."

"I do remember her."

"Really? That's hard to believe; you were only a few years old, and she'd already run off with that man who killed her."

"She would visit us every few weeks. And I have a pretty decent memory."

"I'll never forget the times we spent together as kids. Vanessa was truly an innocent. I was broken up at her passing. If it's any comfort to you, she's still with us in some form. Remember, we can see ghosts. We're seeing a number of restless ones wandering right now. Energy cannot be created nor destroyed." Julius put an arm around Lillian, pulling her close as she flinched at the unexpected touch. "We should get going soon. I admit that part of the reason I brought you here was to test you. Seems like you have great self-control so far, as you haven't tried anything. However, I am trembling with urges, and my self-control isn't as good."

As they left in a hurry, Lillian noticed a slight shake in Julius' hands. Julius stopped to take calming breaths when they were finally out, glad to be away from the dead, even those buried deep underfoot.

A couple of days later, Julius had company. Mandy's sister, Jana, arrived in the late afternoon in her red minivan after driving down from Michigan. Jana gave Julius a quick half-hug and an air-kiss at his cheek. The girls were given a break from their endless chores to spend time with Jana, a woman as lean and bony as the teenage sister in her custody, all sharp angles. Her aura was strong, like Mandy's. Jana's black hair was cut razor-sharp all one length at her protruding jawbone. Black mascara bordered her cold, steel-gray eyes.

Before dinner, Jana helped herself to a cigarette on the flagstone patio, her hollow cheeks sucking into her teeth when she inhaled. At the nearby umbrella table, Julius relaxed with aged red wine from the special refrigerated drawer in the kitchen.

"Care to have some wine?" Julius asked Mandy and Lillian. "We won't tell on you."

"Yuck," Lillian refused. But Mandy was interested, and Julius poured her a goblet. Afterward, both she and Julius pressured Lillian to down a glass. After gagging down the first alcoholic beverage of her life, dry and sour, Lillian felt a bit tipsy and loose, as if her belly was dully on fire.

"Why didn't your boyfriend come?" Mandy asked Jana.

"I just needed a little break from him. Whatever you do, don't tell him I'm here. I told him I went to visit Jerrisene."

Jerrisene? What an unusual name. It sounded like kerosene. Lillian was never thrilled about her own name, which reminded her of an old lady, but was glad her name wasn't Jerrisene.

"Who is that?" Lillian asked, unable to hold back her curiosity.

"Our sister," Jana quickly explained.

"Why are you lying to him?" Mandy demanded.

"So he wouldn't ask questions. When you grow up someday, you'll understand that having to explain things isn't worth the trouble."

After dinner, the two adolescents were told to go to bed a bit earlier than usual. Lillian was not tired at all, so she put on her headphones, hoping music from her portable CD player would eventually wind her down. While lying awake and restless in the darkness, she could feel the presence of Julius making his way down the hall toward his bedroom, and Mandy's sister following him. Their voices begin to murmur through the wall. Wondering what they were discussing, Lillian took her headphones off to eavesdrop. The words were too muffled to make out.

Julius and Jana went quiet. Lillian didn't hear or feel Jana leaving her cousin's bedroom. Why was Jana sleeping in his room? Didn't she have a boyfriend back home? What would he think?

Other sounds began to filter through the wall. Creak, creak, creak. The springs in the bed squeaked faster and faster. It finally registered in Lillian's mind—Julius and Jana were doing it in the next room. A sound Lillian had never heard before, except in movie and television scenes. Lillian was torn between disgust at that woman getting naked with her cousin, and a bit of shameful curiosity.

The bed stopped squeaking. Lillian's imagination filled in the scene that might be going on next door. The two of them on their backs under a thin sheet, Jana perhaps smoking a cigarette, but not sharing it with Julius the way actors did on screen as he did not smoke. After several minutes, Julius' footsteps shuffled down the hall, and the pipes rattled to life as he showered. He went back to bed and all was silent for the rest of the night.

After great difficulty falling asleep, Lillian found herself in a space that had appeared in dreams all her life: a small desolate graveyard surrounded by dry corn stalks, the caws of winter crows in the distance echoing through the gray sky. Gargoyles crouched over black, mossy stone tombs.

A couple of details had changed. Something glowed behind the doors of two tombs, an unseen voice urging Lillian to choose one. Lying on the ground at her feet was a familiar figure who'd also been in her dreams for as long as she could remember. A man in a ripped T-shirt and worn black jeans, tattoos on his arms and hair in a disheveled black mohawk, face covered in dark stubble. As always, the stranger was dead but still warm, with a handkerchief tightly knotted around his upper arm and a needle in his vein. This syringe couldn't be the first; both of his arms were marred with track marks.

Lillian had never figured out who this man was or why the corpse always appeared to her, starting when she was too young to understand that some people injected drugs into their veins. She walked past the body.

Lillian chose the tomb on the right, and when she opened the heavy door, she spiraled into a gruesome scene—burning buildings with shattered windows, riots in streets running red with blood. From the rooftops, hideous things roared. She woke up with a start, unable to fall back asleep until the pounding of her heart slowed.

The next day, Lillian and Mandy were assigned to a solid schedule of chores while Julius and Jana left the house, not revealing where they were going. Lillian burgeoned with the juicy secret that she could not wait to tell Mandy, but their duties kept them separate all day. By the time Lillian ate her tuna sandwich for lunch, Mandy had already gobbled up hers and gone back outside. Once the adults returned, they all shared a dinner and again the girls were told to go to bed earlier. Lillian overheard Julius' bed rhythmically creaking in the night.

Early the next morning, Jana left, giving her little sister a quick hug goodbye before strolling out to her minivan in her clicking high heels.

The next day, Lillian finally had a chance to speak with Mandy. They worked on rows of tomato plants, crouched down on their grimy knees.

"I have something to tell you," Lillian brought up.

"What's that?"

"Julius is doing it with your sister."

"Really?! Gross!!" Mandy's dirty hands flew up near her face in shock. "But now I know why she spends so much time with him."

"I could hear them in his room."

"Ew! Stop talking! I don't wanna know."

"Doesn't Jana have a boyfriend? Are you going to tell him?"

"I don't think I'll say anything. I don't want to start drama. Let's talk about something else before I upchuck. I'm so over this stupid summer. Last summer was cool. I got to hang out with my friends. But I hate this. I think Julius sees us as slaves."

"I guess so."

"And, like, how he makes us wear these stupid, ugly dresses! I'm so mad at Jana for making me stay with this weirdo just so she can screw around with him."

"How long has Jana known Julius?"

"I don't know. I met him in eighth grade, when he came up to visit us. Then sometimes Jana would be, like, gone for a weekend, and say she was at her friend's. Now I know what she was really doing. Or who. Ugh! I don't want Julius going out with my sister. He has a temper and you just never know about him. Sometimes I catch him, you know, looking at me, and I'm thinking you're not supposed to look at me like that... you're way older than me, you know?"

"I've seen him watching me too. Just staring. You think he's looking at us in a way he's not supposed to?"

"Of course! He's just... ewww."

This affirmed Lillian's suspicions. Julius was possibly a bit of a pervert. For as long as Lillian could remember, he'd been one of the darlings of her family, that nice cousin who wrote the sweet letters, spoke to her for an hour on the phone, and sent expensive presents every Christmas. But this summer she grew increasingly uncomfortable with him. The inappropriate question he'd asked, the way he sometimes stared.

Though as Lillian thought on it, she had doubts. Lillian could never be sure whether such things were intentionally creepy or a clueless accident on a well-meaning person's part. She had the powers of perception that let her see auras and feel the cycles of life and death, but reading the finer points of human behavior had never been a strength of hers. Mandy bringing up that something was not right about Julius added new fuel to Lillian's increasing anxiety.

"I want to go home," Mandy complained, "but my stupid sister won't let me."

"I wish I could go home too, but I'm kind of scared to ask, and I want Julius to pay me so I can get a PS2. Hey, you want to hear something neat?"

"What's that?"

"Did you know that humpback whales don't even eat for most of the year?"

"Uh, I don't really care about humpback whales, but that's kind of cool, I guess."

When the Fourth of July came, Julius took the day off. They had no plans to watch fireworks, just to celebrate Lillian's birthday. Now she officially became a teenager, and her father and sister called with heartfelt birthday wishes. Julius, Mandy, and Lillian baked a cake with a beloved recipe from Lillian's father, layered with crushed candy bars.

Julius' own birthday came a couple of weeks later. He took some more days off, promising his young guests that tomorrow, in celebration, he would take one of them out for a surprise. "Whichever one of you has been the biggest help so far will get to enjoy tomorrow afternoon's treat," he told them over cake and tea. "Which one that is, I'll keep secret until tomorrow. Hopefully this will motivate both of you to take good care of my gardens."

Julius chose Mandy, offering to take her to play miniature golf and then visit a friend of his. He commended Lillian's efforts, but said she was a bit too slow. After weeks of trying her best, this came as a blow to her fragile self-esteem. Lillian was overcome with the all-too-familiar sense of being left out, not being good enough. The shame that hung over her whenever she got picked last for a team in gym class. Walking beside Julius to his car, Mandy kept her head down, not saying anything. They left Lillian behind to finish her chores alone.

They were still gone when she completed her afternoon watering and set the food bowls out for the cats. Most of them gathered eagerly around their dinner, but one stood in the distance, eerily still, like a shadow. The other cats gave it a wide berth, acting fearful at the sight of it.

"Hey, kitty," Lillian called out. "Don't you want your dinner?"

It appeared to twitch, but then stood so motionless that she wondered if it was a statue of a cat instead of a real one. Unlike normal living cats, it displayed no aura.

She approached the thing, which gave off a strangely magnetic vibe she'd felt hints of since her arrival, as well as a putrid smell. The cat's tail was up, its body rigid. Patches of fur were missing. When Lillian knelt down to get a closer look, pieces of its face had fallen away. Its one eye was open and shining, marble-gray. Yellow teeth snarled out of a mutilated mouth.

With a trembling finger, Lillian reached out and gently poked the badly injured cat. It was as cold as a block of ice, marble-hard, and from her touch it tipped over and fell on its side. The tail and head remained up, the legs straight.

Lillian ran into the house, shivering. "It's dead, it's dead," she whispered to herself just as she started to realize what must have happened. Reanimation. Lillian's father strictly forbade her from exercising the power to revive a body, and would not even explain how it worked. Now for the first time, Lillian might have just seen the family secret in practice. She didn't know what to do.

Lillian looked for something in the cluttered house to distract herself. After flipping on the living-room television and finding no shows that interested her, she shut it back off. Lillian got out her notebook and tried to start writing a short story, but could not focus well enough to complete a paragraph.

Julius kept his home computer in the study next to the living room, the slatted doors left open. A marquee screen saver rolled across the screen. Though Mandy had begged for weeks to send instant messages to her friends back home, Julius had not allowed the girls on his computer to play even a single game of solitaire.

The impulse to snoop overtook Lillian now that she was alone. She pried a sleeping cat out of the computer chair and sat down, moving the mouse to reveal the plain green desktop. Julius had the ugliest kind of monitor, which blinked at a slow, eye-straining rate.

Listening for the return of the car, Lillian went into the files, searching for anything interesting. What she looked for, she did not know. Lillian found data and salary spread-sheets for the car dealership. Julius also saved letters he'd typed up, and after glancing at a few boring ones to friends and the kindhearted one he'd sent her for Easter, she found a letter intended for Mandy's sister Jana, dated April of this year. Lillian's stomach turned as her eyes skimmed the fantasies about tying Jana up and smearing whipped cream all over her naked body.

Lillian did not see any pornography. Either Julius didn't have any, or he kept it well-hidden. Mandy believed that Julius liked underage girls too much, but he had scarcely touched Lillian at all. She told herself to stop worrying that her cousin might be a sexual predator. Her fiercely protective father would never let her spend the summer with a man if he had even the slightest suspicion that man was a pedophile. Dad trusted Julius a hundred percent.

Just as Lillian opened a game of Minesweeper to give herself something to do, the car pulled up. She scampered into the living room. Julius came in with Mandy at his side, the extensions of his green aura brushing and swirling all over her. He described their great time going out to eat, playing miniature golf, and even letting Mandy spend time alone with a cute boy she had recently met. A boy? They had lived in isolation all summer; how could Mandy possibly find the opportunity to encounter one?

Now, all of a sudden, Mandy wasn't feeling well. Julius thought she had eaten something bad at lunch, and he sent the quiet, dazed-looking Mandy straight to bed.

Later, Lillian went to change into her pajamas. Julius stomped up the stairs a few minutes later and banged hard on Lillian's door. Red-faced, he threw it open.

"You were messing around on my computer, weren't you? I thought you'd be smarter than that. You knew I'd be able to tell. I could see you'd sat in the chair, and felt your touch on my mouse."

"I'm sorry."

"You'd better be. You should have asked permission!"

"I was just bored."

"Part of growing up is learning to suck it up when you don't have someone entertaining you every second. Do I need to give your father a call?"

"Julius, I promise I won't do it again."

His voice softened. "Okay, I'll let this slide. Stay out of trouble and I won't tell anything to your old man."

"Thanks."

"Holy... what's that?! A spider!" Julius backed away shrieking, and there Lillian saw it, the long-legged creature inching its way up the door jamb.

"Kill it! I hate spiders!" Julius ran to his room and slammed the door.

Instead of smashing the spider, Lillian took it in a cup and compassionately nudged it out the window.

The next day, as they ate their lunch sandwiches, Lillian asked Mandy about her outing with Julius.

"We played miniature golf. It was fun," Mandy said with a shrug.

"What about that boy you spent time with? What's his name?"

"I don't know," Mandy replied between bites of her bologna sandwich. "I don't remember."

"You forgot already? But it was just yesterday!"

"I don't know, but I don't remember seeing a boy, okay? We just did miniature golf and rode in the car. Then I didn't feel so hot."

A couple of days later, Julius took more vacation time and stayed home. He donned a dirt-stained T-shirt and sweatpants, so unlike his usual fancy, rich-guy style. Sweat streaming from his thin coppery hair, he ran between his plants and his flowers. Mandy was out at the edge of the property, watering vines.

"The bird feeders are getting empty," Julius hinted in Lillian's direction as she wolfed down a tuna sandwich for her late lunch in the kitchen.

"So why don't you get moving?" he sighed a few minutes later.

"Doing what?" Lillian asked between bites.

"Refilling the hummingbird feeders like I just said?"

"Oh, okay."

"I used to not believe in ADD, but I think I'm seeing it before my very eyes. Argh."

"Sorry. I'll get on it."

As Julius went back out with gardening tools in hand, Lillian removed some of the sugary stockpiled powder from the labeled bag in the pantry. With a large bucket, she collected the empty plastic hummingbird feeders while greedy little birds dive-bombed her. In the kitchen, she mixed the powder with water and heated it up to turn it into a blood-like suspension, just as Julius had taught her. After cooling the water and filling the feeders, she set about hanging them back up.

As she dangled a feeder from a branch by the greenhouse, something long and thin advanced from behind, as rapid as a striking tree snake. Suddenly, Lillian could not move. An outside entity controlled her muscles with crushing force, keeping them locked in place. She could not part her lips to scream as she took steps that were not her own, shuffling away from the house. Was she having a stroke? Was she possessed?

Lillian's body marched against her will toward the greenhouse, through the door with Julius following her close behind. But he was not touching her; it didn't make sense how she moved like this. She was like a prisoner chained up, rattling frantically against her muscles that were, for the first time ever, not obeying her orders.

Once inside, Lillian's body went down onto the grimy floor of the greenhouse as her mind screamed to get up and run. Julius' shadow fell over her.

One of Lillian's earliest memories, a vignette, took place in an old family friend's indoor swimming pool underneath slanted, green-tinted glass. She was a baby, maybe not even a year old yet, in a little inner tube with a rubber seat inside. Most things didn't have names yet, just stark shapes and colors. The blue water went on and on. Lillian's parents, still together at the time, and her sister were far off, though in reality probably a few feet away. Her petite mother in a pink string bikini, her gray-haired father rising tall over them.

Heeeeere kittykittykitties floated to Lillian's ears from outside the greenhouse, jolting her back into the present. For the past several minutes or so, she had been dazed, frightened. But now she slowly began to shift, back in control of her body. She straightened her crooked glasses. The greenhouse panes hovered overhead, reminding her of that early, much happier memory. The air was thick and wet. Everything had lost its name again, just an overwhelming jumble of objects and sprays of green.

From somewhere outside the greenhouse, Julius called his cats for their meal again in that high-pitched tone. Lillian's whole life became consolidated in her most recent horrible memory on that wet grimy floor, for several minutes unable to move, and then simply afraid to move after the supernatural hold let up.

Lillian raised her head, looking down at her yellow polka-dotted skirt bunched up around her hips. Her mind replayed the scene of him moving it out of the way and pulling her panties down, and them carefully replacing them on her body. Julius' cologne, seeping from his body even on days like today when he wore sweats, mingled with the earthy odor of the soil. The smell of the air, the disheveled dress exposing her legs, made it real. It wasn't a dream.

Lillian sat up as dread tightened in her chest. Lost and dizzy, she could not bring herself to make the littlest sound. Her thoughts nearly ground to a stop as a cold, empty sensation, like outer space, filled her head. She curled into a ball, hugging her knees.

Mandy came inside the greenhouse, and then crouched beside Lillian. "What are you doing in here? I thought it was my turn to water the greenhouse plants."

"Mandy, I... I..."

"Did you, like, fall asleep and wake up here?"

"No," Lillian whispered, finally starting to cry.

"You look like... did he do something to you? Is he drugging us? Sometimes I'll wake up somewhere, super-groggy, and not remember what just happened. And then there's that time he was in my bed, and he kissed me and said to be quiet..."

Lillian just stared at Mandy, who had never before let on that Julius had crawled into bed with her and kissed her. Lillian scratched red welts into her arms with her fingernails.

Lillian sensed Julius coming down the cobblestone path leading to the greenhouse entrance, and she grabbed Mandy's shoulder. When Julius opened the door, they both scrambled backwards away from him like crabs.

"What's got you so worked up?" Julius stepped into the aisle, facing them as they buried their heads in their arms. "Was it... our relationship?"

"Why?" Mandy shouted, her face as red as the garden's ripe tomatoes and wet with salty tears.

"I'm feeding and clothing both of you and paying your families generously. You owed me something in return."

"You drugged us!" Mandy accused.

"Mandy, sometimes I gave you a downer—but Lillian, I forgot to put that in my pocket today; I apologize for that oversight on my part. As for how else I made it easy, it is the family secret. With Mandy here, I am not allowed to say any more. If I did, my father would be very put out with me."

The family secret? Had Julius exercised a power Lillian didn't know they had, one of the things they were forbidden to mention around regular people? It seemed inconceivable right now that such a creature had a father—Uncle Gerald—and like a child, Julius was afraid to anger his parent.

"Lillian," Julius prodded, "you were out, right? At least until I lost my focus... the ability isn't that easy to keep up. You may as well get it over with while you're effectively unconscious."

Lillian looked down. She had seen and felt everything, forcibly awake, immobile, and subjected to all of the tearing, burning pain.

Julius herded them closely into the house. Too afraid to disobey him now, Mandy and Lillian ate dinner in silence in his English room. The past and present monarchs watched from their picture frames as the girls stared down at a pot roast that had been in the slow cooker all day, a recipe that Julius got from Lillian's father, of all people. Even though this was a meal from home, Lillian had absolutely no appetite and did not touch her plate. Neither did Mandy.

After Julius left them alone to take the shower that was part of his evening routine, Mandy whispered, "Go pack your stuff. Quick. We're leaving."

Lillian rushed to her room and grabbed her luggage bag, which held her return plane ticket, some loose change, and the jeans and shorts and T-shirts that Julius had not let her wear all summer. After fetching Stimpy from the bed, Lillian went back downstairs and found Mandy pacing restlessly in the living room, her own bag slung over her shoulder. Lillian wished that she could jump into a hot shower right now and scrub and scrape in a powerful stream of scalding water until her skin was raw and throbbing, and then scrape some more until her muscles were stripped from her bones. Only then could she wash this day down the drain. But first, they had to hurry away while they still had a chance, before Julius finished his shower.

"Where are we going to go?" Lillian quietly asked the teary-eyed Mandy as they headed for the front door.

"I don't know. But we'll find a phone, or take a taxi."

Mandy's words faltered as Julius came downstairs, dressed in nothing but a violet towel around his waist. "Both of you come with me," he ordered. "If either of you tries to leave me, I *will* find you."

Julius dragged the girls up to his own bedroom by their wrists. "If either of you struggles," he threatened, "I'll take possession of you."

Taking possession? This must have been his name for whatever mind trick he used to get Lillian to lie still in the greenhouse—a necromancer talent she didn't know existed? After intimidating both the girls into entering his bedroom, Julius shut the door, asked Mandy to get down on one side of his bed, and physically pushed Lillian down on the side next to his nightstand. He slapped her across the face when she squirmed. Tears gathered in her eyes as she was shocked into silence. Next to her, Mandy lay frozen and quiet as a mouse.

"Now that we have an adult relationship, there are some things I require of you both. You must not tell anyone what we've been doing. Not even family members. They wouldn't understand our intimacy, and likely wouldn't believe you anyway. Lillian, being a writer, you've already got a reputation as quite the storyteller. If you let it slip, I will have no choice but to hurt you to protect us. I have some pets, some very bad, very vicious pets, that I could send after either of you in a heartbeat. They can travel long distances and they will tear you to bits, do you understand? Keeping quiet about our new arrangement is very important. Someday when you both start having children, you'll be grateful to me for getting you used to this."

Eventually, Julius fell asleep on top of his blanket, like a baby or one of his cats in a ray of sun. Lillian beckoned for the wide-awake Mandy on the other side of the bed, and both tiptoed out of the room, anxious that he would wake. Like phantoms, they floated down the stairs and grasped the bags Julius had forced them to drop on the floor earlier. They sped up into a fearful run, bounding toward the gate. Branches hit them in their faces; flowers and juicy stems crunched under their feet.

The gate would not open. Lillian had seen Julius opening it from the inside with the push of a button. Her state of panic muddied her mind as she felt frantically around on the wall, trying and failing to find it. Beside her, Mandy shook like a leaf.

Julius approached from the other side of the trees, draped in shadow, wearing his blue pajamas and sandals. A faintly glowing green snake shot forward into Mandy's skull, spreading through her head. Her arms flapped down against her hips, dead weights.

"You girls think you can get away? Think again!" Julius barked. "Lillian, you look like you've seen a ghost. Didn't your father ever teach you about taking possession?"

Lillian stood, speechless and confused.

"I've gotten decent at it; I can multitask now. It's our most subtle, yet most useful, talent. Your target doesn't know what hit them, and they're all yours, doing everything you want. You could break out of any prison, or even hijack a plane. You could assassinate the President. Just have one of his Secret Service men turn his gun on him, and nobody would know it was you. I don't want this to get ugly. Promise me you won't leave."

Mandy did an almost-jumping-jack, hopping around sideways to face Lillian as Julius remotely controlled her movements. Mandy's clammy hands shot around Lillian's neck, gripping it as she choked and gasped for air.

"I will release you if you come back to the bedroom with me," Julius promised as the pressure tightened. "If you cooperate, this ends now."

His concentration deteriorated then, and his mouth gaped open. "Why, you little..." Julius gasped before going silent.

Lillian brought her focus to a point and aimed it at Julius, with no idea if she was doing it correctly. A long tube she could not see plunged out of her and through the air, a strange new sensation, and reached Julius. Though Lillian had learned of this ability just today, she could manipulate it with shocking ease that blew her away. A claw hooked into Julius, penetrating his neurons and muscles, sliding down through his tissues. Lillian felt the firings of his nerves and the flow of his blood.

Mandy fell away from Lillian, stumbling and confused. Julius stood motionless. Lillian viewed herself out of Julius' eyes as well as her own. Two pairs of eyes, one seeing her with her pale, frightened heart-shaped face and disheveled hair in front of the gate with Mandy, one seeing him in front of the house—this left her terribly disoriented. She had to remind herself that she was in control now. And this gave them a window of opportunity.

"What happened?" Mandy screamed, weakening Lillian's concentration.

"Shhh. Open the gate."

"It's weird... he doesn't look like himself anymore."

"He can't move. Hurry!" Even speaking made Lillian's focus waver, and right now, keeping Julius frozen into a human statue was important.

"I can't find that stupid button for the gate! Darn it, darn it!"

Lillian's grasp on Julius became tenuous with Mandy's nearby frenzy. The fragile string snapped. Julius regained himself, grumbling and pumping his fists. "Flexing your mental muscles for the first time, huh? We are not amused."

"I found it!" Mandy hollered. Just before her dainty finger reached the button, Julius struck fast, taking control over her again. The Mandy who was not Mandy chased Lillian, twitching and jerking abnormally through the grass. Julius curled Mandy's hands into twisted claws that grabbed at Lillian's dress. She wrenched away from Mandy and bounded through the dewy grass as fast as she could, sucking in an insect and coughing. Wildly, she ran into the house and slammed the door shut. Before she could lock it, the puppet that was Mandy threw it back open, thrashing at her. She pursued Lillian into the kitchen, groping unsuccessfully for the knife drawer. Lillian scraped her way out of the kitchen and through the living room, tripping and skidding her knees across the floor, rubbing them raw on the wood. She got up and dashed into the backyard as the remotely controlled Mandy still tore around within, searching blindly.

Nearby, plants grew visibly fast as Lillian reached out to them with her mind and prayed that it would do something, anything, to stop Julius. She could not tell exactly where he was right now, or else she'd possess him again. The green cells split and elongated as the roots ripped through the soil, leaves unfurling and twisting. Lillian crept around the side of the house, fixing to sneak up on Julius and act before he could. He lost his grip on Mandy, who ran back to Lillian's side, sobbing.

Through her intense trembling, Lillian pressed the button. The gate finally opened, squealing slowly. Waiting for it to open wide enough to pass through was like an eternity.

Behind them, Julius squirmed in his green prison of Lillian's making. Tree branches reached out to hold him, and so did vines, clamping themselves around him like handcuffs. Grass wove itself all over his legs and feet in a net. The blood drained from his horrified face as spiders began to crawl up his legs.

His two young hostages rushed through the gate.

Too exhausted to continue running, Lillian and Mandy walked down the side of the dimly lit road, panting, both of them looking over their shoulders. For a long time, Lillian was too stunned to speak, her nerves still on fire from the escape, her head still spinning from these powers she hadn't known about until tonight.

Mandy was the first to say something, while Lillian struggled to listen to her plan through a fog of distress. "You don't have a cell phone, right? Neither do I. We need to find a pay phone or go to somebody's house where they'll let us use their phone. I'll call Jana, you'll call your dad or whoever, and we'll ask them to come get us. If anybody asks why, we'll just say that we had some stupid fight with Julius, he lost his temper, and he kicked us out. Don't say any more than that."

"Why do we have to say that?" Lillian asked, glancing over her shoulder yet again. She was ashamed and horrified at the thought of telling anyone the whole truth, not to mention fearful of Julius following through on his threats, but the extent of Mandy's proposed lies confused her.

"I don't want anybody to know what he did to us. If Jana found out, she'd call me a slut."

"Why would she say that?"

"I bet she won't even believe me. She never believes me. My other sister got date raped, and Jana said it was her fault 'cause she went to a party wearing a short skirt and got drunk. I don't want to get yelled at about how this shit is my fault."

"Jana sounds like a bitch. But I don't know... was this our fault? Did we flirt with him or something?"

"I don't know. We should have run away as soon as we figured he was a creep. But we let this happen," Mandy said with a shrug.

"He said he'll kill us if we tell anyone," Lillian added in a meek voice.

"Yeah, and he knows where I live."

"And where I live."

"We just have to lie. We have to take this to our graves, you understand?"

"Yeah."

"My period's late," Mandy confided in a tight, nervous tone. "I'm getting scared. I hope to God I'm not pregnant."

"I hope not too."

A new round of fear sank like a rock in Lillian's stomach. What if *she* was now pregnant? It could happen; a fellow seventh-grader at school had a baby in the spring. She could barely wrap her mind around that nightmarish thought.

They spotted a house with lights on in the windows.

"We've got to stop crying," Mandy urged. "Look calm, and we'll go ring the doorbell."

After the two of them wiped their eyes and took some deep breaths, Mandy rang the doorbell and waited restlessly. A heavyset woman in a faded pink bathrobe opened the door.

"What do you want?" she asked, staring past and around the two girls. Behind her, a colossal television was turned up to a near-deafening volume. She pointed with the remote and hit the mute button.

"We're in trouble," Mandy told the woman in a breathy voice. "We have to get away from the guy down the road."

"Which one?"

"Julius," Lillian told her.

"That one who runs that fancy car dealership?"

"Yes."

"Oh, I hardly know him. He's a strange one, keeps to himself. What were you doing at his house?"

"I'm his friend's sister," said Mandy, "and she's his little cousin, and we were staying with him. We had an argument." Her speech devolved into a mumble.

"How old are the two of you?"

"I'm fifteen, and she's, um, she just turned thirteen."

"Oh, my goodness, you kids are so young. Has he been hitting you?"

"No."

"Did he... interfere with you at all?"

"No."

"Well, come in. I'm Mamie. Gosh, you two look so scared. Must've been a bad fight you had with the neighbor. You want me to call the police?"

"No, no, don't call the cops!" Mandy begged. "It wasn't like that!"

"You're sure?"

"Yeah. It was just a fight and he kicked us out. But can I just call my sister? I can make her come get us, but it'll be a long drive."

Mamie shut the door behind the girls, locking and bolting it, though that did not make Lillian feel any safer. She knew very well that locks did not always stop a mage with the telekinesis they were all blessed with or even a non-mage with a little bit of knowledge about picking locks. If he broke free of the plants and spiders in time, Julius could simply follow their aura trails here, especially Lillian's like a line of faint green fire. She wished she and Mandy could both grow wings and just fly away.

"Jana, come get us now! Or buy us a plane ticket!" Mandy demanded over the phone, wiping her nose as she paced, her eyes pink. "I know it's late… what do you mean, Jerrisene can't come? Okay, I'm sorry! I don't know about trains! What about the bus? So Tyler's coming to get me? Okay, then. Thanks, Jana! I love you!"

Mandy clarified the plan after hanging up. Her sister, Jana, claimed to be too busy to pick her up. Jana's boyfriend, Tyler, was assigned the chore of driving down here to fetch Mandy, and only Mandy, tomorrow. Jana did not want to be responsible for Lillian. For finding a ride, she was on her own. Besides Julius, Lillian knew of no nearby living relatives except for his niece and sister, too closely aligned with him.

"Can you guys drive me somewhere?" Lillian asked Mamie.

"Oh, we won't be able to take you anywhere tonight. I had some beers and my husband can't drive because of his medical condition. Where are you from? Not from around here, are you?"

"I'm from Maryland. I was just here for the summer."

"Oh, goodness, both of you are from out of state? Call your parents. You need to get back home, kid. You're far too young to be running around on your own and I'm not too comfortable getting involved in this. We can let you stay a night or two, and that's it."

Lillian dialed her home phone number, though she did not want to talk to anyone about this day. Evelyn answered. "What are you doing calling so late?"

"I need to come home."

"Why?"

"Um… me and Mandy and Julius had a fight, and we, uh… we left his house."

"Left his house? In the middle of the night?! Where are you staying?"

"With some nice people who live down the road. Can you come get me?"

"Come get you?! Look, you're in the middle of Ohio. That's a long drive."

"But it was a big fight. Can I speak to Dad?"

"He went to bed early because he has a cold, and I'm not about to wake him. Not for something like this."

"But..."

"Just be a big girl and go back to Julius' house. Talk things over with him instead of being immature and running away. And you definitely owe him an apology because I'm sure he's worried sick." Evelyn hung up.

As they got ready for bed, Mandy snapped at Lillian for forgetting to tell Evelyn the version the story in which Julius actively threw them out. But Lillian's head was too mixed up to keep a fiction straight right now.

During the hot shower Lillian finally got to take, she anxiously scrubbed away the blood and other fluid she didn't want to think about that had dried on her legs. She scraped and scratched until her skin turned bright red, imagining holding one of the long skinny brushes used for scrubbing out beakers and test tubes in science class. Lillian wanted to cover one in bleach and then put it up inside her until every last trace was gone, until she had no guts anymore and was left hollow.

After Lillian dressed in the pajamas she'd packed in her bag, Ed and Mamie went to bed. Lillian's sense of fear and vulnerability increased exponentially as they shut off the lights in the main area of the house.

Outside, the aura trails would remain down the road for some time, as incriminating as footprints in snow until they faded. Sleep was almost impossible as Lillian laid on a soft mattress in a room that had once belonged to a high school cheerleader who was now grown up, full of ribbons and flags and pom-poms. Glow-in-the-dark sticky stars turned the ceiling into a night sky, the same way Lillian had decorated her bedroom ceiling back home. Every time a breeze rattled a tree branch outside, or something creaked or snapped inside the house, her entire body stiffened. When she finally managed to drift off in her exhaustion, she tumbled headlong into a disjointed world of nightmares.

Lillian could not be sure if she was asleep or awake when she found herself walking on bare feet through the dark house. Her glasses were back on. The luggage bag she had escaped with was once again slung over her shoulder. Disoriented, Lillian tried to bring her hands up to her face to rub her eyes. But she couldn't even do that, much less change direction back to the bedroom.

Lillian was trapped, the same force that had led her into the greenhouse now controlling her body again. Like appendages belonging to someone else, her feet carried her through the open front door.

Lillian crossed the painfully rocky path on the front lawn, out to the street. Like a puppet, her body was turned, headed toward the BMW parked deep in the shadows. Even without the wisps of green aura waving nearby, she would have recognized that car immediately. Her heart pounded and her stomach lurched with nausea.

Just before getting into the car, her body stopped, and the force controlling it pulled out of her. Before Lillian could move of her own volition, a sharp cool edge pressed against her throat. The dreadfully familiar voice whispered into her ear. "Don't move. Don't make a sound. If you scream, you're dead. Do you understand me? Nod if you understand."

Eyes pooling with hot tears, Lillian nodded.

"Don't you dare take possession of me again, or pull any tricks with plants or spiders," Julius whispered. "I've been up all night and I'm not in a good mood. I won't make the mistake of letting my guard down again. Did you tell these people what we did?"

"I... I..."

The knife lifted off her throat, immediately replaced by both of his hands wrapped around her neck. "Did you or did you not tell the Roths?"

Lillian shook her head no as far as his grip allowed, gasping for air.

"Now we are going to close the Roths' front door before they call me in the morning, complaining that you carelessly left it open and their dog or cat or parakeet escaped. Then we are going to walk back to the car. Don't you try anything." Keeping Lillian's wrist in a painful iron grip and brandishing his knife in warning with the other hand, leaving her too scared to scream after he let go of her throat, they trudged back to the door. And then once it was shut, back to his car.

"Get in," Julius ordered. "If you try anything crazy, like opening the car door and jumping out, I'll take possession of you before you even hit the ground. Don't make me do that."

Defeated, Lillian slumped into the passenger seat, all of her progress to escape now in retrograde as Julius started the drive back to the house. Every house she had walked past hours earlier was a signpost of increasing hopelessness. And Mandy was nowhere to be seen. Was she okay? Had Julius recaptured her too?

"I... I just want to go home," Lillian stammered, eyes filling with tears.

"And you will. You've just got to be kind to me until your departure date."

"I—I promise, I won't tell anyone, I swear, I just…"

"Do as I say and this will be easy for you."

Soon she heard the familiar creak of his gate as they pulled into the carport. The sun just started to turn the horizon orange as her passive, limp body was led back into his house, back into his bed. Again, she was warned not to move.

A while later, after most of the rest of the world around their isolated island of greenery had woken up, Julius sat at the edge of the bed, dialing a number on his cell phone.

"Yes, hello, is this Mrs. Mamie Roth? Hi, it's your neighbor Julius. Yes, yes, yes. She decided to come back. Don't be alarmed. I don't know why she ran off in the middle of the night like that. She decided to make amends with me. Don't listen to what those girls say. Everything is under control. The other girl, Mandy, just has out for me because I didn't let her get her way. Just call me if you have any questions. Oh, Mandy has a ride back home? Phew. What a relief. She left some of her things here—please let her know I'll ship them to her house. Yeah, I have her address. You have a beautiful day, Mrs. Roth."

Lillian waited all day for Julius to drive back to the neighbors' home and search for Mandy, in case her sister's boyfriend hadn't shown up yet. Instead, he stayed home, making his employees work overtime and blaming his absence on a "family emergency."

Julius followed Lillian closely, supervising her chores as she did them in silence. To deny Lillian the time or privacy to plot another escape, he insisted on eating each meal together, and then showering together that evening. Lillian stood in a tiled corner, facing away from Julius and squeezing her eyes shut, though his wandering soapy hands made it impossible to ignore him completely.

That day blended into the next. Julius coerced Lillian to drink multiple goblets of wine during each dinner. At bedtime, he ordered her to do things she never thought she would do until she was much older and married, if ever. To endure it, Lillian kept her eyes shut and did all she could to not be here, with this man sweating on her. She made believe that she was a ghost leaving her earthly body and put herself high on an imaginary mountain, counting the trees and then every needle on every pine and fir bough.

On the third evening after Lillian's return, Julius' teenage niece Katrina came over for another visit. Rather than accompanying her mother, she took her own car. Throughout their shared dinner, Katrina was chipper, talking a mile a minute, like Lillian was her long-lost best friend. It thrilled Katrina to freely speak about "necromancer stuff" without her mother or Mandy around.

"Tomorrow, he's going to show you something amazing," Katrina informed Lillian. "Something really cool that's out of this world!"

"That's right," Julius nodded, smiling. "I've got big plans for us. I won't tell you just yet, because I've gathered that your father has withheld a lot of information from you, and you'll have to see it to believe it. I don't want to spoil the surprise."

"Aren't you the least bit curious?" Katrina prodded Lillian, poking at her shoulder as she sat quietly in her chair, her body tight and closed in. "The least bit excited?"

"Yeah, sure." Lillian put on a fake smile. Forced some more of the bland casserole down so that they wouldn't ask where her appetite had gone.

"I really wish I could be there, man," Katrina sighed. "I always love to see it happen. But I just got a job at the mall. I have to work tomorrow."

After Katrina left and they went to bed, Lillian waited for Julius to fall asleep, snoring with his paw on her bare stomach. She got ready to possess him, hoping that in his unconscious state he would never know what hit him, giving her a chance to leave for good. But somehow Julius felt her flinching, or sensed the gears changing in her mind, and within seconds his eyes fluttered awake. He grabbed her wrists and pinned her down, his heavy weight on top suffocating her. "You'd better not be planning anything," Julius snarled into her ear, "or else you won't be going home."

Terrified to move so much as an inch again, Lillian laid awake until the sun came up. By now, she was leaden with exhaustion.

After they ate some quick bagels for breakfast, Julius took Lillian back to the greenhouse for the thrilling event Katrina had tried to build anticipation for last night.

"As you probably know, we have the power to make any creature do our bidding, living or dead," he explained, squatting down between two tables of vegetable plants. "You've already tried the former when you knew damn well that you weren't supposed to, but I must teach you to do the latter. Your father never schooled you in it, correct?"

Lillian nodded, looking down and refusing to see his face.

"And neither did our cousin Denny? I know you hang out with him a lot."

"Nope." Denny had promised to help Lillian practice some telekinesis tricks when she got a bit older. But he had warned her away from trying "zombie shit" on her own, saying it was hazardous.

"Well, today, you'll be practicing on Boots. Bootsie, won't you come say hi?"

A cat moved, as robotically as Mandy did under Julius' control, and shuffled in their direction. It was still decomposing, its teeth glinting, an ear wilted. A piece of its leg was gone. Lillian remembered that cat.

"It's simple. Simpler than manipulating a live human. You don't even really have to focus your energies. All you must do is look at Boots in front of you and think about what you want her to do. And she will do it. Bringing a corpse back isn't hard either; it's much the same. You just have to think about the dead creature moving once again. And it will respond to your will."

Lillian's mind fragmented into scared little pieces. This was so taboo, so against the rules. Boots stood as eerily still as the day Lillian first laid eyes on her. Lillian willed the cat to turn away, to stop looking at them with that one eye. A few seconds later, the cat twisted sideways like a mechanical toy until her tail end faced them.

"Good job! Now there is something we don't do, not until the time is right," Julius continued. "After being reanimated, any creature, including a human being, is going to be just like her. A pet. A robot awaiting our orders. But with another power of ours, and a little help from a friend, we can turn them into efficient killing machines."

"Dad... Dad never told me about this." Lillian was petrified—of herself, of Julius, of Boots, of everything. Cloudy with tears, her eyes stared back down at the ground.

"That's a shame that your father kept so much from you. I believe he is a bit too overbearing, yet he also does not trust you. Did you know that? You make him uncomfortable, because he knows what you can do."

Did Lillian's father not love her as much as he loved his firstborn, the one who'd turned out normal? Was Julius right that Lillian put Dad ill at ease? Was that why he didn't tell her things?

"I have something else to show you. I'd rather be doing it at night, but there are so many trees around us that we won't be seen. Let's come inside for a brief moment first."

Her spirit broken, Lillian obediently followed Julius into the house. He reached into a closet and took out a rifle she hadn't known he owned, as well as a manila envelope. After they went back out, Julius had Boots walk out of the greenhouse. The cat stood rigid in the grass.

"Watch and listen carefully," Julius instructed, setting his gun down, pulling a yellowed old paper and a small glass tube of dark dried flakes out of the envelope. "You are about to learn the crown jewel of our abilities. Don't try this at home unless you either have a strong firearm in hand or you are absolutely certain that the time is right. Today, I will turn Boots into a higher form. This isn't as simple as dealing with a mindless zombie. We require a little... outside help. Our ancestors all knew how to summon the help, and they knew how to control the higher forms. But over the generations, we've lost a lot of our skills. We forgot how to control the creatures' every move. But the spell on this paper and the recipe for these herbs survived, hidden away by our ancestors. My father found it in a locked box and gave it to me. I will give you your own copy when you're older."

Something in Lillian's belly screamed that this was dangerously wrong as Julius walked around the undead cat, sprinkling the mixture of dried leaves and possibly some type of mineral out of the glass tube onto the ground. Once the cat was enclosed in the circle, Julius stood back, paper in hand, and began to chant in a language Lillian had never heard. Latin? Or was it something more guttural, more primitive? He slid out his green mind extension toward the cat, closing his eyes to sound out commands to himself, muttering them under his breath.

Sulfur-smelling wisps rose from the ground, like a rotten egg cracked open. The circle began to glow a faint red as a snarl resonated through the air. A semi-transparent, faceless horned being rose up from the grass, through the cat. Sinking into its body.

"What is that?!" Lillian gasped, too scared to speak above a whisper. "Is that a... a... demon?"

"Shh," Julius quieted her, handing her a pair of foam earplugs. "Put these in."

After inserting his own earplugs, Julius raised the gun, finger on the trigger. Transfixed, Lillian watched Boots change.

The cat began to struggle and wiggle, like a person slithering out of a tight leotard. Its skin trickled with cold violet blood as it split open down the back. The teeth lengthened into sharp razors like a barracuda's as the jaw expanded. The writhing cat grew to the size of a bobcat, fur falling out as it became unrecognizable. The little toes expanded into skeletal hideous red fingers, and the claws thickened into wide gray blades.

The skin peeled away, dividing over the marble of decaying muscle and bits of bone underneath. Some sharp bony projections grew upwards, out of the shoulders. The mouth, now long and nasty, parted its jagged rows of barracuda fangs to let out a high screech. Lillian protectively clamped her hands over her ears, even with the earplugs in. She had seen things like this before in her worst nightmares, and here she was, watching such a monster come alive for the first time. The creature crouched its hind legs, ready to pounce.

Julius fired his rifle, stopping the thing before it charged at them. It jerked, still mindlessly moving. He fired another round. Blood exploded in a thin cloud out of the creature's back, and it fell into a glistening pinkish heap.

Lillian tore out her earplugs and turned away to throw up. Julius put the gun down and put an arm around Lillian. Wiping her mouth, she shrunk away from him.

"My dear," Julius said softly, "take deep breaths. It's dead. There is nothing to be afraid of."

"It's... it's so gross. It's horrible!"

"It may not be pretty to look at, but it's where so much of our power lies. The mages with fire powers can conjure up their hell-hounds, but they only last a few minutes at most before the power weakens and the creatures dissipate. However, our creatures can last indefinitely. And God help anyone who gets bitten by one. We're immune, but anyone else will turn into a very similar creature in about twenty-four hours. Now do you see why the other mages have feared us for centuries? They almost completely killed us off because they wanted to stop such a thing from ever happening. But we cannot be stopped."

Lillian wished more than ever to be normal, to be innocent, and to have no idea that these mutants even existed, much less that she and her family—even her beloved father—could make such ugly things. Julius turned, his arm sliding off her, his sweaty yet perfumed smell drawing away. He kept the rifle lowered.

Lillian thought she saw the creature squirming in the grass. She screamed, turned, and ran inside as another gunshot cracked through the air.

As she rushed past the kitchen, a cold presence came up from behind, along with a slight squelching sound. She turned cautiously and there it was, that pinkish meaty enlarged thing with the fangs. It hobbled toward her, snarling a silent show of teeth as she backed away, terrified.

The thing cornered Lillian into the kitchen, staring her down with its empty eye. She was too frightened to turn away and run a second time, in case she enticed the monstrosity to chase her. Even if she was immune to whatever zombie disease the mutant carried, it still had a set of sharp fangs that could slice any person clean open.

Lillian kept her body as frozen as possible, holding back the violent trembling that threatened to overtake her. With her telekinesis, Lillian reached toward the nearby wooden knife block and slid out the biggest, most menacing butcher knife. After it floated through the air, she wrapped her shaky fingers around the handle, never taking her eyes off the creature.

The thing leaped at her from two strong hind legs, lunging through the air, snapping its jaws, flying straight at her throat. Scared she did not have enough time to use the knife, Lillian tried to turn and run, only to slip and fall. Her palms slapped onto the polished gray floor and her breath was knocked out for an instant. The knife slid away, out of her reach. She struggled, trying to get back up, heart hammering so hard that it hurt and burned behind her ribs. She grabbed the edge of the stovetop to support herself back to standing.

Julius was nearby, standing still—she could not see him, but she felt him. Why wasn't he doing anything? Did he still have that gun?

Earlier, Julius had cooked omelets for breakfast in the greasy cast iron skillet that still rested on the stovetop. Lillian picked up the heavy black skillet, raising it protectively in front of herself. The monster crept along the kitchen counter, leaving little smears of blood from the ragged bullet holes in its body. It crouched again, and in its position was a vestige of the small furry cat it used to be. It hissed, and then a loud bang echoed through the house. Jumping at the gunshot, Lillian almost dropped the skillet.

The thing collapsed as Julius stood in the kitchen doorway, the rifle still trained on it. "There, that should take care of it. I apologize for that little scare. These beasts are hard to kill."

This was just a "little scare" to him? Shaking violently, Lillian put the skillet back on the stove. Julius fetched a garbage bag and wrapped up the foul-smelling mutation. He asked for Lillian's assistance dragging it back outside. They both sat and watched to be sure the trash bag did not stir.

"Like I've warned you, I don't want you trying this at home," Julius repeated. "Not until you're older; not until it's time. And today you saw why."

Lillian shook her head. "I'm not trying that ever."

"You will, dear. You will. It may be a shock; it may seem disgusting; but look at the sheer volume of the power you can harness. One of these days, it will be simply irresistible."

Nope, Lillian thought firmly to herself.

After the sun went down, Julius took matches and lighter fluid to the dead creature and set it ablaze in the middle of his back yard, just as Lillian's father had burned her puppy's virus-tainted bed, blankets, and toys on a sad day that now seemed eons ago. The greasy black smoke fouled the air with an awful smell.

The next morning, it was time for Lillian to go home. As they pulled through the gate, this didn't seem real, Julius voluntarily letting Lillian leave. Taking her on the first leg of the journey home.

Julius was quiet during most of the drive into the city, but as he took the turnoff to the airport, he gave her a stern reminder. "Remember, our adult relationship is no one else's business. If you tell anyone else, I will have no choice but to put an end to things—permanently—for you and that person. Please don't force me to make that choice."

Julius accompanied Lillian right up to the security line. "I love you!" he called as he walked away, waving goodbye and blowing a kiss. "I hope to see you next summer!"

After getting on the plane, Lillian made a vow to herself as she sipped from a plastic cup of 7-Up, sparkling in the warm sunlight from the oval window. She decided it was the safest way, particularly after Julius' threats to kill her if she told. Lillian decided to lock this whole summer, this terrible dirty secret, away forever. If she could set it on fire and float it out to sea, she would. It would never be mentioned again, never thought of again. Lillian would reclaim her old life, wiping this summer the way one wiped a hard drive to install a new operating system, and from today onward, she would never think about it. No one could know, not her father or sister or cousin Denny, not her future husband who would probably divorce her if he knew she'd been soiled.

Lillian had always pictured sex as a far-off thing in the future, something to gently explore on her wedding night if she ever got married, in a cozy bed scattered with rose petals and surrounded by lit candles. At a religiously-influenced summer camp last year, her camp counselor had encouraged all of the children to save themselves for marriage, as no man would want a woman who'd sullied herself with premarital intercourse. The staff preached that you were not just sleeping with your sexual partner, but everyone else they'd ever slept with. By this standard, Lillian was intimate with Jana and heaven knew who else, a thought that made her want to vomit. The counselor had dotted the girls' arms with a marker to demonstrate that the more times you'd had sex, or the more people you'd done it with, the more stains it left on your body and soul that would never wash off like the ink eventually did.

Now that future joy of bringing a virginal body to her wedding, discovering lovemaking for the very first time after the ceremony, had been taken away. Lillian had occasionally imagined her wedding day, sometimes with a grown-up version of Adam, her friend and crush, as the groom. There was no way Adam, or any other guy, would want to marry her now, not if he knew what happened. The things she'd had to do. She felt damaged and defiled now, but if she split the secret off from the rest of herself, she just might restore an illusion of purity again.

Excerpt from The Autobiography of Gerald Frazier: Architect of a New World

When I started school, it hit me like a sledgehammer. Though my sister Sarah tried to prepare me, she couldn't. No one could have!

For a five-year-old who could read minds, sitting in a classroom full of small children wasn't just noisy. It was also mentally overloading. I hadn't yet figured out how to filter or ignore thoughts, so they assaulted my head day in and day out, like a conglomeration of radio stations with multiple people yapping at the same time.

During the first couple of years, I was a poor student, too overloaded to learn my reading, writing, and 'rithmetic. My teachers came to the conclusion that I was slow and wouldn't amount to much. Little did they know that I'd be near the top of the class when I graduated from high school! By then, I found it ridiculously easy to ace final exams without studying. All I had to do was scan my teachers' heads for the answers while they sat at their desks and my fellow students broke into a fearful sweat all around me. If I was less lazy about turning in assignments, I could have been valedictorian.

My first and second grade teachers wouldn't have guessed it, but like most mages, I have a very high IQ. I have the theory that necromancers and other mages possess more neurons to facilitate our powers. Many years later I did an under-the-table study with a little help from a doctor friend, performing MRIs on myself, my son Julius, and my granddaughter Katrina. All three of us had unusually thick white matter. My doctor friend said he'd never seen anything like it, and he'd stared at hundreds of brain scans. Not knowing the true reason behind my study, he couldn't explain it. I believe this deserves wider study, and it's further evidence that mages are more evolved than the rest of the human race!

In my early childhood, our natural brilliance did not make itself known in my schoolwork. I started throwing tantrums in the classroom. The other children made fun of me for being a crybaby.

It took continued exposure and experience to stop feeling so miserable, and to get a handle on my tantrums. By third grade, I was only having about one breakdown per month. Still, my classmates considered me ill-tempered. My sister Sarah and I were both teased for our red hair and our weight. Unlike our two beanpole siblings, we were the fat kids. The teasing truly got under Sarah's skin. But I never let myself forget that Sarah and I were superior to these ordinary, less intelligent children who didn't know we existed as we hid in plain sight! I learned quickly to harden myself.

Hard Times

After giving Lillian a ride from the airport and pulling up to their home, Evelyn stepped out of her car, sneezing furiously and itching with the beginnings of hives. Lillian wore a pink sundress, the type of thing she usually resisted putting on, and stayed quiet as Evelyn ran inside and straight for the shower, anxious to wash off the cat dander that lingered from Julius' house.

Lillian had grown a couple of inches just in the time she was away. Lou wished now that the visit with his nephew hadn't lasted all those weeks, guilty that he'd missed Lillian's birthday and had to set aside the gifts he'd gotten for her return. He hugged his daughter and then let go as her body went stiff as a board. Lou felt a little hurt, accustomed to her being a daddy's girl who liked to embrace him, but she was officially a teenager now. It was only natural for kids her age to push parents away.

Julius had called a couple of times to complain of difficult behavior. It was nothing major, yet it caught Lou off guard to hear of his happy, obedient daughter acting out. Normally, she followed rules to a T. Lou decided to broach the subject with her gently.

"Did you have a good time with your cousin?" he asked Lillian. "I sure missed you."

"You did?"

"Yes, of course I did! It was an awfully long time to have you gone. Too long. Julius did tell me that you gave him a little trouble. Is that true?"

"I guess."

"Is there something that we need to talk about? Are you maybe going through some rebellion right now?"

"What did he say I did?"

"He didn't go into specifics; he just said something about you getting onto his computer without permission, and sneaking out. I told him, 'Are you sure we're talking about the same kid?'"

"I guess that happened, yeah."

"Wasn't there another girl there with you? Julius mentioned something about her sneaking out too. Do you suppose she was a bad influence?"

"Maybe; I don't know."

"Just remember that it's impolite to go through someone's things without permission. And just because another kid is doing something that seems cool, it doesn't always make it right. Other than those little bumps in the road, Julius sounded pleased with the help. He says the check is already on the way. And just out of curiosity, why are you wearing that dress? I've never seen it before."

Lillian shrugged slightly. "Julius made me."

"Huh, that's odd. Does the dress belong to him?"

"Yes."

"I'll mail it back to him. I also need to give you your overdue birthday presents."

"First, can I take a shower?"

"Of course."

As soon as Evelyn finished washing the cat dander off, Lillian ran straight for the shower, not waiting for the hot water to refill the way she normally would have. After she changed into a tank top and cutoff shorts, Lou found the pink dress crumpled in a corner of her bedroom. He picked it up to put it in the wash.

As the days went by, Lillian seemed a little down, a little quiet. "Are you missing Julius?" Lou gently prodded over breakfast one morning.

"Yeah... I guess."

A couple of years ago, when puberty set in, Lillian had difficulty adjusting to the increased personal hygiene demands of a growing body. Lou had to remind her to shower more often, not wanting her to suffer embarrassment at school, and sometimes she forgot to put on deodorant. But now the pendulum swung the other way. The water bill went up as Lillian showered every day, sometimes twice a day. She brushed her teeth over and over, scrubbing her tongue to the point of drawing blood. Her over-washed skin dried out until it developed rough patches. Lou grew a bit concerned. Could she be developing obsessive-compulsive disorder?

One day, Lou brought Lillian to his nursery to assist him. She began watering the plants in one of his three greenhouses. As Lou organized his inventory of fertilizer and seeds in his main store, he spotted Lillian through the window, running frantically out of the greenhouse and into the parking lot.

Lou rushed outside to find Lillian on the ground, kneeling down and hanging her head, breathing hard.

"What's wrong?" he asked, crouching beside her. "Are you hurt? Did something happen?"

Lillian did not answer. When he put a hand on her shoulder, she flinched away as though he'd just hit her.

"I... I'm not feeling good," Lillian whispered at last. "I'm nauseous. I think I have a stomach bug."

"I'll take you home. You rest so you'll be healthy enough to start eighth grade."

In the days that followed, Lillian seemed recovered, but still withdrawn. Lou's nephew Denny privately pointed out after a shared family dinner that Lillian had "lost some of her pep." In Lou's opinion, this slight shift in her personality was nothing out of the ordinary. Lillian had always been a happy young optimist, excitedly engaged in the world around her, chattering her family's ears off with science facts or the latest book she'd read. She would occasionally come home crying from school after being picked on, but bounced back and smiled again.

Now Lillian had metamorphosed into a sullen teenager who wouldn't hug her beloved father anymore. But that was just what kids her age did. At thirteen, Evelyn became a terror, yelling, sassy, slamming doors. Any parent of a teenager would tell you that they were moody balls of hormonal rage, writing off their parents as dorky embarrassments. A sixty-three-year-old homebody who liked world music, easy listening, and history books, Lou was the first to admit that he was dorkier than most dads of teenagers.

Lillian could not stop wondering what had ultimately happened to Mandy, her companion at Julius' house. More and more, she longed to speak to Mandy, the only one who would understand their shared ordeal. And she hoped that Mandy wasn't pregnant. When Lillian's time of the month happened shortly after her return home, it came as a huge sigh of relief. With any luck, Mandy had gotten the same reassurance.

One afternoon, while home alone, Lillian went to her father's small study and dialed up to the internet, searching phone directories on the old, dim, blinking monitor. She found a Jana Kreider in Ann Arbor, Michigan. Mandy's hometown. Even though phone calls intimidated her a bit, Lillian wrote down the area code and number, logged off, and grabbed the phone from the kitchen.

"Hello?" asked a raspy, flat male voice on the other end.

"Hello, is Mandy there?"

"Yeah, just a sec."

Mandy's high-pitched voice came on the line. "Hello, who's this?"

"This is Lillian."

"Why are you calling me? Are... you're still at *his* house?"

"No. I'm back home."

"How'd you get this number?"

"I looked it up online."

"Why?"

"Because I wanted to talk to you."

"Look, there's nothing to talk about, okay? I want to just forget about that whole thing."

"How did you get back home?"

"My sister's boyfriend came and picked me up, like he said he would."

"Is your sister still seeing... you know who?"

"I'm going to whisper because Tyler is here. She's thinking about dumping him. I bet she'll be leaving Tyler for... oh, crap."

In the background, a female voice yelled sharply.

"Gotta go," Mandy muttered before hanging up.

The next day, Lillian called again. This time, Jana answered. When Lillian asked for Mandy, Jana recognized her voice.

"Please leave us alone," Jana demanded. "Mandy doesn't want to talk to you."

"Why not?"

"You're younger than her. You have nothing in common. Just because you worked on a garden with someone, it doesn't mean you're friends."

"How is Mandy doing?"

"She's doing very well. She's doing great. Now let us be." Jana hung up on Lillian.

A couple of days later, Lillian called again, more desperate than ever to cling to Mandy. Again, Jana answered, threatening to complain to both Julius and Lillian's father if she ever called again. With no knowledge of a cell phone number, an email address, or any other way to contact Mandy, there was little hope of Lillian breaking through.

The weekend before school started, the family got a surprise visit from Uncle Gerald. There was hardly any other kind. The relationship between Dad and his brother been polite but strained for as long as Lillian could remember. Since Dad did not invite Gerald over that often, this wealthy uncle, who owned a medical supply company and lived in the well-to-do Washington, D.C. suburb of Potomac, liked to show up unannounced.

Gerald, a tall, stocky man with thinning gray hair who wore a nicely ironed polo shirt and khakis, asked to borrow Lillian and take her on a walk. Lillian grew sick with fear and worry. Her uncle was not only a necromancer like his son Julius, but also blessed with the rare power of omniscient mind reading. He saw all. Gerald probably already knew what she did, how perverted she was when she led on his own son. Incest, fornication. He would never forgive her.

Don't think about it, Lillian ordered herself for the hundredth time. *Don't think about it*. But as they strolled side by side in the summer heat down the sleepy green tree-lined road, she couldn't keep it off her mind. Any thought quashed here popped up there, like in a Whack-a-Mole game.

"I know that some things happened with my son," Gerald said at last, confident that they were alone. "You need to understand that you're a very pretty young girl. You've developed a nice figure for your age, and that will attract men. But I still think you are too young for such things. I've had a stern talk with Julius. I don't recommend telling your father about the events of this summer. It would upset him needlessly, if he even believes you, which he likely won't. Your father adores Julius, after all."

"I won't tell him," Lillian promised, looking down and unable to meet her uncle's eyes.

"Good. We'd all like to forget the whole business. It's just water under the bridge."

"Water under the bridge? What does that mean?"

"When you think of a bridge, the same water doesn't pass under it twice. From one minute to the next, every water molecule is fresh and new. The minute an event is over, it no longer matters. You must focus only on the here and now. You're not the only person who's had an unpleasant thing happen to you. Just about everybody has. Your father and I had a lot of strife in our childhood, and he's shielded you from the worst of it. My first wife, Enid, left me and then died of cancer. Tawny, my second wife, took her own life last year and I found her body. I put it behind me. People make mistakes; let's leave them in the past. Just focus on succeeding in school, and being proud of who you are. You'll keep on trucking, and you'll forgive and forget. Deal?" Gerald raised his fist, and Lillian stopped on the sidewalk and cowered.

"Hey, we do the knuckle bop. Has anyone taught you that? That will seal the deal."

"Deal," Lillian reluctantly agreed, knocking her fist against Gerald's large one with its fine white hair and liver spots. "Hey, do you know anything about Mandy, the girl who…"

"Oh, I don't know much about her. I hear she is doing well. Julius wishes to marry her older sister. Once Julius has a wife to come home to every night, I am certain that he will be satisfied by her alone, and his deviant behavior will stop. Oh, and promise you'll never call and pester that poor family again. Deal again?"

Lillian met his fist, mumbling, "Deal again."

"The next time I come and visit, I might bring my granddaughter Katrina. She really, really likes you. She is busy, starting her senior year of high school, but I'm sure we can coordinate something."

"Cool." Lillian tried to fake an enthusiastic tone. She had never really bonded with Katrina the two times they'd met over the summer. Katrina overwhelmed her. Even scared her a little bit.

After they walked back to the house, Dad and Uncle Gerald stayed inside to talk while Lillian headed to the backyard, where an old tire swing hung from a tree on a thick rope. She squeezed her legs through it, kicked them outward, and hung upside down, feeling a rush of blood in her head. She spun mindlessly, trying to drown out her thoughts with the green blurring of her surroundings. *Water under the bridge. Get over it.*

Kristin, one of Lillian's two close friends, pulled away as eighth grade began, finding an inroad with the popular girls. They encouraged her to "ditch that nerd" as Lillian watched from a separate lunch table.

Kristin had been one of the few people who did not roll their eyes and tune out when Lillian prattled on about *Star Trek* or ancient Egypt or Princess Zelda or whales. But now, that changed. Kristin stopped returning Lillian's calls and stopped coming over to do crafts.

Lillian took her friend's rejection very hard, crying herself to sleep at night. Every other human in the world now had a label stuck on them as far as she was concerned: *Don't trust me. Don't tell me anything. I would never understand anyway.*

Lillian stopped visiting her other friend, Adam, just as Kristin had ceased seeing her. He was not only male, but her longtime crush. Any romantic urges overwhelmed Lillian so much, and felt so unsafe, that she could not get a handle on them. How could Adam ever want her, now that she was tainted like spoiled food? She could not even make words come out when Adam approached her at school and asked why she had started eating lunch alone on the grass. Like Lillian after Kristin cut her off, Adam was hurt. The pain rolled downhill until it hit him in the face. The guilt of wounding the boy she still had feelings for haunted Lillian. But she saw no other choice.

Lillian also avoided her local cousin Denny. When he invited her to tag along on a weekend hunting or boating trip, or join him to check his crab traps in the water, she said that she had to stay in and do homework. Lying and making up excuses went against everything in Lillian's nature, but after a life of hiding her powers, she was used to keeping secrets. Now she carried a truth deep inside that seemed just as dangerous as the mutant that had almost killed her in Julius' kitchen. If Lillian let anything slip about that summer and Julius then followed through on his threats, there might be more of those hideous things. The same things Denny was also capable of unleashing. Denny had never touched Lillian outside of pats and hugs, or taken clothes off other than his coats and socks in front of her, yet in her mind, any man could snap and turn into the next Julius. Even her father.

During a checkup, Lillian's dentist found that she brushed to the point of making her tongue bleed. He warned her that over-brushing could wear away a person's tooth enamel. Still, Lillian brushed and brushed, trying to erase the rubbery feel and taste of Julius shoving himself into her mouth, still imprinted even as the weeks and months went by. She showered and showered, water scalding hot, skin and hair drying out from all the soap, never clean enough.

One afternoon at home after school, with her father still at work, Lillian wandered aimlessly around the house, deep in her loneliness. She found herself standing over the open knife drawer in the kitchen, her hand wrapped around a serrated steak knife.

Lillian poked at her fingers with the tip of the blade. The pain distracted her a little bit from the emotional torment swirling inside. Something else rested on the kitchen counter. A utility knife her father had used to open a package, and then forgotten to put away. Lillian picked it up and clicked the blade out, running her fingertip over it. The sharp metal cut into her skin like it was butter.

Minutes later, Lillian's right hand still gripped the knife, while a row of parallel cuts beaded with blood on the underside of her left arm. She had just done something forbidden, an act people associated with angry, disturbed teenage girls. Now she had yet another secret to hide.

Panicked, Lillian cleaned herself up in the kitchen sink, wrapping her arm in a paper towel and pressing it down to try to stop the bleeding. Once it slowed, she went up to her bedroom, threw on a sweater to conceal the wounds, and tucked the utility knife away in her desk drawer. Since Dad had a couple of others in the garage, Lillian was confident he wouldn't miss it.

One October night, a terrible vision overtook Lillian as she laid in bed, unable to sleep. Mandy, the one she'd gardened with at Julius' house, fell through space as tears streamed down her cheeks. Her body hit hard, cold ground. Her neck snapped like a twig, leaving behind television static. And then came the desolate graveyard under the gray sky that had been a part of Lillian's inner landscape her whole life, the crows cawing off in the tall, dry grass and cornstalks. A light shone around the doors to one of the tombs, calling to Lillian, before the vision dissolved.

Some news had Lillian's father smiling in excitement. Julius and Mandy's older sister Jana were getting married the following summer, and Dad bought tickets to attend the wedding in Julius' backyard. Not just for himself, but for Evelyn and Lillian. Evelyn would stay in a hotel at night to shield her from the cat dander, but he and Lillian would sleep in Julius' house. The flatline of Lillian's private despair alternated with moments of white-hot panic. Within months, Julius would close in on her again. She had once believed in God and still obediently went to church with her father, but now she had trouble buying the theory of a caring deity up in the sky who looked out for his flock of sheep on earth and never gave them more than they could handle. Lillian's pain snowballed into a bigger load than she could take. Thoughts of suicide came to roost in her head like winter crows.

Sometimes Lillian's only antidote was the utility knife tucked away in her bedroom. The pain on the outside of her skin distracted her from the pain on the inside, from her failure to erase that summer spotlessly from her mind and happily move on as Uncle Gerald wanted her to. The blade and the blood it brought forth turned into an addiction. Lillian adopted a new look to hide the marks: a sweatshirt worn under a T-shirt nearly every day, with a thick tangle of hand-woven friendship bracelets on each wrist. One morning, she took off her long-sleeved pajamas and paused somberly in front of her bedroom mirror before getting dressed for school, her arm and legs crisscrossed with cuts in various stages of healing. Lillian had mostly shied away from mirrors after the stay with Julius. Disgusted at her reflection, she threw a blanket over the mirror.

When the trees started to give birth to pale spring blooms, Lillian wished that the warmer weather would just switch off, that the seasons would stop changing, and the trees would never sprout leaves again, even if it meant staying in school eternally. School was not going well. Lillian's grades slipped; she no longer turned in her homework. She'd become a ghost sitting in the back of her classes.

When the weather warmed up enough that her classmates wore T-shirts and shorts, Lillian stuck to the longest-sleeved shirts in her closet. With the humidity, the insides of her sweaters and jeans turned into a miserable sauna, but Lillian was anxious to hide the scars that weren't there last summer. Dad could never find out, and neither could the kids at school—imagine the teasing then.

One warm sunny day, when the tulips in the moist grass in front of the school grounds were opening in a shower of color, Dad picked Lillian up. In the car, he brought up a topic that had yet to go anywhere productive. A couple of weeks ago, Lillian's school progress report had come in the mail, full of mediocre to failing grades.

"You were always an A student," Lillian's father pointed out yet again. "You're in the gifted and talented program, for heaven's sake. You can't be getting such low grades! What have you been doing to bring them up?"

Lillian simply shrugged.

"Do you want to repeat the eighth grade? Don't you realize how much that would set you back, and how embarrassing it would be?"

"I don't know," she said in the passenger seat, looking down, rocking gently back and forth. "I don't know."

"What's happened to you? You haven't gotten into drinking or experimenting with drugs with your friends, have you?"

"Friends? What friends? I'm not on drugs, Dad."

"Do I need to take those video games away? I'll consider it if you cannot fix your grades." Dad pulled into the shady driveway of the house, cutting the ignition. "Oh, before I forget—while I was at work, Julius called. His wedding is still on for the end of May, and we're still going, of course. He called to finalize the arrangements."

"What about Mandy... Jana's sister... will she be there?" Lillian meekly asked as they paused on the steps up to the front door. It was difficult to work up the courage to get that question past her lips. Mandy who'd shared her suffering last summer, and then wanted nothing to do with her after their return home.

"Oh, that." Dad grunted uncomfortably. "I will need to tell you something, since we'll see the family soon. Mandy is... no longer with us."

"What?! What happened?"

"That poor young lady. I guess she suffered from depression or something along those lines. Back in October, she committed suicide."

"Oh my god! How long did you know about this?"

"Julius called me shortly after it happened. He was quite broken up."

"This happened in October and you didn't tell me?" The night terror from months ago came whooshing back into Lillian's memory—Mandy tumbling in the night, her neck snapping. Yes, that restless night had struck just two weeks before Halloween.

"I didn't feel it was a good idea to tell you. Young minds are delicate. But with the wedding coming up, now you need to know."

"I wish you'd told me sooner!"

"I didn't want to bring you down or distract you from your schoolwork. That will be one bittersweet wedding, without the bride's sister there. Enough about that business. Julius made an offer today. He's staying home all summer, not going on his honeymoon until the fall. He is interested in having you help him out again, and like last year, you'll get a nice monetary gift. He said you were a great big help last summer."

"I don't want to go," Lillian whispered as the blood drained from her face.

"What?"

"I don't want to go." The words came out again, just a little louder.

"To the wedding, or to help your cousin?"

"Neither!"

"What? Your cousin has been nothing but kind to us. He gave us such a generous gift so that you could get nice new things and we could add to your college fund, and this is the thanks he gets? You don't have any other big plans this summer, right? So there is no reason not to assist him."

"I'm not going."

"Yes you are, young lady, and I won't take any more of this attitude you've been getting. You've got an obligation to your family, and you've got to learn that sometimes we help people even if we don't feel like it. You need to celebrate your cousin's special day, and he needs your help."

Dad's decisions tended to be final. Though an overall caring man, he was also a no-nonsense type, a father from the old school. There was no hope of escaping another summer with Julius. Not unless Lillian ran away from home, but who would she run to?

Katrina, in the final semester of her senior year of high school, kept to her word in staying in touch with Lillian. She occasionally called, wrote letters, and after Lillian's father let her open up an email account, she sent emails with the understanding that he had the password and monitored her exchanges. Not trusting that he wasn't also opening letters before his kid got them, Katrina chose her words carefully. Kept it toned down, asking about clothes and hobbies and summer plans. Avoided the topic of the girls' shared powers.

Lillian replied to each letter and email, but her writing was stiff, a bit forced. With the formal language, Katrina got the impression that an adult, probably Lillian's father, coached her on what to write. Their phone calls were awkward and brief; Lillian sounded shy and uncomfortable.

Katrina had to get this girl out of her shell, and get them close. But how?

Things were not going fantastically in Katrina's own life. She lived with her garden slug of a mother in the trailer that Uncle Julius had bought for them years ago. Her mother did little but watch television, sleep, drink, and get high on her pain pills. When Katrina brought home nice clothes or other expensive gifts from her grandfather or her uncle, they quickly disappeared as her mother sold them for pills and powders. Uncle Julius, understanding the situation, kept Katrina's most prized possessions at his own house.

But Katrina wasn't allowed to actually live there. After years of misery at home, she came right out and asked if she could. Her uncle had more than enough space, and he was a bachelor, just him and his army of cats. He'd given a vague answer over the past few years, promising Katrina he'd think about it. After he started seeing Jana, the woman he was about to marry, that "maybe" turned into a firm "no." Jana wouldn't allow it. Julius' fiancée had been icy to Katrina since the two of them met, and the closer the wedding grew, the more they flat-out hated each other. Jana behaved like Katrina was competition. What did she think, that a teenager was going to sleep with her own uncle?

"Setting boundaries," Jana called it, limiting how often Katrina could come over for dinner, how much time she and Julius spent together. Yeah, that woman was clearly jealous. And of course, she did not know of the magic that closely bonded Katrina to her uncle. She never would.

One dewy March morning, Katrina showed up for another day at school, looking forward to each of these days less and less. She pulled into the student parking lot in the beaten-up 1985 Pontiac Grand Am she had inherited from her mother, the model from the year she was born. Julius had offered to buy Katrina a nice new car, but Jana, in her increasing control over him, wouldn't allow it. Why did Julius give her full license to run his life?

Just a few parking spots away was a shiny Mercedes-Benz, purchased at Julius' very own dealership, complete with the Frazier Motorcars frame around the license plate. In a parking lot full of parental hand-me-downs, that luxurious car stuck out like a sore thumb. It belonged to none other than Megan, the classmate who'd given Katrina a hard time since elementary school.

It started out as teasing over Katrina's pale red hair, underweight frame, and cheap thrift-store clothes. And the body odor she sometimes had when her mother didn't pay the water bill. Part of it, Katrina was sure, was the other girls' jealousy over her being so skinny. Megan came up with the nickname "Little Orphan Annie," which stuck well into middle school. Along with the label that still persisted: "trailer trash."

Being "Little Orphan Annie" was one thing. Fairly easy to shake off. But as the kids grew older, the bullying got more sophisticated. Crueler. As Katrina walked into the hall toward her homeroom, she kept a vigilant mind's eye out for Megan's aura—Megan liked to sneak up from behind sometimes. It was too late. Megan was too fast. Her group of rich, blonde, well-dressed friends created a clot in the flow of students past the lockers, holding Katrina up. Just as Katrina heard "I smell trailer trash," Megan rushed up behind her with the speed of a fox and pushed her. Laughter rang out as Katrina fell on her face. She'd forgotten that the zipper on her backpack was partly broken, and many of her books and folders spilled out.

"Get up, you idiot," Megan sneered as she ground her strappy, high-heeled shoe on one of Katrina's textbooks, which had fallen open. For good measure, she gave Katrina a quick kick in the ribs before she and her friends scurried off.

Tears of humiliation beading in her eyes, Katrina quickly gathered her things and stuffed them into her backpack. She would not go and tattle to a teacher or the principal;

she'd tried that before and it only made things worse as the bullies retaliated away from adult view. Megan was a straight-A student and head cheerleader. Who would they side with, the golden girl or Katrina with her mediocre grades and utter lack of interest in sports and joining clubs?

After homeroom, Katrina went to her locker to grab her notebook for her next class. A piece of pink paper had been shoved into the slits on the locker door, fluttering down to the floor as she swung it open. Though there was no name on the letter, Katrina could recognize that handwriting a mile away. Megan must have bought a whole pad of that pale pink stationery just for the purpose of ragging on Katrina. Why couldn't Megan get a life?

Today's love letter was particularly vicious.

Why don't you run your shitty ugly car in the garage tonight, while you sit in it? That'll put you out of your misery, you ugly bitch. The world will be a better place. Oh, right, you're living in ur mom's piece of shit trailer. It probably doesn't have a garage. Why don't you just get a rope and hang yourself? Everyone would be happier.

Though Katrina tried not to give them the satisfaction of seeing her cry, a tear trickled down her cheek. She wiped it away and twisted her face into a snarl before she went back out into the fray of kids in the hallway.

Katrina knew she was better than them. Of course she was. No other student at this school was a mage, though a few had the trait and probably didn't know it. No classmate could possess another human being. No other kid could move things with their mind alone, or raise the dead. If Katrina wanted to, she could make Megan and her friends soil their pants in fear. But it wasn't allowed. The code of the mages demanded secrecy, of course, to the point where Katrina's own mother had no clue she had an unusual daughter. Ever since she was young, Grandpa and Uncle Julius had come to visit just to impress upon her the grave importance of the code.

Uncle Julius knew about the bullying, as Katrina had cried in his arms a couple of times. And so did Grandpa, of course, reading those painful scenes in Katrina's mind during his now rare visits. Both men sympathized with Katrina more than her mother did. Mom just grumbled that she was tired of the whining, and that if Katrina ignored the bullies, they'd eventually quit—advice that never worked. Katrina's grandpa and uncle reminded her that if she fought back, she had to use her fists as weapons, not her powers. Unless Megan put a gun to her head, the abilities were verboten.

When Katrina hit back during a couple of scuffles in middle school, she was blamed and suspended from school, her mother later punishing her with a wooden spoon at home. Since then, Katrina had gritted her teeth, counting the days to graduation and coming close to dropping out until Uncle Julius pushed her to stay in school.

As she ripped up Megan's cruel letter and threw the pink confetti in the trash, something inside Katrina snapped. What did she ever do to Megan to deserve this? What sort of sick person would pressure their target into suicide? As Katrina sat through her next couple of classes, her brain turned with a scheme. Her scowl slowly lifted into a private, satisfied smile. Today, Katrina was going to disobey Uncle Julius. And she'd probably get in trouble later on if Grandpa visited and read her mind. But Katrina wanted just one victory. One thing for herself.

When the bell rang and signaled lunch hour, Katrina had her plan all figured out. She grabbed her lunch, a paper bag containing a plain white-bread bologna sandwich, nothing like the organic vegetables and protein shakes and homemade granola that Megan brought to school each day. Katrina blended into the crowd and sat at the table beside the one where Megan and her friends gathered. Megan, her blond hair pulled up into a perfect bun, had her back turned to Katrina. Oblivious that her target was nearby, Megan nibbled delicately at a celery stick from her sleek lunch box as she laughed with her friends. Katrina looked down, taking bites of her sandwich and giving the impression of minding her own business.

Katrina snaked her powers over to the neighboring table. Stealthily, she took possession of Megan.

Seeing out of Megan's eyes, Katrina felt her heart pounding and speeding up. Tasted her fear as she did not understand what was happening to her, why she suddenly couldn't move and the world went dark.

With Katrina as her puppet master, Megan stood up from her bench. Doing it from a table away was tricky; Megan's body almost fell. Megan's friends shot her concerned looks. "Are you all right? Meg! You're being so quiet all of a sudden! Everything okay?"

Struggling to not let Megan trip and collapse, Katrina manipulated her body, slowly and carefully, until she was standing on top of the table. By then, her buddies were gasping, their jaws dropping. "Meg! Come down from there! What the hell are you doing?!"

Katrina glanced up only periodically from her sandwich, like the goings-on at the next table were a passing curiosity. Flying under the radar was important, even in a cafeteria full of kids who did not know the ways of magic.

Megan's clothes began to come off. Undoing her bra clasp behind her back was such a challenge that Katrina had Megan's hands simply rip the bra off. Simple to unzip, her skirt fell away.

The whole cafeteria hushed into an almost complete shocked silence. Katrina had Megan rummage through her open lunch box. Feeling its contents through Megan's fingertips, she found the dill pickle that was part of her everyday fare.

Fingers curled around the large pickle, Megan stood back up. Katrina drew the pickle down, between her parted legs.

Screams and horrified laughs broke out. Some students gawked, and some fled from the cafeteria in disgust. Megan's friends shrunk away from her in embarrassment, scrambling from the table. A teacher ran to the principal's office to call the police.

More teachers rushed in and tried to shoo everyone out. "There's nothing to see here! Go outside until this is resolved!" some of them yelled as a few others, along with a couple of campus security guards, tried and failed to coax Megan down from the table.

Katrina to continued to blend in as the classmates next to her refused to leave their front-row seat. Putting her sandwich down, she feigned the shock that was genuine on everyone else's faces, as much as she wanted to grin. This was the most fun Katrina had had in a long, long time, intertwined with a special, delicious satisfaction. Getting revenge at last. A whole public circus that Megan would never be able to live down.

Quick to arrive, the cops joined the small crowd of teachers and security guards that had formed a ring about Megan as Katrina made her dance on the table. All of the students sitting nearby were ordered to leave. Even though Katrina wished she could keep going, the cord connecting her to her bully could only stretch so far. As the crowd slowly nudged her away, Katrina let go, unwinding herself from Megan's head.

"What happened?" Megan screamed, falling to her knees on the table. "What's happening to me? What the hell is wrong with me?! My clothes... why are my clothes gone?"

A wave of laughter and murmurs rolled from the audience lingering near the doors as Megan grabbed for her clothes and jumped down from the table, tears streaming down her face and streaking her mascara on her cheeks. A teacher brought a blanket and wrapped it around Megan, who shouted and sobbed as the cops led her past the gawking onlookers and escorted her out of the cafeteria. "What happened? I blacked out! What did I do?! The devil made me do it! The devil made me do it; I swear!"

That afternoon and evening were just like a lot of the others in Katrina's life. Katrina's mother started a screaming argument about her forgetting to wash one of their few dishes the night before. Katrina screamed back. But she still went to bed in a wonderful mood, almost unable to sleep from the high. This was just a taste of what her powers could do!

After that day, Megan was never seen at the school again. Plenty of gossip went around, of course. Though she wasn't there to suffer the teasing, classmates made fun of her, imitating, "The devil made me do it!" in a whiny tone. Any lewd public act had a new slang term: "pulling a Megan." Guys also joked about how much they'd like Megan to "tickle their pickles."

Rumors filtered their way to Katrina's ears about Megan's fate. After she was sent to a psych ward for a night or two, her parents hired a top-dollar attorney to make the situation go away. Even though she was so close to graduation, they helped her to start fresh at some private boarding school. If this was true, and somebody, somewhere, knew where Megan was, then word of that debacle in the cafeteria had probably already made its way to the new school. Though Katrina wasn't around to see it, the thought of the truth being discovered, and her new classmates giving her hell, made Katrina smile.

In their shock, Megan's friends practically forgot Katrina existed, and they left her alone until graduation.

When Katrina's grandfather visited, taking her and Julius out to a lavish dinner to celebrate the end of her high school years, he kept mum about Megan even though he had to know. Maybe Grandpa understood why Katrina did this. She never spoke of it. She just wanted this private victory to hoard closely like a precious jewel.

Gerald brought up a topic Katrina did not expect, and from the slightly startled look on Julius' face, he might not have seen it coming either. "So, Katrina. I know you don't have any plans, except perhaps finding a job that pays slightly better than that part-time job at the mall you have right now. And you didn't apply to any colleges."

"Katrina, dear, I thought you told me that you'd applied to Ohio State and that community college," Julius cut in.

Katrina was busted in that particular lie, even if Grandpa never breathed a word of what she'd done to her classmate. There was no backpedaling out of this now. "I'm so sorry," she uttered in a mousy whisper. "I guess I never did get around to it."

"But you're so smart, and you sounded so determined. Why did you lead me to believe you were going to college?"

"She's been dealing with a lot," said Grandpa. "Juggling a part-time job, her invalid mother, and full-time school. Her grades haven't been great... she's been dealing with depression and lack of motivation, not to mention she shielded you from the worst of the bullying she has suffered. Son, did you know that the bullies were placing notes in her locker urging her to kill herself?"

"No! Katrina, I wish you had told me it got that bad!" Uncle Julius gasped.

"She was ashamed," his father answered. "Katrina, how would you feel if you knew that all of your bullies—I mean, *all* of them, not just their ringleader—were going to get the ultimate payback someday? And at the center of that payback would be you. Us."

Katrina shrugged. "It's a nice thought, but I don't see it happening. Aren't we supposed to keep our powers a secret?"

"What if you didn't have to live in fear, disguising your incredible abilities from almost everybody you know, including your own mother? What if you could just live freely like our ancestors did many centuries ago, without fear of retribution from the water people or fire people or air people, without fear of the ordinary folks finding out and persecuting us? What if we were in charge? How would that make you feel?"

"Well, that would be nice, I guess. But I know it's not gonna happen."

"You don't have much going for you, Katrina. No plans for college, no long-term plans really. But you know you're better than all of those people who have looked down on you. We've told you that before, but it bears repeating. Imagine a world where college degrees, or lack thereof, were a complete non-issue. Imagine a world where everybody knows our worth and we are no longer in hiding. Instead, we're in charge."

"Umm... okay." Even Katrina's grandiose grandfather didn't always go on a power trip this extreme.

"Before I get too far ahead of myself, let's talk about plans for your immediate future. I know that you've felt on the fence about having children someday."

"Yeah, I'm not really sure. Kids are loud and annoying."

"There's no denying they are, but... I'm not sure if I ever made you aware of this before. Did you know that when a mage woman gets pregnant, and the baby she's carrying is a mage, her powers increase substantially?"

"Oh, wow! No, I didn't know that! Does this mean my mom got powers, or felt something, when she was pregnant with me?"

"Since your mother is a mere half-breed, she cannot attain our powers, even while pregnant. But if your mother was a necromancer like yourself..." Gerald lowered his voice a bit, even though they were tucked away in a remote corner booth, where other guests were unlikely to overhear them or even understand what they were talking about. "Her powers easily would have doubled. She may have even gained new powers that she did not have before, like mind-reading for instance. I saw this increase in powers when my sister, Sarah, was pregnant. Sarah never appreciated her powers, and the surge in her abilities made her so miserable that she became a shut-in. But it was one of the few times I wished I could be a woman. Doesn't that sound good to you, Katrina? Wouldn't pregnancy be worth it?"

"Well, there's the whole raising the baby thing."

"Don't you worry about that part. The two of us would be there to assist, every step of the way. I think you wouldn't be like your great-aunt Sarah during her pregnancy at all. I think you would love it, and make good use of it while the powers last."

"But the baby would have to be like me, right? How would I make that happen?"

"By choosing a father who's a half-breed. It would only give you a partial chance at a mage baby, but the only other options would be incest or finding a mage of another sort to have a child with. They've hated us for centuries, so that's not happening. Half-breeds are considerably more common than mages. You should be able to find one, no problem."

"I don't even have a boyfriend. And no, hooking up with that guy at work doesn't count. I'm sure you saw that one, Grandpa. There were a couple of half-breeds at school, but not anybody I'd want to date."

"Don't you worry about struggling to find a suitable young half-breed man on your own. We'll keep our ears to the ground for any."

"Wait, Grandpa, are you saying that you want me to, like, find a guy and start having kids right away, just to boost my powers?"

"The sooner the better, yes. That way, your odds are the greatest, since it may take more than one try to produce a mage child."

"But I'm not ready to have a baby right this minute. I'm not even eighteen yet!"

"Again, don't you worry. Should you find the right male, we'll help you out. We'll get you an apartment somewhere. No trouble at all."

"Still not sure I'm ready for kids, but moving out of Mom's sounds like a good deal. A really good deal. And if you find me a guy, you'll make sure he's cute, right?"

"Oh, of course. I can't promise you Fabio, but I won't set you up with an ugly one. You deserve great things in all areas of life; never forget that."

As summer break neared, Lillian had the sense of being an inmate on death row. She managed to pass her classes, while putting in a fraction of what she had once been capable of. There was no point in trying too hard at anything anymore. Lillian would have to help Julius and be his slave again, in his garden and in his bed. Julius would be a newlywed by then, but his bride-to-be, Jana, clearly did not think highly of Lillian after how she'd snapped at her on the phone. There was no promise that Julius would not take advantage of her again, or that Jana would help her in any way. Lillian saw no way out.

The week after school let out for summer, two nights before the flight, Lillian's father reminded her that she needed to pack. After a day of Lillian dragging her feet and putting off the task, her father dropped a carry-on bag on her bedroom floor, the same bag that went to Julius' house last summer.

Evelyn was home from college, staying in her bedroom next to Lillian's, her own pink suitcase already neatly arranged. She'd have just enough time to attend the wedding before starting a summer internship, before she and her father both left Lillian at the mercy of Julius. As Dad went to hunt in his closet for his nicest suit, Lillian grew dizzy with the gripping, terrible urgency of her situation. Unable to bring herself to pack, Lillian stared at the empty bag, and at the nice new dress hanging from her mirror, in a hopeless daze.

Over the past several months, Lillian had thought about ways to run from both Julius and from the torment inside herself. She could drink poison. Or take pills. Dad had a few guns, but he kept them locked in a safe. Unable to read minds like her uncle Gerald, Lillian had no way of finding out the combination.

With the wedding closing in fast, Lillian's current idea, the one most likely to work without getting interrupted, was already planned out. She hastily wrote her final letter to her family on a cutesy pink notepad on her desk. Even though it would be her last communication with anyone, she held back the truth about Julius, not wanting her father to know of her shame and not wanting Julius to target other family members after her death. Lillian expected that her family would be sad, at least for a while. They might shed a few tears at the funeral. But they would get over it before too long, going on with the rest of their lives as memories of her faded.

After composing the second draft of the letter and leaving it on her desk, and checking to be sure Dad's and Evelyn's bedroom lights were turned off and they had gone to sleep, Lillian slid out a book from one of her shelves. A razor blade, never used, was tucked inside. She fanned out the pages to find it. Shuddering with fear of how much this might hurt, she knelt on the circular rainbow rug on the hardwood floor, gripping the blade in her trembling fingers.

No! a faint voice, a whisper, called to her. *You must live!*

A faceless hooded figure rose from the shadows, wrapped in loose cloth. With the lack of an aura and the faint green dots in place of eyes staring down at her, it was a ghost, not a rare sight to the eyes of her kind.

As far back as Lillian could remember, this cloaked man had appeared in the shadows of her bedroom once or twice a year. One night when she was an infant, an eerie hiss came from the baby monitor and roused her father out of bed. Dad came to investigate and found a dark figure standing over her crib, placed where her bed was now. Terrified that he'd caught a kidnapper in the act, Lillian's father demanded to know who this shadowed man was, and he silently dissolved into thin air.

And there he was again. Probably harmless, like most ghosts. If she just shut her eyes for several seconds, he would be gone when she opened them.

But the shadow-draped man had never spoken to her until now, his dry groan of a voice coming from the black void that was his face.

No!

Lillian squeezed her eyes shut and counted to three. When she opened them again, she had a clear view of her wall of bookshelves. She was alone, the figure gone. Now came the opportunity to open her wrists and get it over with—the nerve was already dissipating. What waited for Lillian on the other side? The God she wasn't so sure she believed in anymore, or that graveyard dreamscape she'd always carried, or the fires of hell? Which was worse, death or Julius?

Lillian dug the blade into one wrist, and then the other, biting her lips to keep from crying out. She crouched on the floor, not the bed, so that her father could sell the clean mattress for some extra money once she was gone. Soon, if things went according to plan, her bloodless body would lie in a shining sanguine lake, finally at peace.

Terrible pain burned from Lillian's wounded wrists into the rest of her body. Her hands curled into claws as she gripped at herself, writhing and attempting to stifle her screams. She could not afford to wake her father or sister. But it was too late. The bedroom door opened, Dad's shadow falling over her.

"No!" Dad screamed in horror, scooping up Lillian in his arms, her twisted hands slick with red. "What have you done? I will *not* lose you!"

Excerpt from The Autobiography of Gerald Frazier: Architect of a New World

I learned how to fish and hunt squirrels at a young age. I shot cans with my BB gun, climbed trees, and nailed together a clubhouse in the backyard to share with my sister Sarah and my few friends. As my brother Lou got older, I included him in a few more of my games and adventures.

Lou spent a lot of time in the backyard sandbox, playing pretend that his small dunes were mountains. When he was about six years old, Sarah witnessed something startling, even miraculous. While our kid brother sat in the sandbox, a clump of the sand lifted into the air and moved over to the other side. My brother had levitated it with his powers! Which would have been more challenging than a solid object, with the countless individual grains. At so young an age, he should not have been able to lift a single speck. It seemed as if God gave Lou twice the amount of telekinetic power that He gave to Papa, me, and Sarah. Though ironically enough, Lou could read minds about as well as an ordinary person could. That is to say, not at all.

Lou's sandbox stunt led to a stern lesson from Papa and Sarah on the code of the mages, which demands discretion. I became jealous of my brother's accelerated development, since I couldn't do anything yet except read minds and push a pencil a quarter of an inch on my desk. I simply could not wait to go through the changes of adolescence and reach the pinnacle of my power.

Until then, I sometimes lived vicariously through Lou. If I wanted a toy, a comic book, or candy for free, I made him do it. I figured it was fair enough, since life had deprived me of his precocious powers.

In 1945, when I was nine years old and Sarah was twelve, she woke up crying in the middle of the night and came to me for comfort. She'd had a nightmare about a pair of blindingly bright bombs, like no bomb humanity had ever seen before, burning and vaporizing thousands of people. We were at the tail end of World War II. Folks had been anxious for years, and I figured that all of the news about bombings and Nazi concentration camps had tainted Sarah's dreams.

A couple of evenings later, as my family wound down and got ready for bed, all of us got a strange feeling, except for my oldest sister Violet, who looked at us like we were crazy. The feeling hit each of us differently. Anxiety made my skin crawl while Sarah and Lou both cried, claiming they felt death on a large scale happening somewhere. My father panicked and sweated, but did not admit to it. When we turned on the radio the next day, every channel buzzed with the news that we had dropped an atomic bomb on Hiroshima, Japan! My father, Lou, Sarah, and I got that same unsettled feeling when the second bomb hit a few days later.

About a year after the nuclear bombs fell, Sarah woke up hollering. Our father was in too much of a drugged haze to assist her, so I ran to her bedside. My sister was covered in sweat and clinging at bunches of her nightgown.

"I had a bad dream," Sarah sobbed. "It was the future."

In my comic books, the 1980s and 1990s would see an influx of flying saucers and little green men from outer space. But the future in Sarah's dream had a disappointing lack of space aliens.

"There were airplanes full of people," Sarah told me as I watched the action unfold in my own head. "And then the airplanes were taken over by bad men. They crashed them into buildings. These two tall buildings that fell down. And one of the planes crashed into the ground because some good folks tried to stop these men. All of the passengers died!"

I could see it all, planes crashing and plumes of smoke. It appeared exactly as it would on my television screen, when the whole world was watching, fifty-some years later.

"It was just a nightmare," I reassured Sarah. "That's all it was. Just a nightmare."

"It was so real, I could hear and see everything! It was horrible!"

"Nightmares are like that. But it was all just a dream. Go back to sleep."

Oh, how ignorant I was back then! Why hadn't I paid this dream more mind after Sarah's premonition of the atomic bombs?

A couple of years later, Sarah had a dream that a man down the street, whose name I cannot remember, would be shot during a trip to Maine. Six months later, that's exactly what happened. He died in a hunting accident.

Aftermath

❧❧ · ◆ ◆ ◆ · ❧❧

The near-loss of Lou's daughter became his worst trauma, walking into a sight in her bedroom that he would never wish on any parent.

The shadowy figure had stood over his bed that night, waking him up with an icy, skeletal hand on his shoulder. When Lou jumped out of bed, the cloaked man dissolved, just as he did over a decade before when Lou caught him standing over Lillian's crib. If not for that ghost, whoever it was, Lou probably wouldn't have woken up until it was too late. And now he'd still be in every parent's worst nightmare, outliving their child. And wondering how he failed so badly that she didn't see her fourteenth birthday. With that outcome, Lou would have had a hard time holding back the urge to reanimate Lillian in his grief, though she would have still been dead.

That grim chain of events was now a blur in Lou's memory. Evelyn woken by his terrified screams, grabbing her cell phone to call 911, the paramedics rushing up the stairs.

While Lillian was in the hospital, Lou took a quick break from her bedside and called his nephew Julius, apologizing for missing the wedding. Julius sounded clogged with tears, though as gracious as ever. He told Lou how sorry he was about the horrific circumstances, how hard it had been when Jana's sister died months before, and how grateful he was for Lillian's survival.

Lou's other nephew, Denny, volunteered to clean up Lillian's bedroom so that Lou and Evelyn wouldn't have to. That round rainbow rug had added a bright splash of color to the room ever since it was an infant nursery, but the bloodstains forever marked the cheery colors with tragedy. Denny rolled up the rug, threw it in the bed of his pickup, and took it to the dump. He never spoke of it again.

After Lillian was discharged from the hospital with bandage-wrapped wrists, Evelyn had to get ready to leave for her summer internship. Denny came to stay for a while to keep an eye on Lillian. Now was not his busiest season as a tax accountant, so he had the time. Lou brought his daughter to a psychiatrist, who diagnosed her with bipolar disorder after hearing Lou's quick summary about the happy little girl with a zest for life unexpectedly spiraling into a suicidal state.

The psychiatrist prescribed a cocktail of medications that turned Lillian into a confused, drooling, wiped-out mess. Before these side effects, she'd read a new book every week or two. Now the light in her eyes dulled and she could not follow a paragraph or carry on a conversation without falling asleep. Concerned that Lillian could not learn anything at school in this state, and not sure what else to do, Lou made the difficult choice to take her off the antipsychotics. He feared this would lead to another attempt, but also felt that she got worse instead of better on the medication.

When Lou read about the highs and lows of bipolar disorder, the description never seemed to quite fit. Bipolar or not, something must have snapped in Lillian's head, and Lou wished he had recognized the red flags instead of dismissing them as normal teenage moodiness. The increasingly quiet, withdrawn attitude. The slipping grades in a previously good student.

And then a new dog just might have saved her life.

Lillian had never stopped wishing for a dog even after the brutal death of her puppy when she was seven. Those memories of cleaning the house with bleach, burning Buster's toys and bed, and the veterinarian's warning to wait at least a year for the virus to die to get another dog were still fresh.

When Lillian started high school, Lou stumbled across a rescue organization that found new homes for displaced blue heelers. A one-year-old dog, Astrid, was placed with Lou. Astrid was a lovely dog with a blue-flecked spotted coat, huge pointed ears, and a bushy tail. With all her energy, she needed rowdy play sessions and two walks per day. Astrid's positive effect on Lillian more than made up for the exhaustion of trying to keep up with her. Lillian smiled more again. She laughed with joy as they played fetch and tug-of-war. She walked with Astrid for miles, and the dog slept on her bed and grew protective of her. Astrid even had a sneaky sense of humor. Her favorite prank was chewing the plastic squeakers out of her plush toys and leaving them inconspicuously on the floor, waiting for someone to step on them and get startled by the squeaks.

Lillian's grades climbed back up as she joined the photography club, the orchestra where she learned to play the upright bass, and the yearbook staff. This got Lou's hopes up that Lillian had permanently healed from the crisis, whatever it was.

One day in the fall of Lillian's freshman year, as the trees began to turn brilliant hues of red and gold, Denny convinced her to go fishing at a nearby river. Without the company of her father, who was busy at his nursery. For the past year, Lillian had avoided spending time alone with Denny. Missing the fun they used to have, she finally caved.

"I've been meaning to talk to you about something," Denny brought up as they sat on folding canvas chairs and waited for the fish to nibble. This phrase always shot fear through Lillian's heart—what if she was in trouble? Had she done something bad? "I know it ain't your favorite thing to talk about, but that... thing that happened in the summer. The attempt."

He was right. Lillian did not want to talk about it, still swirling in a cloud of shock and confusion that she'd even done it, that she was alive afterward when still surviving today was not in her plans. She swallowed hard, looking down.

"You really scared your poor dad when you did that. And me. You know that my mom did that, and succeeded, when I was a kid. My mom struggled for years. My dad had custody. The last few times I visited Mom, she was damn near incoherent. I know it's not easy being like us. Having these powers, feeling weird and different. You can't tell your sister; I can't tell my wife. It's at least a part of what did my mom in. And I was a troubled kid. But you used to cope with it fairly well. I think I told you my mom had visions of plane crashes and nuclear meltdowns and shit. Some if it came true, years or decades later. You don't have those visions?"

"I don't think so. I get weird dreams sometimes. Like this graveyard, or this fox in a meadow, or this guy who just died of a drug overdose. I still don't know what any of it means. And I've never had them come true, like your mom's visions."

"I never thought you're manic-depressive or whatever it is that doctor said you have. I figured maybe something happened. I brought out my cards and did some readings. You know what card kept showing up? The King of Swords, reversed. A lot of the time, those court cards are talking about a person. The first guy that comes to my mind? Julius."

Another lump clogged Lillian's throat.

"I always thought that guy was pretentious, a bit of a prick. That's why I didn't bother going to his wedding. But you all were just about to go when the attempt happened. Right?"

Lillian nodded, body running cold and numb.

"It's Julius, isn't it? You got quieter after you visited him. Something happened?"

Lillian shook her head violently, Julius' threats echoing in her ears as she tried her hardest to hold back tears. She saw the gruesome mutant infused with a sulfuric demon from down below, and his promise that he'd send more of them after her if she confessed to their "adult relationship."

"If anything did happen, you can tell me. And you should tell your father too."

Lillian took deep breaths, willing the tears gathered on her eyelids to not fall.

"Nothing happened? You sure?"

"Yes," Lillian said, her voice almost a whisper.

"If that changes, let me know."

Two years after Katrina's high school graduation, Grandpa and Uncle Julius held to some of their promises. Though she was unable to find anything that paid better than the tech support call center where she worked nights, her uncle covered a good chunk of the deposit and rent on the apartment Katrina shared with her boyfriend of the past several months. Drawing from a bank account his wife Jana was in the dark about, Julius bought them new furniture. Jana demanded that Julius not treat Katrina like a charity case, or like his own child. When Jana became pregnant, she tightened the leash further.

Jana gave birth to a son, Robert Julius, in December of 2004, a year and a half after Katrina's graduation. Even with a newborn at home, Uncle Julius vowed to keep himself available.

Katrina's live-in boyfriend was pretty much what Grandpa and Uncle Julius had promised, a man with mage blood who happened to be quite handsome. They'd moved into the apartment within weeks of their first arranged meeting; neither could turn down the money or the halfway decent roof over their heads. Other than his attractive face, she found her partner boring. After getting off from his construction job, he tended to just watch sports until bedtime, with little to talk about.

Within a few months, Katrina conceived a child. After the first trimester transitioned into the second, Julius got around his wife and stopped by the apartment. Looking closely at her rounded belly, he predicted what Katrina also suspected from the first green wisps of an aura coming through her skin. This baby on the way was most likely a necromancer. She had become lucky on the first try. What a blessing!

Katrina began to feel the baby fluttering and kicking at her from the inside. Just as Grandpa and Uncle Julius promised, Katrina's abilities increased. Her brain zapped with new synapses every day. She began to see ghosts and shades of them more frequently, almost at every corner, it felt like. Katrina's senses of her surroundings expanded. While she could not read minds, at least not yet, the same force of telekinesis that had once moved a pencil an inch now crushed it into splinters.

Katrina grew thirsty with power, picturing all the things she could do if she lived openly as a necromancer. Raising the dead at an increased rate. Perhaps creating even more vicious monsters than the one her uncle had showed her before he married. Maybe instead of just embarrassing her former classmate Megan with that lewd stunt in the cafeteria, Katrina could have seized hold of Megan and all of her friends and done the same to them simultaneously. Or just rid the world of those bullies, flinging them into the ceiling or out the window. Katrina still had months ahead to grow this baby. Imagining what she'd be capable of at forty weeks made her heart quiver with the greatest excitement of her life.

Less worried about Lou snooping, Katrina wrote letters to Lillian, bragging about her pregnancy. Though Lillian was still in high school, Katrina saw no reason why she couldn't get started having babies after her graduation.

When you get pregnant, and if it's a mage baby, you are going to feel so amazing. You're gonna want ten kids! You just have to make sure the baby's dad is a half-breed for any chance at it happening. Don't worry, we can find you a cute half-breed guy. Uncle Julius helped me find one, and he's REALLY hot, so I don't see why he can't help you, too! And my boyfriend has a brother. I don't know if he's a half-breed or not, but maybe I can set you up with him!!

Lillian's responses were shorter, their tone guarded.

That's really nice that you're having a baby and you're enjoying your increase in powers. I'm happy for you that things are going well. I want to get a college education. I don't want kids. I'm not super interested in looking for a boyfriend, but I appreciate the thought.

Katrina wrote back—*Aw, how can you say you don't want kids? You hate kids? That sucks! You're too young to even know if you want kids or not! I wasn't even thinking about kids in HS.*

Lillian wrote back, explaining that she did not hate children, and babysat for a couple of families. Full-time responsibility for a baby did not sound like her cup of tea, however.

One afternoon, Katrina woke to get ready for her night shift while her boyfriend was away at the construction site. She sat up in bed and gasped. Something was not right. The power that burned in her brain and surged through her veins before she went to bed had diluted back to its pre-pregnancy levels.

Panicked, Katrina called her uncle Julius, the only person close by who would understand her concerns. His wife Jana picked up his cell phone, her voice groggy as their baby wailed in the background. Was Jana so jealous and controlling that she answered her husband's phone for him now?

"What do you want?" she grumbled. The cries of little Robbie increased the urgency of Katrina's worry. Robbie was alive and well, with the pair of lungs to show for it. Was Katrina's own baby okay? Please, please let it be okay.

"I really need to talk to my uncle, please."

"Can't you tell we're busy?"

"I know you are, but this is an emergency. It's about my baby."

"Look, we have *our* baby to worry about."

"Just, please..."

Julius snatched the phone from his wife, and Katrina overheard him scolding her. "My niece obviously needs me. What are you doing? Please let me speak to her."

"Okay, whatever." Jana let out an exasperated sigh.

As soon as Julius got on the phone, Katrina told him she'd lost the gains in her powers.

"Oh, no, that's not good," Julius' voice dropped.

"Could it mean something is wrong with the baby?" Katrina began to cry.

"I hope not. You should get checked out to make sure. Do you still feel the baby kicking?"

Katrina thought back, rewinding over the minutes since she'd woken up. Paid attention to her belly. "No, I don't think I've felt anything since I got up."

"I'm sure everything is fine, but call your doctor or head to the ER, and immediately let me know what they say."

On Julius' advice, Katrina drove herself to the nearest hospital. They brushed aside her worries, trying to reassure her that at seventeen weeks of gestation, she could not expect a baby to kick every day, every hour, or to even feel all of the kicks. But at her insistence, they did an ultrasound.

As the wand glided over Katrina's swollen belly, she looked at the screen, biting her nails in anxiety. During the last ultrasound, a heartbeat had throbbed throughout the room while the little arms and legs wiggled. This time, there was silence. No discernible movement.

The ultrasound technician's face went ashen and quiet. She rushed to get a doctor, who manipulated the wand herself until her own face fell. "I'm sorry. There is no heartbeat."

"It's dead?!" Katrina screamed.

"I'm so sorry."

Katrina barely listened as they told her the next steps, things she'd never known or thought about before. She'd always figured that if an unborn child passed away, it simply dissolved. Instead, it had to be delivered, just like a full-term infant. Katrina was instructed to come back tomorrow to induce contractions. Seriously? After this gut-punch of an announcement, she had to go through the pain of labor, with nothing to look forward to at the end?

Katrina called her boyfriend. He answered his cell phone in a huff, asking why she was bothering him at work. When she broke the news through her tears, his only words were, "Oh, fuck!"

He hung up.

Next, Katrina reached out to Julius, who rushed to the hospital to collect her. Urging her to brush off any grumpiness from his wife, he brought her to his house for a while and let her cry on his shoulder. Julius promised to give Katrina a ride back to the hospital tomorrow for her tragic induction.

Another cruel surprise hit Katrina in the face as she stepped into her apartment. Her boyfriend was gone. And so were his few possessions. When she called him, she found his phone turned off, going straight to voicemail.

"Asshole!" Katrina screamed as Julius held her once again. "How could he just leave me high and dry?"

After Julius went home, Katrina called in to work. Her boss showed no sympathy, only grunting, "You'd better be back by the end of the week." There would be no maternity leave. She'd have to return to her dreary cramped cubicle, headset strapped on like nothing happened, before she even healed.

The following night, Julius stood by Katrina's hospital bed as she gave birth to a child she was too frightened to even look at. Once she pushed the baby out, a deafening silence fell over the room, instead of the first cry that should have filled the space. One nurse announced that it was a boy. The other nurses, avoiding Katrina's eyes, furtively covered the child with thin blankets and rushed him away. Mind fogged with confusion and depression, Katrina could not think of a name for her son.

So much for having a necromancer baby, or even a living, breathing baby at all. After learning how easily one could die, for no reason at all, Katrina was not only single again, but too nervous to have another child.

High school hadn't been so bad. The girls who'd teased Lillian years ago still occasionally whispered in each other's ears as she walked past them in the halls. Now, Lillian found these catty classmates easier to ignore. They did not devastate her the way they used to in middle school.

Signs of Evelyn's achievements were still scattered around the main school hallway, pictures of her sports teams, a portrait of her as the homecoming queen in her crown, and a few lacrosse trophies in a glass display case. Though she had graduated in 2000, she'd left quite a reputation behind. Evelyn's senior class voted her both "Prettiest Girl" and "Most Likely to Succeed." Teachers still extolled Evelyn's virtues, like she was a hero. It threw them off that Lillian stood five inches taller than her older sister, was never the center of attention, and lacked interest in athletics, not the bubbly, sporty, petite girl they fondly remembered. Busy with her clubs and activities, Evelyn had somehow found the time to bring big crowds of friends home, and date one athletic boy after another. Home was a much quieter place after she left. It still hurt a bit to live in Evelyn's shadow, but Lillian was comfortable not being the crown jewel of her school, staying out of the spotlight.

Evelyn now blossomed into a bright future, surprising no one. After graduating from Georgia Tech with high honors, she studied for a master's degree. She and her college sweetheart, Jonathan Gundersen, both found well-paying petroleum engineering jobs in Houston, Texas, where they purchased a home. They got engaged. Everything fell neatly into place, step by step. The degree, the healthy income, the white picket fence, the muscular and handsome soon-to-be husband.

When Evelyn brought Jonathan home, the first thing to stand out to Lillian, her father, and Denny was not his dark-haired good looks, but his mage blood. He was just the kind of boyfriend that Katrina encouraged Lillian to find in those long letters about her pregnancy. But Evelyn was not a mage. She could not see her fiancé's stronger-than-average aura. She could not know. Lillian wondered if mage blood drew couples together like a magnet, even if they had no conscious clue. Her mother had it too, and had left her home city to start a family with a man almost twenty years older.

Lillian started spending a little more time with her old friend Adam again, making up for the distance that grew between them in eighth grade. By now, he'd found a serious girlfriend. When Lillian hung out with the two, her former closeness with Adam was gone, replaced with a sense of being the fifth wheel.

During her sophomore year, Lillian made a friend, Christian, who was new in town, and they befriended a third misfit named Ethan. The three briefly formed a garage band. Christian, in particular, got a lot of funny looks for his long hair that was usually black or green, and the piercings stretching his earlobes. When Lillian's father met Christian for the first time, he was visibly startled, but soon came to like him. Dad was less happy when Lillian began to practice a pagan religion and stopped attending church with him.

Lillian kept herself busy with the jazz band she joined at school, the bass guitar she practiced in the evenings, and her school clubs. In her free time, she wrote on her computer and blasted gloomy, post-punk music that came out before she was born.

A couple of boys at school asked Lillian out on a date. She regretfully declined, dreading the possibility of making out in parked cars or being pressured to go all the way on prom night. Lillian still could not admit to the events of that one summer. There was no telling how her body might react to a physical relationship, or what a boy would think of the self-inflicted scars that still kept her afraid to wear shorts or a swimsuit. Would he write her off as crazy? Go tell the whole school that she used to cut herself?

Lillian lived with the constant fear that Julius had left her with a silent sexually transmitted infection. She'd learned from the scary videos in health class that many of these infections were asymptomatic, including the ones that shortened your life. If Lillian gave someone a disease, she would have too much explaining to do. Getting tested was not an option; asking her father to make an appointment at the gynecologist would raise unanswerable questions.

Lillian met a boy her age, Pieter, online. They shared many of the same nerdy interests in books and music and video games, and had fun exchanging emails until they called themselves boyfriend and girlfriend. Getting together in person would not happen for quite a while, if ever. He lived in South Africa. Lillian had no passport, and both of their parents were not comfortable with their kids meeting foreigners from the internet.

Though Lillian got lonely, wishing she could invent a teleporting device to sneak past their cautious families, she also felt safer in this relationship. Pieter was across an ocean and in a different hemisphere. He would not lay eyes on Lillian's scars, or take her clothes off only for her to panic. He didn't have to know her dark secrets.

Julius talked about visiting, which got put off with his and Dad's conflicting schedules. Dad wanted to fly out sometime and meet Julius and Jana's toddler, Robbie, whose pictures ended up on the refrigerator. Even with the delays in meeting up, the man was an ever-present threat. He wrote letters to Lillian, asking innocent questions about how school was going, and she dutifully wrote back so her father would not get suspicious that anything went sour. When Julius called, and when Lillian was pressured to phone him on his birthday every year, she feigned the excited tone she knew Dad expected to hear.

Despite Lillian's nightmares that had her bolting up breathless in the dark, she convinced herself that she shouldn't still be anxious over Julius. What happened could have been worse. Maybe she had even imagined it outright. She was just exaggerating. Things weren't that bad; compared to a lot of people, Lillian enjoyed a good quality of life, with a roof over her head, attractive surroundings, nearby beaches, a caring dad, a beloved dog, an overseas boyfriend, and at least one good friend. She needed to just get over it, like Uncle Gerald said to do years ago.

One day, Uncle Gerald stopped by. And this time, he had a surprise guest. His granddaughter, Katrina. Lillian's heart sank as she watched out of the living room window while Katrina got out of the passenger's side of his polished silver Bentley.

If Katrina tagged along for this journey, then who else would be with him? Of course, the relative Katrina visited and occasionally referenced in her letters. Julius might pop out of the backseat! Lillian was not prepared for this at all.

But no one else got out of the car. Gerald and Katrina came up the porch and rang the doorbell.

Hadn't Katrina had a baby? Where was that child? After Katrina sent a flurry of letters boasting about her pregnancy and the enhancement of her necromancer abilities, the mail from her abruptly stopped. When Lillian wrote to her once, asking how he was doing, she did not get a reply. She and her father had both chalked it up to Katrina being overwhelmed with a newborn.

There'd been no birth announcement either, while Julius had sent a custom-printed page filled with glossy hospital photos right after his son Robbie was born. Maybe Katrina was just more private. Not one to put on an ostentatious display like Julius.

"I would have brought my son," Gerald told Lillian's father. "He was dying to come. He really, really wants you all to meet his little one. But he was tied up with work and couldn't join me."

"That's a pity. We've been missing him. I hope we'll see him soon enough."

Even without Julius present, Katrina served as an unsettling reminder that he was alive, thriving, and that he could still show up whenever he wanted. As Uncle Gerald and her father sat down to chat, Katrina urged Lillian to join her on the back porch for "girl talk."

Katrina was quick to inquire about Lillian's love life. Her face lit up at the mention of Lillian's boyfriend, only to fall a bit when Lillian explained the long distance.

"That's a bummer, that he's some dude from another country," Katrina said with a bit of a sigh. "I mean, you must know nothing about him, really."

"He tells me a lot."

"Still, there's a lot you don't know until you meet someone... I mean, *really* meet them. Like, for all you know, he's a mage and he'd kill you on sight."

"Mages are super rare, you know. That's extremely unlikely."

"Or hey, maybe that guy is a half-breed, like my ex was, and it'll be your lucky day! They don't know they're half-breeds. He wouldn't have to know anything about mages."

"Yeah, my mom carried that mage trait and I'm sure she had no clue, far as I can tell. I'd love to meet my boyfriend, but it's not happening anytime soon. So your ex-boyfriend... is that the same boyfriend you were living with and had the kid with?"

"Yeah, unfortunately. He dumped me. Moved out in a hurry without telling me. That's why I'm back to living with my mom, taking care of her."

"That sucks! By the way, how is your kid doing? You didn't take the baby with you...?"

Katrina went quiet. Her lip quivered as tears glittered in her eyes. "The baby... the baby died."

"Oh no! I'm so sorry! I had no idea!"

"I closed up after it happened. Couldn't tell hardly anyone. One day when I was almost halfway along, I woke up and that extra power I had was gone. The baby's heart stopped when I was asleep. I never found out why. The doctor said babies die in the womb sometimes and it's just one of those things."

"That sounds really heartbreaking. Now I know why you went quiet. You just didn't want to talk about it?"

"Yeah, it was hard to talk about. And my boyfriend skipped town right after I found out there was no heartbeat. Guess he was a fairweather type."

"And an asshole! You're better off without him!"

"Totally. Uncle Julius was there for me the whole time. Even though his wife is such a cunt. I have no idea why the hell a nice guy like him married her. You know what she said to me? 'That's what you deserve for getting pregnant at nineteen.'"

"What a nasty thing to say," Lillian sympathized. After her own frosty encounters with Jana, she'd never liked her, though Lillian did not have the heart or courage to tell Katrina that Julius was not the sweetheart everyone else saw.

"Jana's own kid is just a half-breed like her, and he got to live. It's not fair. That sister Jana was raising, Mandy, the one who killed herself? She was pregnant too."

"Really?! Is that true?" If Katrina told the truth about this, was Julius the one responsible?

"Yep, I heard she was knocked up when she died. She jumped off the roof and her neck snapped. Sounded brutal. Mandy wanted an abortion and Jana wouldn't let her, as punishment for having sex. Jana kept that girl out of foster care, but she was mean to her. My grandpa told me that a few years ago, you, like..." Katrina's voice lowered to an awkward whisper. "...tried to kill yourself or something. Did you?"

"I'm not really comfortable talking about that." In her shame at the fear and stress she had put her family through, and the sheer horror of the razor in her wrists, Lillian really did not enjoy bringing this up. She just wanted to bury that bloody night like the summer with Julius.

"Well, if you really are suicidal or something, you need to snap out of it and be proud of yourself. You know why? Because you're one of the last necromancers in the world. Like Grandpa said, we're the chosen ones."

"Chosen ones? Chosen for what? Or is he on some ego trip?"

"Don't be afraid to have a bit of an ego. You deserve it! I'm not sure exactly what we're chosen for, but we survived this long, and we have these amazing powers, so that has to count for something, right? Don't let anyone, or anything, beat you down! You're a rock star! A superhero!"

"Okay... I guess."

Uncle Gerald came out to the porch. Everyone went in to snack on some sliced pineapples Gerald had brought in a basket. Gerald left at sundown with Katrina, who stayed with him at his house for a few nights. Like most of his visits, this one was short-lived. Lillian was relieved at their departure. Though Lillian's heart went out to Katrina for the loss of her baby, that young woman still put her ill at ease.

One quiet Saturday, in the fall of Lillian's senior year of high school, Denny invited her to his house while his wife was out with friends.

"I want you to practice some of your powers," Denny said. "Now it's time."

Lillian nearly bolted out the front door. After the gruesome things Julius had shown her, which she was still too scared to even speak of, she used her powers only for minor conveniences. Turning the light off without getting out of bed. Stirring pots simultaneously in the kitchen. Pulling a snack into her hand when she lazed on the couch.

"What's wrong?" Denny asked.

"Oh, I just, uh… I really don't think we should be doing this."

"Don't worry. We'll go slow, since it's easy to mess up. When I was young—about twenty, twenty-one, thereabouts—I went out duck hunting by myself. After I had a duck, I got curious. You know, young people love taboo stuff."

"You brought the duck back?"

"I did. No one had even taught me how, but it was easy. Stupid easy. As soon as that duck started flapping, I panicked. I ran back into my truck and grabbed my twelve-gauge shotgun. Had to pretty much disintegrate the thing to get it to quit flapping." Denny laughed, his characteristic deep belly laugh. "It sounds funny now. Gallows humor, I guess. But I was scared shitless. Don't try that at home."

"Don't worry. I won't."

"Not much good comes of zombies, except maybe self-defense. It's like having a gun. You have to use the power responsibly, and know exactly what you're doing. We'll get there."

"We *will* be making a zombie?"

"I wasn't going to show you, but I decided it might be safest. Only for a split second, so you've got the knowledge, and then we'll get rid of it. Like with a gun, pulling a trigger is easy. You'll want to try that gun with the muzzle aimed downrange, so to speak, so you can see what happens when you do it, how it feels."

"Are we going to turn it into... something else?" Lillian got ready to run again. She could not face another monster.

"No, no. I've heard a little bit about changing the zombies into vicious animals, but I don't even know how to do that, or how we would control them. That's just too dangerous. We'll start with the telekinesis. It could get you out of serious trouble someday. This is why I want you to fine-tune it before you leave home."

"Like, in case somebody kidnaps me?"

"Exactly. Or other situations. These lessons might be even tougher than when I taught you to drive a standard. I'll be right back." Denny went out to his garage. *Telekinesis would save me if someone kidnaps me*, Lillian thought, *as long as it's not a mage.*

To Lillian's excitement, Denny came back with a large tackle box, just one of many he owned. Lillian had always loved exploring his fishing lures and baits, holding them up to the sunlight whenever they went fishing or canoeing together and admiring how some of them shone and some of them glittered. But this green tackle box did not look familiar. Denny opened it up, revealing things Lillian didn't expect, much less sparkly than his lures and fake worms: plastic beads, needles, fish hooks, padlocks, string, and other random bits.

"Are we making beaded necklaces?" Lillian asked.

"Yep. Except we ain't gonna be using our hands."

This became the first of multiple lessons, which started out fun but eventually caused a headache. Lillian learned to draw up a needle out of a slit, pick locks, and thread a string through a plastic bead, but try as she might, she could not narrow her telekinesis enough to thread a needle or fish hook. Denny could accomplish these after decades of practice, but only if he really focused.

Aside from straining their brains with the little bits and pieces in the tackle box, Denny had Lillian practice with something she found a lot more interesting: divination. She tried reading a bowl of water, getting only the vaguest of visions. Denny gave her a tarot deck, which she kept quiet about with her father, anxious that he might disapprove.

While these private afternoon lessons took place, Lillian's biology class dissected fetal pigs. The teacher assigned each pig to teams of four or five. In group projects, most of the work usually fell on Lillian's shoulders, and this was no exception. Her team members gagged in disgust and made Lillian wield the scalpel. As she cut through the tissues, it took strength for Lillian to hold back her instincts.

If you think this formaldehyde-preserved pig is the grossest thing ever, Lillian thought to herself in her frustration at the classmates who refused to help, *you should see the things I've seen.*

When Lillian vented to Denny about the class project, he decided, "It's time. You're gonna go to college next year, and I'll bet they'll make you do even more dissections. Time to get it out of your system while you're safe with me."

The opportunity came by accident when Lillian hung out at the park with Astrid one day, letting the dog run off-leash while she took photos. The dog bounded off into a stand of pine trees, rolling on the ground and making snorting sounds. Lillian picked her way through the trees to investigate what disgusting thing Astrid might be wallowing in this time. A skunk had hosed her with its musk last week and they'd just barely managed to wash the last of that stench out of her fur. What would she and her father have to shampoo out now?

Astrid rolled on a squirrel. It hadn't been dead for long enough to become malleable and slimy, but it was dead enough to stink. Dingy fur wired out from the bloated body. Lillian ordered Astrid to walk away from her prize. After getting her back on the leash, Lillian took her pink cell phone out from her bag, flipped it open, and called Denny.

After he arrived, he put on gloves and collected the corpse in a plastic bag. "It's deteriorated, but it should still work. I'll put this in the freezer until the weekend. You go home and give that pooch a bath."

The weekend came. Denny gave Lillian a ride out into the woods, storing the bagged dead squirrel in the bed of his truck along with a loaded shotgun. Though Lillian did not like keeping secrets, already burdened with too many of them, she had not told her father what they'd be doing.

They found a small, damp clearing, well out of view of the road. After dumping the squirrel out of the bag onto the ground, Lillian and Denny both stood back. Denny pumped his shotgun.

"What do I do now?" Lillian asked.

"What you feel like you oughta do," Denny suggested. "Don't overthink it. Just do it."

An excited thread of power leached out of Lillian, scanning the squirrel's body. She usually pulled back when this happened, but this time, she allowed the thread to linger. Even with Denny's permission, this felt so forbidden, so naughty.

The animal stood up on its hind legs like a prairie dog, staring her down with its one intact eye.

"That was so easy!" Lillian gasped.

"Yup, you caught on right away. Now try getting it to move toward us."

Move, Lillian sounded out in her mind. In robotic, rigid motions, the undead squirrel hopped stiffly, its remaining eye glittering like a marble.

After they both put ear protectors on, Denny was quick to dispatch the creature with his shotgun.

Even though most of the lessons happened with Denny, it was her father who showed Lillian the one thing that truly blew her away.

For her seventeenth birthday, Dad had given Lillian an emerald-green crystal that had been handed down through many generations of the family, making her promise to keep it safe. Her paternal grandfather had wrapped the talisman in wire, making it into a pendant. As a child, Lillian loved to hold the crystal in the palm of her hand, sensing it pulses as they spread warmly through her. Dad instructed Lillian to tell anyone who asked, including Evelyn, that it was just a rock that went on a necklace.

Yet no one had ever explained what that crystal could do, exactly.

One afternoon, Lillian's father took her out to the backyard, bringing the crystal. He glanced around, making sure that no neighbors were visible over the fence.

"Hold the crystal," he instructed in a soft voice as Lillian wrapped her hands around it, chain and all. "Close your eyes. Now imagine yourself going to another realm. Sinking through the ground. Don't focus on anything but the crystal. Deep breaths. When you're ready to come back, you do the same thing; just ask the crystal to bring you up. There you go! There you..."

Gravity gave way beneath Lillian's feet, and her eyes shot open in surprise at her free-fall. She screamed as a dark void enveloped her.

The blackness dissolved into mist, giving way to a familiar dream sight: the little graveyard that always felt like a stop on the way to somewhere else, with the time-worn gargoyles standing sentry over tombs and a few crosses sticking up from the ground nearby. The door to one tomb fell open, allowing a warm, soft purple glow to spill out. Something strongly drew Lillian to pass through that door.

She fell slowly in a column of glittering light, drifting down like a petal, like Alice descending into Wonderland. Wondering if Dad had drugged her, Lillian landed softly in a grassy grove. Not one like any she'd ever seen on Earth. The house—the whole neighborhood, the whole town—was gone, replaced with a velvety meadow. The warm, moist air was perfumed gently with purple, glowing flowers. Fireflies bounced all around.

"Dad?" Lillian called. "Dad? Dad!! Where are you? Dad!! Anybody?"

In the distance was a huge lake of mirrored waters. Closer, from the nearest meadows, rose large-scale versions of the crystal Lillian held in her hands, like the spires of some slanted castle. The light of a dim pink setting sun pierced them, setting the crisscrossed fibers alight against a purplish, star-twinkling sky.

Lillian spotted something that looked manmade: a columned structure carved of the smooth green stone. She had a strong sense of déjà vu. As though she'd been born remembering this building.

Completely disoriented, fearing she might throw up, Lillian followed through on some of the last words she'd heard from her father, before his voice faded out. She squeezed the crystal and closed her eyes.

Her body went weightless again, elevating through the thick, sweet-smelling air.

The next time she opened them, she was in her father's arms, gasping for air. Back in her own yard, the air warmer, the sky brighter, the neighborhood where it should be.

"What was that?" Lillian demanded. "Was that a dream?"

"No, sweetheart. That was not a dream. That's one of the best-kept secrets of mages."

"Why didn't you tell me about that place?"

"Because you have to see it to believe it."

"What... I went to another dimension?!"

"Sssh, not so loud. Yes, in a way, you did. That's our special world. The world in between."

"First, I went to a graveyard."

"Really?! That's unusual. That hasn't happened to anyone else that I know of."

"It's a graveyard I've seen in my dreams. Then I walked into a tomb, and that's when I fell again and went into this really pretty area."

"And you saw a building, yes?"

"Yeah. A green building. It seemed familiar, somehow. Have I ever been there before?"

"No, you haven't. That's our temple. Did you see anyone there? A large, dark figure?"

Lillian shook her head in confusion. "No. I was too overwhelmed to go in the temple. But I didn't see anyone. I felt like I was totally alone."

"Huh. Maybe it would have taken a bit more venturing, but I was hoping you'd see him, since I haven't in years."

"See who?"

"We're not exactly sure who he is. He is our leader in the spiritual realm. Some call him Samael, which is also what some folks call the devil. I can't imagine he's really the devil. Some call him the Angel of Death."

"The Grim Reaper, or something like that? That's our leader?"

"Yes. Wearing a black robe, his face a skull. Looking how you'd expect. When I was younger, each time I journeyed to that world, he was there. Watching with those glowing skull eyes. He scared the daylights out of me as a boy, but then I learned he tried to keep us safe. Sometimes he would speak, and I got overwhelmed just from the power of his voice. He warned me to not abuse my powers, and said he would come to Earth. To help us."

"With what?"

"I don't know; he never explained. I haven't seen Samael, or the Angel of Death, or whatever you want to call him, in a long time. It's strange. He vanished about seventeen or eighteen years ago. Denny hasn't seen him since then, either. And I was hoping maybe he would appear for you."

"Where do you think he went?"

"I haven't the foggiest clue. If he did come to Earth, I wouldn't know where to find him. But if we keep looking, hopefully we shall learn something. Each of the four types of mages has a temple. The only ones who can reach their temples are ones who are lucky enough to have crystals, or who know how to do a really deep meditation few can master. Now you see why your uncle Gerald wanted the crystal so badly?"

"Yeah, I guess. So that's the only crystal we have?"

"Yes. Means we're alone down there each time we go."

Phew. No chance of running into Julius in the other dimension. "Is there anything there that can hurt me?"

"No."

"Not even Samael or Death or whoever it is, if he comes back?"

"Very unlikely. I don't think he would hurt his own people. Unless he really is the Angel of Death and it's our time to die."

"I want to do it again."

"Of course you do, sweetheart. Just be careful and don't do it too often. You know how our neighbor's son is a recluse, holed up in his room, playing that computer game day and night? You could get even more lost in the other world than that boy does in his game. Don't let it become a distraction."

Lillian's next foray into that world happened just a week later. Her father suggested that she enter the temple to honor her ancestors. The journey through the graveyard and then down below frightened her less. Once again, there was no deity in sight.

Lillian set foot on a winding, glowing path through the sparkling air. The path led to the temple, which cast off faint green light filtered through its semi-transparent stone structure. She ascended the massive steps to enter between the pillars.

The central hallway was lined with bones from floor to ceiling, black eye sockets staring out from the skulls. Some of the skulls were human, others animal with long fangs. All of the skulls looked to somehow be at peace, green and coated with patches of moss. The hallway gleamed with diffused light cast gently from a green stone pedestal in the center. Doors diverged off the main hall, opening to foggy unknowns. Lillian's instincts led her to a massive room at the end, also walled with skulls and a mesh of crossed tibias. Orbs hovered in midair, some of them coming together into humanoid forms. Their communal sound was sometimes a whisper, sometimes a roar.

Scenes unfolded of shamans who had lived in isolated huts at the edges of their villages, clad in furs and necklaces of bone, sometimes called upon to revive dead loved ones or exact revenge upon enemies.

Lillian grew a bit wistful, watching the ancient ones who had existed before the other mage types turned on the necromancers and set out to kill them all. What would it be like to be respected for her powers, even if people kept their distance, rather than having to live carefully and fake a mainstream exterior or risk her life?

And still, there was no mysterious hooded figure. Just ghostly views of the distant past.

The sun got lower, hiding behind the trees. Some sort of luminescence lit this place up at night in a softly glowing rainbow. Lillian was tempted to stay, but did not want to worry her father. She clasped her hands around the crystal on its chain, and concentrated until reality shifted back to the mundane.

As Lillian's graduation came up, Lou did not hesitate in making plans. He wanted to throw a meaningful party to celebrate this life milestone, just like Evelyn's big bash seven years before. He sent invitations to everyone he could think of.

When Lou called his nephew Julius to invite him, he confidently asserted, "Mark my word, I'll be at the party. It's been too many years since I've seen you and Lillian, and I think about you often. I'll bring a very nice gift."

Lou could not wait to see his nephew and meet Julius' son Robbie at last. It seemed like the birth announcement came in the mail just yesterday, and now that little boy was already two years old.

To drum up Lillian's excitement, Lou told her over dinner one night about the celebration in the works, how he, his friend and former wife Roberta, and Denny would make an epic crab feast followed by cake.

"Who's coming to the party?" Lillian asked. "You've been inviting people, haven't you?"

"Yes, I've already invited everyone I can think of."

"Like who?"

"Denny and Mona, of course. Roberta. Evelyn and Jonathan are coming for sure. Your aunt Violet, if she's feeling up to it. Some folks from work. And of course, you're welcome to bring anyone from school that you please. I invited Gerald, even if the two of us have had our ups and downs. I tried to invite your uncle Victor on your mom's side, the one out in California, but he can't make it. And last but not least, I invited Julius and his family."

"Is he coming?" Lillian's eyes widened just a bit as her fork hovered, trembling, over her food.

"Oh, yes. I'm so excited to finally meet the little one... aren't you?"

"Yeah... I guess."

"You don't sound too convinced."

"Oh, yes, I'm excited. I'm so glad you're throwing this huge party for me, Dad."

Once they finished eating, Lou offered to make strawberry shortcake for dessert. Lillian declined, saying she had homework to finish in her room.

As Lou got ready for bed, he glanced around. The large fleece dog bed beside the fireplace lay empty. It was Lillian's job to bring the dog and her toys inside for the night, and it looked like she had forgotten. Lou went upstairs and knocked on Lillian's door. "Did you remember to let Astrid in?"

"No. I forgot. I'll do it in a second."

When Lillian finally came out of her bedroom, her face was red, streaked with tears.

"What's wrong, sweetheart?" Lou begged as she ran down the stairs.

"Nothing. I just... I'm going to let the dog in."

"Please tell me what's wrong." Lou gently grasped Lillian by the arms to stop her.

"No!" she screamed in an unusually loud volume, shrinking away.

"What's wrong? Did something go wrong with a friend?"

"No! It's nothing."

"Tell me what's wrong!"

"You can't have that party!" Lillian wailed.

"What? Do you mean your graduation party?"

"Yes! Cancel the party!" Lillian backed up and winced, her expression surprised like her own words had frightened her.

"What... I can't cancel the party. I've already put a lot of work into planning it!"

"Then I'm not coming!" The tears began to flow again.

"Please. Something is wrong, isn't it? Tell me what's wrong!"

"If you want me there, you have to disinvite someone."

"Who?!" Alarm bells began to go off in Lou's mind.

Lillian started to shake, her face blanching. "Julius."

"What in the world?! What is this grudge against Julius all of a sudden?"

"He just can't come!"

"Why? Care to explain to me..."

"He just can't!"

"Did you have an argument on the phone?"

"No." Lillian shook her head violently.

"Then why can't he come? Please tell me. He's so excited and I can't just tell him he's not allowed to. It'd break his heart."

"Nothing... it's nothing. He just can't come, okay?"

"Please tell me what's wrong!" Lou insisted.

"I just... I can't tell you. I can't."

"Can't tell me what?"

"Leave me alone!" Lillian raced up the stairs and slammed the door to her bedroom, leaving Lou terribly confused. He was not only frustrated, but scared at this point.

After the dog was in and he tucked himself into his bed, Lou kept his nightstand lamp on, trying to read a book and failing to concentrate. Why was Lillian acting so strangely tonight? She had never demanded that someone be excluded from any social event before. And to cut out a favorite relative for no reason?

Ever since the suicide attempt, Lou really worried whenever Lillian seemed unhappy.

That summer she stayed with Julius nearly five years ago, hadn't he called with a couple of complaints about her behavior? Maybe Lillian didn't like him because he was too strict, or had a different set of rules at his house?

A slight noise caught Lou's attention. As he got out of bed to find a couple of folded pieces of notebook paper slid under the door, footsteps scampered quickly down the hallway.

Lou picked up the papers from the battered hardwood floor, filled with Lillian's small, backward-slanting print handwriting. He sat on his bed and started to read.

Dear Dad,

I am not supposed to be telling you this. But I don't know what to do anymore.

Remember that summer I turned 13, when I went to help out Julius? Things were fine at first, except that me and Mandy Kreider, the other girl there, were overworked. He was working us way too hard, for hours and hours, and we were tired and having no fun. We just kind of wished we could go home.

Weird stuff started to happen. He was having an affair with Mandy's sister Jana, even though Jana had another boyfriend. He asked me about my period and asked if I was a virgin. Later Mandy told me Julius crawled into her bed and kissed her. She had holes in her memory and felt like she was being drugged...

Lou continued to read, his breath catching in his throat, his stomach feeling like it was ripped straight out of his body. His devastated shock turned into homicidal rage toward Julius. His shaking hands nearly tore the letter apart; yet he could not take his eyes off these poisonous words.

Lou read about Julius showing Lillian the family's riskiest, most gruesome power: the monsters. Bile rose in his throat as he found out about the abuse, about being threatened and chased. It made immediate sense to Lou now, why Lillian attempted to take her own life shortly before Julius' wedding and the next scheduled visit that never happened. She could not go back to that awful situation. Who could?

As Lou clutched the letter damp with sweat from his palms, he was overcome with simmering anger toward himself, along with the urge to tear apart his perverted nephew limb from limb. How could Lou have been so naïve? Why hadn't he put the pieces together sooner? The graduation party fell to the back tier or Lou's mind. If Julius showed up, he might not be able to hold back from murdering the man on sight.

Though Lou did not even know what to say, he could not leave Lillian by herself after she poured her heart out in this letter. She wrote in its pages that she was still scared of getting hurt in retaliation for spilling the truth.

When Lou knocked on Lillian's door, it swung open. Still awake, Lillian sat in her chair with her legs drawn up, fidgeting nervously.

"Did you read it?" she whispered, looking down. "Don't read it. Throw it out."

"I read it," Lou admitted in a low rough voice, his throat closing up as a tear spilled down his cheek. "Lillian, I wish you had told me these things sooner."

"But I was too scared."

"I know you were threatened into keeping quiet. But if anybody needs to be scared right now, it's that piece of scum I once called my nephew. I'm... I'm just devastated right now!"

"You believe me?"

"Of course. Why wouldn't I believe you?"

"I don't know... sometimes I kind of feel like maybe it wasn't that bad. Or maybe Julius really is a good guy. Or maybe it was my fault. Like I should have..."

"It was not your fault! That man is a beast, a brute. And yes, it was that bad. I was foolish. I trusted him with my child, who it is my duty to protect. And in doing so, I failed. When you came back from that visit and then those other things happened, I failed to make the connection. I'm very sorry I let you down and did not protect you."

"But you didn't know, and they kept saying I couldn't tell anybody."

"They? Who else was involved in this... this hideous abuse?"

"Uncle Gerald talked to me after I came back home from Julius' house."

"Gerald knew about this?! Of course he did. He must have seen it in your heads! Why didn't he say anything to me?"

"He said that Julius made a mistake, and that I just had to put it behind me and it was water under the bridge."

"That was an awful thing for Gerald to say. Julius belongs in prison. If it were an option, I'd call the cops on him right now."

"Please, no! Then he'll really kill me!"

"I won't. I can't. We are not people you can contain in a jail cell. Julius would take possession of the guards and break right out. We can't involve government; mages have always handled things on our own."

"What about Gerald?"

"Deep down, Gerald is afraid of me because my powers are stronger than his. But I'm not sure how to handle this. I have to think. I'm just..." Lou put his head in his hands as the sobs overtook his body.

"Are you okay?" his daughter asked.

"Of course not."

"I wasn't even expecting you to believe me, or take it seriously."

"Of course I'm taking it seriously. This is a parent's nightmare!"

The next morning, the start of a much-needed weekend, Lou called his brother Gerald, unable to hold in his anger any longer.

"You knew about it," Lou shouted into the phone. "And you didn't do anything, couldn't be bothered to tell me even when that suicide attempt happened? You didn't even try to stop him!"

"I am so, so sorry, Lou. I gave Julius the third degree, but I just felt it wasn't my place to intervene. Now I feel that I should have."

To Lou, this was too weak of an apology. A paltry excuse.

Next, Lou called his older daughter Evelyn. Lillian wished Evelyn did not hear about this, but she understood the reason for this call.

Evelyn and Julius had deepened their bond over the years, talking on the phone every month and exchanging letters and gifts. When Evelyn pleaded to know why she suddenly had to cut Julius off, Lou told her point-blank what had happened, though he left out the details. Evelyn gasped and went quiet.

"That summer, she called the house in the evening," Evelyn confessed. "I picked up. You were sick in bed. She said she'd tried to run away from Julius and she wanted us to come get her, and I just told her to get over herself and go back to him! I never even told you about that call. Why did I just shrug it off? I feel like crap over it now!"

"I didn't understand what was going on either, and I should have known," Lou sighed.

"Why did she wait so long to tell anyone?"

"He'd threatened her. She was afraid to tell anyone. Then when I insisted on inviting Julius to her graduation party, that put her between a rock and a hard place. Trust me, I'm feeling guilty too."

Evelyn insisted that Lou report Julius to the authorities. As much as Lou hated to deceive anyone, he lied to Evelyn out of necessity, promising her he would. He could not possibly explain to her why the officials could not get tangled up in the affairs of mages.

The following week, a letter from Uncle Gerald arrived, written in his nicest hand on thick cream-colored paper.

Dear Lou & Lillian,

I am very deeply sorry for the pain your family has endured. I am aware of the abuses my son committed, and that he is sick in the head. In fact, I no longer have contact with him due to his perverse sexual tendencies, and I have personally ordered him to stay away from Lillian and other young women. He always defers to me in the end, so I have every confidence that he will obey me.

I made some very poor judgment calls. I did not make you aware of Julius' actions, and I really should have. This was a very awkward situation and I thought it was not my place to tell you, because I believed Lillian would soon. I did not expect these years of silence from her.

Again, I hope you will accept my apology for my inaction. I was also unaware that Julius was planning to visit you again. Rest assured that it will not happen, as I will not let it.

Sincerely,

Gerald

Lou seethed as he crumpled the letter in his hands. The mere thought of Julius, or the mention of his name, made Lou's blood boil with fury. After giving himself some days to continue processing everything, Lou told Denny, who reacted with rage and offered to go on a joint mission to kill Julius right then and there. Lillian talked Denny out of it, pleading with him that she did not want anyone dying in her name.

Joined by her father, Lillian visited another psychiatrist, steering clear of the last one who had diagnosed her as bipolar. Dr. Lucy Carlson quickly determined that Lillian was misdiagnosed. After learning more of the story, minus the magical aspects, Dr. Carlson was quick to diagnose post-traumatic stress disorder instead. She prescribed a couple of medications to help with Lillian's anxiety and lessen her nightmares.

Lillian also made an appointment with a gynecologist, terrified, trembling, and pale by the time she reached the waiting room. As she laid on her back with her feet in stirrups, tears streamed down her face while a nurse held her hand and attempted to soothe her. It was a relief when all of the tests for sexually transmitted infections came back negative, though Lillian still felt dirty.

Lillian and her father cancelled her graduation party, letting all of their friends and loved ones—except Julius—know that they were more than happy to receive gifts in the mail. Normally a teetotaler, Lou began to fall asleep with the help of bourbon. His guilt was a physical ache.

They let Denny break the news to Julius that he was no longer welcome to even speak to their branch of the family. During the unpleasant call, Denny made threats, alluding to wood chippers. Julius angrily denied wrongdoing, blustering until Denny hung up on him.

The last day of school, Lillian tracked down her friend Adam in the hallway, finally apologizing for pushing him away in the eighth grade and hurting his feelings. She did not explain anything about Julius, too locked up in her embarrassment and shame to tell any of her friends. All she could get out was, "I was going through some personal shit." With a nod, Adam accepted the apology and promised to keep in touch.

The week after Lillian's commencement, her uncle Gerald arrived unannounced and uninvited. With a sigh, Lou let in his brother. In Gerald's beefy arms, he held a wrapped graduation gift.

"That's top-of-the-line," Gerald remarked as Lillian opened up the box containing a new Apple PowerBook. "College students need a good laptop computer these days. I ordered the professional model with the most advanced features, and I got you a full suite of graphics programs because I know you have an interest in photography. There's ample room for your photos, music, and those science fiction stories you keep writing. This will also be perfect for chatting with that overseas boyfriend your father does not approve of."

Gerald knew exactly what gifts made people the happiest, one of the benefits of full mind reading. In her surprise over the expensive gift, Lillian almost forgot to thank him.

Gerald nodded toward Astrid, the dog, who whined and thumped her fuzzy, wiry tail on the rustic hardwood floor. "Your pup wants Milk-Bones and a romp around outside.

Yes, you don't have to be human for me to read your mind. But that much is obvious by her body language anyway."

"We plan on taking her for a walk this afternoon. She's always filled with energy," said Lou.

"I'd better be on my way. I wanted to pass along my best wishes. Take care. Have a good time at college, Lillian, and don't drink too hard and abuse your liver the way I did. Don't let your father's worries keep you from going, and use your gifts—by that, I mean our inborn gifts—wisely." Gerald took a graceful little bow.

After Gerald's silver car left the driveway, Lou gave in to Astrid's demands and leashed her. With his daughter, he walked the dog down the quiet tree-lined road from their white clapboard house. Unable to contain her excitement, Astrid frantically yanked at her leash like a desperate prisoner rattling against shackles in a dungeon. She zigzagged as Lou's arms strained to hold onto the leash.

"I'm a little concerned about Gerald getting you that fancy machine, though for him it'd cost about as much as a bag of popcorn, relatively speaking," Lou confided. "I'm pretty sure there's strings attached."

"What do you mean, there's strings attached?"

"I'm concerned Gerald might use it to manipulate."

"Should I give it back? Should I not use it? Though to be honest, I'd be disappointed."

"It's yours and it shall come in handy at school, but don't let it turn into an obligation for something you aren't comfortable with. If he tries to make you feel guilty or like you owe him a favor, don't do it. Let me know."

"There's stuff that happened that I don't know about, isn't there?"

"Can you take this dog before she yanks my arm out of its socket?" Lou handed the leash to Lillian. "I suppose I never told you much... Gerald used to blackmail me when we were boys. Someone who reads your mind knows how to exploit all your weak spots."

"That's awful. But do you think that he might have outgrown it?"

Lou shook his head. "I question how he's made a lot of his money over the years. I still don't trust him. Lillian, I know that you've wished you were one of the mind readers."

"Yeah, it would make it a lot easier to spot scammers and fake friends."

"But I think it's for the best that we aren't. I'm not sure that any mind reader comes out normal."

It was time to feed the dog her dinner, and eat dinner themselves. They turned around and headed back home in a more comfortable silence.

Later, setting up the new laptop, Lillian found an envelope tucked deep into the bottom of the packaging. A narrow, capped plastic tube, filled with dried herbs, was taped to the envelope. As she opened it, the contents were hauntingly familiar. A thick, creamy paper was covered in Uncle Gerald's neat cursive handwriting, in a language that looked almost like a poem of nonsense words. It wasn't German, the language Lillian studied at school.

Beneath, Gerald wrote:

To make the circle, combine the following ingredients. I included a small vial to get you started, whenever the time is right.

2 bay leaves

1 teaspoon salt

1 teaspoon dried rosemary

1 teaspoon dried wormwood

1 teaspoon poppy

1 teaspoon deadly nightshade

Distribute in a circle around your target, and chant the above spell. As you've had demonstrated to you before.

Lillian's stomach turned as she ran to get her father. Knowing of that day when Julius transformed his deceased cat into something not of this world, he agreed that this was not good knowledge to have or to pass on. They unanimously decided to burn both the paper and the contents of the vial in the sink. Lillian did not rest until there was nothing but smoldering ashes, washed down the drain.

Excerpt from The Autobiography of Gerald Frazier: Architect of a New World

Papa had something I wanted, a precious artifact passed down in the family. The green crystal, which allows us to pass into the other world, our very own kingdom, where our temple stands and our mysterious leader, who might be Death himself, used to reside! No one really knows where these ancient crystals come from, but it is a possibility that the divine entities who oversee us entrusted the first mages with them.

My father never allowed the children to touch the crystal. I wanted it more than anything. I stole it twice to experiment with travel between the two worlds, and it blew my mind out of the water! The other world is a beautiful place filled with glistening water and glowing trees, and I had a grand time swimming in the pristine ponds. The chaotic noise of the world up above turned into almost a lullaby down below. One of the times I took the crystal, I was about ten years old. I returned it to Papa's desk, and with his powers he was able to tell that I'd recently touched the crystal. When I ended up on the business end of Papa's belt, it only made me want the crystal more.

Hopefully, if you're reading this, you now live in a world where this same treasure is now passed around and shared by all of us chosen ones, who deserve to participate in the joy!

When I was twelve, a lonely, childless war widow named Mrs. Donnell moved from New York City to live with her aunt down the street from my home. When this good-looking blonde woman spotted me riding my bicycle down the street one day, she invited me in for a cup of tea. I didn't even have to ask her to tell me stories about life in the Big Apple. All I had to do was read her mind, of course, to see the busy streets and taxicabs and exciting, bustling shops. To a boy growing up in a more rural area, it was a whole new world! I was definitely intrigued by the view of the skyline from the apartment she'd shared with her husband before he went off to fight in France and never returned.

The widow invited me over on more than one occasion when her aunt stepped out. When I offered to bring my siblings, she declined, only wanting my company. And then she started making advances. Though I saw it coming, this still threw a bit of a monkey wrench into my young mind. I wasn't the first adolescent boy she'd developed an appetite for, since fully grown men simply did not excite her enough. Not long after, Mrs. Donnell remarried and moved away, leaving me alone in a confused and somewhat embarrassed state. Sarah and Lou grew suspicious that something had happened, and I threatened them and told them to shut up when they asked.

After entering high school, Sarah wanted badly to fit in. With her plump figure, she worried that boys would not want to date her. She wrapped her hair tightly around painful curlers every night and went on a series of unsuccessful starvation diets.

Sarah's looks and weight were not her only worries. She wished she could wave a magic wand and make her powers and visions go away. She would cry and moan, "I just wish I was normal like all the other girls!"

I couldn't believe Sarah's desperation to give up her incredible powers and be an ordinary person! I suppose we were becoming opposites. To the best of my knowledge, Sarah never willingly used the powers at her disposal, not once. To her, they were an unwanted demon, possessing her since birth.

During my freshman year of high school, Sarah had another vivid nightmare about the distant future. She woke up screaming like she had several times before. As Lou and I comforted our shaking sister, Sarah told us, "A rocket ship was going up to outer space, and it fell apart in the sky! The people on it died!"

"There were people on the rocket?" Lou asked. "Really?"

"Yes. They did not make it. They fell in the ocean!"

She was too shaken to go into further detail about the dream, but of course I saw it anyway. After the explosion, a president spoke on a color screen, and it wasn't any president we'd had before. Though I might have recognized a younger version of him in his acting days if we had a television or went to the movies more often.

I almost forgot about that nightmare. I put a lot of them to the back of my mind, until they came back to haunt me.

Though she didn't know it, and neither did we at the time, Sarah predicted John F. Kennedy's assassination years before he was elected president, recounting details right down to the First Lady's blood-splattered pink dress. She would also dream about tsunamis and major earthquakes, even picturing herself standing helplessly on the beach in the path of some fierce wave. These natural disasters would make the news decades later and only then trigger a vague memory of some night terror my sister had and wrote me a letter about.

Since Sarah could not tell us exactly when these tragedies would happen, we disregarded many of her dreams. She did sound like a bit of a loon, babbling about plane crashes and rocket ships. Just think of the disasters we could have averted and the money I could have come into if we'd taken some of Sarah's dreams seriously!

I do remember Sarah keeping a diary or two, on top of the letters she wrote to me that I still have. But for the life of me, despite my combing people's minds and memories for clues, I have not been able to nail down where that damned diary is. I think whoever does have it has forgotten it's packed away in a box somewhere. It could be extremely useful to me, so if you, the reader, might know where it is, and I'm still here, please provide it to me.

Katrina and Julius

A time-worn car pulled into a driveway in the dim gray sunlight. Exhausted, Katrina stepped out and went inside the white trailer where she lived during her high school years, where she'd moved back to take care of her mother. Her reddish-gold hair was shorn in a ragged pixie cut. Underneath her almost colorless gray eyes, dark circles evidenced her strain from her long night shifts at the call center.

Katrina's mother slept in the battered recliner in front of the television set. A wisp of smoke curled out of an ashtray nearby. On the screen, bikini-clad young women screamed bleeped-out curses at each other. Katrina stood behind her mother and silently concentrated. The television shut off as the power button depressed. The gentle plume of cigarette smoke died as Katrina, without moving, quashed the lit embers. Katrina's mother, still unaware of her daughter's abilities, snored on.

Katrina went to her childlike pink bedroom and wiped her makeup from her face. Before changing into her nightgown and getting into bed, she glanced at the photographs tacked to her ribbon-edged bulletin board of nostalgia. In a favorite picture, a beaming, pigtailed six-year-old Katrina had her arms around her uncle Julius, who'd come to deliver gifts for Christmas. If not for Julius and her multimillionaire grandfather, Katrina's memories of Christmases and birthdays would have been painful ones, since her mother would have spent money on drugs and cigarettes instead of celebrations or gifts.

When Katrina turned twenty-one last summer, Julius took her out for her first drink. A photograph from last year's birthday celebration, the two of them giving thumbs-up signs over their Bloody Marys, was the centerpiece of the bulletin board.

At the bottom corner of the board, Katrina's eyes paused at one image. Two adolescents sat on a wooden bench in a wonderland of flowers. The girl on the left was a teenage Katrina, her hair longer back then, pulled back in glittery butterfly clips. The kid on the right was her mother's younger cousin Lillian, in unflattering plastic-framed glasses and a white sundress. Her fine hair fell in a choppy cut on her shoulders.

Hidden behind this snapshot was one that trickled down to Katrina just this year. One of Lillian's high school senior pictures, taken in tall grass as she posed with her panting, pointy-eared dog. She apparently loved that animal so much that she insisted on the dog's inclusion in the photo shoot. How could Lillian be that obsessed with a slobbering animal? What a weirdo. Katrina did not understand why people found dogs so special; to her they were just barking, smelly annoyances, though they intrigued her with the possibility of becoming scary sharp-toothed zombies. Dressed in a black top with a heavy load of necklaces, Lillian smiled her pretty smile as her much longer hair covered her shoulders. The geeky childhood glasses were gone. Contact lenses, probably.

In their younger years, Katrina had wanted to be Lillian's friend, partners in action. But now she considered her a traitor, almost not to be spoken of. Lillian had humiliated Katrina's dear uncle. She'd accused him of being a pedophile and turned her father and their other cousin against him. How could Lillian hurl such a serious and sickening accusation against the most incredible man Katrina ever had the pleasure of knowing?

Julius was no rapist. If he really was such a monster, Katrina would have been his easiest target, with lots of time alone together and a mother who didn't give a shit. Yet he had never touched Katrina in any way that made her uncomfortable. The same couldn't be said for some of the men her mother used to bring home from the bar. Men who would creep out of Mom's bedroom in the middle of the night to molest Katrina, or even offer her mother some extra cocaine in exchange for copping a feel on her daughter. Katrina was grateful once she gained the power to take possession at the age of twelve and could stop the drunken perverts in their tracks. She turned them around and made them walk outside naked, and once she left their heads, they just stood there, so confused that they forgot what they were trying to do.

Julius was a gentleman, nothing like those sloppy-looking creeps. He had class. And if Katrina could protect herself from disgusting men with her powers, why wouldn't Lillian have done the same to fend off Julius?

Lillian was a liar. How dare she?

Both Julius and Katrina's grandfather, Gerald, had decided to stand down on the issue for now. Gerald could go visit Lillian occasionally, but Julius had to just keep his distance, not contacting her even to defend his reputation. Katrina was also under orders to not do anything, but she really wanted to meet with Lillian, alone, and give her something to really whine about. It angered Katrina that nobody else wanted to punish this bitch.

"Pow," Katrina whispered to herself, turning her hand into a gun and aiming her index finger at the two photographs of Lillian. When that was not enough, she ripped them off the cork and tore each one in half, tossing the slick pieces into her heart-covered wastebasket.

Just before plopping into bed, Katrina checked her small silver cell phone to find a text message from Julius. *I know you're stressed lately. Hang in there.*

Katrina replied with a thank-you and the phone vibrated with a response. *Don't forget that you won't be stuck in your lousy dead-end job forever. Things will improve.*

Her spirits lifted a bit as she crawled into her narrow bed, turning on the delicate music box on the nightstand, a gift Julius had given her when she was five years old. The crystalline music lulled Katrina to sleep as the little ballerina twirled.

Not far from where his niece Katrina was getting ready to sleep, Julius laid in bed with his cell phone in his hands, having just finished texting with her. His wife, Jana, still slept soundly below their high carved headboard, her bony form curled on its side. It was always best to contact Katrina at moments like this, with no chance of Jana complaining.

Dressed in silk pajamas, Julius got out of the bed and did his morning stretches in the thin sliver of light that crept around the edges of the window shade. He brushed his teeth, shaved, dabbed on cologne, and tugged on a snug gray suit. He was combing his hair when Robbie, his son, escaped from his room and babbled down the hall. Without emotion, Julius fetched the chubby little boy and carried him down the stairs. He sat Robbie in his booster seat at the dining room table. Tuning out Robbie's impatient calls of "Daddy, Daddy, Daddy!", Julius went into the kitchen to prepare cereal and a sippy cup of juice. After he brought them to the table, Robbie dug in, scattering brown chocolate balls of cereal all over the floor and splashing milk onto his pajamas. His father sighed.

Julius had an ulterior motive behind growing his family and even behind marrying Jana, one that she would never be able to wrap her ordinary mind around. She simply wanted to be a mommy. He wanted power.

Julius had hoped that after all the trouble of marrying a woman he pretended to love, he would get in return a necromancer child just like himself. From watching the patterns in his family, Julius' father had figured out that the powers stemmed from a recessive genetic trait that Julius and Jana both carried. The powers came through in Julius as he had two copies of the gene, while Jana just had one. Having never met Jana's estranged parents, Julius had no idea if one of them was a full-blown mage. Some families passed that trait down through the generations, unaware that mages even existed.

From his rudimentary understanding of genetics, Julius got his hopes up that he had a real chance of a necromancer baby. But instead, Robbie was only a person with simple mage blood, a "half-breed" as Julius' father would say. What a waste of money and flesh! When Julius spent time with that disappointment of a son, fed him, or took him places, he did it impersonally. It was Jana who showed the boy more affection with kisses, bubble baths, and bedtime stories. To her, Robbie had every trait he needed to be a lovable human. To Julius, he was an empty shell.

Julius had wanted more children, but that was not to be. Not unless they adopted. Jana was deeply unhappy with the side effects of her pregnancy, most notably the weight gain, and she developed preeclampsia that put her health in danger. Terrified of another baby, she had her tubes tied without consulting her husband first. Julius was so livid that he nearly divorced her. And if he found a suitable woman with mage blood willing to have his child, he still would leave Jana in a heartbeat.

At this rate, he would never get his necromancer child.

Excerpt from The Autobiography of Gerald Frazier: Architect of a New World

L ike my sister Sarah, my brother Lou wished to fit in, be ordinary, and live a carefree youth. He no longer had any desire to use his powers, the way he did as a small boy. I got frustrated with both Sarah and Lou. I reminded them that they had something very special that made them better than our eldest sister and the ordinary people roaming around us, and that nobody else could ever take away! I assured them that they should be proud instead of feeling miserable and like freaks of nature. They ignored my assertions.

My sister Violet moved out at sixteen and married Gene Ryder, an auto mechanic who was a nice enough man, though less than handsome. She married the first man who proposed in her hurry to move out. Sarah got jealous, also wishing to be married.

We would visit Violet and her new husband for dinner. Lou and Gene took a liking to each other, and soon Violet's new husband was teaching my brother how to fix cars. Gene spent days with Lou underneath engines, with wrenches in their fists. They'd come home all streaked up with black grease. I believe this was the first time Lou felt like he had any real father figure.

In the parlance of today's psychology books, Violet was a "parental child." With a dead mother and an inattentive father, when our aunts weren't around to help, she raised us and cooked our meals, somehow never picking up that something was unusual about her three siblings.

Violet was vehemently opposed to having children. Papa and our aunts on our mother's side pressured her to get pregnant, since it was expected of women back then, unless they were nuns. As Violet's years of married life ticked past and no baby came, people pitied her, assuming she was barren. She and her husband only made love once in a blue moon, using the pull-out method. Or they went in through the back door, so to speak. See the things I know about people? All I have to do is go near someone to step right into their bedroom.

You can only imagine the happy dance Violet did when she reached the change of life in middle age and no longer had to worry about babies. At least she was a fabulous cook after all of her practice growing up.

Fleeing the Nest

The August after her graduation, Lillian got ready to transition to Northern Colorado University, where she had won a nice scholarship. Though she did not have a chance to tour the campus, Lillian fell in love with the college through brochures in the mail. The university had a renowned geology program and she hoped to eventually go to graduate school to study the science of volcanoes.

Lou was reluctant to let the baby of the family leave the nest, especially to a faraway place that he was unfamiliar with. He encouraged Lillian to go somewhere close to home. Among his worries was the possibility of gangs of mages living in other parts of the country—the reason he had not let Lillian go on the senior class trip to Europe. And they knew never to travel to New Orleans, Louisiana. Uncle Gerald had warned them for years that the city was the "mage capital of the world."

In a fed-up gesture of stubbornness and a bit of rebellion, Lillian clung to her Colorado idea, not wanting to live in such fear of seeing new places or getting a fresh start. Besides, Dad had no problem with Evelyn going to school out of state. Julius and Katrina lived in Ohio, and Uncle Gerald used to as well. Even though they were definitely not Lillian's favorite people, it comforted her a bit to know they hadn't had trouble in that densely populated area. At least not as far as she knew.

As the time drew closer, the jitters began to set in. Dad and Evelyn, who'd come back home to help with the move and give freshman-year advice, embarked with Lillian on a road trip in the hand-me-down Jeep Cherokee that Denny gave to Lillian when she got her license. This vehicle could be nice for off-roading adventures in the mountains. Denny stayed behind and watched Astrid. Leaving the dog in the rearview was the single hardest part of going away to school.

After days of changing scenery, they arrived in Fort Collins, Colorado. Cornfields and soft pastures gave way to peaceful streets with Victorian houses and brick-lined downtown avenues under canopies of greenery. Mountains rose in the distance.

Throughout the school grounds, buildings towered over green lawns speckled with fir, pine, and cottonwood trees. A clock tower at the center loudly struck the hour. Late-summer flowers were everywhere. This campus was so pretty that no brochure could do it justice.

After getting registered and getting her student ID card, Lillian found Bailey Hall, the women's dormitory where her new room awaited. Lillian studied the other parents and students rolling televisions and computer monitors and trunks on dollies, clothing slung over their shoulders. They all looked refreshingly typical. So far, there was no evidence of magical people. But this was only the beginning.

According to a packet she had received in the mail, Lillian's roommate on the second floor would be Tara Nicholson, a sophomore majoring in business administration. When they spoke on the phone a couple of weeks ago, Tara had promised from her parents' home in a suburb of Denver that she would supply bookshelves, curtains, and a microwave. Lillian agreed to bring a television. Hopefully Tara would be as nice as her voice sounded. But Lillian's social anxiety kicked in as the situation got real. Going into the white-walled building, her stomach knotted in fear of the unknown.

A short, dark-haired student approached the three, introducing herself as Mallory, the residential assistant in charge of the second floor. "You'll be Tara's roommate!" Mallory gushed after shaking their hands. "She's my cousin, we grew up together, and she's a real sweetie."

A sticker-covered piece of construction paper was taped to the green door of Lillian's room, triggering childhood memories of summer camp crafts. Glitter puff paint spelled out the two names: *Tara N. + Lillian F.* The roommate was not there, but she had been in the room not too long ago. Fresh streaks of an unfamiliar aura swirled on the scratched hardwood floor in one side of the room, already cutely furnished with Betty Boop memorabilia. The other side waited empty for Lillian, with the school-issued furniture pushed up against the cinderblock wall. One half of the walk-in closet was filled with expensive-looking clothes and a panoply of shoes.

"I know what could brighten up this space," Evelyn grinned. "Flowers! Maybe get a floral blanket for your bed. You could get a vase, pick some flowers, and put them on your desk. It would complement your roommate's decorations perfectly!"

After bringing Lillian's boxes up to the room and taking her out to dinner at a steakhouse, Dad and Evelyn checked into a motel room. Evelyn, who'd nudged Lillian into taking her first steps as a baby, helped her with her homework, and showed her how to apply makeup when she was ten, once again made herself the older, wiser mentor. "You should go back to your dorm by yourself and meet Tara and the other girls in the hall. Making friends with your roommate should be one of your first priorities, because she could give you important connections. A strong social network in the dorm is your second priority."

"I'm actually really nervous about meeting my roommate," Lillian confessed.

"Don't be nervous. Positivity makes a great first impression, so *always* remember to smile! Once you've got that support network, everything will work out great. You all can study together and swap tips for doing well in your classes. A big group of friends who had my back was crucial to my success in college. And if there's tutoring, don't hesitate to take advantage of it. Have you thought about joining a sorority?"

"No, I haven't. That sounds even more terrifying."

A dark, quiet room greeted Lillian after her return to the dorm. She set up her bass guitar in the corner and put up posters. She lined her collection of model pyramids on her desk, arranging them from biggest to smallest, and beside it she carefully set up her small stash of quartz crystals. She opened up her new laptop from Uncle Gerald and tossed sheets and blankets onto the bed. All black, with none of the flowers that Evelyn had recommended. Beside the pillows landed Stimpy, the plush doll of the cartoon cat that Denny gave her for Christmas when she was small, and a few other stuffed animals. After years of being clung to, Stimpy's red fur had dulled.

The card-key lock finally clicked open. The somewhat dilute, orange-and-gray aura of a typical person approached. Tara was tall and skinny in low-cut jeans and a midriff top. Her long, highlighted brown hair was scraped back into a tight ponytail. A belly button ring glittered on her tanned, board-flat stomach. Lillian felt the same way she did around her tiny, athletic sister. Out of proportion, with a bottom too big, thighs too thick, and breasts too small.

"Oh, hi," Tara said in her smoky voice just as her cell phone rang in her pocket, drowning out her new roommate's hello. Tara pulled her phone out and flipped it open, making arrangements to meet with someone and leaving the room in a flash.

Alone again, Lillian got ready for bed, took her nightly dose of the antidepressant that Dr. Carlson back home had prescribed, and attempted to fall asleep. Although the medication helped to reduce the nightmares, it did not get rid of them completely, and a stressful change in surroundings tended to set them off.

Lillian found herself in her adolescence years ago, back in Julius' garden. Her hair, shorter back then, hung around her face. An undead, slimy hand clamped firmly on her ankle, like a shackle.

The scene changed. Her old acquaintance Mandy, alive again, ran through wet grass and water-beaded tulips. Vines gripped Mandy, twining around her arms as she dissolved into thin air and her scream turned into a silent whisper.

Mandy got free from the vines. She wrapped her small, fine hands around Lillian's neck in a thorn-lined pit of purplish blackness. Mandy was dead but not dead, her neck broken, her silvery eyes dull as her head, filthy with soil and dried blood, hung limply to one side.

Lillian woke with a start, thinking more about Mandy than she had in a while. Though Julius' niece, Katrina, hadn't written to Lillian since the ugly truth came out, Lillian still wondered if she'd told the real story when she claimed Mandy was pregnant at the time of her death.

And if so, who had put her in that state.

An intimidating new world opened up for Avery Joseph as he set foot on the grounds of Northern Colorado University. He'd taken a campus tour back in January when it was cold, the trees bare that were now so green, bits of snow on the ground. Things had been a lot quieter then, without all these freshmen and families showing up.

Avery and his mother walked past posters advertising freshman orientation and rushes for fraternities and sororities. Greek life did not sound like his thing. Even outside of that culture, Avery had no idea if he would find a niche.

Avery had not attended a school since eighth grade, from which he was pulled out early. He had spent the past four years homeschooling. His single mother, busy with her career as a midwife, determined that he had the maturity to stick to mostly self-directed studies. She chose and bought the books, scoped out good correspondence courses, and let Avery take care of the rest, so long as he could demonstrate his knowledge and pass an exam every now and again.

During those years, Avery made more friends than he ever had before, finding a good and loyal group of fellow teens in a tabletop gaming club. And now he was leaving all of that behind in Albuquerque, moving hundreds of miles north for school, the biggest leap of faith he'd taken in his life.

Even though his mother and his best friend both encouraged him to be his true self, Avery had toned down certain aspects as he packed. His clothes and decorations were carefully chosen, socially acceptable stuff, though he would not go so far as to pretend to love sports. A favorite family activity, knitting, would stay under wraps just for safety. When Avery was in elementary school, he brought up knitting when the teacher asked the children what they liked to do for fun. Laughter rang out, and the other boys called him "gay" and a "sissy" and gave him hell. Avery left his yarn stash back at home, terrified of what his roommate might think.

Avery did bring a couple of the sweaters he was most proud of, thick for the winter ahead. He didn't have to tell anyone he'd made them.

As they strolled to the administration building, the two of them noticed something on the sidewalk that stood out jarringly among the thousands of aura trails left by the other students and parents. The sorts of trails that mages, like themselves, would leave behind.

Instead of red-orange like their own, the aura remnants were green.

Avery and his mother both grew up not knowing of mage society, history, and rules, until they made a new friend—Adelita, an air person—when he was around ten years old. When Adelita briefed them on the code of conduct, she brought up a type of mage called necromancers, so hated and feared by the other three mage types that they'd killed the last ones hundreds of years ago. Some speculated that necromancers were a pure myth, never existing to begin with.

What was this on the ground? Could their family friend be wrong? Or had someone, maybe a family with the mage blood, have just walked past?

Avery's mother nudged him, whispering, "Did you see that?"

"Yeah. I see that."

"That... can't be, right? Necromancers?"

"I thought Adelita said they were dead. It's impossible. And I'm not sure what they'd be doing here. They might be some other type—or maybe it was just regular people and there was just a big crowd. There has to be another explanation."

"Avery, if you ever see anything unusual at this school, you tell me right away. And if you ever see a necromancer, run. Please."

"Sure, but I'm not going to worry about that right now." Avery already had enough weighing on his mind.

Avery had one mage classmate, Wyatt, during his short tenure at a private middle school. Wyatt, who had water powers, was popular, surrounded by throngs of admirers.

When he played sports, his telekinesis gave him a secret boost getting balls into hoops and goals. Wyatt never spoke one word to Avery, in spite of what they had in common.

Now, was he about to have a potentially dangerous classmate who should not exist?

To tone down his worries, Avery decided to believe that trail meant nothing.

Avery met his new roommate, Anthony, a smooth-faced, clean-cut eighteen-year-old who had been homeschooled his entire life. For a whole different reason. Avery was raised completely without religion, except for the occasional eclectic Yule ritual and trees at Christmastime. Anthony grew up in church. His parents had shielded him from public schools, fearing they were too secular.

Avery learned this within seconds of meeting his roommate. He could read some minds, yet could not see into Anthony at all. Anthony's mother, hovering nearby, had a mind as transparent as a fish bowl. If Anthony had a partner or a social life or a rebellious streak, he kept it well-hidden from his parents. Some months back, Anthony had stood up to them for the first time in his life, putting up a fight to apply at this school. And now here he was, knowing what to expect even less than Avery did. Avery hoped that Anthony, and himself, would not end up bullied, or fall flat on their faces under the demands of this new place.

Avery's mother took him out to dinner, and then dropped him off for his first night sleeping in the dorm room. Anthony and his parents were absent, maybe eating a meal out themselves. Avery's mother gave him an embarrassing final parting gift that he saw coming in what he could read of her mind, a box of condoms. Why did she have to buy that? Did she really think that her painfully shy son, who'd never been on a date, would magically turn into Casanova now that he'd left home? Cringing, Avery put the box away in the bottom drawer of his school-issued dresser.

Anthony came back. His parents lingered until it was almost nine and they went to their hotel room, unable to take their eyes off the son they still thought of like an over-grown toddler. Avery was bombarded with his new roommate's mother's catastrophizing about the life of drugs and wild sexual orgies that might commence as soon as they got in their van and left for home.

Avery struggled to speak to Anthony through the constraints of his nervousness. Meeting new people, even this smiling and unfailingly polite roommate, was always the worst. Knowing he tended to make a bad first impression only heightened Avery's fear.

As they tucked themselves into the bunk bed, Anthony made conversation, inquiring about Avery's hobbies. Still protecting himself from being laughed out of the room, Avery only disclosed one pastime: art.

"That's really neat," Anthony said. "I'd love to see your art when we're more awake."

As Anthony snoozed above him, Avery laid on the bottom bunk, struggling to switch his brain off after the shock of this transition. Even more intimate than brushing his teeth and changing into pajamas with someone he just met was falling asleep in his presence. Avery kept his mind on the education he hoped to achieve, the main reason for coming here. Not to make friends or impress people. To get a degree.

And what about the necromancer, if there even was one? What would happen if they ever crossed paths?

After waking up to her first morning on campus, still alone in the room, Lillian attended a long, dull freshman orientation in the performing arts center. After getting back to Bailey Hall, she found signs on the walls announcing an ice cream social for the whole dorm. After Evelyn's encouragement to quickly forge friendships, she went upstairs to get ready and came down to the television lounge wearing a dress she had sewn herself from discarded black fabric. And underneath, a pair of red-and-white striped leggings funneling into black combat boots.

Most of the other residents wore cutoff shorts and tank tops. They gathered around low tables and on the sofas, spooning melting ice cream out of plastic bowls. Lillian sat next to her new roommate. Tara and the group she was talking with to went silent as Lillian tried to introduce herself.

As if Lillian were invisible, Tara turned away and asked the others, "Did you hear? The swim team's having a party tonight. Let's go and get hammered!"

Losing her appetite for ice cream, Lillian went to a corner and lingered alone for a while, too shy to talk to anyone else. She went back up to her room ashamed, as if she had already socially failed. Evelyn would not approve of this at all.

Lillian ate another dinner out that night with her father and her sister, who spent the meal rattling off study tips. Since they had to catch a shuttle to the airport early in the morning, Lillian's father gave her a long, tight hug and implored her to let him know as soon as possible if the first semester went sideways. It was obvious how much he did not like her attending this faraway school, even more so after accompanying her on the long road trip.

Tara stumbled into the room after midnight, waking Lillian. The strong smell of alcohol hovered around her like a cloud. Tara vomited loudly into her wastebasket, thumped onto her bed, and started to snore. After she gagged a few times, Lillian tiptoed over and gently rolled Tara onto her side for fear of her choking to death on her own puke. More chunks spilled from Tara's mouth onto her pillow. Lillian hoped that she wouldn't spend the whole school year babysitting a drunk. As she tried to go back to sleep, the smell turned her stomach.

Classes began the next day. When Lillian woke up with her alarm, Tara was already gone, leaving behind fresh blankets and sheets and pillowcases on her empty bed. The vomit-stained bedding was stuffed into a laundry basket. It blew Lillian away that someone could get up and start her day after drinking so hard and sleeping so little. Totally overwhelmed, Lillian had had difficulty locating some of her classrooms, and nearly missed a class.

A letter from Evelyn arrived a week later. Lillian made her way to the inner circle of the post office building, where wide windows scattered yellow-white light all around the tiled floor. She sunk into a couch and tore the envelope open, finding a printed, doily-edged wedding invitation and a photo. The wedding was planned on South Padre Island, Texas, for the coming spring, and Lillian would serve as a bridesmaid. In the picture, Evelyn's petite hands rested on her beau Jonathan's brawny shoulder, and her auburn hair was flawlessly curled. Everything looked perfect, as always.

Lillian went back to her dorm and put the photo on her desk. As usual, it was hard not to be a bit jealous of Evelyn's charmed life.

During meals in the cafeteria or the dormitory kitchen, Lillian's aloneness became painfully obvious as she strolled silently with her trays of food, surrounded by chatter. Most of the other freshmen in her dormitory already belonged to cliques, impenetrable circles of friends who sat around tables as they studied and ate. Lillian wasn't sure how to break through. Even her own roommate had barely said two words to her since moving in. What would Evelyn think? With no telekinesis, telepathy, or other magic, how did these people connect so effortlessly?

Lillian was not totally friendless. She still kept in touch with a few people from high school, though distance separated them now. And she had a diverse group of contacts on the internet, including her boyfriend in South Africa. Yet making local friends seemed beyond her.

Lillian started to go out for fast food instead of facing the cafeteria, wolfing down her meals as she hid in her vehicle. The passenger's side, and then the backseat, started to fill up with discarded cups and bags and burger wrappers. The trash embarrassed Lillian, but having no friends to ride around with, she did not feel motivated to clean it up.

Homesickness set in painfully. The further the big move fell into the past, the harder it was to face. Lillian's father sent care packages with snacks, letters, and his homemade peanut butter cookies. Lillian saved a few cookies in a plastic bag, tucking it away in her nightstand. When she needed a pick-me-up, she brought them out and breathed in their aroma.

One evening, after a furtive drive-through dinner, Lillian rushed back to her room through the shadowed halls. Not thinking of the hot vibrations issuing from the room, Lillian opened the door and turned on the light.

Two bodies, shining with sweat, joined on Tara's messy bed. She and a man bucked and moaned, slapping violently together. Lillian mumbled an apology, shut off the light, and ran to the study pod down the hall. Trembling with panic and flashbacks to that summer with Julius, she sat down on a couch, closing her eyes and digging her fingers into her arms.

When Lillian finally calmed down and returned to the room, Tara's lover had left. Tara slept alone in her bed, though the room was still pregnant with the stenches of sex, sweat, and hard liquor. When Tara's alarm clock woke Lillian in the morning, she was foggy-headed after nightmares and broken sleep.

As Tara stood at the sink, combing her blond-streaked hair, Lillian spoke with her roommate, the first real conversation in their weeks of living together. "Uh, next time you're, well, with a guy, could you please put a hat or a hair tie or something on the doorknob?"

"What?" Tara asked, speaking to the mirror as she swiped mascara onto her lashes. "Don't tell me you're some kind of prude or a virgin or something."

"I don't care what you do when I'm not here. I just would like some warning before I walk in."

"My last roommate didn't care. She got laid too."

"I'd rather not see your private moments. Please put a hair tie on the door next time."

"Whatever," Tara sighed under her breath. She capped her mascara and walked out, shutting the door hard.

A few days later, Lillian came into the room to find a tall, brawny black-haired male whose face was dark with stubble. He wore tight, faded jeans. The visitor turned to Lillian and shook her hand, introducing himself as Tara's boyfriend Kolby Cooper, bragging that he was the son of a famous rodeo cowboy. Uninterested in rodeos, Lillian had never heard of this family.

This was not the same man who'd been in bed with Tara the other night. No, that guy had very pale whitish hair, not Kolby's pitch-black mop.

"Come on, Kolby," Tara urged in an almost whiny tone, tugging at his hand. "Let's go to dinner."

Kolby said goodbye to Lillian, looking over his shoulder at her as he and Tara left the room.

Tara ignored Lillian's request to hang something on the doorknob during intimacy. A few days after meeting Kolby, Lillian opened the door to find her roommate naked with another unfamiliar guy. Startled when the hallway light spilled in, he spun his head around and yelled, "Oh, shit!"

"Keep going, baby!" Tara urged underneath him.

Lillian slammed the door and ran down the hall, embarrassed, angry, and sick to her stomach. Did it thrill Tara to be caught in the act?

Lillian began spending much of her time in the upstairs study pod, doing her homework there. Most of the other dorm residents were not interested in that room of mismatched couches, going instead to the downstairs lounge to watch sitcoms on the large television and snack on bowls of popcorn and paint each other's toenails.

When Tara was gone, Lillian spent time relaxing, lying belly-down on her bed with her laptop as the golden fall sunlight warmed her back. She chatted with her boyfriend Pieter and posted heartfelt, sometimes angst-ridden entries in the online diary she'd maintained since her sophomore year of high school. The best nights in that room were spent alone. When her roommate's bed was neat and undisturbed, Lillian didn't know where Tara was, and she didn't care.

One day, something changed with Pieter. He stopped responding to Lillian's emails and instant messages. For days she told herself he was busy at his new job. The more days went by with no word from Pieter, the more she worried that he was in the hospital, or simply ignoring her.

Lillian went looking for a distraction, wearing the family-heirloom green crystal around her neck. After wandering the campus in the late afternoon, Lillian found a quiet spot beneath a large elm tree near the sciences complex. She glanced quickly around to make sure that no one was near enough to see her, and then knelt down as her long coat and button-covered book bag draped over her. She closed her eyes and directed her energies into the crystal, and then swiftly vanished. The only sign of her left behind was a patch of drying, tamped-down grass.

After passing through the dreamscape cemetery and opening the door in the tomb, Lillian landed on soft grass. The warm, moist air, not dry and chilly like above, was perfumed gently with flowers. Glowing fireflies bounced all around. The crystals she remembered from her first forays into this world were present in the background here too, set against a pastel sky glittering with stars. There were purplish, snow-capped mountains on the horizon, unlike the flat marshy land of her hometown. The temple, as always, stood nearby.

Lillian put down her book bag and ran off like she was five again and at the park, through a cloud of twinkling fairy lights. The air dimmed as Lillian stopped at the lip of a pond swirling with blue and black water. She took off her clothes, except for the crystal and her striped headband, and hung them on a branch. Skinny-dipping was utterly out of the question in the world above. But here, with not another soul around, was the only place she felt safe stripping down. She dove into a warm paradise, and briefly underwater, she saw visions of twirling flowers and of her own pale body suspended, long ruby tendrils of hair unfurling in the black water. After coming up, Lillian floated on her back for a while, looking up at the blue, black, and purple montage of the sky and stars.

The sun got lower, hiding behind the trees. As night fell, the world lit up in a softly glowing rainbow. Lillian was tempted to stay, but did not want to miss her evening photography class. She got out of the water, shook herself dry, wrung out her hair, and put her clothes back on. Still giddy with happiness and peace, she grabbed her book bag, slung it over her shoulder, clasped her hands around the crystal on its chain, and concentrated until she levitated.

On the campus, the sun was similarly setting and the light came not from plants but from lamps lighting the paths. Guessing she was already running late, Lillian decided to skip the class. As she walked back toward the dormitory, diamonds of water dripped from her chilly wet hair and made small spots on the ground glow ever so slightly.

As always, the ground was interwoven with the trails left behind from others' auras as they walked, a bit harder to see now in the setting sun. Halfway to her dormitory, Lillian stopped short.

One of the trails pulsated, taller and brighter and wider than all of the others. It was the sort of strong trace that a mage would leave behind, yellow-orange. The color of fire.

Don't panic, she told herself. *You don't know who left that trail behind. Maybe somebody walked past here just a minute ago and that's why it looks so bold. And let's hope that person is ordinary.*

The next evening, Lillian reclined on her bed, studying for her first pre-calculus test the following morning and a bit tired from donating blood earlier that day at a school blood drive. A bright green band was still wrapped around her elbow, holding gauze in place.

Disrupting the peace, Tara came in with a shaven-headed young man, possibly drunk again, her eyes wide and her stare unbalanced.

The guy gave Lillian a side-eyed glance. "Um... your roommate?"

"Don't worry about her." Tara quieted him with a sloppy kiss.

Just a few feet away from Lillian, the two of them wriggled out of their clothing, as if they didn't have an audience. Or what if Tara wanted her to see? Wanted to rub it in her face? Not once had Lillian wanted to watch her roommate go at it, but Tara clearly did not care. Lillian gathered her books and her iPod and rushed to the study pod.

She returned later, hoping to go to bed, though was little hope of sleeping right now. Tara's bedsprings still squealed as her headboard banged against the wall. Lillian tried and failed to ignore what went on behind her in the mirror as she brushed her teeth, removed her contact lenses, and swallowed her pill. She slammed a pillow over her head and turned up the volume on her iPod. When those combined measures did not drown out the noise, she finally tore her ear buds out, sat up, and demanded, "Please cut it out! I'm trying to sleep."

"Go fuck yourself," Tara said sharply, followed by a short laugh.

When it ended, Tara and the man sat on the edge of her bed, still naked. Tara lifted up a small plastic bag full of pills, and they each swallowed one.

And they were at it again.

Lillian escaped the room in her pajamas. Desperate to get some rest, she tried to fall asleep on a couch in the study pod, kept awake from the bright fluorescent lights that stayed on in the room twenty-four hours a day. Vulnerable and out in the open, Lillian could not fully drift off. Tempted to escape to a much nicer place, Lillian was disappointed to find that she had left the green crystal in the room.

That morning, in a haze of anxiety and exhaustion, Lillian could hardly concentrate on her math test.

Two days later, the professor handed it back with a D minus. After heading back to the dorm, Lillian caught her roommate sitting alone at her desk, tapping away on her keyboard.

"Tara, I need to sleep sometimes. You really kept me up the other night."

Tara ignored her, slouching in her chair and typing with one hand as she ate a candy stick with the other.

"Couldn't you go somewhere else if... you know?"

Tara sighed and spun around in her chair, her eyes cold. "Sometimes his place just doesn't work. I never see *you* bringing home guys."

"You affected my grade on my test."

"*You* affected your grade because you didn't work hard enough. Just sleep somewhere else."

"I paid for this room. This is my room."

"Well, so did I. And I have the right to do what I want. I wish I had my old roommate back. You're lame."

Lillian wearily left the room, going down the hall to see the residential assistant, hoping she was in. She knocked on the door of Mallory's room.

"What do you need?" Mallory asked.

"I want to be moved to a different room."

Mallory leaned against her door frame, shaking her head. "I'm sorry, it's too late in the semester to change your room. If you move out of the dorms, you won't get a refund. Oh, and while you're here, there's something else we need to talk about. There have been recent complaints about noise coming from your room."

"You think?! Tara's keeping me up at night. I don't feel safe in there."

"I need to be frank with you. According to Tara, you are the one who's been making the noise."

"That's not true! How could she say that?"

"I went to your room yesterday to discuss these noise complaints. You weren't in, but Tara was. She told me you like to bring your boyfriend home late at night and she's been really upset."

"She's lying!"

"You should get a hotel room next time. I can't have you disturbing our neighbors and making Tara uncomfortable."

Even though Lillian almost never lost her temper, heat rushed to her cheeks. "That's utter bullshit! It's Tara!"

"I'm really disappointed that you're pointing fingers. Tara is my cousin and we grew up together. I know her better than anyone and I know she's telling the truth."

"No, she's telling a bold-faced lie."

"Care to tell me what's really going on? We are both adults and you can tell me about your boyfriend. It's just that this noise late at night needs to stop."

"Let me tell you about my boyfriend, then. He's in South Africa, okay? He's never been in my room, or even been to this country."

"Some internet thing, I'm guessing? He doesn't visit, so you're hooking up with other guys?"

"What? No!"

"Come on. Tell me the truth."

Lillian could only withstand these embarrassing accusations for so long before her mind began to shut down, like a computer hanging up and crashing. She ran from Mallory. Not wanting to face Tara in her fragile state, she darted down the hall to the communal bathroom. Lillian closed herself in a stall, slapping the walls with her palms and crying. After getting back to her room later, and thankfully finding herself alone, she wrote another email to her boyfriend, spilling her guts and venting her frustration, though she hadn't heard from him in two weeks.

The next morning hit Lillian like a punch in the gut, even after a night of peace and quiet without Tara. She woke up to an email from Pieter, apologizing for the long delay in getting back to her. While he felt bad about Lillian's friction with Tara and wished he could help, he'd found a local girlfriend, leading to the revelation that things with Lillian were unlikely to go anywhere.

If Lillian was honest with herself, Pieter was not wrong. Though they'd talked about meeting, money for the flights was an issue and Lillian still did not have a passport. If they visited and then went back home, how long would they have to wait for their reunion? Pieter was eighteen; he deserved to expand his dating horizons. And in her fear of intimacy, Lillian might not have been ready to meet him in person.

Yet it hurt to get hit with the break-up email when Lillian's living situation was well on its way to hell. Lillian headed out of her room to go to class, eyes patched up with a bit of makeup after shedding some tears. As she passed the downstairs television lounge, a few residents sat on a couch in there, giggling, whispering, and pointing at her.

Was Tara spreading gossip about Lillian now?

Now too raw to go to class, Lillian turned and ran back up to her room, digging through her plastic tub of self-care supplies until she found a razor. She broke open the plastic and took one of the narrow blades. After grabbing alcohol wipes from her first-aid kit, Lillian rushed to the bathroom to hide, not wanting to chance Tara walking in on her.

Crouched in a locked shower stall, Lillian pulled back her sweater sleeve and exposed the pale underbelly of her arm, marked with a few silvery, faint scars dating back to eighth grade, the most prominent being the slash on her inner wrist from the suicide attempt. The blade bit into her skin and opened a clean line. Blood came up, forming perfect round beads. She incised another line and then another.

If Lillian's father or her psychiatrist back home knew about this moment, they'd be very, very unhappy. She had reassured them both that this habit was long behind her.

Lillian wrapped her arm in paper towels, carefully pulled the striped sleeve of her sweatshirt over it, and returned to her room, hiding in a thick cloud of shame for the rest of the day. Tara burst into the room that night, quiet resentment dripping off her as she avoided meeting Lillian's eyes. Lillian immediately left for the study pod and laid down on the couch, even though those fluorescent lights buzzing overhead made it so hard to rest.

"Why the hell are you sleeping out here?" someone asked early the following morning as Lillian's eyes fluttered open. A pair of students who lived down the hall, who had never spoken to Lillian before, stood over her.

"She's weird," the other one said, raising her eyebrow. Chuckling, the two of them turned and walked away.

In the days that came, snow began to fall, a glittering lightweight dust that turned even the tiniest tree branches an icy, twinkling white. Breezes blew plumes of snow off the mountains and out of the nearby trees, and it rained down like fairy dust. Lillian enjoyed the pretty views, but she seldom denied to herself that coming here was a mistake.

Avery sat at his desk in his dorm room, taking advantage of some alone time while his roommate was out to catch up on some homework. He put on his headphones and got into the zone.

When Avery got tired of looking at the assignment sheet, he got up, stretched his arms over his head, and peered out the upper-floor window over his desk at the soft white landscape. Sometimes, people-watching and letting the sunlight hit his eyes refreshed Avery and gave him that last boost of energy to finish his homework.

A few people were off in the distance, milling around and walking to late-afternoon classes. One of them made Avery freeze up.

What arrested his attention, laying eyes on that far-off figure in a long black coat, was not her fiery autumn-red hair, some of the reddest hair he had ever seen.

It was her aura.

Large, waving and far-reaching. Green.

Impossible.

Even from such a distance, something about this girl pierced Avery. Chilled him right down to the bone.

Avery had spotted those green trails on the campus when he first moved in. Trails were one thing. The aura radiating out of an actual person was another. As Avery stood glued to the window, the student walked out of sight, giving no signs of awareness that she was being watched. Even from here, her trail still glowed softly on the sidewalk.

Avery knew one thing. In case this truly was a necromancer, he had to be careful. He had to stay away from her, and to run if she ever confronted him.

There still had to be some other explanation. Avery decided to hold off on telling the two other mages in his life, his mother who shared his fire powers and her friend who had air powers, about this strange sighting. Best not to worry them unless things got bad.

After he finished his homework, Avery took out his sketchbook to start a drawing, a fun activity to reward himself a little. Finishing off tedious schoolwork with something relaxing was one of the most valuable tricks he'd found in his years of self-directed studies.

Avery's roommate came back from a club meeting. While Anthony was friendly and pleasant to live with, sometimes Avery needed a little space. He left for a student café and sat down alone at a corner table with a hot tea.

When he glanced at his watch, time had jumped. How did it go from 5:10 to 5:43 in the blink of an eye? How did this café get busier and noisier all of a sudden with students buying quick bites for dinner?

The sketchbook page that had been empty when Avery sat down and first sipped his tea was now full of smudgy black images he could not remember, his hand smeared as it gripped the charcoal pencil.

This hadn't happened to Avery in years. Lapsing out of reality, only to find he'd drawn ghosts that haunted a place, or something that occurred in the past, or perhaps the future.

What populated the sketchbook page was more frightening than most of Avery's drawings, even the unintentional, automatic ones he'd poured out as a kid. Monsters, hideous glistening things, opened mouths full of barracuda fangs connected by strings of saliva. A few of these creatures had wings like a dragon's, sailing through the sky. Corpses lay ripped apart in pools of black charcoal blood.

"What the heck?!" Avery whispered to himself. "Ew. What is this?"

Unsettled that he'd drawn such a scene, even if he had no recollection of doing so, Avery almost ripped out the page and threw it away, not wanting to scare his roommate if he saw it later. But Avery decided to keep it, just in case he figured out what, if anything, the drawing meant. He closed his sketchbook, tucked it into his backpack, and walked back to his dorm.

Excerpt from The Autobiography of Gerald Frazier: Architect of a New World

Like our sister Violet, Sarah married a man she was not particularly crazy about, simply because he had asked her on a date and she was anxious to leave home. Shortly before her twentieth birthday, Sarah married a classmate, Frank Mackenzie. Sarah worried that her weight would hold her back from finding other men. Extra padding does not limit your options as much as Sarah believed. I was never skinny, and look at how many women I got later on in life! I did hope for Sarah to stick with Frank, so I did not say anything to boost her self-esteem and urge her to look elsewhere. If anything, I lowered it. I would hint to Sarah: "You'd better treat that man well because you don't have a lot of other prospects." I never said I wasn't a bastard.

Sarah felt uncomfortable getting hitched to this man, and not just because he was not the best-looking, did not shower often, and had a quick temper. Being the last surviving Mackenzie, he was distantly related to us and carried the mage trait. Sarah already made the connection about my mother's aura, stronger than most. She had married a necromancer, and three out of her four children were also born necromancers. And now Sarah was entering the same sort of pairing, anxious about creating another generation like us.

Sarah wanted children, very much so. And she would have preferred ordinary children, since she loathed herself for her powers and still equated them with demonic possession. Sarah had the same dreams of domestic bliss that a lot of girls did. The white picket fence, little feet running around beneath the Christmas tree, warm apple pies in the oven. Sarah wished that she could simply produce children without any doubt that they would live out the rest of their lives never knowing what a necromancer was.

In spite of his genetics that she found less than desirable, Sarah decided that marrying Frank was better than being alone.

Two days before the wedding, Sarah had a dream of dying young. By now, I was taking her dreams a little more seriously, and it frightened me.

Within months of the wedding, Sarah was pregnant!

Lillian's First Winter Away

A mid all the excitement about Evelyn's upcoming wedding, one person had his reservations: her cousin Denny. Evelyn's fiancé Jonathan had never given him a warm, fuzzy feeling, though he had only met the young man in person a few times. On Halloween night, he decided to take in everything the universe might have to say about the springtime event. He asked his wife, Mona, to linger downstairs in her lacy black witch costume to give handfuls of candy to trick-or-treaters. Even after more than thirty years, Mona did not know that the outdoorsy, rough-around-the-edges man she had married was a witch in the literal sense.

Denny took time to himself in the spare bedroom after feeding his wife a white lie that he was going to take a nap. Tonight, with the veil between the spirit world and the living world at its thinnest, was a good time for divination. Closing the door behind him and drawing the window shade, he lit a semicircle of candles and unwrapped his brutally honest companion, his well-worn tarot deck. Finding the cards would give Mona the creeps, so he kept them locked up in a drawer when not in use.

Shuffling the large cards, he closed his eyes, took deep breaths, and visualized Evelyn and her beau Jonathan beneath a rose-covered arch. What would happen if they married? Denny laid out a spread of cards and turned them over one by one, unveiling paintings of despair and damnation, and a heart pierced with three swords.

If the cards had any accuracy this time, Evelyn should definitely not marry that guy. What could Denny do about it, though? His uncle Lou, who was footing a chunk of the bill for that wedding, would not listen, especially if Denny brought up the tarot reading. If Denny called Evelyn in Houston right now, there was no way she would take it seriously, either. She'd always viewed the world through a critical, skeptical lens. Not only that, Denny could not predict exactly what might go wrong.

Sometimes people had to learn painful and disappointing lessons on their own, the hard way. Such a shame it should be Evelyn, Denny's lovely, bright young cousin who had nearly every conceivable thing going right in her life.

On Halloween, Lillian dressed up as a green Martian and went to a dance in the student union building. After she got sick of sitting on a bench to the side, not working up the courage to talk to a single person, she went outside in the chill, under a steel-colored sky that would soon release snow. Lillian grabbed a bag from her room and decided to go trick-or-treating in the dormitories, whose outer doors were propped open just for tonight.

Growing up, Lillian had a blast collecting candy in the quaint neighborhoods of her hometown. Tonight's solitary excursion was much less satisfying. Lillian knocked on a few doors in the building next to hers and held out her bag. Strangers dropped in candy and a couple of hard squares of ramen noodles. She lost interest, feeling anxious and awkward that she walked alone while the other trick-or-treating students stayed in groups.

After returning to her room, Lillian washed off her green makeup and microwaved a bowl of water and one of the ramen packets she'd received tonight, hungrily licking the last grains of salt out of the flavor package. Tara was gone, probably living it up at some epic Halloween party after she'd left earlier wearing devil horns and a silky red dress.

What would it be like to live Tara's life, days full of partying and sex and fun? The loneliness, the excruciating sense of being a social failure, overwhelmed Lillian.

She fumbled in her nightstand until she found the tarot deck Denny had given her. After smoothing out the blanket on her bed, Lillian sat on the bedspread, shuffling the cards. She asked the powers that be if she should stay at this school or just drop out, already miserable in her first semester.

The spread came up laughably positive. Cups running over with the clear waters of love, happiness, and The Sun, illuminating all it shone on. Even The Lovers appeared, nude figures joining hands.

"Pshaw," Lillian said to herself, gathering the cards and putting them away. She was not sure she had much skill with these cards, and did not want to call Denny, in a later time zone and probably in bed, to talk it over.

Lillian found her crystal on its chain, and set back out into the frigid night. She found the portal beneath the tree and held the crystal until the little cemetery came, and then the peace and stillness that followed.

Brilliant stars blinked in a sky much clearer than the one above, some of them purple and some of them a bright burning red. Lillian headed into the softly glowing temple, wandering and deep in thought as she watched her ancestors. The shamans. The ones who came on the ship. The Confederate soldier who took his own life.

A faint shadow appeared on the floor, below the ghosts of necromancers past. A man with his aura fading, an ordinary aura. Lillian was confident this man had no powers in life, making it odd that he'd appear in the necromancers' temple. In the dreams she'd had her whole life, she stumbled upon him right as he died, pushing the final overdose into his blood from the needle still sticking out of his arm.

Who was this man? Lillian had never even known anyone who had a drug overdose. Yet somehow, deep in the clutter at the back of her mind, she remembered this fellow with his hair sticking up in a mohawk. Finding his body. Taking his ghost out of its shell.

Drawing the light from his just-dead corpse, and bringing it to... where?

As usual, when Lillian tried to chase these incomplete memories, they dissipated into fog, just like the image of the man before her eyes.

Once Lillian was back in the ordinary world, remnants of the ground's past glided by amid the falling snow flurries. This being the most supernatural time of year, lots of ghosts were out, most of them invisible to the ordinary people. Faint images of folks in old-fashioned attire with corsets and coattails soundlessly traversed the whitening ground. For Lillian, these were a common sight, and she had learned to mostly ignore them. They paid no attention to the living, and one could pass right through their cold bodies.

The following evening, Tara was gone, thank goodness. Someone knocked on the door to Lillian's room: Tara's boyfriend, Kolby. A resident must have let him into the front entrance.

"Hey, is Tara in?" he asked when Lillian opened the door.

"No, she isn't."

"Do you know where she is, by any chance?"

"Nope. She never tells me anything."

Kolby frowned. "Hmm. She's been hard to reach lately. Not answering her phone, lying about where she's been. I think something's going on."

He came into the room without being invited, shut the door behind him, and sat down at Tara's desk, running his fingers through his tousled dark hair and tipping the chair back a bit. "Me and my buddies are having a party tomorrow night, a typical Friday-night get-together. Want to come?"

Lillian stood in a dumbfounded silence. She couldn't make friends here, and now she was so casually invited to a party?

"Yes," she confirmed, desperate for someone to treat her kindly. "Is Tara coming?"

"Nah. It'll just be me and some friends. And you. By the way, do you have a boyfriend?"

"No. Not anymore."

"Oh, sorry to hear that. But I think you'll have fun. I'll see you Friday. Oh, and Tara doesn't have to know. Don't mention it around her."

"We hardly speak to each other anyway. She doesn't like me. Even though she hasn't bothered to get to know me."

"I think she's just jealous of you."

"Jealous? Why?"

"Well... you're not bad-looking. Pretty hot, actually."

"Thanks," Lillian said shyly, not quite believing him. "Do you guys have an open relationship?"

"Huh? No, we don't. Why did you ask that?"

"She keeps bringing guys home. Doing it in front of me."

Kolby gritted his teeth as his face flushed red. "I *thought* she was cheating! Who are these guys?"

"I don't know any of their names."

Kolby verged on shouting. "The next time you see some loser who's balls deep in my girlfriend, please tell me!"

"I will. I'm sorry I had to tell you this. Are you going to break up with her?"

"I don't know. God, I was gonna propose to her and everything. I felt kind of sorry for her, with her messed-up childhood. You know how her parents used to drink."

"I don't know anything about her parents."

"They're sober now, but it was rough. Tara's done drugs. She told me she'd stop."

"What kinds of drugs?"

"Uppers. Pills like Adderall and stuff. Ecstasy. She tried cocaine. She took stuff to stay up and study, or dance all night. Then she promised me never again."

"I'm not so sure about that. I saw Tara taking pills with one of those guys. Not sure what it was, but it seemed to give them energy."

"Might have been ecstasy. I need time to think about where the relationship with Tara is going. I'll meet you outside at seven tomorrow to give you a ride to the party. We could both use some fun."

"Where is it? I can drive myself there."

"Parking gets pretty tight in that neighborhood, especially when there's a party. Better to go together."

The next day, Lillian hemmed and hawed about what to wear to the party. When she had arrived in rather gothic attire to the ice cream social at the start of the semester, the other dorm residents, including Tara, did not say a word to her. With the sting of that memory still fresh, Lillian decided it was safest to wear something boring, since Kolby hinted he'd bring her to a casual gathering. After putting on jeans and a black-and-gray raglan top, she still had reservations about getting in Kolby's car, as she barely knew him. Still, her future friends might be waiting for her tonight.

Kolby tried to make small talk during the ride in his shiny silver new Jetta. Lillian asked if he had any interest in science fiction, hoping to find common ground, but he shrugged that topic off dismissively.

After Kolby parked along a curb, the presence of a party was obvious from well down the shadowed, icy street. Even out in front of the house with broken shutters and dulled paint on its frilly trim, blaring music nearly drowned out the loud hoots from the people standing in heavy coats, exhaling their speech in puffs of vapor. Lillian wanted to crawl up a tree like a squirrel, or run and hide.

Kolby slipped through the front door so fast that Lillian lost sight of him and his grayish aura. She tried to follow him inside. The main room was too bright and cramped and chaotic, swirling with people and a cloud of cigarette smoke above. The speakers throbbed at a volume that hurt Lillian's ears. A scruffy young man in a fraternity sweater motioned for Lillian and led her through the tightly packed crowd. She bumped into strangers' shoulders as their voices turned into one prolonged, deafening shout.

Someone nudged Lillian into a room down the hall and shut the door. A lava lamp and a few candles cast soft reddish-orange light. It was a bit quieter, though music still thumped through the door and walls.

Kolby reclined on a battered brown couch with two other young men. Smoke curled out of their nostrils and from the glass pipe they passed around, sucking on it as they held a lighter to the top. It registered at last in Lillian's mind that they were getting high. Something Lillian had never done, as she did not like to lose control.

"Hey, you," Kolby said, nodding toward her. "You want to take a puff?"

"Uhh... no, thanks."

"What's wrong, you ever done this before?"

"No," she admitted as all the anti-drug scare tactics in school during her childhood came rushing back. And she wanted to keep a clear mind, remembering how Julius used to pressure her to drink wine, how he'd probably drugged Mandy.

"It's okay," said the one in the fraternity sweater. "You don't have to if you don't want to."

Lillian stayed in the room to shield herself from the noise and suffocating crowd, among guys too high to have much of a conversation. She perched on the end of the couch, not knowing what to say or do and wishing she could just go home. Not back to her dorm room. Back to the cozy and peaceful home she grew up in, thousands of miles away.

"Kolby told me about you," said the young blonde man next to her. "He said you're pretty nice."

"Thanks."

"I like your hair. It's a pretty color."

"Thanks."

"Does the carpet match the curtains?" he asked with a flirtatious smirk. "Got a fire crotch?"

Lillian tensed up. This was not the first or even the third time she'd been asked that obnoxious question. "That's private. Can we talk about something else?"

"Here, would you like the rest of my beer?" He thrust a half-empty bottle in front of her.

"I, uh... I'm underage."

Every man in the room began to giggle, and then laugh outright. Increasingly uncomfortable, Lillian made her way to the door, but Kolby got up and blocked her way. She bit her lip and looked down.

"Hey, it's okay," Kolby said. "Who gives a shit if you're underage? What are we gonna do, call your mommy and daddy, call the cops? I'm not twenty-one yet, and neither are half the people at this party."

"I just... except for wine, I've never had a drink."

"Come on, then," Kolby encouraged. "Try a beer."

Giving in to her people-pleasing instincts, Lillian was persuaded to take in some hoppy, bitter beer, choking it down. As her resistance weakened, the men pressured her into smoking the bowl. The smoke burned harshly within her lungs. She coughed violently. Why did people think this stuff was fun?

As the music outside the door blended into one with the mellow chatter, Lillian's awareness dimmed. The group of boys essentially waited on her, putting fresh new cold bottles of beer in her hands after she'd finished the last, refilling the bowl and encouraging her to take the first inhale. Lillian giggled uncontrollably as her skull filled with an empty helium sensation. Her body grew floppy and loose, not jumping as much as she normally would have when a furry male paw draped across her shoulder. Kolby's lips moved closer until they were on hers.

Was this real, her first kiss, or a hallucination? No hand-holding, no romance, no setting sun? And with her roommate's boyfriend, of all people! Lillian put her hands up futilely as Kolby leaned toward her again. As he jammed his slimy mouth onto hers, she instinctively tried to shove him off by other means. But a mind that could move objects and possess people was now as useless as a paperweight. Kolby's wet, unwelcome tongue pushed into her mouth as his hand wiggled up her shirt like a spider.

Frightened and disgusted, Lillian shoved at Kolby's chest as she tasted his beer-soaked, smoky spit. Light spilled upon the pair, with a shadow in the center.

"You slut!" a hauntingly familiar voice screeched. "What are you doing?"

"Tara!" Kolby's voice faded in and out. "What are you doing here? This isn't what it looks like!"

"That nasty freshman whore!"

Loud crashing ensued as Tara stormed into the room. She grasped Lillian by one of her twin braids and yanked her upright, and then shook her by her shoulders. Terror overwhelmed Lillian. The room alternated with Julius' moist, grassy yard, and Mandy's hands around her throat as Julius controlled her body.

"Tara!" someone screamed. "Calm down!"

"Fucking skank trying to steal my boyfriend!"

Kolby wrapped his arms around Lillian and spirited her through a blurry hall to a too-bright bathroom. He sat her on the closed toilet seat and asked if she was all right. Now crying, Lillian threw his arms off of her.

"I'm so sorry," Kolby apologized. "I didn't know she'd be here! She had no right!"

"Let me go home!" Lillian sobbed. "I wanna go home!"

Kolby led her by the hand across the lawn, now an unrecognizable snow-caked moonscape filtered through the goggles of beer and marijuana. Lillian suddenly giggled again as Kolby sat her down in his car. As he drove off, drunk and high himself, Lillian started to pound on the window, screaming and halfway certain she was in Julius' BMW instead.

Once they reached the campus, Kolby quietly led Lillian, tipsy and stumbling, to her dormitory. She was too trashed to remember the way at the moment, vacillating between gasping laughter and choking sobs.

"Look, I didn't even know Tara would be there," Kolby sighed. "I'm so sorry, man. It's just... I don't get why a hot chick like you doesn't get out much. So I thought I'd fix that."

Kolby took Lillian's card key from her pocket and brought her into the dormitory, up to her room. Tara was not present. But something about the room had changed—Lillian was not alert enough to know exactly what. Kolby laid Lillian down on her bed like a sick child and left without another word. She buried her face in her pillow and cried herself to sleep.

In the morning, Lillian woke early, finding herself alone. Her head pinged and pounded with a fierce headache while her stomach turned. Rubbing her temples, Lillian propped herself up. The sunlight spilling through the window assaulted her throbbing eyes. She shuffled to the sink to take some ibuprofen.

After gulping the pills and hoping for them to stay down, Lillian finally looked around. Her music posters lay in shredded, crumpled balls on the floor. Robert Smith of The Cure was torn in half, right through his white face and wild hair. The plush Stimpy, who usually rested between her pillows, sat on his head in a corner of the room. The drawers of Lillian's nightstand hung open, contents ransacked. Ground into crumbs and dust were the peanut butter cookies sent in a recent care package from her father. Some books were tossed from the bookshelf, pages ripped out. From the orange and black streaks of aura, Lillian knew exactly who had wrecked her things. Tara, in a rampage that must have taken place shortly before Kolby brought Lillian back here.

Tara must have done something worse to Lillian's laptop, she realized with worry, as she pictured it stomped and broken into a mangled mess of circuits and dislodged keys and shards of screen. She had left it turned off in her book bag in the closet. When she frantically went to check, the computer was unharmed inside the bag, and her camera, not cheap, hung intact beside it. Lillian breathed a sigh of relief that Tara had overlooked that equipment, and hadn't touched the bass guitar either. But the torn textbooks had cost money too, and the smashed cookies brought tears to her eyes. Their scent always soothed her, and now they were gone.

Trying to ignore her nausea and piercing headache, Lillian put what she could back in order. Most of her wall posters were not salvageable and went into the trash.

Earlier in the semester, Lillian would have gone straight down the hall to Mallory, the residential assistant. But after Mallory accused her of lying and sided with her cousin Tara, Lillian did not wish to speak to Mallory ever again.

Curled into a ball on her bed, Lillian called her old high school friend Christian, now going to college in North Carolina, for advice. They didn't talk often, but she valued his blunt feedback.

"Tara's cousin is your RA?!" Christian snarled. "What a crock of shit. Report that to the dean. Maybe there's a rule against it. Tara's probably on drugs and it's making her moody. Maybe you can look through her stuff. If you find a stash, you can get her ass expelled. Don't go to her worthless cousin; go to the campus police. Stay away from the assholes at the party. They were counting on you getting trashed."

"Kolby didn't do anything to me when he brought me back to my room. Even though I was pretty out of it."

"Maybe he thought it would make him look too bad. But still, he forced a kiss on you. Be careful."

Lillian took her friend's suggestion and searched the room for drugs, keeping her ears and aura senses carefully tuned for signs of Tara walking down the hall. After checking Tara's nightstand drawers, Lillian peeked at the sides and undersides of the drawers for possible bags of powders and pills taped into hiding places. She found love letters from Kolby and several other men, each of them thinking they were Tara's one and only. After going through the shelves and desk and lifting Tara's mattress, Lillian did not find so much as an empty beer bottle. Tara was keeping any chemical use hidden, probably well aware of dormitory rules.

Tara never appeared that night. Or the night after. Lillian made an appointment with the Dean of Students in his fancy, sleek upstairs office, hoping that if she complained way up the chain like Christian had recommended, she might finally get help. When she described her wrecked possessions and the noise issues, the dean showed no reaction. Learning that Tara and Mallory were cousins, he shook his bald head.

"Mallory must not have disclosed that she is related to one of her residents. That's against our policy. Unfortunately, I can't help much on the other issues without proof that your roommate is the offender. But we will get the situation with your RA taken care of."

Late the next morning, after another night thankfully free of Tara, Lillian found Mallory crying in the hallway, moving cardboard boxes out of her room. She did not look Lillian in the eye.

Angela, the tall slim blonde who was the residential assistant on the ground floor, posted signs around the dorm and made phone calls, summoning everybody to an "emergency meeting" in the television lounge that evening. As the girls gathered for the meeting, Tara showed up, her eyes cold as she stood in the corner and crossed her arms.

"You guys, Mallory had to move out today," Angela announced in a grumpy tone. "I don't know the reason why, or where she went, so don't ask me. They'll look for a new RA for the spring, but it's too late to replace her for the fall. I'll have to manage both the upstairs and the downstairs until the end of the semester. I know we'll all be very busy studying for our finals. I'm going to have my hands really full. So I am asking all of you, please, *please* don't bother me unless it's something urgent."

Terrified to spend the night with Tara after she showed up glowering at the meeting, Lillian transferred herself to the other world, remaining there for a day and no longer caring about the homework she had fallen behind in. Lillian lived in happy denial, skinny-dipping in the diamond-water lake, and watching the stars and the pink filtered sun come and go. She did not even come up to eat, with her appetite ravaged by stress.

In her deep cave of avoiding the world, Lillian currently did not know her grades. Having not done her homework in a while, Lillian also missed a math exam and would probably fail the class. She wished to drop out and move back home and maybe get a job restocking shelves at her father's nursery. So much for becoming a scientist.

Lillian only returned because if she did not, she might die in the other world and trap the crystal there, her spirit sliding to the bone-filled temple while no one knew what had happened to her. She could not, in good conscience, doom her family to a lifetime of searching for a body they could no longer access.

After coming up to the dim evening light, Lillian walked down the cleared, salted path through the snow to Bailey Hall. The dormitory's hulking dark profile in the setting sun gave her a panic attack.

Lillian's heart raced even faster as she came through the door to her room, knowing instinctively that Tara was in. Her roommate sat cross-legged on her bed next to some friend of hers Lillian did not recognize, giggling.

"Oh, there she is, that ho," Tara hissed. "I don't know where she's been. Yuck, let's get out of here."

Tara and her friend bumped roughly into Lillian as they left the room.

College was nothing like Lillian had pictured, a peaceful place roaming with mature intellectuals who sat serenely under trees or in library study carrels. Instead, this was the cliques and bullies of middle school all over again. Did people just never grow up?

Lillian hid in the shower stall she chose out of habit, with the razor in hand. After bandaging and cleaning up, she went back to her room and crawled into bed, with her roommate's absence her only consolation.

Lillian was shaken from sleep deep in the night. Her body stiffened, frozen in fear, as Tara hovered over her in the dim glow of the night light.

"I don't want to ever catch you looking at my man again, you understand?" Tara snarled, her long nails digging into Lillian's shoulder. Lillian tried to wrench away. Tara flipped her over to face her again, wrapping her long, cool fingers around Lillian's neck.

"And you know what?" she barked. "I know you're the one who got Mallory fired. Who the hell do you think you are, bitch? How could you do that to her? We have a lot of people looking out for us. If you ever mess with me or Mallory or my man again, I'll make you wish you were never born. Because you know what? I hate your ass."

Tara tightened her grip as Lillian choked and gasped, reaching up and grabbing in a futile attempt to pry Tara's fingers away.

Suddenly, the pressure on Lillian's throat was relieved.

Tara wavered and levitated a few feet into the air, screaming and helplessly flailing her long thin arms and legs. How unexpectedly easy it was to pick up a whole human! As Lillian released her telekinetic hold, Tara fell on her behind on the floor. She glanced around with her wide brown eyes, stunned.

"There's something you don't know," Lillian growled, sitting up. Despite the terrible tension gripping her throat almost like Tara's hands did seconds ago, she tried her hardest to speak clearly. "You think you can push me around and make my life hell, but you don't know what you're dealing with."

Stuffed animals lifted from the top of Tara's bookshelf and hurtled through the air, landing around her like a shower of asteroids from the sky. Tara's head spun around, her mouth agape. Her books flew down and fell open, pages feathering out. Nightstand drawers slid out and slammed back in. Tara's polka-dotted Betty Boop clock fell from the wall.

"Oh my God!" Tara shrieked, getting up and clapping a hand to her bloodless face. She dashed out the door. Her footsteps thumped loudly, fading down the hall.

Lillian knew what a mistake she had made. In showing her roommate just one of her powers, Lillian had very uncharacteristically violated the code of ethics most mages followed. The normal people, even those married to mages, weren't supposed to have a clue; but now Tara had seen it. Now it would probably get out, and Lillian would have to contend with the consequences.

Lillian returned to her classes, though some of the damage to her grades was irreversible. She no longer fully understood the lectures or quizzes, and it was too late in the semester to drop classes or withdraw. The other students still came to class looking so put together and prepared, dutifully taking notes and quickly finishing their quizzes and tests. *They all have their shit together, unlike me,* Lillian thought to herself in her shame.

When Tara occupied their room, Lillian spent uncomfortable nights on the backseat of her vehicle, curled under a mound of coats and shiny thermal blankets to keep warm in the bitter weather. After those neighbors down the hall had called her "weird" for lying on the couch, she was too self-conscious to sleep in the study pod. Having no friends in this city, no private couches to snuggle up on, she became woozy from the cumulative stress and sleep deprivation.

One day, walking past the room she'd come to avoid and sensing her roommate's presence inside, Lillian caught snippets of a phone conversation, muffled through the door that was open a crack.

"Yeah, I saw the craziest thing. Can't explain it... stuff flying all over the place."

Lillian stayed in place and held her breath, quiet as possible.

"That's impossible, right?" Tara went on. "Happened a while back... I think you're right, I must have been drunk. Can't remember if I partied that day. Or maybe it was, like, a dream or something."

Please keep on thinking that, Lillian said to herself as she slid down the hall to the empty study pod.

After struggling through her finals, Lillian discovered her grades: Cs, a D, and an F, even though she had started the semester with obsessive, perfectionist homework and high test scores. She was punished with academic probation and a revoked scholarship that she would need to write a letter of appeal to get back. After weeks of pleading with the residential office, they granted Lillian a room change for the next semester. However, so many bad experiences in just one semester solidified her decision to drop out.

The day before Lillian's flight home, Tara still had not left for the winter break. Lillian hid out in the driver's seat of the Cherokee, making the call to her father that she'd been dreading and putting off. When Lillian disclosed her poor performance, he reacted with much less anger than she had expected.

"I was anticipating that your grades might not be stellar. I've been told that it is common for first-time college students to get overwhelmed. But I'm confident that you can turn it around."

"Evelyn didn't get overwhelmed. She was an A student the whole time, wasn't she, while playing sports and working?"

"Most of us aren't like Evelyn. And you know what? That's okay."

"Maybe it's from growing up in Evelyn's shadow, but I always wondered if maybe I was not hardworking enough, or just not that bright. I think I can't handle college. It's for smart people like Evelyn."

"Sweetheart, you were in the gifted and talented program, remember? There's no lack of intelligence. Evelyn is always running on a hamster wheel of stress. Even in high school, she missed a lot of sleep and made herself sick to get those straight As. I never could get her to step off that hamster wheel and relax a little."

"Yeah, that's true. But sometimes I can't do things that are easy for other people and when I get stressed out, I shut down. I've been having problems with my roommate and it's really been frying my brain. But I wonder if something is wrong with me. I'm sorry, Dad."

"I'm sure your roommate had a lot to do with it, and nothing is wrong with you. We can talk about that when you get here."

When he and Lou picked Lillian up at the airport, Denny's salt-and-pepper hair had grayed a little more since August, when Lillian saw him last, and his belly paunch had expanded a bit. Dad still looked the same, tall and slender with a full head of silver hair and his signature wire-rimmed glasses.

"My goodness, you look like you've lost weight. Not on a diet, are you?" Denny observed as they walked through the cold parking garage.

"You do look thinner," Dad agreed, pausing to examine how Lillian's clothes hung off her. Lillian's jeans had fit snugly back in August and now needed a belt to stay up. "Have you been eating enough?"

"I guess I just got too stressed out," Lillian meekly explained. She'd barely noticed the changes: going from wolfing down fast food to nervously nibbling on handfuls of Chex Mix to almost completely losing her appetite. "I wasn't on a diet, or trying to starve myself. I just started... forgetting to eat."

As they crossed the Bay Bridge, Dad discussed the plans for the next few weeks. Evelyn and her fiancé Jonathan would visit for Christmas, bringing Lillian's sleeveless bridesmaid's dress so that she could try it on and ensure that it fit. Lillian began to worry in secret, staring into the darkness out the window that would be an expanse of water by day. Some of her recent self-inflicted wounds, hidden under long sleeves and her old friendship bracelets, had not healed into obscurity yet. She would ask for privacy when she tried the dress on.

At the wedding itself, that would not be an option.

They pulled up the familiar driveway and dragged Lillian's luggage up the steps to the door. Hysterical with joy, Astrid, the dog, knocked Lillian down when the three came inside. Lillian rolled happily around with the wriggling dog on the living-room floor.

The following day, after sleeping in, it still didn't feel real to be back home. Lillian helped her father to set up the Christmas tree and she twined a gold garland around the stair railing. With their lights and decorations, they created one of the beautiful holiday scenes Lou was famous for. With no one else around to watch, they both got lazy about concealing their telekinesis. Ornaments appeared to levitate independently from their boxes. The garlands unfurled themselves like snakes charmed from baskets. The TV flicked on and off, doors opened and closed, and dinner was stirred in its pot from the next room.

Lillian thought of her mother, absent from gathering around the Christmas tree. If that boyfriend had never shot her, how would that change the course of the family's lives? Vanessa was spoken of rarely, a shadowed memory in the past, though the albums still held photos of the scrappy little brunette woman with her characteristic owlish glasses. The watercolors she'd painted of local landscapes, water, and birds in the grass hung on the walls.

"Why didn't you two get married?" Lillian asked her father as they sat beside the crackling fire in the living room. Something had always seemed odd about the story of her parents' on-again, off-again relationship. "Why didn't she stay?"

"Oh... I don't know. I think it's just that I had already been divorced, and we didn't see the point. People would ask about it, and also about our age difference. Vanessa preferred older men."

A few years ago, Lillian had stumbled upon newspaper clippings from the murder, saved in a shoebox. Her mother's partner, Karl Thiessen, had pled not guilty by reason of insanity, claiming that he did not recall shooting her. He told the police that he lapsed into a "fugue state" and the next thing he knew was the horrifying sight of Vanessa lying dead in their living room and his old revolver gripped in his hand. Karl was the one who called 911, screaming, "Somebody shot my girlfriend!"

A medical and psychological evaluation found nothing wrong with Karl, no explanation as to why such a healthy man would enter a violent fugue state and lose a chunk of his memory. Especially damning was their rocky relationship. Friends and neighbors testified that Karl and Vanessa argued often. The prosecution and jurors did not believe Karl's side of the story, and he was found guilty, rotting behind bars to this day.

His claim of a blackout never sat right with Lillian. Especially after she'd learned from Julius about their power to take possession.

No. It was impossible that any necromancers were involved. Lillian's mother had simply run into rotten luck, leaving her father for the wrong man, a move that cost her her very life.

"I am sincerely pleased to be here today."

Gerald raised a glass of red wine to the large conference room full of his employees, who sat at round tables littered with artificial holly leaves. The windows overlooked the city skyline. The Washington Monument glowed white in the setting sun. "This has been a very productive year for Frazier Medical Supply, and I'd like to thank each and every one of you for all of your hard work. It is with great regret that I inform you that while this was a profitable year, it was not as profitable as I would have liked, due to some circumstances beyond our control. Unfortunately, this means we will need to eliminate a small number of jobs. I will inform the affected employees after the holidays, so you are all promised your jobs through Christmas and the new year. I urge you not to panic. With this wonderful company on your resume, you will have no trouble pursuing new career goals."

As the employees turned to one another to whisper and speculate, Gerald sat back down and retreated into his head, reviewing the underlings he had decided to prune. Several folks were committing timecard fraud, thinking they got away with their absences and long lunches. Mick Mahoney, a dead weight, spent most of his time either surfing the internet or texting his girlfriend. Rosemary Brass just found out she was pregnant, and after that kid was born, she wanted three more, burdening others with her maternity leaves and then missing a lot of work to care for sick children. Joseph DeLeo had cancer, a diagnosis he kept secret from everyone at work, and took frequent sick time for his chemotherapy and radiation treatments. Gerald, of course, read his mind and knew of his many disappearances to come. Gerald would keep the most necessary, useful, healthy people without things like young kids muddling their lives. Even those who complained about him and the company as they drank their stress away during happy hour. As long as they did the work competently, they could gossip about him all they wanted. Gerald had a thick enough skin to take it.

After excusing himself from the party, Gerald went to a nearby luxury hotel. In the lobby waited a platinum-blonde woman wrapped in a long gleaming mink coat. She'd already met with Gerald plenty of times. At the sight of him, she spread her full ruby-red lips into a magazine-worthy smile. She wanted Gerald to think she was called Lacey, but Gerald, of course, knew her real name: Marit Blom, the granddaughter of Norwegian immigrants. She grew up on a farm in Minnesota. After joining the cheer squad in high school, she went to Sarah Lawrence College, dropping out after a couple of semesters. Marit thought in words, not in pictures, and she regularly had nightmares about the sun burning the earth to a crisp. She lived near Rock Creek Park and, like many of the local high-dollar hookers, had slept with members of Congress. From their pillow talk, she knew a lot of political secrets, and Gerald knew them too.

When most people hired call girls, they didn't want to know much about them and just indulged in a fantasy, turning them into substitute girlfriends or dehumanizing them into blow-up dolls. Gerald, of course, couldn't escape being bombarded with their dates of birth, deep dark secrets, and the fact that they were just as human and complicated as anyone else. He had to make an effort to detach himself from each girl he hired.

They took the elevator to a fancy suite with a generous king-sized bed. Gerald sat at the edge of the bed, still in his black business suit, as Lacey, or Marit, let her mink coat fall to the floor, unveiling a skintight red negligee and stiletto heels. She did a striptease for him before enticingly tugging on his silk tie and removing it with her teeth. This certainly was simpler than being married, the reason Gerald never sought another wife after the death of his last one. Services were available when Gerald wanted them, and no one was at home to put her noise in his head day after day.

The day before Christmas Eve, Evelyn arrived with Jonathan. "How was your first semester of college?" she asked Lillian.

"My first semester was honestly... tough." During their few short phone conversations, Lillian had told Evelyn nothing about her roommate situation, or her poor grades. She felt as if she were letting her sister down, not living up to Evelyn's expectations that she'd immediately befriend her roommate and neighbors and study together.

"Oh, everyone has a tough first semester. I'm sure it took some adjusting, being far from home like that. It'll get better."

After Evelyn and Jonathan settled in, they unrolled Lillian's bridesmaid's dress from a suitcase, urging her to try it on. Lillian said she didn't feel like it today, but promised to wear the dress soon. She was going to put this off for as long as humanly possible.

A couple of days after Christmas, Evelyn came out of her bedroom with a big smile on her face and the sleeveless bridesmaid's dress dangling from her small, French-manicured hands. "You're going to try this on. I don't want us to forget about it before we leave."

Attempting to hide her panic, Lillian took the dress into her room to change, using her telekinesis to pull up the back zipper when her hands could not reach it. She would do whatever it took to not ask for help.

Lillian studied herself in the full-length mirror. The glossy floor-length dress looked stunning, a rich sea-glass green that almost perfectly matched her eye color. She rotated her arms outward. Just as she feared, some of the more recent cuts were still visible, faded purple marks.

Most people were oblivious to signs of self-harm. No one at school had said anything, at least not to her face. Lillian feared that Evelyn, still skittish about wounds after the suicide attempt four years ago, would notice no matter what.

Evelyn knocked on the door. "Do you have it on yet? Come out!"

"I have it on and it fits. I think I'll just take it off."

"No, no! We all want to see you in it!"

Lillian grabbed a shawl from the closet and came back downstairs with it draped almost completely down to her hands.

"It looks pretty," Evelyn said, squinting her eyes and circling around. "Looks like it fits okay, a bit loose—but breathing room is better than it being too tight. Once you're all made up on the wedding day, you'll look fantastic. But you won't be wearing a shawl. I want to see you without it."

The shawl fell soundlessly to the carpet.

"I want to see you from the back. Wait, what's that?" Evelyn grabbed her sister's wrist and twisted her arm to get a closer look. "You've been cutting yourself again, haven't you?"

Their father sunk into the couch, shaking his head sadly.

"I... I had a rough semester," Lillian mumbled.

"I had rough semesters too! I live by the saying: when the going gets tough, the tough get going. I just don't understand why you would want to hurt yourself. You'll humiliate me on my wedding day."

"She will not ruin your wedding, sweetheart," said their father as Lillian escaped up the stairs. She overheard snippets of the argument brewing: "...her coping skills," "forget coping skills, it's just sick," and a final yell of "Well, you just try getting married and dealing with all the stress!"

Lou came up to speak with Lillian in her bedroom. Still wrapped in her green dress, she was lying on her back on the bed, hands to her eyes, holding back tears. After taking a seat at her desk, her father asked why the cutting had started again. Had something terrible happened at school?

As she usually did, Lillian finally decided that it was best to tell the truth, no matter how embarrassing and painful. She took deep breaths, tried to stop the tears that stung her eyes, and took him back to the beginning: Tara's behavior, the suffocating loneliness, and that party with Kolby and his friends. She was honest about Kolby's forced kisses, and the group pushing their beer and weed on her.

Lou surprised Lillian again when he directed his anger toward the boys, not toward her. "I know you. You drink much less than I did at your age. Yes, it's true... your old dad had a bit of a wild side. I'm sure those boys were trying to take advantage of you."

After going over Mallory's firing, Lillian went into the part she beat herself up the most about: the demonstration of her powers in a moment of panic as Tara threatened her, without fully thinking it through until the worry hit later.

"I'm so sorry," Lillian said in a near-whisper. "I just wanted Tara to leave me alone. I guess I was like a skunk spraying someone in self-defense."

"While I am a little concerned that you let the powers show, I agree, you were defending yourself. That rotten girl was choking you, for crying out loud."

"I was really stressed after that. I thought now I had screwed up really badly, even though Tara told someone over the phone that she thought she might have just been drunk and imagining things. And I'd just reached my breaking point with everything going on and it was hard to focus on my classes. I didn't want to be there anymore."

"I'm not sure it is a good idea for you to go back to the school. Why don't we sleep on it for a while, and see if you still want to withdraw."

"I feel like Evelyn hates me. It hurts that she thinks I struggled because I wasn't tough enough."

"Evelyn does not hate you, sweetheart. She's stressed about the wedding, she's scared, and she doesn't understand because she hasn't walked in your shoes."

Over dinner, Evelyn apologized to Lillian and their father for her comments earlier. Saying sorry did not come naturally to Evelyn; the words came out halting and awkward. Both Lou and Lillian accepted the apology, though damage was done, Lillian's trust in her sister eroded.

Evelyn and Jonathan left the next morning on a road trip to see friends. That afternoon, an unexpected guest pulled up the driveway of Lou's house in his sleek silver car, the engine luxuriously quiet. Uncle Gerald appeared on the doorstep, ringing the doorbell and peeking through the screen.

"Did I invite you here?" said Lou from the other side.

"Pardon me for rudely coming uninvited. But if I waited for you to invite me, I'd be waiting until all that's left of me is a skeleton. I've been wanting to see the girls."

"You just missed Evelyn, I'm afraid."

Lillian sat at the sewing machine, patching together the remains of a couple of T-shirts. She paused, watching them from behind her father's back, as Gerald stepped inside.

"What a shame that I missed Evelyn, but I look forward to watching her tying the knot in a few months. I've got my toast memorized. Hey, Lillian, merry Christmas. Spend it, put it in your savings, do whatever you want with it." Gerald reached into his leather wallet and handed Lillian a check for a thousand dollars.

After Lillian got done thanking Gerald profusely, he asked, "How was your first semester?"

Uncomfortably, Lillian put her hands in her lap as Uncle Gerald read her like a barcode scanner with his large, sea-colored eyes.

"Oh, dear, what a nasty semester you had. But I'm sure you can bring your grades up and hang on to your scholarship as long as you stick it out. I encourage you to return to the school with fresh determination. It will get better. And don't worry about Tara Nicholson. She is just one of the nobodies. They're no match for us."

"Now, Gerald," said Lou, laying a long, elegant hand softly on his brother's arm. "I've been trying to discourage her from using her powers."

"For too many generations, we have lived in hiding like cowardly little church mice. We weren't born the special ones, the chosen ones, for nothing. Lou, it's a shame you never use what you have except for quiet household chores."

"Gerald, it isn't good to get carried away. I know I was born powerful for whatever reason, but nothing good could come of it."

"I disagree with you, but I know how set in your ways you've become."

A few minutes later, Lillian's father urgently had to use the bathroom and left them alone. Gerald knelt beside Lillian, breathing loudly and invading her space. She drew back as he patted her shoulder. He spoke in a low, rough growl of a whisper.

"Hey, hey. No matter what your father told you, I don't bite. Just between you and me, don't let Tara stop you from going back to school. You're going to move into another room, and she is worthless. If she ever bothers you again, you have plenty of options."

"Like what?"

"What would you like to see happen to her?"

"Well, I'd like people to see how nasty she is... and I just want her to leave me alone."

"Do you think the world would be better or worse without her?"

"Well, the world would be better without people like her."

"Obviously. The girl is a mean-spirited whack job and she's going to cause headaches for a lot of people. What if this was something you could change? There are possibilities for dealing with Tara. Things you could easily get away with."

Lillian tensed up, less and less comfortable by the second. What was Gerald getting at? "I don't really want to 'deal' with her. I just want her to stay out of my life."

"I'm just giving you some food for thought."

Finally, Lillian's father came out and the uncomfortable conversation stopped as he asked Gerald and Lillian what they were up to.

"We were just chatting," Gerald answered. "I was giving your daughter a pep talk so she won't feel discouraged. I really think she needs to go back to school. She shouldn't worry about that god-awful roommate for another minute."

After making some small talk with Lou and drinking a lemonade from the fridge, Gerald declared, "I should be off—got a few things to take care of at home. I do appreciate the two of you having me for a little bit. And Lillian, don't let any bullies get you down. You're better than that." He nodded to his two relatives and was out the door.

The following morning, Lou drove his daughter to the airport in the icy blue-gray dawn. At this point, Lillian was on the fence about giving it another semester, or simply packing up her things and driving back home. Upon dropping her off, her father gave her a quick embrace and reminded her, "I'm just a phone call away."

"And thousands of miles," Lillian said, tight-chested with anxiety.

After getting through the shoe-removing, coat-unpeeling chaos of the security line, Lillian ran to a restroom to throw up, sick with panic.

A letter from the school residential life office had arrived at her father's house just a couple of days ago. Lillian would live with Bridget Shin, someone she'd never heard of, in the basement of Johanson Hall. If she even made it that far before bolting from the campus.

That afternoon, after fetching her vehicle from the airport parking garage in Denver and going north, Lillian pulled onto the campus, stomach lurching again. Fewer cars than normal were around, as some students had not yet returned. After parking next to a dumpster, Lillian threw away the old fast-food trash, making room to pack her boxes.

Lillian walked into Bailey Hall, darker and quieter than she'd ever seen it. Tara was still absent from the chilly, dusty room, though most of her things waited for her return. Lillian gathered a bag of possessions and nearly went to pack it in the back of the Cherokee. Instead, something compelled her to find the new dorm. Just one peek to satisfy her curiosity, and then she'd be out of here.

Johanson Hall was a building of light brown brick, comfortingly far away from Bailey Hall. After going down the stairs and finding her newly assigned room, Lillian felt the essence of a stranger from the other side of the door. Damn, the new roommate was already here. Lillian knocked, since her card could not unlock this door yet. She braced herself for the sort of icy reception she'd gotten in August.

The room was lined with punk rock posters. A plump young woman sat at one of the desks, wearing a black Pantera shirt. Her black hair was clipped short, with a longer blue blaze swept aside over her round face. Like most people, she was typical, with no evidence of powers.

"Hello. You're my new roommate?" she greeted.

"Yes," Lillian said, remaining guarded.

"Your name is... Lillian, right? Am I remembering right?"

"That's right."

"I'm Bridget. Nice to meet you. Are you moving in from another dorm?"

"Yes. From Bailey."

"Is your stuff still there?"

"Yeah."

"Want me to help you carry it?"

"Sure!"

As Bridget put her coat on, she gave Lillian a choice of which bunk she preferred in the bunk bed. Lillian picked the bottom, and Bridget had already put her blankets on the top, so it worked out. Lillian decided to have faith that she might be staying here after all.

As they walked to Bailey Hall, Lillian asked Bridget if she'd had a roommate last semester.

"Yeah, I did. She decided to switch schools."

"Was she nice?"

"Yeah, nice enough. We didn't have any problems, but we had nothing in common."

If Bridget was telling the truth, what a relief—the roommate's departure had nothing to do with her.

"Why are you leaving your last room?" Bridget wanted to know. "Did something happen?"

"I had problems with my roommate."

"Are you okay telling me what happened?"

"Oh, it was a trainwreck. She thought I was trying to steal her boyfriend and took it out on me, while she was cheating on him. She kept having sex when I was in the room, even after I told her I didn't want to see that."

"Oh, Christ! That's so gross."

"When people complained about the noise, she said I was the one having loud sex."

"Oh, how embarrassing!"

"Yeah, I was angry and embarrassed. And that's not even the whole story."

"What a piece of work. What was her name?"

"Tara Nicholson."

"Name doesn't ring a bell, but I'll try to watch out in case I run into her."

Another private sigh of relief. Bridget didn't know Tara, assuaging the fear that they were friends.

"I almost dropped out," Lillian revealed as they entered the quiet, echoing Bailey Hall and took the stairs up to her old room. "Even today, I'm fifty-fifty on dropping out. I want to just pack all my stuff and go back home with my tail tucked firmly between my butt cheeks. I think Tara turned the other girls in this dorm against me. When they saw me, it was like somebody farted."

"I hope you don't drop out. This is a great school and I've met awesome people here. I'm not sure if you realize, this dorm has a reputation for being the most stuck-up one on campus. And your roommate was a bully. I bet she was jealous of you."

"Her boyfriend thought that too. I'm not sure what she'd be so jealous of. And since I came here from back East, I had no way of knowing this dorm has a reputation. Now it makes sense."

Lillian let her new roommate into her old room. After Bridget ogled the guitar for a while, it was one of the first things they carried to the new room, along with the amplifier.

"What type of music do you listen to?" Bridget asked. "You like Type O Negative?"

"Yes! Got it running through my veins, too. Peter Steele is dreamy!"

Bridget laughed. "Here's a bit of a tougher one. How about Revolting Cocks?"

"Yes, awesome!"

"My last roommate never heard of any of those bands. I think we're going to get along just fine."

For the first time at Northern Colorado University, Lillian was warmed from the inside with a little sense of belonging. As they went back and forth to pack things, Bridget asked Lillian where she was from. And then Lillian turned the question around on her.

"That's an easy question with a complicated answer. Want me to tell you a novel about my life?"

"Sure!"

"My dad is a first-generation American. He joined the Army, and then he was stationed in South Korea, where his folks are from. That's where he met my mom. Then they moved to Germany, and that's where I was born. My little brother, Brandon, was born in Italy. You get the idea... we were Army brats. We lived in different states, different countries."

"That's fascinating that you've moved so much! I've lived in the same town my whole life until I came here. But I can't imagine... was it also rough? Starting over so frequently?"

"Yeah, it was rough having to meet new people and make new friends every few years. And now my family lives in Colorado Springs. Are you getting hungry at all? Want to do dinner? I know a place that has the best New York-style pizza."

"Mmm. Pizza!"

The semester began after a few evenings of gorging at that little pizza place Lillian had never heard of until now. Lillian felt confident about staying at the university and getting back on track. Bridget still acted warm and accepting, a big difference from Tara's detached snobbery. They were both night owls and stayed up late, talking and laughing. When Bridget brought home occasional dates, she did Lillian the courtesy of putting hair ties or rubber bands on the door handle.

After having no safe person around during her first semester, Lillian gushed about her interest in geology and volcanoes while her roommate listened patiently. Though she majored in something else entirely—journalism—Bridget took it in stride. When Bridget learned that Lillian was a writer, she begged to see her work until Lillian shyly emailed her a finished draft of a science fiction novel featuring a war between three space stations. During her free time, Bridget ate it up, praising Lillian for her skills. "You're really good! You should get published!"

This gave Lillian a badly needed confidence boost.

Through Bridget, Lillian made another new acquaintance, Tim Whitman, an extremely friendly and bubbly sophomore. He happened to be friends with Laura, a downstairs resident in Bailey Hall. Laura confirmed that Tara had spread rumors about Lillian, accusing her of boyfriend-stealing and calling her a "slut." The residents also shunned her simply for being "weird." After meeting Lillian face to face, Laura went back to her connections in the dorm and refuted the gossip. There were rumblings of trouble between Tara and her new roommate, a pre-medical student. Neighbors overheard screaming arguments.

One January day, Lillian walked into the cafeteria to grab lunch. As she headed toward the counter to get her food, she froze and let out the faintest gasp of fright.

There it was again. The aura of a fire person, not a rudiment of footsteps on the ground but attached to an actual person maybe a hundred feet away. They sat behind a partition that hid them from Lillian's view, but she saw, clear as day, the long, thin, glowing orange extensions extending skyward.

Chest-tight fear gripped Lillian. Whoever sat behind that barrier could burn her to a crisp or bring forth what Uncle Gerald described as black "hell-hounds" with long razor fangs. The fire people's guardians, which sliced and killed and then vanished in a flash, had Lillian wondering why the other mages gave her people such a bad rap instead of addressing the horrors that the fire people could unleash instead. Fifteen years ago, a menacing mob of them confronted Uncle Gerald during a business trip to Singapore, and he survived only by the grace of his masterful talking-himself-out-of-trouble skills. He stopped traveling abroad after that close call.

After turning and leaving the cafeteria without eating a bite, Lillian ran, not walked, down the sidewalk. She slipped on ice, bruising her knees, but got right back up again and continued to run until she burst, panting, into her room. She leaned against the closed door, and it took a long time of calming down before she was confident that no one was after her.

Bridget was out, which came as both a relief and a disappointment. Though Lillian didn't want to explain to her roommate what had her scared and out of breath, the fire mage would have preferred not to expose themselves to an ordinary person. Depending on how closely they followed the code.

Lillian would not eat in the cafeteria during peak hours again, she decided. Lillian, and her nervous father, had expected that a student population this big might include one or two other mages, despite their rarity. But dodging the enemy for possibly the next three years sounded so daunting. This certainly would not be the last time in her life she'd have to hide from another mage.

Groups of people were everywhere. Crowds, cities, corporations. It sunk in for Lillian. Dodging the other mages was a train ride she could never get off.

Excerpt from The Autobiography of Gerald Frazier: Architect of a New World

S ome months into her pregnancy, it grew obvious that my sister Sarah carried a mage baby. And you know what happens when people like us are carrying babies with powers. Her power doubled. She was capable of so much more!

Since Sarah was determined to never use her abilities, she struggled, holding back the urge to bring up the dead left and right. I dreamed of walking in her shoes, thinking of how amazing it would feel, how much control I could gain. This one thing had me wishing to be a woman, in spite of their considerable social disadvantages.

Sarah retreated into a deep state of misery. The constant sight of ghosts tormented her. In her third trimester, she became a complete shut-in, jabbering and going mad. Her husband Frank was on the verge of having her committed. I did my very best to talk him out of it, reassuring him that I knew my sister better than anyone and that she'd recover from this temporary mental illness once she saw her precious baby. Thank heavens Sarah was not put away. Back in those days, people who went into insane asylums rarely came out. Lobotomies were popular, especially for unruly women. If some doctor had hammered an ice pick into Sarah's brain and stirred it around, she might have lost her powers, her visions of the future, or both. She might have lost everything.

In March of 1954, Sarah delivered a baby boy, Denison Michael. My brother Lou and I hopped on our bicycles as soon as school let out and rode straight to the hospital. While we lingered at Sarah's bedside, she cried tears of relief that her perceptions came back down to normal, rather than tears of happiness over the newborn in her arms.

"I was seeing so many things," Sarah confided to us in a whisper once a nurse finished poking and prodding at her and left the room. "So many horrible things. I dreamt of that destruction I saw in my dreams as a girl. I also dreamt of things you don't want to know about, even though I know you can see it, Gerald. Monsters. I couldn't get it to stop. Ghosts talking to me everywhere when I was awake. I was about ready to throw myself out the window. I was hanging on by a thread."

I left for a college in Ohio not long after the birth of my baby nephew. Aside from the handsome scholarship they offered me, I couldn't be sure what drew me to that not-so-glamorous-sounding state where I had never been, where I had no family or friends. I acted upon a hunch that something big waited for me there. When I came back home for Christmas, I discovered that Sarah became pregnant again and caught a ride to Baltimore for an abortion, not telling her husband. The procedure was illegal, and women went to questionable practitioners who often used dirty instruments. Sarah could have been killed, and she knew it, but such was the depth of her desperation! After reading her mind and stumbling upon this secret, I was very disappointed in Sarah. When I caught her alone, we got into our single worst argument. I told her it was a waste of a perfectly good child. Sarah shot back that if it was another necromancer pregnancy, it might have driven her permanently mad. But I had faith that she was strong enough to handle another such child, as long as she was careful to lock herself away like last time. Pregnancy is always temporary, after all.

Even though we'd been close to one another as children, we did not speak as much after that fight. I didn't see anything wrong with the birth of a necromancer. I lamented that we were raised with such shame over who we were, such a fear of our own power. I wished Sarah could adjust her outlook, the way I did.

Sarah never got pregnant again. I suspect that the abortion made her sterile. Little Denny was doomed to be an only child.

Evelyn's Wedding

Tara's boyfriend Kolby, of all people, changed his schedule and transferred into Lillian's evening psychology class. She sat toward the front and did not spot him until it was over and the students filtered out of the building. Startled, she froze in her tracks as he greeted her.

"Hey, I was hoping I would see you again," Kolby smiled as they stood in a cone of orange light cast from a lamp above the sidewalk. In the light, the hard planes of his masculine, stubble-darkened face lost dimension.

"You look like a deer in headlights," Kolby added when Lillian did not respond in her surprise. "Hey, it's okay. Me and Tara are history. We finally broke up for good."

"I'm surprised you didn't do that a hell of a lot sooner."

"I know, I know. I was stupid. Anyway, what are you doing later?"

"Homework."

"What are you doing this weekend? Why don't I take you out to a nice dinner?"

"Are you... asking me out?"

"What does it sound like? Of course I'm asking you out."

"I'm sorry but I'm not interested." After that forced kiss at the party last semester, Lillian wasn't sure she wanted to be his friend, much less date him.

"I would be really happy if you gave me a chance. And I also wanted to apologize about that party. I know I was a bit of a creep, and I'm sorry. How about Saturday?"

"Sure, I guess," Lillian tentatively agreed. Maybe she should give it a shot with Kolby after his apology. After only dating someone in another country over the internet, never letting a man get physically close to her, Lillian questioned if most marriages and long-term relationships began with a soup of lukewarm feelings, anxiety, and hoping for the best. Lillian insisted upon taking their own cars, and Kolby agreed.

On Saturday evening, Lillian combed her hair back into a barrette and pulled a fuzzy scarf from the closet as her roommate Bridget blasted music and worked on a report at her desk.

"Where are you going?" Bridget asked.

"Oh, I forgot to tell you! I'm going to see Kolby. He asked me out to dinner."

"Kolby? Wait... is he the one who's your old roommate's boyfriend?"

"He was, but they broke up, thank the gods."

"Eek! That guy! He kissed you in a super-creepy way."

"He did apologize to me about that stuff last semester."

"Are you attracted to him, like, at all?"

"He's cute, I guess."

"It sounds like maybe you don't want to go on this date."

"I'm not enthusiastic about it."

"So don't go!"

"Isn't it considered rude to stand someone up? I already said I'd meet him." Lillian checked her watch and panicked. "The date is in fifteen minutes! I don't have time to think about it, so I might as well go."

"Good luck. Don't be alone with him."

Lillian arrived at the same place where her father and Denny had taken her to dinner in August, a dimly lit restaurant filled with the thick aroma of roasting steak. She sat on the wooden waiting bench, jumping when a hand descended on her shoulder. Kolby sat right next to her, pressing his leg against the edge of hers. "Hi. Glad you could make it."

After being seated, they did not talk about much—Lillian was not sure which topics to bring up. She looked down at the menu and played with her fingernails, covered in blue polish that was beginning to chip. Kolby asked if Lillian wanted to go get a drink later. He knew of a bar where his friend worked and would agree not to check their IDs. She declined.

After the plates of medium rare steak were set down enticingly on the knotty wooden table, Lillian remembered her previous dorm room again, the hardwood floor, the dust motes swirling in the squares of light, the dreaded footsteps and creaks approaching the front door, Tara sliding her card into the lock.

Newly arrived guests, a group of young women in high-heeled boots, held their hands out in the waiting area as the hostess gave them menus. At the front of the group was a tall brunette with a fake-fur coat hanging over her skinny jeans. Lillian knew that coat and that orange-black aura, all right.

"We have to leave," Lillian whispered to Kolby. "Tara's here!"

"We've hardly started eating yet; I have to pay for this meal. Don't worry about her. She won't even see us. We're at the back, and they put big groups where the booths are."

"But Kolby, look! They're coming our way!"

"Calm down. It's over between me and her. If she sees us, she'll just have to suck it up."

As luck had it, the hostess seated Tara and her friends at the long table next to the small one Kolby and Lillian shared. Nausea washed over Lillian. She put her silverware down as Tara stared at her, eyes narrowing. Tara turned to the friend next to her and whispered into her ear through cupped hands.

"Kolby, can we ask for the check and leave?" Lillian pleaded.

Kolby ignored her and turned to the neighboring table. "Hi, ladies. What's up? Do you remember Lillian?"

"Why wouldn't I?" Tara groaned with a roll of her eyes.

"I'm really happy to announce that we're now dating." Kolby took Lillian's hands in his, tightening his grip when she tried to yank them away.

"Kolby, I'm not..."

Before Lillian could finish her sentence, Kolby leaned his torso over the table, fast like a striking snake, grabbed her arms, and tried to kiss her. She wrenched away, tempted to make the potted plant hanging up above fall on his head and knock him unconscious in a shower of soil.

But she wouldn't use her abilities in front of schoolmates. She wouldn't make that mistake again.

Desperate, Lillian twisted her arms until Kolby released her hands. When free, she kicked her chair behind her and started to run for the exit.

"Lillian! Where are you going?" Kolby called sharply. He ran faster than her, catching her when he locked his arms around her waist. "What's wrong with you?"

"I can't be here."

"Sorry, girls!" Kolby called to Tara's table. "We had a little fight earlier. I think she's a little mad."

"Mad?" Tara scoffed. "How about batshit crazy? Hope you're having a fun ride."

"Oh, no, this isn't what it looks like. Hey, honey, let's go back to the table. I'm paying, remember?"

Badgered and guilted, Lillian stayed. Kolby continued to brag to the table next to them, exaggerating the perks of the love relationship that did not exist and worsening Lillian's confusion as to why he was making this all up. Whenever she tried to speak, he reached across their steaks and put a finger to her lips.

At last, Kolby paid for the meal and let the two of them leave Tara and her group behind. As they walked out the front doors, Kolby stopped and turned to face Lillian, who stood ready to bolt from one of the most awkward situations of her entire life.

"I didn't know they'd be coming. The way I acted in there, that's... I guess that's my way of putting Tara behind me. I'm sorry if I weirded you out. I'll get you a coffee tomorrow to apologize for everything. You owe me some time together after I paid for your meal tonight. And that wasn't cheap. Right?"

Lillian reluctantly agreed to meet for coffee, even as the thought of ever seeing Kolby again twisted her stomach.

When Lillian got back to her room, she wanted to vent to Bridget, but her roommate was gone. Lillian tried to take that horrid dinner date off her mind and focus on her homework, and eventually fell asleep.

Evelyn's wedding, a couple of weeks away, was already taking place, her sister the white bride on the breezy beach. Backed by the turbulent gray Gulf of Mexico, she and Jonathan held hands beneath an arch of roses and vines. Each long, dagger-like thorn was coated in blood, dripping thick and red, splattering Evelyn's cream-white gown and rolling down in streaks. A tidal wave rose up in the background, waters gathering together in a tall, frightening shape that defied gravity. This hulking bluish mass curled menacingly before slamming itself down on the couple. It claimed them, sucking them in, and when the wave flattened and receded, nothing was left on the beach, not even the bleeding arch.

Lillian woke with a start. A humanoid shadow stood beside the bunk bed, wrapped in a dark shroud, its eyes faint green pinpoints peering down at her out of blackness.

Lillian recognized this man, the figure who'd appeared in her bedroom back home every so often, even watching over her as an infant and begging her in his whisper of a voice not to kill herself. Now he was here? Ghosts rarely traveled from the places that bound them. Had he appeared to reinforce the message of the bad dream?

After rubbing her eyes, the man was gone. Lillian put on her slippers and coat, grabbed her hot pink flip phone from where it charged on her desk, and left the room so as not to wake Bridget, now soundly asleep in the top bunk. Going outside, Lillian called her father's cell phone, knowing he'd be sleeping with the sound turned off, and left him a message. Uninhibited from a half-asleep brain, she groggily told him that she did not think a beachfront wedding was a good idea for Jonathan and Evelyn, and that they ought to change their plans if at all possible. Lillian did not really think about what she was saying until she decided to listen to the voicemail before sending it. Embarrassed at her disjointed rambling, she deleted the message and did not leave a new one.

The following afternoon, Lillian walked off the campus in her snow boots and arrived at a downtown coffeehouse to see Kolby, already waiting at a booth tucked into a corner. She ordered an iced latte at the counter and sat with him.

"How was your week, sweetie?" Kolby asked, as if talking to a spouse.

"It went fine. And I'm not your girlfriend, so I'm confused about you calling me 'sweetie.'"

"What? I thought there was something between us. Be a little nicer, will you?"

After an exhausting trial of strained conversation, Kolby told Lillian that he needed to use the restroom. Lillian waited in silence for his return, but the next shadow to fall over her was not his. She looked up, speechless, at none other than her former roommate. Running into Tara at the restaurant last night was more than enough. And now here she was again?!

"You stole my man!" Tara hissed. "You'll pay for this, bitch!"

"I wasn't... he's..."

"Shut the hell up!"

In a wavering voice, Lillian begged her, "Please don't come near me, or I'll report you for harassment."

"I know the cops. I know lots of people. You'll be sorry you did this to me!" Tara picked up Lillian's latte, most of it still in the cup, and threw the liquid into her face and her long loose hair.

"Too bad it's not hot! Would have loved to see it burn your skanky face!" shouted Tara as she stormed out the door.

Other guests stared as Lillian fumbled around for napkins. Her face dripped with foam into her lap filled with melting ice cubes.

"Again, I didn't know she'd be here! I swear!" Kolby called after Lillian. She ignored him as she ran as fast as she could through the exit, down the sidewalk, nearly bumping into a passing stranger.

When Lillian reached her dorm room, she wiped tears from her sticky, cold cheeks. Bridget looked up from her desk, eyes wide. "Whoa, what happened to you?"

"I got a drink thrown in my face!" Lillian sobbed.

"Who did that?"

"Tara."

"Should have known it was her! Let's get you cleaned up and calmed down, and you can tell me what happened." Bridget dampened a towel with warm water. After Lillian went into the bathroom to change her shirt, Bridget sat down with her and helped to wipe the latte from her face.

"Every time I meet up with Kolby," Lillian said once she managed to stop crying, "Tara shows up like clockwork. It happened last night, and it happened today. He says he didn't know she'd be there. I don't know if it's a coincidence."

"I'm sure it's not a coincidence. I think it's a setup. Kolby knows where Tara is going to be. Maybe he's hacked into her email; a lot of exes do that. Or maybe he even invites her there. Then he lies to you. He wants her to see you together."

"And what's the point of that? To make her mad?"

"Kolby hasn't gotten over Tara, or he wants revenge, or both. He wants to make her mad, or make her so jealous she'll take him back. Sorry to break it to you, but Kolby does not care about you. He's manipulating you because Tara's the one on his mind. I recommend you stop talking to him. Every time he asks you out, just walk away. Refuse to be part of their drama."

The night after flying to Texas for the wedding, Lillian stayed with her father at Jonathan and Evelyn's one-story brick house. She'd been here a couple of times for previous visits. The interior, festooned with black-and-white decorations, was clean, contemporary, and, as always, immaculate from Evelyn's compulsive housekeeping. Evelyn was antsy with nerves and excitement. She had gotten her dark red hair layered and highlighted with golden streaks.

The next morning, the sisters left with their father and the groom-to-be on a monotonous road trip to South Padre Island. Some guests arrived in a fleet of rental cars, and those in the wedding party put on their suits and dresses for the rehearsal. Lillian got anxious wearing the sleeveless green dress for the second time, though she had not harmed herself since the fall semester and those cuts had faded. Now that Lillian was eating more regularly, the dress did not hang off her as much as it had when she first tried it on. The waves rolled gently in the background. They faced a sea of empty chairs while the bride and groom stood underneath a flowered, rosy arch nearly identical to the one in Lillian's recent nightmare, except bloodless and clean.

Lillian could tell where the groom-to-be had inherited the mage blood he unknowingly carried: his father, a leather-jacketed man with a long white beard who had the same thickened aura. Though like all of these individuals, it was impossible to tell what sort of mages ran in their family, if any. What if Jonathan and Evelyn had children someday? Would the children be born with powers?

The following morning, the family helped Evelyn into her dress and veil. Repeatedly, Evelyn panicked, held her stomach, and brought a hand to her lips.

Jonathan's mother, a professional hairstylist and makeup artist, dolled up the bride and bridesmaids. She circled around Lillian with a curling iron and a can of smelly hairspray. Because Lillian's hair was too straight and fine to hold a curl very well, Jonathan's mother thickly layered on the spray until the scented cloud made Lillian light-headed. Evelyn's soon-to-be mother-in-law put on a coating of non-oily sunscreen to keep Lillian's milky skin from turning lobster-red in the sun. "I know how it is with you redheads. Y'all don't tan, you burn."

Lillian stood up, aiming a hand mirror at the full-length mirror behind her. Her hair fell down her back in elaborate, vivid spirals. A rhinestone-studded clip adorned one side of the fancy hairdo. As Lillian twirled in front of the full-length mirror in the shining green dress, she did not feel so weird-looking and insecure. For one of the few times in her life, she saw a beautiful, almost confident young woman looking back at her.

Guests filtered in, each of them picking up a wavy-edged paper handout commemorating the union of Evelyn Brooke Frazier and Jonathan Jacob Gundersen on this temperate day of March 19, 2008. The wedding party made its appearance, pair by pair. Lillian almost tripped on the aisle of hard-packed sand as countless digital cameras aimed their unforgiving lenses at her and one of Jonathan's brothers, whose slick, sweaty hand gripped her arm. No longer did she feel self-assured, put on display like this. Now she grew anxious about falling or doing something else to embarrass Evelyn.

Lillian looked vigilantly around, making sure she saw no signs of her cousin, Julius. Evelyn had kept her word in not inviting him, soothing the fear in the back of Lillian's mind that Evelyn might lack an understanding of the abuse he committed and try to force them to mend fences. That other cousin, Katrina, did not show up either. No letters or emails had come from Katrina in over a year.

Lou walked down the aisle scattered with rose petals, his hand hooked around Evelyn's arm. Gold and chestnut curls peeked out from under her veil. He presented her to Jonathan and took his seat in the front row, sniffling into his scarlet handkerchief as Jonathan's mother wiped her teary eyes, careful not to smudge her eyeliner.

The aggressive tidal wave from Lillian's dream never crashed down as they posed for a drawn-out, tiring photography session and then finally left the beach to fill their table at the head of a crepe-paper-strewn banquet hall. Lillian was overloaded; she couldn't wait for this hectic day to slow down. After Uncle Gerald, her father, and some friends delivered toasts, the eating and dancing began.

One of the guests was a man with hazel eyes and salt-and-pepper hair. It took Lillian a few moments to place his identity: Victor Christensen, her mother's brother, a software engineer living in California. Victor wanted to speak to the bride, but she was too caught up in the center of attention. He sought out Lillian, introducing his grown son Jason, who looked like a younger, bearded version of himself. Neither had seen Lillian since she was a baby. Victor did not share his deceased sister's mage-blood trait, and neither did his son. Their auras were as weak as most people's.

Lillian shyly asked Victor to tell her about her mother's family. He chatted almost nonstop with stories even from before his time, about his grandparents on his mother's side who had fled from Russia, escaping the Bolsheviks. His father's side of the family grew oranges in a southern-California orchard.

"My parents—your grandparents—met on a blind date. I'm not sure what brought my dad to Cincinnati, where my mom's family settled once they came to the U.S. My dad died when we kids were little. We grew up poor, and we got picked on at school. It was rough. Your mother was all about horses and had a collection of figurines. She could tell you all about pintos and white horses and whatnot, while I barely know a thing about them. Nothing would have made Vanessa happier than a real horse, or even just some riding lessons, but my mom couldn't afford it. My mom worked for minimum wage at a meat packing plant. If there wasn't enough food, she'd let us have it and she'd go hungry."

"That sounds hard." Lillian hadn't known how much poverty had impacted her mother's childhood.

"It was. It still affects me; I get nervous with every grocery I buy, even though... not to sound like I'm bragging... I can afford a home in Silicon Valley and I'm making six figures. I remember one time as a little kid when we weren't struggling so much. When my mother had the baby."

"You mean, when she had my mom?"

"Nope, your mom was born when I was too young to remember."

"There was another kid in the family?"

"Apparently so. After my father passed away. When I asked my mom why her stomach was growing, she'd just yell at me. Mom came home from the hospital empty-handed. I never saw the baby or knew if it was a boy or girl. You just didn't talk about stuff like that back then... the whole taboo against 'bastard' children born out of wedlock. I think she must have given it up for adoption. For a while after that, we were doing much better. Enough food, plenty of toys, plenty of treats, and a new car. Mom hadn't changed jobs, so I think she might have been paid for the adoption. Then that money must have run out because we were struggling again later on."

"Did you ever ask your mom what happened to the baby?"

"I asked her in my twenties, and it went nowhere. She said it never happened and I was imagining things. I also asked Vanessa, and being little at the time, she couldn't remember. I have a theory, though. My mom was friends with your uncle Gerald, that one over there. I don't know when or how they met, since he lived over in Columbus at the time. Every now and again, he'd pay Mom's rent or buy us a meal when we were desperate. I don't remember any other men coming around when Mom got pregnant. Just between you and me, I think it was his."

"Wasn't he married at the time to his first wife?"

"Yeah, he was married. I think her name was Enid, don't remember for sure. They would bring their kids, Theresa and Julius, over to play. I remember when those kids were little. They must be about fifty now—wow, time flies. Theresa was a brat. No one liked her. Not even her own parents, I don't think. Julius was sweet as can be. He and your mom were two peas in a pod."

Lillian nodded, trying to conceal any reaction, reminding herself that her uncle Victor was just one of the many well-meaning people who didn't know of Julius' transgressions. Julius had once admitted to a childhood crush on Lillian's mother, who later turned him down. Was that his motive for assaulting Lillian?

"Are Gerald's kids here?" Victor asked.

"No, they're not. I have a hard time imagining that Uncle Gerald got my grandmother pregnant. But I guess it could have happened, because Uncle Gerald has a reputation. He can't keep it in his pants."

"Yeah, the man always struck me as a womanizer. We'd better change the subject, because here he comes."

Gerald appeared beside them, patting Victor on the shoulder. "Hello there. I remember when you were just a little tyke. I haven't seen you in ages. It looks like the two of you are having a good time bonding. But I'll need to borrow Lillian for a bit, if that's okay."

Lillian's maternal uncle waved goodbye as her paternal uncle grasped her arm and led her outside. Unsure of Gerald's intentions, and well aware that he would know every word she'd just exchanged with Victor including Gerald's skirt-chasing habits, Lillian stayed silent as they ambled down a grassy path between shrubs. Almost no one else was around. The salted scent of the water penetrated the thick air.

"Don't listen to Victor," Gerald chided as he smoothed the sleeve of his black suit. "That man never shuts up. He's a worse gossip than a sixteen-year-old girl talking to her friends on the telephone. I don't want you thinking I impregnated your grandmother."

"Was she actually pregnant during that time?"

"Yes, she was. And a hush-hush adoption took place. I even helped your grandmother with the adoption process a bit. But I don't remember the name of the baby's biological father; it was over forty years ago."

"So it wasn't you?"

"Oh, no," Gerald chuckled. "Victor was only about six years old. He remembers a few details, but he's not a reliable source. Speaking of pregnancies, I'll let you in on a little secret. Just between the two of us. You're going to be an aunt this fall."

"Evelyn's having a baby?!"

"She found out about a week or so ago. It's very early on. Jonathan's in a hurry to have kids and he finally talked Evelyn into trying about a month ago. She got pregnant on the first try, lucky her. She's keeping it from everyone. Even your dear old dad doesn't know. But I thought you should be the first to know that you'll have a niece or nephew to spoil. Isn't that exciting?"

"Yeah, that is."

"By the way, I see that Tara Nicholson continues to harass you. And you have done nothing except making a weak threat to contact authorities. You need to not be so afraid. There are... more effective ways to take care of her."

"Taking care of her? You mean..."

"She is a thorn in your side. She makes people's lives needlessly hard, and you could fix that so easily."

"Are you suggesting I do something to her?"

Gerald took on a firmer tone. "Let's face it, Lillian. You have incredible skills, and you need to practice them. You've mostly done laughable things, like threading strings through beads and traveling into that flowery dimension. But you need to practice the real stuff. The stuff that isn't always pleasant. And what better target is there? Tara is a loose cannon. She treats you horribly, and instead of fighting back, you simply lie down and take the abuse. Even after you moved out of that room, you still let her terrorize you. Although I'm not sure anyone would believe her, she knows too much. Just something to think about."

"I don't know about this. To be honest, Uncle Gerald, I'm not sure I want to know what you're hinting at."

"I will leave that decision up to you in the end. And know this: being born a chosen one, you are every bit as valuable as that rare crystal. Carry on our legacy, will you? I'm no spring chicken and I know my own days are numbered; yet you're so young, with so much potential. Let's go back in before people start wondering where we are."

"My goodness," the man said out loud to himself in a near-whisper. He had been walking along the street past the banquet hall, rumbling with the noise of yet another wedding reception. He stopped at the sight of two figures in the fiery orange evening light, standing and talking: a hefty older man in a black suit and a young woman in a green gown with long, curled red hair. Though dimmed in the deep shadows, their auras were unmistakable, green, faintly glowing tendrils that waved out. Clearly, these were no ordinary out-of-towners.

The man turned and rushed away before he chanced getting spotted.

At the recent conference he'd attended for the council of mages he belonged to, whisperings circulated of the necromancers' continued existence right here in the United States. He hadn't believed the rumors. It was common knowledge passed down through the generations that the necromancers had been dead since the 1700s, and he found it extremely unlikely that they could somehow come back. But now the very proof of the unbelievable stood before him, and they were unwise enough to attend a wedding right here, in his own family's territory. Or was it intentional, the precursor to an assault on his clan?

The man wished that auras showed up on film—which they never did—so that he'd have proof. Instead, he ran away before being spotted.

The next morning, Lou put on his favorite pair of broken-in blue jeans with a belt around his long, narrow waist. His daughters were also much less fancy today, with no makeup, glasses instead of contact lenses, hair in messy ponytails, and comfortable jeans and flip-flops. Lou's new son-in-law took them out to brunch at a seafood restaurant near the hotel. Denny was also invited but he stayed behind, buried under pillows and blankets as his head throbbed with a hangover. Uncle Gerald and Uncle Victor had already left to catch their flights home.

While they finished eating, Lillian got up to go to the restroom, turning down a long hall. When she came out of the single-occupancy bathroom, a line had formed. A petite woman with corkscrews of brown hair dominated Lillian's attention. The blue of her aura extended much further than most. The woman's eyes widened as the baby in her arms, dressed in a yellow onesie, looked up from its little starfish hand. The baby was the same, with sapphire eyes as blue as its aura.

Lillian guessed what they were, these two people wrapped in the hues of the ocean. Water mages. According to her father and Uncle Gerald, these people could mold fluid to whatever shape and function they pleased and could stay under water forever without drowning.

What could Lillian say to this woman? Or should she bolt, and then go warn her father? What would happen to her if she tried to run?

The infant innocently held a toy up to Lillian, a plastic ring with big bright keys, and smiled a wet smile with two tiny teeth. Instead of meeting the baby's eyes, Lillian rushed out of the hall as people stared openly. She glanced backwards once. The woman jogged toward the front entrance instead of the restroom, the baby in her arms now red-faced and crying. The glass door slammed shut as the bells hanging from the door jingled discordantly.

"That woman had just shown up," said Lou as Lillian sat back down in their remote corner booth, badly shaken. "Right after you left, she came in and they took her drink order. She didn't notice us at the table. May we go outside?"

"What was that lady's problem?" Jonathan asked. "She was acting like Lillian was going to kidnap that kid."

"I'm not sure what's going on. We'll figure it out," Lou lied to his new son-in-law before walking with Lillian out to the parking lot.

"You didn't say anything to that woman, did you?" Lillian's father wanted to know.

"No. I just left."

"I'm glad you said nothing. You remember what we've told you. You just don't talk to other mages, no matter what. Maybe we ought to start packing as soon as we're done eating."

"But it was just one person and a baby."

"Look at the baby, though. There could be a whole family, a whole clan. It's inevitable we'll see mages every now and then, but I'm concerned this woman thinks you're a threat. I shall ask Evelyn and Jonathan to take us home today, instead of tomorrow like our plan was."

After they went back inside, Evelyn and Jonathan enthused about their upcoming honeymoon in Cancún. Lou dropped hints, claiming he'd had his fill of the beach, while Evelyn and Jonathan would spend next week frolicking on the white sands of the Mexican coast. When they did not pick up on the suggestion, Lou began complaining that his slight case of arthritis was bothering him and he wanted to relax at Evelyn's house before his flight home.

Evelyn didn't want to leave just yet, standing by her original plan to linger for another day. Besides, couldn't her father rest his aching joints here? They had perfectly comfortable beds at the hotel.

After the uncomfortable brunch, Evelyn and Jonathan took a walk by the beach. Lou and Lillian returned to the hotel and sought out Denny, who felt a bit better after taking some painkillers and napping his hangover away.

When Lou told Denny in a hushed tone about his daughter's encounter with the woman and her infant at the restaurant, Denny was quick to agree that they should all escape this place. Denny went back to his room to pack. Lou and Lillian did the same so their bags could be grabbed at a moment's notice. Lillian fought anxiety as she stuffed her items away with trembling hands.

A knock at the door made Lillian and her father both jump. The green tendrils creeping through and under the door told them it was Denny. He thumped his fully packed luggage bag onto the floor.

"I think they might be looking for us," he warned. "Out the window, I saw a group of 'em walking down the road."

"What do we do?" Lou asked. "Should we make a run for it?"

"Don't. It'll call attention to us. Just stay in here and hopefully they'll leave us alone."

"I hate to break it to you, Denny, but the trails we've been leaving behind are more than enough to call attention to us."

"I know. But maybe if they see we're staying inside, they'll know we're not looking for trouble and they'll cool their jets."

Several tense minutes went by. Someone rapped at the door. Rays of shimmering, semitransparent blue pierced the wood and slithered around its edges like snakes.

"We know you're in there," said a man's muffled voice from the opposite side of the door.

"I think we should just answer," Lou whispered.

"No," Denny mouthed at him.

"Open up," a woman's voice called as the knocking got louder. "We're coming in regardless."

Denny got up, raked his fingers through his short graying hair, and unlocked the door.

The mages stepped inside, one by one—a tall dark-haired man with piercing azure eyes; the woman from the restaurant with the baby; and a paunchy man about Denny's age with a long gray ponytail hanging down the back of his Hawaiian shirt.

"I can't believe this," the eldest one growled. "I thought you'd all died out. And now you're on our territory."

"Sir," Lou replied gently, "I was not aware I was on anyone else's territory. I came for my daughter's wedding. She chose this place, not me."

"I wish you'd tried checking with your know-it-all brother Gerald," said the younger man, reading Lou's mind without doubt. "Maybe he knew this is our place."

"Sir, my brother never said anything, and he left this morning. I don't think he knew. I'm sorry."

"We protect this land, this coast."

"Fellows, we apologize. My daughter who chose to get married here does not have the powers, as you can probably see. She couldn't have known. Our bags are already packed. You'll never see us around here again."

"What makes you think you'll be leaving?"

"We are not here to cause trouble," Denny insisted. "Read our minds all you want and you'll see that."

"But here's the thing, Mr. Mackenzie. You people can do terrible things. Things that can spread, things that can kill. And if we let you out of here, you'd be a public health risk."

Lillian jittered with adrenaline as she became aware that a careless mistake, a wrong word, could cost them their lives. And so could doing nothing. No longer desperate to die as she had been at her lowest point, Lillian wanted to leave this place and be free. Alive.

"We're... we're people," she said as they all turned to face her. "You guys are people, and as you can see from our deep, dark secrets you're reading, we're people just like you. We're very careful to not hurt others."

"Well, let me tell you a little something about Denny that you don't know," the younger man shot back. "He hasn't always followed the rules. Does the name Andy Brentwood ring a bell?"

"Who's Andy Brentwood?" That name did not sound familiar at all to Lillian.

"A guy I went to school with," Denny mumbled, rubbing his thumbs over his hands.

"And is he dead or alive?" the visitor demanded, nodding toward Denny.

"Dead—he passed away in high school."

"He didn't just 'pass away.' Somebody or something killed him, right? And that something was *you*."

"Did you really?" Lou gasped.

"It was just... we were fighting. I was a stupid teenager, and it was an accident. But I haven't hurt a fly since; I swear."

"See, that's the thing. When your kind is a hotheaded teenager, or someone who's not good at controlling their impulses, it costs lives. You don't know what'll happen if your young girl loses her cool. I can't read her well, but something is very strange about her. She gives me some intense heebie-jeebies."

The walls bled. No, they wept. Steel-gray water tumbled down the plaster in silent rivers and began to pool on the carpet. It also bubbled from the sink, overflowing. A waterfall ran thickly over the counter's edge.

"Look, I'll cut you a deal," Denny negotiated, his tennis shoes getting wet from the fluid expanding across the carpet. "We won't be any bother again. As long as..." The woman suddenly found her baby ripped from her arms, hovering in the air. She reached futilely for the infant, who floated into Denny's arms. The baby began to whimper.

"Give her back!" the mother screeched. "What did you do to her?"

"Nothing, but why'd you bring the baby if we're so dangerous? Why didn't you leave her with a babysitter?"

"Because we can protect her better than any babysitter who's not a mage! Give her back *now*!"

"Not until you let us out of here," Denny told her in a careful monotone. "Let the three of us out and you'll get her back safe and sound, no trouble."

"Give her back *now*, you monster!" the woman hollered, lunging at Denny. Just before her balled fist could meet his jaw, the green line of possession shot into her head and she was thrown backwards onto her bottom, into a shallow puddle.

After knocking her down, Denny released her.

"Deal for you, Mr. Mackenzie," the dark-haired man said as he put a hand on the panting woman and helped her back up. "We'll leave, and you can meet us down at the beach and give back our daughter. If you try to run away, or you lay a hand on the baby, you die. Give her back unharmed, and you live. Fair enough?"

"Yes, sir. We'll bring her immediately."

"No, no!" screamed the woman as the younger man clenched his arms around her waist and dragged her kicking and flailing out the door. "How could you?! Don't let those monsters be alone with her!"

"It'll work... I promise, honey..."

Once they were gone, Lillian asked, "Should we just run away and get Evelyn and Jonathan in the van?"

"No, we shouldn't," her father sighed as the infant started to squawk unhappily. Denny bounced and cooed at her. "I wish we could, but we can't leave with someone else's child. Denny, why did you take the baby?"

"I didn't really plan it out. It was just an impulse. Now I wish I hadn't."

They left the wet, glistening hotel room and took the elevator down as Denny ssh-shhed at the angry, red-faced baby. The rank smell of poop filled the small space.

"Is that true about the boy you went to school with?" Lou whispered to Denny.

"I don't want to get into it. It was two teenagers thinking with our fists and nuts instead of our brains. I made a mistake, but I never got caught. Uncle Gerald surely knows, but he's never ratted me out as far as I know."

"How, precisely, did you kill the boy?"

Denny sighed. "I don't want to talk about it."

"If these water people didn't do what we told them to, would you hurt the baby?"

"I wouldn't hurt a baby. I'm not that much of a bastard and I hope you know that. Even though the kid stinks to high heaven. I wish we had a clean diaper."

Once out of the building, they quickened their pace toward the beach, turning corners around a couple of empty buildings in the quiet, bright, humid midday. As promised, the water people waited for them, standing side by side on the pale sand. The necromancers ran up to them as the grit filled their dampened shoes and flip-flops.

"Here you go," Denny reassured them, offering up the unharmed baby, whose chubby legs dangled out of her onesie. "Alive and well. Just needs to be changed. Now off we go."

"Not so fast," the gray-haired man insisted as the baby's mother snatched her back. "You all stay right here. We will leave, and we will keep an eye on you. When we're out of sight, you're free to go."

Obediently, Lillian, Lou, and Denny stood, their feet close to the softly lapping water, as the others walked away, leaving indented footprints in the sand with residues of bright blue.

Something cold hit Lillian like concrete, knocking the breath out of her lungs. Black and gray filled her stinging eyes as the tart taste of salt swelled in her mouth. Something hard and sharp impacted her leg through her jeans. Her head broke above the surface of the water for an instant, and the clouds were sideways, blurry because her glasses had been knocked away. Waving blue blended with the fuzzy edges of a humanoid figure in the distance. And then another wall of water rose and slammed Lillian back under.

Lillian bumped into someone. Recognizing them as her father, she wrapped her arms around his waist and kicked hard toward the surface, or where she guessed it was, because the world had turned upside down and she had lost her sense of gravity. Their heads popped into the air, both of then choking and coughing.

"Swim to shore!" Lou gasped out.

"But Denny!" Lillian screamed, glancing around and seeing no sign of her cousin in the tall, roiling waves.

"Swim to shore!" her father commanded again, gripping her wrist in his hand as he paddled away, straining at the waves. Wanting to find Denny, Lillian broke from his grip and turned back in the other direction. Another wave, unnaturally huge, smacked down upon her, forcing her upside down into confusion.

Lillian counted on the ability she'd practiced as a child to dive deep into swimming pools and hold her breath for long periods, but eventually her body burned and ached from a lack of air. She kicked through the sandy depths, a red cloud leaching from the rip in her jeans, as she felt with her powers for obstacles and for Denny up ahead. No matter how hard she kicked, he slipped further and further out of reach. Something rumbled up above, its roar muffled, and Lillian's face was shoved into the sand, the last of her oxygen forced out in a few bubbly coughs. With a mouthful of grit, she dug herself out and carried on, ignoring all of her pain and discomfort.

Denny dragged lifelessly along the sloping floor. Grabbing him, she flailed in the direction that she thought was up, now close to drowning and desperate to take a breath. Where was the glittering surface? The waters swirled and the dim filtered sunlight shifted from side to side in the sea of gray. A whirlpool of some sort caught the two of them and rotated them for a few rounds, and then Lillian thought she saw something through her blurry, salt-burned eyes and the frothing of the water. A dark, decayed, skeletal hand, reaching for her from the tattered sleeve of a robe. The cold, sharp hand wrapped around Lillian's arm and tugged upward.

Their heads burst out of the skin of the water. Lillian spat out water, so dizzy she nearly passed out. Nothing was touching her arm now—she must have imagined that bony, rescuing hand in her confusion. Her arms were hooked under Denny's arms and around his barrel chest. His head lolled into her shoulder. The skin of his motionless face looked disconcertingly gray, though his aura suggested he was still alive.

She used one arm and her legs to glide through the water, gasping for the breath she desperately needed and fighting against the drag of Denny's weight. The white strip of sand neared, and there her father was curled on the ground. Lillian's knees and feet hit the shallow mud, and she crawled out of the water and onto the land, pulling Denny by his arms behind her.

Lou hugged his drenched body, coughing and shivering. His shirt was stretched and disheveled and dirty, but somehow, his glasses were still on, not washed away like Lillian's. Together they rolled the limp Denny onto his back. His drenched white T-shirt stuck to his skin like tissue. He was not breathing.

Lillian, who had learned CPR in her high school health class, placed the heels of her hands on Denny's chest and hoped that those practice dummies had prepared her for this day. After a few presses on Denny's sternum, a cough came up from deep inside him. He twitched as clear water sprayed from his mouth. Lou and Lillian rolled him onto his side. He coughed more fluid out of his lungs.

"What happened?" Evelyn's voice called from the distance. "Are you okay?"

Evelyn ran to their side. Jonathan trailed behind her, shirtless, his muscles bulging.

"I believe Denny almost drowned," her father spoke in a rattling whisper. "We need help—we need to get out of here."

"Oh, no!" Evelyn cried. "Do you need to go to the hospital?"

"Lillian's hurt. She's bleeding," Jonathan pointed out. They all looked down at the red wet slit on Lillian's thigh, staining the tear in her soaked jeans.

"Come on," Evelyn urged. "There's an urgent care place near the hotel. We're taking you there."

"Evelyn, we need to leave town," her father pleaded. "We need to get in the van and go."

"But you need some medical attention. None of you look good."

"We can worry about that later," Lillian said, her voice a painful, burning, salty rasp. "There are people here who tried to hurt us. Let's leave."

Finally convinced, Evelyn and Jonathan helped them off the beach and into the back of their van in the hotel parking lot. The newlyweds went inside to get their things and check out on behalf of all of the rooms.

As the others waited in the hot van, Lillian pressed a towel to the oozing wound on her thigh. Denny coughed, complaining that he felt drained. The three of them tried to figure out what to tell Evelyn and Jonathan if they asked for further details, and speculated as to whether the water people searched for them this very minute.

As Evelyn loaded up the last of the suitcases, Denny said in a voice still weak and scratchy, "We need to go now!"

From behind the van came a figure. Though the individual was unrecognizable to Lillian without her glasses, the aura was obvious. As Evelyn and Jonathan raced to the front seats and Evelyn started the engine, water spread around the tires, splashing as they drove off.

"Oh my God!" Evelyn screamed as the puddle gave way to a lake engulfing the van. Water swirled and churned on the outsides of the windows.

"Just keep going!" Denny ordered. "Foot on the gas! Go, go!"

"I can't even see anything!" Evelyn raced through the water, shaking, knuckles going white on the steering wheel. Bubbles blew past through the amorphous gray water, and a few drops began to leak inside.

"Evelyn, watch out!" Jonathan shouted. A black shadow, the roundish shape of a car, advanced directly in front of them. A horn blared, its sound dampened through the water.

Jonathan reached over, grasped the steering wheel, and jerked it to one side. The tires squealed and a bump came up underneath, something with a hard edge.

Another dark thing swept past in the murky water, a corner of a structure, and Jonathan turned the wheel again. Evelyn pressed the accelerator harder and the van sped up, nearly flipping.

A figure appeared at the side, and a dull impact vibrated throughout the vehicle. Evelyn pumped the brakes, sending the van into a spinning, skidding arc. All of them squeezed their eyes shut, bracing for rolling, before the van lurched to a stop.

The outside was bright, too bright. The sun shone unfettered through the windows. Pale-faced and trembling, Jonathan and Evelyn looked out onto the suddenly dry street. One of the water people, the younger man, staggered across the asphalt, holding an arm that hung listlessly.

"I just hit that guy!" Evelyn said in a low, tight whisper. "I should go help him..."

"No!" Denny demanded. "That man is trying to kill us. He's the one that made that water go everywhere. Get out of here before the cops come and keep us here!"

"But..."

"Listen to Denny," Lou pleaded. "We leave or we die."

Evelyn stomped on the gas, swerving the van out of the little beachfront town and embarking on the bridge that led to the mainland.

"Baby, you can't do this!" Jonathan implored as they raced above the speed limit, sailing past car after car. "You don't just hit somebody and run! This is a felony! And with how you're speeding, this is gonna turn into a police chase!"

Evelyn's body rattled in fear. She did not answer.

Jonathan turned and gave everyone in the backseat a hard look. "Why did you make her do this? Where did the water come from? Who was that man?"

"Jonathan, it's all very complicated," Lou told him. "It has to do with things that we cannot talk about."

"Why not? I can't make sense of this and I'd kinda like an explanation."

"If I were you, I wouldn't try to make sense of it. Just know that there are dangerous people there."

"But if they're dangerous and they're after you, why couldn't you just call the cops on them?"

"They could simply drown the cops."

Jonathan finally talked the silent Evelyn into slowing down. All of them kept glancing over their shoulders and out the back window, watching for flashing lights of police cars, or, worse, a person or wave chasing after them.

Evelyn pulled to the side of the road to throw up. Jonathan took the wheel.

When they reached a coastal town along the way back to Houston, Lou finally let Jonathan stop at an urgent care clinic. Lou and Denny were told they looked pretty good for two men who'd almost drowned that day, while Lillian got stitches in her leg, apparently cut when it rammed into a sharp underwater rock. As soon as they got released, they wasted no time in getting back on the road as the sun got lower.

"I have no idea what happened," were Evelyn's first words spoken in hours, "but I never want to talk about it again. I just want to forget it."

"Could we be living in the Twilight Zone?" Jonathan said, half-joking.

"I said, don't mention it again!" Evelyn snapped.

"Gee, sorry. I was just trying to lighten up."

"Well, I'm too traumatized to lighten up! This couldn't have been good for the baby either."

"What baby, sweetheart?" her father asked from behind her.

"Ummm...." Evelyn groaned, hesitant. "Right before the wedding, I had a positive pregnancy test. I wanted to keep it quiet for a few months. Now I'm sad I spoiled the surprise."

"I wish you'd told me as soon as you found out! When are you due?"

"I just took the blood test last week and we've been busy with the wedding, so I haven't been to a doctor yet. But I'm guessing sometime in November. Now, if you don't mind, I'm not in the mood to talk much."

After they reached Evelyn and Jonathan's house that night, Evelyn stormed off to the bedroom as Jonathan lingered in the driveway, inspecting the van for damage. A trace of a blue glow remained on the slightly dented side of the van. Feeling trapped in an extended nightmare, Lillian walked around in a numb haze, unable to sleep that night.

After Denny fell into an uncomfortable, contorted sleep on Evelyn's pull-out couch, dreams of Andy Brentwood haunted him, the boy forever fifteen years old with his tangled long blond hair, leather jacket, and the hand-rolled cigarette always pinched between his thick fingers. His cigarette was found floating near his body. The police ruled that Andy Brentwood had drowned in a creek by accident.

Denny had tried so hard to forget the day he and Andy brawled over Mona Wise, the girl they both loved, in a fistfight. After nearly blacking out while Andy caught him in a chokehold, Denny decided to punish Andy a little, below the surface of the water. He hadn't meant for things to get this out of hand, and could still hear himself screaming, "Shit, shit, shit!" as Andy bobbed back up, not breathing, aura gone. Wiping his bleeding, punched nose, Denny hopped on his bicycle and fled the scene in a panic.

When his father later asked at the dinner table where he got his black eye, Denny made an excuse: "Got hit by a baseball." Denny's father, and the stepmother who sat scowling at him in disapproval, probably did not buy that lie. When his mother died, Denny started to get into fights, taking out his anguish on other kids. After his father married the overly strict stepmother he hated, Denny found himself suspended from school more often, while their file on him thickened. The principal said he'd spend his adulthood behind bars.

But no one made a connection between Denny and Andy, whose body was found floating the next day. Denny got off scot-free that time. Even at the angriest point in his youth, he never once had the desire to take another human life. He'd meant for Andy to walk away from that fight, wishing he'd never crossed him.

Having just about died from water-filled lungs himself that day, Denny finally understood the agony he had caused in Andy Brentwood's final moments. Mona, who became Denny's high school sweetheart and later his wife, was a very bitterly won prize.

Terrified of flying, Mona did not attend Evelyn's wedding. That was probably for the best. He might have lost her that day if she'd gotten caught in the middle of the battle.

The son sat on a stool. A blue plastic sling and a white cast surrounded his arm. He stared blearily at his father, who placed himself like a thick plug between his son and the softly babbling television set.

"Terry, how could we let them get away?" the father barked, his deep voice seemingly making the wood-paneled walls rumble. "How could you let it happen?"

"I'm sorry," his son mumbled, his tone slowed by the narcotics they'd given him in the emergency room. "It's kind of hard to concentrate when you just got sideswiped by a car, so I lost my focus. Aren't you at least glad I wasn't run over and killed?"

"Of course, but they shouldn't have been able to even get out of the gulf."

"These people are very tough, Dad. Especially that kid. There's something weird about her for sure. And maybe I didn't have enough nerve to finish the job."

"Where did they go after you got injured? Were you able to get a read on that?"

"I wasn't able to get a read after I got hit. But here's what I got before that. They were planning to go to Houston, where the ones who just got married live. And then the two older guys will fly back to the east coast, where they live. I couldn't read the girl that well, but she's going to Northern Colorado University."

"Ah. Other than the college student, where do they live?"

"The family lives in Maryland. The ones we saw, anyway. The family's scattered over a few cities—there's a few of them who did not attend the wedding. I got a lot of names, a few fragments of addresses. I'll tell you when my head clears up a bit so you can write 'em down. I'm sure finding them again won't be any problem."

"Come to think of it, I'm not sure chasing them across the country is the best idea after what happened, Terry," growled his father, stroking his thin white whiskery beard. "The next confrontation could be a lot worse, especially if they decide to fight back instead of flee."

"Suppose we should still try to do something about them? Catch them by surprise?"

"We'll study them. We'll find out as much as we can. We'll stay behind the scenes."

Excerpt from The Autobiography of Gerald Frazier: Architect of a New World

I n high school, my brother Lou was athletic and quite popular with his classmates. He enjoyed stardom on the track and field team and the baseball team. Lou was good-looking, with nice strawberry-blond hair that did not stand out to bullies the way my red hair used to. He dated a pretty, equally popular majorette named Roberta, and everyone expected they'd marry right out of high school. They were right.

Here's what nobody knew except me. The relationship with Roberta was a sham from the start.

When I was in the first grade, I started getting crushes on girls. When Lou was in the first grade, he started to get crushes on boys. And these weren't just the fleeting, bi-curious types of crushes that most people get, whether they admit it or not. He consistently had a thing for a boy in his class, year after year. Like my attractions toward girls, these crushes got a lot more interesting once puberty began.

Lou knew better than to tell anyone. Back in those days, if people thought you were a queer, you would end up a social outcast if you were lucky, dead if you were unlucky. Our father might very well have beaten Lou to death with his bare hands if he ever found out, which—God rest his soul—he never did. Lou tried to fit in, becoming very convincing in his flirtations with girls.

Lou's secret gave me control. Even though his powers trumped my own, I held my brother in the palm of my hand from the time we were young boys. If I wanted him to shoplift candy, do my homework for me, steal watermelons off a farm, or any number of other petty crimes, all I had to do was threaten to leak the truth. Lou obeyed me, dodging farmers' shotguns filled with rock salt and using his telekinesis to sneak candy from store shelves.

In high school, Lou had a best friend, Walter. They cheated on their girlfriends with each other, meeting in hidden locations. They rendezvoused in tool sheds, Walter's parked car on dark streets out in the woods, and Walter's bedroom, to which Lou climbed up a lattice after everyone else went to bed. Of course, they kept it all a deeply buried secret, but as a mind reader, I witnessed everything during my visits home from my university.

Our house was a mess because our father was often indisposed. Lou, embarrassed about the conditions at home, often stayed with our aunt Lillian. Dr. Lowhorn, the doctor who delivered us and enabled our father's addictions, was so burned out from his job that he spent evenings at the house to drink and inject with my father. You would not believe how many doctors struggle with addictions. Dr. Chu, my current physician, has a secret Vicodin-popping habit.

Everyone has a secret.

Water and Fire

For the first week after returning to school, Lillian called her father and Denny daily. When they didn't answer their phones, she worried, picturing them gray and twisted on their floors as water puddled. Even though the death-feeling never came, it was hard to restrain her haywire imagination.

Almost drowning had added a new layer to Lillian's trauma. She kept watch on the locked door and the small window beneath the ceiling of the basement room. Taking a shower became a challenge when the water splashing her eyes and mouth took her right back to that day after the wedding.

For the rest of the semester, Lillian carefully dodged Kolby, Tara, and the fire mage, whoever it was. She spent nights in the library studying feverishly for finals. Vivid tulips sprang up on the campus and the trees sprouted pale green leaves. The lawn mowers started to run daily, filling the air with the damp, organic scent of cut grass.

Despite the stressful spring break, this semester ended with much better grades, including the class Lillian had to repeat. She earned her scholarship back.

Right after finals, Lillian and Bridget hung out with their friend Tim in their dorm room, listening to music and eating cupcakes to celebrate the end of the semester. As Lillian sunk her teeth into a soft, sugary cupcake, the death-feeling came on. The foreboding and finality whenever someone Lillian knew passed away. Worried, Lillian called her father and her cousin Denny, who both answered their phones and assured her they were doing fine.

This time, death must have come for someone else.

Katrina pulled into the parking lot and dug the printed campus map of Northern Colorado University out of her glove box. Katrina's grandfather Gerald had marked the route to Bailey Hall with a ballpoint pen, ending with a big star at the dorm and the room number scrawled beside it.

Katrina parked within walking distance, but not too close. Just as Grandpa had suggested. She pulled out the papers tucked under the map. Photos of Tara posing with her friends and puckering her lips, printed from her MySpace profile.

"That girl is in love with herself, and I'm grateful that the internet provides a place for such self-absorbed people to show off their photos," Grandpa had told Katrina when he met with her in secret and walked her through her job to come. "You are fortunate that I did not have to draw a sketch of her features. I'm a crappy artist."

Katrina still nursed a massive grudge against Lillian for what she did to Uncle Julius. It was tempting to find her as well and come up with some kind of punishment. Grandpa forbade it. No one could know Katrina was ever here. She had one job alone, the thing Lillian, that pansy, could not follow through on.

Watching the sunset through her windshield, Katrina chugged the rest of the energy drink she'd purchased at a gas station in Kansas. During the road trip, she'd subsisted on a lot of those. Grandpa padded her wallet with cash for all of the food and hotel rooms and fuel, and then some.

Once the sun slid behind the horizon, Katrina tucked her short hair under a slouchy hat to disguise the pale red color. Though she had no need for glasses, she put on a big, chunky pair of frames with no lenses to make herself even less recognizable. Katrina got out of the car, vigilantly watching her surroundings. A few students walked by, none of them giving her more than a passing glance. No Lillian. Good. Looking enviously at the pretty campus, Katrina thought to herself of just how privileged Lillian and Tara were to be here. Though Katrina could have gone to college, and maybe Uncle Julius or Grandpa would have paid for it, if she'd gotten it together enough to apply.

Grandpa had passed along from Lillian's memory that a big tree stood just outside the window to her old dorm room, which faced the back of the building, toward the adjoining parking lot. An expert tree climber since childhood, Katrina shimmied up the trunk and perched on a branch that held her slight weight, just outside the window. The light was on, and the window was open.

Alone in the room, Tara paced and talked on her cell phone. With no roommate or friends present, now was the perfect time.

Katrina hesitated. Could she do this? Did she have what it took to end a human life, especially one so young?

Then she thought of Megan, the high school tormentor she'd gotten the best of. Tara sounded like she and Megan had a lot in common. Both were nasty young women who picked on the wrong family. When Katrina controlled Megan's body to humiliate her in the cafeteria, that was one thing. Megan's reputation lay in ruins, but she walked away alive, and her parents helped her start over somewhere else. For Tara, that would not be an option.

Katrina channeled her anger over a lifetime of injustices into her aura. It converged into a snake and then slid through the window opening. As Katrina took possession of Tara, her cell phone clattered to the floor. Katrina's skill was getting better. As Tara turned and walked to the sink, she moved in an almost natural gait.

Under Katrina's command, Tara filled the glass of water on the counter, opened the medicine cabinet, and grabbed for every bottle of pills Katrina could just barely see from her vantage point. Pushing down on the child-safety lids of each pill bottle was tricky, but Katrina pulled it off, spilling only a few tablets. She shuddered from the scratchy discomfort echoing in her own throat as Tara gulped down handful after handful of pills.

After every pill was down, Katrina kept her hold on Tara for a while, to make sure they took effect. Wooziness and nausea began to surge through Katrina's body, reflected from her target. Katrina withdrew when Tara vomited down the front of her dressy blue shirt. Taking possession could not stop that bodily function.

Oh, no, was Tara puking up all of the pills before they killed her? Was this all for nothing? Katrina's fingernails dug into the branch as her whole body broke out into a cold sweat. She glanced around the room for anything to use as a weapon.

Tara fell to her knees, and then collapsed as her breaths hitched and gasped to a stop. As her body went still, foamy vomit pooled around her head, and her aura faded.

Her stomach sinking, Katrina wanted to run away from the gritty reality of a stranger dying a terrible death. She lowered her head, squeezing her eyes shut. The only thing keeping her up in the tree was the need to make sure Tara was dead before she left.

At last, Katrina opened her eyes and checked. Like every inanimate object in the dorm room, Tara had no aura. She was gone.

Getting revenge on Megan in high school had Katrina walking away smugly satisfied. Taking a life, even some mean girl she'd never met, was a whole different experience. Darker. Heavier, leaving a stain that would last forever.

The door opened. A young woman stepped inside, letting out a piercing scream. She fell to her knees at Tara's side and shook her, pressing two fingers into her neck.

The roommate dialed 911 on her cell phone and put it on speakerphone as she began performing chest compressions on Tara.

It was time to get out of here. Katrina slid down the tree, hit the ground, and broke into a run, wanting to be out of sight before the ambulance came. Unaccustomed to the high altitude of the Rocky Mountains, Katrina was out of breath when she reached her car.

When guilt and disgust started to consume Katrina, she covered her eyes with her hands to block it out, to forget what she had just done. She pulled a cheap, prepaid cell phone out of her pocket and quickly punched in a text message to her grandfather, the code that the job was finished. *Pink whale.*

And then Katrina sped away, starting the first night of her journey back home.

The day after their late-night celebration, as Bridget and Lillian packed their things to move out for the summer, Tim called, saying he had news he wanted to break in person.

"Girls, you're not gonna believe it!" Tim announced after they let him into their room. "Tara Nicholson is dead!"

"What? Seriously?!" Lillian gasped.

There was no doubt now in Lillian's mind that Tara's passing had given her the death-feeling yesterday evening. She did not even see this coming.

"What happened to Tara?" Bridget asked.

"OD'd on pills, it sounds like. Tara's roommate found her dead and tried to bring her back, but it was too late. My friend Laura saw the body bag being carried down the stairs. Everybody's freaking out, of course."

"Oh, I bet," said Bridget as Lillian, in her surprise, had difficulty thinking of any words. "What was this, a suicide?"

"Maybe. Or Tara was trying to get high and she overdosed."

"I think it's the latter," Lillian finally squeaked out. "Maybe it was suicide. I have no idea if she was depressed; she was a miserable person at any rate. I wished she'd drop out and go away, but I didn't wish she'd die." She hesitated for a moment, sitting down on her bed as it sunk in. "Shit."

The timing of Tara's death, just a couple of months after Uncle Gerald had last dropped sinister hints for Lillian to harm her, raised red flags. It seemed too strange. Could

Gerald be behind it? Traveling here without telling Lillian, maybe sneaking into the dorm and taking possession? Lillian did not even want to think about it.

Later that afternoon, Lillian took a private walk past the front of Bailey Hall. Freshly picked bouquets of flowers rested on the steps and front porch. A small crowd of Lillian's former neighbors, including the one who'd called her "weird" for sleeping in the study pod, held each other and sobbed. Even with Tara dead, that dread and anxiety from last semester came rushing back.

Since Lillian's card key could no longer access the building, she followed the crying group as they went inside, not even appearing to notice her. Lillian caught the front door just before it latched shut. Quietly, she crept around downstairs, and then upstairs, checking the aura trails. For what, she didn't know—Uncle Gerald? Or maybe even that fire mage she'd been dodging for months?

Lillian found no unusual auras inside, though she recognized Tara's fading trail from yesterday, the last day of her life. As Lillian walked past the room she'd shared with Tara, closed and empty and quiet with the coldness of fresh death, the bad feelings from last semester strengthened until they became flashbacks.

Lillian hurried out and made her way back to her own room. She wanted to be done with all of this.

A couple of weeks after Lillian went home for the summer, Tim emailed her the link to Tara's obituary. She had died just a month before her twentieth birthday in June, survived by two siblings Lillian didn't know she had. Tara had played soccer and loved snowboarding, facts also new to Lillian. Her many friends remembered her as kind, warm, fun-loving, and a great listener. Like most obituaries, there was not a negative word anywhere. People really did not speak ill of the dead.

In August, Lillian returned to Colorado. She was placed on the top floor of Stephenson Hall, a coed dorm, again rooming with Bridget Shin. They got along well enough that they had requested to stay together. When Lillian first arrived at her new home, it left her in awe. Gothic gray stone coated the outside of the three-floor residence hall. Red-and-white checkerboard tiles covered the floors on the main halls, and the top floor ended in arched windows overlooking the mountains. Recessed lights cast soft rays from the sloped wooden ceilings. This certainly was more attractive than last semester's basement home.

Parts of the building felt cold, too cold, to Lillian, who heard rumors of a few suicides in years past and possible hauntings. When her invisible feelers melted into the structure like the roots of a tree, sliding through the halls and rooms out of her view, she picked up things. In a few of Stephenson's rooms, vortexes swirled, places that might bring ghosts.

Still, Lillian and Bridget both loved their new room. Lillian lined her windowsill with plants and cacti and gave them names. Lillian got a job reshelving books at the library.

Determined to avoid the melodrama of her first year, even with Tara now dead, Lillian still kept on the lookout for Tara's former boyfriend Kolby as she walked from class to class. After not seeing Kolby anywhere, she heard that he'd dropped out in his grief.

Walking past a knoll one cool September day, Lillian stopped when something round tumbled down the slope of browning grass and rocked to a stop at her feet. She bent down to pick it up. At first she thought it might be a rock.

It was a cantaloupe melon.

At the top of the hill stood a guy from her English class, the one who wore a leather jacket every day. Though she had never spoken to him and did not know his name, she recognized his pretty-boy looks and the aura more visible than the average person's, showing that he had mage blood. It was a montage of different colors, brownish here, reddish there, greenish there.

"Hey, is this yours?" Lillian called up at her classmate, cradling the rough-skinned melon in her arms.

"It's for you," he replied, coming down the hill toward her.

"Why?"

"Just, uh, to get your attention." He smiled. Up close, he was even more handsome, with lustrous brown hair and bright blue eyes ringed with thick lashes.

"Well, thank you. What's your name?"

"Zachariah. Call me Zack." He extended his hand with long fingers like a pianist's. Tentatively, she shook it. "And you are?"

"Lillian. But you can call me Lil."

"You want to get coffee or grab a bite to eat sometime?"

"Uh, sure," she agreed.

"Tomorrow at five work?"

"Sure."

After returning to her room, Lillian cut Zack's gift into wedges and split it with Bridget. The following evening, Lillian arrived for her date with Zack—if it was a date—in one of the student cafés. They each got a coffee and sat down. Zack's leather jacket was open, showing off a beaded shark-tooth necklace against his white shirt.

Zack revealed that he was twenty-one years old and hailed from Michigan. He majored in psychology. They asked about each other's favorite colors, with Zack's being orange, Lillian's being cobalt blue. Zack's favorite movie was *The Terminator*, while Lillian's was *Donnie Darko*.

"You like that evil bunny, huh?" Zack said with a laugh. It was the closest thing he made to a joke. After that, failing to establish a rapport and find things to talk about besides their basic favorites, they sat through a long, awkward silence.

Lillian expected Zack to lose interest in her after that evening of forced conversation. Before the next class they had together, Zack approached Lillian and asked her out again.

Lillian might possibly have a boyfriend now! He seemed nice, probably just a little shy, and it didn't hurt that he was cute. This all happened so fast. Other nineteen-year-old women already had years of firsthand experience with dating, which Lillian did only online, where the boys she never physically met seemed safer. Zack might be good and healthy for her. He presented an opportunity to grow and learn. After worrying over the years that finding a partner might be difficult, or that she was just too odd for most guys to want her, Lillian told herself to appreciate this opportunity.

For their Thursday night date, they went to see a film in the campus theater. And then Zack insisted on giving Lillian a ride to his house.

No! her voice of warning cried. *Don't get in the car with him!* But, trying to keep her hopes up about the budding relationship, she got into the passenger seat of his aging Buick.

Zack rented a cluttered off-campus house with two roommates, both tucked away in their rooms with their subwoofers booming. Zack encircled a couple of Lillian's fingers with his and led her to his bedroom, where he tossed his backpack to the floor.

Lillian had never seen such a bare bedroom, with not so much as a picture on the pebbly-textured wall. Her own room was decorated with color and glitter to match her vivid mind. A thin green blanket neatly covered the uncomfortable-looking twin bed, and the desk had nothing on it but a closed laptop and a pencil. What few clothes Zack owned, identical outfits of light blue jeans and white T-shirts and gray boxer shorts, lay folded next to the only other piece of furniture: a hamper.

They sat beside each other on the hard mattress. Lillian figured out what Zack expected next when he closed his eyes, puckered his lips like a fish, and leaned toward her. Though fireworks had yet to happen, she hoped to experience them in a moment as she closed her own eyes. His wet lips slimed her face as she waited for it to end. Lillian lacked the experience to know whether Zack was a bad kisser, or whether she simply wasn't ready. His saliva carried a hint of tobacco.

When Zack let go, Lillian was quick to pull away. "Do you smoke?"

"I do, but I'm trying to cut down. Why, I have a little smoke on my breath?"

"Yeah."

After rinsing with mouthwash, Zack wanted to kiss more. Lillian quietly sat through it. She had to stretch her imagination when she crafted the romantic scenes in her stories where characters melted in one another's arms, a bliss unlike this slobbery reality. Zack swung her legs on top of his own and put another arm around her lower back.

"Do you want to?" he said.

"Do I want to what?"

"Uh, you know... do it."

Do it? Already?! Lillian couldn't speak, her mind blanking out. While she wanted to try lovemaking eventually, she was not ready, not sure if she'd healed enough for her mind to handle it. Lillian did not intend to tell Zack about that summer with Julius. Even her couple of close friends did not know. Pain and embarrassment locked those memories deep inside. Lillian was too scared of what people might think. Zack could judge her as damaged goods or figure that too much emotional baggage weighed her down.

This sudden suggestion put Lillian between a rock and a hard place. How could she explain her reticence without giving away her past?

"Hey, you seem nervous," Zack told her, pulling her close again. "Haven't you ever done it before?"

"Sorry, I... I just can't right now. I'm not ready."

"You have nothing to worry about. I'm clean. I don't have any diseases. I'll pull out so you won't get pregnant."

"I'm not up to it right now. I'm sorry."

"Okay, then, we'll do it another time."

"Thanks." Relief washed through Lillian's body. When she mentioned she had home-work to finish, Zack gave her a ride home.

Lillian and Zack continued to see each other as September melded into October and the leaves on the trees turned brilliant yolky gold and orange. Bridget gave her advice that every relationship started with a honeymoon period when both parties felt fantastic, unable to get enough of each other. And that Lillian ought to not be surprised when the passion cooled down.

Still, no sparks erupted. This was not the amazing high Lillian was told to expect with a new relationship. She rigidly went through the motions with Zack, watching movies and eating dinners.

Zack was harder to crack open than a walnut. From questioning him, Lillian found that he had a brother, a sister, and two separated parents, but he did not let her in on their personalities or occupations. Beyond his favorite color, his major, and his favorite movie, Lillian still knew very little about her boyfriend. Whatever made Zack richly unique—his hobbies, his favorite childhood toy, his best and worst memories, his secrets, his wishes—he never revealed. When Lillian asked Zack what he liked to do for fun, he shrugged and said, "I'm not sure." These painfully boring conversations never got easier.

Curious, Lillian asked one day for the names of Zack's siblings. Zack grumbled, "You've never met them, so why does it matter?"

"I just want to learn about you and the people in your life. I already told you about my sister."

Zack sighed. "Their names are Nicholas and Chelsea."

"How old are they?"

"Uh... I can't really remember. Nick is, like, three years older than me, I think. And Chelsea's two years younger."

"What do they do? Are they in school, or..."

"I don't know."

"Are you not on speaking terms with them?"

"I just don't remember, okay?" Zack snapped. "Why are you so curious?"

"I'm just trying to get a sense of your family. Is it a sensitive subject? Do you not get along?"

"We get along fine, we just don't talk much. Now can you just drop it?"

That was Lillian's first glimpse of Zack's quick temper, watching him get snippy and frustrated when Lillian asked questions that she thought were perfectly innocent—but maybe there was some bad blood in the family that he did not wish to bring up. Besides, Lillian had not told Zack about the split between her own relatives last year. And since he never asked, he did not know that half these relatives existed.

The second display of Zack's anger happened on the way to the movies one evening, when a slow driver up ahead sent Zack into a fit of road rage. He laid on his horn, rolled down his window, and yelled and cussed as Lillian sank down in the passenger's seat. Though Zack's temper made Lillian increasingly uncomfortable, she told herself that she should be grateful that he never hit or pushed her, and that maybe he just needed to work a little on regulating his emotions.

Lillian described the dull relationship to her father during their phone calls. "Dad, I feel like I'm going on dates with a cardboard cutout."

"I hope that sparks will fly soon enough as you warm up to each other more. Maybe he's just painfully shy. I wish I could meet him myself to get a feel for him. I hope he has good intentions."

Lillian was not hearing from Evelyn often, but she and Jonathan sent out monthly mass emails updating family and friends on their pregnancy. Evelyn posed sideways in pictures attached to the emails, showing off a belly round like the moon in her billowing maternity tops. After learning they were having a girl, they hinted that they had chosen a name, but refused to make it public.

Days before Halloween, Lillian and Bridget sat in their messy dorm room with their friend Tim in the inviting circle of light spilling from Bridget's floor lamp. They merged parts of their costumes together with Lillian's sewing machine. The three planned to dress up as the Powerpuff Girls from the cartoon, with long dresses, white stockings, and shiny black shoes. Now that Lillian had a couple of people to hang out with, Halloween was certain to be more fun than that lonely night last year.

Lillian's cell phone rang, and Zack's name popped up. Again.

"Where are you?" he asked.

"Like I mentioned, I'm in my room with my friends, making our costumes." It got annoying when Zack asked where she was going, who she'd be with, and then called an hour later with the same questions, like he hadn't listened the first time.

"Which friends?"

"Bridget and Tim."

"It's just Tim, right?" Zack acted increasingly threatened when Lillian spent time around any young men, except for Tim, who was openly gay.

"Right."

"When will you be done?"

"It will probably be a while, since we're working on sewing."

After Lillian hung up, she sighed, "Zack's getting to be a pain in the ass."

Bridget frowned. "I'm surprised you haven't yelled at him yet. And how he's always asking who you're hanging out with? He seems possessive and insecure."

"Hopefully he just wants to know what I'm up to."

"Honestly? I don't have a great feeling about that guy."

"Hey, Lil," said Tim, changing the subject. "Weren't you going to show us your Blossom hair?"

Lillian took her comically large red bow and wide-toothed comb into the bathroom. She stood in front of the sink and started to comb her hair to the top of her head, gripping it into a high ponytail.

Lillian froze, her hair still in her fist, when a loud snap popped a couple of rooms down the hall, echoing. And then silence fell all around her.

"Are you done in there yet?" Bridget called.

Lillian stepped out cautiously, asking her friends if either had heard the sound. They hadn't. Lillian came back out with the bow jutting from the top of her head.

"Perfect!" Tim clapped. "You look just like her, except your hair's not quite the right color and you don't have bangs. Well, I guess Blossom sort of has red hair. Now let's try on the dresses."

Lillian's dress fit a little bit tightly, but not restrictive enough to keep her from breathing. The three laughed as they pranced out of the room in their black shoes.

Just as they turned to go back into the room and change out of the costumes, a blue-green mannequin floated toward Lillian from the shadows of the hall, nude and glowing and crackling. The unmoving feet skidded silently over the floor. The hair was long and shaggy, and its eyes gazed through her like piercing green lasers. Half of the head was reduced to reddish pulp.

Lillian blinked hard and counted silently to herself. *One. Two. Three.* When she opened her eyes, there was nothing but a faint green trail of vapors seeping up from the clean floor like a mirage.

Every now and again, the afterimage of a death was harder than usual to forget. Like this vision, a possible aftershock of one of the long-ago suicides. Violent deaths resonated most deeply with Lillian, almost as if she could read their minds in the grave.

Two days before Halloween, Lillian called Evelyn to wish her a happy birthday.

"I'm sorry I haven't called more often, and didn't invite you to come visit and rub me on the belly," Evelyn apologized. "It's just that right now, you're reminding me of the wedding. Of those crazy things that happened the next day."

"Yeah, I understand. Trauma can be complicated... been there myself."

"I'd rather not talk about it further."

"How are you doing? How are you feeling?"

"Awful. I've been sick and passing out. It keeps getting worse. I had to go to the ER when I fainted at work."

"Oh, no! I didn't know that! That's terrible!"

"I hadn't been telling Dad everything because I didn't want him to worry. The doctor isn't sure what's wrong with me, and she put me on bed rest just to be safe."

"For how long?"

"Until I have the baby. I'm already tired of living on the couch. I'm telecommuting on some days, but it's just not the same as keeping busy at work. In the evenings, I'm passing the time by watching football. I'm bored out of my skull."

"Oh, man, that sucks." Lillian had hardly any memories of Evelyn indulging in quiet downtime, besides hanging out with friends. She'd forced herself to go running with the flu or a sprained ankle, and now she couldn't stay in motion and keep busy. This had to be difficult for her.

"At least I'm a bit better when I'm resting. And it makes me realize just what a champ our mom was when she spent those nine months sick as a dog, going to the hospital for dehydration, when she was pregnant with you."

Lillian helped to decorate a haunted house in the student lounge near her room, putting up flashing strobe lights and stretching fake cobwebs over the furniture. Papier-mâché dead bodies were dismembered on the pool and foosball tables, and gory plastic heads hung from meat hooks. A student in a hockey mask, splattered with fake blood, menacingly held up a plastic chainsaw.

Bridget, Tim, and Lillian excitedly got into their costumes on Halloween night. Tim slicked his wavy blond hair with waxy yellow gel and pulled it into two knobs at the sides of his head.

Zack would not be joining them tonight. Instead, he helped his roommates turn the home they rented into a dark haunted house with buckets of slimy grape eyeballs and spaghetti intestines for neighborhood kids to plunge their hands into. Zack grumbled that Lillian would go out with friends, and called her cell phone in between putting up decorations. When Lillian, Bridget, and Tim set out into the night, the calls stopped as Zack became busy with visitors.

After milking heaps of candy out of a few residence halls, the trio went on to Hollander Hall, a small dormitory tucked beside the golf course on the far edge of campus. Lillian had never set foot inside this building until now.

A fire person had been here. Recently. Their trail glowed in a braid winding in and out the main door, up the stairs, tamped down by all the feet of the students trick-or-treating, but still unmistakable.

Hopefully that person had just left. But they had walked in here repeatedly. Just today.

Lillian and her friends made the rounds on the ground floor before climbing upstairs. The trail of the fire person stood out on the upper floor, up and down the hall. Lillian would have left immediately if she did not have companions who would not understand her concerns.

Tim knocked on a series of three doors. The first opened and a student in a Guy Fawkes mask gave them Twizzlers. At the second, there was no answer.

Tim knocked on the third door. When it swung open, the breath left Lillian's body. Her belly filled with a hot liquid sensation of pure fear.

The fire person stood just inches from her, surrounded by radiant orange extensions. A lean young man, he wore a ribbed blue sweatshirt instead of a costume. He had smooth, golden skin and wavy black hair, slightly messy on his head. As Lillian stared, dumbstruck and waiting for something terrible to happen, to be burned or torn to pieces, he briefly made eye contact, dark brown eyes piercing into her from behind a thin pair of glasses. He smiled slightly at the group, showing a set of large, straight oval teeth, as he dumped handfuls of hard candy into all of their bags. Including Lillian's.

Heart pounding and afraid to even move, Lillian prepared to die. The last encounter her family had with other mages almost ended up that way. And now, less than a year later, here was yet another one. Probably the same one she had carefully dodged for months.

Tim nudged Lillian as she stood frozen, her breath caught in her throat. "Hey, look, they're giving out Pez dispensers next door! That's so awesome! C'mon!"

Lillian almost forgot that she saw things invisible to Bridget and Tim and most of the population. As Lillian's friends dragged her away, she glanced over her shoulder once again at the fire person, infusing him into her mind one last time so that she could recognize his face. As another trick-or-treater came to him, he glanced at her again. Some of the doors had glittery signs with the students' first names, but his had been taken down, removing the opportunity for Lillian to learn his name.

"I'm sorry, we have to leave," she confessed to her friends.

"What's wrong?" Tim asked. He and Bridget then noticed the tears of terror welling in Lillian's eyes. She blinked them back hard.

"I can't explain—we just need to leave."

"Okay, let's go," Bridget agreed.

After they left, pulled their coats back on, and walked several yards away from Hollander Hall, Lillian took deep breaths of night air to try to calm down, though her heart still hammered against her sternum.

"Did either of you know that guy living upstairs in there, the one with glasses and black hair?" Lillian asked after she evened out her breathing.

"Which one?" Bridget wanted to know. "The Asian-looking one in the blue sweater?"

"Yes."

"Never seen him before," Tim shrugged. "But he was kind of hot!"

"He looked vaguely familiar," said Bridget. "Might have been in a couple of my classes, but I've never talked to him and don't know his name. Lil, do you know him?"

"No."

"Oh, good. You seemed a little nervous when you saw that guy. I was afraid he'd done something to you. But you've never seen him before?"

"No, I haven't. I guess I... I don't know... he reminded me of someone."

"You just had a panic attack in there. Everything's going to be okay," Bridget soothed.

As they continued across the campus, and then went out for a dinner at a 24-hour restaurant, Lillian could not forget what she saw as Tim reminisced about his wild Halloween nights in high school, getting drunk and toilet-papering houses. Lillian tried to keep her attention on the conversation, telling herself, *Just smile and nod. Act like everything is normal. Because to Bridget and Tim, it is. Don't talk to them again about the fire mage. To them, he's just a nobody and they've probably already forgotten about him.*

After Tim went home and Bridget and Lillian went back to their dorm room, they both changed out of their costumes and went to bed. Bridget fell asleep; Lillian did not. She thought of doing a private tarot reading by candlelight, or a Halloween ritual, but her mind spun too much for her to focus. Now that Lillian found herself lying awake in the bottom bunk with no one to talk to, her dread and fear levels crept up. The fire mage could be searching for her right now. If he really wanted to locate her, it might not be difficult if he stumbled across just the right building, saw just the right greenish tracks she had recently left on her way into the front door.

If Lillian was unlucky enough, he might even be a mind reader. The mere possibility chilled her down to the bone. If he was as gifted as Uncle Gerald, he knew exactly where she lived already. Along with all of her secrets.

Suddenly not wanting to sleep on campus, Lillian hid in the bathroom so as not to disturb Bridget and called Zack's cell phone. He answered after three rings, snapping, "It's late."

"I'm sorry to call so late."

"You know I'm not a night person! You shouldn't be calling and waking me up like that!"

"I just... I figured you might still be awake because of the haunted house," Lillian said in a faltering voice, starting to cry.

"No, that's over."

"I was just wondering if... if... I could stay the night there," Lillian pleaded.

"What, are you crying or something now? Jesus!"

"Rough night..."

"Oh, all right, come on over."

"Thank you. Maybe I could sleep on the couch?"

"What's wrong with my room? You are my girlfriend, after all."

Lillian arrived at Zack's house, where the haunted house props lay in cluttered piles. Zack sat on his bed in his T-shirt and boxers, waiting for her. Staying fully dressed in the shirt and leggings she'd put on after removing her costume, Lillian tucked herself in and squeezed against the cold wall, uncomfortable on the concrete-hard mattress. As Zack crawled in next to her, she realized just how slim the bed was. There was no way to get around their bodies touching.

A couple of weeks ago, Lillian had brought up cuddling, thinking it might be a nice way to slowly work up to a more physical relationship. "I don't like to cuddle," Zack had protested. "I like to fuck."

So here they were, going from hardly touching to hopping in bed together. Though curious, even a bit sexually frustrated, Lillian was still not ready for intimacy.

Zack reached around and clamped his hand onto her breast, squeezing it painfully hard.

"Ow, stop!" she gasped. "What are you doing?"

"Ah, you're so sexy," Zack cooed. His hand squeezed and kneaded her breast like it was a gel-filled stress ball. Julius had done the exact same thing during that horrible summer.

"Seriously, stop!"

"Fine, then. If you don't like being touched there, I'll touch you somewhere else." Zack groped her bottom with almost bruising force.

"Stop that!"

"What's your problem? You don't like being touched?"

"Not that rough, and not out of nowhere like that. Please stop." Lillian's heart pounded as hard as it did earlier that evening, when she found herself face-to-face with the fire mage.

"That's how my ex-girlfriend liked being touched. She liked me to take charge." Though Lillian figured Zack had dated before, he talked so rarely about his past that this was the first mention of any former girlfriend.

"Sorry, but I'm not your ex. All of us are different."

"You've been frigid this whole time."

"I just want you to be more gentle."

"How?"

"Maybe start by holding and caressing me, I don't know. I just want you to take things more slowly."

"Maybe I can get you in the mood somehow."

"Zack, I've had a stressful evening and my nerves are shot. I'm not ready tonight."

"How much longer do I have to keep waiting?"

"I don't know. I'm sorry."

With a grunt, Zack went to sleep, snoring in her ear. Lillian was awake all night on the painfully hard mattress, pressed against the wall.

After leaving Zack's house, Lillian arrived in her dorm room to find Bridget still out cold in the top bunk. Grateful it was a Saturday, Lillian tried to nap, but she had spun enough anxieties for herself about the fire mage that the sleep still would not come. After Bridget woke up and went out, Lillian called her father to vent and ask for advice.

"I had a feeling this would happen," Lou said with a sigh when Lillian informed him about the student she saw last night. "There's thousands of people going to that school, and there was a chance there'd be one or two mages. Don't say you weren't warned about that possibility when you insisted on going there."

"Should I switch schools, just to make sure I'm safe?"

"Sweetheart, a lot of the schools are even bigger than the one you're at now. If you went someplace else, you could run into an entire group of them. You're lucky you just saw that one by himself. If I were you, I'd keep an eye on things, especially since you haven't seen any others."

"What do I do if he comes after me or I run into him again?"

"Remember what we've talked about? Just not saying anything to them and leaving as quickly as possible?"

"Yes."

"And if he does attack you, which I hope he won't, remember that our powers are the sneakiest. You use them only if he or someone else tries to hurt you, you understand? Tell me immediately if you run into trouble with that boy, and we'll decide what to do."

As they continued talking, Lou revealed that Denny had gotten a strange phone call in a vaguely familiar voice, ordering him to watch out for himself and not threaten anyone. They believed it may have come from the water people they had barely survived that spring.

"Aren't you worried?" Lillian asked her father. "What if they come after you? I'm still afraid they'll come after me, on top of my worries about that guy I saw last night!"

"I think they might be a little afraid of us after we got away, but I cannot say for sure. It's been months and they haven't shown up, so hopefully they won't."

On the early morning of Sunday, November sixteenth, Natasha Cosette Gundersen came into the world, six pounds and eight ounces, red-faced and screaming.

Even after all the exertion, Evelyn felt better. Stronger. No longer lightheaded or sick to her stomach.

Natasha was a bundle of newborn awkwardness, just barely filling Evelyn's arms. Scrawny and wrinkled, she had swollen eyes open just a slit and glistening with slimy antibiotic ointment. Thin wisps of brown hair, the same shade as Jonathan's, poked out from underneath her white cap.

Jonathan sat on the nearby rocking chair, calling friends and family members with the news. Not long afterward, Jonathan's parents arrived, squealing like pigs in their excitement.

His mother immediately got on Evelyn's nerves, snatching the baby away and aggressively pinching her cheeks until she started crying. "You actually had the baby? Your hips are just so narrow. I was sure you'd need a C-section!"

"Yes, I actually 'had' the baby." Evelyn rolled her eyes at her mother-in-law.

"You're not really going to try to breastfeed, are you?"

"Yes."

Jonathan's mother laughed condescendingly. "Look at how flat-chested you are! I'm going to be worried sick that baby is going to starve."

Sensing Evelyn's anger, Jonathan made an excuse that Evelyn needed a nap in order to shoo his parents out.

After Evelyn came home, her life fell into messy-house, sleepless-night chaos. Her past infant care experience, helping to teach her sister to walk and talk and babysitting other folks' kids, had not prepared her for full-time parenthood and the brain fog that came with it.

Despite her fear of them carrying in germs from their flights, Evelyn allowed her family to visit at last. Evelyn's now semi-retired father arrived a couple of days before Thanksgiving to meet his first grandchild. When he arrived, Evelyn was on the couch, holding Natasha, dark bags under her eyes. The breasts her mother-in-law complained were too small to feed a baby now ached and leaked.

Oddly, Lou did not outstretch his arms to receive the yawning, gurgling baby. Instead, his jaw dropped a bit, his eyes widening as he stepped back a few paces.

What on earth offended Evelyn's father? Was Natasha less attractive than the hormonal rose-tinted goggles of new motherhood let on, even though he'd already been emailed pictures and her appearance should come as no surprise?

Feeling almost personally rejected, Evelyn cradled the infant against her chest. "Does she smell?" Evelyn asked her father, who stood over her, strangely quiet and clenching his jaw. "Does she need to be changed? I thought I just changed her."

"No, no, there's no bad smell," Lou assured, finally adopting a slight smile. "Why don't you let me hold her?"

Cautiously, he sat beside Evelyn on the sofa and took the baby in his arms, rocking her a bit.

The day before Thanksgiving, Lillian arrived. When Jonathan brought Lillian to the house, Natasha was off in the nursery, napping. Lillian was instructed to not go peek just yet, however curious she might be about her brand-new niece. Even lingering quietly in the doorway made the baby stir. When someone set foot nearby, even if they tiptoed, she could tell.

The family members all sat on the white couch to talk for a little while. When Lillian went to the kitchen to pour herself a glass of water, her father also excused himself and joined her, leaning down a bit to whisper. Evelyn watched through the doorway out of the corner of her eye as her father and sister muttered quietly to one another, saying things she couldn't quite hear. She guessed that they were discussing Natasha, that Lou thought something was wrong with the baby and he wanted to warn Lillian before she saw her. Or did Lou think that the baby did not resemble Jonathan and suspect Evelyn of cheating? Ah, that could be it. Evelyn felt hurt and excluded, the latest wound after years of sensing that her father favored Lillian, that those two shared a special bond from which Evelyn was permanently shut out. Quietly, she buried her anger.

The four of them put on a movie. In the middle of it, a high-pitched cry arose from the nursery. Evelyn shuffled down the hall and came back out with Natasha held up against her chest, all wrinkled pink skin with sparse hair on a large, bulbous head.

Lillian had also seen the pictures Evelyn and Jonathan sent out in the emails and posted on Facebook, but she, too, appeared a little surprised. She stared at Natasha, taking a long time before she finally reached out to cradle her.

"How did this happen?" Lou said in the remote corner booth of an Italian restaurant after he and Lillian had left for a bit, telling Evelyn they wanted to let her rest. "No mages—other than our kind—have ever been born in this family. I just don't understand."

Surrounding Natasha were long waves, tentacles of color so big for someone so small, an unbelievable thing that would never show up in any baby picture. And they were the sapphire blue of the ocean.

Even after noticing the pink-laced blue remnants of the aura on the baby's car seat and then in the living room, Lillian had still frozen up involuntarily in her surprise when Evelyn brought the newborn out of the nursery. They could not deny it. Natasha was a water person.

"I don't get it either," Lillian agreed. "But could it be from Jonathan's side of the family? He's got mage blood too."

"Maybe, but I'm worried it's something worse than that. Maybe Evelyn had an affair."

"But what are the odds of her sleeping with a water person?"

"Not likely. You don't suppose that when we were down south for the wedding, one of those men could have taken advantage of her? You think the timing's right?"

"She got pregnant right before the wedding. That's what both she and Uncle Gerald said. And I didn't see any signs at the wedding of being raped or having an affair. But you never know."

"I hope to God no one hurt her. But if Jonathan isn't the father, then who is? A few years from now, Natasha will start wondering why she's different, why she sees things no one else can. And she'll start asking questions. Evelyn and Jonathan won't have any idea. They'll be in over their heads."

"Should we make an exception and break the code? Should we just tell Evelyn about the powers, so she won't be blindsided later?"

"Not just yet. That could be risky. She may not understand, or may not believe us."

"Or maybe she would go bragging to people that she has a special baby."

"I believe Evelyn would be wise enough to not do that, but when we break it to her, it must be done delicately. I'll handle it."

"Dad, I don't know if it's the trauma from what happened after the wedding, but I have a weird sense that we haven't been alone since we got here. That we might be followed."

"Followed? By who?"

"I don't know, but I keep imagining the worst. That it might be... them."

"The water people? Remember, they're a long distance away. I think we're safe. I hope."

"You don't sound too convinced, Dad."

"They're probably afraid to get tangled up with us again. Let's head on back to Evelyn's."

The crowd at the restaurant, light when they first arrived, had thinned to almost nothing. They left the nearly empty building to a desolate parking lot with just a few cars. A black car was parked along the curb, just down the street. Something about that vehicle was not right.

"Dad," Lillian whispered, gripping Lou's arm tight. "There's someone getting out of that car over there."

"What car? Oh, that one over there? Oh, no. Oh, no! Run!"

They raced toward Lou's rental car. There was no mistaking the glow, even in the faint light cast from a dim street lamp. The man stepping out of that black car was one of the water people, his aura rising high, bright, and blue.

"Stop right there!" a voice commanded. Just as Lou's hand reached the car door, water slicked down its side, coating his fingers.

The two men, one younger and one older, who had attempted to kill them months ago now had them cornered. Absent were the woman and the baby, but these were more water people than Lillian hoped to see again in her lifetime. Lillian's heart leaped into her throat, as if she were near drowning all over again.

"Leave us alone!" Lou begged. "We simply want peace. We want to be left alone!"

"We've been watching you," the younger man said. "We found where your daughter lives. Tell us how it happened."

"How what happened?"

"The birth of that child."

"I don't know! That's what we're trying to figure out too!"

"Whether she had an affair or whether it was just funny genetics, the child is one of us," the one with long gray hair cut in. "Born into a family that isn't safe."

"You say that my grandchild is one of you," Lou replied. "We only want what's best for her, too. The best thing you can do for her, and our family, is to leave us alone. Let us live our lives and we won't bother you again."

The older man's face remained stony, but the younger one's finally relaxed. "Dad," he urged, "maybe they're right. We can't hurt the baby. Maybe we should just leave all of them alone. Come to an agreement."

"Are you serious?! Terry, do you hear yourself right now?"

"Yes. I'm serious." The son turned back toward Lou and Lillian, who stood frozen, anxiously anticipating the next act of aggression. "I already broke my arm this spring trying to come at these folks, and maybe it's time to stop all of this before things get even worse and we risk our lives further. Dad, please, let's just stop."

The father grumbled. "Oh, okay, Terry. Maybe you have a point there." With a sigh, he looked back toward Lou and Lilian. "Here's the conditions. Y'all must look after that child, keep her safe, and make sure that nothing happens to her and she's got some support with her powers. And you must leave us alone. As long as nothing happens to that baby, we also stay in our lane."

"That sounds... more than reasonable," Lou agreed. "And my condition—you owe us an apology for the terror you've put us through."

"We're sorry, then. We may not have thought it through, and we went too far. Here's another condition. You must not hurt anyone with your powers. And make sure that Denny behaves himself too."

"Absolutely. Though you must understand that these powers can happen out of pure reflex when we feel the need to defend ourselves."

"We can make an exception for self-defense when your life's in danger, then. But no creatures and no zombies. Shall we shake on it?"

Lillian was nervous about touching these people, and from her father's spine going straight, she sensed that he was not in a hurry to trust them either. But all four of them extended their hands for firm shakes.

"If you ever need help with the little girl, look us up," were the father's parting words. "I'm Lonnie Jenkinson, and this is my son, Terry."

Lou and Lillian waited to leave until the water people's car was long out of sight. As they stepped into Lou's now-dry rental car, they both peeked behind them all the way back to Evelyn's house, vigilant for signs of being pursued.

Lillian got almost no sleep that night, though she woke dry and alive, the house undisturbed. Still, whispering amongst themselves, neither she nor her father fully trusted the words of the water people. Or that they'd let Evelyn and Jonathan live in peace when they inevitably had to go home. With the new baby in the mix, the stakes were that much higher.

Thanksgiving was a gloomy, rainy day spent lazing around the house and holding Natasha while the turkey cooked aromatically in the oven. Thick rivulets of rain coated the windows and sliding glass door, and soft gray light was cast through the house. It triggered frightening memories of what the water clan did to the family that spring.

During Lillian's first date with Zack after her return to school, he asked far more questions about baby Natasha than about the rest of her Thanksgiving experience. It was unusual for Zack, who generally did not seem intrigued by anything at all, to fire away so many questions. Was the baby sleeping and feeding well? Any glimmer of a budding personality?

"Why are you so curious?" Lillian asked as they picked at their salads.

"Okay, I'll admit it. I love babies. I would like children someday. You want children, right?"

Yikes—this was a glaring incompatibility. Lillian had to get the truth out, giving it to him straight even if she risked being dumped on the spot. "I don't."

"You sure?" Zack prodded, his face falling a bit.

"Yeah. I've never been interested."

"Why not?"

"I just never had that instinct, I guess. I think I would make a good mother, but I just don't feel it's the right path for me."

"Haven't you even been around kids?"

"Yes, when I was in high school, I used to babysit. Most of the kids were fun, except for that one who reached into his diaper and finger-painted brown art on the walls. I like kids, don't get me wrong, but sleepless nights and lack of time to myself just doesn't sound like the life I want."

"It's different when it's your own. If you don't have kids, you will regret it."

"I don't know about that. My cousin Denny didn't want kids, and now he's in his fifties and still doesn't regret it."

"I think deep down, you want to be a mother."

Once the food came out, things went back to the usual, uncomfortable silence, with little to talk about between the couple. They parted without a goodbye kiss. Lillian went back to her dorm feeling frustrated. She'd expressed her desires only for Zack to invalidate and gloss over them.

A couple of weeks later, after they were done with finals, Lillian, Tim, and Bridget went to a shopping mall just to walk around and unwind. Zack tagged along, and when they passed a jewelry store, he urged them to step inside. They tried on expensive diamond rings for fun, and Lillian made her friends laugh, getting on bended knee and pretending to propose marriage to them.

That night, Bridget went out elsewhere. Zack visited Lillian alone in her dorm room as she packed her luggage, preparing to go home for the winter break.

"There's a reason I wanted to look around in the ring shop," he informed Lillian.

"You're not telling me you're going to... propose?"

"What, you're not ready?"

"Whoa! Zack. We've only been together a few months!" Lillian was surprised to the point of fear.

"Sorry, I didn't mean to frighten you. I just thought girls liked it when a guy showed commitment."

"I'm sorry, but I don't think I'm ready for that kind of commitment."

"Well, then, I might get you a gift. Not quite to that step, or whatever. But just to show we are committed."

Though the conversation unsettled her, Lillian allowed Zack to make out with her before he went home. He sucked painfully hard, groped and pawed clumsily, and filled her mouth with his saliva.

When Bridget learned later that night what had just transpired, she gasped in shock. "Whoa, shit, that guy needs to pump the brakes! That would have freaked me out so much, I probably would've dumped him."

"I'll think about it, since the relationship doesn't give me a lot of joy and I'm not sure if that's normal. But I don't know when or if someone else will come along. What if I end up alone?"

"Dude, you're only what, nineteen? It's too soon to worry about ending up alone. People this age are playing the field."

"Ever since she was thirteen, my sister could practically snap her fingers and a boyfriend would appear. And I was a late bloomer, even though I wasn't always looking. Maybe I'm just a little insecure because of my sister. Feeling like it's better to have someone than to be alone."

"But ask yourself if you'd be happier alone than with Zack."

"Honestly, maybe I would. He bugs me with his calls. He makes me nervous. But I'm not sure I'm ready to break up with him. That's a hard conversation to have and I'm not even sure *how* to dump him."

"I've been through a few breakups and can give you pointers. If you don't feel ready for that yet, keep an eye on him. Wait and see if he'll bring up the ring again. Maybe he doesn't understand really well how relationships work."

Once she arrived home, Lillian was delighted to be back with her father and her beloved dog. Her father and Denny spoke little of that spring's incident with the water people and the later promises they made in the fall, though baby Natasha's powers became a hot topic.

Uncle Gerald invited the three to his New Year's party at his mansion. Lou treated Gerald more kindly, since the two brothers weren't getting any younger and wished to bury their past resentments toward each other. Denny, who considered Uncle Gerald a pretentious ass, decided to stay behind and dog-sit Astrid for the night.

After Lillian spent the afternoon riding in the car with her father, wearing a surprisingly nice black sequined top she'd found for five dollars at a thrift store, they reached Potomac, a quiet area where manorial estates rested well behind fences and trees. They pulled up Uncle Gerald's long driveway to his brick mansion, where pure white columns bordered the porch. So much living space for a widower with a long-empty nest.

The immaculately clean home had hardwood floors that gave a soft reflection of all things above them. A mirror image: a world above, a faded reverse world below in the soft brown. Instead of being frightened into hiding by the visitors, Gerald's orange striped cat was out, padding noiselessly across the floor. In the center of the living room was a marble fireplace, and above it hung an oil painting of Gerald when he was younger, wearing a black suit, back when silver had just started to infiltrate his deep red hair. Now it was all gray.

Delicious smells came from the kitchen as Gerald and his friends prepared a pasta dinner. People began to gather in the massive kitchen. The center island was covered with plates of appetizers. Once the pasta was ready, it smelled rich and savory. Lillian heaped a serving onto a plate.

More guests rolled in. After she finished eating, Lillian went back to the kitchen, spooned another serving of pasta onto her plate, and wandered around, seeking quiet from the older couples she didn't know. She went down carpeted stairs into the recreation room with a ping-pong table, pool table, dartboard, and home theater. She ate half the plate alone on the overstuffed couch and then practiced throwing a few darts.

Gerald descended the steps, finding Lillian checking out the titles on the wide bookshelf. "What are you doing down here when the other guests are having fun up there?" he inquired.

"I'm having fun too."

"All by yourself?" Gerald glanced at Lillian's half-eaten plate. "You know, this being your second serving, that pasta will go straight to your hips. It is simple carbohydrates. You do look like you've put on a bit of weight, and I hate to say it, but your backside has always been rather large."

Lillian stared, shocked that her uncle would speak to her this way. Was he trying to put her down, targeting the body part that made her the most self-conscious—her rear end—just to make her feel bad? Much to Lillian's embarrassment, her eyes filled with tears. Gerald walked over to comfort her, putting his arms around her. She flinched.

"That was rude of me. You've always been such a sensitive girl. I should have been more gentle. I'm so, so sorry, but given my own recent heart trouble, I think we could all stand to improve our diets. Why don't we talk about something else, to help cheer you up?"

"Sure. Thanks for apologizing."

They sat together on the couch as Lillian dabbed at her eyes. Gerald began to chat, responding, as usual, to the things she did not come out and say.

"You're doing really well lately. I'm glad that you've made friends at your college and brought up your grades. I think you have increased your confidence and study habits by leaps and bounds. And Tara is dead. That problem took care of itself. Try not to worry about that boy you saw in the dormitory on Halloween night. I know he's a terrifying sort of mage, but he doesn't look like the type who has the guts to attack you, so long as you avoid him. You know the rules; don't talk to them, don't provoke them. If he does give you any trouble, just let me know and I'll get it taken care of. Try not to worry about those water people either. I can't be sure how honest they were when they vowed to leave you and your father alone, but if they seriously wanted you dead, then one or the other party would be dead... and if any necromancer were dead, it'd be a huge, huge loss. If they ever make trouble again, or if that boy at your school does the same, please do not hesitate to use your powers. Throw all of that shame your father taught you right out the window. Oh, and I would like to congratulate you on the new gentleman in your life. He is quite handsome."

"Thanks."

"I know you feel you're not that into him, but remember that outside of the internet, which in my opinion doesn't count, you've never had a real relationship before. I believe you are nervous due to lack of experience. I'd suggest sticking it out, and I promise that the love will bloom. Anyway, come on out to the party. Socialize. Have fun."

Lillian took a breath and came up to where the other guests were gathered. Gerald introduced her to a few coworkers and golfing buddies, including the vice president of Frazier Medical Supply.

Later, Lillian went up the gracefully curving stairs to put her overnight bag in one of the bedrooms. The space of the huge, yet fully furnished, bedroom stretched emptily around Lillian. She remembered this room well, on those occasional childhood outings when Dad would bring her and Evelyn to visit Gerald and his second wife, Tawny, when she was still alive. Tawny had been a sweet woman, energetic and fun and a great cook, inviting the girls to swim together in the backyard pool or go on walks with Tawny and Gerald's dog along a nearby canal.

Tawny died when Lillian was eleven years old. A suicide by overdose, the same manner in which Tara had lost her life, whether intentionally or not. It came as a total shock to everyone who knew Tawny. If she had been depressed, she'd hid it well.

Uncle Gerald appeared in the doorway. "Party's not over yet. If you are feeling shy and want to hide, keep in mind that this is a small, intimate, quiet gathering, compared to some of the galas with a hundred guests that I find myself invited to."

After rejoining the party, Lillian hung around her father, the only person there that she felt comfortable with, and grew bored. Everyone rang in 2009 with bubbly amber champagne and confetti. Tired guests started to leave. Lou went upstairs to tuck himself in, as did a couple of other guests who had decided to spend the night.

As she got ready to climb the stairs, Lillian paused by Gerald's study. The door hung wide open. Usually it was closed.

Curious about this room she'd barely ever laid eyes on, Lillian crept closer to the doorway. Though Gerald claimed to be estranged from Julius, faded old baby and childhood pictures of his son still hung on the wood-paneled wall.

A thick stack of printed papers sat on the mahogany desk next to Gerald's desktop computer. Nearby was a large safe, or possibly a gun cabinet.

Gerald stepped right behind Lillian. She spun around, already feeling guilty like a child with a hand in the cookie jar.

"Didn't your father teach you it's impolite to snoop?" Gerald said quietly.

"I wasn't snooping—I just was..."

"Curious. And if I hadn't shown up, you would have snooped. You would have walked in there. The temptation would have become too great. Curiosity killed the cat, as they say. Let me tell you a little something about your mother. She sometimes attended parties and spent the night here. And I hate to say it, but she was nosy. Where you hesitated to walk into this room, she just waltzed right in. I know you want to remember her fondly, but she was a rather childish woman. I want you to be careful. Don't end up like her."

"I'm sorry, Uncle Gerald. I won't go in there."

"Good."

As Lillian brushed her teeth in the marble-trimmed bathroom adjoining the bedroom where she would sleep tonight, she turned over Gerald's last sentence. *Don't end up like her.*

Karl, the partner who had murdered Lillian's mother, swore he'd kept his gun in his nightstand only in case of a burglar, never dreaming of using it against Vanessa. Yet one day, he just woke up standing with the weapon in his hand, confused and horrified at the sight of Vanessa dead on the floor. No one had believed his testimony that he could not remember the crime, and the medical evaluations found no physical or mental illnesses.

What if... no, it couldn't be Uncle Gerald. Why would he?

Or would he?

Excerpt from The Autobiography of Gerald Frazier: Architect of a New World

M y years at the university were quite an experience. I realize what a risk it was, being one of the very few members of my family to leave home and venture out of state to attend school. After the boyhood thrill of seeing the lecherous war widow's memories of the big city, I grew anxious to explore the world. During high school, I had applied to Columbia University in New York City, and did not get in. Another way the fates seemed to call me to Ohio instead.

Dare I say that I remember less of my higher education than I should because I drank rather heavily. I joined a fraternity, where I eventually became vice president. We engaged in cruel, yet almost erotic, hazing rituals. To prove my worth, I had my bare bottom whipped and paddled. When we weren't bruising our new members' buttocks, we drank until we passed out.

I cut down a bit on the partying when I met Enid Richardson, a beautiful classmate from Cleveland. Enid had her flaws, like everyone else. She was a kleptomaniac who got sexually aroused when she shoplifted makeup from department stores. But she wasn't nearly as screwed up as some, and her mind was more at peace than those of my most troubled family members. I found Enid's company refreshing, and we got engaged.

I never encountered a mage not of my family until college. But I'll never forget the day, my senior year, when I ran into a new freshman, an air mage. She was a tiny girl of eighteen, but tough as nails after her parents, both mages, had secretly taught her that she could conquer anything. She threatened to fry me on the spot with her lightning powers!

"You might want to think twice about that, Miss Marilyn Wilson," I chastised her, doing my best to sound intimidating while quaking in my boots, watching it dawn on her that she had not revealed her name and I was reading her mind. "If you take me out, I have a family of people like me. They'll come after you."

Marilyn went white as a sheet in the worst fear she'd ever experienced after eighteen years of believing herself to be invincible. At a younger age, I might have felt guilty for causing a lady such a fright; but by then, I was learning to not care about another's fear. If I let myself get emotionally involved, I'd go off the deep end.

"Don't worry so much," I reassured Marilyn after giving her that good scare. "If you leave me alone, and say nothing, I leave you alone. Do we have an understanding?"

"Yes," Marilyn mumbled before she ran away.

Even though we saw each other on campus from time to time, there were no more problems, and Marilyn gave me space as promised. Thank God Marilyn did not tell her parents back home in Indiana about me. Marilyn's grandmother, the family's mind reader, likely had Alzheimer's. She'd lost her powers and could barely speak.

Sometimes a little fear goes a long way in negotiating and saving your own skin. And believe me, I would get more practice in chance encounters in the years to come. Most of the other mages are scared to death of us, as they well should be, and in the end would rather flee than fight. But there still is definitely a threat that we must keep mindful of, which is why we avoid them if at all possible. If you're reading this, hopefully, this sort of threat is now a thing of the past!

I married Enid shortly after we graduated with our business degrees. We rented an apartment for a while to save up the money for a house, and we both found office jobs.

I received a letter from my eldest sister Violet informing me that our father had died from a stroke. I'd had a gut feeling that he was gone, like I did when other relatives passed away. My younger brother Lou inherited our childhood home. He gutted and renovated the house, hoping to share it with his girlfriend Roberta when they married. And much to my consternation, Papa left the green crystal to Lou in his will. I had no idea why it had to be him! Why not Sarah, the firstborn necromancer child in the family? Or me, since I was the most ambitious of my siblings? I was far angrier about the crystal than the house or anything else. I felt betrayed.

A Forbidden Friend

T he spring semester began. In addition to her geology classes, Lillian was signed up for a literature course she shared with Zack, and a technical writing class. When she arrived for the first session of technical writing, the strength of the yellow-orange aura hit her as soon as she entered the lecture hall. It poked up from one of the back rows.

The fire mage was in the class!

Terribly flustered and not knowing what else to do, Lillian ran to the front row. During the introductory lecture, she kept her eyes fixed on the podium, not risking even a quick glance toward the back of the room. When the time came to leave, Lillian waited until most of the other students were gone before she dared to peek behind her and get up.

The mage had left with the crowd.

The second day the class met was a Thursday. Lillian again waited until most of the class walked out before she left, and then rushed through the empty lobby and out of the building. Even in the safety of her dorm room, with Bridget right there, Lillian lived in fear of being tracked down. The same fear she'd had since Halloween, now flared up again.

The following week, Lillian once again hurried out of that class and across the sun-splashed tiled lobby toward the exit. She timed her departure a bit earlier than she had last week, before she was confident that the fire person had left the building. As she walked briskly toward the exit door, his unseen presence encroached upon her. Heart speeding up in terror, she broke into a full run for the glass door.

"You don't have to run," a voice said behind her.

Lillian froze and spun around. There he stood, dressed in a silver coat and black jeans. Up close, he was an inch or two taller than her.

Not one hundred percent confident that he was the one who'd just spoken, Lillian looked around. The two of them were alone in the lobby.

"You don't have to run," he repeated in a barely audible voice.

Lillian was tempted to turn and barrel away at full speed anyway, but running could trigger a predator's chase instinct. As far as she was concerned, a beast stood just feet away from her, no less of a threat than an angry grizzly bear rising over a hiker. A situation where running was the first instinct, but the worst idea.

Both of them looked down at the tile floor, caught in an awkward stalemate, avoiding eye contact. Why wasn't Lillian taking off, even if it might induce him to chase her like a dog after a squirrel? She had to get away!

"What's your name?" the classmate asked.

Against her better judgment, Lillian told him. If he was like Uncle Gerald, he already knew it. "Lillian. What's yours?"

"Avery."

"What year are you?"

Run. What in the world are you doing, making conversation with this person who will kill you?

Yet her stomach-lurching fear competed with mounting curiosity.

"Sophomore," Avery answered in a near-whisper, fidgeting his hands together nervously.

"So am I. What's your major?"

"Communications."

Silence fell again. As her instincts warred against each other, Lillian wanted to keep him stalled here while she had the chance to either befriend him and save herself—a notion she quickly threw out, since they could never be friends—or make sure that he was not poised to kill her the moment she turned her back.

Lillian glanced around again to ensure that no one was close enough to hear them. "Are you one of those mind-reading ones?" she asked in a low voice.

"Yes."

"How much?"

"I can't see everything," Avery said in his shy whisper.

"Stop!" Lillian demanded, feeling caught in the recurring nightmare she had of finding herself back in high school and stark naked, laughed at in the halls. He said he couldn't see everything, but he could see some things, and that was more than enough. For all she knew, her scars, physical and emotional, could be exposed right now; her weak spots that could easily be exploited. What did he know? This was worse than dealing with Uncle Gerald.

Before this Avery could possibly see another thing, Lillian turned at last and ran, book bag slapping against the curve of her hip. She glanced anxiously over her shoulder to be sure she was not being followed.

Lillian skipped that class for a couple of sessions until she had to be there for a quiz. Again, Avery sat in the back, and she looked down, waiting for an especially long period of time for the classroom and lobby to empty out before she felt safe leaving.

Burning curiosity still got the best of Lillian. She logged onto Facebook and searched the university's network for people named Avery. Two results came up. Avery Allen, a blonde sorority girl with nine hundred Facebook friends and a timeline filled with photos of herself chugging beer, was clearly not the person of interest. She'd been Tara's friend. Lillian's former roommate grinned in some of the drunken party photos, and this Avery openly vented her grief over Tara's death. *Eight months since you've been gone,* said the most recent memorial post.

The second result might have been the right one, though his profile picture did not provide a clear look at his face, taken from a distance as he sat cross-legged under a willow tree. The black hair, glasses, and slim build did match. His last name was Joseph.

Unlike the sorority girl, this Avery had his privacy settings tightly buttoned down. Lillian could not access his posts, photos, birthday, hometown, or any other details. Though she longed to find out more, she did not want to attract his attention by sending him a friend request.

They had one mutual Facebook friend, Max Jansen, a recent acquaintance Lillian had made in her elective glass blowing course. When Lillian went to that class the following afternoon, she asked Max if he knew an Avery Joseph.

"Yeah, he's in the anime club," Max explained.

"That's how you met him?"

"Yeah, I'm the vice president."

"What do you guys do?"

"Watch anime, of course. And every fall, we go to a con down in Denver."

"A con?"

"A convention. I guess you're not familiar with anime and cosplay and that kind of stuff?"

"I'm not into it, no. Are these the conventions where people dress up as characters?"

"Yeah, that's what cosplay is."

"Does Avery go to these cons?"

"Yeah, he's come with us the past couple of times."

"Where is he from?"

"I think he's from Phoenix. Either that, or Tucson. Someplace in Arizona. Don't quote me on that."

"How well do you know him?"

"Not well. That dude's one of the shyest ones in the club. For a group of geeks, that's saying a lot. Why are you so curious?"

"I just... I have a class with him and wanted to know where he was from."

"I could have you two meet up. I'm not sure how far it would go, since he doesn't talk much."

"That won't be necessary, but thanks."

To Lillian's relief, Zack had dropped the subjects of engagement, marriage, and babies. Yet he never stopped pressing the topic of sex. "We've waited long enough. I can't take it anymore. What's the holdup?"

Lillian still had not told Zack about her past. Even after therapy and healing to the point of discontinuing her medication, Lillian could not predict how she'd handle intimate physical contact, even the willing kind. She did want to try it, but not right now. Not with Zack and all the pressure he put on her. Before going to bed with someone, she wanted what this relationship lacked. Love that felt good, pleasant touching, kisses that didn't resemble making out with an aggressive eel.

But Zack wouldn't back down. He kept whining.

When Lillian set a date in February, Zack resented the wait as he counted down the days. As the day came, her stomach churned with anxious nausea all day in her classes. Still, she did not want to disappoint her boyfriend.

To set a cozy, romantic mood and soothe her jangled nerves, Lillian shut off the lights in her room, turned on a scented oil diffuser, and lit up the multicolored Christmas lights strung on the walls. Then it was time to head to the front door of the building and let Zack in.

They took off their clothes, barely touching one another. Zack's belly pooched a bit from his otherwise solid, surprisingly furry body. Lillian's stomach clenched at the sight of the first penis she had seen up close since that summer with her cousin. Years before then, her kindergarten classmate had whipped his little thing out on the playground during recess. She'd poked and pulled it in her curiosity, regarding it as scientifically as she did the ants digging their tunnels in her ant farm at home. Now, she felt almost as if she was peering down the barrel of a gun.

Lillian looked down at her pale form, horrifically self-conscious about the rippled cellulite that she wished she could carve away from her buttocks and thighs. With that and the self-injury scars, she had not worn shorts or a swimsuit in years. And now here she stood, unveiling the naked body she was ashamed of.

Without a word, Zack pushed Lillian slowly backwards on the bottom bunk of the bed.

"Wait," she said. "Can we do… other stuff first? Work up to it?"

"You're not telling me to eat you out, are you?"

"I didn't say that."

"Good. Because you women all smell. And you never even blew me."

"You want me to try that?"

"Not right now. There's just one thing I want."

"Can we at least… kiss? Hug? Touch?"

"But you kept me waiting this long!"

Zack put his hands on Lillian's knees and pried her legs wide apart. Almost out of instinct, Lillian clamped them shut, clenching her fists. He wedged his fingers back in between her knees and forcefully wiggled his hand down.

"Stop!" Lillian screamed. Cologne filled her nose, though Zack wore none. Flashbacks of tearing, burning pain rocked her.

"Whoa, whoa. Sorry. What's your problem? I'm so turned on… can we put it in?"

Lillian decided to just get it over with. She closed her eyes like she did during pelvic exams at the gynecologist, taking deep breaths. Her chance had finally come to do the thing most people craved. If she could just relax, maybe she would have fun and fully get over her trauma. Zack fumbled with the condom wrapper. He hadn't wanted to wear a rubber, but with no other birth control method, Lillian insisted. As he lowered his hairy body onto her without a kiss or caress, she tried to quell the increasingly anxious pounding of her heart. While he thrusted in a rhythm like a metronome, staring straight ahead at the wall instead of at his girlfriend beneath him, she zoned out from the chafing and pain, attempting to detach.

It was over in perhaps a minute, or even less. Zack got up, tossed the spent condom in the wastebasket, and started to tug his clothes back on.

Seriously? This was it?! This was the activity that people obsessed over and paid prostitutes to experience? This was the magical, transcendent wedding-night soul union that the counselors at the childhood camp said was worth waiting for? How overrated!

Bridget got in later that evening. Eyes gleaming expectantly, she wasted no time in asking, "How was it?"

"Well... I don't know." Lillian sighed.

"Sometimes, a couple's first time can be a little awkward."

"He just shoved it in, and then it was over before I knew it."

"Did he at least try to give you some fun beforehand?"

"No. I asked him to at least kiss me or touch me or something. He wouldn't do that, and just complained. Then he tried to pry my legs apart."

"Jesus! Did he not know what he was doing?"

"I'm not sure. He pounded like a jackhammer, it was kind of painful, then he got up and left."

"Were you at least turned on at all?"

"No. I was nervous and dry as a bone."

"Oh, Lil, no wonder it hurt! Zack was supposed to warm the oven first. Either he's never gone near a woman in his life, or he's incredibly selfish and just wanted to ram a blow-up doll. I'm sorry you had that experience. Not cool at all."

A couple of nights later, Zack pressured Lillian again and came over to her room. She gave in, hoping that this time Zack would try a little harder to please her. No such luck. She laid there with eyes squeezed shut, counting the seconds through the repetitive, passionless pounding and grateful that it was again short-lived. Like the previous time, Zack got dressed and left in a hurry. That night, she had nightmares.

After waking up tired with her alarm the next morning, alone as Bridget had an early morning class, Lillian noticed something peeking out from under the bed. A worn leather wallet. It couldn't be Lillian's shiny homemade duct-tape wallet. Or the glitter wallet Bridget wore on a chain. This one must have fallen from Zack's jeans pocket last night, forgotten when he left. Lillian called Zack's phone, and when he didn't pick up, she left a message that she would bring it to his house after her morning class.

Lillian, who was supposed to be getting ready for class, succumbed to the temptation to snoop. She opened the wallet, inhaling its musky animal smell. Zack's Michigan state driver's license was behind a window of foggy, beaten-up plastic. Lillian pulled out the license to get a closer look, sensing that something was off.

The full name was Zachariah Douglas Dunaway. Lillian hadn't known his middle name until now. In his picture, he wore the exact same outfit as always, right down to the necklace. She focused on a bold line that she did not understand. DOB: 09-04-1981.

Zack claimed to be twenty-one. Yet according to his license, Zack was twenty-seven years old, her sister Evelyn's age. Why did he lie to her? What did he have to gain?

Or maybe he was actually underage and this was a fake ID. If so, he'd found someone who could make a very authentic-looking false license. That possibility did not add up either. Some people used an older sibling's license to get into bars, but any sibling in that photo would have to be Zack's identical twin in a matching outfit. And Zack said he didn't drink, not liking the taste of booze. Lillian had never seen him touch any of the beers that his roommates kept in their fridge. Why would someone with no interest in alcohol carry around a fake ID?

Or could it be fake for other reasons? Was Zack Dunaway even his real name?

The wallet did not hold anything else remarkable, just a debit card, a few twenty-dollar bills, and a receipt from the last restaurant where they ate together.

Lillian did a web search on how to spot a fake ID. When she turned the card, colorful holograms gleamed in the light as a sign of authenticity, just like they did on her own driver's license. The websites suggested flicking the edges of the card to see if any laminate came off. None did, another sign that Zack's ID was real.

Now too distracted and wound up to go to her class, Lillian decided to dump Zack after catching him in this brazen lie. Relief more than sadness washed over Lillian. After months of pushing herself to spend time with Zack and feeling obligated, she had a good excuse to escape this relationship. Today.

Though Zack had yet to return her phone call, Lillian went straight to his house. She pulled into the freshly snow-shoveled driveway, behind Zack's car. Finding the front door unlocked, Lillian pushed it open. Zack sprawled on the couch, talking on his cell phone.

"...It's been going very well. Whoops, there she is. I'll have to call you back." Flipping his phone shut, Zack looked up at Lillian. "Hey."

"Hey," she said, stepping inside and closing the door. "Have you listened to your phone messages?"

"Haven't had a chance just yet."

"You left your wallet in my room."

Zack sat up, stiff as a rod. "I've spent all morning looking for that thing. You have it?"

"Yes."

"Thank God! Can I have it back?"

"First, I'd like you to explain something." Lillian held up Zack's driver's license. "If this is right, you're the oldest twenty-one-year-old I've ever met."

Zack sprang up from the couch and charged at Lillian, grasping her by the wrists and slamming her up against the wall. The license fell from her fingers.

"Why did you do that?" he yelled, spittle splashing her in the face. "Don't you know how rude it is to go through someone's wallet?"

"Take your hands off me!"

"Why did you have to go and snoop like that?"

"Just please, let go of me!"

"All right, fine," Zack growled, releasing Lillian's wrists and backing away as she panted and fought back tears. They stared at each other for several seconds before Zack spoke again.

"Sorry, I'm just pissed right now. But here's your explanation. If a twenty-seven-year-old asks a nineteen-year-old out, it just doesn't look right. You're legal, but I would've looked like a creep, you see what I'm saying? Forgive me. Please."

"Forgive, maybe, but the trust is gone after you… you lied to me and then assaulted me. I've got to go. Please don't call." Lillian set Zack's wallet down and turned to leave.

"Oh, come on! You're overreacting! I didn't even hit you! You're one hell of a cold fish anyway. It's no wonder you were single."

Ignoring those final barbs, not confident that he wouldn't flat-out punch her the next time, Lillian sped out of the driveway. Her phone vibrated in her pocket with repeated calls from Zack as she headed back towards the campus. Once back in her room, Lillian wiped away tears, took several deep breaths, and then listened to his messages imploring her to come back. But she did not plan on it as she erased the voicemails. Though weak and trembling from the shock of the final confrontation, she was free. Already lighter.

Lillian went over the relationship and its end with her roommate Bridget that night.

"You should only sleep with someone because you want to," Bridget pointed out when Lillian mentioned the second bedroom encounter she had endured rather than enjoyed. "I'm not even sure that was totally consensual. You just 'put out' because he nagged you. After he assaulted you today, I'd say you dumped this assclown not a minute too soon."

"I think a big part of why I didn't break it off sooner... I was worried about hurting his feelings. Pressured to spend time with him. Obligated. Sure, he's good-looking, but his looks don't matter if his personality is shit. I was a bit lonely when he asked me out and also felt like I 'should' have a boyfriend, because I'm behind most people my age in the dating game. But you know what? There's no 'should.' I don't need a boyfriend."

"Exactly. I've been dating since I was thirteen, breaking my parents' rules, but I know some people older than you who haven't started yet. There's no race. No requirement to be with someone."

Though she had no desire to talk to Zack again, Lillian grew concerned when he never returned to their shared class. She was nervous to go to that class, prepared to time her exit to dodge him like she avoided Avery in her other class—but she did not spot Zack anywhere in the lecture hall or in the crowd. It was not like him to ditch class.

After a week, Lillian got worried enough to try calling Zack to ask if everything was all right. Instead of ringing, she heard a jarring tone and then an alert. *This number has been disconnected or is no longer in service.*

What timing for Zack's phone to go dead. Was he taking this breakup so hard that he'd changed his number?

Imagining that Zack had become despondent enough to harm himself, Lillian visited the literature professor, Dr. Reddy, in her office to ask if she knew anything. Was he at least turning in his homework?

"I don't have a student named Zachariah Dunaway," Dr. Reddy insisted. "I have never heard that name. Perhaps you are confusing him with someone else?"

"He was in your class," Lillian explained. "We were dating, and then we broke up, and I haven't seen him since. I'm getting scared that he's in a bad state."

"Most of us have had relationships end, and most of us recover. I'm sure he's fine. Let me check my class list just to be sure." Dr. Reddy slid her finger down the list of students registered for the class. "No, that name is not on my list."

"But surely you saw the guy with brown hair and blue eyes who sits next to me, even though it's a fairly big class and all."

"Was he the attractive one who wore a black leather jacket?"

"Yes, and he wore jeans and a necklace with a shark tooth every single day."

"With my volume of students, I don't always put names to faces. Come to think of it, I don't remember him taking tests or turning anything in, and it should have dawned on me that he wasn't participating." Anxiously, Dr. Reddy twirled a lock of her wavy black hair.

"I had another class with Zack last semester. He told me he was dyslexic and they let him take tests in a separate room."

"In my class, no one is getting that accommodation. He lied to you about having a learning disability so you would not figure out he was pretending to be in the class. The nerve! I'm busy with a lot of students, but now I'm mad at myself for not noticing that something was rotten in Denmark."

"I just... I'm shocked... I can't believe he was pretending to be your student! And to lie about a thing like that! It makes sense that he would have gotten lost in the shuffle."

"I know, but this was my class, my responsibility. I wish I'd been paying closer attention, and I'm sorry I didn't."

Lillian poured out much of the rest of the Zack story to the professor, including the lie about his age and his shoving her up against the wall when she confronted him.

"I am very glad, for your sake, that you are away from this young man," Dr. Reddy said. "Wait here. I'm calling the campus police."

"Really? I don't think you need to get the police involved."

"What this man did is significant. I'm concerned for your safety."

After making the call and describing the details, Dr. Reddy waited for a call back. After her desk phone rang a little while later, they both learned that no one named Zachariah Dunaway had ever been enrolled at Northern Colorado University. One of the cops had driven out to Zack's house, only for no one to answer when he knocked on the door. They promised to keep an eye out for him in case he ever returned.

After leaving Dr. Reddy's office, Lillian walked across the campus to get to her room, hurt setting in over just how extensively Zack had deceived her, and shame that she'd believed him. Like the professor, she was embarrassed that she'd never suspected he was not actually taking the classes. Zack had brought in spiral notebooks and taken notes during the lectures, but never once had Lillian spotted him doing homework or studying after class. She'd never seen a textbook in his room or backpack, either.

After spending some time in her room to decompress, Lillian headed to Zack's house herself, more angry than frightened. His car was gone from the driveway. One of Zack's roommates answered the door, wearing only pajama bottoms and holding a colorful glass bong in one hand. "Hey, what's up?"

"Is Zack around?"

"He's gone, man. He split, like, a week ago. He just packed up his shit in the space of a few minutes and sped off."

"He didn't give anyone any notice he was leaving?"

"Nope. Our landlord is really pissed. We're pissed too, because Zack paid a third of the rent. His number's disconnected. We think he left town, but we have no idea where he is. I'm really sorry, dude."

"Well, thanks for telling me what you know."

"No problem. Wish I knew more. Oh, and one weird thing I noticed when Zack was still here. He had wads of cash. Like, thousands. Would you know anything about that?"

"Seriously?!" Zack had never struck Lillian as someone who had much money, with his old beater of a car, the few identical changes of worn-out clothes he owned, and his barren bedroom.

"There was, like, this duffel bag in Zack's closet. One day when I was in Zack's room talking to him about something, it came open, and tons of cash spilled out. Zack flipped out, man. He shoved it back in the sack and said, 'You did not just see that.'"

"Maybe he was a drug dealer?"

"If he was, it wasn't pot he was selling, or else we probably would've been his top customers." The roommate laughed.

"I spotted that duffel bag in his closet. But I never saw what was in it. And I never saw any drugs."

"He was definitely hiding something, dude."

"Did he leave anything behind?"

"Not much. He took that duffel bag, of course. He took his laptop, his clothes, and shit. But the bed and desk are still in there. We lent them to him because he moved here with no furniture. If you want, you can go in and look around, see if there's something we missed. If you find out where he is, that'd be awesome."

Lillian went to the bedroom. The desk, wiped down and gleaming, held no signs of Zack, and when Lillian pulled open the drawers, all she found inside was a pen and pencil. She lifted the bare mattress and peeked under the bed. If Zack had stashed any secret items there, he'd taken them. The closet was an empty white cavity, with nothing but a few coat hangers. Zack had been gone long enough that only the faintest smears of his aura were left behind, no reverberations of any recent movement.

After that visit to Zack's house, Lillian looked elsewhere for information. Web searches turned up people who shared Zack's name but not his description. He seemed to have no social media presence. Lillian felt foolish, ashamed, and completely confused as to why anyone would pull off such a deception. None of this made any sense.

When his daughter Lillian called and revealed the shocking news about the ex-boyfriend posing as a student, Lou asked if she knew the names of Zack's family members. Lillian did not know his parents' names, but he'd told her of two siblings, Nicholas and Chelsea. Now Lillian wondered if this brother and sister were even real. Concerned for Lillian's safety, Lou wanted to know just what this Zack had been planning. Did he simply want to date Lillian that badly, or did he have more sinister intentions? Did this count as stalking?

Once he got off the phone, a very angry Lou combed through online phone directories. He called each Dunaway family in Grand Rapids, Michigan. The fourth person he reached was a Douglas Dunaway.

"Do you by any chance have a grown son named Zachariah?" Lou asked.

"Yup," the man replied in the rough sort of voice that might belong to a heavy smoker.

"Mr. Dunaway, do you have other children named Nicholas or Chelsea?"

"How do you know all my kids' names? Who the hell are ya? Some sort of scammer?"

"No, I'm not a scammer. I am a father too. My name is Lou Frazier."

"I've never heard of you. Really, who are ya?"

"I have a daughter named Lillian who dated your son Zachariah while at school."

"I never heard of your daughter either."

"Where is your son? Is he living with you now?"

"I honestly don't know where that boy is. This ain't the first time he's run off and told nobody where he was going."

"When did you see or hear from him last?"

"'Bout six months ago. He went to school in Colorado, and I thought he'd finally make something of himself. Then I heard he up and quit school. Might've ran down to Mexico again, but I can't be sure."

"My daughter did some detective work after your son vanished," Lou informed Douglas. "He lied. He was not even enrolled at that school. He just rented a room in town and sat in on classes to try to impress my daughter. He even lied about his age."

"Yeah, hate to say it, but Zack just ain't stable. I'm sorry your daughter fell for it. If he weren't a grown man, I'd look for him and whip his ass. I had to do that plenty when he was a boy; too bad he didn't learn nothing from it. Sorry I can't be of more help."

Douglas hung up.

A couple of weeks after Zack fled, a paper was due in technical writing. With the upheaval in her life, Lillian procrastinated on writing the bulk of it until the day before it was due.

When she handed back the papers, the professor made the students line up single file in the same order as the stack. To Lillian's horror, the lottery forced her to stand directly behind Avery Joseph.

Why couldn't everyone just line up in alphabetical order, leaving a safe cushion of people between them?

When a student glanced at her paper, frowned, and started an argument with the professor in her displeasure over her grade, the line went stagnant. Lillian's heart raced and her palms sweated. She tried her hardest to show no outward signs of distress.

Avery stood still and quiet, not glancing behind him, though he had to know Lillian was there. Lillian could not be sure whether it was her nerves or some deep-rooted self-sabotage instinct that opened her mouth.

"Hey."

Lillian wanted go back a few seconds in time and clap her hands over her lips. Did she have a death wish? Or maybe she was a little curious about him. Drawn like a moth to literal flame.

First there was silence from Avery, who cast a sideways glance behind him. And then he said, "Hey."

A few moments passed as other students chattered in the standstill line. Avery whispered, "You can hide your thoughts."

"Really? How?"

"I'll tell you somewhere else."

"Sure," she said, still aghast at the words coming out of her mouth. She reached into her book bag, wrapping her fingers around her small can of pepper spray. Like pepper spray was going to be any match against his powers. "Where do you want to go?"

"Dunno."

"What about Stevie's Coffee?" Stevie's, the same place where the now-deceased Tara Nicholson had thrown a drink into Lillian's face a year ago, was the first to pop into her anxious mind.

"Sure," Avery agreed.

"You know where it is?"

"Yeah."

"What time?"

"Uh... six."

"Six tonight? That works for me."

The line started to move again as the angry student at the front stormed away, grumbling that she was going to call a lawyer. Avery and Lillian took their papers, and then parted ways in silence as they returned to their seats, hers in the front of the room, his in the back. Lillian dashed out of the class as soon as it ended, and then could not focus on her homework after returning to her room. As her appointment with Avery drew closer, her fear mounted.

Simply not going was a possibility. Maybe the impolite way was also the safe way to get out of this trap she had foolishly locked herself in.

But that could also draw Avery's ire when the two of them returned to class. Maybe it was best to just head to Stevie's, see if Avery even showed up, get the conversation over with quickly, and ensure they stayed in public view at all times, where both would remain bound by their code of secrecy against using their powers.

Lillian drove the short distance rather than walking, in case a quick getaway became necessary. Once inside, she ordered a hot herbal tea and secured a booth by the front window, well within other customers' line of sight. She looked out the window at the wintry street misted with white fog as she waited for Avery.

It did not take long for him to arrive. After walking in, he glanced at her once, expressionless, and put in his order at the counter. After he came over to the booth with a steaming tea, took off his thick silver coat, and sat down across from Lillian, neither of them seemed to know what to say. Both struggled to meet each other's eyes.

"Can you see a lot in other people?" Lillian asked, making a conscious effort to keep her voice down.

"Depends on the person."

"What about me?"

"Not much."

"Whatever you saw in me, please don't spread it around."

"I don't."

"So, that trick you were going to show me?"

"Picture metal closing off your whole head."

Lillian tried it, focusing hard on a visualization of encasing her head in a thick armor of protective metal, hoping Avery had not lied to her to extract her secrets. This was deceptively simple. Just too easy.

"Do you think it's working?" Lillian asked.

"Yep."

"Can you see nothing at all, then?"

"Yeah, but there wasn't much before."

"Good. If you're not lying."

"I'm not."

A long, fidgety silence passed by as both of them looked down at their laps. Lillian broke the pause at last, checking over her shoulder to be sure no one was too close. "What can you do?"

"Powers?"

"Yeah."

"Not here." Avery shook his head.

"Where are you from?" Lillian asked, struggling to keep them talking instead of just sitting there, nervously staring at their hands.

"New Mexico."

"What town?"

"I grew up in Albuquerque."

"I've never been there. I want to check it out sometime."

"Ah."

"I heard they have this hot air balloon festival there. I bet it's pretty nice."

"Yeah."

Injecting life into this faltering conversation was a challenge for Lillian, who had never been skilled at small talk. Apparently, Avery was even worse at it.

"Do you have any brothers or sisters?" she asked.

"No."

With no siblings to inquire about, Lillian struggled that much harder to find the next thing to say. "I have one older sister," she revealed to Avery. "And a niece."

"Oh."

Another silence passed by. Even the wooden Zack Dunaway had been a more engaging conversationalist than Avery. Lillian looked forward to leaving. Not because she feared for her life like she was supposed to, but because she found this meeting awkward to the point of torture.

She thought of one more random question. "Do you like any video games?"

"Uhh... yes, actually."

"Which ones?"

"I like *Legend of Zelda* stuff."

"Cool! So do I! Did you ever play *Ocarina of Time*?"

"Yes. That was my favorite game."

"Mine too!"

Surprisingly, Avery was the next to ask a question. "Do you like role-playing games?"

"Never tried them. But I've always wanted to."

"At my house, there's, uh, gamer parties on Fridays."

"Are you inviting me?"

"Sure." Avery shrugged a bit.

"Will there be a lot of other people there?"

"Some. Not a lot. It's low-key."

"Do you live by yourself?"

"No. I've got three roommates."

"You said it was a house. But when I saw you last semester—I don't know if you remember me on Halloween—you were in the dorms."

"Yeah, I remember you. I moved in December."

Avery took a notebook from his backpack, tore a page out, and jotted down his address and cell phone number. Underneath, he wrote in bold capital letters, much stronger than his speech: *STARTS @ 6. CAN BRING FOOD AND/OR VIDEO GAMES.*

"I'll think about it." Lillian made no promises.

"I've got to go." Avery sipped the last of his tea. Nodding toward Lillian, he got up and left. Lillian put the piece of paper in her pocket and watched through the window as Avery walked to a 1980s-model pickup truck with a camper shell parked along the other side of the street and rode off into the fog. Once the truck was well out of sight, she headed home.

The following evening, without really thinking about it at first, Lillian got ready for the gaming party that Avery had invited her to. Her few friends on campus were busy and she did not have much homework for the weekend; she found herself bored. She purchased a box of chocolate chip cookies, stuffed it into her bag, and packed her portable Nintendo DS.

As Lillian took off with a printed map to Avery's house, she suddenly balked at her plan. This was supposed to go no further than a brief, noncommittal meeting. Maybe there was no party, and like a spider with a web ready to catch prey, Avery had set a trap.

Lillian wanted to at least look at the house from a distance so she could remember exactly where he lived. If she stayed in her vehicle, he didn't have to know she'd been near. Somehow, after she'd spent months turning Avery into the bogeyman, he seemed less threatening than what she'd already been through with the water people and her cousin Julius. And she hungered for more information. Had Avery been ordinary, Lillian might not have bothered heading to his house at all. His flat personality reminded her a little too much of Zack.

Lillian got lost. Not wanting to call Avery for help, she circled around until she finally found the right street and recognized his truck in a driveway. She parked down the street, scoping out the two-story Victorian-style house with lit windows and a small cluster of cars parked outside. A young couple, both with unremarkable auras, walked inside, carrying a large salad bowl covered with tinfoil.

Heart speeding up, Lillian finally made her way down the wet sidewalk and rang the doorbell. A fool, what a fool. Why didn't the fear that had been instilled in her from early childhood protect her from walking straight into dire mistakes such as this?

A middle-aged, large-bellied, bearded man opened the door. "Hello, you don't look familiar. Have you been here before?"

"No."

"My name is Richard." He stuck out a hairy hand for her to shake. "And you are?"

"Lillian."

"You're the one Avery told me about! Come on in, if you don't mind taking your shoes off and leaving them in the shoe rack by the door. I'm kind of funny about dirt. Ever play *Dungeons & Dragons*?"

"No, but I've heard of it."

"Our main dish tonight is pasta. We have meat sauce and vegetarian sauce. Serve yourself."

The living room was warm and casual, scattered with mismatched couches and futons and plants. Some people were gathered around the Wii console. Others mingled in the kitchen, ladling red sauce onto their dinner plates. A few others sat around the dining room table, rolling many-sided dice. The mellow mood comforted Lillian.

She was quick to spot Avery, the only person she recognized. In a voice still quiet, Avery encouraged her to help herself to dinner. "I made the veggie sauce."

Richard, the homeowner, led Lillian around, introducing her to all the strangers. Richard rented out rooms to three college students: Avery, who had a large upstairs bedroom to himself, and an engaged couple named Jared and Heather, who shared a room downstairs. Jared and Heather looked so similar they could pass for brother and sister with their curly brown hair and blue eyes.

Richard left Lillian's side and went into the kitchen to fix himself a plate of seconds. Lillian ate by herself, sitting on the bottom step of the stairs, feeling too shy to go up and talk to anyone. Just in case, she made a conscious effort to keep her guard up with the mind trick Avery had taught her yesterday.

Avery appeared with a plate balanced on his hand. "May I sit?"

"Yeah."

"I didn't expect you to come."

"You got me curious," Lillian admitted.

"I'm sorry if I sounded like a goof yesterday," Avery sighed. "I'm just really shy around new people. Tend to make a bad first impression. And, well, I was nervous."

"So was I. Contrary to what you might have heard, I don't bite. How did you meet all these people?"

"I met Jared during freshman year, and now we're pretty close. Richard hosts game nights at this comic book store we go to. I met the rest through them."

"Is Jared your closest friend?"

"The closest I have here at school. I also have a best friend back home."

"This bestie back home... is he, or she, you know... like you?"

"No. She has no idea."

Already, they knew things about each other that their closest friends didn't. Yet they hardly knew each other at all.

Avery helped Lillian to fill out a character sheet for *Dungeons & Dragons* so that she could learn to play if she came to the following week's game night. Avery was not surprised when she chose a druid for her character. His was an experienced sorcerer.

Lillian found it easier to get on with Avery than during their last meeting. If anything, she stuck close to him, the only familiar face. Now that he was less anxious and more responsive, talking to him rattled her less.

Tonight, a different person made her skin crawl.

A tall dark-haired guest named Ryan doggedly followed Lillian around the house. When she, Avery, and his roommate Jared played a quick board game, Ryan joined, bragging arrogantly about his skill and annoying everyone else. After the game ended, Lillian could not shake off Ryan.

"Do you have a boyfriend?" Ryan asked, following Lillian into the kitchen while she looked for a snack.

Lillian attempted to scare him off with her deadpan humor. "Yeah, I do. He runs on double-A batteries."

Ryan laughed uncomfortably. "Seriously, would you like to go on a date with me? I could take you out to dinner."

"No, thank you. I'm not dating right now." Even if Lillian weren't seeking time to herself after the roller coaster ride with Zack, she would not want to go out with someone who acted like this.

Ryan asked her out again just a few minutes later, like he hadn't heard her when she turned him down the first time. Even after Lillian rebuffed him, he would not take his eyes off her.

Avery took Lillian aside, still within earshot of Ryan. "You want to come upstairs and check out some of my stuff?"

No! the voice in her head warned. *He'll hurt you! He could rape you up there!*

Hopefully, Avery was hearing none of these thoughts, but he possibly sensed her balking. "No pressure," he added.

Ryan came toward them, his gaze set straight on Lillian like a lion on the prowl. Her skin prickled in discomfort again.

"I'll go up with you," she told Avery before she had a chance to think twice about her words. As they reached the top of the stairs, frightened thoughts barraged through her head again, the stories of rapes happening at crowded parties while the victim's friends remained oblivious to what went on in the next room. A perpetrator could press down on your windpipe so you couldn't even scream.

"That guy keeps asking me out and won't take no for an answer," Lillian confided once they got to Avery's room and shut the door.

"That's why I suggested we come up here. I could tell you were uncomfortable."

"I said I'm not looking for a relationship and that didn't stop him. Maybe I should have told him I have a boyfriend to make him leave me alone."

"You shouldn't have to lie. He should have stopped at 'no.' I'm going to tell Richard."

"You don't have to do that." As much as Lillian wished Ryan would back off, she was afraid to request that someone intervene on her behalf. She was a first-time visitor, not expecting these strangers to take her concerns seriously.

"Richard's already warned Ryan to stop being creepy to women, and honestly, I've wanted that guy gone for a long time. You can wait here. Lock the door if you need to."

After Avery left the room, Lillian locked the door and leaned against it. Here she was, alone in Avery's personal lair. Curious, she could not help but glance around. The large bedroom looked cozy, cluttered, and richly lived in, lit with holiday string lights and a pink salt crystal lamp. A mountain of scrunched-up blankets was piled on the wide bed, underneath a sloped ceiling. A scroll depicting a blue-haired anime character hung on the wall over the bed. A plastic bin contained balls of yarn, which caught Lillian's attention, as she'd learned to crochet a few years ago.

Drawings and paintings also captured Lillian's interest. Some were done in the manga style with huge-eyed, almost noseless characters, while a few of the watercolors were realistic, beautifully detailed. As someone who could barely draw stick figures, Lillian stared at the pictures with fascination and a bit of envy over the talent she did not inherit from her mother. The few times she'd tried painting with watercolors, they ran together and turned into mud. Crisp and clear, these paintings practically glowed.

A loud voice came up from downstairs, muffled through the floor. Someone yelled angrily.

Avery came back up several minutes later, and Lillian could tell, through his aura shining around the door, that it was him when he knocked. She put her mental defenses back up, unlocked the door, and let him in.

"Ryan is gone," Avery advised.

"Thank you."

"No problem."

"That artwork on the wall is really good. Did you draw and paint those?"

"Yes."

"I see you do watercolors. My mom used to do those, too. She sold some of them, and had some in an art gallery." Lillian paused before adding that last line about why her mother no longer painted. "She died."

"I'm sorry to hear that. My dad died too. Before I was born."

"You could make a career out of this talent."

"It's hard to make a career out of art. That's why it's my minor, not my major."

"I'd ask you to teach me how to draw, but I'm pretty hopeless at it."

"I think I could teach you. It takes some practice and changing your perspective."

"What can you do? I'm sure I already know. And now we're behind a closed door; no one is going to hear us."

"Fire. Create fire out of nowhere, basically. I'm also immune. I can't get burned. When I was little, I ran through a burning building. I don't remember it, though."

"Those hell-hounds I've heard about—like dogs—are those real?"

"Yes. But they last only for a few seconds. They tend to be a self-defense thing."

"That's amazing that you're immune to fire. If I had that talent, it would work out well for my future career goal."

"Which is?"

"I want to be a volcanologist. We'll see if that works out."

"That sounds like a cool job. What about you? Your abilities? Is it what I think it is?"

"What do you think it is? I'm not one of the mind readers, just so you know."

"My mom's friend talked about these people called necromancers. But she said they're all dead, so I was confused when I saw you. To be honest, I'm still confused."

"Did your mom's friend say they were bad and evil?"

"Yes. She told me they were dangerous."

"Most mages, if they find out we're still around, are either terrified of us or they have it out for us. And they're the ones who killed most of us to begin with."

"You're saying that you really are a necromancer?"

This could be the death of her. "Yes."

"What are you able to do?"

"It's hard to explain. If you're a fire person, I can best be described as an earth person. I'm good with plants. And can reanimate things that are dead."

"It really is true. You can create zombies."

"In a way, I guess. But don't worry. You won't see zombies lurching around, like..." Lillian imitated a B-rated horror movie zombie, shuffling with arms held rigid in front of her body. "Braaaains!" she groaned.

For the first time, she made Avery laugh.

Someone else's weight creaked up the stairs. Richard, the homeowner, knocked. "Everything okay up here?"

"Yes," Avery told him.

Richard turned toward Lillian. "I wanted to tell you how sorry I am that my guest was bothering you tonight. He's gone now. I told him to leave and not come back."

"Seriously, he's banned for good? I heard yelling. Was he mad?"

"Yes, he was very angry and it took two guys to escort him out. No one was hurt. I don't want you to worry. We'll keep an eye out to make sure he doesn't come back. If he does, we'll call the police."

"I feel bad that all this shouting and drama happened because of me."

"Don't spend one second blaming yourself. Ryan was already on his last chance in this house. I want all of my guests to feel safe and have fun."

After the three came back downstairs to mingle, Lillian found herself sitting on barstools with Richard and Jared in the kitchen. Most of the leftover food was put away, and the space had grown quieter.

"Lillian, there's a pitcher of iced tea in the fridge," Richard pointed out. "Can you grab that and put it on the counter?"

Lillian got up, reached into the refrigerator, and pulled out the glass pitcher filled with amber tea and clinking ice cubes. Just as she shut the door, she slipped in her socks on the linoleum and fell. Still in her hand, the pitcher hit the floor along with her body and shattered. Struggling to get up on the slick puddle of tea and ice, Lillian skidded on her palms and felt a stinging sensation in her right hand. Ignoring it, she grabbed at the refrigerator, swiping with her wet hands until she got them around the door handle and pulled herself up. Richard rushed to her side as a greater sharpness bit into the sole of her foot. Numbly, Lillian looked down. A triangular piece of glass jutted out.

"Don't pull that... out," Richard said too late as Lillian did just that. Blood bubbled out from the cut in her blue striped sock as she limped across the slick white linoleum toward the kitchen counter. She slipped and fell again in a pink mixture of tea and blood as Richard caught her by the arm. More guests rushed over, urging Lillian to sit down and lean against the wooden kitchen cabinets, pressing rags and towels to her hand and foot. A voice asked if she needed to go to the emergency room, and she mumbled that she did not think so.

Avery was the next to come and kneel beside Lillian, checking if she was okay.

"I think I'm okay. I can't believe I'm so clumsy that I can't even get a tea pitcher without slicing myself into pieces."

"Can I try putting something on those cuts?"

"Sure."

Lillian figured that Avery would go get some ointment, but instead, he applied gentle pressure through the wrapped towels, closing his eyes and going still. Not sure what he was doing, Lillian grew a bit unnerved at his touching her, even through the towels. A faint, tingling warmth penetrated first her foot, and then her hand.

Richard ordered almost everyone to stay out of the kitchen until it was cleaned with bleach and cleared of glass shards. Despite his house rules against indoor shoes, he put on a pair of boots, as well as rubber gloves.

Avery wrapped Lillian's hand and foot in gauze from the household first aid kit. "Maybe driving home isn't a good idea," he suggested. "I could give you a ride home in your car. Then somebody could pick me up."

Though she had taken the risk of entering his bedroom and he was nothing but respectful, Lillian hesitated at the idea of sitting in a car alone with Avery at night. At the wheel, he would be in complete control. But there might be a simple way to get out of this.

"Can you drive a stick?" Lillian asked him. Most people her age didn't know how. Inheriting Denny's Jeep had left her with no choice but to learn.

"Yes," Avery affirmed. Now declining his offer was going to get more complicated.

"Um, I'm not sure if I'm comfortable getting a ride from you. I hope you don't take offense."

"None taken. Would you be okay with Richard taking you home? I'd have Heather take you, but she can't drive a stick."

"Yeah, Richard can take me."

Richard interrupted his cleaning to give Lillian the ride back to campus. She was apologetic while he reassured her, "We're only human. Accidents happen." He got out and asked if she needed assistance as she limped to her dorm, confirmed once more if she would be all right, and then waited outside for his other tenant, Jared, to pick him up.

Lillian awoke late the next morning and removed the bandages, intending to replace them, only to discover well-healed silver slits on her hand and foot. She had not expected the cuts to join back together and fade this quickly. Walking barely hurt at all. How strange.

The following week, Lillian watched for Avery in class. On Tuesday, he did not show up. Lillian had decided not to go to another game night at his house. She had a few reasons, the first one being her concern that the creepy man who'd followed her around might come back. Richard had claimed to ban him permanently, but people too often said things without meaning them, and nothing was stopping him from relenting and giving Ryan another chance.

Another deterrent was Lillian's embarrassment after turning the kitchen into a bloody mess last week. Though the broken pitcher was purely a freak accident, Lillian might have left Avery and his roommates with a bad impression.

When Lillian went to class on Thursday, Avery was there. He walked up beside her as they left the building, asking if she'd be coming to the next evening's game night.

"I was afraid you guys wouldn't want me there again," she replied.

"Why not?"

"That whole incident in the kitchen. Making a mess."

"Look, everyone knows it was just an accident. It's fine. How are you healing up?"

"Strangely well!"

Lillian decided to go over to the house a second time, just to keep things friendly and smoothed over.

After finding a lot of meatless foods in the kitchen, Lillian learned of the two vegetarian regulars at the parties, including Avery. Lillian, a staunch meat-eater who loved nothing more than a good Philly cheesesteak, had to restrain herself from teasing Avery, the way she would a close friend.

Lillian had fun that night playing her first-ever game of *Dungeons & Dragons*, with Richard serving as dungeon master and Avery helping to teach her the guidelines.

The man who had been kicked out last time never came back. No other guests crossed any boundaries.

Though she had not wanted to make this a habit, Lillian attended the next party, and then the next, craving more chapters of imaginative play. As she got to know a few of the regulars, she felt more at home, and the Friday night stress relief gave her something to look forward to at the end of the week. Lillian tried to interest Bridget and Tim in the game nights, but neither of them liked role-playing games. Even without her friends coming along, she enjoyed herself.

The only thing that kept her from relaxing one hundred percent was keeping her guard up around Avery and shielding her brain with the visualization of metal, though he said he could hardly see anything in her mind without it. It slipped from time to time, and if he noticed, he didn't say anything.

Avery's unlikely new friend kept making it back to the household game nights. They said hello to each other after their shared class, but found themselves more at ease chatting through instant messaging. Avery had the sense that Lillian relaxed a bit more behind their screens in the comfort of their bedrooms, not having to worry about placing imaginary metal around her head despite his assurances that she was nearly impenetrable. It came as a relief that she was no longer afraid of him, and that he finally had someone at school who truly got it, who knew the intricacies of mage life. And it didn't hurt that she was kind, and a good listener. They shared enough about themselves that Lillian edged from the acquaintance zone into a forbidden friendship.

Most of their chats revolved around the basics, what movies, music, and games they enjoyed. They had a few things in common, besides their favorite childhood video game and their biggest shared secret. They'd both been raised by a single parent who had them late in life, with the other parent dead. While Lillian carried some fond, if vague, memories of her mother, Avery had never met his father, who got drunk and crashed his car into a wall, never finding out about the unintended pregnancy. Avery only knew his father through the stories from his mother and the relatives he connected with online: born in the Philippines, raised in the Aleutian Islands of Alaska, and orphaned at a young age. He'd worked on a fishing boat and then relocated to California to join a rock band. This father had carried the mage trait. Whether there were any full-blown mages on that side, Avery did not know, not wanting to ask through social media. Maybe if he someday visited his uncle in Alaska or those cousins in the Philippines, he'd find out.

Avery's mother's family history got disturbing, like the stuff of Southern Gothic horror stories. As he told Lillian these tales in person, walking from class, she got more and more curious. Avery's grandmother in South Carolina, the wealthy descendant of a once-famous tobacco dynasty, was a cruel, racist, and hypocritical woman who had kicked his mother out at the age of sixteen. She'd recently passed away, and hardly anyone had shed a tear. Avery had met his grandmother only once, and it was not a nice conversation. From reading her mind clear as day, and also speaking with one of her former servants who resided in the same nursing home, Avery knew the truth. While his grandmother claimed to have been raped by the servant's brother, it happened the other way around. This drunken use of force led to his mother's conception, and later, the gossip and racism directed at her with the biological father's mixed Black and Native American ancestry. He and Avery's grandmother had both had the mage blood.

Though he had fun getting acquainted with Lillian, another female classmate dominated a much bigger chunk of Avery's thoughts. Susannah Garcia was in his figure painting class. A short young woman with long, flowing, curly dark hair and thick lashes, she also had a nurturing personality. Warm and extroverted, she put people at ease right away. Avery saw through her very well. Mind reading could give the false impression of being someone's best friend, and in this case, it led to unrequited love with an excruciating twist. When models posed nude in their painting class, Avery thought more about Susannah standing behind her canvas a few feet away than about the naked people right in front of them.

Crushing on Susannah was a mistake. She barely noticed Avery. His face registered in her mind as only a blur. She didn't know his name. And that hurt.

Avery never did approach Susannah, much less introduce himself. A bigger factor than his shyness was the small, glittering diamond ring on her finger. Though Avery had never met him, he knew all he cared to know about Susannah's fiancé. Controlling and manipulative, he scarcely allowed her to talk to other people. Many of her friendships faded into nothing; she rarely went out anymore except to go to class or work. Susannah mistook this jealousy for sweetness and concern. Avery had no way to warn her to get out of the relationship without sounding like a stalker or giving away his powers to ordinary people. It ate at Avery that he could not give Susannah his advice. She would likely not want to hear it even from someone close to her, and she'd already been pressured to shut most of her friends and family out.

One afternoon, Lillian came by the house to visit. She was curious to learn the basics of knitting, a hobby Avery had stopped hiding from his friends and classmates. All of Avery's roommates were out, leaving the two of them alone in the residence for the first time. Lillian still did not fully trust him. Though he did not try to pry into her mind, he sensed the opaque visions of metal she still guarded herself with.

They sat together with some needles and cheap yarn, and after a bit of confusion, Lillian managed to get started on a simple dish rag pattern. As she needed less and less help to keep going, they talked about other things.

Mind reading came up, and Avery revealed his feelings for Susannah, though it embarrassed him to let that hit the air.

"You think you and Susannah would make a great match?" Lillian asked.

"Definitely. But she doesn't even know my name. To her, I'm just some random dude in the background. And even if she knew me, that doesn't mean she'd be interested in me."

"Have you thought about saying hi to her? I mean, as a shy person, I know that saying hi isn't easy. But she'll notice you."

"The problem is, Susannah is engaged to a guy. And he's a jerk. He's possessive. She hardly has any friends left, thanks to him. She thinks that kind of jealousy is normal and he's just being sweet. I hope she gets out, but there's nothing I can do since she doesn't know me."

"Oh, man. That's really rough, that you have to watch her in that awful relationship and your hands are tied."

"Exactly."

"Zack, the one I just broke up with, was jealous too... not wanting me around men unless they were gay, constantly calling. It got really exhausting. And you know how that ended in a dumpster fire. I really hope Susannah figures out that it's not normal or sweet and gets that guy out of her life. Until she sees the light, there's no easy solutions."

"Yeah, it sucks. That isn't the worst part about being a mind reader, though. You wouldn't believe the kinds of twisted things people do and the awful secrets they have.

And no matter how nice they are, people think a lot of hurtful things that they keep to themselves, stuff you're better off not knowing."

"I can understand how it would get hard. You would say everybody has secrets?"

"Of course. If I can get a good read on them, I see their gross habits that they do when no one's looking. Their trips to the bathroom, what they do in the bedroom. The worst part is people who've gotten away with terrible crimes—like killing someone—and can't even admit it to themselves. When I see it, I can't report it because that person was just some stranger I walked past at the mall and I don't have any evidence."

"Yikes."

"I've called an anonymous tip line a couple of times, but I don't know what happened to those people. Even when there isn't something horrible, sometimes books and movies get spoiled before I get the chance to watch or read them. I see things that are just... disappointing. Like that my roommate Heather is a habitual liar, and Jared's kind of in denial about it, since they've been together since they were twelve."

"I barely know Heather, since she kind of acts like I'm invisible during game nights, but that sucks that she's like that. This is totally off the subject, but I'm not sure how our families would react to us hanging out. I don't think they would like it. How do I tell them about this?"

"I just wouldn't tell them."

"But unlike Heather, I feel bad if I'm not telling the truth. So I don't know."

"I'm all for honesty too, but sometimes, what people don't know won't hurt them. Think of it this way: us mages are lying all the time anyway, hiding our powers from the world. I would wait."

"What do you remember about Mom?"

The question didn't quite feel safe as it left Lillian's mouth.

Evelyn and Lillian sat across from each other in in a restaurant booth. Tucked beside her, baby Natasha was strapped into her car seat, sucking on her chubby sausage-roll fingers. Evelyn and Jonathan had brought her to Colorado on her first road trip, staying in a hotel for a few nights.

It was the first time the two had ever discussed their mother except in passing, during that ominous attempt with the spirit board when they were kids, or that one time when they both acknowledged that Mother's Day got harder for them year after year, watching other people take their mothers out to dinner and buy them flowers. Evelyn and Lillian were always ignored on that dreaded holiday. No one knew what to say to them.

"I remember Mom spent a lot of time painting, of course," said Evelyn. "And she was sweet. But she seemed a bit like a fun aunt or babysitter who came and went. It was weird compared to other families. She actually moved out before you were born, and then came back. She bounced around, and stayed someplace in New Hampshire. Some artist colony."

"Whoa, I knew she'd drifted around some, but I didn't know she'd been in an artist colony. Or that she ever lived in New Hampshire."

"The colony didn't work out and Mom decided to get back with Dad. Then I begged for a brother or sister and you were born. After she had you weaned, she found that new... boyfriend... and started going back and forth before she moved in with him."

"It sounds like maybe she didn't know who or what she wanted."

"Maybe she was just a wandering spirit, but I always had the feeling that there was something our parents weren't telling us."

"I do have some memories of her. But you had a lot more time with her than I did."

"Wow, you can remember that far back? You were so little."

"I even kind of remember it like you described, that fun lady who would come visit and bring presents, and then go back to D.C. to be with Karl."

Evelyn swallowed hard. Took a gulp of her iced tea and swallowed again. "I remember the last time I spoke to Mom."

"What happened?"

"She called. I was at home, downstairs. I think you'd been put down for a nap. Dad was on the porch with a cigarette. I answered the phone."

"What did she say?"

"She said, 'Evelyn, I have something really important to tell your father. Is he there?' I said he was outside having a smoke and offered to go get him. She said, 'Nah, I know he won't come inside.' Dad was so careful about shielding us from secondhand smoke. Then Mom said something like, 'Just tell him I want to see him as soon as I can. I want to talk in person.' It was the last time I heard her voice. I forgot to tell Dad until it was too late. Just two days later, she was dead. The very next day, Dad quit smoking, saying he didn't want to die on us too."

"I remember his story about quitting cold turkey, doing it for us. You never found out about the important thing Mom wanted to talk about?"

"No, to this day, I have no idea. I still beat myself up with the what-ifs, and wonder if it would've changed anything... probably not."

After Lillian returned to campus that night, that conversation nagged at her like a splinter in her skin. What was their mother calling about, so close to her death? What did she know?

On Friday, Lillian skipped a few not-so-important class periods and spent much of the day with her sister and brother-in-law. They drove out into the mountains and had a picnic. Later, they window-shopped and enjoyed some downtime in Stevie's Coffee, drinking tea as Evelyn bounced Natasha in her lap.

A text message came in on Lillian's phone. Richard, Avery's roommate, announced that tonight's gaming party would be a special one with traditional board and card games only. He asked if she was coming. Lillian typed a response that she had company and could not go. Richard replied that Evelyn and Jonathan were invited, baby and all.

Lillian asked if they were interested, expecting them to say no, since Evelyn was not into games of any sort. After giving it a few moments of thought, Evelyn surprised Lillian and agreed to go. "Who knows, it might be fun."

Later, as they pulled up to Richard's house, Lillian's stomach hardened into a bowling ball of anxiety. Here was a branch of her very own family, about to meet some of her new friends, including the one person who should be expressly forbidden. In Evelyn's eyes, Avery would look no different from anyone else there. The only one who could tell was Natasha, four months old, unable to talk, and very unlikely to remember this night. Just a couple of months ago, Lillian would not have even let Avery near her baby niece. Now she trusted him just enough to not hurt her family. And she'd mentioned Natasha's unexpected abilities once or twice.

But what if Avery could read Evelyn's mind? If he saw into her well enough, he would discover lots of details, including the thing Lillian had never told him about and hoped he'd never seen hints of: Julius. She would be embarrassed if any of her friends found out about the abuse. They could start treating her differently and looking down upon her as a fragile, broken porcelain doll. Lillian did not want their pity.

When Lillian and her family members arrived at the party, the living room filled with delighted screeches and squeals, the high-pitched kind that only happened when a baby appeared in the room. Once the initial wave of excitement subsided, Lillian found herself holding Natasha as Jonathan and Evelyn socialized with guests. Avery walked over to say hi. Natasha noticed him, craning her chubby head to follow him with her huge, fascinated green-flecked hazel eyes.

Evelyn played poker with Richard and some of the guests, but Natasha soon started fussing, cranky and tired. Richard offered to let her nap up in his bedroom, away from the noise of the party. Evelyn fetched a collapsible playpen from her van, went upstairs, fed Natasha, and put her to bed. This allowed Evelyn and Jonathan to stay later than their normal bedtime. Evelyn admitted to Lillian that she hadn't had fun like this since before her daughter's birth.

Jonathan and Evelyn left with a groggy baby, only to reunite the following day. Lillian could not remember when she had last bonded with her sister like this. They met Bridget, Lillian's roommate.

On Saturday evening, the two sisters went out to dinner alone while Jonathan stayed behind at the hotel to watch Natasha. Evelyn gave Lillian her personal opinion on the friends she'd met. "I'm not sure what I thought of that Bridget, with her blue hair and that ring in her nose and all. But I guess that's not my kind of fashion."

"Yeah, I remember you freaking out when I showed you pictures of my high school friend, Christian."

"Oh, yeah, how can I forget that green hair and those stretched earlobes?"

"And what if I told you that when Bridget got her nose pierced, I tagged along and got a piercing too?" Lillian lifted up her shirt a bit to reveal the blue-jeweled barbell in her belly button.

"What did you do to your stomach?" Evelyn gasped, laughing a little. "Don't let Dad see that. I guess I shouldn't judge people so hard for their personal style. But if Natasha starts getting nose rings when she's a teenager, I think I'm going to tear my hair out."

"By the time she's a teenager, I bet poodle skirts will be back in style and you'll be missing blue hair and nose rings."

They laughed.

"Those people I met last night... Richard seemed like a nice guy, pretty gregarious, a lot of fun, if a little weird."

"I like how quirky he is."

"Jared—that's the young brown-haired guy, right? He seemed like a boy-next-door type. He and his girlfriend looked like they make a good couple. And that guy with the black hair and glasses... what was his name again?"

"Avery?"

"Yeah, that's the one. I talked to him a little. Tasha seemed really taken with him. He seemed really shy, but friendly. Is he single?"

"Yeah. Why do you ask?"

"He's kind of a cutie. Maybe you two are interested in each other?"

"No, we're just friends. He's not my type. We don't have much in common." Lillian had already gone against the rules pounded into her all of her life by hanging around Avery. Even if she wasn't on a break from dating, she would not cross that red line. She and Avery had no glimmers of physical or romantic attraction. And that was for the best.

"That's understandable," said Evelyn. "Once you're in the friend zone, you stay there. And didn't you just recently break up with someone?"

"Yeah, that too." Lillian told Evelyn more of the story about Zack, his lie about his age, and then his disappearance.

"God, what an ass!" Evelyn exclaimed. "Promise me that if this man ever tries to contact you again, keep your guard up, and do not get sucked back in."

After Evelyn's departure, Lillian wanted to see Avery alone. He readily agreed, hinting that he had a lot to tell her. She was antsy with curiosity about whether he'd read Evelyn's mind. Though Avery was cramming for a test right before spring break, he found time to meet in the middle of the week, visiting Lillian in her dorm room while Bridget was in class. He lounged on her bed while she relaxed in her desk chair.

"Just curious, were you able to read Evelyn? Don't tell me all her secrets and everything, but I'm wondering."

"It wasn't the clearest read, but I was able to get the basics. She's pretty smart. But she is chronically stressed out because she pushes herself way too hard. The inside of her head is like well-organized chaos."

"Pushing herself, making herself sick, not getting enough sleep... she was like that in high school too, and it worried my dad to no end. Were you able to pick up anything from her past? Like my teenage years?" Lillian really hoped that the answer would be no.

"Not really. When someone is harder to read, I mostly get what they're thinking in the moment and a few foggy memories."

"I am going to ask if you did see one thing, which both me and my dad have wondered about, but can't ask. Who is Natasha's father?"

"Definitely Jonathan. It was actually on her mind at the party. She feels like you and your dad have talked about her and acted kind of suspicious around the baby. I'm guessing Jonathan has water people in his family and that's why it happened."

"Evelyn doesn't know anything about mages, does she? I was always told to keep it from her."

"As far as I could tell, she doesn't know. But she feels the rest of your family has some kind of secret. Evelyn had other stuff on her mind, too. Problems in her marriage."

"Oh, no! I thought they were a happy couple. And they just got married a year ago!"

"They're fighting. Jonathan's not helping out around the house. Evelyn doesn't want any more kids because she got so sick when she was pregnant. Jonathan wants more, and he doesn't want to adopt."

"Why would he pressure her to get pregnant again? She was on bed rest. It affected her health."

"Jonathan doesn't want Natasha to be an only child. He hates only children. He thinks all of them are spoiled brats, and kids need siblings to be normal."

"Seriously? That's so silly! Having, or not having, siblings is out of our control. You're an only child, right? So that means that you would be on Jonathan's shit list?"

"Yeah, I would've been. I'm an only child unless you count the babies my mom lost. She had four miscarriages, I think, before she had me."

"The poor lady. She must have been really grateful for you."

"Yeah, she was pretty shocked when I came along. Jonathan is ridiculous. He has lots of biases. And Evelyn thinks he's cheating on her."

"Dare I ask... were you able to read Jonathan? Is he cheating?"

"I could see Jonathan all the way through." Avery's expression grew tense. "If I tell you, you'll keep it between us, right?"

"Of course."

"I don't even know where to start. Jonathan's cheating with his coworker and having an emotional affair with some girl online. I really just wanted to take Evelyn aside and tell her everything, but I couldn't prove it to her, not without breaking the code. She's going to have to find out for herself."

"That's so sad. Maybe we could mail her an anonymous envelope with Jonathan's passwords, or maybe she'll find out on her own. She is going to end up hurt."

"What have you heard about how they met?"

"They met in college in Georgia, and he took her out to dinner. That's all I know."

"You don't know anything about your uncle being involved?"

"Huh? No. Which uncle?"

"Gerald."

"You're saying Uncle Gerald has something to do with the relationship? Did he set them up?"

"Yes, he did, and Evelyn doesn't even know."

"What the hell?! Do tell me more."

"Jonathan had a class with Evelyn, but figured she was out of his league because lots of guys were after her. He was also really stressed out about money and student loans, and just feeling lonely. He was eating at a fast food place one day. Then guess who came and sat down next to him?"

"Uncle Gerald? In a fast food restaurant? That's not a place you'd normally find him. He must have been following Jonathan."

"I'm sure he was. Gerald introduced himself and made some chit-chat. Then he brought up Evelyn, saying they'd make a great match. Jonathan brushed that off, telling Gerald that such a hot girl wouldn't want him, and that he'd watched Evelyn turn guys down because she was so busy. Gerald coached him on how to talk to Evelyn and recommended a place to eat that she really liked. Then Gerald gave Jonathan his phone number and said the thing that really blew his mind. If Jonathan dated Evelyn and the relationship worked out, Gerald would pay for his education."

"Holy shit! Gerald's not even paying for my education. Didn't pay for Evelyn's, either. Did Gerald hold up that end of the deal?"

"Yes, he did. But if Jonathan tells anybody that Gerald was behind it, the deal's off and he has to pay Gerald back."

"But... *why?* That's so strange. Did Gerald set them up because Jonathan has mage blood? Was he hoping they'd have kids? Mage kids?"

"It's a possibility. Gerald didn't tell Jonathan the reason. Like Evelyn, Jonathan has no idea that mages are even a thing."

Excerpt from The Autobiography of Gerald Frazier: Architect of a New World

On September 1, 1959, I became a father! My daughter, Theresa Marie, was born. Enid and I had been married for about a year. A survivor of childhood polio, Enid was in delicate health, and the pregnancy and delivery were hard on her body. The doctor warned her to have no more children.

Theresa was not an easy baby. She had colic. People have been puzzling for ages about why some infants scream for hours on end, but at least in my daughter's case, I got the answer. It was stomachaches from the doctor-recommended homemade formula we mixed for her, and general infantile feelings of frustration. While it was a relief to always know why she was crying, it also frustrated me when I couldn't do a damn thing to make her feel better.

Most people in those days began having children quite young. We were in our early twenties, and most around us had babies, but now I see just how young and unprepared we were, particularly for a high-maintenance baby and the exhaustion that came with it. Enid fell into a depression and broke down in sobs several times when she could not cope with the crying.

Though she carried the trait in her blood, Theresa was not a mage. If I understand the genetics right, there was no way she could have been, since Enid did not carry the trait. Both parents need the right genes. I'm certain it is recessive.

At the time of Theresa's birth, my understanding of inheritance and genetics was poor. I went to the library and began doing research in order to change that.

One day I took a walk in the park down the street from our apartment complex, away from the incessant wails of the screaming baby. I sat under a tree raining down yellow fall leaves, relishing the peace and quiet, with no one else nearby to disrupt my thoughts with their own.

At that very moment, it occurred to me. Enid and I would likely never have another child. After I had studied enough Punnett squares in the library, which show the likelihood of children inheriting genetic traits, I knew we would probably never have necromancer children even if we bred like rabbits. Even among most of my cousins on my mother's side, the trait had already been bred out.

Why did I want a mage child, unlike my sister Sarah who already had one? Sarah wrote in her letters to me about her misery and overwhelm with her little boy, though he was too young to come into his powers. Denny was a destructive, furniture-scaling child that ten wild horses couldn't keep up with. But I'd be proud to have a necromancer child, even one as energetic as my nephew. I wanted to repopulate the world with necromancers so that we could return to the power and glory we once had!

I wanted to get back at the world for decimating our numbers and then trying to cruelly stamp out the last of us. After the rushed emigration from our homeland, stowing away on that ship, a few of us had been surviving for centuries. That was all we'd been doing. Just trying to stay under the radar and survive, even as a couple of us fought in our new country's wars. We had never really belonged.

For me, this wasn't enough. I didn't want us to live in obscurity like we did for the past two hundred years, and then die out and be forgotten. I wanted our numbers to swell. I wanted an army. I wanted a revolution! I wanted it to be payback time for our centuries of suffering and being misunderstood.

How was I going to accomplish that?

Exposed

❖⟫ ·◆· ·⟪❖

"Orbie?" Avery called, holding the handful of Milk-Bones tighter and tighter as he walked through the tall, fragrant trees. "Orbie, where are you?"

He was enjoying a low-key spring break at the same place where he'd spent his early childhood, and where he'd been born, literally. The expansive ranch where his mother's longtime friends, Ralph and Mindy, had lived for decades, a cozy house surrounded by green, dry forest and tall grasses. Grateful to be back here, Avery had so many happy memories of these grounds, of exploring the surrounding nature and spotting deer and revealing bugs under rocks.

Upon arrival yesterday, he had a few wistful thoughts of his crush, Susannah. A nature lover who enjoyed hikes, she'd be in heaven if he showed her this place. Like anything with Susannah, that would never happen. She was still engaged to that possessive man, and still did not know Avery's name. Avery stayed in his own lane.

Right now, Susannah fell to the back of Avery's mind. He'd been uneasy since yesterday, when Ralph and Mindy said they'd recently dealt with a prowler on the property. Their friend, the midwife who had delivered him, decided to rehome her dog, Orbie, and Ralph and Mindy took him in the hopes that he would guard the ranch. They'd gotten a phone call in the middle of that conversation yesterday, revealing that the strange man was arrested for sneaking around on a neighbor's property.

Still, something was not right.

Today, Avery came outside to take Orbie for a walk, a little concerned when he did not see the dog anywhere. He searched further and wider from the house, calling the dog's name with a handful of treats to lure him. "Hey, Orbie! I have bones!"

The dog's aura trail, circling all around the house and weaving through the nearby trees, was difficult to tease apart at first. But as he widened his own circle, Avery found the freshest spot where it branched off. As he followed the trail, headed toward the back of the property, a chill washed over Avery's body. He did not have a good feeling about whatever lay ahead. A dead silence smothered the woods. The birds in the trees had stopped chirping.

As he continued calling for Orbie and the dog didn't come, not so much as a rustle off in the trees, Avery's unease intensified. And so did the sense of nearby humans. Ones he didn't know. The hair stood up on the back of his neck.

"Hello? Orbie? Who's there?" Avery reached the low fence that divided the property from the surrounding forest. Where Orbie's trail crossed it, the rusty old barbed-wire fence had collapsed into the grass. Avery stepped over it.

He clamped a hand to his mouth, stomach turning.

An animal hung from a tree, throat slit. A dark circle was soaked into the soil beneath, blood so fresh he could smell it.

Orbie. Some monster had killed him. Who would do this to an innocent dog?!

The essence of other people, strange people, rushed up from behind. Before Avery could turn around, something cracked sharply at the back of his head, splitting the skin. He saw stars as his glasses fell and his legs liquefied, giving way under him. A hand brought a chemical-smelling cloth to his face.

As Avery's eyes opened, the world was blurry, upside down. His head, throbbing and aching terribly, hung beneath his body.

Like the murdered dog he'd stumbled upon, he hung from a tree branch by a rope fastened painfully tight around his ankles. Another rope pinned his hands behind his back. Standing in a semicircle around him were figures in white robes.

It was like a bad dream—the cult that had haunted the area a long time ago, back in the 1950s, killing people and animals to collect their blood for rituals. Avery's mother had seen long-gone visions of them during her pregnancy with him. While he'd only read about them in a few old newspaper articles, he'd always had an intuitive knowledge of this group. They'd all been arrested decades ago, the members either dead or still rotting in prison.

They didn't exist anymore. If Avery closed his eyes, he'd wake up from this nightmare.

Opening his eyes again unveiled the same vision. This was no bad dream; this was real life, happening right this minute. Blurbs of thoughts filtered from a few of their heads as they shuffled around, murmuring and grabbing a bowl and a knife for their next ritual sacrifice: him. The grandson of the group leader arrested decades ago had decided to revive his ancestor's cult. Here he was, with his small but growing army. The New Men of Krokpa, a once male-only group who now recruited women too.

With his disoriented mind, Avery sent out silent distress calls to his mother, hoping against hope that she'd receive them and that they hadn't already killed her. Their powers had given the two a mental connection since birth. One knew when the other was in trouble.

Yes, she was alive! And getting closer! But not quickly enough. The leader of the ritual grabbed the long knife, approaching Avery with his face drawn.

If Avery wanted to get out of this alive, he was running out of options, unable to shake himself loose from the rope binding his legs unless he wanted to lose time fumbling around with his telekinesis and risk falling and breaking his neck once the knot was undone.

The firm words echoed through Avery's head from the day after he prematurely left the eighth grade. *You must never, ever use those powers ever again.*

Without hesitation, Avery had made that vow. The powers were dangerous and unpredictable; even something intended to be a small push could quickly spiral out of control.

But as the knife drew closer to his throat, he struggled against the mental block of that years-old promise.

Screams of pain broke out.

Spring break was over too soon. Once again, Lillian looked forward to the weekly gaming party on Friday. But to her disappointment, she received a mass email from Richard, the homeowner, informing the regulars that his elderly parents had come to visit, forcing him to cancel the parties for the next couple of weeks.

After those two weeks had passed, the regularly scheduled game nights came back into effect.

As Lillian got excited to return, she realized she had not heard from Avery since before spring break. As they did not speak on a daily basis, it took a while to notice his silence. And she'd seen him in class only once since the break ended. When Lillian got held up talking to the professor after class, she did not get the chance to say hi to her newest friend until he was already gone.

Did he get sick? It was not like him to skip class.

When Lillian arrived for her first game night in weeks, she glanced around the house. Fewer guests than usual gathered around board games on the floor, and Avery was nowhere to be found downstairs.

As Lillian put together a plate of food, Richard placed a hand on her shoulder. "Were you looking for Avery?"

"Kind of, yeah. I haven't talked to him lately and I'm just wondering how he's doing."

"Not that great, I'm afraid."

"Is he sick? Did something happen?"

"Something happened. He kind of wants it private and doesn't want the whole world to know, but you've been a good enough friend to him that I think I can tell you. He had a pretty rough spring break. I don't know the whole story. I gather that he and his mom were visiting somebody down in New Mexico, and then they were all kidnapped and attacked. Thank goodness they all managed to get away."

"Oh, no! That's awful! Who kidnapped them?" This really alarmed Lillian. Was this a mage conflict, similar to what had happened after Evelyn's wedding?

"You're not gonna believe this—it was a cult. This group of weird people who were wearing white togas or something like that. They were hiding out near his friends' house. I think they all got arrested after that. I hope."

"Did anybody get hurt?"

"Yeah, Avery and his friends got bopped on the head. Avery got a minor concussion. But they all recovered just fine. His professors are giving him some breaks. He said he might try to come out tonight if he feels ready, but apparently he isn't. I'd give him some space if I were you."

Lillian played video games on her own for a little while, feeling a bit guilty for enjoying herself while Avery was holed up in his room, recovering from something scary. Promising to return soon, Lillian drove back to the campus to gather a couple of her self-help books about healing from trauma, recommended by her psychiatrist back home. With her favorite blue glitter gel pen, she wrote on a piece of paper: *I have found these helpful in the past. Borrow them for as long as you need, or not. If you want me to take these back, it's no problem. Lil.*

After tucking the note into one of the books, Lillian hurried back to Richard's house and crept up the stairs, going a bit against Richard's advice. Lillian quietly set the books down in the hallway outside Avery's bedroom, determined not to disturb him. Just as she turned to go back downstairs, Avery opened his door.

"Did you need something?" he asked.

"I was just leaving some books you might be interested in. You can borrow them, or you can give them back."

"I'll check them out."

"Richard told me some of what happened, and said to give you space."

"There's part of it that Richard doesn't know."

"What's that?"

Avery waved her into his messier-than-usual bedroom and shut the door behind them. "That's the part I can only tell you. In order to get free and keep myself and my mom and her friends from being killed, I used my powers. I saved us."

"Did you burn those people that had you trapped?"

"Yes. Not enough to kill them. Just enough to hurt. A little goes a long way, so I've got to be careful."

"You've got to do what you've got to do."

"But I promised a long time ago not to use the powers. So never again."

"Why did you make that promise?"

"Because these powers are really dangerous. Really bad things happen if they get out of hand. I'm sure you know that."

"Yeah, my cousin Denny always said the powers are like a gun. A big responsibility."

"It's a responsibility I never asked for."

Shifting the subject a bit, Avery opened the laptop on his desk and pulled up news articles. The nomadic cult members, who shaved their heads and wore white sheetlike robes, now sat in jail awaiting trial, while some of them had been treated for what the articles termed "unexplained burns." Investigators suspected this small group in a few unsolved murders around the country, in which the victims were strung upside down with their throats slit.

"Do you think they caught all of these people?" Lillian wanted to know.

"I sure hope so. But just in case, we're keeping an eye out for anything weird. This cult was actually a revival of an old cult that used to live in the wilderness near our friends' ranch, the same place we were kidnapped from. I sure hope I don't see or hear about these people ever again!"

In May, a couple of days after Lillian arrived in Maryland for a summer break at home, Uncle Gerald dropped by Lou's house for a visit. This time, he called first, giving Lillian time to mentally and emotionally prepare. She showed her father the metal visualization trick that Avery had taught her, and he practiced and hoped for the best as he waited for his brother. Much to Lillian's relief, he assumed that she had come up with the trick herself. She was spared from telling a bold-faced lie about her friendship with Avery.

Gerald became frustrated after his arrival, throwing his hands up. "Why can't I read either of you? I just want to know what you've been up to, and how work and school is going!"

"My daughter has figured out a little trick to keep your head out of ours," Lou explained to his brother.

"Why? All I want to know is that you're happy and you're doing well."

"We are. But the two of us would also like a little privacy. Why don't you find out how we're doing the way normal people do, by asking us?"

Gerald demanded to know what this trick was, and when Lou explained, he finally calmed down a bit. "That should be useful in case I ever encounter anyone I shouldn't," he remarked with a smile. "It's ridiculously simple. Can't believe I didn't discover it on my own."

After returning to school in the fall, Lillian once again roomed with Bridget in the same beautiful building, looking forward to more fun and late-night conversations in their cozy little space. Lillian would have a fairly busy semester loaded with hardcore science courses.

Avery's crush, Susannah Garcia, happened to sit near Lillian in environmental science class. Long curly dark brown hair hung down around Susannah's round, soft face. She had a slightly plump figure and pendulous breasts.

Susannah grinned at and said hi to Lillian a few times, though they were strangers. Yet Susannah did not speak to any of the men in the class, avoiding their eyes and not returning their smiles.

One afternoon, after class let out, Lillian ran into Susannah in the shadowy hallway. Susannah smiled sweetly at her.

"I know someone you might want to chat with," Lillian suggested.

"Who?"

"I can introduce you to him. He's a friend of mine. A really nice guy."

"Why?" The smile fell away from Susannah's face.

"He said you had a class together. He thinks you're... well... a very nice person, and he'd like to get to know you better."

Susannah backed away slowly, clinging to her backpack strap. "This is more than a little creepy. I'm about to get married, you know. I can't be talking to other guys."

"I'm sorry; I didn't mean it like that..."

Susannah did not respond as she turned and rushed down the hall. Lillian had blown it. She replayed the conversation in her head as she walked away, red-faced at how unsettling she must have sounded.

Since Lillian and Avery had no classes together this semester, she did not see him often except during game nights. She still checked in with him over instant messages, asking how he was holding up after the assault during spring break. The next time the two hung out alone was a few weeks after Lillian's failed encounter with Susannah, a Saturday in an emerald-green park. They sprawled on their backs in the velvety grass in the shade of a fir tree as they caught up.

Avery had gone on a date a couple of weeks ago. Though he usually had no luck in this area, single his whole life and too bashful to make a suave first impression, the chemistry heated up and the girl said she wanted to meet again. But after they parted ways, his date never called him back, increasing his fear that he'd never find someone at this rate.

"It really sucks that she stopped calling. I wish she'd at least tell you if she changed her mind. But this doesn't mean you will be alone for the rest of your life," Lillian reassured him.

"Yeah, but I'm one hell of a late bloomer. I still feel like Susannah, the one I told you about, would be right for me. But there's no point in even thinking about her."

"Did I tell you she's in one of my classes?"

"Wow, you didn't tell me! Are you sure it's the same one?"

"Yeah, I'm pretty sure. Average height, long curly dark hair, busty?"

"Sounds right."

"I talked to her recently, and I mentioned you. I said you might like to meet."

"What?!"

"I didn't mention your name. I guess I was kind of... hoping she'd get to know you. And then it would at least make her think, if not dump that jerk she's with. But it didn't go over well."

"What did she say?" Avery propped himself up on his arms, going rigid.

"She said it was creepy, that she's about to get married and can't talk to other men, and then she walked away from me. We haven't spoken since."

"What I told you was supposed to be in confidence! Susannah was not meant to know about any of that! I just... I need a break. I need time."

"I'm sorry... I didn't tell her about the mind reading or anything..." Lillian mumbled, getting up from their grassy haven of shade as Avery walked away. Her words fell silent.

Lillian was angry with herself, and embarrassed. Why did she try to meddle in affairs where it wasn't her place to say anything? She should have known better. Not only that, getting on a fire mage's bad side could be an incredibly dangerous thing. This was one of the major risks of forming an alliance: the friendship turning sour. If they ran into each other again, what would Avery do to her?

Not sure what else to do, hoping to smooth things over, Lillian emailed him with an apology: *Avery, I'm truly sorry. I did not mean to piss you off. I realize I made a mistake. I should have known that whole situation is none of my business and there is nothing I can do. I promise to be more careful what I tell people. Sincerely, Lil.*

Avery sent a reply saying that he appreciated and accepted the apology. Lillian breathed a sigh of relief, though this did not assure her they were still friends. Her worries held her back from reaching out again or going to the weekly gaming parties. When no one called or texted from the parties to ask if she was coming, as they had in the past, this fully convinced Lillian that she was no longer welcome.

One crisp, golden Saturday afternoon, Lillian had her dorm room to herself. Bridget was spending the weekend off campus, sleeping over at her new boyfriend's house. Lillian spoke on the phone with her old high school friend Christian for a while. He asked if she'd ever found out what became of Zack. Lillian did not know anything beyond that call her father made to Zack's father, and didn't really care much either, wanting to move on from that lousy charade of a relationship.

"Why don't we look him up on Facebook?" Christian suggested.

"I searched for him on the internet after he skipped town, and found nothing."

"Let's try again, just for laughs if nothing else."

With her friend still on the phone, Lillian opened her laptop and searched on Facebook for Zack's name.

"I'm getting a hit this time!" she announced. "He must have made this profile after we broke up. Jeez, that picture looks like a mugshot!"

Taken with a bored expression in front of a cinderblock wall, the profile picture was out of focus, yet unmistakable. Zack wore the daily outfit she photographically remembered: the black leather jacket, white T-shirt, and beaded shark-tooth necklace.

"I think I found him," Christian said. "The black jacket dude, right? Holy shit, that picture is awful."

After Christian had to end the call to go to work, Lillian probed deeper, unable to discern Zack's current location or much else. Out of halfhearted curiosity, she scrolled through his small friends list, not expecting to recognize anyone.

Her eyes first landed on a few friends with the familiar surname Kreider. That had been Mandy's last name. Mandy, the one who took her own life after that summer with Julius.

And then Lillian's own last name jumped out at her. Her first thought was coincidence. The name was common enough that she shared it with Anya Frazier, a classmate growing up and now a Facebook friend. Like a set of twins, their photos appeared side by side in their school yearbooks, though Anya was Black and they were not related.

But these friends of Zack's were indeed relatives, people in the estranged branch of the family that Lillian never wanted to see again. First, there was Jana, Mandy's older sister who'd married Julius and had a kid with him.

And then Julius himself in a business suit.

They looked as Lillian remembered, except with a few more wrinkles, a bit more weathering in their skin. Jana still had a gaunt, sharp face and dyed black hair cut to her chin. Julius had the same short, light reddish hair and the blunt face with a firm chin, those features so painstakingly etched in Lillian's memory after seven years.

The room spun and tilted. Lillian's stomach dropped. She came close to throwing up, unable to accept the reality that her ex-boyfriend knew Julius and had some sort of relationship with Jana's family. And that he'd kept all this hidden, like the cash-stuffed duffel bag in his closet. None of this made any sense.

Lillian ran out of the room, shaking all over, trying to escape from her past, from everything. She nearly ran into the guy who sat playing his guitar on the bottom stair, and screeched across the floor. She bounded out the door, past the group of friends who sat under a nearby willow tree smoking pot. They glanced curiously up at her through their stoned haze.

After she stopped running and panted for a while, Lillian hid herself in a remote thicket of trees and began to beat them mercilessly from a deep well of rage she didn't know she had, whaling on them as the leaves trembled gently above. She watched, detached, as her fists slammed the bark over and over until they went numb, leaving dark smears. Lillian was angry at Julius, at Zack, at her uncle Gerald for telling her to get over what his son did to her.

Other feelings, tucked away beneath the rest, roared to the surface in a volcanic eruption. Lillian was also angry at her father. What if he knew, deep down, that something bad had happened with Julius, yet stayed in denial for years until she spelled it out in the letter she wrote? Resentment seethed towards Evelyn for brushing off the signs and refusing to help Lillian during that desperate phone call from the neighbors' house. Julius had groomed her father and sister with his long letters and gushing phone calls and pricey gifts and kind words, yet it was Dad who trusted Lillian's care to him. Dad who failed to make the connection between the suicide attempt right after eighth grade and his refusal to let Lillian opt out of Julius' wedding.

Distant from herself as if floating into the air, Lillian wiped the hot tears from her face and walked back to Stephenson Hall in the darkening night, hands tender as she reached into her pocket for the student ID that doubled as her key. She trudged up the stairs past the young man on the bottom step. He stopped strumming chords on his duct-taped-together guitar and stared at Lillian's hands. She shut herself into her room, broke open a razor to fish out the blade, and carved into her arm for the first time since living with Tara. Her fingers trickled and bled along with the incisions.

When Lillian fully realized what she was doing, she threw the blade across the room. Injuring herself had once helped to center her in times of distress. But now she felt even worse, about to explode from the anxiety that shielded the long-hidden pressure cooker of built-up fury.

Now, Lillian faced no choice but to clean up. Holding a pair of tweezers slippery with blood in her trembling fingers, she plucked splinters out of her scraped knuckles. She washed the wounds as well as she could, put ointment on them, and wrapped bandages around her hands.

Lillian was desperate not to be alone tonight. She did not know what she would say to any friend; she just needed a distraction. Bridget, the first choice, did not answer her phone. Their friend Tim did not answer either. And neither did Christian, who probably had his phone put away on silent while he worked his evening shift at a restaurant.

Lillian's deep shame held her back from calling any family members. As far as Dad and Evelyn were concerned, Lillian had recovered from her years-old trauma. Though she'd apologized, Evelyn's past comments about Lillian harming herself because she was not tough enough still stung.

Lillian sat at her computer and looked through her list of buddies available for instant messaging. Not many people were signed in this evening. Out of those few active names, the person Lillian knew the best was Avery. After a couple weeks of avoiding him, he was certainly not the top choice for talking about something as delicate as tonight's breakdown.

But he was someone. And she didn't have to tell him everything or let him see her bandaged hands in person. Maybe they could talk about trivial topics, even smooth things over a bit more, and it would distract her and help her feel better. Or he might still be a little mad after the argument over Susannah, and could say something snippy, sending her spiraling down again.

After Lillian said hi, Avery replied, *How have you been?*

They talked a bit. With Lillian's unusually terse responses, Avery suspected that something was amiss. He asked if she was all right. Lillian typed back, slower than usual with her stiff throbbing hands. *Not really, but it's fine, really.*

Are you sure?

After chatting for a few more lines, Avery said that he was a little worried and would come by to check on her. Before Lillian could stop him, he logged off.

Frantically, Lillian cleaned up the best she could, hoping to convince Avery to leave as quickly as he came. The guy with the guitar was now gone, and Lillian found herself alone in the quiet lobby. As she waited, jittery, beside the locked front door of the dormitory, another fear popped into her head. When Avery saw the injuries, he might make assumptions about a suicide attempt or psychotic episode and call the campus or city police. If the cops came, Lillian might be committed in a hospital psych ward and then possibly expelled from school. She'd heard of colleges kicking out students who struggled with depression, not wanting to deal with the liability.

She should never have talked to anybody.

By the time Avery knocked on the glass of the double doors, Lillian had begun crying in her fear of what might befall her whole education. She wiped her face the best she could with a tissue, trying to suppress her sniffling, before letting him into the building.

When he stepped inside, Avery glanced at the bandages on her hands and arm. "What happened? Are you okay?"

"Yes... I'm... I'm fine." Lillian broke down in tears, a blubbering, raw, mortifying mess. She fell straight into his arms, unable to speak for a few moments.

"Let's get you to your room. Is your roommate there?"

"N-no..."

Once they got to the room, Avery sat with Lillian on the bottom bunk of the bed.

"Just breathe deep and slow," he encouraged her. "Sit down. Breathe. Can you tell me what happened?"

"I... uh... I'm just having a rough night, and uh... It's just... please don't call the cops on me. It's not that serious."

"I won't. You sure you don't need to go to urgent care?"

"I'd rather not. I don't want a doctor asking questions. I don't think you should be here."

"You seem like you might need someone. But if I need to leave, I can."

"No... don't leave. I just... I thought I needed someone to listen, but I don't like people seeing me like this, and..." Lillian shyly looked down at her hands. Spots of blood were coming through the white bandages. "I did this to myself," she admitted, fresh hot tears leaking down her cheeks.

"Let me see your hands."

Lillian drew them away.

"I won't unwrap them. But I can heal you up a bit."

"Heal? How?"

"You didn't know that we have a bit of a healing power?"

"No. I had no idea we could do that!"

"Remember when you fell and cut yourself on the glass at my house? Did you notice the cuts healing really fast?"

"Yes, I was surprised. That was you, when you were touching my hand and foot?"

"Yes. If you want me to try that, I'll be gentle. Hopefully it'll keep you from getting infected."

"Sure. It wouldn't hurt."

Avery took her wrapped hands into his and focused. His rays of orange converged into her injuries, hot like the fire he represented, yet not painful. Already, her aches dulled as his power tingled just under her skin.

"You want to talk?" Avery said after he finished.

"Let's talk about you. Because I don't want to think about myself right now. How have you been?"

"I've been doing okay. Still mentally recovering from those attacks in the spring."

"Did anything more happen with those cult people?"

"Still in jail awaiting trial, last I heard. Sorry I've been out of touch; I was wondering where you were during game nights."

"I was afraid things were strained between us. I felt bad about what I said to Susannah, who's been avoiding me since that day I gave her the creeps. Again, I'm sorry that I don't have enough of a filter sometimes."

"That's okay. You were just trying to be a good friend. But it was for the best. I had to move on. Because guess what? I met someone."

"Really? Who?" Lillian's mood perked up at this good news.

"Her name's Chrissy. We met on *World of Warcraft*. We've really hit it off."

"Does she go to school here?"

"No. The hard part is the distance. She lives in Delaware."

"Any plans to meet her in person?"

"No, not yet. We've just been talking for a couple of weeks. I'll see how things develop."

"That's a good plan. Move slow. I'm so happy that you found someone."

"Thanks, me too. Are you sure you don't want to talk about what's on your mind?"

"I don't know… maybe I should just let it out. There was this ugly thing in my past. It happened years ago. I hardly ever talk about it because it's hard to talk about and I don't want people to feel sorry for me. But I saw something tonight, something I wasn't expecting, that just brought all these feelings back. There was a ton of anger that I didn't know I had. So I guess I just freaked out."

"If you want to tell me, I'm here."

"It's some disturbing stuff. I'd want you to keep it between us. And I might have to stop. You sure?"

"I'm sure."

Lillian completely unrolled the imaginary metal from her head, already feeling like an exposed nerve, though she knew·he could not see into her very well, even in this unprotected state.

As Lillian told the story about Julius, it poured out of her more and more painfully, searing like hot lava. Yet even during the parts she still felt ashamed over, it spewed out like uncontrollable word vomit.

The whole time, Avery listened, watching her patiently as her eyes filled with more and more tears. A few times, he asked gently if she needed to stop. But she went on, ripping the whole story out of herself like a giant parasite. She included the parts she could never tell her psychiatrist, where Julius showed her the most terrifying aspects of the magic, turning his dead cat into a grotesque creature.

"I wish I could go back in time and tell you none of this was your fault," Avery said once the violent flow of words finally trickled to a stop. "You were just a kid, and you didn't ask for it, or seduce your cousin, or anything. It doesn't mean you're dirty. It means he is an abuser."

"I know that now, but I had no one to tell me that back then. And even if my brain knows one thing, my body feels another. I feel defiled."

"I can understand. Those feelings are hard to shake. He's such an awful person... I'd love to punch him. What a piece of shit."

Lillian let on that the pain never truly ended, even after getting out of Julius' slimy grasp. She described the plans the next summer to see Julius again, and her hopelessness that led up to attempting suicide. She went over the misdiagnosis of bipolar, the years of having to feign cheer when she called and wrote letters to Julius, the dread that it was only a matter of time before they met again, and how much the truth later shattered her father and caused a rift in the family. Lastly, Lillian connected the whole ordeal to tonight's discovery of Zack's Facebook profile and connections.

"I'm still waiting for Julius to come into my life again, to come and hurt me," Lillian confided to Avery, her voice raspy from the anguish of reciting her worst memories. "It's been years. I've gotten therapy, I've been on some pills for anxiety, and then I weaned off them. I'm doing a lot better than I was, and my dad and I have tried to get our lives back. But then there's times like tonight."

"Lots of molesters use threats to keep a person quiet, like Julius did. But often they're too much of a coward to follow through. I know about some of that from reading minds.

But I can understand being scared all over again, and it must have been really freaky to find out your ex is connected to Julius."

"Back then, I thought Julius was dead serious about his threats. I didn't know I had so much anger still, until tonight. I'm angry that it happened. Angry that he's gotten away with it and he's living a good life. We didn't get the police involved because the police would lose against a necromancer. I wasn't able to even tell any of my friends until tonight. I never told Zack. Of course, I figured back then that he wouldn't know Julius, yet somehow, he does. If I got another boyfriend, I'm not sure I could tell him either."

"You are not what happened to you. And someone who truly cared about you would know that."

"Thank you, it actually really helps me to hear that. Meanwhile, Julius is still living his life, still married to Jana, and they have a kid now."

"I sure hope Julius isn't abusing his kid, but I guess that's out of your hands. It must be really hard, knowing he's still free."

"Yeah, it is. I worry about who else he might be hurting."

"There's something going on in your family, Lil. I don't know what it is, but I can feel it. Be cautious. Do you mind if I have a look at Zack's Facebook friends?"

Lillian took her computer off her desk and handed it to Avery.

"Didn't you mention someone named Jerrisene, Jana's sister or something?" he asked.

"Yeah, Jana and Mandy's sister."

"I'm seeing a Jerrisene Kreider."

"Probably the same one; that was Mandy's last name."

"Her stuff is public. Her birthday was a few weeks ago. Look what Zack wrote on her timeline!"

Lillian peered at Zack's post on the screen. *Happy birthday, Cuz!*

Jerrisene had replied, *Thanks so much, cousin! We've got to get together soon!*

"Jerrisene is Zack's cousin?!" Lillian gasped. "Jana and Mandy are *related* to Zack! What the fuck!"

"I'm so glad you broke up with Zack. If you didn't, this wouldn't have ended well."

"I wish I'd dumped him much sooner than I did. Why do you think Zack was after me? What did he want?"

"The whole thing might have been set up by Julius himself, to bring you back to him."

"Zack's roommate said he had a duffel bag in his closet that was stuffed with cash. I wonder if he was paid to snag me? Was I paid for?"

"I don't doubt it."

"That makes me really angry, even if Zack was just a pawn. As soon as I saw Zack's friends, I knew that couldn't be a coincidence. And that's a big part of why I broke down tonight. Betrayal. Feeling like I'll never be free of Julius. Never."

"You got Zack out of your life before it reached that point. You've got friends and family who have your back. But I can understand how you wouldn't feel safe after this."

"What do you think of me now that I told you about all this?" Lillian asked. "I'm still not sure why I told you. Are you afraid of me?"

"No, I'm not afraid of you. You're my friend, and you are very strong. You've survived so much. I can tell you're worn out emotionally."

Lillian glanced at her watch. "It's midnight. You must be getting tired."

"I'll stay for as long as you need. Or if you want, I'm sure Richard would let you stay over at my house."

"No, go. I'll be fine. We should get to bed."

"Are you sure? You okay with being alone tonight?"

"I think I'll be okay."

"If you need anything, just call me. I don't care what time it is."

Once Avery was gone, Lillian shut off the colored lights strung along the walls and laid on her back in bed, not sleeping. Instead of being relieved to have her friend so kindly listen to her painful story, she was terrified. What had she just told him? What the hell was she thinking? How dangerous could this get, now that it had left her lips?

The part she hadn't told Avery, figuring he would not want to hear about it, was those two terrible sexual encounters she'd been pressured into with Zack, the passionless jackhammering and painful dry chafing. Zack's connection to Julius put it in a horrific new light.

Rape by proxy.

"Gotcha," Gerald whispered to himself, peeking out from behind a stand of bushes surrounding a one-story home. For weeks now, he had been stalking the home's sole occupant, a bald middle-aged man he had first encountered at a subway station.

Norman Woodley was a soft-spoken electrician who did not stand out. In his private time, he had a hobby that would horrify just about anyone. Gerald knew not only where he lived, but that he had claimed six lives, burying the bodies in his backyard garden after a couple of hours of listening in delight to their screams. Norman chose street prostitutes and drifters, people whose disappearances were unlikely to make the news, whose families didn't care about them and wouldn't even notice if they were gone.

Norman was not busy killing anyone in his soundproofed basement tonight. Instead, he went outside to rake leaves, turning on the porch light. Before he had the chance to go to his toolshed to pick up his rake, Norman went limp, his arms falling down. Stiff, a puppet, he shuffled out of his backyard, waddled down the street, and slumped down in the passenger's seat of Gerald's car.

Since Norman lived alone, with no love life, no close friends, and no family nearby, Gerald felt confident that it would take a while for anyone to notice the man's absence. And Norman did not socialize with his neighbors. As long as his car stayed in the driveway, they wouldn't miss him.

Gerald removed a syringe from his bag, uncapped it, and injected the neck of the still-possessed Norman, wincing a bit at the tiny sympathy sting in his own neck. Once Norman lapsed into unconsciousness, Gerald started driving, now that he no longer had to multitask. As Gerald left the Virginia suburb where Norman lived and headed back home, Norman was still out cold, his head leaning against the window. Gerald was pleased that he'd gotten the dosage right, allowing enough time before Norman emerged from the fog later tonight.

Norman slowly woke up. As he blinked his eyes to clear them, he found himself surrounded by an unfamiliar wood-walled room, lit by a bare ceiling bulb dangling above his head. As Norman tried to move, painfully tight plastic zip ties cut into his wrists and ankles. A rope around his waist confined him to a wooden chair. He grunted and struggled, alarmed to find himself tied up the exact same way he always bound his victims.

"I know what you've been up to, Mr. Woodley," a man's gruff voice said from behind him. "I know that you enjoy tormenting them with a knife before finally snuffing them out using strangulation."

Norman tried to protest. How did this man know any of that? Norman had always been wise enough to not tell a single soul, and careful enough to secure his basement and cover his tracks. Groans came out through the duct tape wrapped around his head. He wrenched his body again as the man who had him trapped paced around his chair in circles.

"The tables have turned. Now you are like a fly caught on flypaper. There is no escape. It's time to think about how your victims felt in their final moments—not that you'd care in that emotionally deficient brain of yours."

Something dragged and scraped painfully along Norman's flesh. He looked down as a knife floated in the air, moving mysteriously along the skin of his arm like the planchette on a spirit board. What he saw made no sense. The adrenaline of terror spurted into his bloodstream as the knife left behind thin red scratches.

"I'm not going to cut any deeper, not just yet," said his captor with a cruel smile. "I just love seeing the fear in your eyes. Like you did with your victims."

After what seemed like an eternity, the knife clattered to the floor.

"Now, Mr. Woodley, meet my pets," said the old man, reaching down to a large wooden crate on the floor and sliding a panel open. Two unkempt coyotes stepped out, smelling so terrible that Norman gulped back vomit behind his duct-tape gag. To Norman's horror, bits of fur and flesh dangled from their ragged bodies.

"Have at him, boys! Sic, sic!"

Baring their yellowed fangs, the animals lunged at Norman. He slammed his eyes shut and rattled futilely against his restraints as the teeth tore into him.

Later, Gerald was worn out, panting and sweating after dragging a large plastic-bagged bundle out of his basement, up the stairs of the recreation room, and out the back door, where he buried it. He then burned the reanimated wild coyotes so that they would not continue to stink up the secret room that adjoined his recreation room. After the hard labor of digging, Gerald splayed out on his living room couch, red-faced and wiped out. His cat jumped onto his belly and curled up.

"I need to get in shape, kitty," Gerald gasped as he petted the feline. "My back's killing me now. You know what would have been quite amusing? If I had reanimated that man to dig his own grave. But then I would have had to dismember and burn him, and it still would have given me a workout."

In the days after her revelation to Avery about all of the pain and trauma of her adolescence, Lillian was angry at herself. *That's just supposed to be between you and your family.*

And telling Avery about the hideous animals, as well as the other powers, was probably a form of treason. Once you told someone a secret, it was a secret no more. Hoping for Avery's memory of that teary and bloody night to fade, Lillian avoided the next Friday-night gathering. The next day, she got an instant message from Avery, asking if she was okay. He assured her that he'd keep their conversation private, and that folks missed her at the gaming parties. The *Dungeons & Dragons* campaigns just weren't the same without her character.

That night, Lillian got into a deep conversation with Bridget as they lay in their beds, not sleeping. Against her better judgment, Lillian told a condensed version of the story about Julius, leaving out the family's powers. Bridget surprised Lillian, showing much of the same empathy and compassion that Avery did.

"There's something that I never told you," Bridget revealed. "I got raped too. I was fourteen. I'd just moved to Texas and started at a high school where I didn't know anyone... story of my life as a military brat. Somehow, I got invited to a party. All the kids were drinking. I had a few beers. This guy, a star football quarterback, convinced me to go down to the basement with him. Turned out I'd been drugged. I started to fall asleep on the couch. I woke up to find him pulling my clothes off. I couldn't move."

"Oh, shit. Oh, man." Not used to other people sharing tales such as this, Lillian was at a loss for words, terrified of saying the wrong thing and even a little sheepish that she was handling this situation with less finesse than Avery had.

"That same guy drove me home after he put my clothes back on. I barely remember that either. He told my parents that I got sick. They believed him and I got in trouble for being out past my curfew. Then word spread around at school that he'd given me roofies. He told people he couldn't have raped me because I was too fat and ugly for him to get it up."

"That's so cruel! I'd love to find that guy and kick him in the nads until he coughs them up. And how horrible the anxiety must have been when you went to school, being scared of running into him and hearing people saying those hurtful things."

"Yes, you nailed it about the anxiety. I pretty much learned his schedule just to avoid him. Every morning until the asshole graduated, I did not want to get up for school."

"Did you ever tell your parents? Or report it?"

"No. I was never comfortable telling my parents. They're strict and I was scared of how they'd react. I didn't report it because high school football is like religion in that place, and I knew they would accuse me of ruining his bright future. I just stuffed it down."

"Like I did. And I ended up hurting because of it."

"So did I. It messed me up for years. I didn't avoid sex like you did. Instead, I got promiscuous. And drank way too much. I figured, since I was damaged goods, I might as well sleep with everyone. I got a reputation at that school. Embarrassing to think about now."

"But you were acting out because you were hurting. I hope you've found some healing."

"Yeah, some. But that's not to say I don't still have nightmares."

"Like me."

"Point being, you are not alone. Far from it."

"Thank you. There's this part that I was too embarrassed to tell Avery or my shrink... and I'm really embarrassed to tell you too. I feel so disgusting because of it, so confused." Lillian's voice lowered to a mumble. "Even though it hurt, even though I was dissociating as much as I could and I couldn't look at him, there was one time when I... I had an orgasm. Does this mean I was secretly attracted to him? Did he turn me on?"

"Oh, no, the asshole absolutely did not turn you on. You're not attracted to him. Your body was just trying to protect itself. You are not disgusting!"

Hearing that Bridget had survived an ordeal of her own helped Lillian to feel more connected, less apart from everyone else. With each person Lillian told, the pressure lowered inside her, like steam released.

A couple of weeks later, Lillian went over to Avery's house for an afternoon visit, where he caught her up on the details of his new relationship. Chrissy lived with her parents and attended a community college. Avery hoped to go visit her on the east coast during the winter break.

"I'll be seeing my dad for winter break," Lillian said. "We're a couple of hours away from Chrissy, and if I could, I'd love to hang out with you and meet her. But I won't have a car since I'll be flying, so I'd probably have to ask my dad for a ride, and unfortunately..."

"Yeah, I understand. That's okay. You want to meet Chrissy? I'll see if she's around."

Avery sat at his desk and Lillian leaned over his shoulder as Chrissy's face filled his computer screen, offset by a background of pink striped wallpaper. Chrissy had corkscrews of shoulder-length brown hair and sweet freckle-dotted round cheeks. Sharing a class with his former crush Susannah, Lillian figured that Avery must have had a thing for bubbly, curly-haired brunettes.

"Hi!" Chrissy waved enthusiastically after Avery introduced the two. "I've heard a bit about you! That's a cool, stripey shirt you're wearing. What does that shirt mean?"

"It's a Joy Division shirt."

"Like, that old band?"

"Yeah."

"Cool! I've heard a few of their songs. Not my thing, but love the shirt!"

Loud noises erupted in the background. Crashes, bangs, and children's shrieks.

"Settle down! Get down from there!" Chrissy shouted, turning toward the side. She excused herself for a few moments, walking offscreen.

"Watching your nephews again?" Avery wanted to know once Chrissy returned.

"Yep. I'm stuck babysitting a lot these days. Oh well, at least my sister's paying me. They're being little terrors today!"

"Will you need to babysit when I visit?"

"No. Carrie is taking her boys to Florida. Thank God!"

The three of them chatted for a while, and then Lillian began feeling like the third wheel on a date. As Avery and Chrissy talked more intimately, exchanging sweet nothings, Lillian suddenly found herself in a strangely bad mood, on the verge of stomping from the room.

She was jealous.

As Avery got lost in the sugary conversation, Lillian took deep breaths to center herself, sealing her mind once again in visions of metal to keep her storming emotions a complete secret. Lillian had gotten a bit lonely, though she was nowhere near the stark isolation of her first semester. And maybe she wished, just a tiny bit, that she was on the other side of that screen.

No. It couldn't be possible. She could not think such taboo thoughts about Avery, not now, not ever. She did not like him like *that*; they were just friends. Any closer feelings were strictly forbidden.

Lillian just wished she had a real relationship of her own, that was all. And maybe Avery's recent kindness in supporting her through an extremely vulnerable moment, his acceptance of her whole truth, got her emotions confused, imagining an intimacy that didn't exist.

When she got back to her dorm room, Lillian decided to set up a profile on a dating website. Bridget looked over the profile and the pictures before giving the thumbs-up to let it go live.

The following week, Avery's plan to visit Chrissy hit a roadblock. Chrissy's mother was hospitalized after a stroke, requiring Chrissy to devote the next few months to helping out her family. They hoped to reschedule their visit for spring break. Avery was let down, of course, yet his sympathies went out to Chrissy's mother. Lillian asked him to send along her own good thoughts for a speedy recovery.

Evelyn paid for a plane ticket for Lillian to see her over Thanksgiving. Their father would not be joining them this time, but Evelyn admitted over the phone that she was desperate for a little company. It surprised Lillian that someone as socially adept as Evelyn could feel alone. But maybe more people knew that pain than Lillian assumed.

When Evelyn picked Lillian up, she pushed a pair of sleek sunglasses from the top of her head over her reddened eyes. Natasha, a year old, looked so much bigger in her stroller than Lillian remembered, her brown hair filling in. After outgrowing the wrinkled awkwardness of the newborn stage, Natasha was cute, with the elfin features that ran in the family.

When they arrived at Evelyn and Jonathan's house, the toys sprinkled around the carpet did not startle Lillian, but stranger were the signs of adult sloppiness. Coffee rings marred the glass coffee table, and dirty dishes stunk up the sink. For as long as Lillian could remember, Evelyn was a neat freak, the kid with the tidiest room on the block.

"When does Jonathan get home from work?" Lillian asked as Evelyn lowered Natasha into a playpen.

After slowly turning back around, Evelyn held up one hand and pointed at it with the other. "Notice that? Notice anything missing?"

Lillian examined her sister's elegant little hands, fingers ending in points with long translucent nails. "Where is your wedding ring?"

"Bingo!" Evelyn shrieked. "Life as a single mother... it sure is swell, isn't it?"

"Are you serious? What happened?!"

"He moved out at the start of this month, moved in with his girlfriend, and filed for divorce. And guess what twists the knife in even deeper? Tasha has a half-sibling on the way."

"Jonathan got his side chick pregnant?"

"While we were still married! Tequila has been my best friend lately." As Evelyn started to shake and wipe at her eyes, Lillian watched something she'd almost never been privy to before—Evelyn breaking down in tears. Usually, she was quick to blink them away and recover her composure. But this time, the tears went on and on. Lillian put her arms around the hard muscle and bone of Evelyn's short, slim body.

"I haven't even told Dad," Evelyn moaned into her sister's shoulder. "I don't know how to tell him. It'll break his heart."

"Remember, Dad's been through a divorce, too. I think he will understand that none of this was your fault." As her mind righted itself from the shock, Lillian chose words similar to the ones Avery had comforted her with during her recent rough night. Words to deflect shame and blame away from the one who was hurt.

"Dad got divorced way before we were born. He and his ex are good friends, and they didn't have kids together. Jonathan is no friend of mine. He's taking me to court. Battling me over custody, even though he barely lifted a finger to help with Tasha. He wants to make this divorce hard on me."

"I'm so sorry he's being an ass and making it worse. Though you can't keep this divorce from Dad forever."

"I know... but I'm ashamed that this is happening! It's awful knowing I wasn't good enough for Jonathan. I couldn't keep him happy..."

"Maybe it had nothing to do with you. Maybe he just happens to be a jerk." *And Uncle Gerald paid him to go out with you, just as Zack was probably paid to go out with me. Men who are paid for your relationship don't love you. But I'm not allowed to tell you that.*

"It's hard not to blame yourself when it just happened, though... it's hard not to wonder what you could have done differently..." Evelyn sniffled.

"Don't blame yourself."

As Lillian slept on the couch that night, she had a dream of sitting at the lip of a mirrorlike pond under a row of cherry trees in bloom, whose soft pink petals fell around her and into her hair like snow. A petite woman sat down next to her, dressed in a pink blouse and tight jeans. Thick owl glasses sat on the woman's face, surrounded by straight brown hair. Lillian at first thought it was Evelyn before realizing it was her late mother. A ghostly glow reflected from her forest-green eyes. When Lillian said hello, she did not respond. An attempted hug had her dissolving into wisps from Lillian's empty arms.

As Lillian gazed into the water, it revealed a more grisly sight: her mother lying on a rug, blood pooling around her head from the final gunshot wound. Yet she looked up, confused and blinking, rising from herself with lit green marble eyes. A little girl in pink overalls with a long red ponytail stood in front of her, extending a tiny hand. Lillian took a few moments to recognize that child. Herself at age three, calling out, *Mommy? It's time to go.*

Lillian's memory of that life-changing day when her father got the phone call was jumbled with time and trauma. One minute she'd been watching Barney the purple dinosaur on TV, and then the next she was confused, blanked out of reality, convinced she'd just seen her mother even though miles separated them. And then came the hours of inconsolable crying that had Dad worried her appendix might have just burst.

This was the first time Lillian could remember the death-feeling smacking into her, dark and cold.

As Lillian startled awake from the dream, feeling not alone, a humanoid shadow rose over the sofa, above her. That cloaked, hooded man, with green dots for eyes, a lifelong sight. As Lillian blinked, he faded away.

Even with that figure gone and out of her sight, something still unsettled Lillian. She felt watched, as if the picture window at the front of the living room had eyes peering at her through the blinds. Lillian got up, shuffled in her pajamas toward the window, and peeked through two of the thick blinds at the street, lit only by cones of orange light cascading down from a few streetlights.

A man stood well down the sidewalk, his features indistinct in the darkness and his body turned toward the house. Lillian knew this was no ghost. With the waving blue spires in the streetlight's glow, this was, instead, a water mage.

They had promised Lillian and her father to leave them alone, so long as Natasha was safe. But could they be trusted? Still watching the family like this?

As the man began taking steps toward the house, fear rose further up in Lillian's throat, sour and bitter. Her body tensed, preparing to rush to the bedroom and wake her sister, grab the baby, and run. Though running would not keep them safe.

The man stepped into a black car parked along the street and sped off. As she watched the car go around the bend and disappear, Lillian began to cry with relief. She returned to the sofa and could not sleep for the rest of the night, curled up but hyper-alert, waiting for something bad to happen.

"Son," Gerald pleaded with Julius. The two faced each other in Gerald's massive study, tense and a bit angry. "We can't keep dragging our feet, dragging this on for years."

"But we've got to wait until the time is right, Dad," Julius insisted. "And the time never seems to be. There's always something going on."

"Julius, I am not going to live forever. I want to see everything play out before I die."

"All right, all right, Dad. I'll start looking for a place. After that, I'll worry about gathering up the family. Even though it won't be easy after people stopped speaking to each other. I'm afraid it might take some drastic measures."

"What about your wife and son? Will you be bringing them?"

"No. They are both half-breeds, and you know my wife cannot have more. They're of no use to us."

"I still would encourage you to bring your son. Once he gets older, he could be quite useful."

"I'll have to wait years for Robbie to be useful in that way." Julius walked away to pour himself a glass of wine. Meanwhile, Gerald took his cell phone from his pocket and called his brother Lou at home.

"Come and join us," Gerald urged. "Our family is bringing together a wonderful plan, and I want you to be a part of it."

"What plan?"

"I'm afraid I cannot divulge all of the details just yet. But believe me, you won't regret it."

"Gerald, I can't jump into something if I don't even know what it is. Can you please stop being so cryptic?"

"Oh, you're so stubborn, brother, so set in your ways."

"If you could explain what's going on, then I'll consider it."

"Would you like me to tell everyone your dirty little secret?"

"Excuse me?"

"Your refusal to commit to our family's mission may have dire consequences for you."

"Gerald, first, I do not know what the hell is going on; and second, I will not let you have power over me. You got away with blackmailing me when we were kids, but we're too old for this now. I will not play your games. Tell people whatever you want to tell them."

"Wow, brother. It's not like you to be so careless. You might want to think hard about all this." Gerald chuckled before he hung up.

Excerpt from The Autobiography of Gerald Frazier: Architect of a New World

I put a lot of thought into my idea, plotting how I was going to give us necromancers a good, booming, healthy comeback.

The answer to that particular question started to come into focus while I was in Cincinnati on business. I was saving up, hoping to start my own company. Out of impatience to accumulate wealth faster, I used my powers to pickpocket some extra cash while I strolled on the streets between meetings. With the beauty of telekinesis and taking possession, I didn't even have to go near them. My wife was quite an accomplished shoplifter even without my special toolkit. We all stretch the rules and the law a little bit.

As I took a break and window-shopped, I spotted a woman just down the street. The first thing to get my attention was not her pale ginger hair, but her mage blood. She had a decently attractive face and would have been a lot sexier without her cheap, stained blouse and short, utilitarian haircut. The woman held the hands of her two small dark-haired children, who wore almost threadbare clothes. The children had huge, desperate eyes.

The boy did not have mage blood. The toddler girl was a half-breed like her mother.

I could tell this mother was downtrodden even before I got close enough to read her mind. Recently widowed, she worked in a meat-packing plant that paid barely a pittance. Paying the rent this month was uncertain.

"How do you do?" I asked as I approached, pretending, as always, that I knew nothing about her. She could write an interesting memoir if she wanted to! Irina Christensen, formerly Petrova, was the youngest child of a large family from St. Petersburg, Russia. The father, Vladimir Petrov, was a published novelist. You can still find translations of his historical war novels in special-interest bookstores. The family fled from the Bolsheviks. Irina was born in Paris while the family took refuge there, and she knew three languages as a result. The whole family fell on difficult times since making their final move to our country. Being a published writer does not promise wealth, and Irina's father did not leave a dime of his royalties to his youngest daughter.

"I'm... well," Irina said in her slight Russian accent, staring at this man who was a stranger to her, even though he already knew all there was to know about her. "Who are you?"

"My name is Gerald. And you are?"

She told me her name even though I already knew it.

"And your kids? These are some cute kids you have here."

"This is Victor. Very bright boy. And this is Vanessa."

"You all look like you might be hungry. Would you like a hot meal?"

"I don't need anyone taking care of me."

Despite her chilly demeanor, Irina was lonely and would be delighted for a man to pry into her business. So away I pried, walking with her. Finally, I cracked the ice, and Irina not only opened up, she broke down and wept. Knowing what a turn-on it is for women, even tough ones like her, to have someone play the sensitive guy and offer a shoulder to cry on, I let her sit on a bench with me and sniffle on mine.

I began making regular trips to visit Irina, writing her checks, and taking her and the kids out to dinner. She vented to me more and more about her problems. Life as a widow was hard, though she'd already been unhappy with her husband, George, when he suddenly died of a stroke. Irina found out after the wedding that George was the product of his mother's affair with a Mexican man who worked in the family's citrus orchards in California. The family attempted to cover it up. Living in a time when racial stigma ran high, Irina worried that her children might stumble upon the family secret. As far as I know, those kids never found out that their grandfather was Guadalupe Hernandez, not Elmer Christensen.

Race was not Irina's main reason for getting fed up with George. The man was socially inept like his mother. George embarrassed his wife at parties and never held a job for long before he said the wrong thing, angered the boss, and got fired. With his lack of earning power, he left her nothing when he died.

After that marriage, Irina was grateful for the attentions of a man with well-honed social skills! Little did she know that I'd learned them in the most brutal ways possible.

As Irina sought comfort from me, this opened up a chance to begin my army. I seduced her. It helped me that mind readers are such good lovers. Instead of fumbling around and irritating our partners like a lot of men who have learned only from the body-slamming in pornographic films, we know what women actually want in bed. No matter what we look like, once we get them seduced, we can pretty much have any woman we want.

I reserved hotel rooms and paid for babysitters to watch Irina's children for the night. I wasn't sure what exactly I'd do if we had a love child, but I hoped that we would!

One evening, the phone rang. Enid answered it and yelled for me, saying it was someone calling from the bank. I brought my voice down low when I recognized Irina's voice and knew she was no lady working at the bank.

"Gerald, I don't know what to do. I'm late," Irina whispered. I wondered if she'd been late to work, but quickly, I figured it out. She hadn't gotten her monthly period.

I almost jumped for joy until I reminded myself how terrified Irina must have been. For a single woman at the time, a pregnancy was very bad news, socially and financially.

"Don't worry," I reassured Irina, thankful that my wife had gone off to give Theresa a bath and couldn't hear me. "I'll get it taken care of."

"Aren't there doctors who will, well, get rid of it? Do you know any such doctors?"

"No, no, don't get rid of it. That's dangerous. Those doctors are butchers."

"I cannot afford a baby. You're a married man."

"I'll think of something. Until then, you just sit tight and relax. I will find a home for the baby. I'll do all the work. I promise."

The Catfish

A fter that tense holiday visit with her freshly divorced sister, Lillian returned to school. Avery turned twenty-one on the fifth of December, and Bridget's birthday came just three days later on the eighth. In the dorm kitchen, Lillian baked trays of cupcakes for them both. Immediately after these back-to-back birthdays came hellish final exams.

The reward was the flight back home to see Dad, and all the homemade cookies, dog snuggles, decorations, and warm apple pie that Lillian had looked forward to for months. Lillian's father had finally decided to retire and sell his nursery business.

During the late afternoon of Christmas Eve, the smooth sound of a luxury car came near as headlights swept over the front window. They knew exactly who knocked. Astrid, sprawled on the floor before the fireplace, laid her large pointed ears back in mistrust, tensing her body. Lou opened the door to Uncle Gerald, who stood on the front porch bearing a basket stuffed with cheese and fruit and summer sausages.

"Hello, Gerald," Lou greeted. "Unexpected visit, but I appreciate you bringing all those snacks."

"I wanted to present this basket as a gift, and also an apology for being difficult during our phone conversation not long ago."

Gerald sat down at the table with them to feast on sliced pineapple from the basket. "I see you both are keeping your thoughts from me again, so I'll do this the old-fashioned way. How are you both doing? Lillian, how is school going?"

They chatted about mundane things for a while, until Lou went to the kitchen to clean up some dishes and then stepped outside to straighten up the porch and check on the dog who'd been let outside. Gerald lowered his voice. "Lillian, have you ever felt like there's perhaps something your father isn't telling you?"

"No? I'm not sure." Lillian shrugged.

"I know that you've wondered about your parents' living situation. So has Evelyn, who's old enough to remember your mother's comings and goings. Don't you wonder why they seemed only loosely committed? Why they never married? Why your father was married at a young age to his high school sweetheart Roberta, and they didn't procreate? She had kids after leaving him, so you know infertility wasn't the problem."

Lillian nodded reluctantly. Yes, she had wondered, especially after that childhood summer camp her father paid for that preached abstinence before marriage, while her own parents had children out of wedlock. Dad later regretted sending her to the camp and the shame its teachings caused.

"There's something you don't know, and I feel it is time that the truth came out. Your cousin Katrina and I have been testing out a technique called mind transference. We haven't fine-tuned it yet, but I think it shall work with you, and I'd like to experiment. Take my hand."

"Why?"

"We need physical contact to make it work. Your father's still outside, but I believe he's close enough, and he has just let down his guard. His mind is no longer blocked."

"What... why?"

"It won't take but a second. Take my hand." Gerald reached over and squeezed Lillian's hand in his wider, beefier one. She flinched. He held a finger to his lips.

A string of foreign images and impressions whizzed through Lillian's head, flowing side by side as they reflected from her father just outside the open back door and through Uncle Gerald, like light bent by a prism to burst into a full rainbow of colors.

They say high school is the best four years of your life, and Lou is certainly savoring the best years of his so far, basking in the glory of being part of the in-crowd. It boosts his self-esteem when people smile and nod as he walks down the hall, or when he wins a race, and he is crowned the homecoming king on the football field while fireworks go off. His girlfriend, Roberta, is the queen, like a fairy tale.

Lou's popularity has inflated his ego a little, yet it also puts him on edge that they adore what they see the outside, not who he really is. Being some sort of a witch or wizard isn't the only thing he keeps beneath the surface.

Lou is best friends with his baseball teammate, Walter. They often go out on double dates with their girlfriends. Roberta wants to marry Lou. Walter's own high-ranking girlfriend is Susie, a beautiful blonde majorette. Neither boy has gone any further with their girls than kissing them goodnight on their doorsteps. Other things can wait until their wedding nights. Little do Roberta and Susie know what their boyfriends have done in the privacy of Walter's bedroom after Lou sneaks out of his house at night and climbs a trellis up to Walter's window.

Thank God Gerald is away at college, Papa cannot read minds, and Sarah has only limited insight.

"Lou," Roberta tells her husband, blocking his way to the kitchen so that he cannot check up on his simmering pot of soup, "we have a problem."

"What problem, honey?"

Roberta's brown hair is wound into tight pincurls, her ribbed sweater fitting snugly on her skinny body. They've settled into their wedded life in the childhood home Lou has worked so hard to renovate, the walls painted, most of the furniture new. The couple have talked about filling the upper rooms with babies, anticipating the pitter-patter of little feet down the stairs.

"Has it occurred to you that it's been three months and we have hardly been intimate at all?" Roberta brings up.

"I'm too tired when I arrive home from work, I'm still grieving my father's death, and it's been hard work getting this house fixed up. I promise that on a Sunday afternoon, when I have the energy, I'll..."

"It's always a different excuse. What's wrong with me, Lou? Do I smell bad? Is it my crooked teeth? Am I ugly?"

"No, no, there is nothing wrong with you, Roberta. You're beautiful! It's not you. It's me."

"Why don't we try it right now? Let's make a baby."

"Don't get me wrong, I would love to have ourselves a family." Here, he speaks the truth.

"Nothing's stopping us."

"Except the soup on the stove. It'll burn." And his best friend Walter's impending arrival. He and Susie moved to Kansas City after their wedding, but soon he'll be coming to visit, and Lou wants to conserve his libido.

Roberta, now remarried with two children, walked out on Lou years ago. Lou isn't sure how Walter keeps his own wife satisfied, but he must, since they have four children. Lou takes a vacation and boards a train to Kansas City to visit them.

Susie takes the kids to the zoo, leaving Lou and Walter behind. They jump at the chance for some private time, heading to the bedroom as rain begins to patter the windows. Distracted, Lou does not sense Susie coming back into the house until her footsteps approach the bedroom door. When it flies open, Susie stands in the doorway with the baby on her hip, the two-year-old clinging to her skirt, and her beehive hairdo messy and flattened from the rain. Walter pulls the blanket over their naked bodies.

"We got... rained out," Susie's voice drops. Face going white, Susie lets out a bloodcurdling scream. The baby begins to cry along with her.

"This isn't what it looks like," Walter tells her in a rushed tone, keeping the blanket over himself as he reaches to the side of the bed for his pants.

"This is disgusting! Can't you see, Walter? This man isn't your friend." Susie points at the silent, solemn Lou, face going from white to purple. "He is a pervert. He's trying to turn you into a... a homosexual. Get out of my house, and never come back!"

Vanessa sits on the bed, pulling up the sheets over her bare chest. Lou turns away from her, hunting for his shirt that has been tossed onto the floor beside the bed. She has lived here for a month now, sleeping in one of his spare bedrooms down the hall, ever since she wrote him that letter.

Despite their nearly two-decade age difference, Vanessa confessed to a longtime crush on Lou since meeting him through his brother Gerald. But now that the young woman is here, things are becoming more and more awkward. Each time they attempt something in the bedroom, the mood dies before their pants come off, each hug and caress feeling stiff and unnatural.

After pulling his pajama shirt back on, Lou turns toward Vanessa. Her nightgown falls back over her body.

"Vanessa, I'm so sorry, but this isn't working out," he admits.

"Do you find me unattractive?"

"No, no, not at all. You're a very attractive girl. It's just that... I don't know... there is a lack of chemistry. I'm so sorry."

"Don't you want children, though?" Vanessa cuts straight to the point. Lou has inquired with adoption agencies, but each one is awfully suspicious about placing a child with a single man.

"I'm not going to force anything on you if we can't make it work. I may want children, but no one actually needs them."

"I have an idea! We just have to get the baby-making ingredients into the right place."

"And how are we going to do that if we're sleeping in separate bedrooms?"

"I saw this thing in some of your plant supplies. This plastic dropper. It was still in the wrapper. Do you still have it?"

"I think so—I haven't brought it into work yet. Would that even work?"

"I don't see why not. I heard that a woman can take her temperature to learn when she's most fertile. I'll go to the library to do some research."

Vanessa stands over Lou as he sits on the couch with his evening tea and reads the paper. She has been working on her watercolors since she arrived home from visiting her brother in California. The walls are covered with scenic, blue-skied paintings of grass, water, ducks, and geese. Vanessa is no longer so small-waisted. Her belly, five months pregnant, lays full in her striped sleeveless shirt.

Vanessa knows by now that they probably will not marry, yet she's still held up her end of the selfless offer. She knows that if she moves on after the baby is born, it won't go with her.

"Got a question for you," Vanessa says, sitting down, supporting herself with her hands like she's afraid to quash her rounded belly.

"What's that?"

"Lou, are you gay?"

He takes in a breath, taken aback by the bluntness of her question. "What makes you think that?"

"Well, you couldn't really sleep with me."

Their trick to bypass sex worked in only two months. They have not told anyone that they made this baby outside of the conventional method; Lou reminds Vanessa that it's no one's business, not even the doctor's.

"I talked about you with Victor last week," Vanessa goes on. "He asked if you dress neatly. And he thought you might be in the closet."

"Why did you go telling Victor? Who does he think he is to say these things?"

"It's a yes-or-no question," Vanessa challenges Lou. "Are you or aren't you?"

"Please don't tell anyone; I've got friends, I've got a business. I haven't even told my nephew. Please keep it a secret."

"Have you really and truly been with men? Are you with one right now?"

"No. Not in years. But since you must know, there have been a few."

"I'll keep it a secret, I promise," Vanessa vows. "But my cousin Billy, who Victor and I visited, doesn't keep it a secret. Billy lives with his boyfriend. And I think it might do you good to not keep it a secret either."

"Billy's in San Francisco, right?"

"Yes."

"Most places are not like San Francisco. In most places, people don't take kindly to people like me."

As Lou stepped in through the back door, Gerald dropped Lillian's listless hand, and the stream of memories stopped abruptly. When Lillian snapped back to the present, only a few seconds had gone by, packed with decades of her father's life.

Lou faced the two, asking his brother, "What are you doing?"

"Just testing out how well my mind transference ability works on your daughter."

"Mind transference? What is that?"

"It is a technique for swapping information and memories. And I'm pleased to see that it works. I think most mages can learn to do it, and if you're a mind reader like myself, you can draw memories from a third person."

"Gerald, really. What are you doing?"

"In this case, not much, except perhaps telling your daughter the truth about certain things."

"About what?"

"The reason why you and Vanessa couldn't manage to fuck, so you used the turkey baster method to conceive your children."

"What? That's private! Why did you show her that?" A crimson color rose in Lou's face.

"Does the name Walter Haverford ring a bell? It was a name Lillian was unfamiliar with. Until now."

"What did you do?! Lillian, what happened? Surely I told you about my old friend Walter."

"You never mentioned him before," Lillian said, her voice flat in her confusion. "Is it true his wife walked in on you?"

"Gerald, what did you do?!"

"All I did was show her the truth," Gerald answered smugly. "As the old saying goes, the truth shall set you free."

"Gerald, how dare you? That was cruel! Get out of my house!"

"But you let me stay to have some food."

"Get out now! Leave or you'll wish you were never born!"

"Okay, okay…" Gerald put his hands up and backed away. "Don't hurt me, brother. I apologize for offending you. I'll be on my way."

After Gerald's car left the driveway, Lillian sat on the sofa, dizzy from the fresh foreign vignettes that filled her mind against her will, pictures of her mother, of Walter and his furious wife with the 1960s beehive hair.

Lou paced back and forth, putting his head in his hands, digging his fingers into his white hair. "You saw things you shouldn't have seen," he acknowledged in a muted voice.

"Yeah," Lillian replied as she processed the jumbled movie she'd just been made to watch in her head all at once. Her father had been through so much pain and shame, carrying heavy burdens that hardly anyone else knew about. Even though Gerald showed her things she didn't want to see, she was overcome with empathy for the seventy-one long years he had spent closeted.

"What else did he show you?"

"Besides Walter? Stuff about my mother. I couldn't make it stop."

"I hope you understand why there were certain things your mother and I didn't tell anyone. I hope that you don't think less of me now that Gerald did this."

"I understand why it was private. But if you'd just told us, I would have loved you just the same. I don't think less of you."

"You say that, but I could have lost everyone else in my life. Growing up in my generation, it was not friendly for people like me. It still isn't. Gerald invaded my privacy. And I'll probably never forgive him. I've gone too easy on him… but not anymore. Though living with a secret such as this, all these years… honestly, it's been killing me."

"I wish Gerald didn't do that, though," Lillian sighed. "It should have been your choice. I had always thought Mom was really your girlfriend. But it seems like she pretty much agreed to be a surrogate?"

"Yes, there was no real commitment there, to be honest. Nor did she seem to expect it once she found out the truth. She had you two purely out of the kindness of her heart. That was another thing that I hadn't felt like explaining, but now you know."

Lou and Lillian both took a couple of days to sit with the thing Gerald had done to them both. Lou invited his ex-wife Roberta over for a visit to give her some closure. She was no longer the slender, smooth-faced young brunette in his and his daughter's now collective memory. Roberta had grown into a pudgy and gray-haired grandmother, wearing a gold cross necklace and an oversized T-shirt with a teddy bear on it.

Roberta remembered their former classmate, Walter, well. Though Lou never heard from Walter or his wife Susie again after she caught them in bed together, and Susie kept her lips sealed about that day, she still spoke on the phone with Roberta occasionally. She had divorced Walter about thirty years ago after she caught him visiting gay bars. He later died of a heart attack.

Upon hearing of Lou and Walter's long-term relationship, Roberta gasped, "Oh my goodness, you didn't! I would never have guessed! The two of you just seemed so… normal—that isn't the right word, is it? Well, I guess that explains a lot."

Once she overcame her surprise, Roberta took the news better than Lou had expected, thanking him for telling her. Roberta understood why he'd been so secretive for so long, the things he'd had at stake in his younger days.

After Lillian returned to college, Lou began the risky task of disclosing his orientation to more and more people. Their reactions, like Roberta's, were not as bad as he had feared. Denny and even Evelyn had wondered off and on about him over the years, noticing little hints and clues; but others claimed they'd had no idea.

Lou did not give credit to his brother Gerald for giving him the courage to come out. That choice should have been Lou's alone, not forced upon him before he was fully ready. Lou vowed never to speak to Gerald again.

After casting out some bait a few months ago on the dating website, Lillian reeled in disappointing results. Some of the conversations dried up before any opportunity to meet in person. The handful of dates ended without a second date when they never called again or claimed they "weren't looking for anything serious." Lillian left one date early when the man came on too strong, hugging her aggressively.

One February evening, Lillian hung out with Avery. She had not seen much of him outside of the gaming nights lately, as he spent a lot of time chatting with his girlfriend. As they walked around campus, Lillian got an idea.

"Remember when I told you about the other world?" she brought up.

"The one you can go to with the crystal? Yeah, it sounds amazing."

"I'm wearing the crystal right now. You want to see if we can both go down there? Together?"

"Let's try it. I'm game. Hopefully the worst that would happen is me standing by myself while you disappear."

"If you don't come through, I'll come right back up. If it works, you might feel disoriented. You'll feel like you're falling. But it's a slow fall. Nothing will hurt you. Not even the creepy graveyard you'll see before we get there."

Once they stopped under the snow-heavy limbs of an isolated tree, Lillian glanced around to be sure that no one lingered nearby, and then instructed Avery to close his eyes. As he did, Lillian took his hand, molded it into her paler one, and put the crystal between them. Her heart fluttered at the warmth of his hand in hers. Lillian squeezed her eyes shut and descended.

"Open your eyes," Lillian said. Somehow, they had bypassed the graveyard. Was that little scene for her eyes only?

Trees rose here and there, tall pines with sagging branches. Scattered throughout were rolling bluffs of desert with spiky plants. The lavender sky dyed the grassy sands pink. This was no place Lillian recognized, even with the familiar temple nearby.

Avery pulled away and spun around, his mind blown to see the other world for himself. "It worked, didn't it? It freaking worked! This is beautiful!"

"It worked, but this place has changed. I think you influenced it somehow. Is this what it looks like back home?"

"It does look like some parts. Except dreamier."

"Follow me and I'll show you something." Lillian led him past the glistening pond that was still there and toward the softly glowing emerald temple, rising above a large rock glittering with green crystals. Explaining the temple's purpose to Avery, she went up the steps, and after hesitating for a few moments, he did too. They walked to the back room, the space of bones and ancestors.

"This place feels intense." Avery shivered a bit at the sight of the glinting bones that walled the interior surfaces, some human and some unrecognizable.

"Remember, there's nothing in here that can hurt you. Even our leader isn't here. My dad said he's been gone for years. No one knows what happened to him, and I've never even seen him."

"You have a leader?"

"All mages do. I think. Ours looks like Death, wearing a black robe. I don't know if any of the others are MIA like ours."

"Since there's no crystal in my family, I have no clue who mine is."

For a while, they watched the foggy room of swirling ancestral spirits, who shaped themselves into ancient, fur-clad human forms before dissipating into fine mists.

After they walked outside, Avery wondered out loud who had built this green temple in the first place or if it had arisen by itself. Lillian, who'd questioned the same thing, did not know the answer. And neither did her father.

"Look over there." Avery pointed toward a horizon where the sharp rocky outline of a ridge met the swirled blue and pink cap of a sky. They walked down the path to investigate and looked down on something Lillian had never expected to see here—other people. A small group dotted the lower landscape beneath the ridge, sitting on desert rocks or bathing at the rim of a large steaming pool. Orange sheaths surrounded them; they were all fire people. Faint voices came up to Lillian's ears.

Just beyond a stand of evergreen trees, a radiant yellow and red temple rose up. Its columns continually changed color like the heart of a flame, or the roiling magma inside a volcano. On the front step, behind a thin glowing orange river, sat a large black beast with oversized pointed ears like a jackal's, protectively watching the people.

"I think that's your leader," Lillian whispered, heart pounding.

"I think you're right. I can feel it. I'm even hearing it speaking to me in my mind now! Like it's giving me a blessing."

"What's it saying?"

"Telling me I'm powerful. And that I have a huge destiny. I can't make sense of all of it... I know there's more, but I can't even hear all of it, and I'm only at the edge of understanding it."

"Incredible! Are you still hearing it? Or feeling it?"

"It's stopped for now."

"And those people down there?"

"Those must be people with crystals. Probably not even from around here. I can hear a few of them. They're speaking Japanese."

"What if they notice me?"

"That could be bad. We should leave."

They took the crystal between their fingers and brought themselves back up to the earth's chilly surface.

Though it would be a deep gesture of trust, Lillian almost offered to let Avery borrow her crystal, to see if it worked if he used it alone. He could explore a space made just for him and the other fire mages visiting from around the world. Lillian held back. Lending something to a person might end in a falling out, or the object going missing. She'd lost books in this manner. Most books were easily replaceable. The crystal was more precious to herself and her family than any diamond ever would be.

"I've never actually seen your powers," Lillian said as she and Avery walked back toward where he'd parked. "I'm curious about what it's really like for you. What exactly you can do."

"Let's talk about that some other time."

"I'm not asking you to burn a house down. Maybe you could just light up a little kindling in the fireplace at your house, or just tell me about it..."

"I can't do any demonstrations for you."

"Why not?"

"I can't do it again unless I really have to. I made a promise."

"When was the last time you did it? When you were kidnapped?"

"Yeah. Those people wanted to cut my throat, I was tied up, and I was running out of ways to escape. So that one time, I was forgiven."

"I'm not sure why anyone would need to forgive you; it was obvious self-defense. Did you ever use your powers before you saved yourself?"

"I'd rather not talk about it. If I did, then you'd see how I could hurt you and you wouldn't want to be around me."

"I already knew that, and I still choose to hang out with you."

"Sorry, it's just a bunch of bad memories."

They walked on in a hushed, uncomfortable silence. Lillian had the sense that she'd dug too deep, upsetting the balance of the friendship.

Lillian flew back home to visit her father on the Saturday that marked the beginning of spring break. The following day, Avery would land in the neighboring state to see his girlfriend, whose mother had recovered from her stroke.

Lillian brushed aside little pangs of jealousy as she waited to hear about Avery's much-anticipated visit. The couple stayed on Lillian's mind as her father took her out to dinner on Sunday night. For all she knew, Avery might be making out with Chrissy at this very moment. Lillian wished him the best. Chrissy was truly lucky to have found someone so kind.

Late the following morning, as her father puttered around the house, Lillian sent a short text message to Avery, asking how it was going, curious but half-expecting him to not reply.

His response chimed in immediately. *It's complicated. Can I just call?*

Now getting worried, Lillian gave the go-ahead to ring her number. All her father had to know was that a friend called.

"Is everything okay? Are you having fun with Chrissy?" she asked.

"No, I'm not having fun." Avery's voice sounded rougher than usual.

"What's wrong?"

"I haven't even seen Chrissy!"

"What? Didn't you arrive yesterday?"

"Yeah, I got in last night. She said she'd pick me up, and she never did. I took a cab and I'm in a hotel. I hardly got any sleep."

"Maybe there was a misunderstanding?"

"I don't think so. I've called her a million times and she didn't pick up. I think she blocked my number!"

"What?! Why would she do that?"

"No idea."

"Did you try going to her house?"

"I took the cab to the address she gave me. It's a dry cleaning place, not a house. I checked my phone, saw she was online, and sent her an IM, since I couldn't call her anymore. Then she blocked me there too!"

"What the actual fuck?"

"She found someone else? She's embarrassed about something? Or she got cold feet? I don't know."

"If she changed her mind, why didn't she say something? Why would she just disappear and leave you stranded in a place you don't know? What is that?"

"I can't believe someone would do this. There damn well better be a good excuse."

"Since she's blocked you, you might never hear an excuse. Do you have a phone number for her parents or her sister?"

"No, I don't have their numbers. I really don't know what to do. Any ideas you have, throw them at me."

"Have you tried Googling her name to see if you can find her real address or another number?"

"I tried that, and I didn't come up with anybody in this city with her name."

"Can you try messaging her friends on Facebook to find out if they know anything?"

"Yeah, I'll do that. That's the only place where she doesn't have me blocked, not yet. I don't know what I'll do until Saturday. It will be lonely and expensive."

"Can you try to get a flight back home sooner?"

"I checked. The flights are booked. I'm stuck."

"What about a standby ticket?"

"If the flights are full, I could be trying for days. My mom offered to come get me, but she'd be driving for days. I told her there's no point."

"I feel so bad for you. Since we're not far away, if it weren't for... you know, I'd have my family help you."

"Don't worry about that. I'll think of something."

Once the conversation ended, Lou, who had just set a stack of fresh hotcakes on the dining room table, turned toward his daughter. "Sweetheart, who were you talking to? Do you have a friend who's in trouble?"

"Yeah. My friend went to visit his girlfriend and she never showed up. She gave him a fake address. Something is definitely fishy."

"That's terrible! I hope he is able to get in touch with her. Oh, did I hear you saying something about having your family help him?"

"I don't think we can."

"Did I hear you say we're not far? Where is he?"

Oh, no. Lillian had said too much within earshot of her father. "He's in Wilmington," she admitted.

"Delaware?"

"Yeah. But I don't think there's really anything we can do for him."

"Where is he staying? He doesn't know anybody there, besides that girl?"

"Nope. He's staying in a hotel."

"Staying there alone is going to be bad for him. Any friend of my daughter's is a friend of mine, and I'm happy to let him stay here. I just retired. I have more than enough time to help entertain your friend. We could put him up in Evelyn's old bedroom."

"I don't think you'd want him to stay here. We'll just have to think of something else."

"It's almost selfish not to help that young man, don't you think?"

After dinner, Avery called again. Desperate to vent, he'd tried reaching a couple of other friends, and Lillian was the first to answer her phone. He broke news that had Lillian's blood boiling.

Through some sleuthing and a terribly awkward phone call earlier that day, Avery found that his girlfriend, Chrissy Meyers, did not exist.

The woman behind the farce was Cassidy Searcy, a married thirty-one-year-old home-maker who lived in Massachusetts. With her baby-faced features and squeaky voice, she looked and sounded a decade younger. Her mother did not have a stroke over the winter; she'd been dead for years. While Cassidy grew up in Wilmington, she hadn't been back since her mother's funeral.

Carrie, the older sister, was a fictional character. Cassidy had no sister, just a brother who'd gotten sick of her lies and cut her off. The children who'd sometimes played in the background during webcam chats and phone conversations were not Cassidy's nephews. They were her own sons, ages five and three.

Avery learned the unthinkable truth from a man who still kept the "Chrissy Meyers" Facebook profile friended to monitor Cassidy's schemes after she had a fake romance with him and told him she lived in Florida. Cassidy loved to start emotional affairs with young men while her husband worked two jobs, basking in the attention, telling them she lived in a different city each time. This man sent Avery a link to Cassidy Searcy's real profile. Avery clearly recognized the woman in brown boots and skinny jeans, smiling with her two young boys and a tall, brawny husband against a background of fall foliage.

Avery was put in touch with Cassidy's husband, Liam, who wanted to gain more information by phone. Avery struggled with his usual shyness when talking to strangers, giving initially halted answers that started to come more easily in his growing anger. When Liam caught Cassidy in her online affairs, she insisted it wasn't cheating, as there was no sex. He'd wanted a divorce for years, but stayed married in his fear for the children's well-being. Cassidy was not a good mother. When she didn't scream at their sons, she neglected them in favor of her computer games. Liam was terrified of the family court giving her custody, but Avery's experience pushed him over the edge and solidified his decision to leave her.

"I feel embarrassed and violated." Avery's voice was on the verge of tears. "I just can't even... how could anyone do this? And why? Putting someone's feelings through the shredder just because she's bored? Or likes the thrill of getting attention?"

"I can't wrap my mind around it, either. I can't imagine what she was thinking, stringing you along and taking it this far. It's so cruel and twisted! I'm so sorry she did this to you."

"Now you see how being able to read people doesn't keep you from getting screwed over? I should have seen the signs something wasn't right. Even though she never hid her face. I've heard of those fakes... catfish, I think they're called... but they usually steal a picture of some good-looking person and always have an excuse not to video chat or meet up. But this was different; she showed me her real face. Sometimes she wouldn't get back to me for days, and then got snippy and said she was 'busy.' I mean, I'm a full-time student and I work in the payroll office, but I try not to blow off the people I care about. Sometimes I'd ask a simple question and she'd make me feel guilty, accusing me of not trusting her. When I wanted to send a card or a gift, she always had a reason not to give out her address. Her parents snooped in her mail, or she didn't want them to ask too many questions, or someone was stealing from her mailbox, or she might move out soon. She didn't give an address until just a few days ago, and it turned out to be that dry cleaning place."

"She's very manipulative. She was playing on your emotions and didn't want you questioning anything. Please don't beat yourself up. We want to think the best of people we love. We don't want to think somebody could be that much of a liar."

"I wasn't even in love with a real person. Just a character. If I got dumped, that'd be one thing... but finding out the person I put love and time and energy into doesn't even *exist*... the rug's been pulled out from under me."

Lillian spent most of that call in her bedroom. Once it ended, she came back downstairs to fix herself some dessert. Shocked and heavy-hearted, she was also increasingly worried about Avery. Even if it made her jealous, she would have much rather seen him happy, coupled up with a real girlfriend, than going through this.

"Was that your friend who called this morning?" Dad asked.

"Yeah."

"You were talking for quite a while; it sounded emotional. Did he find out what's going on with that girlfriend? Is she okay?"

"She was a fake. She's some woman in Massachusetts who's married with kids, posing on the internet as a young, single college student."

"My goodness! It was all a hoax?! What a heartless thing to do. I'm sure that young man feels like a fool. Frankly, I'm concerned about his well-being. We're going to get him. It's a bit late for me tonight, but we can leave in the morning."

"I'm still not sure that's a good idea."

"I really think he should not be alone. You care about your friend, don't you?"

"Of course." Lillian did not realize until today just how deeply she cared.

"It's truly no problem for me to have company, and I don't understand your hesitation."

"Normally, if this happened to a friend, I'd go get them in a heartbeat. But I'm not sure... I'm not sure he'd want to come over."

"You won't know until you ask. Want to give him a call and let him know about my offer?"

"I could, but... Dad... there's something you don't know. Something I can't tell you."

"I don't follow. This has me worried. Please tell me."

"You promise not to completely flip out? Or go on a rampage?"

"Why? Is this friend of yours a criminal?"

"Of course not! He's really nice. Evelyn's met him, and she liked him."

"Then what could be so wrong with him? It seems selfish to not offer to help, and I can tell you are hiding something. I don't like that."

Feeling backed into a corner, Lillian finally said the words she could not take back. "He's a fire mage."

"A... a what?!" Lou's face blanched.

"I'm sorry, Dad. I know we are not supposed to talk to them; but we had a class together, got curious..."

"Have you ignored everything I have taught you?"

"I was afraid of him. I avoided him for months. And then we ended up in the class, and I still avoided him. And then, somehow, the walls came down."

Lou put his fingers to his forehead for a few seconds, taking deep breaths. "The walls came down, you said. And then what did you start doing together, you and this fire mage?"

"I started going to his house."

"His house? Were you not thinking at all?!"

"He has roommates. They have parties there on most Friday nights where people play games. It gives me something to look forward to during the week. That's where Evelyn met him when she was in town."

"She brought the baby too, didn't she? He was around my granddaughter?!"

"Yes, and nothing happened. Everything was fine. And we just started hanging out."

"Hanging out alone?"

"Yes, we've hung out alone."

"Jesus, Lillian! Doing what?"

"Just talking, or doing crafts together, or walking between classes." She stopped short of revealing that she'd shown Avery the crystal and the other world.

"That's an awful lot of trust you must have."

"He's supported me. He's a good listener. He's the one who taught me the trick to hide our thoughts. And he gets me in a way that regular people don't. But now that you know the truth, I'm sure you've changed your mind about letting him stay here."

"You hid this friend from me. It makes me wonder what else you're hiding."

"I'm not hiding anything else."

"No other mage friends?"

"No. Just him. I knew you'd freak out. But before you knew this, you said any friend of mine is a friend of yours, and you were pressuring me to have him stay here."

Lou sighed. "Okay. You have a point. If this young man stays here, he would mind his manners?"

"Of course. I'm sure he will."

"Go ahead and call him."

Avery wept in the thin-blanketed hotel bed, with a pillow tight over his head and the blinds closed. The previous spring break was a horror, being hit in the head and then strung up from the boughs of a tree, dangerously close to being murdered.

But that day had been more straightforward. All he had to do was defend himself. He'd read some of their minds, and like members of any cult, they were lonely and unstable people fleeing from difficult lives, brainwashed by their leader into committing despicable acts.

Traumatic as that was, it made more sense than what was happening to him now. Somehow, this trickery stabbed Avery in the heart even worse than the physical assault and attempt on his life last year. And brought back painful memories of middle school, when a girl feigned romantic interest just so her friends could get a cheap laugh at Avery's expense. It confused him that a grown woman a decade older than him had just pulled a similar illusion, costing him time and money in the process. How could he fall for this? He was ashamed.

After spending much of the evening on the phone with Lillian, his best friend Alexis, and his mother, Avery had to hook it up to the charger as he looked for something to occupy his time. Avery rarely drank, and had only one glass of wine on his twenty-first birthday. His mother had overcome a drinking problem before he was born and she never drank a drop in his lifetime, leaving him with a healthy fear of alcohol. But some liquor might be just the right prescription for such a rotten day. Avery was just about to look up the nearest bar when his cell phone vibrated with an incoming call from Lillian. He picked it up, still attached to the charger.

"We can come get you tomorrow if you want," she informed him.

"What?!"

"You can stay with us. My dad's offering. You can stay in Evelyn's old room."

"Whoa. You know why I can't do that, right?"

"I told my dad."

"You told him what? Back up. You told your dad... about the powers?!"

"He overheard us talking, and heard where you are. He got concerned about you and started asking questions. When I said we couldn't go get you, he kept asking why not. He said it was selfish not to help you. I didn't want to explain, of course. But Dad figured out that I was hiding something. It put me kind of between a rock and a hard place. So I told."

"And then what happened? Was he angry?"

"I'm afraid so."

"Then you guys probably shouldn't come get me."

"Here's the thing, though. When my dad first mentioned putting you up at the house, he told me, 'Any friend of my daughter's is a friend of mine.' After the truth came out, I brought up again what he'd said. And it made him think. That's when he changed his mind. The round trip would take a few hours, so it's a bit late to go tonight. Oh, and my cousin Denny wants to ride along too."

"Because they're nervous and they don't trust me."

"Would you rather we stay home?"

"The options I have aren't great. Since you guys are willing to go to the trouble... why don't you come get me?"

After giving Lillian the address for the hotel, Avery came down with a migraine, brought on by crying and stress. He took one of his prescription pills to numb the pain that drilled into the side of his head and then fell into a deep, black sleep, not waking up until late the following morning. He finished packing his suitcase and paced around the room, jittery with anxiety.

A knock came at the door. Extensions of green shone through and around the edges of the frame. Hushed into silence, Avery slowly got up to open it.

Lillian stepped inside, wearing a thin ribbed jacket. Avery fell into her arms and struggled to not weep against her shoulder. He pulled out of the hug before the dam had a chance to break.

Two gray-haired men stood in the doorway, one of them fairly squat with a round belly. The other one was tall and thin. Avery recognized him as Lillian's father with the family resemblance, the same luminous green eyes behind his bifocals. Both men were using the mind-blocking trick at the moment, so if either was readable, Avery could not get through. They stared him down, suspiciously and almost aggressively. Lillian's father had a dog on a leash, straining at her collar, whining and trying to get a sniff at Avery. He recognized this dog from Lillian's stories and photographs. Astrid, the blue heeler that she missed whenever she was at school.

"Know this, kid," the shorter man remarked in a hoarse voice. "You'd better behave yourself. If you try something, we'll shoot you, bring you back to life, and shoot your ass again." He laughed, a hard-edged cackle that suggested he might not be one hundred percent joking.

"Denny, don't say that," Lillian admonished. "You're scaring him."

In his deep discomfort, Avery almost asked the family to go home without him, but instead, he gathered up his suitcases. They escorted him to a red SUV, put his two bags in the back littered with well-chewed squeaky dog toys, and then Lou accompanied him to the front desk to check out while Denny walked the dog to a grassy area to pee. As they all got into the vehicle, Avery slid in the backseat and Lillian sat beside him. The two men up front glanced back at him frequently. The dog affectionately nudged him from behind the seat with her cold nose.

"What do you think of seeing wild ponies on the beach?" Lillian asked as they pulled out of the parking lot.

"Really? Sounds nice. That's near here?"

"Yeah. We could go sightseeing this week; might take your mind off of stuff. Have you eaten?"

"Not today."

"When did you last eat?"

"I can't remember. I've lost my appetite."

"I stop eating when I'm going through a bad time, so I know what that's like. You need to eat, though. It won't make this situation go away, but taking care of yourself will take the edge off a little."

"Want to hit a McDonald's or something, Uncle Lou?" Denny suggested.

"Sure," Lou agreed from behind the steering wheel. "Avery, do you want me to get you a sausage McMuffin?"

"I don't eat sausage."

"Don't care for it?"

"I don't eat meat."

"What?!" Denny protested. "How in the hell do you get any nutrition?"

From a drive-through, they ordered hotcakes and hashbrowns. As they got on the road, Avery balanced the food in his lap and picked at his hotcakes with a plastic fork. With his stomach in knots, he could barely get these simple carbohydrates down.

Later in the afternoon, they reached Easton, the town where his friend grew up. Avery was impressed with its pretty charm, yet it was not enough to cheer him up in any way. They pulled up to the family home, whose shady porch and front steps looked slightly familiar from the vague, intermittent flashes he'd gotten from Lillian's mind on those few occasions when she had truly opened up to him.

Once everyone was inside, Lillian led Avery up the stairs to show him Evelyn's old bedroom, where he would sleep. The loft bed Evelyn had as a teenager was still there, with a metal frame and a desk tucked underneath. Up the ladder, fresh bedding waited for Avery.

The room was set up like a shrine for a high school queen bee. Lacrosse trophies lined the shelves; first-place ribbons hung on the wall. Decade-old photographs of a teenage Evelyn at school dances with her massive group of friends decorated a bulletin board on one wall. After glancing around her superstar sister's room, it was little wonder to Avery that Lillian felt insecure about a lot of things.

Avery set up his laptop on the desk as Lillian gave him the wifi password. He called his mother to let her know where he was staying, keeping her unaware that he was going to sleep in the lair of necromancers. She did not need one more thing to worry about.

His appetite still strained, Avery chose only oatmeal and cinnamon as they ate dinner. A thick, awkward air hung around the table as Denny and Lou peered over their silverware at Avery. Denny would be sleeping on the sofa tonight, just to "keep an eye on things." Avery began to feel like he was under arrest.

After Lou and Denny went to sleep, Lillian and Avery spent some time together in Evelyn's old room, sitting on the mattress of the loft bed and leaning against the purple wall, keeping their voices quiet.

"Denny is probably staying over because he thinks I'll burn the house down," Avery said. "I'm glad I don't have to stay all alone in a hotel, and thanks for going out of your way to get me, but this is still uncomfortable."

"I'm sorry about that. I'll try to get Denny to lighten up. If you want, we have some movies here we can watch. You might want to avoid Dad's record collection except for the reggae, which is pretty decent. He's into Barry Manilow. Yep, I was raised on easy listening."

"I think we should stick with movies. And reggae."

"It doesn't feel real that you're actually *here*. In my house."

"I'm sure we both thought I'd never visit here."

"We can do some sightseeing tomorrow. There's plenty to see."

"I'll go, since I really should get out, but I might seem a bit out of it. I'm really down about what happened."

"I understand. I'd really like to meet up with that Cassidy Searcy, or whatever the hell her name is, in a dark alley. She is garbage."

After Lillian went to bed in the adjacent room, Avery got on his computer and tried in vain to keep himself distracted. He crossed his arms on the desk and laid his head down.

A knock came at the door, and Avery knew it was not Lillian. Lillian's father rapped gently again. The door creaked open.

"Would you like me to make you something to help you sleep?" Lou whispered.

"Um... sure."

Lou tiptoed downstairs, yelping when he stepped on a noisy plastic squeaker that the dog had chewed out of one of her toys. He came back up with a cup of chamomile tea.

"You feel pretty heartbroken right now?" Lou said in a low voice, sitting on the one other chair in the bedroom as Avery sipped his tea at the desk.

"Yeah, I do."

"Well, I don't understand you kids having these internet relationships these days. Maybe it works sometimes and I can't understand it because I'm from a different generation. But you did what you did expecting the best of people."

Astrid, the dog, walked into the room, and Avery reached down to stroke her head between her large triangle ears.

"Astrid is fond of you," Lou commented. "That dog is smart as a whip, and a good judge of character. I am wondering something. Were you brought up by mages? People like you?"

"Just my mom."

"Did your mother have a pretty good background knowledge on the matter?"

"No. She wasn't raised by mages."

"You heard nothing about the code? Or people like us?"

"Not until I was about ten. Then my mom found a friend who told us all that stuff."

When Lou left, Avery climbed up to the mattress and crawled under the purple blanket and stared up at the shadowed ceiling, decorated with glow-in-the-dark stars. He thought of Lillian asleep in the next room, picturing her waking up and changing her mind about which bed she wanted to be in, crawling up the rungs of the ladder to lay beside him. As soon as that thought crept up, Avery stuffed it deep down into the recesses of his mind. He just needed a hug from someone. Anyone. That was all.

The next day, after he got up and showered, Avery overheard Denny downstairs, questioning Lillian. "Why did you hug him like that when we picked him up? That was quite an embrace. Is there something going on between you?"

"We're just friends! It lasted, like, three seconds. If you were in his situation, wouldn't you need a hug too?"

After Avery cautiously came down the stairs, Lou offered him a stack of leftover pancakes.

"I still think you're either very brave or very foolish to keep this boy here, Uncle Lou," Denny said from the couch, as if Avery weren't nearby.

"I can find somewhere else to go," Avery offered, anxious to leave this house and a bit irritated with Lillian for caving in and revealing the truth to her father, even if she meant well. If he'd stayed at the hotel, he would have a lonely week and the cost would add up night after night, but at least no one would treat him as the enemy.

"I'm sorry that my nephew is being over-cautious," Lou apologized. "Denny, can you tone it down?"

"Hello. You have a fire person in your house. Don't you realize that's unheard of? But I'll try to shut up now. I'm sorry."

Avery ate a pancake, hoping to make it to his departure date without being possessed, attacked, or shot for a misunderstanding about his motives.

Lou gave Avery and Lillian a ride to some nearby attractions, including quaint little towns and the beach. Denny did not ride along, and everything felt more relaxed without him. Later, around the dinner table, after Lillian got up to get seconds, Lou tried to reassure Avery. "Once you've put that impostor behind you, I'm sure that a real woman will come along soon enough."

"As long as it ain't Lillian," Denny added, laughing a bit though his expression was serious.

"We're just friends," said Avery. People often asked if he was dating Alexis, his best friend back home, though she had a boyfriend and there was no attraction.

After dinner, to Avery's relief, Denny left.

Lillian invited Avery into her bedroom, pointing out the books and rock and crystal collections on her bookshelves. She pulled out photograph albums and school yearbooks, telling stories of classmates and her favorite teachers. This was just what Avery needed. Distraction. Stepping into someone else's life to forget his own. He enjoyed the yearbooks and pictures, finding out what his friend looked like as a long-haired, bespectacled child and as a teenager. She trusted him with photos of her most awkward stage in the sixth and seventh grades with short, shaggy hair growing out after a pixie cut, huge "birth control glasses" as she called them, and mismatched clothes.

Lillian got flustered when she turned the page of an album to a photo of herself as a small child in a pink dress, and the adolescent Evelyn with a mop of frizzy permed hair and stone-washed jeans, both sitting on the couch. Their visiting cousin Julius sat between them, putting an arm around each sister and pulling them close. To Avery, his smirking face dripped with slime.

"I thought Dad burned all the pictures of him! He must have missed this one!" Lillian slid the photograph out of the plastic holder and minced it, tossing the shreds into her bedroom wastebasket.

"Are you okay?"

"Yeah. It's gone. Whenever I see a picture of him, it just feels like he's staring at me and my skin crawls."

"He's the one I'd like to meet in a dark alley."

After getting up the following day, they went on a drive with Lillian's father to Washington, D.C. They walked around, showing Avery the columned buildings and monuments, reflecting pool, and pink-blooming cherry trees. As they sat on the white steps of the Jefferson Memorial, Avery struggled to keep his mood up, unable to forget that this was not where he had planned to be or the people he had expected to be with.

"You okay?" Lou asked.

"I'm glad I get to see all this for the first time. But I'm still feeling hurt. I'm so mad at myself that I fell for those lies."

"I fell for it too," said Lillian. "Please don't beat yourself up. I talked to that atrocious woman a couple of times, remember? I could even hear those kids. I thought Chrissy was real, her sister was real, and those were her nephews. I never doubted her for a second."

"But you weren't dating that character. I should have seen the signs."

"We want to think the best of people."

"Sorry if I seem down," Avery apologized. "I really appreciate you guys taking me out to see all this. I'd be a lot worse off otherwise."

"Just give yourself space to feel what you need to feel."

The unlikely trio looked on in silence at the blustering blue-gray March day. A breeze sent ripples through the reflecting pool and the soft pale pink cherry blossoms.

They went out to dinner. After they returned to the house that evening, Avery and Lillian talked and played board games. Most of the tension from the past days was gone. Though Avery still grieved over the relationship that never was, a warm, cozy, slumber-party feeling enveloped him, reminiscent of late nights playing *Dungeons & Dragons* with a childhood friend.

After Avery went to bed, he laid awake, his mind drifting. He thought of Lillian walking beside the reflecting pool earlier, with her long ruby hair falling straight over the back of her jacket. He daydreamed about her climbing up into the loft of her sister's bed to lie next to him. Having her in his arms.

No, stop, Avery ordered himself before the fantasy progressed any further. *You can't think like this. You thought you'd be holding your girlfriend this week, she isn't real, and you're so confused.*

As he struggled harder to chase the unwelcome thoughts out of his head, Avery admitted to himself that while he was wrapped up in his smoke-and-mirrors love affair with "Chrissy," he did not have a chance to dwell on his growing fondness toward Lillian, an attraction that nagged like a dull muscle ache for months. It wasn't just her looks. A kind, straightforward, and honest personality, with a good dash of creativity, also had Avery liking her more the longer he knew her.

But anything besides friendship with Lillian was never meant to happen. Avery would scare her away if he opened up about these feelings. She had never shown hints of a crush on him, not from her behavior or what little he could read into her mind: vague images, at most. Not to mention how much it would horrify both of their families if they dated.

Their parents' reaction wasn't his only concern. If Lillian got any closer to Avery, she might find out something that she would not like. A dark chapter of his past that he hoped to keep closed and locked. Fireballs streaking through the sky. Wild dogs lunging, shadows through the air. Blood staining the dirt. Screams.

They could not be anything more than friends. Period.

Avery asked Lou to return him to Wilmington the day before his departure date, insisting that he would be fine sleeping in the airport for one night. He wanted to ensure that he got out of the house before they had to drive Lillian to a separate airport for her own flight back, and told Lou that he did not wish to keep imposing on him. Avery made himself scarce so that he would not be alone with Lou or, worse, with Lillian's cousin Denny. These men had become cordial enough in Lillian's presence, but there was no telling if they would turn hostile after she departed and could no longer stick up for Avery.

After Avery returned to Richard's house and his whole social circle found out what happened, some of them sympathized like Lillian and his mother had done. But not everyone was so understanding. Avery's roommate Heather hurt his feelings with her criticism. "How could you be so stupid? You should have known!"

Cassidy's husband Liam convinced Avery to send him the chat logs with his wife for evidence in divorce court. Avery forwarded the email chains and instant messages from his sham relationship. Laying eyes on the lovey-dovey chats again was purely mortifying. Avery removed a few intimate photos Cassidy had pressured him into taking, figuring Liam would not want to see them. Avery had not even wanted to take these pictures, but she'd begged and pleaded. Did she have a whole collection of men in vulnerable poses, trophies from her exploits?

Avery's friends did not know about those evenings of taking clothes off in front of their webcams after "Chrissy" claimed her parents went to bed. She never showed him her lower half, hiding her C-section scar while dropping erotic hints that any further exposure could wait for their visit. Through his mind reading, Avery had unintentionally seen and felt plenty of encounters. He knew the soft, fleshy curve of a breast. He knew the taste of a woman. Many of them, in fact. But physically, Avery had never gone further than a few kisses on dates, and he'd confided in "Chrissy" about his inexperience, feeling behind his peers. Along with the rest of his emotions, this woman had played his sexual frustration like a violin.

Still slammed with physically painful waves of heartbreak, Avery found a bottle of tequila in Richard's liquor cabinet one night and drank himself sick.

The week after that very strange spring break unexpectedly spent with Avery, a letter landed in Lillian's mailbox at school. It had no return address and was postmarked in Columbus, Ohio. This immediately put her on edge, but she cautiously opened it, as the messy handwriting on the envelope wasn't Julius' fine cursive.

The greeting card had a silly picture of a squirrel and a flower. The message scrawled inside was from none other than Katrina.

Hey, Lillian.

I know it's been a real long time since we've talked. Sorry if this is weird for me to be sending you this. My grandpa gave me your address. I remember we had a lot of fun together, years ago, and I miss those days. I hope to hear back from you, and it will just be between us. Here's my number...

Lillian tucked the card into her book bag. At first, she was on the fence about writing back, since she didn't like to simply ignore someone who had taken the time to reach out to her. But did Katrina still eat dinners at Julius' house? Were they still close? Did Katrina perhaps even buddy up with Zack?

Lillian decided not to respond.

Avery requested to visit Lillian when she was alone the following evening, wanting to talk about something.

"Thanks for letting your dad help me," he expressed after she let him into her dorm room. "It was kind of nerve-wracking, but it saved me money and I got to see neat stuff."

"I'm sorry that Denny was making scary comments. I wish he didn't do that."

"It's okay; he has reason not to trust me. You know, I've been thinking... and I think maybe you don't want to get too close to me."

"What?" The statement took Lillian by surprise. Weren't they good friends?

"You seem to think I'm harmless. But I'm not."

"Neither am I. We've already discussed this."

"When I was younger, I had to promise not to use my powers. And if you knew the reason... well, it might be best for you if we just spent less time together."

"I like hanging out with you! What is this about, really?"

"Are you sure your roommate won't walk in anytime soon?"

"No, she's not coming back tonight. She's with her boyfriend."

With the need for careful secrecy, this had to be bad. Lillian grimly resigned herself to getting cut out of Avery's life. "Can we get to the point?" she asked. "You're making me nervous."

"First, let me ask you something. Have you ever let go, lost control, and used your powers? Or felt close to it?"

"Other than using them against Julius?"

"Yeah."

Lillian confessed to her urges when she had to dissect a fetal pig in high school, while the squeamish classmates in her group made her do most of the cutting. She went back to the day when Denny encouraged her to purposefully reanimate a dead squirrel, to get a handle on her abilities.

Lillian admitted to striking back when the late Tara Nicholson threatened and choked her, picking Tara up off the floor and flinging her things around to frighten her bully of a roommate into fleeing. Lillian was quick to assure Avery that she had nothing to do with Tara's death the following semester.

"That's all pretty tame, to be honest," said Avery.

"What is this private discussion we are about to have?" If Lillian was about to be dumped as a friend, she wanted to get the hurt over with as quickly as possible.

"I told you I was homeschooled, right?"

"Right." Lillian had never thought to ask why. She attributed it to his mother, who sounded like the type to go against the grain of society.

"I went to public schools and one private school before then. I was picked on at every school. The kids thought I was effeminate, or they thought I was gay, or they thought I was just a nerd, so they gave me hell. I was called names, beaten up, spat on."

"I'm so sorry! That's awful! Bullies suck."

"Yeah, they do. I don't remember all the details. I blocked some of it out. My mom kept switching me from school to school to try to protect me, but sure enough, it'd start up again. One day... my memory of that day is fuzzy, since I've tried to block that out too... I finally lost it."

"How old were you?"

"Fourteen, I think. I was in eighth grade. I... I don't think I want to tell you this. I don't want to scare you."

"You can tell me."

"It was lunchtime. I'd had it pretty bad at that school for a while. They kept calling me a 'faggot.' I'd been called that for years. In PE class, they'd steal my clothes and put them in the toilet. They even made a nasty website about me and kept harassing me over instant messages. I was getting to the point where I thought I'd be better off dead."

"Oh, no. You did not deserve to go through that," Lillian sympathized. Middle school was not easy for her either. On some days she was teased or picked last in gym class. After that mortifying day when she bled through her pants, her peers laughed and chucked tampons at her in the hallways for months. But Lillian could not imagine this level of persistent torment, cyberbullying a kid could not escape from.

"On the day that I lost it, somebody taped an embarrassing sign on my back. It was a girl sitting behind me in class, and I couldn't read her mind. She just acted like she'd poked me by accident. I'd had 'kick me' signs put on my back before, but that sign said I would do a sexual thing because I was gay. At lunch, they gathered around to beat me up. I was mobbed. A bunch of kids were on top of me all of a sudden and I couldn't even breathe. My face was smashed into the dirt. I felt like I was going to die. All I was thinking, in the moment, was that I was about to suffocate, and I had to defend myself. I had to do something to distract them. Then before I knew it, there was chaos. I heard screams. People were burned, people were bleeding, and the building was on fire."

Behind his glasses, Avery's eyes glistened with tears.

"Did you know that was going to happen?"

"No. I just wanted to do a little something to get them off me. I wanted to scare them, not hurt them. I didn't know it could get that bad, that easily."

"Did anyone know it was you?"

"Everyone was sent home early. My mom brought me home, she turned on the TV, and of course the fire was all over the news. Then I 'fessed up. She would have figured it out anyway. She was very upset. And so was I... the most depressed I've ever been. Suicidal, even. She pulled me out of school. Her friend, who's a mage, found out too. Nobody else knows I was behind this. Except for you. Most people thought it was just a fire, but they couldn't explain the dogs. They couldn't explain why fireballs came from the sky."

"Was anyone killed?" Lillian asked before she thought twice about whether such a question was a good idea while Avery fought back his tears, his voice weak and strained. Could his answer change how she cared for him?

"No, but it came closer to that than I like to think about."

"Did they recover?"

"I think so. A few of the kids have scars for the rest of their lives. All thanks to me. I've wondered if I'm a horrible person. If I deserve to have bad things happen to me, like that bullshit with the fake girlfriend."

"You didn't deserve that."

"I figured you would be a lot more shocked. That you'd be angry at me."

"Well, I am surprised... and saddened... but you were a kid being mobbed, and I can totally see how it would happen if you weren't experienced with your powers and you underestimated them. And some mages have great abilities. I'll bet you're a really powerful one, and you didn't know it. Did your mom or anyone ever have you practice your powers before that happened?"

"No."

"With no practice, you'd be out of touch with the level of your strength, and you wouldn't have known."

"Now that you know I did this, do you want to keep hanging around me?"

"To make you unleash that harm, I would have to torture or threaten you, right?"

"Pretty much."

"You made a mistake when you were a kid. You were under duress. I could just as easily make a mistake and cause a catastrophe."

"I feel like I was fourteen and I should have known better."

"But it's only natural to fight back when you're in danger. Like you did when those guys in togas kidnapped you and almost slit your throat."

"Thanks for being more understanding about it than I expected. Please, please don't tell anyone."

"I'll take it to my grave."

"I guess I told you this because I wanted to give you the choice. To decide whether you want to walk away now."

"I'm not walking away. I'm staying. If you'll let me." Lillian put an arm around Avery, and then drew back when he flinched.

"I should probably get back home," Avery said after an awkward silence. He wiped his eyes and left.

The busy semester headed toward its finish. Lillian struggled to keep her mind off of her increasing attachment to Avery. That unexpected spring break together, those memories of playing board games and sightseeing, held a special, cozy magic. But since his heavy confession about the explosion back in eighth grade, he'd withdrawn, casting a shadow over the friendship. He was cordial during the game nights, but she did not hear much from him during the weeks.

Lillian's roommate Bridget was on the verge of moving to Oregon with her boyfriend. As they began to pack up their things in their shared dorm room, Lillian's heart sank at the sight of the cardboard boxes. She and Bridget had truly enjoyed living together for the past two and a half years, becoming great friends. Not wanting to risk another bad roommate after Tara's impact on her mental health during her first semester, Lillian had reserved a single room for the following year, just down the hall from her current one. Though more expensive, Lillian thought it was worth it. If all went as planned, she only had another year left.

Before leaving for the past couple of summers, Lillian had deposited many of her things at the house her friend Tim rented with a couple of roommates. But he, too, was about to graduate and move away for a job. Lillian did not know many other local people she trusted to store her stuff. When she reached out to Avery, he agreed to hold her things. Richard could water her plants while he was gone for part of the summer.

When Lillian arrived at his house, Avery wore a deep blue button-up shirt she'd always admired, with an elegantly coiled dragon printed on the front. She had trouble taking her eyes off him as they carried the boxes up to his bedroom closet and set the plants on the kitchen windowsill. They placed her bass guitar on its stand next to his desk.

Lillian sensed that Avery might urge her to leave. Not wanting to go just yet, she tried to engage him in a conversation, which settled on Uncle Gerald and how he had outed Lillian's father during the winter—a transgression that now had the two brothers completely estranged.

"That technique your uncle used to put your dad's memories in your head... how did he do that?" Avery asked.

"I'm not exactly sure. But he held my hand the whole few seconds the memories poured in. I'm guessing the person has to touch you for it to happen."

"And what did he call it?"

"Mind transference, I think. You want to try it? Just with our own thoughts, not anyone else's. Stuff we want to pass along. It seemed like Gerald could control what went into my head and what didn't."

"I think I've done it once before, with my mom, without knowing what it was. I guess we could try it."

Sitting beside each other on the edge of Avery's bed, they wove their fingers together as Lillian tried not to let her body shudder or get excited at his touch. Injecting a controlled flow of memories and thoughts seemed to work, and they told stories without speaking. Lillian saw fuzzy, scant, yet pleasant early childhood impressions from the first home her friend lived in, where he was born. Most things were wooden, worn, old and dusty, yet perfect. Avery played in cardboard boxes and sat in columns of sunlight from windows. Warming fires burned in the fireplace. Avery's mother, a tall woman with curly brown hair, crouched down beside him to draw and color together with markers. They explored the woods outside.

With that came the double-edged sword of his mother's own painful memories from before he was born, too much for him to process at such a young age—the scariest being her marriage to a domestic abuser in the 1970s, an ordeal she'd barely gotten out of alive.

Later came the vaguely remembered apartment in the city after his mother's decision to leave country life in the hopes he'd make friends, and then the brown flat-roofed stucco house where his mother currently lived. Lillian saw long stretches of time alone, with his mother busy and frequently absent, dropping him off with a babysitter before rushing to the births she attended. Sneering faces and shoves in school hallways came along.

That much-regretted eighth-grade day was a blur. Avery tried to temper the worst day of his life, glossing over it while showing just enough snippets. Fireballs zoomed from the sky, crashing down as demon dogs snarled before they vanished and the taste of gritty dirt filled his mouth. After the glimpse of that dark day, good times and bad whizzed by in fragments—guilt and grief, making friends, and the nervous excitement of leaving for university.

Avery tired out and stopped the stream of memories, asking Lillian to take over and give it a try. She showed him bits and pieces of her mostly slow-paced childhood, the gifts Mom would bring before she died, the immediate alarm bells in Lillian's gut the moment she was murdered. Out of Lillian's mind came the smooth purple skins of eggplants growing in the garden, the excitement of the trip to Disney World that her father very reluctantly took the girls on after years of begging, and the deeply satisfying afternoons reading book after book in her sunny bedroom.

The two friends felt each other's emotions. The colors and atmospheres that inhabited their heads began to intertwine. As they grew less careful of what they shared, their borders as two separate entities merged and melted together and swirled and faded.

Lillian wanted to pull Avery against her and meet his lips with hers. She went weak with ecstasy just thinking about it, tingling with an electricity she had only known in her private fantasies, never with another human being. Because their minds were still linked, she knew, wordlessly, that Avery desired the same. They began to lean in.

Avery yanked his hand out of hers, turned away, and stood up from the bed. The moment shattered.

"This wasn't a good idea," he said, not meeting Lillian's eyes. "We're confused. We're heading in a direction where we shouldn't be going. We should cool it. I'll have Richard bring your stuff when the break's over."

"I'm sorry." Overwhelmed and embarrassed, Lillian began to cry. She got up from the bed and fled from the house. When Avery did not chase after her or call for her to come back, she took that as a further cue of rejection. Though they had just held hands, she felt as if she'd been thrown out of bed in the middle of making love.

Lillian spent the rest of that afternoon hiding in the alternate world, the liminal space she had once shared with Avery. Now she wished she had kept this magical place, with all of its bioluminescence and slanted crystals and star-streaked skies, a secret, her very own sacred space. She laid on a bed of glowing flowers, gloomy over the destruction of the most intimate friendship she'd ever had. *Why are you attracted to him like that? You already knew you weren't even supposed to be friends. Of course you scared him off. What did you expect?*

The following day, Lillian went to Tim's house for a graduation and going-away party for both him and Bridget. Trying to lift her own spirits and make herself feel a little bit attractive, Lillian wore a glittering shirt and her favorite leggings, dabbed on a bit of makeup, and braided a silver ribbon into her hair. But upon arrival, all of the laughing and socializing got to be overwhelming for Lillian as she still mourned the moment lost with Avery. She went outside, sitting on the back step and watching the night sky with a cold, frosty root beer in her hand as she tried to compose herself.

"What's wrong?" Bridget asked, sitting next to Lillian and putting an arm around her.

"I'm that obviously sad?"

"Yeah. I can tell when you're sad."

"I'm trying not to mope around at your party. Sorry if it seems that way. I've just got something on my mind."

"What is it?"

Maybe Lillian would feel better after opening up to someone. "It's Avery."

Though Bridget and Avery did not know each other well, they'd gotten pizza with Tim and Lillian a couple of times. Back in January, the four of them went ice skating together. Bridget and Tim no longer recognized Avery as the one who had caused Lillian such a panic attack during Halloween trick-or-treating a couple of years ago.

"Something happened with him?" Bridget asked.

"He said he'd take my plants and things for the summer. Yesterday, I dropped them off. We hung out. And then..."

"And then what? You have a crush on him, don't you?"

"I guess so," Lillian admitted. "That's why they call it a crush... you get crushed. We, um, we were on his bed and there was this moment between us."

"On his bed? You guys boned, didn't you?" Bridget grinned hopefully.

Lillian burst out laughing. "Haha, no. Nothing that exciting. We, well... we almost kissed."

"Almost kissed? There wasn't even any lip-to-lip action?"

"No. He put a stop to it and said we need to cool it. I don't even know if we'll ever speak again."

"What?! This really sweet girl, who happens to be a hot redhead, is into him, and he rejects the opportunity?"

"Thanks, I'm glad you think I'm hot. I guess we just wouldn't be a good fit. And it's complicated." More complicated than Bridget would ever know.

"And some horrible person pretended to be his girlfriend. That whole thing was beyond messed up. It happened only a couple of months ago, and maybe Avery's just not ready for a relationship. Give him time and space. He might come around."

"He's also the one who saw me right after my self-harming breakdown last semester. I'm sure no one would want to go out with me after seeing me like that."

"Don't worry. As you know, I've had some trauma, some depression issues, and it doesn't stop me from dating. Avery seems like the type to understand nobody has a perfect life."

"It wasn't meant to be. I need to put him behind me."

"Yeah, one way or another, things will work out. When you're ready, why don't you get back in and have fun?"

As Lillian came back into the house booming with music, she was not so sure about Bridget's reassuring words. Being an ordinary person, Bridget was unaware of the centuries-old animosity dividing Avery and Lillian.

After Bridget downed a number of drinks, she confessed to having had a crush on Lillian ever since she moved into her room. Instead of disgusted or offended, Lillian was surprised and flattered to hear this, even if the attraction was one-sided.

Bridget's boyfriend was not jealous of this crush. If anything, it turned him on.

As Lillian hugged her friends and told them how much she was going to miss them, she started to cry, feeling vulnerable at the tears leaking down her face in front of other guests. Lillian had a lot of fun times to reminisce about, those late nights spent laughing with Bridget so hard their chests hurt and they could barely breathe, and those drives with Tim in the mountains as they listened to music. If Avery and his gaming parties were a thing of the past, she would be left with almost no local friends during her senior year.

"This is just the perfect retreat," Gerald exclaimed, throwing his arms out grandly as his son Julius and granddaughter Katrina stood by his sides. They looked around at their rocky, tropical surroundings. A few palm trees swayed in the breeze on the small, undeveloped island. Frothy waves crashed against the beach nearby.

"Yes, it's gorgeous, Dad," Julius affirmed, putting an arm around his father. "Perfectly isolated. Safe."

"You did good picking this out, son," Gerald complimented him. "The only problem I'm having is that it's going to become a little bit cramped. But if we plan carefully, it'll be okay."

"What about Jana?" Katrina asked Julius. "Does she know you're gonna be moving? And what about Robbie?"

"I'm not telling my wife a thing until we're absolutely ready. Then I'll make up some sort of excuse. I decided to take the boy here, in case he's of some use. She won't know where to find us."

Katrina breathed a sigh of relief. She and her uncle's wife never got along, and she was grateful to not have to share an island with that woman. "What about Lou, Lillian, and Denny?"

"Oh, we'll find a way to talk them into joining us, somehow," Gerald mused with a shake of his head. "It won't be easy. I am not their favorite person right now, and Lou hasn't even spoken to me since December. But even if I cannot change his mind, there are the others."

"But they're still mad at Julius over those stupid lies, right?" Katrina asked.

"Yes. Lies and baseless rumors, as you know. But I still think forgiveness is possible with long, hard work. Although the forgiveness may have to be forced, since I likely will not be around much longer." Gerald paused before going on. "I advise both of you to watch your backs carefully. Other mages do know about us. I told you about the water people who made a truce with Lou and his daughter; but I'm not sure I trust them, and I have the sense they are still spying on our family. The one who read my brother's mind may well have set me as a priority to watch. The house on this island will obviously take months to finish, but once it is done, we must be prepared to retreat if and when it becomes necessary."

"Fully understood, Dad," Julius acknowledged with a nod.

"I have another question, Grandpa," Katrina cut in. "What do we do about Evelyn's kid?"

"For now, nothing. But once she reaches the age where she begins to harness her powers, we need to keep a close eye on her. Hopefully, we'll be here before that happens."

The three of them fell back into silence, admiring the wind-swept, endless ocean views.

Excerpt from The Autobiography of
Gerald Frazier: Architect of a New World

With quick thinking and ingenuity, I whipped up a plan to deal with my mistress's pregnancy. Irina would give the baby up for adoption, and I'd pull some strings to make sure the baby landed in my house. Enid had been asking to adopt a child anyway. I informed my wife that I knew of an unwed, knocked-up teenage couple over in Cincinnati, and in several months, their baby would be ours.

Irina told me during our secret phone calls that she felt very sick, fainted during work, and had some deeply troubling episodes of bleeding. Her hard labor at the meat packing plant frightened me. It was terribly unhealthy for anyone, more so for a pregnant woman. I absolutely did not want to risk her losing the baby. I wrote a check for Irina that allowed her to stay home and eat well until her due date. Though Irina still felt sick, her health improved a bit. After she was finally able to rest, the bleeding ceased, thank God.

Finally, that summer day came in 1961 when a baby boy was born perfect and healthy at eight pounds. And better yet, when I first laid eyes on the bundle of joy in the hospital nursery, he was just what I'd been hoping for—a child with powers like mine! My prayers were answered!

He had Irina's pale red hair and looked a little like me, but not enough to raise any suspicion that I was his biological father. We named him Julius Gerald Robert. The name had a powerful ring to it, and it also fit since he was born in the month named for Julius Caesar.

Julius was the perfect baby. While all babies cry, Julius was so much quieter than Theresa had been. He slept through the night sooner than she did, and walked and talked early. As he grew older, Julius continued to be a delight. Obedient and polite, he had smiles for us every day. Only once did I ever feel the need to spank him, around the age of three, when he threw and broke the cookie jar after I told him to stop eating cookies. Julius learned his lesson immediately, and the pain he felt, both physical and emotional, softened my heart enough that I never laid a hand on him again. With Theresa, it was a different story.

Theresa was only twenty-two months old when we brought Julius home, but from day one, she became jealous of him and turned into a little monster. On multiple occasions, Enid and I had to stop her from hitting him, drowning him in the bathtub, or doing something else nasty. When Julius was four years old, Theresa pushed him down the stairs, breaking his arm. This was not a fun thing to explain in the emergency room, where doctors were suspicious that we had committed child abuse, not the sweet-looking little girl who played innocent.

The fighting between the children eventually simmered down with age, but resentment sometimes bubbled underneath the surface.

Julius was so much easier to raise than Theresa, who had challenged us from the start and frequently went to bed with a hot butt. Julius also had the intellect that most mages are blessed with, scoring forty points higher on the childhood IQ test than Theresa. She was in the average range, but dumb as a rock compared to her brother. Julius learned things the first time, while we could tell Theresa something ten times only for it to not sink in. Julius rarely needed help with schoolwork, while we had to sit down every weeknight after dinner to get Theresa's homework done as she struggled through her math problems at a snail's pace and threw her pencil in frustration.

We could seldom deny that Julius was our favorite. Any parent who tells you they don't have a favorite child is pulling your leg.

Irina took it very hard that she could not raise Julius, as most mothers do when they are separated from their child. She became obsessive, calling my home in tears at three in the morning and risking our affair being discovered. To calm Irina down, I made a compromise. In exchange for her continued silence, I would let her visit Julius. Our kids played together when we met up at parks, and Vanessa and Julius became close from an early age, unaware that they were half-siblings. Julius couldn't read minds. I kept Victor and Vanessa happy with gifts that their mother could not afford. Victor, a born scientist, enjoyed chemistry and building sets. Vanessa loved horse models and any books about horses.

I had very high hopes for my boy's future. Meanwhile, I had started my medical supply company and we were starting to rake in the profits. We bought a nice house in the suburbs. My life was definitely on the up and up.

I had my precious boy, but it wasn't enough. I wanted more!

Love and Attraction

Abustling summer waited for Lillian, who left for California the day after Tim and Bridget's party. Victor, her mother's brother, offered her money in exchange for help with repairs and renovations around his home. With her past, it was a little hard to stomach the notion of staying in a house with a male relative she didn't know that well, even if he had no powers. Yet she agreed to go, to keep her mind busy. It would be a long drive, some of it through hot deserts, but Victor paid for the gas and Lillian did not mind long trips. Blasting music on the open road always recharged her batteries.

Lillian arrived at Victor's clay-tile-roofed home a couple of evenings later. This being her first visit, the thing that immediately stood out in her uncle's living room was an old black-and-white family photograph of her grandmother with curled pale hair and grandfather with pitch-black hair and olive skin. Victor was a toddler in his father's lap, Vanessa an infant in her mother's arms, chewing on a toy.

Victor took Lillian out for a dinner of sushi. He yammered on about his son Jason's job in software engineering, and the second grandchild Jason and his wife were expecting. In the days that came, Lillian worked in the yard and cleaned out the accumulation of junk in the garage, a manageable workload, nothing like Julius' crushing demands when she was twelve. After revealing the story of Julius' abuse to more and more people, she thought about telling her uncle, but decided against it. Though Victor had not spoken to Julius in years, he fondly remembered the boy who was his sister's best, and sometimes only, friend. What if he didn't believe Lillian?

Lillian slept in late each morning, luxuriating in the lack of tests and deadlines. On weekends, Victor brought her on fun trips to nearby attractions and to meet his cousin Billy, who lived in the same San Francisco apartment where Vanessa had visited him over twenty years ago.

During breaks between chores, and late at night, Lillian curled up with her laptop and began writing a new novel to pass the time. It was hard to get the sentences out as she struggled not to dwell on the ever-present fear that she'd ruined her friendship with Avery. He still had her friended on Facebook and a blogging site, making occasional, brief posts that never mentioned her and not commenting on her own posts. Did he have her filtered on those sites now? Anticipating a cold or rejecting response, or no response at all, Lillian held back from reaching out directly. She clicked on Avery's screenname a couple of times, closing the window before she could type anything and send it his way.

It was hard not to let her mind wander to that last encounter and the mutual surge of emotion that came with it. If they gave into their cravings that day and their lips had joined, how far would it have gone? She still wanted him, felt confused and in love, and they might never speak again.

One evening, after sundown, Lillian and Victor sat and talked on the raised chairs at his kitchen island. Her skin prickled with a strong sensation of being watched. Sometimes this feeling tingled throughout Lillian's body when ghosts appeared, but when she turned around in her tall metal chair, there were no apparitions. This house was peaceful, with less aftershocks of death than many other homes. If something was there, it was something alive.

As Lillian gazed at the kitchen and dining room behind her, she pinpointed where that edgy feeling originated—beyond the sliding glass door to the backyard. On the other side of that door, the glass black from the night outside, something lurked. Something sinister.

"Are you okay?" Uncle Victor asked.

"I feel like someone is watching me. From the yard. I'm feeling a little spooked."

"Let me go check it out." Victor walked across the tile floor in his pajamas and comical bunny slippers, peeking out through the glass and turning on the porch light. "I don't see anything out there. Still got the weird feeling?"

"Yes."

Victor grabbed a flashlight, slid open the glass door, and stepped out onto his back patio. He swept the beam from his flashlight around his yard. Near the gate, a bush shook slightly.

"There's nothing out there," Victor concluded after coming inside, "except for a little critter in the bushes. Probably just a rabbit."

The next day, late in the morning, Lillian watered the plants out back. As she rotated around to the bushes near the gate, she froze, dropping the still-spraying hose as it soaked the slippers on her feet.

Around and underneath one of the bushes, along part of the yard's perimeter, rose softly waving, semitransparent green tendrils, an aura trail that someone or something had left behind within the past twenty-four hours. This same trail was smeared like glowing paint on and underneath the closed gate.

With the strong, unmistakable protuberances of green, it was almost without doubt the remnants of a necromancer's footsteps. Not her own, of course, since she could not see her own aura. It wasn't her father; she knew his colors well enough to recognize them anywhere and he would never visit without telling her, much less creep around in the yard. Neither would Denny.

This left few other possibilities.

Shit. Julius. He's stalking me. No.

And Victor had gone to work. Lillian was alone. Victor could come back in the evening to find her missing. And being ordinary, he would not have any magical trail to follow. Those green traces were all invisible to him.

Heart racing, Lillian peered cautiously around, opening the wooden gate. The necromancer had passed through it; the trail wound its way along the grass beside the driveway and took a turn down the sidewalk. She walked along the trail for a short distance, but did not want to risk following it all the way to the end, in case none other than Julius himself waited at the terminus of this green line. But curiosity mixed in with fear, and Lillian took one more step, and then another.

Several yards down the sidewalk, the trail ended abruptly. The person who had left it behind must have gotten into a vehicle, making them impossible to track down.

Severely shaken, Lillian returned to her uncle's house. She kept a sharp knife from Victor's wooden knife block within easy reach, often resting her fingers on the handle. Lillian listened for any unusual noises in the house, or any cars going down the street at a suspiciously slow pace. Her body stayed ready to fight or run for her life. Lillian wished Victor had a dog to bark at the first sign of something not right.

"You seem like you may be feeling just a bit twitchy today," Victor observed when he got home from work that evening and found Lillian in the kitchen, hurriedly sliding the knife back into the block.

"I'm just, uh, still nervous from the other night."

"Just so you know, this is a pretty safe neighborhood. A lot of my neighbors don't even lock their doors, even though I do. Everything is going to be fine."

Lillian breathed a little easier when they went out to eat that evening, and found distraction in Victor's nonstop chatter. But after they returned home, and particularly when her uncle went to bed, Lillian's sense of safety eroded again. She took the knife from the kitchen and tucked it into the top drawer of the nightstand. Lillian got little sleep that night, and kept imagining the creaks of doors opening when they should not. When footsteps thudded loudly down the hall, Lillian bolted upright in bed to find her uncle getting up to use the bathroom.

In the days that followed, Lillian anxiously kept an eye out for any other evidence of nighttime prowlers in the yard. It came as a relief when Victor set aside a long weekend and accompanied Lillian and his son and daughter-in-law and young grandson on a road trip down south to Disneyland, staying at a hotel in the evenings. The vacation took Lillian's mind off of a lot of things. The necromancer stalking her. Avery.

Once they returned to Victor's home, the worries came back. Sleeping at night was difficult, knowing that if that necromancer wanted her, they could easily get her—like Julius had once done.

Lillian left the house one day, not wanting to be there alone. She brought her laptop to a coffee shop a few blocks away.

A familiar air, something from long ago, filled the space just after the front door swung open. Lillian glanced up and had a jolting sense of looking upon a long-lost sister. A skinny young woman with hair clipped short in a sleek red-gold pixie cut, eyes surrounded in smoky black makeup, walked up to the counter to order. Hoop earrings swung from her ears.

Katrina.

Lillian wanted to run, yet she was glued to her booth, frozen.

As soon as she finished ordering, Katrina spun on her heel and confidently walked toward Lillian's booth.

"What are you doing here?" Lillian asked, almost at a loss for words.

"I just wanted to say hi. I hadn't seen you in such a long time and it's just not fair."

"How did you know I was here?"

"Long story short, my grandpa read a little bit into your dad's mind and found out your summer plans. I'm lucky he caught that when he did, now that your dad won't let my grandpa go near him."

"Nobody came with you, did they?"

"No, just me, myself and I. I just got let go from my job, which sucks, but now I have freedom. I got to go on an exciting road trip."

"Do you have a place to stay?"

"Don't worry about where I'm staying. I can take care of myself. We're tough. We can survive just about anywhere."

When Katrina's steaming cup of coffee was ready, she swiped it from the counter and then boldly shoved herself into the booth next to Lillian. Though Katrina's trendy sequined shirt and snug skinny jeans looked clean and new, her body odors suggested that she had not showered or brushed her teeth in some time.

"So, how's life treating you?" Katrina wanted to know.

"It's treating me okay at the moment. There's something I have to ask. By any chance, have you come onto my uncle's property?"

"I was just trying to figure out if it was the right house and if you were there."

"Could you please not do that again? It kind of scared the shit out of me."

"Oh, okay. Sorry."

"And did you follow me here?"

"How else would I find you?"

"If you wanted to visit me, why not call, or shoot me an email?"

"Grandpa gave me your number. But silly me, I lost it."

"What about Facebook? Or Twitter?"

"I'm not on those sites. I'm a low-profile kind of girl. Besides, I wrote to you, and you never wrote back."

"Sorry, it's just that it's been so long..." *And I don't know if you still hang around Julius.*

"Write back to me next time. Hey, there's not a lot of people here, and I don't think anyone will hear us. Do you ever practice your powers?"

"Not much. Just small stuff for convenience when I'm alone."

"Just telekinesis, it sounds like. You don't practice the other things?"

"No. It's not safe."

"It's sad to see all that stuff going to waste, man. You can do incredible things if you just take the time to practice. I really wish I was pregnant right now so I could feel what it's like to have that surge in power for the full nine months. But I'm single, and I never felt ready after that baby died. Too scared it'd happen again. I remember you saying you didn't want kids. Is that true?"

"Still true."

"Why are you wasting the chance to have even bigger superpowers? You could have a baby, take advantage of those powers, and then I could raise it."

Lillian did not answer. She was more than a womb; she had so many hopes and dreams for her life aside from the unpleasant-sounding process of pregnancy and birth. And if she ever had a baby, she would not be comfortable giving it away like an inanimate doll to this cousin she barely knew and had never quite trusted.

"Oh, and everybody's still wondering what's up with your sister's kid. That water thing," Katrina brought up.

"I've wondered the same, but I think it was just a genetic accident. Both Evelyn and her ex-husband have mage blood."

"We just aren't sure how the future will turn out with her. Nobody expected her to be born like that."

"My sister has no clue that her daughter has powers."

"Of course not, and it's safest that way. I might pop by and give your sister a surprise visit too. Don't worry, my lips are sealed. Oh, and you still have that green crystal, right? I was wondering if I could borrow it."

"Well, to be honest, I don't know you that well, and I don't think I'm comfortable letting you borrow it."

"Really, now?" Katrina sneered, her eyes turning dark. "We're family. Blood is thicker than water. Don't be selfish."

"I, uh... I don't mean to be selfish, but we haven't really talked in years."

"Okay, I guess I understand. We need to work on getting to know each other. I do have some cool things I'd like to show you."

"Like what?" This turn of phrasing clenched Lillian's stomach. The last time Katrina had promised her she would witness something great, it turned out to be gruesome and deadly. Julius' mutant.

"I'd like it to be a surprise. Sometime soon, I'll have to take you on a trip. What do you think of a nice summer vacation?"

"I have stuff going on for most of this summer. Then I have two more semesters of school."

"Aren't you graduating?"

"Not until next spring, as long as I pass all my classes and I can get into them before they fill up."

"Anything after that?"

"I'm going to try to get into graduate school."

"I don't know much about that stuff. I never went to college. I don't think we even need it. But we'll totally have to do a road trip to celebrate your graduation. I also have a gift from my grandpa, just for you. Take it." Katrina reached into her pocket and handed Lillian an envelope thick with cash. "I've gotta go. See you later, alligator!"

After Katrina left, Lillian peered out the tinted window. Oblivious to being watched, Katrina got into a boxy 1980s-model Pontiac with scuffed gray paint. Lillian stared at the car until it disappeared into traffic.

"I wouldn't trust Katrina," Lillian's father warned when she later called him to tell him of the encounter. "I don't like how she stalked you across the country to surprise you. No doubt in my mind that she's after the crystal. Gerald used to try his darndest to get his hands on it. Somebody is clearly trying to butter you up, since Katrina gave you an envelope with five hundred dollars in it. I'm concerned that Gerald or... perhaps someone else... put Katrina up to this."

"Like Julius?"

"Just keep your wits about you, and keep a close eye on that crystal. You still have it on a chain?"

"Yes."

"Keep it close. Wear it around your neck at all times."

After that conversation with her father, Lillian followed his advice and stayed diligent about wearing the crystal on its chain, keeping it on when showering and tucking it into her pajamas when she slept. Now that she knew what sort of car Katrina had, Lillian glanced out the window when a motor hummed through the neighborhood. And she stopped going to that coffee shop.

One day, sitting at Victor's dining table after finishing her chores, Lillian could no longer stand to refrain from contacting Avery. She wanted to confirm if they'd had an irreparable falling out or if he would talk to her again. After deep-breathing her panic away, Lillian opened a chat window on her laptop and said hi. The minute that followed, waiting to see if he'd ever reply, dragged on like excruciating hours.

Avery said hi back. This didn't mean they were still friends, but at least one line of communication had reopened.

Nervously, Lillian typed her next line. *I just wanted to reach out and tell you I'm sorry things got so weird between us.*

I'm sorry too. I panicked, then after you left I just didn't know what to say. I've wanted to talk to you, but I was kind of scared to.

So was I.

I feel bad. I'm not mad at you.

Thanks. That sets my mind at ease. I have a confession to make. I haven't been able to stop thinking about you.

I can't stop thinking about you either.

What exactly is our relationship now?

I'm not sure. We'll have to keep talking. Take things one day at a time.

Lillian was overcome with almost full-body relief, though still not certain where she stood. While she now trusted Avery to not use his powers against her, he could hit her in the emotional gut if his skittish state of mind led to a rejection.

They spoke again the following day, airing their confusion about the new direction of their friendship. Currently visiting his mother, Avery promised he'd tell her the truth about Lillian soon, though he hadn't just yet. During the week before school started, all of Avery's roommates would be away on vacations. Avery would have the house to himself. He invited Lillian to come and stay with him after her geology field camp ended, while they sorted things out at their own pace.

For the sake of Lillian's comfort levels, Avery offered to sleep on the living room futon, leaving his bed for her. The thought of holing up alone together made Lillian's heart jump a bit, even if they bedded down in separate rooms. There was always the chance, however disappointing, that the chemistry that had built up so urgently in May might now be broken or gone completely.

A week after her twenty-first birthday, before she was scheduled to hit the road again for geology field camp, Lillian returned to her uncle's house after taking some of his old things from his garage to the dump. Something in Victor's home was amiss.

The first thing to stand out was the strong green trail, freshly deposited along the red tile floor, coming and going from the open sliding glass door. Katrina had picked the lock on the back door and walked uninvited through the house so recently that her vague green footprints were still fresh.

"Get out!" Lillian shouted into the living room, standing cautiously in the doorway. Her voice echoed through a silent house.

Upon closer examination, Katrina had already left, the trail doubled over on itself out the back door and through the yard and gate.

Lillian ran down the hall, checking the bedroom where she was staying. The drawers on the dresser and nightstand hung sloppily open, still pulsating with the green remnants of Katrina's hands that had just rummaged through Lillian's clothing. The closet door was thrown wide open as well, hangers and clothes swiped aside. Katrina had visited to search stubbornly for one object and one object alone.

Katrina had gone through the other rooms. Uncle Victor's drawers were open and disorganized, several pairs of his boxer shorts thrown in a polka-dotted heap on the floor. Katrina had also whirled through the bathroom, her fingers crawling into Victor's bag of razors, shaving cream, and toothpaste, her fingerprints still smudged on the mirror of the medicine cabinet. Katrina hadn't even thought to cover her tracks.

Lillian called her uncle, who left work immediately and phoned the police on his way home. Lillian was bound by the code to not tell him the truth—that she knew who did it, what they were looking for, and that a necromancer could render an armed police officer helpless. In case Katrina hung around on the street, Lillian hoped the sight of some police cars might still send a strong message that she and her uncle would not play games.

After looking through his things, Victor reported to the two police offers who'd arrived to investigate that nothing was missing. That stood out as very odd after how thoroughly the intruder had ransacked his underwear drawer. "Even my ex-wife wasn't that interested in my underwear," Victor quipped.

The last time someone broke into Victor's house, back in the early 1990s, he came home and stumbled upon a teenager running scared across the driveway, hoisting his stereo on one shoulder. It stumped him that nothing was taken this time.

Concerned for their safety, Victor called a friend who agreed to let the two of them stay over at his house for a few nights. Though she was confident that Katrina could not track her down after the car trip to a different suburb, Lillian found herself restlessly tossing and turning at night on the stranger's splayed-out sofa bed.

When she could not sleep, Lillian opened up her laptop, finding what she'd hoped to see: Avery still up and available to chat. Talking to him, venting about the break-in, and joking around a bit raised her spirits and finally helped her relax enough to fall asleep. In case Katrina followed Lillian to his house, Avery promised to keep an eye out, and hoped his existence would intimidate her into staying away.

After arriving in the mountains of southern Colorado for geology field camp, Lillian set aside a chunk of time on her first evening to walk to a private spot with halfway decent reception and call Avery from her cell phone.

"I'm excited to see you soon," Lillian confessed, "but I'm also nervous."

"Nervous about what?"

"Lots of things."

"Me too. Depending on what happens, I'm anxious about what your cousin Denny might say or do. Your dad is a nice enough guy, but he might not be thrilled either."

"Denny's likely to be upset, but he doesn't own me. I won't let anyone harm you. My dad knows I'm coming to see you. I think he's putting the pieces together. What about your mom? She always sounded pretty laid back."

"Honestly, she was shocked when I told her everything, but I think she's going to be okay with it."

"What about the catfish? That's still fresh in your head, and if it were me, I'd be messed up and afraid to trust anyone for a long time. I'd say it was a trauma."

"It was."

"Are you sure you're ready to get involved with anyone?"

"I needed time to move past it. I'm still embarrassed. I wonder if I deserved it."

"You don't need to be embarrassed; you were dealing with a highly skilled manipulator. And why would you deserve that?"

"I don't know. The thing that happened in eighth grade. I wonder if no one should get close to me because of that."

"That was a kid who was scared and trying to defend himself. This was a grown-ass woman who carefully and deliberately played with your head. It's your guilt talking."

"I can't let that woman ruin my life, or stay single forever because of her. But the guilt is tough."

"I don't know if I should say this. I'm afraid of getting hurt, if we see each other and then we're not ready. I'm afraid of hurting you. I've probably still got some PTSD from what happened when I was younger. And last year, when I had that breakdown, it must have been scary for you to see me like that. I worry that you might look down on me and think I'm really unstable. That I'm batshit. I don't want you thinking you have to fix me."

"No, I don't think that you're batshit, or you have to be fixed. You got triggered that one day when you found out something horrible about your ex and your cousin."

"Since you're a twenty-one-year-old guy who's never been in a real relationship, I'm guessing you want certain things. I worry about how I'd react. I'm scared of being too broken for a healthy adult relationship."

"There's no pressure to do anything. Like I've been saying, we'll see how it works out. We'll do what we're comfortable with."

Those weeks of field camp were a grueling ordeal. Lillian spent hours of every day outside, digging through the soil and jotting notes. Even though she generously slathered on sunscreen and wore bandanas to protect her fair skin, the sun turned her a bit pink. During what little free time the students had, they ate and slept in a stuffy set of barracks.

When field camp ended, it was time to finally go and face Avery. Alone. Lillian's stomach flip-flopped with a mixture of nerves and anticipation as she yet again packed the things she had brought along on her exhausting summer of road trips. Before leaving, she showered, brushed and flossed every nook and cranny of her teeth, popped a powerful breath mint, and put on an extra layer of deodorant. Blasting music to distract herself from her unease, Lillian headed toward the unknown, even in a familiar house with a person she knew well.

Avery paced, waiting in the house empty except for Richard's cat sleeping the day away on the sofa. He took out pillows and blankets to convert the futon into a bed for himself later that night. Avery washed the blankets and sheets on his bed and decluttered his room. He showered for longer than usual.

After drying off, he put on his blue button-up shirt with a golden dragon on the front. Though she had never come out and said it, Avery got the impression Lillian liked this shirt on him. After dressing, Avery shaved, though he grew little facial hair, and brushed and flossed his teeth multiple times in a row. Like they were going to make out when she arrived. No, they probably wouldn't. Why was he overdoing the hygiene?

As the minutes ticked down and he cooked a quick dinner of stir-fry, Avery decided that it was best for them to just remain friends, after struggling not to fall in love with her for months. After he terminated the near-kiss in May and Lillian fled the house, he'd smacked himself in the forehead and cursed.

While his mother had come to terms with their bond, there was no telling how his mother's good friend Adelita, an air person, might take it. She was the one who had first informed them of the gruesome, supposedly extinct necromancers. Avery already knew that cousin of Lillian's who'd stayed at her father's house would not react well at all to their having a relationship. Her father, though friendlier, might turn on him at that point, too.

Avery's brain went in one direction, his heart in another, as Lillian pulled up the driveway. He opened the door while she carried in a duffel bag of her belongings. She wore a snug, glimmering shirt, her hair tied into two long braids.

They kept their bodies distant from each other, the passionate momentum of that encounter in May when they had mingled their minds and wanted each other desperately now long gone. They ate at the dining room table in a disappointing near-silence.

"You want to put on a movie?" Avery suggested once they finished with their plates, looking for something, anything, to fill in the quiet.

"Sure," Lillian agreed. They chose a film from Richard's shelves and sat beside each other on the couch, inches between them that stretched into miles and hands tucked firmly into their laps.

As they watched the superhero movie, Avery could not be sure of the plot or the characters' names. All he could think about was the warmth radiating from Lillian's body, so close, yet so far. He weighed the pros and cons of being bold, reaching over and taking Lillian's hand. His hand twitched toward her arm, and he drew it back in when she made no reciprocal gestures. The last thing Avery wanted to do was make Lillian uncomfortable with unwanted touch, though she'd said she did not want anyone to handle her like a fragile, broken doll.

Many people would already be taking their clothes off by this point, and like a shy young teenager sitting next to his crush in a movie theater, Avery couldn't even hold Lillian's hand. As he tried to train his eyes on the television again, Lillian's hand crawled toward him. He reached over, and their hands joined. A trickle of the warm excitement from that moment back in May began to flow again.

Lillian did not turn to face him, instead still watching the television—though he got the impression she wasn't really watching, her body stiff, her mind a blank. While he could barely read her anyway, he did not detect the wall that she always used to put up.

Lillian was the one to shift positions next, leaning her head on Avery's shoulder. He relaxed his own body. Their hands reached around to frame one another's faces as her eyes glowed with desire. The first kiss was a bit tense and short-lived. With the soft delight of the second one that immediately followed, the moment in May came roaring back into their veins. Urgently, they embraced as they succumbed to their hunger for touch. The rest of the movie played in the background, ignored.

Once the movie ended, they had dessert, frosty balls of mochi ice cream. They cuddled on the couch, making out again once there was nothing left of the mochi but a slight chill on their lips.

Late that night, as Avery got ready for bed, he went to his bedroom to change and came back downstairs to the converted futon. Though he normally slept just in boxers, he covered up, putting on an old T-shirt and pajama bottoms. He did not want to give the impression he was hinting at anything sexual. But with this modesty and sleeping on separate floors, did he go too far in walking on eggshells? After climbing under the covers on the uncomfortably thin futon mattress, Avery grew too warm in his pajamas.

A light flicked on upstairs. Lillian descended the stairs, wearing pajama pants and a worn-out spaghetti-strap top Avery had never seen on her before.

"Having trouble sleeping?" Avery asked.

"Yeah."

"So am I."

"Maybe it's because I'm in that bed alone."

Avery went upstairs. They both slid under the blanket and their lips met again. Lillian put her whole body into it, curling her fingers into his hair, wrapping her legs around him. Though Avery had her in his arms, he was afraid to let his hands brush over her breasts or between her legs, even as the loose pajama top twisted and revealed more than he'd expected to see.

They listened to each other's hearts and did a little of what they had done a few months ago, lacing their fingers together, directly exchanging thoughts and memories and feelings that words could not describe. They drifted off to sleep in a warm nest of joy.

A slow-paced, heavenly day followed. They went out to breakfast and walked around in a park, watching a music festival. That evening, they both spoke to their parents, breaking the news that it was more or less official now. Tempting as it was to put these calls off and focus only on their happiness in the moment, they decided to get it over with. Neither Avery's mother nor Lillian's father were especially surprised. Lou wished her the best, letting on that he'd grown to like Avery, who'd been kind and gracious during his stay at their home. Yet he reminded Lillian to "be careful." He would handle telling Denny, who just might flip tables when he found out.

That evening's attempt to watch a movie resulted in another makeout session. Once the movie ended, they ended up in the bedroom. Lillian encouraged Avery's hand to slide up the inside of her shirt, to cup the swell of her breast. Their shirts both fell away, and they lay skin to skin, warm together. They reached for the waistbands of each other's pants. Lillian hedged, gently stopping Avery before he could tug her pants down.

"You okay?" he asked. "You want to stop?"

"I'm afraid of you seeing my legs."

"Why?"

"Well... scars from cutting myself. I'm afraid they'll scare you. My body image isn't great. I'm self-conscious about the cellulite on my butt and legs."

"Every part of you I've seen is beautiful. I'm sure the parts I haven't seen are also beautiful."

"You're the fox," Lillian mumbled later, just as she began drifting off in Avery's arms.

"I'm the... what?"

"I just figured it out. These dreams I have every once in a while. Where I'm in a meadow and I see a reddish-orange fox in the woods. Then he comes out and starts looking sort of human, and takes my hand, and I just feel peaceful. I feel loved. The fox doesn't have a face, but I feel the same with you as I do with that fox."

"How long have you had these dreams?"

"Since I was little."

"You think we have dreams that predict the future?"

"I've had them before, but they're symbolic. I can't figure them out until later. I heard that my dead aunt had dreams that showed things exactly as they'd happen. Like even John F. Kennedy's assassination."

"That's incredible. Now I'm going to pay closer attention to my dreams."

"Yeah, look for patterns. When I was with Zack, even before I knew about his shenanigans, something in me was screaming that I didn't want to be with him, that something was wrong. And he was a pretty lousy 'boyfriend.' But now my instincts are saying this is right."

The following evening, back in the bed, in the soft glow of the nightstand lamp, their shirts and pants came off. The few faint scars on Lillian's legs did not stand out nearly as much as she feared, though in the heat of the moment, Avery was not looking too hard. Both pairs of underwear were tossed to the floor as their hands explored what was underneath. Lillian took Avery's hand and gently guided it to the silken wetness between her thighs.

"Do you have any protection?" she asked.

"Really, you want to?"

"Yes."

"I'd love to... but I've never done this before. I don't know if I'll be very good."

"Everything we've done so far is amazing."

Avery turned to his nightstand where he had an unopened box of condoms stored, the same box the woman posing as his girlfriend asked him to pack when he went on his doomed trip that spring. He'd almost thrown them away in anger after getting home. As he grabbed one, performance anxiety set in.

Avery turned back toward Lillian, taking her hand as she wrapped her legs longingly around him. He slid in as she gasped and clung to him, trying to go slow, be gentle. What began as slightly awkward, inexperienced motions ended with both of them breathless.

"I'm happy," Lillian sighed later, her head on Avery's chest. "I'm not sure if I ever told you, Zack pushed me into it. Twice. It was horrible. This was exquisite. This is how it should be."

In the days that came, they had one long, ecstatic session after another. While in bed on the second-to-last-day of the visit, Lillian reached down with an open hand. "Take my hand," she urged Avery. "Feel what I feel." He entwined his fingers with hers, his head buried between her thighs. Her climax surged through two bodies instead of one, nearly driving him to the brink.

The last day of Lillian's stay at the house, they dried off with towels after a lengthy shower together. As they returned to the bedroom, Lillian's cell phone buzzed on the nightstand. She answered it, flipping aside her wet hair. Denny's voice came through, loud and sharp enough that Avery could make out his words.

"Have you entirely lost your mind?" Denny barked as Lillian held the phone away from her ear. "What has gotten into you? You on a suicide mission? If you aren't, you need to stop this foolishness right now!"

"I'm looking beyond our differences," Lillian tried to assure him. "We're having a wonderful time. We..."

"You might be having fun now, but it'll change! You're smarter than this! You need to run from that guy right now!"

"I'm sorry, but we can't just stop seeing each other."

"Fine, then! Don't come crying to me when you end up in the hospital, or worse!" Denny hung up.

Lillian put her phone down, taking deep breaths. Avery wrapped his arms around her. "Let's try not to worry about him right now. He's angry, and he's reacting. Let's give him time to cool off."

"No matter what he says, I'm not going anywhere."

The next day, Avery helped Lillian to move into her new dorm room, carrying her plants and boxes of things over, spending the night. Back in May, he'd talked about Richard delivering her possessions so they wouldn't need to see each other. Lillian was so grateful for the very different end to the summer, the relationship taking a turn she wouldn't have even dreamed of a year ago.

After that glorious week together, Lillian found herself practically going into withdrawals sleeping alone again. They had no classes together, and even a few days seemed too long of a wait. Avery's roommates returned from their vacations, unsurprised to learn about the outcome of the relationship. They saw it coming more clearly than Avery and Lillian themselves had.

As Lillian started her classes, she hoped that she wasn't just riding the high of a surreal honeymoon phase that would crumble into dissatisfaction in a few months' time. When Lillian went to the Friday night gaming events at Richard's house, she brought whatever homework or projects she was working on and spent the night. If she had time, she stayed through the weekend with Richard's permission. Avery stayed in Lillian's dorm room a few times per week. How quickly the clothes came off when the door closed behind them made Lillian glad to have no roommate and lots of privacy.

As the late summer turned into fall, the lengthening shadows from the reddening autumn trees became connected to the magical times with Avery, to the richness and warmth he brought to Lillian's life. When they were apart, Avery did not inundate her phone with calls demanding to know where she was or who she was with, the way Zack had. He trusted that they would see each other again soon enough. Lillian spent time with her partner because she wanted to, without any dreaded sense of obligation.

As the weeks passed, they both noticed something new: a weak connection between their minds when they were apart. One could vaguely sense how the other might be feeling, even across town. When Avery came down with a bad migraine and had to spend the day shut up in his room with the curtains drawn, Lillian became a bit dizzy, her head a bit sore.

Lillian tried calling her cousin Denny every now and again, hoping he had cooled off enough for a rational discussion, and unusually for him, he never returned the calls.

"Do you think Denny will speak to me again?" Lillian sighed on the phone with her father. "I never thought he'd stoop low enough to do the silent treatment. I don't like it. It hurts."

"I'm sure he will come around. He just needs some time to think things through. This relationship of yours is nerve-wracking for both of us and he's not taking it well."

"It's still nerve-wracking for you too?"

"Yes. I know I cannot stop you. But I cannot help but have... certain worries."

"Worries? About what?"

"I'm a little bit worried about how other mages might react if they see the relationship. And I know that you have said in the past that you don't want children. Is that still the case?"

"Yes, it is."

"In case you change your mind in the future, that's another worry of mine. Your child would be born with powers. It would be inevitable. It would just be a question of which kinds of powers."

"Seriously, don't worry about it, Dad. He doesn't want kids either."

As the Thanksgiving break from school approached, Lillian grew increasingly nervous over her holiday travel plan with Avery. On Wednesday, the two of them would drive down to Albuquerque, where Lillian had never been, and spend four nights at Avery's mother's house.

Lillian was thankful for one thing: that Avery did not come from a big family and his relatives all lived so far away. A noisy litter of siblings and cousins and aunts and uncles would have scared Lillian that much more. One mother to size up her worthiness as her precious son's girlfriend was more than enough.

Some friends would come over for the evening feast. They sounded like laid-back people, less daunting than Avery's mother. And better yet, everyone else who attended, as far as Lillian knew, would be ordinary. The one mage friend had other plans.

During the hours-long drive, the weather was arid yet cold, the scenery ever-changing from mountains to farms to plains. They arrived in the glittering city after nightfall. They stepped out into the evening, dry and chilly but not as cold as Fort Collins, and Lillian got a stomachache, as if someone had tied her guts into knots. From within the small square house, warm light filled the living room windows.

Avery draped an arm over Lillian and they took a few deep breaths together before going inside. That red cluster of dried peppers hanging near the front door, the painting over the living room sofa, that woven rug with the blue zigzag pattern, that shining wooden coffee table, the fluffy orange cat that came to inspect them with a pink nose—she'd seen all of these things, in whole or in part, through Avery's memory.

Avery's mother, Deborah, was a tall woman. Lillian, at five feet seven inches, was on the tall side, but Deborah rose above them both. She did not look like Avery except in the upward slant of her eyebrows, and a little bit in the face shape. Her skin was an olive shade, and her curly graying hair was tied back into a braid with ringlets escaping. She had piercing yellow-amber eyes, and her embroidered top hung loosely over a slightly pudgy middle-aged figure. Her aura ranged from red to yellow, like Avery's, fiery yet warm, welcoming, and open.

"I've heard so much about you." Her voice held a slight vestige of her Southern childhood.

"Likewise," Lillian replied, not sure what else to say.

"I made some soup for dinner. I bet y'all are hungry."

They sat down with bowls of a spicy soup filled with potatoes. Deborah let on that she was frustrated after her car key had broken off in the ignition. Lillian offered to try prying it out. She put to use the skills that Denny had taught her, the cousin who still was not speaking to her. She slowly nudged and wiggled the key out, giving herself vertigo as she made her telekinetic extension as skinny as possible. At last, the broken piece of key slid out.

Impressed, Deborah asked Lillian to pick the lock of a fireproof box containing some of her important papers, to which she had lost the key. When Lillian successfully got it popped open, Deborah was very grateful.

While this meeting got off to a good start, Lillian remained quiet, her nerves on high alert. To ease Lillian's mind a bit, Deborah brought out old photo albums. Lillian had fun paging through vintage photos of a young, slender, brunette Deborah, as well as Avery's baby pictures. Avery gave Lillian a tour of his bedroom, with wall-to-wall built-in shelves of books, comics, games, and the Pokémon cards and artifacts he grew up collecting. Deborah went to bed in her room on the other side of the house, relieving Lillian of the pressure she put on herself to carefully watch her behavior.

After shutting off the lights, she and Avery tucked themselves into the bed that hadn't been slept in for months, talking and cuddling, though too self-conscious to get any more amorous with his mother's proximity. For the first time in the grainy darkness, Lillian began to feel a little sense of being home.

The next day, Thanksgiving, was filled with activity. Deborah's old friends Ralph and Mindy arrived. Ralph was tall and skinny, his gray hair balding, while Mindy was short and plump with long, wavy steel-colored hair. She wore a long tie-dyed dress. This couple owned the ranch where Avery spent the first part of his life. They laser-focused on Lillian. The attention made her anxious all over again, though she found common ground with Ralph, an appreciation for the band Pink Floyd. The couple asked question after question about where she was from, her family, her interests, and her zodiac sign—Cancer, the same as Mindy's.

"A Cancer and a Sagittarius," Mindy enthused, bringing up Avery's sign. "I think those two can make a good, long-lasting pair. Water and fire to balance each other."

All of them helped to cook. Lillian mashed the potatoes and whipped up the vegetarian gravy. In the middle of the day, she and Avery took a break from food preparation and he brought her on a ride to show her around in the daylight. The sky stretched wide and pale over a rocky ridge of bluish mountains on the horizon. Bare spindly trees dotted the quiet streets of brown stucco houses that evolved into sprawling horse farms and fancy compounds set down long driveways. Fascinated, Lillian looked out the window at the scenery of Avery's past, before they met.

After they got back, more and more guests started to filter into the house, most of them Deborah's friends, a few of them Avery's. Lillian needed to take a quick solitary walk to head off getting overwhelmed.

Later, in the backyard, Deborah approached Lillian and led her to a quiet corner of her winter-dry grass. "My friend Adelita had told me she wouldn't make it," she confided in a low voice, "but she just changed her mind. She's coming. Has Avery told you about her?"

"She's the one who's a... you know what, right?"

"Yes, she is," Deborah whispered. "I just don't want there to be any surprises."

"Did you tell her about me?"

"I told her not to worry. I'll keep everything under control."

Later, as Lillian lingered in the yard and chatted with Ralph and Mindy, the people she felt more comfortable around than most of the others, she felt it before she saw it—the bright hot aura of an air person. There she stood, the tall, dark-haired family friend Adelita, with her husband, an ordinary man, and their two adolescent kids who had no powers.

"What is this?" Adelita cried out, staring straight at Lillian. The orange of Deborah appeared, mingling with Adelita's blue-white colors. The two women vanished from view for an extended period, and Lillian hung back, sticking close to Avery, afraid to go looking for either of them. Avery took Lillian's hand and squeezed it to comfort her, streaming soothing thoughts into her. *Don't worry. Mom is going to get Adelita calmed down; I'm sure of it.*

Later, when everyone was called inside to eat, Lillian spotted Deborah and Adelita in the living room. Adelita very deliberately kept her distance from Lillian, also shooing her children away with subtle hints. Like Lillian was going to harm her kids. How insulting. Once they sat down to eat the turkey, Tofurky, hummus, cranberry sauce, and casseroles, Lillian's anxiety upset her stomach. Adelita was seated across the table from her, glancing at her repeatedly as Lillian stared down at her plate. If Lillian had known this change of plans would happen, she wouldn't have come.

Two more unexpected guests showed up, an opera singer named Stardust and her mother Jess, another longtime friend of Deborah's. Lillian had heard a few stories about these people, and they were both quite friendly. Stardust sang a couple of songs for the group.

After everyone filled up on dinner, they helped themselves to pumpkin pie, played board and card games, and flowed in and out of the house. As some of the guests left, Deborah put a few of her old vinyl records on her turntable: Leonard Cohen, Neil Young, Johnny Cash.

Lillian breathed a sigh of relief when Adelita left with her family. Avery quietly consoled her when they took a break in his bedroom, assuring her that Adelita was a nice lady and would eventually soften to the idea of Lillian, just as he felt certain her still-silent cousin Denny would. Until then, he and his mother would continue talking to Adelita and help her to eventually understand their relationship. Like a lot of other mages, she had been warned against necromancers from birth, while convinced they were long dead. It would take time to undo this programming in her mind.

"And your mom seems really chill with me," Lillian said.

"Remember, she didn't know what mages are even called until she was in her forties and met Adelita. As a kid, she had to figure it all out on her own. It was scary for her, but since she had nobody to talk to about this stuff, she had nobody to teach her to be afraid of necromancers."

The rest of that extended weekend was much quieter and less stressful, with the crowd reduced to Deborah, Avery, their friends Ralph and Mindy sleeping out in the living room, and the couple of other friends staying in a hotel for a couple of days. They spent that Saturday wandering in a historic district. Deborah took the whole group of friends out to lunch at a café rumored to be haunted. Just as she was about to eat her aromatic, sizzling fajitas, an apparition, a woman in a long dress, floated along the periphery of Lillian's vision. The ghost stories were true, but nearly every place was haunted if you looked hard enough.

"My mom really likes you," Avery assured Lillian during the drive back the next day. "She thinks you're very sweet."

"Well, that's a relief."

Excerpt from The Autobiography of Gerald Frazier: Architect of a New World

After my father's death, my sister Sarah and I grew closer again. We wrote to each other and occasionally visited. But sadly, Sarah cracked up mentally as the years went by. She still loathed herself for being a necromancer, to the point where she prayed for death to come and take her. The downward spiral worsened after Sarah's husband grew tired of these mood swings he did not understand, and divorced her. Sarah stayed in a mental hospital for a while as her ex took care of their son. From the hospital, she wrote me a letter stating that she'd been haunted by terrible visions of a future taken over by zombies and monsters that tore up everybody in their path.

I believe she was predicting a future when we come to power! And it will not be terrible, like she believed. Since many of Sarah's predictions came true, it gives me confidence, looking back!

I still have a strange letter that Sarah wrote to me in 1962. After her discharge from the hospital, she was on her own. With few people willing to hire a woman as heavy as she was, Sarah did not find work. She moved to Salisbury, a city not far from where we grew up, to stay with a cousin on our mother's side. Sarah was napping in the spare bedroom one afternoon, and then came a recurrence of a dream she'd had as a girl, in which a wall was torn down. When Sarah woke up, she screamed as a strange man in a tattered robe stood right next to her bed. He spoke to her in an unusual accent, introducing himself as Armand, revealing that "the one who decides" would be born close to the time that this wall would come down. This man did not tell Sarah who this person was, or where or when he would make his appearance.

"The signs are falling into place," Armand said. "We have waited centuries for the one who decides. He has an important job with the dead, but soon, maybe in ten years, maybe in thirty, he will come to earth in the body of a man. You are the prophet. After he is born, you must watch over him. He shall walk the earth in a body that will carry great power, but will be mortal."

When Sarah asked this man to clarify what this heroic unborn figure was supposed to "decide," he just said, "Fate." Armand disappeared into thin air, and only then did Sarah snap that she'd been speaking to a ghost! This was no ordinary spirit. Most of the ghosts we see are echoes of the past, not someone you can hold a conversation with.

When I first read that particular letter, I could not figure out whether it carried an important message, or if it was just Sarah going further off the deep end. During my next visit with her, I read in her mind that she honest-to-God saw a bearded man in a beaten-up robe and was convinced they had spoken!

Sarah spent the rest of her life obsessed with this encounter. She kept a close eye on television and the newspapers, watching for any stories about a big wall coming down, a sign that some special baby boy was about to be born or perhaps had been already. When I came to Salisbury to check in on Sarah, I found our cousin's spare bedroom plastered with photographs and drawings of stone walls, brick walls, the Great Wall of China, and every other type of wall you can imagine from around the world. I looked around, shook my head in disapproval, and encouraged her to stop fixating so much on walls. Even if that child was born, locating him would be like finding a needle in a haystack.

That man in the robe came to visit Sarah again. He told her a couple more details: that on the day the momentous child was born, there would be explosions. That didn't make it easier to pinpoint. Since we're a long way from world peace, there are bombs exploding somewhere in the world pretty much every day. Sarah told me about this during the Cuban Missile Crisis, when tensions were sky-high and people lived in fear that they didn't have much time left. Despite Sarah's assurances that life would go on and no nuclear missiles would fly, anything could have happened.

It is my hope that by the time you are reading this, bombs and tanks and silly wars are a thing of the past!

I never saw my sister again after that visit. I allowed three years to lapse between trips back home. Lou called me crying in 1965, informing me that Sarah had taken her own life with an overdose of pills, leaving her boy motherless. Sarah, who'd revealed so much of the future, did not live to see the first man on the moon. I was frustrated; I was furious at both her and myself. I'd never been able to talk my sister into appreciating her powers. And she never will.

Our brother Lou didn't get angry so much as grief-stricken. He stepped in to help care for poor Denny. The boy was staying with his father when it happened, and this spared his young eyes from seeing the body. Still, this impacted Denny terribly, and he became a very angry child.

Lou, who now had his own business that I'd gifted him some money for, ended up divorced. Roberta, his high school sweetheart, walked out on him, and he did not protest. They told the relatives that they had "irreconcilable differences," that vague phrase people use to weasel their way out of explaining what really destroyed their marriage. Of course, I knew the truth. Roberta was fed up with the lack of sexual intercourse, particularly frustrated as she had hoped for children. After that, Lou remained single in our childhood home, carrying on the occasional homosexual affair behind closed doors. It was really too bad. I would have been happy to find a lady with the right genetics.

Lou and I had a chilly, distant relationship as adults, though he accepted my financial help in opening up his nursery. He held on to resentment towards me, feeling that I'd manipulated him relentlessly when we were young boys. But sometimes in life, you've just got to step on toes, and that's something Lou never understood. He also refused to give me the ancestral green crystal when I asked. But I knew that I would gain his trust one of these days. I kept my hope alive that I'd think of something to help my lonely brother have children, the right kind of children for my ultimate mission. I trusted that the answers would come to me eventually.

We still had our eldest sister Violet. She was still married to that man with ordinary genes and dead set against having children, and also getting a bit older by then. The thought crossed my mind of somehow getting the proper genes in her, by force if need be. The ends justify the means, right? But if she were to get pregnant, I knew she'd immediately do as Sarah had done, get an abortion. Or, another terrible option—give the child up for adoption. Imagine the frightening experience of growing up a severely misunderstood necromancer in a family of ordinary people, having no idea what you are or exactly what your powers are!

It was no use, since I was living in another state and too busy with my work and my children to watch my siblings like a hawk. I had to find other avenues.

The Truth About Natasha

It was a Friday evening, pouring down rain, kicking off one of those weekends that Evelyn dreaded: her daughter Natasha's court-ordered visits with Jonathan. This also meant leaving her with his girlfriend, Kendall, and their infant son, Colton. The baby who had been conceived while Jonathan was still married to Evelyn.

Kendall never looked Evelyn in the eye when she dropped Tasha off.

Evelyn and Jonathan at least agreed on one thing: to indefinitely delay telling Natasha that baby Colton was her half-brother. Tasha, who'd just turned two, was too young to understand.

During the long drive in the heavy rain to the suburb where Jonathan shared an apartment with Kendall, Tasha slept in her car seat in the back, with a doll clutched in her hands. A rustle came from the backseat as Tasha stirred awake.

"Almost there!" she chirped.

"Yes, Tasha. We're almost there." It was the exact same thought that just went through Evelyn's mind. Tasha had a strangely good grasp of how far they were from their destination during car trips. Evelyn wondered how Tasha could possibly know how close they were getting this time. Surely she could barely see anything from the rear-facing child seat in the back. The windows were smeared and pelted with pouring rain as the atmosphere darkened outside.

"Daddy. Kendaw," Tasha mumbled.

"Yes, we're on our way to see your daddy and Kendall this weekend."

"Colton." Tasha could not quite pronounce her L's yet. The baby's name always came out sounding like *Coat-in.*

"Yes, and Colton. That's Kendall's baby."

"He brother."

The words washed over Evelyn like a pitcher of ice water. "What? What did you say, Tasha? What?"

There was no response. In the backseat, Tasha looked down, stroking and tugging the hair on her doll.

"Tasha, who told you about Colton? Who told you that? Can you tell me who said he's 'brother'?"

"Mommy... Mommy fought..."

"Mommy thought what?"

"Coat-in Tasha's brother."

"Did anybody ever tell you he is your brother? Did anybody ever tell you?"

No answer came.

When Evelyn pulled into the parking lot of her ex-husband's apartment complex, she was still cold and numb all over. No, no, there was no way Tasha had somehow read her mind. Nobody could read minds; Evelyn could not believe such a ridiculous notion had even popped up.

As Evelyn unstrapped Tasha from the car seat and carried her up the stairs to the apartment, she came to the conclusion that Jonathan must have told their daughter that he fathered the baby. And Tasha could not find all of the words to accurately tell her mother how she knew the truth. Jonathan had done it on purpose, looking for ways to hurt Evelyn, to get the last laugh. By the time she knocked on the apartment door, Evelyn whipped herself up into a state of fury.

Kendall, a skinny woman with bleached blond hair and fading tattoos on her arms, opened the door, looking down and avoiding eye contact with Evelyn as usual. Colton was sprawled in a baby swing near the door. Jonathan, watching football with a beer in one hand, got up as Evelyn shut the door behind her and put Tasha down. She pattered toward the baby swing and placed her little hand on the infant's nearly bald head.

"Brother," she said in her tiny voice.

Jonathan's eyebrows shot up, and then his eyes hardened. Kendall continued to look down, chewing her lip.

"You told her," Evelyn accused. "One or both of you broke the agreement and told her, didn't you?"

"No, I didn't," Jonathan insisted. "Babe, did you say anything about it?"

His girlfriend meekly shook her head.

"Well, somehow she knows."

"You must have told her, then!" Jonathan shot back at Evelyn. "Because there's no other possible way for her to know."

"I did not tell her. She started talking about it in the car. She said it out of nowhere."

"It wouldn't be the first time she said something out of nowhere. Evelyn, I hate to say it, but there's something up with Tasha. She kind of creeps us out, to be honest with you. It's the things she blurts out."

"What sorts of things?"

"Well, I didn't want to get into this, but the last time you dropped her off here, Kendall and I had just had a bit of an argument. The argument was over before you even showed up. I started wondering if you'd bugged this place."

"Of course not! Why would I bug the apartment? That's illegal!"

"Then how was Tasha parroting words of our fight? Parts of it were even word for word. It was very weird."

"I don't know how she does these things. I really don't." Evelyn shook her head.

"Well, neither do I. It's starting to feel like she's reading our minds!"

"There is no such thing as mind reading, and anyone who says they can do it is a fraud."

"Well, then, maybe she's just playing a trick on us."

"Do you hear yourself? A toddler who's still in diapers, playing magic tricks?"

"Let's all just back off and try not to think about the whole issue, how about that?" Jonathan suggested. "Just simmer down."

Evelyn felt anything but relaxed after leaving her daughter behind with her ex-husband. Tension wound her up tight. She had never heard of another parent in a situation like hers, and decided that she had an unusually perceptive toddler, skilled at reading social cues—both a blessing and a curse. What would Tasha blurt out next? Something even more sensitive and embarrassing?

Lou encouraged both Evelyn and Lillian to come and visit for Christmas. Six months ago, the last thing he'd expected to happen at his age had happened. Lou met someone, and now they decided it was an appropriate time to introduce him to the kids.

Lou and Derek Goldberg, a retired veterinarian living in southern New Jersey, had run into each other by chance during a summer trip to a nearby beach. They walked for a while on the sand, chatting until Derek asked the shyer Lou if he could take him out to dinner. Still getting accustomed to life outside of the closet, Lou accepted.

They commuted to one another's homes for visits. With the newness of it all, they took things slowly and cautiously in the beginning. Though their personalities meshed well, they did not have everything in common. Lou had children and Derek did not. Lou was a dog person and Derek preferred cats. Lou was a homebody while Derek had a passport full of stamps. Lou was Episcopalian and Derek was Jewish. After being out for twenty years, Derek had a lot more experience in the gay social scene.

And like most people, Derek had no supernatural abilities. To him, mages would be something out of a fantasy book, if he even had any inkling that they existed. Lou had to hide that side of his being from Derek, making him feel a bit wistful, even jealous, that Lillian had someone she could be her whole self with.

Once Derek arrived in his car for his winter visit, Evelyn was the next guest to show up with her daughter. "Flying with a two-year-old isn't fun," she said, visibly frazzled, after she pulled up in a rental car with a very hyperactive Tasha.

Once they came into the house, Tasha shrieked, "Derek!" The two hadn't even been introduced, and already she ran toward him, climbing to get on his lap.

Derek shifted in a bit of discomfort as the toddler wallowed on him. "My nieces and nephews are all grown up, and I haven't had a little kid Velcroed onto me in years," he laughed.

"She is usually shy around strangers. She must really like you," Evelyn brought up as she lifted Tasha into her arms.

The following evening, Lillian arrived. She did not bring Avery, who stayed with his mother. And Lou got the impression that the tension with Denny made him uneasy about returning.

With a bit of smugness, Evelyn told Lillian, "I *knew* you and that guy were going to end up together! And you said he wasn't your type! What took so long?"

Like Evelyn, Lillian got along fine with Derek. In spite of Lillian's somewhat reserved nature with new people, he got her to open up a bit. It made Lou grateful that his daughters were so accepting of his surprise relationship.

After Derek left a few days later, Lillian and Denny spoke tersely on the phone. Once they broke the ice, Denny agreed to come and pick her up so they could talk for a bit. The two mended fences, coming to a cautious acceptance over Lillian's situation.

While they were out, Lou was left alone with Evelyn and Tasha, who napped in her playpen in front of the warm fire.

"Tasha is such a smart little girl," Lou pointed out. "You must have told her everyone's names. She knew Derek's name on sight."

"I don't see how it was possible," Evelyn said, biting her lip. Her eyes began to glisten. "There are a lot of things that shouldn't be possible."

"Like what?"

"Dad, I don't know who else to talk to about this. I'm concerned there is something strange about Tasha—no, there isn't. It's just my imagination."

"Something strange?" Lou asked, hiding his alarm and trying to keep his voice steady. "What do you mean?"

"Sometimes she just blurts out things that she's not supposed to know. For one, she knows the baby Jonathan had with his girlfriend is her brother, and Jonathan and I both agreed to keep it from her. Jonathan still could have told her; he denies it, but we know he's not trustworthy. But here's the thing. Someone who works at Tasha's daycare claimed that Tasha said he was going to propose to his girlfriend. He swore up and down he didn't tell anyone. It was his secret plan, and somehow it was blown open by a two-year-old! It's starting to feel like she's reading our minds. But there's no way."

"Sweetheart, if this is what I think it is, and we don't address it, things will only get worse."

"Worse? Gee, thanks, Dad. That's what I needed to hear."

"Tasha is reading people's minds. And she's good at it, too."

"Seriously?! Look, Dad, there is no such thing. No one can read minds."

"Many things in our family aren't scientifically proven, but they are real. We kept it from you for your own safety. But now I'm left with no choice but to tell you."

"Tell me what, Dad?" Evelyn demanded angrily, her pale cheeks flushing.

"I know how crazy it all sounds. It may be easiest if I just show you."

"This has to be a joke," Evelyn sneered, eyes cold and hard, as Lou walked to the kitchen and grabbed a pot holding a few flowers he had forgotten to water. They'd just died, withering, the petals beginning to fall. He brought it back to the living room, setting the pot down on the coffee table in front of Evelyn.

As the flowers perked up, yellow color flushing back into the now-plump petals, Evelyn's eyes widened. Her hand flew to her mouth. "What trick did you just play?"

"Magic."

Evelyn scoffed. "So you're a magician."

"If you want to call it that. Me, Lillian, Denny, Gerald, and Tasha—all of us are magicians."

"This is a terrible joke, Dad."

"Each one of us has the power to move objects. Except for Tasha. She's too little for most of her powers to kick in. Except for mind reading."

"You expect me to believe that? How would I never notice if everybody has superhero powers except me?"

"Because we're taught to conceal them from people, even family members, who don't have these abilities."

"So you sit there and tell me that you and Lillian have magical powers and I never had any idea all my life, and you expect me to believe you?! This is getting less and less funny." Evelyn shook her head angrily.

"If the flowers don't convince you, I can show you something else."

"What are you going to do, a card trick?"

"Hand me that deck of cards over there, then, and I'll show you a card trick," he sighed, pointing to a box of playing cards on the coffee table. Evelyn tossed it into his hands.

Lou cupped the box in his palms. It rose up into the air and levitated about three feet above his head, silent and still. Evelyn reached above the deck of cards, searching for a barely visible nylon string that might be holding it up. As she attempted to grab the deck, it floated behind her father's head, just out of reach. An indescribably shocked expression crossed her face as the deck coasted forward and into her limp hand. In her state of abject disbelief, Evelyn's fingers failed to curl around the deck, and it slid from her palm and fell to the floor with a soft thud.

"How did that happen?" Evelyn gasped. "Dad, how did you do that?! Did you put a magnet in there, or..."

"No magnets, no sleight of hand. It's telekinesis. Just like you've read about in books."

"If Tasha can read minds, then you're a mind reader, right? What am I thinking about right now? How many fingers am I holding up?" Evelyn extended two fingers and put her hand behind her back.

"Evelyn, I cannot read minds. Only certain folks have that talent. Your uncle Gerald is one of them. That's how he outed me, and that's why we no longer speak."

"I still don't really believe any of it, but what other magic powers do you have, or think you have?"

"You do not need to be concerned about all of my powers. Tasha has a different set of powers than the rest of us in the family, and that's what you need to worry about. As she grows older, you may start to notice she can control water, or create it. She may be sensitive to weather patterns. You may also notice the telekinesis I just showed you."

"How come no one took the time to mention any of this to me sooner? I'm so upset. I've been lied to my whole life. I need a minute." Evelyn stepped out briefly onto the porch to collect herself.

"We live by a special code," Lou explained after she was ready to come back in. "We do not tell folks what we can do. In the best case scenario, they think we've lost our minds; in the worst case, they make attempts on our lives. Or try, at least. That's why the whole fiasco with the water happened after your wedding, when me, Denny, and Lillian were nearly drowned. Some people were after us. People who share Tasha's powers. We later made a truce with them, and they haven't bothered us since. I decided to make an exception to the rules to help you understand Tasha, and so you won't be frightened as she grows older."

"Count me frightened, Dad."

"You'll get used to it. Slowly, but surely, you will. I raised a child with powers and I survived. You will too."

"I always felt like there was something weird about Lillian. Even when she was little. How she always found me while playing hide and seek. Was it the... don't tell me she can read minds!"

"She can't. But she can see things that you cannot. That's how she won those games."

"I can't deal with this. I just... can't even. Tell me, people who read minds, can they see everything? All of your secrets, all of your thoughts?"

"It depends. Most mind readers can only read certain people, and often it's just partial. Your uncle Gerald is a rare type. He can see everything in everyone's head."

"Oh, God! If Tasha is the same type as Gerald, what am I going to do?! I'm sorry, but I can't live with someone like that, even if it's my own child! Having no privacy!" Tears leaked from Evelyn's eyes.

"Types like Gerald happen once in a blue moon. I don't think she'll be quite like him. But, yes, it is concerning. It's scary. I know how you must be feeling. Even having children with your mother, who did not have powers but carried the trait for them, I was terrified. Honestly, I prayed that both of you would be normal, and when your sister came along, I got more than I bargained for. Believe me, I was frightened of what the future might hold.

If you want to mask your thoughts from Tasha, I can teach you a trick that will help. I can't promise it will always work."

"My child, it's been too long since I've seen you!" Gerald warmly embraced Katrina as she came in from the chilly winter night. "I'm delighted to have you here! Please, tell me all about your adventures in that nice new car of yours."

"The adventures have been... well, great. I am so glad you bought me that car! I was terrified of the old Pontiac breaking down with how many miles I put on it."

"Come in. Sit beside the fire and warm up. We've got lots of catching up to do."

After they perched in front of the roaring fire, each holding a cup of homemade eggnog infused with brandy, Gerald scanned Katrina's mind.

"You did a fine job keeping tabs on Lillian during your travels. You were careful not to follow her too closely after she returned to school. I'm sure she didn't have a clue of your presence. That boyfriend of hers, that is just unbelievable!"

"I couldn't believe it either! What an idiot!"

"I'm sure she thinks they've bonded because they're both mages. But that girl doesn't have an ounce of sense." Gerald sighed and shook his head.

"I looked them up on Facebook. His name's Avery Joseph. That's all I know."

"That young man presents a danger to Lillian, and a danger to us. He's a much greater obstruction than a normal boyfriend would be. I think it is a good bet he would resist our plan and fight back. You must return once they're back at school, and you must kill him."

Katrina gasped. "Grandpa, that's risky. You're putting me in danger!"

"What other choice is there? I would go with you, but with my recent heart trouble, I need to remain near my doctor. You've killed before. You know how we can go undetected."

"The only person I've bumped off was Lillian's stupid roommate. And now, you're asking me to go kill another person because of her, and we're talking about a *mage*. A fire mage!"

"Yes, indeed, you must be very careful. But you are clever and I'm certain you can catch him alone. Just stay quiet as a church mouse, keep your distance, and shove him in front of a car. Or hide outside his window and have him grab a knife from the kitchen. Make it quick."

"I think it would be quick and efficient to just put a bullet in his head."

"Please don't shoot him. Guns are loud and leave too much evidence behind with their powder and shell casings. You already know how we can cover our tracks seamlessly and make it look like an unfortunate accident or a suicide. Since Avery is in a new relationship with an attractive woman, his friends and family must assume he's very happy, so an accident would be the most believable scenario. I know you can do this. It has to be done."

"Okay, Grandpa, I'm scared, but I'll do it. Can't I have help? Can't Uncle Julius go with me?"

"I don't think it's necessary. If Julius joins you, it may increase your risk of being seen. Your confidence will only grow after you do away with this young man. You'll need that spine of steel once we're in for the biggest battles of our lives. And while she grieves, Lillian will become more pliable. It will be easy to convince her to join our mission. She'll feel she has nothing to lose."

After they drank down their eggnog, Gerald invited Katrina to come down to the recreation room. "I have something marvelous to show you."

As they went down the carpeted stairs, turned on the light, and Katrina's grandfather headed toward the bookshelf that concealed the hidden room he'd shown her right after its construction, Katrina already knew that they were not alone in the house.

Gerald pulled the bookshelf away from the wall, and then unlocked and swung open the security door.

A woman sat on the cot inside the barren secret room, with a plate of half-eaten chicken legs on the floor nearby. She looked up at Katrina with an expressionless, tear-stained face beneath her stringy brown hair.

She had mage blood.

"Katrina, I would like you to meet Michaela," Gerald introduced the woman. "She has been with me for two months. Julius has already paid us a visit. We will soon see if that visit was successful."

"Grandpa, that's so awesome!" Katrina jumped for joy, even as his captive glared at both of them, hate turning her eyes to stone. "You caught one already!"

"Convincing her to forget about some man that she was going to marry and join our mission has been an uphill battle," Gerald let on after he had Katrina fetch oatmeal for Michaela, removed the plate of chicken remnants, and then latched the door shut. "And she suffers from asthma, so I must be careful to keep a steady supply of inhalers and check on her frequently. I do wish I could have found a half-breed who's in perfect health.

Michaela's not fully on board yet. She has not enjoyed your uncle's visits. But I'm thankful I finally convinced her to stop trying to escape, and no longer need to keep her tied up."

"Just keep trying. She'll come around."

"Katrina, it's also time for you to start thinking of procreating again," Gerald encouraged his granddaughter. "I know you were scarred by that loss you suffered some years back. But lightning doesn't strike twice."

"Then find me somebody. Somebody who won't bail on me if things go south."

"I'm keeping my eye out."

Two nights later, as Katrina slept in a guest bedroom, both she and her grandfather woke up simultaneously with a bad, empty feeling twisting their stomachs. After glancing around the house, they crept down to the secret room to check on Michaela, knowing the outcome before Gerald even unlocked the door.

Michaela lay curled and gray on the floor, dead from a likely asthma attack.

"Damn it to hell!" Gerald screamed, punching the wall, kicking the cot where his captive had slept. "Well, we're just going to have to pick ourselves up, dust ourselves off, and find another one. Katrina, help me bury the body. And whatever you do, no reanimating."

Two months later, Katrina was back in Colorado, just as she'd promised her grandfather. To leave as few trails behind as possible, she hung around remote edges of town in the new white Hyundai her grandfather had purchased, which looked just like so many other cars on the road. Katrina ate beef jerky in the car and slept in the backseat. And when Katrina drove onto the campus, she did not dare set foot outside of the vehicle. She would love to search Lillian's room to look for the crystal, or perhaps steal it right off her body, but on this trip, stealth was more important than ever.

Though Katrina figured out where Avery lived, following him and Lillian and learning their routines was tricky. Katrina could not just walk after them and hide in the shadows. During Katrina's last mission to murder someone in this town, she'd been tense, but now the fear crystallized into a knife edge. Though she would not leave until Avery was dead, Katrina resented her grandfather for putting her in danger. Alone, without so much as her uncle to help.

"You can do it," Gerald had encouraged over the phone during her road trip, avoiding any directly incriminating words about their plan. "This is important for your growth. Once you carry it out, you'll be more confident, and we can all move forward and be ready."

Early one evening, Katrina spotted Avery on a walk in his neighborhood, toting a reusable grocery bag. She slowed her car to a crawl, set back far enough on the street that he wouldn't notice, and followed. Right now, Avery was alone. Good. Catching him without Lillian, or even his ordinary friends, was important.

The sound of traffic filtered through Katrina's open car window, reminding her of the busy street nearby. Avery might be headed there to get groceries. She'd still have to take possession, get out of the car, and walk behind him for a ways. With any luck, his gait wouldn't be stiff and awkward enough to make him stand out to any passers-by. And then into the traffic he'd stumble.

It was going to hurt. Even if a necromancer couldn't be injured by the pain inflicted on someone under their possession, and the sensations came through dulled, sympathy pains could still echo back to the attacker's body. Katrina did not want to connect with someone else's bones snapping under tires, even if it hurt less for her than it would for him.

Suck it up, she told herself as she crept closer to Avery, and then pulled her car over to the curb. *It'll just hurt for a second.*

Katrina got out of the car, shutting the door as gently as possible. She took a few soft steps, deciding she was close enough to take command of Avery several yards in front of her.

Avery looked over his shoulder and stopped as he met Katrina's eyes. He spun around and walked straight toward her, his face stony.

Shit! He's chasing me! Abort! Abort!

Her heart pounding almost out of her chest, Katrina's legs turned to jelly as she ran and pulled her car door open with trembling fingers. On squealing tires, she peeled out of the neighborhood.

Katrina did not stop glancing at her rearview mirrors, reflecting her huge and terrified gray eyes, until she was well on her way to Kansas.

I'm sorry, Grandpa. I'm so weak.

"I'm so glad you got that weird feeling you were being followed, then decided to chase her instead of trying to run away," Lillian sighed as they huddled together. She'd left her class early and came over to Avery's room as soon as he got in the front door and texted her. "If you had run in the other direction, she might have gotten back in her car and taken possession of you."

"It was a split-second decision. Do I run, or do I chase? I remembered how much I could scare her. How scared you used to be to even come near me."

"I'm afraid to ask, did you read her mind? She must have been up to no good, sneaking around town without telling me, following you..."

"I only read a little bit. Katrina thinks in words, not pictures. She was thinking, 'Abort, abort!' And that's when she got in her car and sped away."

"That means she had a plan to do something with you. And she had to drop that plan when you chased her. I'm really scared for you, Avery. What if she comes back? Or even comes back with... reinforcements?"

"She looked terrified. I'm confident... well, sort of confident... that she won't be back. Now she knows I can spot her and I won't back down."

"I'm still concerned. That's why I'm staying here tonight. I can't let anything happen to you. I love you too much!"

"I love you too. I'm so glad something didn't happen and I made it home. Let's just be vigilant," Avery suggested.

"We should stick together as much as we possibly can," Lillian recommended. "Remember that if a necromancer takes possession, you'll be helpless. You can't use your fire, I'm pretty sure. But if it's both of us, hopefully we can scare away anyone who might make trouble."

"You don't have to watch me every second. I really don't think she'll be back. I think I can manage. And we're moving away from here soon. Hopefully she won't find us again."

Lillian had just gotten accepted into a highly regarded graduate program in San Diego. Not wanting a long-distance relationship and having no job lined up yet, Avery planned to go with her. Though they had reservations about relocating to a big city neither was familiar with, not knowing if there might be any gangs of mages there, Lillian could not refuse the opportunity. They would figure out their new living situation and search for work once she started at the school in the fall.

"If Katrina or any of my other creepy relatives come back, I don't care what your mom says. Use your powers if you need to," Lillian suggested, clinging to Avery tightly.

The beginnings of summer warmth hung in the pleasantly moist air of the May morning. Lush tree boughs hung over the sea of mortarboards as the spring graduating class of 2011 sat in rows and rows of folding metal seats. Lillian made sure to yell and clap when the name Avery Francis Joseph was called and he walked proudly across the stage. Later, they got around to the geology department and called out her own name, and the university president handed her the diploma with her brand-new Bachelor of Science. Much to the surprise of the people in Lillian's life, long hair didn't tumble over her gown. Even though the idea of change terrified her, she'd gotten it cut shoulder-length. Already, this hair was so much easier to take care of, so much lighter.

Last night, Lillian had become anxious, disbelieving that this would happen, that she could reach a milestone so momentous that her father, sister, niece, cousin Denny, and maternal uncle Victor had all flown out here to be a part of it. Yes, Denny showed up, having apologized for that angry phone call back in August, and for ignoring her. Now he accepted her relationship.

In spite of how much Lillian had healed, all the years that had passed, what Julius did to her was still immediate in a way, as crystalline as if it had happened yesterday and could repeat itself all over again tomorrow. And Avery's chilling encounter with Katrina brought Julius and everything associated with him too close to home.

Standing on the stage was surreal, like floating above the wooden planks, as Lillian looked out into the audience. Avery's mother was an orange pinpoint in the sun. Faint wisps of green defined her own relatives two sets of bleachers away. There were no tall green spires anywhere else, where they didn't belong.

Once the ceremony was over, everyone found each other. The collective families and friends gathered on a grassy knoll and talked. Little Tasha's hair was tied into brunette pigtails, and her speech skills had shot up since Lillian saw her last. Tasha squealed at the sight of Lillian and hugged her a lot before gravitating straight toward Avery's mother.

Deborah's friend Adelita had come up with her on the drive. After catching Lillian's attention, she asked to speak privately for just a few moments.

"You know... I wanted to apologize for how I acted on Thanksgiving. I was not expecting to see you, and didn't fully understand the situation. I was startled. Now I've had time to wrap my head around it, and I've seen how happy Avery is. I just don't want there to be any more tension between us."

Floored, Lillian accepted the apology.

Though Denny first bristled at the sight of Adelita, they started to make a bit of small talk. With each of these meetings, the age-old barriers between magical people crumbled bit by bit.

Afterward, Richard held a graduation party at his house, where Lillian had just spent the previous day moving her things into Avery's bedroom for storage until the next transition. Evelyn kept a close eye on Tasha, watching everything the child said in their mixed company. Evelyn still struggled to accept and fully believe the truth about Tasha's powers.

Deborah, who'd faced similar challenges when raising her son, sat privately in Avery's room with Evelyn for a bit, shutting the door. They discussed the uniquely distressing situation of parenting a small child who could read minds and who knew too many things, paired with the early-childhood lack of a social filter.

The following week, Avery, his mother, and Lillian went on a road trip to visit her friends Ralph and Mindy. Their ranch was nestled behind trees, with a sprawling wooden house and a nearby stable, and it blew Lillian away with its beauty. Avery had not been here since the members of that cult had assaulted him a couple of years before, and returning was healing for him.

"You're probably wondering why I was imploring you to visit me," Gerald said in a voice weaker than usual, sitting on his bed and stroking his cat, as Katrina sat next to him, listening.

"Are you going to yell at me again for failing to get rid of that guy?"

"No. What's done is done. Since he saw you, we need to pull back and regroup before you even think about going near those people again."

"Something else is wrong, isn't it?"

"I grow weak, Katrina. My heart problems are escalating. My doctor doesn't want to hurt my feelings, but of course I know what she's thinking. I don't have much time left, and my doctor does not think I'll be approved for a transplant. I can feel the life force draining from me."

Katrina took a long look at Gerald, her eyes wide and her face troubled. "Your aura..."

"It's looking duller. Even Julius was noticing that a bit the last time he visited. There's no denying it. Katrina, I am dying."

"But Grandpa, you don't know that. Maybe there's still something you can do!"

"I'm sick and tired of being sick and tired, to be honest. And all of these monkey wrenches were thrown into our plans. Our first captured half-breed died on me, you never managed to get that crystal and now that young man in Lillian's life might be on to you, and the construction on the island hasn't even started thanks to all of that red tape. I'm not counting on living to see things come together."

Tears welled in Katrina's pale eyes. Gently, Gerald wiped them away with his thumbs.

"Don't cry," he said softly. "Even if I'm not here, this is by no means the end. We can still proceed. You and Julius are just as capable of taking charge. I already have my will revised. When I go, the money is split among you, Lillian..."

"Why her?! She isn't even your kid!"

"I'll get there in a second. She'll get less than you, but it should be enough to pay for the rest of her education, pay off any student loans, and then some. I have a small amount set aside to keep your mother breathing for the rest of her natural life. You and Julius get all the rest, and this house is yours."

"Mine?!" Katrina gasped. "I can't take this house. You're not serious!"

"Where else are you going to go? Surely you don't want to spend the rest of your life rotting in your mother's trailer and working miserable low-wage jobs? As one of the chosen ones, you deserve better."

"But why not Julius? He's more accomplished than me."

"Just between you and me, while Julius is a very important player in our family's future, I don't trust him as much as I do you. He is impulsive and does not always think things through that well. He's been a little... reckless, particularly around women. You are of a sharp, clear mind. You will... lead."

"Me? Lead?!"

"Of... course... my dear."

"Grandpa! Are you okay?" Katrina put her hand on Gerald's arm as he leaned forward, clutching at his chest and gasping. His face turned red.

"Just those damn angina pains again. Okay, I'm better now."

"You've tried talking to your brother, haven't you?"

"Yes, without much luck. I perhaps did something impulsive myself and now he's in an unforgiving frame of mind. I have been calling him, trying to make up, and using sly terms to talk him into our mission. But he cuts the calls short. And at this point, I don't want to risk another surprise in-person visit. At the rate things are going, we'll have to proceed without his knowledge. And he's gotten to the age where he might not be around in another ten years. However, there's still a bit of hope with Lillian."

"Even with that boyfriend?"

"Yes, she's getting a part of my inheritance, so that will stimulate her guilt gland and that wall she's put up might come down."

"But if that house on the island isn't even built yet..."

"Oh, it will be. You'll just have to take matters into your own hands if I'm gone."

"But I can't! It won't be the same without you! It'll be too overwhelming! I've never been in charge before!"

"Stop behaving like a child. You are smart. You are capable of more than you think. You just need to muster up the self-confidence. Sometimes in life we don't have a choice but to take the reins. And you will not be alone. Julius will help you. And I'll leave something else. I've been working on my memoir for the past couple of years. It shall be a gift to our future generations to explain how it all came about, what it took to get to where we're going. Ever since I've been on medical leave from work, I've been doing my best to finish it up quickly. It is in a document on the laptop I keep in the bedroom, and I saved a backup on the desktop in my study. You should have no problems finding it."

"You're telling me in case something happens to you, I should print it out or whatever?"

"Precisely."

"Grandpa, stop talking like this! I don't want to lose you!"

"When Mary Fraser, your great-grandmother several generations back, came over here with that small group who'd survived the attack from the air people, they brought a vast knowledge of necromancy and witchcraft from their destroyed colony. A lot of that knowledge was beaten out of the next generations thanks to churches and religious shame. But you can't beat the whole witch out of the necromancer, and a few spells and potions and divinations have been preserved. Including the spell I've passed along to you, which converts creatures. Would you believe that you can still talk to Mary if you wish? And without just waiting for her ghost to show up?"

"Even without the crystal?"

"Yes, even without the crystal. Come with me."

Gerald led Katrina down to his game room, past the bookshelf that concealed the security door. He removed a still-life painting from the wall and opened a safe concealed behind it. Inside was a small glass vial, its surface rippled, darkened, and too heavily stained to see what was inside. Gerald carefully removed that and an envelope.

"What is that?" Katrina wanted to know.

"That is Mary's blood."

"Ew. I hate blood."

"Katrina, you must get over that fear. Because believe me, you'll be seeing a lot more blood. Mary's is so old and dried, it might as well be a pinch of oregano. My father may have let that crystal go to Lou, but at least I got my hands on this before anyone else could get it. And here's something else you want to guard with your life. I let a phlebotomy student practice on me last week." Gerald removed one of several capped vacuum tubes filled with his own, much fresher blood.

"Gross!" Katrina flinched again.

"You'll save these tubes for when I'm gone. Today we'll take a drop from my body. Both your blood and the blood of the person you wish to contact are required. Now watch carefully."

Gerald led Katrina up the short flight of stairs from the game room the kitchen, stopping to catch his breath along the way. He set a pot of water to a low boil, opened the long-closed envelope, and pulled out a severely yellowed, handwritten piece of paper. He followed a series of steps that looked to Katrina like abracadabra and hocus-pocus, crumbling two dried bay leaves into the bubbling water after seasoning it with black pepper and cinnamon, pricking his finger with a knife and letting a ruby drop fall into the simple tea, pressuring Katrina into stabbing her own fingertip as she winced and grimaced, and muttering an incantation over the steaming mixture in a language so ancient that he could barely pronounce it. As Gerald poured his brainpower into each step, his aura funneled into the pot, his face paled, and sweat broke out upon his brow.

Gerald waved the vial of Mary's long-dried blood through the vapors from the boiling tea. Katrina jumped as floorboards creaked several rooms away. Cold spots came together within the home.

"Mary Fraser," Gerald asked, "please come to us."

The temperature in the kitchen dropped like a rock. Gerald urged the shivering Katrina to turn and look behind her, and there it stood, a figure that hadn't been there before—at first flickering like static, and then solid. Shorter than Katrina, the old woman wore a plain blue dress that flared out and completely covered her legs, and her white hair was a wild halo of waves. Her body looked so solid, so real, that it was almost impossible to guess she had lived in a different set of centuries from the people standing before her.

"Ye both be careful," Mary warned, her green eyes narrowing in an expression somewhere between disapproval and hate. "Not good what ye be doing."

Mary's body dissolved. Her next words faded into something inaudible. As she vanished into thin air, Gerald clutched at his chest, gasping for breath, his face turning red as sweat dripped from his brow. He collapsed, his shoulder slamming into the oven door as he slid down to the hard floor. His aura dulled rapidly before Katrina's eyes. The old vial of Mary's decayed blood fell to the tiled floor and shattered.

Forgetting about the boiling pot on the stove, Katrina ran for the phone and called 911.

Another figure flickered into view where Mary had been standing just a moment before. A taller, younger, more modern figure in a striped T-shirt and blue jeans, that familiar arrow-straight red hair falling to her shoulders, in a style shorter than Katrina remembered.

Lillian. What the hell was she doing here?

Katrina blinked and she was gone. Both she and this ancient great-grandmother Mary had to be illusions. In her state of stress and fear as she clung to the grandfather who'd stopped breathing, Katrina had to be seeing things.

An ambulance arrived after minutes that felt like hours. Crying hysterically, Katrina watched from the kitchen as Gerald was taken away on a stretcher. She prayed that Gerald would recover from this and return home, and continue to be her leader, she the follower who took his orders. She was most comfortable that way.

Gerald never returned home. His funeral took place the following week. Many business associates came, including the COO who would take his place. Julius and Katrina, both wet-eyed and wringing their hands with anxiety, were also present. Julius brought his wife and their six-year-old son, but Katrina's mother, now a complete shut-in, chose not to come.

Uncle Lou and his daughters did not attend. This wasn't surprising with the longtime fracture in the family that had started with those silly rumors of Julius being a pervert.

Oh, how Katrina missed her grandfather. She looked up to Julius too, but his leadership style wasn't as strong or confidence-inspiring; rather more scattered and disorganized. Katrina didn't want to admit this to her uncle, but she had always had more faith in Gerald at the helm of their mission.

After Katrina drove back to Ohio, packed her few things into her car, left her mother's home, and then returned to Potomac and moved into her grandfather's manse, she found herself struggling to clean and care for all of those square feet. She was accustomed to a small space to keep tidy. And Gerald had not warned her of the chunks that property taxes would take from her inheritance.

Well-wishers came by with casseroles for a while, and then the flow of guests trickled to nothing. Katrina made no new friends in this upscale neighborhood where most people kept to themselves. The silence of her life grew oppressive.

Julius, who visited from time to time, also lost his focus, drowning in grief and disillusionment. Julius and Katrina decided to table their plans, not sure when they'd feel ready to set them in motion again.

Months turned into a year, and that year turned into two years. Two years blended into three. Lonely and stir-crazy, Katrina was still too unfocused to begin building the island getaway Gerald had purchased, despite Julius' increasing encouragement that she keep an eye out for women with the right genetics.

Katrina did not deem herself capable enough to take charge. Deep inside, she still carried that scrawny little girl who hadn't come out quite right. The child who got laughed at for her thrift-store clothes and tattered shoes, whose classmates held their noses and gagged when she walked into the classroom. Even though she'd gotten her revenge on the ringleader of the high school bullies with that public masturbation stunt, the damage to her confidence remained. The day that Katrina had humiliated Megan in the school cafeteria all those years ago was the day she had peaked, as far as she was concerned. The one time she really did something for herself, not to satisfy Uncle Julius or her grandfather.

Katrina spent her time escaping on the computer, playing games and chatting on forums devoted to her favorite television shows. Katrina wanted to look for a job to fill her time, but Julius discouraged her. Not only was there no need for her to work, it was good for her to stay under the radar until they managed to get their plan together again.

From time to time, Julius called to gripe about Katrina's mounting inertia and depression. But he had his own distractions to grapple with. The wife, the kid, putting out fires and quashing false accusations of sexual misconduct at work. A vision had a way of falling apart and dissipating like a shimmering mirage when its spearhead died.

Excerpt from The Autobiography of Gerald Frazier: Architect of a New World

I n 1972, my wife Enid deserted me for another man. She left Theresa and Julius in my custody, deciding she wanted her freedom more than she wanted the children. I wasn't exactly faithful in the marriage either, having a love child with Irina and hiring the occasional hooker. Enid's adultery hardly fazed me.

Nine years after the divorce, Enid died of breast cancer. By then, she had almost no contact with me or the children.

Theresa and Julius were both sad and angry about their mother abandoning them. Julius took it especially hard until I finally trusted him with the secret that Enid was not his birth mother. That took a load off his shoulders. During that father-son talk, I told Julius some about my overall mission. See, I don't normally come right out and say it, because I knew most family members wouldn't take kindly to the idea in its rawest form. But Julius tended to accept whatever reality was thrust in front of him. His mind, though smart, was malleable.

I realize now that I may have made some mistakes with my children, but I believed I needed to do whatever it took to make new warriors. Though I did not reveal the full scope of my idea, I hinted to Julius that if we needed to resort to some intra-family relationships, then we could, no matter how taboo by modern society's standards. For instance, I've read some research that came out after my children were grown, stating that every housecat is the world is descended from a small group of domesticated cats in the Middle East. There must have been considerable inbreeding, and now our world is full of millions of healthy, happy pet cats, or was at the time of my writing! Thoroughbred horses and American bison have similar histories, starting out with only a handful of creatures. Every boom has to start small!

I dropped little hints to get Theresa ready for our mission too, even though she never had any clue what a necromancer was. Reproduction could be her only role. I couldn't bring myself to do anything to her directly. Being her father, it felt too wrong.

Not long after my divorce, I bumped into a younger woman named Tawny Roberts at an opera, a half-breed carrying the mage trait. Though Tawny would not be winning any beauty contests, I would do whatever it took to grow my army. After two months of dating, I proposed, knowing she'd be thrilled.

After I married Tawny in the mid-1970s, I moved back to my native Maryland, purchasing a home in Potomac. Tawny was a decent stepmother to my children, and a good cook. Tragically, she had one miscarriage after the other. We sought help from a doctor, who delivered the grim news that Tawny's female organs were a twisted mess, too malformed to repair with surgery. A viable pregnancy was impossible. Back then, we did not have the technology to have a surrogate mother carry one of our fertilized eggs. While I can read minds, I don't have X-ray vision to see a woman's internal organs. Had either of us known, I never would have married Tawny. That's the worst thing about the inability to bear children, how it sneaks up on you after you've made the mistake of being optimistic.

Tawny wanted to adopt. I talked her out of it. There was no point in me having any more children if they did not carry my genetic superiority!

Since my wife was a dead end, I spent free moments on my business trips searching for other half-breed women. I began a long-term affair with a lady named Carol from Oregon. After she became pregnant, she suddenly moved away and stopped contacting me. When you're having extramarital affairs, women get easily spooked. The break was so clean that with all of the mind-reading and sleuthing I did, I couldn't find her. She had not told her friends and neighbors where she went. In the early 1980s, searching the internet was not an option.

If Carol carried to term, her baby is probably not the only child I have out there. It's a terrifying idea, since what if they are necromancers? With no support system and no one to guide them?

To maintain my reputation, I did not divorce Tawny. Kicking her to the curb for an internal birth defect would have made me look a little too bad. And once you've been married more than a couple of times, women start figuring you're the problem and they shy away.

I still had my children, Julius and Theresa, to work with. Usually, people consider this sort of thing sick and abusive. But in this context, I really don't think that is the case. Remember what I said about the cats. And do you think cats and other animals care if they're related to whoever they mate with? Their only goal in mind is satisfying their hormones and the primal desire to procreate and pass on their genes. And cats are by no means brainless animals. During my adult life, I've rarely been without a pet cat or two. I enjoy the company of felines. They are more intelligent and thoughtful than people realize, and even approach the world as a sort of science experiment. Believe me, I know. I can read their minds, too!

The bias against breeding within a family is largely manmade.

Winds of Change

❦ ·•◆•· ❦

"T his place is a mess!" Julius snapped at Katrina. "When was the last time you hired a maid?"

"I don't know," Katrina mumbled. "Maybe six months ago?"

"It smells awful in here. Why don't you care for your living space? What would your grandfather think of you doing this to his nice house?" Angrily, Julius gestured toward the stack of pizza boxes and takeout containers piled in the corner of Gerald's living room, buzzing with flies. A similar mountain of food boxes, as well as dirty dishes, smelled up the kitchen. Dust and grime created a dulling patina on the furniture and once-gleaming downstairs floors. Yo-Yo, Gerald's cat, dashed around, batting at a discarded milk cap.

"I don't know, I guess it feels like it's invading my privacy, having a maid in here," Katrina said.

"This place is going to become infested with pests... roaches, rats. How can you stand the smell?"

"Mom's place is so tiny, cleaning it was nothing. And Mom has hardly any dishes. If you wanted to eat off the plate, you had to wash it. But this house is so damn huge. And there are things that a maid shouldn't see."

Julius smacked his forehead. "That's why your grandfather put hiding places throughout the home. After all of the pride that he took in it, this house is not meant to turn into a dump inhabited by trailer trash."

"I am not trailer trash!" Katrina shouted, her face flushing red. "Fuck you!"

"Then stop living that way. I didn't mean to hurt your feelings, but you've got to get a grip, Katrina."

"Do you think I'm trailer trash?" Katrina demanded to know, jabbing her thumb into her chest. "Do you look down on me like the kids I went to school with, who picked on me? Do you think that little of me?"

"You're a smart girl, Katrina, with a lot of potential. As I told you many times, you're so much more than those children who picked on you years ago. It's time to leave them in the past. Do you want to end up like your mother? Do you want that to be your future?"

Katrina chewed her lip. Shook her head, tears standing in her eyes. "Of course not! Who do you think I am?"

"Your life has stagnated, Katrina. And we've got to change that. I understand that it was sad when my father died. I was crushed, too. But we've got to move on. We've got to do him and his legacy proud. I do not look down on you. By the time you've picked yourself up out of this rut, I will be prouder of you than ever. What do you say we get this thing back in motion? And start today? Yes?"

Katrina nodded, resigned.

Julius beamed and enveloped her in a bear hug. "That's my girl! I knew that spunk was still in you! First, we must start with hired help to clean this place. We'll make calls to the people handling the island construction, and get that going again. And we need to talk about how we're going to grow. You still want to have children, right? That's part of the plan to help us?"

"Of course."

"You're almost thirty. Your time isn't going to run out just yet, but the clock is ticking. I know how upsetting it was when you lost that baby years ago... trust me, I was there... but you want to have a lot. Yes?"

"I want to feel that power again. That was amazing while it lasted. But there's a little problem. I'm single. I don't know any male half-breeds right now."

"Don't you worry about that. I'll figure it out."

"I have a crazy idea. What if you help me? We don't have to have sex. A turkey baster would take out the ick factor. Isn't that what Lou did? I know you're my uncle, but..."

"No," Julius said firmly, shaking his head.

"You know Grandpa said that incest is okay, like as a last resort. We'll be guaranteed necromancer kids every single time."

"We're too closely related. I want to produce a new generation of necromancers just as much as you do. But I don't want a generation of crippled ones."

"It's not like we're brother and sister. The first generation of incest kids usually have nothing wrong with them. I actually looked it up."

"It wouldn't be the first generation. You see, Katrina, I didn't want to tell you this until you were ready... but I'm not just your uncle. I'm your father."

Katrina's jaw dropped. The news hit her like a bucket of ice water after a lifetime of her family staying tight-lipped about her paternity and the big blank spot on her birth certificate. "What?! You and... my mom... did it?"

"Your mother and I are just half-siblings. Different biological mothers. My father had an affair with my birth mother, who so happened to be the maternal grandmother of Uncle Lou's kids, and then staged an adoption to cover it up. But at this point, genetic variety would be healthier. I know where your ex-boyfriend is. After years of aimless running around, he is back home with his parents, working at a hardware store while he tries to figure his life out."

"But he's a jerk. He left me when we lost our baby."

"I know how that hurt you. But he's grown older and wiser. I'll need to sit down and have some serious discussions with him, to talk him into coming back and staying."

A month later, after a team of maids had cleaned the house from top to bottom, a battered sports car pulled up the driveway. Out stepped Zachariah Dunaway, the one who'd pretended to be a student at Northern Colorado University some years back, wearing a leather jacket and his signature shark-tooth necklace. This was not his first relationship with Katrina, not since he had fathered the child she lost at nineteen. Both he and Julius promised this time that he'd stay. That he'd commit.

In the years that followed Gerald's death, Lou dealt with mixed emotions over the brothers' up-and-down relationship and their estrangement at the end. Grief—more the longing for a brother who'd treated him better than for the death itself. Relief that the blackmail and embarrassment was over. Guilt at feeling anything positive about someone passing away.

Rumor had it that Katrina, Gerald's reclusive granddaughter, inherited his mansion. One would think he'd at least give it to one of his children, like his down-and-out daughter Theresa. Or Julius. Lou had a sneaking suspicion that Gerald had never cut his son off like he'd claimed to. Katrina became a hermit in that large home, according to the few whisperings that flew around, but at least now she left Lillian alone. It had unsettled Lou, the way she'd stalked and written to Lillian for a while and then followed Avery that one day until he chased her into her car. Maybe Gerald's house distracted her enough to drop her fixations.

Life went on happily for Lou. His golden years were peaceful ones, almost as if making up for the rough patches in the past. Derek, Lou's partner, talked him into selling his house and moving to a new, smaller place together. Even though Lou hesitated at leaving the house in which he was literally born, where he'd grown up and raised his kids, he finally agreed to relocate with Derek into a nice apartment they found in Annapolis. They married in a small beachfront ceremony, with both daughters in attendance. One of the guests was Lou's former spouse, Roberta. Both of them giggled at the irony of inviting one's ex to their wedding.

A few years later came the crushing day when his dog Astrid's arthritis buckled her legs beneath her, she suffered a stroke, and Lou had her euthanized. Lillian, attending school in California and working on the end stages of her PhD, sobbed when she learned about it over the phone.

Evelyn held up well, at least publicly, in the aftermath of her divorce, juggling the demands of work with single motherhood. She met Gary Roderick, a day trader who had a couple of sons with his ex-wife. After her poor outcome with Jonathan, not to mention that frightening run-in with the water people, Evelyn did not want another showy wedding. They went to the courthouse without any guests, keeping it private until after the fact.

During a visit, Lillian informed Evelyn that Avery had read her first husband's mind years ago, uncovering the secret that Uncle Gerald made a deal with him to pay for his college so long as he dated Evelyn. Even with Gerald dead and Jonathan mostly out of her life, this knowledge unsettled Evelyn down to the bone. Evelyn, Lillian, and Avery all theorized that Gerald wanted them to produce a mage child, perhaps to stroke his own twisted ego.

Tasha's partial mind-reading ability presented some challenges when she started school and around her new stepfather, who had no clue of the family secret. Following her father's recommendations, Evelyn concealed Tasha's powers even from her husband, and trained her daughter to cover it up in a world full of ordinary people, classrooms full of ordinary kids.

Tasha was socially clever, popular with classmates and beloved by her teachers year after year. Occasionally, she slipped up and said something that made someone a bit uncomfortable. But most of the time, her mind-reading ability tortured no one but herself.

Tasha usually wore a smile, but occasionally, at bedtime, she broke down in tears just before Evelyn shut out the lights. Or threw private tantrums in her bedroom once she got home from school, punching her pillow and kicking her stuffed animals.

After Uncle Gerald's death, Lillian was stunned to find herself named in his will, destined to inherit hundreds of thousands from him as soon as it made its way through probate. It shocked her even more that her father and Evelyn didn't get a dime. In her guilt over the preferential treatment, Lillian offered to split the money with them. Other than a small amount Evelyn claimed for her daughter's fund, they declined. They felt dirty taking the money.

Lillian handled the inheritance as wisely as she could. She put much of it in savings, donated to her favorite charities, and set another big chunk aside to pay for her student loans, rent on an apartment for her and Avery, and the resources and time sunk into pursuing her PhD. Also making a little fund for adventure, she traveled with Avery. They embarked on road trips to visit national parks and went camping, just the two of them facing nature, having the time of their lives.

Sharing a living space presented a few challenges. Lillian did not always love Avery's repetitive techno music, and he tired of her often gloomy music. They had rare arguments, mostly about clutter or dirty dishes in the sink. The occasional pile of forgotten laundry or plates on the counter was just a minor inconvenience amid the peace of living with someone they could reveal their whole, true selves around. To make life and household tasks more convenient, they freely used their telekinesis. Mind transference helped them get around the misunderstandings and communication blocks that other couples faced.

After a few years of cohabiting, with Lillian still in school and Avery working as a technical writer and studying online for a master's, they took a vacation from their busy schedules and tied the knot. On Evelyn's advice and their own preference to not do anything ostentatious, they kept the ceremony low-key, inviting an intimate group of family and friends and selecting a scenic mountain location near where Avery grew up. Like her graduation a few years ago, this all seemed a bit unreal, too good to be true, as she gazed into the eyes of the one who'd terrified her the first few times she saw him, now her life partner after those months of struggling not to fall in love and insisting that they were platonic friends. Bridget, Lillian's close friend and former roommate, laughed about it throughout her toast: "These two were stubborn as shit about getting together!"

During Lillian's graduate studies, they learned to cope with long separations. While putting together her dissertation on the shifting of tectonic plates, Lillian had to travel for field work and overcome a lot of fears about doing so, both related and unrelated to magic. Close to the finish line of her program, she spent months in Antarctica, having to fly to New Zealand first. Those months were uniquely challenging with the hikes in rocky, remote locations almost completely untouched by humans, the bone-dry cold air, the sun that never went down in the summer that was winter back home, and the small group of advisers and students she couldn't get away from. And it still made her anxious to leave Avery alone in their apartment, though Katrina had not bothered either of them in years. She came back to a world too noisy, too busy. The thrill of field work gave Lillian's life a purpose other than her late uncle Gerald's fixation on the family's powers. She longed to be more than just a mage cloaked in secrecy. She wanted to contribute to science and do good for the world.

After successfully earning the degree, Lillian spent the next couple of years in a postdoc appointment. As a side adventure, she self-published a series of science fiction novels. The books did not sell a lot of copies, but the few that did sell got rave reviews.

Lillian was offered a well-paying job at a research institute in Alexandria, Virginia, which would require more trips to Antarctica and other remote places. They moved across the country, grateful for the opportunity to live much closer to Lillian's aging father and stepfather and visit them often. They watched their backs a little more carefully after the move, also a bit too close to Katrina for comfort. When Lillian was out of town, Avery's mother stayed with him to help out around the house and give an extra layer of protection and peace of mind.

Excerpt from The Autobiography of
Gerald Frazier: Architect of a New World

I wished that I could put my nephew Denny to use in growing the family. But he presented just as much of a dead end as my second wife! He wasn't sterile as far as I know. He just never wanted children, and married his high school sweetheart, an ordinary girl with not a drop of mage blood, who had the same wishes. Even with our power to take possession, I found it daunting to make a man breed unwillingly and never tried. Denny got a vasectomy in his twenties.

I had another option to work with: Vanessa, the daughter of my former lover Irina. Unlike her brother, she was a half-breed. I had known her since she was two years old, and she had grown up into a pretty, petite woman.

I'd intended for Vanessa and Julius to end up together. She was his childhood crush, an attraction that never really ended. I made the mistake of not predicting her mother's reaction when Vanessa confessed that after pushing Julius on the merry-go-round at the park, the two sneaked into a thicket of trees and exchanged a kiss. Irina got angry at the news, slapped Vanessa, and demanded that she stop spending time with Julius, insisting it was inappropriate for a teenage girl to date a ten-year-old boy.

I had another idea... my brother Lou, who longed for children and felt he was out of options. He still lived all alone in the same house he was born and raised in with those empty bedrooms. When Vanessa came of age, I privately encouraged her to kindle some flames with my brother. Despite her preference for older men, she resisted the idea because of the distance, and because she herself wasn't in a hurry to bear children just yet. But then I found that I had the power to influence certain people's minds, if I put my will to it. After I crawled into her head enough, Vanessa began longing to join forces with my brother. She was headed for a dead end in life anyway, still living with her mother after dropping out of college, let go from her retail jobs when bosses did not like her awkward demeanor and slow performance. Vanessa had gone on some dates, only to find that men used her and had one thing on their minds.

After exchanging some letters, Vanessa left Cincinnati and moved in with Lou. Vanessa's few friends and family members were surprised, as Lou was practically old enough to be her father and lived in another state. But as much as Irina complained about Lou's age, she was relieved to have her late-blooming daughter move out.

Vanessa was happier in her new home. No mother nagging her, no pressure to work in any more department stores or hot dog stands, and she could paint her wildlife scenes in peace. She began to sell her watercolors and display them in art galleries, and made a bit of a name for herself.

They had some trouble in the bedroom, and then got an idea of using a plastic dropper. In their embarrassment, they told no one. But of course, when I visited, I knew what they were up to. I wished I could have cheered them on!

The dropper idea worked like a charm. During Vanessa's first pregnancy, she figured out Lou's homosexuality secret, and he convinced her to keep quiet. In October of 1981, Vanessa had a baby girl, Evelyn Brooke. I had my concerns about such a small woman giving birth to a six-foot-tall man's child, but the delivery was quick and uncomplicated, and she fit right back into her size-zero clothes. As soon as I heard about the new arrival, I insisted on visiting. I was happy to hold the cooing, gurgling little bundle. Baby Evelyn was merely a half-breed, though this is not to say she wouldn't be useful. The two of them would have to try again. I heavily encouraged at least one sibling. The more tries, the better.

When Evelyn was small, Vanessa had an identity crisis and ran off on Lou, moving to New England to join an artists' colony. I drove up there and visited her a few times, persuading her to return to my brother.

By then, my kids were of age and Julius had gone to college. Craving familiarity, he returned to the same city where I raised him, starting a business with the money I'd set up in his trust fund. Theresa moved with him. Despite the city's growing size, we hadn't had much trouble with other mages there, and I hoped for it to stay that way.

By this time in my life, I was doing very, very well. Mind-reading helped me to choose the best business partners and make the best decisions, and now I was reaping the rewards. I bought myself a leisure yacht just to celebrate. My army was slowly growing, even if things often didn't go as planned and I was caught in a childless second marriage with a homely woman. I pretty much had it all. I was on top of the world.

On August 26, 1985, I became a grandfather! Theresa gave birth to a healthy baby girl, Katrina Marie. Julius sounded absolutely thrilled when he called me from the hospital to announce the baby's arrival. Julius was more than happy to tell me that it was official: Katrina Marie was a necromancer! My kids had done me proud, even if Theresa never knew it.

I caught the first plane I could to visit them, carrying a bag full of rattles and blankets for the baby. I wanted to make sure Katrina had people looking out for her from the start. When I arrived at the trailer Julius had purchased for Theresa and the baby, she and Julius were still fighting as they always did, shouting at each other while the newborn wailed in her crib. Theresa confided in me that she "hated" Julius. That she was glad she'd broken his arm when they were small, and wished his neck had snapped on those stairs instead.

"Now, don't hate your brother," I tried to soothe Theresa. "Remember what I told you growing up? Don't go by what the world thinks. Please cooperate with your brother. He gave you a gift." I picked up the baby and gave her a dramatic snuggle to remind Theresa that she was doing the family a favor, though she of course didn't know the reason why. She was filled with anger, unable to understand, much less appreciate, the power of the necromancers that lay just underneath her nose!

Just five months after the thrilling birth of my granddaughter, I had a definite sense of déjà vu when the Challenger space shuttle broke apart and the disaster grabbed the attention of everybody in America. It happened just as my sister Sarah had envisioned in her dreams as a girl, right down to President Reagan's speech on television addressing the nation afterward. Though Sarah was dead for almost twenty-one years, I hung on to all of her letters and notes about "the one who decides," still unable to figure out who it could possibly be.

Within days of the space shuttle disaster, I turned fifty, a stern reminder I wasn't getting any younger. And my army, the idea that I'd conceived nearly thirty years ago, was still small, meager, and in its infancy. If you breed cats for about ten years or so, you'll go from a few cats to a huge mass of the critters. Not so with humans and their longer breeding cycles. I despaired at the thought that my army may never come to fruition in my lifetime.

I threw a big party anyway, trusting that baby Katrina, at least, would carry on my legacy someday!

Growing

Nearly a decade after her grandfather's passing, Katrina still lived in his home, though the quiet and solitude were as dead as he was. She and Zack had two living children. Paisley was a noisy, imaginative three-year-old with auburn hair, freckles, and Katrina's pale gray eyes. Zachariah Jr. was a year and a half old, with his father's dark hair just starting to grow in after a bald infancy. Much to Katrina's disappointment, both of the toddlers had the mere mage blood, like their father. She'd known by the fourth month of each pregnancy, when that delicious increase in powers never came.

Zack never even liked children, and now that she had them running around, Katrina also found how much they turned her off. Zack and Katrina never stopped being disgusted with messes, runny noses, and smelly diapers pouring out of the pail. They couldn't stand the piercing screams that small children let out when they needed attention or simply played. They hit and slapped Paisley and Zack Jr., ordering them to shut up and growing angrier when the children cried in their pain and fear.

Despite their frustration with these two little ones, Katrina and Zack were trying diligently to conceive another. When Katrina ovulated each month, she laid down for another round of mechanical pelvic slamming. Katrina wasn't going to give up until she got a necromancer baby, even if it meant popping out ten non-mages first.

Zack, who still had no idea that mages existed, was in it just for the money Julius and Katrina had promised him so long as he didn't bolt if she suffered another loss. He'd made that mistake years ago in an overwhelmed moment, not liking to deal with crying, emotional women.

Zack did not question the hows and whys of this transaction. He had also not thought it odd when Julius and Gerald approached him years ago with a deal to rope Lillian, a girl he'd never even met, into a relationship. They offered a bonus payment if he convinced her to marry him and start a family, the sooner the better. Zack remained bitter about his falling out with Lillian. That girl had treated him a lot worse than Katrina did, giving him a lot more resistance. And she didn't even like sex; what was her problem? Katrina, at least, put out without complaint.

Katrina updated Zack a little bit about Lillian, now a geologist who studied tectonic plates or earthquakes or something like that, now married. Zack wondered out loud if she was so cold and standoffish with her husband.

When mess accumulated in the house, Zack and Katrina hired two new maids, a mother and daughter working together for the same company. First, the mother came and removed the garbage. The next day, her daughter, Lydia, arrived to finish off the mopping, scrubbing, and finer touches.

It just so happened that this pair shared the mage trait. Convinced that this was her lucky day, Katrina watched Lydia from the upstairs balcony while she bent down to scrub the baseboards. When Paisley and Zack Jr. came up to tug at Katrina's pant leg and plead for food, she snarled at them to go to their rooms. Cowering, both of the children scattered.

The maid who'd shown up yesterday looked to be over fifty and probably past menopause. Lydia, the slim blonde tattooed woman dusting the downstairs today, appeared to be in her twenties, and at a glance, radiated health. If the odds leaned in Katrina's favor, she was fertile.

When Lydia finished cleaning that afternoon and packed up her supplies, Katrina happened to be alone in the house, other than the children. Zack had gone shopping, leaving open a perfect window of opportunity. As Lydia went back and forth putting her things in her car, Katrina locked her children in Paisley's bedroom.

"Mommy, where you going?" Paisley cried from the other side of the door, pounding on it.

"Shut the hell up and play with your toys until I'm back. Mommy has work to do."

Right after Lydia pulled out of the long driveway, Katrina left, locking the gate behind her. She followed Lydia quietly in her car, not closely enough to raise any suspicion. The pursuit went on until Lydia stopped at a gas station.

All that remained of Lydia was her company car filled with cleaning supplies, next to pump number nine.

When Lydia's eyes opened, she squirmed, immediately panicked that she once again couldn't move. Scratchy rough rope pressed her wrists together, while duct tape was wrapped tight around her legs. The last time she'd been awake, she had lain on the floor of a car. Now the ropes and tape bound her to a chair.

The surrounding room carried faint, bad stenches of vinegar and a hint of death. As her blurred vision slowly cleared, Lydia immediately recognized the woman with light red shoulder-length hair who stood towering over her, staring down at her with hard eyes, commanding, "Don't move."

Lydia had sensed something amiss from the moment she had entered Katrina's property. Despite her obvious wealth, the yard was poorly kept and shaggy with weeds. The cluttered interior brought to mind a hoarder's house on those reality shows Lydia liked to binge-watch, though not to the extreme that it would end up on television. And Katrina's toddlers, the ones she'd acted so nasty and impatient with, were sad and dirty enough that Lydia considered calling CPS the minute she got home. Right now these kids were nowhere to be seen. And Lydia would not be calling anyone, her purse and phone nowhere in sight.

Lydia's mother had let on in a text message yesterday—was it yesterday?—that Katrina and her stoic, scowling boyfriend, Zack, had unsettled her. Something didn't seem right about that man, either.

The last thing Lydia knew before someone tied her up was stopping to get gas. And then she'd blacked out at the pump, losing time. What did this woman do to her? She did not remember even being attacked. Had anyone at the gas station seen something? Was help on the way?

Listening to her gut instincts would have meant turning down a wealthy client, a lot of lost revenue, and appearing irrational to all of her coworkers. Lydia had ignored the bad feeling, and now she found herself in captivity, heart thrumming in her fear that these could be her final moments.

"Don't move," Katrina repeated. "We don't plan on killing you, so don't worry. But we expect you to cooperate. You'll see why you're with us in time."

Lydia struggled against the ropes and screamed futilely into the duct tape as Katrina left, locking a heavy metal security door behind her.

"Look, I understand that the perfect opportunity was there and you just couldn't help yourself," Julius scolded Katrina as they sat at the kitchen island. "But with the way that you did it, you were taking quite a risk."

After Katrina had called Julius with an urgent request to talk in person, he caught the soonest flight he could to visit her. They spoke quietly as Zack, still unaware of the abducted woman in the secure basement room, sat in his bedroom playing computer games while the kids wailed.

"I'm sorry, but half-breeds aren't a dime a dozen. And remember about six months ago when I tried to bribe that one half-breed?"

Julius nodded, recalling the homeless woman with the mage trait who'd refused Katrina's offer to move in rent-free as a nanny, insisting, "I don't need no one doing favors for me. I can take care of myself." Since then, young women with mage blood had been hard to come by.

"Then these two half-breeds came right into the house!" Katrina argued, throwing her hands up into the air. "Her mom was too old, but she's young. How could I resist? I think it was a sign from God that this lady came. A sign that it's time we got moving on our mission!"

"But Katrina, it was not that far from the house that you took her, right? About five or ten miles. And you're the last person she was with before she disappeared? In spite of our talents, the cops sniffing around here is the absolute last thing you want. Even if we can easily take out a policeman, you don't want to go on record as a person of interest. Do you understand?"

"Yes, I understand," Katrina said meekly. "The next time I go looking, I'll try to go far from the house. But I can't read minds. I couldn't have scanned her brain like a barcode scanner so I could go break into her house later."

"I understand. It's frustrating that we lack my father's ability. We have to make do with what we've got."

The following evening, a police officer came by to inquire about twenty-seven-year-old Lydia Cooper, whose mother reported her missing last night when she could not get hold of her by phone and found her apartment unoccupied. Taking deep breaths and trying her hardest to look cool and calm, Katrina acknowledged that Lydia had come by to clean the house.

"I don't know where she went after she finished; she just left," Katrina said of the woman who was currently tied up in the secret room.

The policeman thanked Katrina for her time and left. She leaned against the door, covering her face with her hands and blowing out fierce sighs of relief.

Later, Julius and Katrina went down to the secure room. After Katrina tore and cut the duct tape away from her mouth, it took a prolonged period of shushing, begging, and pleading with Lydia to get her to stop screaming. As it slowly sunk into the captive's mind that she was unlikely to get help in this chamber, a hopeless, defeated, empty look filled her teary blue eyes.

Julius waved a plastic blue test stick in front of Lydia, along with a sheet of instructions.

"What is this?" Lydia mumbled.

"This is an ovulation predictor kit."

"Why do I need that?!" Alarm rose in her voice.

"We can't get into all of the details just yet. We don't want to overwhelm you. Please take the test for us and we'll make your evening as painless as possible. Do you promise to not fight us if we untie you? Because if you do fight, you will black out again."

"I... I promise," Lydia whispered fearfully.

"Wait, maybe we shouldn't waste those tests just yet," Katrina suggested. "Lydia, when was your last period?"

"That's none of your business!"

"Please just tell us, and we'll give you some dinner and leave you alone for the rest of the night."

"Why are you asking a question a gynecologist would ask... you're trying to get me pregnant or something?!"

"We get into all of that later," Julius informed her. "But soon, you will be thanking us for taking you in. We're doing you a favor, the magnitude of which you cannot possibly comprehend just yet."

"A favor?! Please just let me out of here!"

"If we let you out, you'll be regretting that. We're saving your life, Lydia."

"I still want out! Let me out, you psychos!"

"Careful what you wish for," Katrina sneered.

Had it been months since the start of Lydia's imprisonment? It must have been, with the growing bulge in her once-flat belly. Katrina, her jailer, was now visibly pregnant herself.

In captivity, time ran together like a muddy river, most of the days identically miserable, one week blending into the next.

Lydia had spent the first weeks of her confinement listening for footsteps, and when she heard none, she screamed her loudest when she guessed that no one was home. *"Please! Somebody help me! Please!"*

No one came to her rescue. Her voice went hoarse.

Usually, the only person to visit Lydia was Katrina, coming to feed her, bring a book to read if she was feeling friendly, or if she happened to hear the hollering, smack Lydia across the face and order her to shut up.

From time to time, the middle-aged man with reddish-gray hair had come to visit as well. Lydia got the impression that he lived some distance away and these visits had to be arranged in advance. At the middle of her menstrual cycle, Katrina had withheld food until Lydia starved and broke down, finally agreeing to pee on a test stick as she hovered over her plastic bathroom bucket.

And then that older man would show up. Lydia did not even know his name. Who was he—Katrina's father? Her uncle? Parts of Lydia's days went black as they drugged her.

After Lydia became pregnant, Katrina began to strap her down to her cot to prevent self-harm, placing an absorbent pad under her bottom now that she could no longer get up to urinate in the bucket when alone. The rough ropes dug into Lydia's wrists as her swelling body sweated, ached, and itched horribly. Katrina only freed her for supervised meals, sponge baths, and bathroom breaks over the bucket.

Katrina brought home a roommate one day. Lydia watched as a short, dark-skinned young woman walked slowly into the room, seemingly in a trance, possibly sedated, before Katrina tied her to a chair.

"Lydia, meet Jessica," Katrina said with a brief hand gesture, like she was introducing a friend at a casual party. Jessica began to tremble in hysterics, struggling in her wooden chair to get away. Its legs scraped and rattled on the floor.

"What did you do with my dog?" Jessica demanded. "Where is he?"

"He's my dog now. We'll take good care of him. Be nice or I'll kill your little doggie and you'll watch!"

Lydia craned her neck as Katrina quizzed Jessica about her last menstrual period. When Jessica spotted Lydia swollen and tied up, she quickly caught on.

"If you're going to try to somehow get me pregnant, it probably won't happen." Jessica's voice shook with the tears she'd been crying off and on.

"And why is that? You on birth control? You're going off it."

"No, I'm not on birth control, bitch. I had cancer. The chemo and radiation damaged my eggs."

"Well, that's unfortunate," Katrina growled, biting her lip in obvious frustration. "You know what, I'm sure you'll be good for something. And whatever you do, don't untie Lydia, or you'll both stay tied up. I don't want to chance her trying to hurt that baby."

After Katrina served bland microwaved dinners, freed and then re-tied Lydia, and shut off the lights, Jessica defied Katrina's warning earlier and undid the knots in Lydia's ropes. The two talked in the pitch blackness.

"I have no idea what happened," said Jessica. "The last thing that I remember is meeting that woman at a park when I was walking my dog. If a man approached me, I would have been wary. But she seemed nice, she told me how cute my Maltese is, and you don't think a pregnant woman is going to hurt you. And then I was here. I think I was drugged. I don't even know where we are. Do you have any idea?"

"I'm pretty sure I know exactly where we are, because she hired me and my mom to clean her house. Remember the address in case we get out." Lydia rattled off the street and house number she had painstakingly memorized.

"We're in Potomac? I live in College Park. About half an hour away. Why do you think this bitch wants to turn us into baby factories?"

"I don't know. I really don't know. Why would she need any more babies? Look at her!"

"It's very strange. I'm sure we'll get out of here soon. We'll think of something."

Two days later, when Katrina came through the security door to serve a breakfast of oatmeal, she was ambushed. Jessica hid against the wall, gripping the one wooden chair. She darted around the door and attempted to smash the piece of furniture over Katrina's head.

In spite of her bulging belly and waddling gait, Katrina dodged the chair like a fox, dropping the food tray to the concrete floor as the bowls of oatmeal splattered.

Jessica's body froze and sunk to the floor as the chair clattered out of her limp hands. Katrina knelt next to her, breathing hard in anger, and pulled open the thin jacket she wore, exposing secret pockets along the inner lining that held syringes. Katrina pulled out one syringe, uncapped it with her thumbnail, and stabbed it deep into Jessica's neck. She injected her with another. And another. Lydia, who'd been waiting to tie Katrina up after

Jessica knocked her out, forgot her original plan and watched in silent horror as her hands squeezed around the loops of rope.

"You're giving her too much!" Lydia gasped at last. "You'll kill her!"

"That's kind of the point," Katrina snarled. She put two fingers to Jessica's neck as her glassy, empty dark brown eyes stared up at the ceiling. "No pulse. If you think that you can just sneak up and attack me, think again. There are things about me that your stupid little brain can't begin to understand. I can make you powerless in the blink of an eye. I really, seriously don't want to kill you in your condition, but now you see that I will do what I have to do. Do I make myself clear?"

Eyes spilling with tears, Lydia nodded.

"We're moving to a nice place where we'll enjoy ocean breezes and relax on the beach. You'll have freedom at last. And after you get there, you're going to be really grateful that I took you in. You know why? Because everyone else on this planet is boned. I know you haven't been watching the news. There's this pandemic now. Like a flu or something going around, and the restaurants have shut down. But what's about to happen is even worse. This world is going to burn. And you'll be in a safe place, away from it all. I saved you! I fucking *saved* you!" Katrina spun around and left, slamming the door behind her before she bolted it.

Katrina left Jessica's body in the little room for at least a day, maybe more, before that male relative of hers showed up and the two of them put her in a black garbage bag and hauled her away. By then, the corpse smelled bad enough that Lydia had vomited up her last couple of meals. The odor lingered after its removal.

The sun hadn't quite come up yet one August morning. A purplish light barely peeked over the horizon as Julius threw a few full suitcases into his BMW. After loading fifteen-year-old Robbie, a lanky boy dressed in a basketball jersey, into the car, he stepped back inside to give his wife a parting peck on the cheek. "Bye, honey," he said in a dry, passionless whisper.

"I hope you boys have a good time in Spain." Jana blew an air-kiss. "I wish I wasn't too busy to go."

"Me too."

"Text me when you guys land. I can't believe you didn't cancel that trip. Don't forget to wear your masks on the plane. I don't want you catching that bug."

"I didn't want to cancel something I'd already spent that money on. But don't you worry. We'll be careful, honey. We've got masks, sanitizer, everything."

The first flight landed in Washington, D.C. Instead of catching the connecting flight to Europe, Julius led the increasingly confused Robbie to the car rental counter.

"Dad, where are we going?!" Robbie demanded as Julius searched for his rental in the parking lot.

"Someplace extra special," was the only answer Julius would give. After driving for a short while, Julius pulled off into a thicket of trees and held out his hand. "Robbie, I'll need you to give me your phone."

"Why?"

"Give it to me, please."

"Why? You haven't explained a single thing to me, Dad."

"Because I said so. Now stop mouthing off and give it to me."

With a resigned sigh, Robbie took his iPhone from his pocket and handed it over. Julius told Robbie to wait in the car. He walked several yards into the lush late-summer trees, turned off both Robbie's phone and his own, and flung them into the water of the nearby canal. They both landed on the murky water with a plop and sunk down.

"Dad, what did you do with my phone?" Robbie pleaded as Julius slid back into the driver's seat of the rental car and took off.

"Where we're going, we won't need them."

"You got rid of my phone?"

"And mine too."

"How could you do that?! How am I going to talk to Mom and my friends?"

"It will do you a world of good to unplug for a little while. I promise I'll buy you a new phone as soon as we're back."

"I want to know why we aren't on the plane to Spain." Robbie sighed in frustration, scraping his fingers through his shaggy brown hair.

"Because we're going somewhere better."

"You haven't explained *why*, Dad. Or where."

"I will. You just be quiet and be patient. I promise this will be worth your while."

After driving through the well-to-do suburbs, they arrived at a place Robbie recognized, his late grandfather's house. Someone Robbie hadn't seen in a long time greeted them at the door: Cousin Katrina. Her hair, longer than Robbie remembered, looked greasy and unwashed, and she wore pink overalls, heavy in front with a pregnant belly.

Robbie gasped. Behind Katrina stood an unfamiliar woman with long, tangled blond hair, wearing dirty pink pajamas. She was also expecting, her hands linked together with handcuffs over her protruding stomach. Who was this, and why was she cuffed like a prisoner?

"Zack and the kids have already left, right?" Julius asked his niece. Zack who? What kids? No one had told Robbie anything about Cousin Katrina finding a partner or starting a family.

"Yep. They're at the island. They took Grandpa's old cat and that one girl's little dog with them. It's incredible. My senses have grown so much that I could feel them even miles away!"

What senses? Robbie wondered, too scared to ask. *What island? What the hell are they talking about?*

"Did you check Lillian's house?" Julius asked Katrina.

"I did take a drive down there several months ago. I hung out down the street. Neither of them were home. I couldn't stay for too long because of the damn kids and having to feed Lydia."

"And you didn't search for the crystal?"

"No. She probably takes it with her. They've got cameras, and I didn't want them to see my trail. And now driving isn't really safe for me anymore. I see too many things. Too many ghosts that look real."

"We'll catch them. We'll check again on the way back from Texas, if nothing else."

Julius turned toward his son with hard, threatening eyes. "Robbie, I expect you to be quiet and follow us. Do not stray. Do not speak. We are going to take a drive, and then we are going to get on a boat. Once we're on the boat, I will explain everything. I promise."

Eyes downcast, the other pregnant woman walked obediently behind Katrina to Julius' rental car.

Julius sat on a lawn chair, facing a roaring brick outdoor fireplace and enjoying a goblet of wine. Near the fireplace on the brick porch pavers, his father's elderly cat was curled up into a tight ball in his custom-made sheepskin pet bed. The sun sunk behind the few palm trees on the island.

Katrina sat on a stool, wrapped in a white cotton dress, swinging her legs anxiously and doing sudoku puzzles in a book propped on her big belly. Periodically, both she and Julius checked their watches. An occasional scream came from within the large building, muffled through the walls.

"Here comes the doctor," Katrina whispered.

Dr. Ronald Matheson, a tall, gray-haired man with mage blood who had abandoned his career and disappeared from a life in the trenches of a contentious divorce and nasty malpractice suit, came out the back door with a white-wrapped bundle in his arms. The doctor knelt down by Julius, giving him a peek at a writhing, swollen-faced newborn.

Katrina got up from her stool and peeked over Julius' shoulder. To both Julius and Katrina, the baby appeared just as it had through the skin of Lydia's stretched belly before birth, with the stronger-than-average but still muted aura of someone who was only half mage.

"Folks, I was admittedly a bit nervous about doing a delivery outside of a hospital setting," Dr. Matheson acknowledged as he gently placed the infant into Julius' lap. "But Lydia's doing fine, and the baby appears healthy. Great vitals."

"I'm glad. You'll want to get used to it, doctor, because there will be plenty of deliveries to come. So what is it, already?" Katrina wanted to know. "Boy or girl?"

"A boy. May I bring him back to his mother, or would you like to look at him a little longer?"

"A little longer, please," Julius requested, extending his arms to hold the baby. As he stared down at the gurgling newborn, his expression changed to an angry twist of disgust. He stood up and flung the baby across the patio, toward the fireplace. The white swaddling cloth fell away. Katrina's and the doctor's jaws both dropped.

The baby went still in midair. Katrina cushioned him and reeled him into her arms with her telekinesis.

"What the hell!" Katrina shouted at Julius, holding the baby protectively away from him. "What's wrong with you?"

"It's no use," Julius snarled. "The thing is a half-breed. We don't need more of those. We need mages!"

"How dare you try to hurt the poor little thing! He's just a baby! And you let your own half-breed son live, didn't you?"

"Okay. I'll let the kid live. Just this once. We're keeping all of our existing half-breeds. That includes you, Dr. Matheson. You're in no danger, sir."

The doctor, who had already had the necromancers' powers explained and demonstrated to him, nodded nervously, face white as a sheet.

"But after this, we will need to begin culling half-breeds," Julius went on. "There's only so much space on this island. We haven't even had a necromancer birth since 1989. It's been over thirty years of half-breeds and nothing else! If we could figure out how to prevent them from being born, that would be great."

"Thank goodness this one isn't a half-breed," Katrina boasted, proudly patting her belly. "And the power... the incredible power... I'm loving it! I can go out miles and see everything! I can grab anything! I can do anything!"

Excerpt from The Autobiography of
Gerald Frazier: Architect of a New World

J ulius wrote and called Vanessa after her departure. Like me, he encouraged her to
return to Lou and to her little girl who missed her mother. Much to my delight,
Vanessa agreed to go back.

During my New Year's party at the end of 1988, I invited Lou and Vanessa. She did not
feel well enough to attend, but Lou came for a short while. Vanessa was pregnant! What
had her vomiting back at home was severe morning sickness. She'd barely had nausea with
Evelyn.

Vanessa became so ill that she required hospitalization. They kept her stable with
intravenous fluids and a bland diet. As the months went by, Lou worried, not just about
the sickness, but because he saw that Vanessa was carrying a mage baby! Though he'd gone
into this knowing it could happen, my brother did not feel ready. Like our dearly departed
sister Sarah, Lou just wanted to be an ordinary man with ordinary children.

Both Julius and I did our best to reassure him that everything would be fine, that he
would know what to do, and that the child's future was secured. I did not reveal the full
scope of my excitement to Lou. He was not ready to receive it.

The day the baby came was not the due date, but instead the Fourth of July. That
coincidence was not lost on me: Sarah's babbling about the "one who decides" told us
that this individual would come on the day of explosions in the sky. I could not be sure
about this. The baby was a girl, while the "one who decides" was supposed to be a male.

Lou named the baby Lillian, after his favorite aunt who took him in as an infant, and
chose the middle name, Margaret, to honor our dead mother. As soon as Lou agreed to a
visit, I excitedly beelined over to his house, bringing my son Julius who was in town. We
showered my brother and Vanessa with gifts, just like the heaps of stuff I'd brought when
my granddaughter Katrina was born a few years earlier. Little Lillian's aura was unusually
bright and vivid compared to most of ours. I wondered if this was linked to interesting
potential. After all my roadblocks, things moved along splendidly!

Vanessa wanted no more children after that miserable ordeal of a pregnancy. But at least I'd gotten results. Even if I'd have to wait into the twenty-first century for our smallest necromancers to come of age, this was certainly a step in the right direction. I had Julius. I had little Katrina. I had Denny, even if he was chilly and distant enough towards me that he had not come to my birthday party. But minds could always be changed if I worked hard enough, I reckoned.

The only way I could make things work out ideally was to raise and keep all of my necromancers in my own home. But I couldn't do that. Julius was the only one I had raised. I was allowed direct access to Katrina, over the phone when I couldn't see her in person, but I had to be much more roundabout with the other family members. Lou, an overprotective dad, allowed me to come over occasionally, but sometimes he turned down my offers, and I was never granted time alone with the girls.

Lou's close relationship with his nephew Julius opened up a different avenue. Julius regularly wrote long letters to the family, and sometimes came to visit, always welcome even if his dad wasn't. If I couldn't get through all of Lou's barriers against me, Julius could.

Taken

After cooling down from her evening workout, Evelyn washed her face and put on her skin cream, getting ready for bed. Her husband Gary was away visiting a relative, leaving Evelyn and Tasha with the house to themselves. Being a school night, it was eleven-year-old Tasha's bedtime. To Evelyn's annoyance, electronic blue light glowed from under Tasha's door.

Evelyn knocked and opened the door to find Tasha sitting at her desk in her Hello Kitty pajamas and talking on Zoom with her friend Evangelina from school. Except for family members, she was not supposed to chat with anyone online without supervision.

"Hi, Tasha's mom!" Evangelina said on the screen with a wave.

"Hi, Evangelina. I hate to be a buzzkill, but shouldn't you girls be in bed? It's past Tasha's bedtime."

After Evelyn cut the conversation between the two classmates short and turned the light on, Tasha pouted. When she admitted that she had yet to brush her teeth, Evelyn insisted, "You go brush right now, and then you get tucked into bed. I'm waiting."

"Dang it." Tasha stormed into her bathroom, and then said little as she crawled under her pink Hello Kitty comforter.

"You've been pushing boundaries a bit lately, Tasha," Evelyn pointed out as she sat at the edge of her daughter's bed. "Is there something going on? Something you want to talk about?"

"I don't know," her daughter sighed as she took her white-framed glasses off and folded them, placing them in the case on her nightstand. Tasha laid her head on her pillow, her thick brown braid thrown over her shoulder. "I guess I'm just sick of being different."

"You feel different from other people? That's why you've been acting out a bit?"

"I guess. When you can't tell your friends what you really are, and you have all this stuff you have to keep a secret, you just get sick of being different and then you get sad and it just gets, I dunno, hard to care."

These words frightened Evelyn. "I care," she reassured her daughter, trying her best to sound calm, not knowing what else to say. Tomorrow, she would call her father for advice. "I care very much."

"I wish Grandpa Lou and Aunt Lillian lived closer. I feel less weird when I'm with them. And I wish I could hang out with my friend Destiny."

"I know. We'll figure it out soon."

Evelyn reached for the pink polka-dotted light switch plate. Out went the light, with only a dim moonbeam coming in through the large window above Tasha's bed.

Tasha closed her eyes, pretending to sleep. Using her imagination, she put herself in a dark room. As it had so many times before, a blue, misty doorway appeared. Tasha walked up to it, her footfalls soundless in the dark, and knocked.

"Come in," said a voice on the other side.

Good. That meant that her friend was still awake. Had she already gone to sleep, Tasha would have been greeted with silence.

Tasha slipped through, finding the tall, plump, dark-haired Destiny Jenkinson, also in her pajamas and her physical body probably doing the exact same thing as Tasha's, lying in bed with closed eyes.

The two girls had first met eight years ago when Destiny popped straight into Tasha's head purely by accident from her home miles away, after their parents put them both down for naps at the same time and they failed to fall asleep, instead lying bored in their beds.

Destiny's parents and her grandpa knew about this friendship. Tasha learned in bits and pieces over the years that before she was born, and when Destiny was a baby, Destiny's family had made an attempt on the lives of Tasha's own family. They later came to a truce, cautiously leaving each other alone, yet staying vigilant, ever since.

Destiny's parents and Tasha's mother did not approve of the girls' bond at first, but grudgingly came to accept it, as long as the two girls interacted only through their minds.

Tasha was three years old, Destiny four years old, when they stumbled into that first astral-projection playdate. Now they weren't so little anymore, both of them in middle school. Destiny was almost thirteen and Tasha would be twelve soon—where had the time gone? Tasha worried that Destiny might become too cool and mature for her. The ability to manipulate water into any way, shape, or form did not materialize for Tasha yet, while Destiny's powers had blossomed a year and a half ago, discovered by accident when she took a bath and a column of water rose up from the tub.

Destiny was a seer, an ability she'd had practically since birth. If she peered into a bowl or even a sink or bathtub filled with water, she sometimes spotted hints and symbols of the future, or the present.

"Tasha, I want you to be really careful this week," Destiny warned as the girls sat in a soft blue cloud-like glow, cross-legged in their pajamas. "When I took my bath tonight, I shut off the light and looked into the water. And what I saw... I don't wanna scare you, but it wasn't good."

"What? Was it about me? I'm scared!"

"Don't be scared; just be cautious. I couldn't see the pictures in the water exactly, but it was something about necromancers."

"Which ones? Grandpa Lou? Aunt Lillian? Cousin Denny?"

"No. It wasn't the good ones. One of them was this pregnant lady with reddish hair and an angry-looking face."

"I've seen... heard... a few things about a lady named Katrina. Was it her?"

"Yes. And there was this man. He's older than Katrina, but looks kind of like her."

"Julius." Tasha's spine tingled as she said the name. No one had ever talked with her about that relative she'd never met. Or even mentioned his name in her presence. But she knew this was a man who'd done horrible things. She just knew.

"Yeah, I think it was Julius. They were in a car, driving at night, I'm not sure where. They were talking about you."

"What were they saying?"

"I couldn't understand most of it because my dog barked at the worst time. You know, she's a Chihuahua and she has this ear-splitting bark. But they definitely said your name. They're up to something."

"Like what?"

"I don't know. I'll try to do another reading in the morning. I hope it'll be quiet then. Please be careful, Tasha. Make sure the doors and windows are locked."

"You know that's not gonna stop them if they... they aren't coming here, to my house, are they?"

"I hope not. Since they don't talk to the rest of your family, they probably don't know where you live. But, just... I want you to stay safe."

After the two friends finished chatting and pulled back into their own heads, Tasha's anxiety made it difficult to fall asleep. But finally, far past her bedtime, she did.

Evelyn tucked herself into the huge king-sized bed. Without her husband here, in the massive void of empty sheets, a sensation she had not felt in a long time descended upon her. Unsafe, skin prickling, hair standing up on the back of her neck as if some-one—or something—was standing in the shadows and watching her. At one point, Evelyn snapped on the lamp and fearfully peeked around, which she hadn't done since she was a kid scared of a creature dwelling in the closet. The room contained no monsters or anything else that didn't belong, and neither did the walk-in closet when she opened it and swept the hanging clothes aside.

When Evelyn's alarm went off just before dawn, she awoke with a headache, sitting up and rubbing her forehead. Determined not to let the throbbing pain stop her morning run on her treadmill, Evelyn put in her contacts, took painkillers, pulled on her snug workout top and shorts, and went to Tasha's bedroom to ensure she was getting ready for school. Though the classes were online after the COVID pandemic had sent the students home that spring, Evelyn expected Tasha to fully dress and behave as though she sat in a physical classroom.

Tasha was nowhere in sight. Her pink comforter was peeled away from her empty bed.

Evelyn went to Tasha's adjoining bathroom, finding it empty, and then the living room to check the couch, where Tasha occasionally migrated in the middle of the night when she couldn't sleep in her own bed. But this morning, the living room held no sign of her, no blanket or pillow on the couch. Evelyn glanced back into her own bedroom. Tasha was neither in the bed nor under it.

Evelyn's heart pounded faster and faster as she rechecked each bathroom in the house, coming up empty. Her stomach twisted in a sick knot as she rushed back into Tasha's room. She opened the closet and laundry hamper and peeked under the bed, though Tasha had never played hiding games.

Tasha's glasses lay folded up in their case on her nightstand. Like most people in the family, Tasha was so nearsighted that she could barely function without corrective lenses. That Tasha would go anywhere without the glasses was troubling.

The glass of the window was slid upward in its frame, the screen removed and tossed aside.

Evelyn dashed out to the quiet, empty backyard, helplessly screaming Tasha's name.

Did her ex Jonathan have something to do with this? Would he stoop this low?

Despairing, Evelyn whipped out her phone and called 911. She'd never had so much trouble breathing before as she gasped her emergency to the operator and gave the address. "Someone... broke in... and kidnapped... my daughter!"

"Ma'am, stay where you are. I'll send someone right there."

Going on automatic pilot, a state in which time stood still in this too-quiet vault of a house, Evelyn phoned her work. Her boss, horrified to hear the news, vowed to assemble a search party himself.

"I hope she'll be back home before you have to do that!" Evelyn told him, her voice quaking.

"I hope so, too. Take the time you need."

When the officers arrived and checked the scene, they reassured Evelyn that, contrary to what she'd heard about missing-person cases, they would not delay the search for twenty-four hours. Especially not for a child. The circumstances pointed to an almost certain kidnapping and every second that passed was a precious second lost.

Suffering through the worst and longest day of her life, Evelyn sat on the couch and wept as police officers interviewed her. She was gripped with a sense of losing all control, the room spinning around her.

"When did you last see your daughter?"

"Last night, when I was putting her to bed, at about ten-o-clock. She was up past her bedtime, talking to a friend on her computer."

"Which friend was she talking to?"

"A classmate, Evangelina Gomez."

"We have to look at all of the possibilities. Do you know the names of Evangelina's family members, or their home address?"

Evelyn struggled to remember names or anything else right now. She pulled up the parents' contact information on her phone screen for the cops to take down.

They asked about Tasha's height and weight, and if she had any distinguishing marks—the birthmark on her left shoulder.

"Tasha has an underactive thyroid. She's on medication," Evelyn said through her tears. "She really shouldn't go too long without it. All her pills are here."

"I understand. Now, we must ask some questions about the family situation. Was there a divorce in this child's history?"

"Yes."

"Can you tell us about the other parent?"

"Jonathan Gundersen is my ex-husband," Evelyn groaned. Though she really didn't want to talk about him right now, she provided Jonathan's address and contact information.

"What's the custody arrangement?"

"I have primary custody. He gets visitation."

"What has your relationship been like with your ex-husband?"

"Rocky, rocky. He pays child support, but we really don't talk."

As detectives cordoned off Tasha's bedroom, snapped pictures, and bagged potential evidence with gloved hands and tweezers, Evelyn put her head in her hands on the couch, blaming herself. If she hadn't snapped at Tasha last night, then maybe she would have gone to just another tedious day at work, knowing Tasha was safe, instead of spending this day in hell.

The couple living across the street had a possible clue. At about three in the morning, several neighborhood dogs, including their own, worked themselves up into a barking frenzy. After the noise woke them, the neighbors turned on their lights and looked out their living room window. An SUV was parked in front of Evelyn's house, dark in color, windows rolled up. Within a minute, the vehicle sped away. While their front door camera captured the vehicle, it was not close enough or at the right angle to get the plate number.

Evelyn's ex-husband and his girlfriend of the moment had solid alibis. Both denied knowing where Tasha was. Search parties began combing through Evelyn's neighborhood, hiking through the streets and the dense tangles of vines and trees between the rows of houses.

Melanie Jenkinson stood at the sink, washing and soaking a few dishes. Nearby, her daughter Destiny sat cross-legged on the linoleum floor, drawing anime characters on a sketchpad. Melanie's husband, Terry, watched television in the living room.

Destiny froze and went slack. Her dark blue eyes nearly rolled up in the back of her head.

"What's wrong, honey?" Melanie pleaded, gently shaking her daughter. For a frightening minute, Destiny did not respond. Melanie was close to grabbing her phone and calling 911, fearing Destiny was having some sort of seizure.

This had happened a couple of times before. Melanie's husband, who could read a little bit into Destiny's mind, theorized that she was getting lost in magical perceptions. When Terry and Melanie took Destiny to doctors, just to be sure, none of them found evidence of any seizure disorder.

Destiny's eyes focused again, losing their foggy sheen, as she met her mother's eyes. Her expression was grave. "Mom," she urged, "go look in the sink."

Melanie rushed to the kitchen sink. In the soapy water, a vision shimmered, and then became crisp. A girl a bit younger than Destiny with hair in a brown braid, dressed in Hello Kitty pajamas, was curled in the backseat of a car, eyes huge and glassy with terror. A male voice snarled, faintly audible in the water. *Please just stop crying. Stop crying! Stop it!*

Shockwaves of dread radiated up from the water. The scene vanished into a rainbow shimmer of soap.

Melanie knew who this was. Destiny's friend Tasha. The one Destiny's parents reluctantly allowed to befriend their daughter, so long as the bond stayed in her head and none of them came into direct contact with the family they'd been watching from afar, cautiously avoiding, for years.

But right now, with a child in trouble, it didn't matter what family she came from. All that mattered was her safety.

Melanie ran to her husband just as he cracked open a beer and started to unwind. "Terry!" she screamed.

Terry scanned her mind, which he could get only a murky read on—usually a good thing, as it avoided too many fights and hurt feelings. "Something's the matter with that other water kid?"

"It looks like Natasha has been kidnapped. And I won't be able to live with myself if I don't try to do something to help her. Call your dad."

"I'm not so sure about that."

"Just call him, please, sweetie."

Lillian was splayed out on the bean bag in the living room of her townhome, practicing on her bass guitar and blowing off steam after coming home worn out, yet strangely anxious, from work. After her travels for field research, she found lab work somehow more tiring, even if it meant the cozy predictability of coming home to Avery each day. He'd just gotten off his shift working remotely as a technical writer from their spare bedroom, and he busied himself layering colors onto an oil painting in the corner that served as his art studio. Avery had gained a social media following for his work, making a bit of extra income selling prints.

A call came in from Evelyn. Lillian had not heard much from her sister, except for occasional texts and Facebook likes, since a family holiday visit eight months ago. Calls, text messages, and emails to Evelyn often went unanswered. After years of this, Lillian put less effort into reaching out. Evelyn claimed she was "too busy" to stay in touch, which hurt. Even when camped out in remote corners of the world, Lillian made the time to contact loved ones in whatever ways she could. For Evelyn to call out of nowhere, this had to be urgent. Maybe there was a reason for the unease deep in Lillian's stomach.

Lillian put the guitar in its stand and picked up. "What's up?"

Evelyn shrieked in a hysterical tone Lillian had never heard from her before. "Tasha is missing!"

"Oh no. Are you serious? Since when?"

"Since last night or this morning! She was kidnapped! Someone broke into the house and… they took out the screen on her bedroom window, and…" Evelyn's voice dissolved into sobs.

"They don't know who kidnapped her?"

"No, I don't know!"

"Could Jonathan have something to do with it?" Lillian had read that most child abductors were desperate parents who'd lost custody, not creepy strangers. Everyone close to Evelyn knew that her ex was a cheating sack of slime. He'd never seemed interested in spending much time with Tasha, though he still could have taken her just to hurt Evelyn.

"The cops supposedly ruled out Jonathan. I slept through it, then I woke up and she was gone! I'm a terrible person!"

"No, you're not. Please don't blame yourself. You were sleeping, and no one expects this to happen! Have you told Dad?"

"Yeah. I called Dad and Derek. They're beside themselves right now. Dad's trying to find a flight out here."

"I really wish I could help! This is awful! If you want, I can make the trip, go over there…"

"Flights might be tough with the pandemic and everything. Just pray for Tasha."

After Evelyn hung up, Lillian sat back down, numb. She had last seen her niece in person over the winter holidays. Tasha was growing up so quickly, and she and Lillian had more fun together with each visit, which didn't happen as often as they wanted. An awful helplessness washed over Lillian.

Avery rushed in and wrapped his arms around her to offer what little comfort he could. He said nothing, knowing no words could un-kidnap her niece.

"We'll get her back," Lillian vowed, beginning to tear up. "If I could get there soon enough, maybe I could see trails. Dad's trying to get there too. But we would all have to fly if we want to get there on time to see any clues. And it would depend on when we can get a flight."

Avery pulled his phone from his pocket, checking local flight schedules, frowning. "There's no flight that'd get to Houston until tomorrow evening at the earliest. I'm scared that the trails will fade."

"What if there's another way?"

"What other way? What are we going to do, drive?"

"No. This." Lillian pulled the chain out of her shirt, dangling the crystal on its necklace. These days, they used it sparingly, either when Avery borrowed it or Lillian traveled to the other world alone.

"You know that's not going to get us there, right?"

"We don't have any good options. Let's throw the kitchen sink at this. We can just hold the crystal, visualize Evelyn's house, and hope that it does... something. Picture everything about her house and her neighborhood that you can remember."

"Okay, it's worth a shot. But in case this works, which I doubt it will, we need to make sure Norma and Daisy are taken care of."

Lillian sent texts to their retired neighbor, summing up the situation and asking if she would be willing to check in and feed Norma, their mixed-breed dog, and Daisy, the lazy calico cat they'd adopted from a shelter a couple of months ago. Always happy to spend time with the animals, the neighbor quickly responded, adding that she would pray for Tasha.

They hugged their pets, just in case they wouldn't be back tonight.

Avery wrapped his hand with Lillian's around the crystal, as he had the one time years ago when they experimented with simultaneous travel to the other world. Squeezing their eyes shut, they mentally placed themselves in Evelyn's house, the way they remembered it from their last visit.

They descended into the other world that lived under their quiet neighborhood, a field of tall trees and fairy-like lightning bugs glinting in the moonlight.

Instead of landing on soft grass, they plunged into a pool of deep azure-blue water, which soon overwhelmed them with psychedelic tunnels of bright colors, speeding past in a dizzying kaleidoscope of shapes.

Lillian gained speed, falling too fast. Never had the other world given her a roller coaster ride like this. Weightless and terrified, she clung to Avery's hand. His own grip tightened. She could not even see him in this world of color zipping past. What if the forces pulled them apart—would it doom them to never find each other again? Destroy them? Lillian's head spun while her stomach turned.

And then her knees smacked into a carpet.

Lillian could spin on carnival rides for hours without getting sick, but this plunge through the tunnel overwhelmed her cast-iron stomach. She bent over on all fours and threw up.

Next to her, Avery fainted.

Evelyn screamed.

Wiping her mouth, Lillian looked up and met her sister's watery, jumpy eyes. Evelyn, dressed in a worn-out T-shirt and ripped jeans she normally wouldn't be caught dead in, shrunk back like she'd just stumbled upon a coiled rattlesnake in her living room.

"What the... how did you suddenly..." Evelyn stammered.

With trembling fingers, Lillian held up the crystal still in her hand. "We just... we just fucking *teleported!*"

"That's a magic power I didn't know you had."

"Neither did I."

"Learn something new every day. Is he okay?"

"I sure hope so." Lillian turned Avery over, shaking and patting him. After coming to, he blinked a few times, just as shocked as Evelyn and Lillian.

"Let me clean up this puke. I'm so embarrassed," Lillian sighed.

"No, you rest. I'll take care of it." Evelyn fetched a small vacuum and filled it with soap and water, insisting that Avery and Lillian both lie on her couch, drink water, and rest.

After cleaning up, Evelyn told them more details. Since word had gone up and down the street about Tasha's disappearance, nervous parents had begun keeping their children inside. Swings hung empty from backyard swingsets. Evelyn's husband Gary, out of town, was currently struggling to make arrangements to come home. Dad and his spouse Derek had purchased plane tickets, but could not arrive until tomorrow evening.

"I don't suppose Dad has another one of those crystals?" Evelyn wanted to know.

"I'm afraid not. Probably not a good idea to have him teleport anyway. It was hard on our bodies; it would be much harder at his age."

Evelyn led her visitors to the site of the crime, left almost exactly as she found it. She flipped on the light.

Tasha's bookshelves and hanging hammocks full of stuffed animals remained undisturbed. The cops had taken her laptop and tablet to determine if any predators had made contact with her online.

The three of them grabbed flashlights and went out to the backyard, where Evelyn showed Avery and Lillian what little evidence had been found. The perpetrator had somehow picked the lock on Tasha's window to gain entry. A set of footprints was tamped down in the dirt just outside the window, probably from an adult male who wore size 10 shoes. Oddly enough, no similar footprints had been found embedded in the carpet inside Tasha's bedroom or anywhere else in the house, even though the investigators could not figure out how the kidnapper could drag Tasha all the way out of her bed and through the window without clambering into the room. The only clues the carpet held were impressions of Tasha's bare little feet, and some unusual dragging marks, possibly from her knees.

Avery and Lillian searched the grassy backyard, where Tasha had presumably been taken though the latching wooden-picket gate by the rose bush. They found glowing remnants of the slightly faded trails, one of them the last that was left of Tasha. The other trail gave off greenish hues. The kidnapper was a necromancer, confirming Lillian's bad gut feeling. That left only a few chilling possibilities.

A mage could have easily undone the window latch without even touching it. And then it would have been a simple matter of pushing out the window screen, snaking out to the unsuspecting Tasha sleeping in her pink bed, taking control of her, and then puppeteering her body out of the window.

"Look over here," Avery said a couple of minutes later as Lillian circled the perimeter of the yard for more clues. She came over to investigate. Another pair of footprints was sunken into the dark pebbly soil of a flowerbed beneath the master bedroom window, smaller than the ones outside of Tasha's room.

Lillian rushed in to borrow a pair of Evelyn's size-six flats to be sure these footprints weren't Evelyn's own. The prints dwarfed the black leather shoes that fit Evelyn's petite feet. At least two people, if not more, had orchestrated this kidnapping. And leading up to these footprints was another illuminated green trail, telling of a necromancer.

A co-conspirator could have possessed the sleeping Evelyn's brain to remove any chance she might wake up and interrupt the kidnapping. Really very cruel.

Avery and Lillian followed the trails, intermingled with the smudged bluish remnants of Tasha, out the backyard gate and along the edge of the front lawn. Just as they expected, the trails ended at the sidewalk where Tasha's captors had loaded her into a vehicle.

Lillian broke the news after they got back inside and sat down with Evelyn. "We saw trails showing that mages—people like us, people in the family—have been here. There were at least two individuals. Honestly, there are only two other mages in the family that I know of, besides Dad and Denny and Tasha. Julius and Katrina."

"My worst nightmare—that pervert!"

"My worst fear too. I was hoping Tasha would never, ever know him."

"I'm so desperate that I called Julius' house, even though I haven't spoken to him in over ten years. I was going to demand answers from him if I had to."

"Did you speak to him?"

"No. His wife picked up and said he is gone."

"Gone?"

"Supposedly, he went to Spain and took their son with him. But Jana said she's getting worried. They haven't called, and their phones are turned off. She thinks Julius might have run off because she found out he's sleeping around and someone he worked with is pressing charges against him for sexual assault."

"So he hasn't changed, and it's catching up to him. Did Jana know anything about Tasha?"

"No. And I interrogated her. I can be intimidating when I want to be. She swore she knows nothing. I think she's telling the truth."

"Wherever Julius went, he doesn't want to be found. He may have discarded his phone so he can't be tracked."

"Oh, don't say that. Now you've got me more freaked out, and I'm already at my limit! The other one—Katrina—didn't she move into Gerald's house after he died and then have a couple of kids?"

"Yeah, I heard that, but I don't know much else. She used to write to me and stalk me, Evelyn. She even stalked me to our uncle Victor's house. She went after Avery too, which freaked us out. She wanted my crystal really badly. Then when Gerald died, she just dropped off the map. We moved closer to her, and still haven't had any issues. But there's always been something fishy about her."

Lydia lived in a heavily armored room, where a barred window gave only a glimpse of a few brushy branches outside. Her newborn son, whom she'd named Michael after her dead father, slept nearby in a bassinet. Though Lydia slowly bonded with the baby, nursing him every few hours and striving to keep him safe, he was also a constant living reminder of her trauma.

Lydia still wasn't sure exactly where she was after a trip tied up in the back of an SUV and then below the deck on a rocking boat that made her sick. Katrina kept promising to let Lydia and baby Michael out of the room soon. But Katrina never followed through, complaining that Lydia still "talked back too much."

Lydia remained determined to not let these people gain any emotional control over her, and to await her chance to escape with the newborn, even if it meant staying calm and quietly defiant for the time being. As long as she shook her head and glared at Katrina during her visits to the room to bring food, the total imprisonment continued.

One day, Katrina showed up with company, impatiently dragging along a hysterically crying girl in her tween years or perhaps a little younger. The child's hands were bound behind her back with rope. Horrified and disgusted, Lydia swallowed back vomit. The last time Katrina gave Lydia a roommate, it wasn't long before she murdered that woman and let her corpse decay on the floor. And now a child!

Katrina shoved the newest prisoner onto a nearby cot, ordering, "Stop crying! Don't you dare try any funny business! We'll be watching you!"

As the girl huddled into a ball, Katrina threw a few crumpled blankets at her and said in a calmer tone, like a hostess with a willing guest: "There are a few clothes in the closet, dresses and jeans. I hope they fit you. Let me know if they don't. I also left a clean toothbrush and a comb and stuff on the counter."

In a flash, Katrina was gone behind the heavy metal door as it beeped and locked.

Lydia rushed over to the girl, dressed in pajamas. Her braided hair was messy and coming undone. Lydia untied the child's wrists and then sat quietly with her for a while, putting an arm around her narrow shoulders, until her crying settled down enough that she could speak.

"What's your name?" Lydia asked in a gentle tone.

"Tasha," she answered in a tired, worn-out voice.

"How old are you?"

"Eleven."

"I'm Lydia. Where do you live? Where are your parents?"

"I live with my mom in Texas. They took me out of my mom's house. They were gonna take my mom too, but they didn't because a bunch of dogs barked and they got scared somebody might see them."

"Did they put you in a backseat of a car and put you to sleep?"

"Yeah, but I was waking up some. I know what they were thinking—saying. It was weird. They said that my mom's almost forty but she's got a couple of years left to have a baby. They might come back for her. I hope they don't!"

"Oh, no," Lydia groaned, perpetually sickened at these captors' obsession with women as breeding machines. "Tasha, do you know these people?"

"No, but I'm related to them. Katrina, the pregnant lady, and Julius are the ones that brought me here."

"Is Julius the older redheaded guy?"

"Yeah. They're, like, my mom's cousins. They pretend Julius is just Katrina's uncle, but he's really her dad. Katrina's parents are brother and sister."

"Oh, gross!"

"Julius is a bad man. So was his dad, who's dead. His dad told him to sleep with his sister, and that's how Katrina was born. Watch out for him."

Lydia did not want to say this out loud, but sadly, avoiding Julius if he decided to pay them a visit was not an option. With the armored rooms and security doors and syringes of drugs they carried to knock out any victims who made too much of a ruckus, this perverse father-and-daughter team had clearly thought out their plan to imprison women down to the finest details.

"Do you have any idea why they're doing this? Keeping us locked up?" Lydia asked.

"You don't wanna know. It's horrible."

"Yes, I do want to know."

"They want to take over the world."

"They must be even more off balance than I thought!"

"Yeah, they are. But you know what's really scary? I think they can do it."

"I really doubt that. How could they possibly take over the world, unless they have nuclear weapons or something?"

"Lydia, they don't have any bombs, but they can do stuff I'm not supposed to tell you about. Stuff you wouldn't believe. We have to stop them. We have to!"

Julius parked down the street, his back aching and his bottom feeling hard as a rock from so many hours of driving. He unfolded the printed paper that listed Lillian's address, or at least her last known address. It was a quaint townhome attached to another unit. Julius' father's money may have been a part of the down payment on this nice little place, surrounded with flowers and a vegetable garden. Katrina had shied away from this home in the past, as they'd put up cameras at the entrances. But now, so close to the endgame, camera footage would not matter as much. Julius walked up to the shady porch and knocked on the door.

Out back somewhere, a dog barked. But there were no footsteps inside. No feeling of human presence, despite the cars in the driveway. Julius turned the doorknob, surprised to find it unlocked.

Patting the hard outline of the pistol in his pocket, Julius stepped inside. If he encountered Lillian's husband, he was just going to get rid of him before taking her. What a deep satisfaction that would be, watching the fire mage who didn't belong in this family go down at last. Covering his tracks, making it look like an accident, would not be so important this time. And Julius could not wait to have Lillian back in his realm, after not even seeing her for eighteen long years. Still, he longed for both her and her sister. Such beautiful girls, though it was Evelyn who most resembled his boyhood love, Vanessa. It was a pity about Evelyn's cat allergy that had kept her from visiting, and how she stopped answering his letters after her father poisoned her against him.

And he still couldn't have Evelyn. They'd had to get out of her neighborhood fast.

Except for a speckled cat who looked up, startled, from a hammock, the house was empty. And the freshest aura tracks, deposited by someone ordinary, did not look familiar. Julius searched each room. The somewhat cluttered kitchen; these people had fallen a bit behind on washing dishes. The living room full of hanging plants. The one bedroom that looked like a work-from-home office combined with an art studio. The other bedroom where they slept, its walls papered with drawings and paintings and prints. Julius remembered that red stuffed animal tossed between the pillows, from Lillian's stay at his home. Over thirty now, and she still slept with that toy?

As he turned to leave and consider his next steps, a furry gray dog, some pointy-eared mutt, lunged at Julius, barking fiercely. An older, gray-haired woman hooked her fingers under the dog's collar as a watering can dangled from her other hand.

"Hello? Who are you?" she asked, startled.

"Oh, I'm, uh... I'm Lillian's uncle. Her uncle Dave. She's expecting me. Do you where she is, by chance?"

"They're on their way to Texas. Their niece is in trouble. It sounds as if the girl was taken from her home."

"Oh, no! I hadn't heard of this," Julius lied.

"It sounds like such a frightening situation. I'm their neighbor. I'm taking care of the pets and watering their plants until they get back. I pray that child is found safe."

"I'll keep the little girl in my thoughts and prayers, too. Thank you for letting me know."

Sighing in defeat, eyes heavy from little sleep, Julius walked out and down the porch steps as the woman tried to calm the barking, growling dog. He pulled a burner phone from his pocket and punched in a text message to Katrina. Plans would need to change. Luck had it that she was already headed back in Evelyn's direction.

Infuriated at the news of Tasha's disappearance, Denny was convinced he knew exactly who was behind it. Once his head cleared enough after the news yesterday, Denny had shut himself away and did a tarot reading, which hinted at his own suspicions. Even if his uncle Gerald was no longer around to cast blame on, Gerald had left a legacy of poison in his wake.

Without even telling his wife where he was going, or discussing it with his uncle Lou who might discourage him, Denny left a couple of mornings after the kidnapping. He arrived in his late uncle's quiet, tree-shaded neighborhood, parking his Jeep Wrangler well down the street.

Denny just knew Katrina had a hand in this. Though they'd scarcely spoken before, he was determined to confront her. And he didn't expect it to be pretty.

Denny unlocked Gerald's front gate with his mind. Because it was so simple to trespass on the grounds, easy as slicing through butter, he imagined that a very tough-to-breach security system lay ahead. Denny strolled up the long driveway. The lawn was not as well-manicured as it had been during Gerald's lifetime. The grass was overgrown with weeds, the shrubs untrimmed.

When he reached the columned front porch, Denny crept up the steps. Glancing around for security cameras and seeing none, Denny rang the doorbell. He knocked, sending hollow echoes reverberating inside. He tried the knob.

The door swung open, unlocked. No alarms went off.

"Katrina?" Denny called, getting no answer. He reached out and swept around with his telekinetic extensions, finding no signs of a human presence inside. Or even an animal, save for a few insects.

Denny stepped inside. His footsteps echoed in the great room, where rectangles of sun spilled from the side windows. The home was not quite clean, with little piles of paper and clutter in the corners, ashes in the fireplace, and dust on the knickknacks.

Putting a hand to his perpetually aching back, Denny decided to search the upstairs and work his way down. After climbing the stairs, he found nothing that could point to Tasha's whereabouts. Just a bunch of small children's toys, half of them broken, and some trash. Struck with a sudden feeling of his flesh crawling, he went back down and peeked into the master suite.

The bed that once belonged to Gerald sat low and wide over thick plush white carpet. Denny peeled back the red comforter. Though the bed had not been slept in recently enough to leave fresh aura remnants, a faint sweaty smell hit his nose. The sheets hadn't been changed or washed in quite a while.

Denny's next stop was the study. Sinking into the massive leather chair, he booted up the desktop computer and looked into the files. Denny inserted his keychain thumb drive into a USB port, just in case he found any clues worth copying over and taking home.

Saved on the desktop was a document called "Autobiography." Denny clicked on it and got swept up in reading the story of Gerald's life, starting from the innocence of infancy, though he stroked his own ego from the beginning.

It stirred Denny's emotions to read about his mother, Sarah, and all the things no one had ever told him about her childhood. Denny remembered her as an anxious woman, loving and kind yet dragged down by the weight of her depressive spells, increasingly withdrawn toward the end as she holed up in a relative's spare room after her release from the mental hospital. When Denny visited her, he asked about all the photographs and drawings of walls decorating her room, and she never produced a straight answer.

When Denny's mother predicted the future with chilling accuracy, had she known that she would end up taking too many pills, leaving her eleven-year-old boy behind with a wound that never healed?

As Denny read on into Gerald's adulthood, his jaw dropped more and more. At last, he tipped backwards in the chair, recoiling in horror.

"Uncle Gerald, you were one sick son of a bitch," Denny groaned aloud as his head churned with anger, his stomach with nausea. It now came as little surprise that Gerald's children were both so deeply troubled. Gerald's obsession with breeding more necromancers had turned him into a pig, an accomplice to rape.

Through his disgust, Denny's eyes fell back on the computer screen. "No, no, I can't keep reading this garbage. Or maybe I should just skim it and figure out what the hell's going on right now. Maybe it even says where Tasha is... let's hope."

After his eyes jumped around through the rest of the unsettling read, not spotting any clues about where Tasha was taken, Denny saved the document on his little thumb drive. At least Uncle Gerald hadn't completely held back about what a despicable piece of shit he was, Denny thought to himself, as much as he tried to justify it. And there were still delusions of grandeur and omissions of truth even in this supposed tell-all book.

After pocketing the thumb drive, Denny continued his canvass of the house, making his way down to the recreation room, mostly empty except for a ping-pong table collecting dust. With the feelers of his telekinesis, he discovered something strange behind the black bookshelf full of outdated issues of dirty magazines. A sort of hollow. Denny nudged the bookshelf at one side. Bolted to the wall with metal hinges, it would not budge. Expecting some hidden vault filled with money or important papers, Denny shuffled to the other side and pried at the edge until it swung away from the wall, unearthing a metal security door. He jiggled the steel handle and was surprised to find it unlocked just like the front door. Denny stepped into a sparsely furnished room with a bare bulb hanging from the ceiling, a chair in the middle, a couple of cots, a roll of duct tape, and a tangle of white nylon rope on the floor. There was a slight bad smell, a hint of feces, a fainter hint of decay. The concrete floor was spattered here and there with old reddish-brown stains, more thickly layered near a drain. Instead of a hidden cave full of riches, this looked like a serial killer's hideout.

Up above, the front door closed. The sound rang loudly throughout the house. Hair standing on end, Denny prepared to hide himself behind the bookshelf, pulling it into place, when he realized from yards away that the visitor was not a maid or servant, but a necromancer. Denny's breath caught in his throat as he tried to stay utterly still.

"Hello?" a male voice called as the footfalls came closer. A voice Denny hadn't heard in years.

Julius, haggard and sweaty with bags under his eyes, face more wrinkled and hair thinner than Denny remembered, appeared right in front of him, no doubt following his trail into the room.

"I had a feeling you would end up here," Julius said, his mouth twisting into a cruel smile. "Good seeing you again."

"Good seeing you too, cousin. You look like shit."

"Why, thanks for the compliment. It's been a very busy week and I've been running ragged. I couldn't find Uncle Lou, or Lillian. But what great timing, just as I was coming by to check that we didn't forget anything. I found you. You're coming with me."

"I'm not going anywhere, except home to my wife."

"You're coming with us. It's the plan. We have been a little afraid to touch Lou; he's powerful. We tried to talk him into it, in a roundabout way, and he refused. Now we do it behind his back and hope we'll have the power to overcome him. Either that, or he'll pass away soon and not be a worry anymore. Lillian will be joining our army next."

"Army? Is this the same one that your father was talking about in that sicko autobiography?"

"Yes. I take it you had a good read?"

"There is no justification for the things you've been doing."

"What must be done, must be done."

"Where are you taking me?"

"On a nice long cruise. Don't give me a reason to kill you, because I really don't want to do that. If you try to take possession of me, I'll bet you anything I can do it faster. Now come with me."

"Hell, no. You try to kidnap me and I'm taking possession first."

"Try me." Julius reached into a deep pocket of his sweatpants and drew out a gun, pointing it straight at Denny.

Why hadn't Denny thought to carry his own sidearm? Today might have been the most important day to do so. Yet among all the stress and confusion, it had slipped his mind.

Denny glared into Julius' eyes, silent for several seconds. Just as Julius' shoulders sagged with the first hint of relaxation, Denny tried to strike him with possession over his body. Having not practiced this skill much, Denny could not do it fast enough. Julius beat him to it.

"I'm glad that I did not have to use this gun. I can't afford to have someone like you wounded, or worse, dead on arrival," Julius said, maintaining his control over Denny and slipping the weapon back into his pocket. Having never been possessed by another necromancer before, Denny was terrified by his sudden helplessness.

Julius removed something else from his other pocket. A syringe filled with clear liquid. He popped the cap off and pushed the fluid painfully into Denny's upper arm.

Denny's lights went out.

As they waited for Lou to arrive, Evelyn, Lillian, and Avery joined the growing neighborhood search party, walking in the thick, spiny brush and the swampy grounds behind the houses, calling Tasha's name. More volunteers arrived on horseback.

A hubbub ripped through the entire scattered group as a searcher dismounted his horse, shouting that he had found something. A stuffed animal half-buried in the muck, its fur matted with grime.

Her heart soaring and sinking at the same time, Evelyn went running to see it firsthand.

The man pulled a large plush cat out of the mud, shaking off a few clods of dirt. Evelyn looked carefully over the filthy toy.

"That doesn't look familiar. It didn't belong to my daughter." A tear of disappointment leaked down Evelyn's cheek.

Everyone set about looking again. Back where they had started, with nothing.

Eventually, Avery needed to walk back to Evelyn's house, though they'd strayed far enough that it would be quite a hike. Dying of thirst in the humid heat, he needed to refill his empty water bottle and use the bathroom. After finding Lillian, Avery transmitted his plan to her with a touch of the hand. Sometimes mind transference was just quicker and more convenient than talking. Within a second, Lillian nodded and gave a thumbs up.

Resting on Evelyn's couch after filling his bottle with water and ice, Avery called his mother, now seventy-one years old, retired, and still living in the home where he came of age.

"How did you get to your sister-in-law's so quickly?" she asked.

"You won't believe how we got here; I'll explain the next time we visit. I'm taking a rest in the nice, cool, air-conditioned house, and then in a few minutes I'll start looking again."

"Do you want me to come and help find that child?"

"It would take you a while to get here... sorry, Mom, I have to go." Dread sunk sharply into the pit of Avery's stomach.

Lillian. Something was wrong. Telepathic distress calls came from a point in the distance.

Forgetting to grab his water bottle, Avery ran out of the house. He called Lillian. She didn't answer. His texts, asking if she was all right, went unread.

Yelling Lillian's name, he ran and ran. The alarm bells in his head grew fainter as she went further and further away. Avery chased in the eastern direction from which the signals came, across the thickly layered network of aura trails from the other searchers and a few horses. The thick brush, filled with spines and obstructive branches, made for a slow journey. He ran into Evelyn, out of breath as he told her he thought Lillian might be in trouble.

Evelyn asked around among the fellow searchers. "Has anyone seen my sister? She's five foot seven, average build, straight red hair about midway down her back. She's wearing jeans, a blue striped tee, and glasses with blue frames."

Despite the hair that made Lillian stand out, no one mentioned seeing her in the past half hour or so.

At last, Avery found Lillian's trail. It had followed the others for a while, and then branched off sharply. Why would she stray so far? Had she spotted a clue in the distance?

His sense of wrongness turning into sheer panic, Avery followed the trail, still fresh as it wove through the trees.

Lillian had ventured in the direction of the nearest street. Sideways on the ground was the half-drunk water bottle she'd been clutching in her hand the last time Avery saw her. The cap was off the bottle, and much of the water had drained into the ground. A few feet away, something sparkled. Lillian's phone lay screen down in the dirt, its blue glitter case twinkling in the sun. Like most people, she would never willingly toss her phone aside. Avery's heart plummeted as he grabbed it, brushed the dirt off, and activated the screen. The most recent activity was the call and text messages he'd sent her. She'd made no outgoing calls.

Avery broke into a run, screaming Lillian's name. He got no answer, just the same unsettling silence. Why had he gone back to the house, allowing himself to lose track of her?

Lillian's trail stopped abruptly at the street. Meaning she had gotten into a car. They had no rental car here, and the only person Lillian might possibly catch a ride with was Evelyn, still in the thick of the search. And never had Lillian just disappeared without first telling Avery where she was going. Even if she was upset, she would never desert him without warning.

This was not good. This was not good at all.

Lightheaded, dizzy, on the verge of fainting in his panic, Avery sank to his knees. Frantically, he sent out psychic signals, pleading for Lillian to give him a sign.

No answer came. She was too far away. Or worse.

Excerpt from The Autobiography of Gerald Frazier: Architect of a New World

Not long after Lou's second daughter was born, a hot news story grabbed my attention. The Berlin Wall in Germany was torn down as the Soviet-era Iron Curtain began falling apart. As I watched the footage of people dismantling that big, graffiti-covered stone wall, I wondered if this was the prophecy from some mysterious, ghostly man that drove my sister Sarah to the brink of madness. A massive wall would crumble around the time the "one who decides" arrived!

But there was that one major inconsistency. Sarah said the mythical figure would be a man, yet baby Lillian was a girl. I believe the birth still has yet to happen and the Great Wall of China, or some comparable wall, will collapse that day.

At one of my parties, Vanessa met Karl, a friend of mine who'd had good fortune on the stock market. Despite Vanessa having an infant and cohabiting with another man, they hit it off well. Karl figured out the little secret about Lou, who allowed Vanessa to call and write him. After she finished nursing her year-old baby, Vanessa decided to move on from Lou. Since they were pretty much roommates anyway, he didn't object too much, just getting a bit concerned that the kids might miss her. After moving into Karl's ornate apartment in Washington, D.C., Vanessa caught rides back to my brother's house to see the kids. Sometimes I took her.

At one of my New Year's parties, Karl got blotto drunk. For their safety, I asked them to stay until morning in one of my guest bedrooms rather than risk their lives on the icy roads. Though sober, Vanessa could not take them home. She was too frightened to learn to drive a car, and never had a license. Vanessa got up early while Karl was still upstairs in bed, hung over. She believed that I was asleep, though I was in the process of waking up, and tiptoed downstairs, intending to look for a snack in the kitchen. I caught Vanessa in the hallway, dashing away from me like a scared animal. From reading her mind and tracing the trail of her aura into my study, I immediately figured out what she'd done.

I had made the mistake of leaving the door to my study open. That was not my only error. When I had rummaged around in there looking for my checkbook and a few papers the day before, I had foolishly left some very private materials sitting out on my desk... a journal and some letters from Julius, as well as a letter to him that I had yet to send.

When Vanessa walked past, her curiosity got the better of her. Intrigued by the sight of that mysterious, leather-bound journal and those handwritten letters, she traipsed into the room and snooped. She had read the letters, as well as some of the entries in the journal.

Vanessa found out things she was never meant to know! Things that were only supposed to be between me and Julius, and eventually, the other necromancers once I either won their trust or bent them to my will. Some of the terms completely bewildered Vanessa. From her perspective, Julius and I were simply out of our minds!

As the things she'd read turned around feverishly in Vanessa's head, she worried about my brother Lou and what I might be planning to do to her two children. She spent that late morning carefully avoiding me.

Once Karl managed to keep some aspirin down for a little while, she badgered him into rushing them home. If she couldn't interfere in what little she had perceived of my master plan, she at least wanted to stop Lou, Evelyn, and Lillian from being a part of it. Karl was about to take Vanessa up north on a skiing trip the next day, but as soon as she returned from Vermont a few weeks later, she wanted to see Lou. Feeling it was major enough to not discuss over the phone, she wanted to sit him down in person. She hoped to talk him into never allowing those little girls near me again.

I had to stop Vanessa!

If you're reading this, you're aware of what efficient killers us necromancers are. It's simple to hijack someone's mind and make it look like they're at fault. And that is why Karl still sits in prison at the time of this writing for shooting Vanessa dead after their return from their trip.

Julius and I were shaken up for a long time. After that close call, I always got in the habit of locking my study or keeping my private materials in a secured cabinet. I burned that journal and those old letters that Vanessa had found. It is easier to lock a door than it is to clean up the mess from knowledge falling into the wrong hands!

Unfortunately, some years later, I slipped on my privacy once and left my things unlocked, and my wife Tawny found out too much. Tawny looked for evidence that I had committed adultery, and she found something else that blew her mind even more than my philandering ways! She "committed suicide" that very day. Once again, I had no other choice.

For the rest of the 1990s, my business empire kept booming, but my personal family life was a waiting game. Waiting for the youngest two necromancers, still children, to grow up so that they could be of use in my army. Once they caught up in age, I judged that we'd be substantial enough to move forward.

My granddaughter Katrina ate up the idea of power eagerly, even as a child. She was about twelve when her father and I finally broke a few more bits of our plan to her, swearing her to secrecy of course. Young Katrina announced that she couldn't wait until we "inherited the world." Gotta be proud of that girl!

Dealing with my nephew Denny, I encountered a lot of walls of frustration. That boy had never been fond of me, and on the rare occasions I got to see him, I did not find his mind malleable. I was still determined that at the right time, we would do whatever it took to get him on our side. In the end, he was not going to have much of a choice.

My brother Lou also brushed off my hints at joining me for something great in the future. I determined that ambushing him with my entire plan would be unsafe at this point in time. But there would come a point when he wouldn't have much of a choice but to be on my side either, even if his power exceeded mine. And that abundance of power would become a great asset to us all.

Though Lou did not allow me much time alone with his two daughters, Julius won all of their hearts from the beginning. I depended on him to someday convince them.

Julius found a family with the mage trait, though I do not know if there were any actual mages in recent generations. He married one of them, a rather controlling woman named Jana, hoping for genetic diversity. They only produced one child, a half-breed son. Not long after, a scandal hit us. When Lillian was almost out of high school, she accused Julius of doing something terrible years before. This came from a teenager so mentally unstable that she'd tried to kill herself. Thank God she lived, unlike Jana's younger sister, who was successful at her attempt and also told crazy stories about Julius. Such a pity; I could have put Jana's sister to good use in the future.

I wish Lou hadn't listened to his daughter's wild tales, but he believed her story, creating a divide in the family and hindering our progress considerably. I had to think fast on my feet to prevent Lou from cutting me off completely!

But I still had every confidence that our army would assemble the way it was meant to, even if it might take more time and effort after Lillian tossed that monkey wrench into my gears.

I still found opportunities whenever possible. Evelyn went to college in Georgia, and I took a trip to see her. I found a down-and-out young man named Jonathan. It was just my luck that he shared a class with Evelyn. She was a very pretty, slim girl, with lots of boys chasing her as always. I wished to strike while the iron was hot and she happened to be single, a condition that never lasted long in her life. I gave Jonathan tips for winning her over, and offered to pay the rest of his tuition should he succeed. Just between us, of course.

There was only one reason I put Jonathan up to this. He had the mage trait. Further increasing my luck, the two of them eventually got engaged and married. I had Jonathan nudge Evelyn into pregnancy as soon as possible. Right before the ceremony, she finally caved, and conceived a child. Immediately following the wedding, a clan of water people who lived near the venue targeted my family, making attempts on their lives. I'd already gotten on the plane back home when it happened, and I am so, so fortunate they managed to escape. I could have lost a huge chunk of my army and my legacy that day. Ah, well. The water people will soon get theirs, along with the rest of the world.

A baby girl, Natasha, came the fall after their wedding. She was born a mage, but the wrong kind! A water mage, just like the ones who attempted to kill members of my family. This shocked myself, Julius, and Katrina. We blame Jonathan's genes for that happening. Though the family members I met at the wedding just appeared to be half-breeds, there must have been a water person somewhere along the line.

As of the time of this writing, we are still debating exactly what to do with that young girl. Her birth was carefully planned, with a shocking and unexpected result. I have no idea whether she would be useful or whether we should just dispose of her when the time comes.

Evelyn and Jonathan have since divorced. Jonathan is an insecure, attention-hungry man, the sort who cheats. I saw his skirt-chasing coming from a mile away, yet I was so eager to marry Evelyn off to a fellow half-breed that I chose the first one who shared a class with her. Such a shame.

We urged Katrina to begin having children as soon as she could. She trusted myself and her father to find her a boyfriend. I already had a young man in mind, a very handsome fellow named Zack, the cousin of Julius' wife who was, like Jana, a half-breed. After his father raised him to be a tough guy, Zack did not have charm, but I hoped his good looks would more than make up for it. Katrina was more than happy, and before too long, she got pregnant. Her baby-to-be was destined to be a necromancer!

But about halfway through the pregnancy, tragedy struck and the baby inexplicably died in Katrina's womb. Zack, angry and emotionally unprepared for a situation like this, left her as soon as he found out. With her now fragile emotional state, and being single again, we had to table our plans with Katrina.

Lou's younger daughter, Lillian, made the choice to go away to college in Colorado. I decided that now was as good a time as any to select a suitable boyfriend. Yet I had a hard time finding anyone willing to move down there except for Katrina's ex, Zack, single, jobless, and again eager for the money I offered. He agreed to masquerade as a student, keeping quiet that he'd ever known Katrina or the rest of us. On the campus, getting lost in the shuffle without raising suspicion was easy.

Like my nephew Denny, Lillian was dead set against the idea of procreating. I never did find her mind as easy to influence as some people's. I was never able to persuade her, either by talking to her or reaching into her head. But Lillian was still quite young, leaving the possibility that her mind might change as she grew older. The right young man might be able to talk her into what I couldn't. I emphasized the importance of this to Zack.

Zack could not pull off the act as well as Evelyn's former husband did. I'd made a mistake choosing him for this role. When Lillian caught Zack lying about his age, he disappeared for a while. I needed to find another young man who was a bit more suave and intelligent, or try another tactic.

While I schemed about my next steps, Lillian did something that startled us all. You'd really think she would have known better. She got involved with a classmate who happened to be a mage. A fire mage!

What's more? Lou, who had stopped speaking to me by then when all I did was the favor of setting his truth free, was stupid enough to host this young man at his house!

Completely unheard of. For who knows how many centuries, they, along with the other kinds, had been out to kill us, and we had avoided each other like the plague, never willingly speaking to one another, treating each chance encounter like somebody wasn't getting out alive. And now she was romantically involved with the enemy? What the hell was she thinking, risking her life like that! How angry I would be if this boy turned on her and she ended up dead, after the work of getting the unlikely pair of her parents to procreate at all. I wanted to personally call Lillian and shout at her, until I found out through the grapevine that Denny had already expressed his own unhappiness with the whole deal. The two young lovers, of course, hadn't listened to him, and then he finally resigned himself to accepting it. Lillian wasn't likely to listen to me either. She might be a smart kid and all, but love is blind.

To my knowledge, Lillian and that young man are still together. Let's hope that whole deal ends as painlessly as possible, for all of our sakes. I have yet to meet him. But one thing is for sure. He would cause nothing but trouble in the implementation of our plans. Thus, he will be among the first eliminated. She'll get over it, I'm sure, once the new world order is established. She will finally appreciate her own importance!

The Fight

⟨⟨・・◆・・⟩⟩

The black tide went out. Lillian slowly surfaced. Her head throbbed with dehydration. She didn't know what time it was as she woke in long, laborious stages, fighting to kick her brain back into action.

Deep sleep still tempted Lillian, but she was terrified to succumb to it again.

Those waves of power that suddenly approached during the search for Tasha had come from the pregnant Katrina, reaching for Lillian from a shockingly far distance and catching her by surprise. Katrina took possession before Lillian even knew what hit her, leading her to an unfamiliar dark gray SUV as she shuffled in that horrifying, helpless zombie state she had not experienced since her abuse at the hands of Julius.

As Lillian's eyes fluttered open, Katrina was in the passenger's seat, silent. Behind the wheel sat none other than Lillian's sham ex-boyfriend, Zack Dunaway, expressionless, saying nothing. Other than a few small wrinkles and silver hairs, he looked just like she remembered, right down to the faded blue jeans and shark-tooth necklace. He'd injected something into Lillian's arm to knock her out while she was still frozen in Katrina's remote grip, unable to defend herself.

Lillian found her ankles bound and her wrists locked together in handcuffs as she lay under a stuffy, smelly blanket on the backseat, her head too groggy to focus her powers and free herself. Zack pulled over to inject Lillian again before she could sharpen her mind enough to fight back.

After that came a brief stint of consciousness on a boat as her nose filled with the salty scent of seawater. By then, Lillian's body screamed from its unnatural position, her arms wrenched behind her back.

Possessed again and walking under external control even as her brain stayed half-asleep, Lillian passed a series of cages in the moonlight, emitting a bad odor she remembered all too sharply from her childhood. The smell of her puppy suffering from parvo.

No, it was the stench of the creature Julius had created from his deceased cat. Like the parvo smell, but somehow even worse, with more hell and more death.

"Avery isn't here," a familiar voice snapped as Katrina's waves of power overwhelmed Lillian, so thick she could hear their sheer, glassy sound. "You've asked for him, like, fifty times. Just shut up."

"Where am I?" Lillian mumbled. Her memories slowly trickled back. Her eyelids felt woven together; it was hard to keep them open. Her blue jeans clung to her legs, wet and smelly. Harsh artificial light streamed down mercilessly from up above.

Tasha was somewhere around here. Lillian just knew it.

"We brought you a long way." Katrina stood over Lillian, grinning. "We got you here as quick as possible. Zack exhausted himself with all that driving."

"What—why did you do this to me?"

"We brought you where you're supposed to be."

"Stop... stop drugging me. I don't want to be here. Let me go."

"I'll stop the tranq for now, but if you disobey us, we'll put you back out so fast it'll make your head spin. And if you try to take possession of me, I'll beat you to it, 'cause in my condition, I'm faster than a speeding bullet." Katrina smirked and proudly rubbed the large bump in her denim dress.

When Katrina handed over her eyeglasses, Lillian put them on, blinking. "Tell me where the hell I am."

"We finally finished building this place after years of setbacks. It's Grandpa's brainchild. A big house for the whole family, and our helpers. Built to stand up to hurricanes. This is Grandpa's private island. The Atlantic is all around us, off the coast of North Carolina. Isn't this amazing?"

Lillian looked around at the bare walls, and the steel door across the room. No ocean was visible, as the room had no windows. For all Lillian knew, Katrina was lying about their very location.

"I just want to go home," Lillian pleaded.

"This is your home now. And you should forget about your precious Avery. He's not one of us. Soon, it will be all over for him and the rest of those worthless people out there. But the good news is, we decided Tasha might be useful. Your niece is safe and sound. You can stop worrying about her."

Lillian struggled to sit up. The handcuffs and rope that had restrained her in the car trunk were gone. Wordlessly, Katrina threatened her, holding up a syringe filled with clear fluid. To illustrate her point, Katrina squirted a bit out the tip. It beaded and dribbled down.

"Don't bother using your powers to try to get out," Katrina warned. "The door's got a combination lock and it's made of steel. The walls are thick. You'll stay until we're sure you'll behave. You have a sink, a toothbrush, a dress to wear, a toilet, and a jigsaw puzzle. And a little shower stall. With no curtain, so you don't get any ideas. You should take a shower. You were out so long that you pissed yourself. Gross!"

"I'm your prisoner, aren't I?"

"You don't have to be a prisoner. Just swear allegiance to us and believe in our family's mission, and you'll be free. You'll be better than free. You'll hold the whole world in your hands."

"I don't know what this mission is, but I'll never swear allegiance."

"Look, Lillian, you don't have a lot of choice. This is God's plan for you. I'll be the one to bring you food. I know you're not my dad's biggest fan, so he won't visit right away, not until you decide to bury the hatchet."

"Your dad? I thought you didn't know who he was. Wait..."

"I can see the wheels spinning in your head. Figuring it out, are we?"

"Your parents... brother and sister..." Lillian came close to gagging. Was he also the father of Katrina's unborn child?

"The family tried to cover it up, but at this juncture, there's no point in keeping secrets anymore."

"You want to keep necromancers alive with incest?"

"Maybe it sounds a little icky, but there's so few of us left. What choice did we have? But look at me. I'm healthy. And we'll patch things up between you and my dad."

"Fuck you."

Narrowing her eyes, Katrina slapped Lillian across the face. "Don't you ever talk to me like that again or I can end you, you understand?"

Lillian said nothing. She kept her expression steely, not wanting to give Katrina the satisfaction of tears.

"Once you've showered and changed, you've got reading to do. Grandpa's autobiography is sitting on that table. You should read it as soon as possible to get real familiar with our history and what's going on. Oh, and we're lucky you had this around your neck. Now it's with its rightful owners." With a cold smile, Katrina reached into the front of her dress and pulled out the green crystal on its chain. Cruelly, she dangled it in front of Lillian's face.

"Give me that!" Lillian grabbed for the crystal. Katrina pulled it out of her reach, and then turned and left, slamming the heavy-duty door behind her. It locked automatically.

Lillian curled up on the hard mattress. She dug her nails into her arms and started to cry hysterically, sinking into hopelessness. Lillian began to think about the most efficient tools in this room to end this dire new reality before Julius had the opportunity to lay his slimy hands on her ever again. Like Katrina had pointed out, there was no shower curtain, nor were there any sheets on the bare mattress. Or any razors. Lillian dissociated. As far as she was concerned, she was dead already.

Down the hall and up a flight of creaky wooden stairs, it was time for dinner. Lydia and the doctor who had delivered her baby both happened to be good cooks, placing them under pressure to serve as the group's personal chefs. They brought out some fried fish on silver platters, and Katrina took one plate back down into the shadows of the hall.

"How is Lillian?" Julius asked when Katrina returned. Beside him sat Denny, submissive and looking down as if in prayer. And Robbie, face twisted in resentment as he forced down every bite. Zack Jr. babbled in his high chair nearby.

"Well, I set Lillian's dinner on her nightstand. She did take a shower and change clothes, it looks like. But she's just lying there like an idiot, not saying or doing anything." Katrina shrugged.

"Let her be. She'll come around. Always remember that being shaken up makes people receptive to change. Now, Tasha, eat your peas or else we'll change our minds and decide to eliminate you."

"I want my mom," Tasha protested, pushing her peas around with a knife. "I'm not hungry. I want to go home."

"You won't be seeing your mom again. We're not going back for her; it's too much effort. This is your home now. Eat!" Katrina ordered.

Julius finished eating and went outside. It was his turn to stand sentry, watching the surrounding ocean for any lights that shouldn't be there, any signs of intruders.

Inside, Katrina and Zack got the children ready for bed. As usual, the parents yelled while the toddlers cried.

Back at Denny's home, his wife, Mona, paced frantically after a sleepless night. Stomach twisted up in knots, she couldn't eat breakfast. Coffee was the only thing that stayed down, increasing her jitters.

Yesterday was one of the worst days of Mona's life. If not the number one most horrific out of her sixty-five years. After an evening of not answering his phone, Denny never came home, and Mona reported him missing. This could not be a coincidence, right around the time two relatives also vanished.

Or what if it had nothing to do with those missing cousins? What if he'd had a heart attack behind the wheel? Or plunged into some water somewhere?

While other friends and loved ones searched around town that morning, Mona flipped through the address book she shared with her husband. Denny had recently said something about Gerald, his uncle who had died nine years ago. The one who'd always given him the heebie-jeebies.

After Mona ran across Gerald's name and contact information written down in the address book, he stuck in her head and would not go away. Though Gerald was gone, some granddaughter of his had inherited the house. Mona had never met this woman, but maybe she knew something? Mona decided to chase every lead and every hunch. Though she was likely wasting her time driving around the state, she set her phone to navigate straight to Gerald's home. Crossing the Chesapeake Bay Bridge intimidated her so much that she avoided it when possible, but today, it felt necessary.

Mona's heart beat fast in shock as she drove down Gerald's street. There it sat by the curb—Denny's Jeep, still splattered with mud from an adventure the couple had both enjoyed the previous weekend. Getting her hopes up that it might contain her husband, Mona parked behind it and rushed over, peeking in all of the windows and pounding the doors.

The vehicle was empty.

Anxious to find Denny, Mona decided to continue her search before calling the police. After getting back into her own car, she found the house, abandoned and left unlocked amid a shaggy, poorly kept yard. The gate hung open, and Mona boldly drove up the driveway before getting out and heading inside. Not the grand space she remembered from her occasional visits during Gerald's lifetime, the interior was a bit messy with some pieces of trash and some dust, as well as broken children's toys. Someone had fled from here, and they hadn't bothered to pack many of their badly-treated possessions.

Mona screamed Denny's name, getting only echoes in response. She tripped over a grungy toy, yelping when it lit up and giggled in an unsettling baby voice.

Apparently, this granddaughter didn't live here alone, with the toddler toys and some men's toiletries and shave cream and scattered beard whiskers around the sink of the master bathroom.

Where were these people? And more importantly, where on earth was Denny? Filled with the same sinking feeling from last night, Mona searched the house thoroughly, going down to the game room. A bookshelf on hinges was pushed away from the wall, a metal security door opened behind it, uncovering a bleak, prisonlike room clearly hidden from public view until now. The room smelled dirty. The sheer wrongness of this space chilled Mona to the bone.

Mona focused her search on the office one level above, rifling through the drawers and an open, yet empty, safe. Any important papers had been either taken or put down the overflowing shredder.

After calling the police to report Denny's vehicle, Mona returned, defeated and deflated, to her home that evening. Mona napped on the couch for an hour, afraid that if she got into bed for a proper snooze, the tears would come and not stop. Or that she would miss something important, sleeping through a clue or a phone call that would change everything.

After waking up and having more coffee, Mona went up to the attic, even though Denny couldn't possibly have vanished up here. He spent little time in the musty attic, except to get holiday decorations in and out of storage.

What was Mona doing in this hot stuffy space? Even she didn't know, but after finding Denny's Jeep, she decided to trust her instincts completely. Something called to her, a faint, tempting whisper. A forgotten cardboard box lay underneath the dust-caked little round attic window.

Mona carefully picked her way across the rafters, enveloped in the strange chemical odor of old mothballs, pushing away cobwebs that clung to her face. She knelt on her aching, arthritic knees beside the box. When she opened it, a puff of dust came out, carrying an ancient dried mummy smell. Nobody had gone through these old clothes and papers in years. Many of the yellowed papers were letters, some of them typed with a typewriter, some of them written in cursive.

It took Mona a few moments to figure it out. These things had belonged to Denny's mother. Some of the letters came from other people, while some were written by her and never sent.

At the bottom of the box was a leather-bound journal. Mona pulled it out and leafed through its yellowed pages, filled with cursive handwriting that got messier and more erratic as the years went by. This was Sarah's private diary. Denny had never shown this to Mona before, and she doubted even he knew it existed. A lot of the entries didn't make sense as Mona read them in the ray of dust-filtered evening sun.

But some things did jump out at her.

1/2/1963

I had the dream again. The same dream I had as an adolescent, from which I woke up in a panic. The airplanes being overtaken by men and then crashing into the two tall buildings in New York City.

Except there was... more to this dream. When I was a girl, I dreamt only of the two tall buildings. But this time, my dream jumped to other places. Another bad man flew a different airplane into the Pentagon.

These men also attempted to steal a fourth airplane. I do not know where they intended to fly it. Somewhere very important, I'm sure. But the plane crashed and burned when its passengers fought back.

This is one of the dreams that will come true. I just know it. Many of my other dreams already have, without fail. It is simply the timing that catches me by surprise.

I never told my former husband about these dreams. He would not have believed me. And after my stint in the loony bin, who would believe me? I only wish that these dreams could help me to stop such a tragedy before it starts. I could see it happening, but I do not know any of the hijackers' names or where they come from. Or when this is going to happen, just in the far, far future. In each of my dreams, the folks carried little telephones in their pockets.

Maybe there's no telling exactly when, or how, to stop it, because the future is set in stone?

"Huh," Mona grumbled after reading that entry. This had to be a joke. It was impossible that anybody could have predicted those terrorist attacks way back in 1963, exactly how they happened. Such an entry could only be written after all of the news reports. What a sick and unfunny prank for somebody to play, referencing those attacks where thousands lost their lives because it made for a compelling fake diary entry.

But who? This wasn't Denny's sloppy chicken scratch. Or any other writing Mona recognized. Denny could be embarrassingly crass sometimes, but he'd gotten emotional on that day in 2001 and this wouldn't have amused him at all. And the diary seemed genuinely old with its yellow pages and slightly acrid smell.

Mona flipped forward a few pages, where a particularly unhinged entry caught her attention.

4/3/1963

The ghost paid me a visit. The man who has been coming in the night to speak to me for some time, and always tells me about "the one who decides."

The ghost seemed weak this time. His voice was only a whisper that I had to strain hard to hear. He still could not tell me who "the one who decides" is going to be. When I asked if it might be my boy, he said no. The one has yet to be born. It might be years still. It might be decades.

He told me the Angel of Death is going to have an important job on earth. He is going to leave the realm of death, where our gathering place is the intermediary, and come to Earth in a human form. That will be "the one who decides."

I asked how the Angel of Death will carry out his duties if he's going to become a human, and the ghost assured me that his supernatural form is present everywhere, while another incarnation will live in the human form. This man will not know who he is as he walks the earth, and will need guidance. The human brain is far too tiny to hold an angel's knowledge.

"And that is where we are needed," the ghost said before he grew weak enough to vanish into thin air. "Once he is born, we must watch him closely."

The night following the ghost's visit, I had an awful dream. It was about my boy. Grown up and older, with gray hair, well after the year 2000. And he was dead, somewhere on an island, while the Angel of Death brought him to the spirit realm. The human body, I did not see. The angel was a huge, terrible thing, a great blob of blackness that somehow shone like light.

I pray that this dream will not come true. But I have the utmost dread that it will, and that this is a clue to when "the one who decides" will walk the earth.

Mona slammed the diary shut, wanting to burn it in the fireplace. Tears began to spill from her eyes. This woman had predicted 9/11, and now she was predicting the death of Denny? Along with some strange, biblical prophecy?

No, no, this diary had to be a joke. Mona would bring Denny home alive if it was the last thing she did. If only she knew where he was! Though she kept her phone in her pocket with the volume cranked up, it wasn't ringing. The cops weren't calling with any updates.

Mona went downstairs, balling her fists, and beat the couch cushions to a pulp while she sobbed.

After washing under a trickle of almost-cold water from the puny showerhead, squeezing out soap and shampoo from tiny hotel-sized bottles, Lillian was a bit relieved to finally be clean, yet no happier to be in this place.

After sitting back down on the cot, now wearing that scratchy dress that looked like something Julius might have picked out just for her, Lillian grabbed the printed stack of papers on the small table, held together with a binder clip. For lack of anything better to do until she figured out an escape, Lillian began to read. If this prison cell really was Gerald's idea, maybe she would learn something, anything, to help her get out of here.

The document held some genuinely interesting bits, including Lillian's father's childhood, her late aunt Sarah's premonitions, and her maternal great-grandmother's affair with a man from Mexico, which shed light on an unexpected result of the DNA test she'd recently taken for fun.

The fascination soured into utter horror as Uncle Gerald impregnated Lillian's maternal grandmother. It took only a second to figure out who that baby would be. Julius was her mother's brother!

Sickened at the things Uncle Gerald confessed to, including her mother's death to dam the truth from being leaked, Lillian ran to the sink to vomit once she finished reading. Her blood boiled with anger that Gerald had confessed to many of his own sins, yet he denied his beloved son's wrongdoing. She wanted to rip the pages, now dotted with her tears, to shreds. Instead, she folded them up into a small square and shoved it into her bra, riding on the small hope that she could flee from this island with evidence.

When Katrina brought Lillian's meal on a tray, she smirked coldly. "Did you read Grandpa's story?"

"I did. Made me throw up, literally."

"You have to get used to our situation. This is going to be the safest place in the world real soon."

"If you're hoping to use me for a brood mare, I have an IUD. So don't bother." She'd had it for years, after trying unsuccessfully to find a doctor who would sterilize a childless woman. She'd been on the pill before, and found the IUD a lot more comforting as she could not slip up and forget to take a tablet, but still wished for the permanent option.

Katrina grinned. "We have a doctor with us. I'm pretty sure he can take those things out."

"He's not touching me. Nobody's touching me!"

"Listen, if you don't stay with us, you die. Think it through and maybe you'll pull your head out of your ass."

Katrina stormed out. The door clicked shut, leaving Lillian alone again, desperate and hopeless, stomach lurching as she thought of her worst fear, Julius. She had to get out of here. To prevent any chance of Julius coming near her, it had to be now.

Lillian put her feelers around and through the walls. They were thick and reinforced. If she punched them, she would just end up with bloody knuckles—though she'd never tested the telekinesis to its limits. Lillian mentally headed for the weakest but still-strong point, the door. Its hinges were bolted deep into the wall. Screws might be possible to undo without a tool, but not these titanium bolts. Lillian crouched on the ground and squeezed her feelers through the tight space under the door, reaching down the edges of the wall, the rough carpet, and up and down the hall. If she searched enough, she might find the keypad on the other side, and then she could begin to guess at the combination.

Familiar orange warmth filled Lillian's whole body. Avery, reaching out to her over a distance—but not as long of a distance as before. He'd somehow figured out how to track her down, and was probably on his way at this very moment. With neither of them knowing exactly where she was, or what might come between them, he might be taking a grave risk.

No, Lillian begged wordlessly, trying hard to throw out her signal with her mind. *Please don't come here. It's dangerous. It's not worth it.*

Lillian threw herself back on the sparse bed and wept, shutting out the light. One light bulb stayed on over the sink.

Out of the shadows, something moved. A figure dimly glowed, shining blurry through Lillian's tears. A man hovered over her bed, a crumpled hooded robe framing the marble green of a dead pair of eyes.

Lillian sat up, wiping her tears and immediately recognizing this ghost. The one who'd made appearances since she was a baby. The one who tried to stop her suicide attempt as a young teenager.

"Who are you?" Lillian asked, knowing that he'd probably just dissipate instead of responding.

A voice came, a dry creak, so faint it was like the wind. "I am Armand."

That was the name of the ghost mentioned in the autobiography, who allegedly spoke to Sarah, the aunt she never knew.

"Why are you here? Where did you come from?" Lillian questioned him.

"In life, I was a magical person, as you are," Armand said, his voice coming in a little more loud and clear now with a thick accent she could not place. "I had air powers. Centuries ago, a prophet named Luther said that disaster would fall upon the earth at the hands of your people, the people of the dead. Luther ordered that all of your people must be killed. With my fellow prophet Adler, I saw other visions. We saw a man of great power and courage. Only this man could change the fate of the world. I was bound to protect him, in life or in death."

"Did you appear to Sarah?"

"Yes. Sarah was a prophet, like Luther. We have waited for centuries, behind the veil of the spirits. The one who decides would never be born if your ancestors were all destroyed. I came to your ancestor, Mary, to warn her of an attack. Mary came to America. We received more signs."

"Who is this one who decides?" Lillian asked, anxious for the ghost to reach the point before he dissolved and left her hanging. "Is he going to help us escape?"

"You don't remember who you were, do you?"

"Who I was? I've always been... me, haven't I?"

"We thought the one who decides would arrive as a man. In our time, we believed women were the weaker sex. We were wrong."

"You're not saying this person... is *me*, are you? This isn't real." Lillian wanted to laugh.

"We watched the moment of your birth. The signs pointed toward that year, that day. And now the time has come upon you to act."

"If you were supposed to watch and protect me all my life, where were you when I was raped? And when I was kidnapped?!"

"As hard and unfair as it may be, there are certain matters in which we've been prohibited from interfering, as they are part of your making the choice. When you attempted to take your own life, it was I who woke your father and urged him to your room. We could not let you die, even if it sapped all of the strength of an old ghost. Even these words are draining me, but it is the power of angels that keeps me talking."

"Angels? Seriously? Is this some biblical thing?"

"No. Angels are not men with halos and wings. They are masses of incredible energy, beyond the human imagination."

"Yeah, and these so-called angels didn't help me either. This can't be for real."

"Do you recall anything from before your birth? Do you recall... death? Bringing anyone home?"

"Death? Just this man I've been dreaming about my whole life... looks like a punk rock type from the seventies or eighties, and I don't know who he is. I stumble across his body right after he OD's on heroin. I'm sure it's nothing. Just dreams."

"That man was real, Lillian. He was the last of the dead that you helped to cross over before you came to earth."

"Okay, I'm even more confused. I used to... not be on earth?"

"The fate of the world rests upon your shoulders."

"What am I supposed to do, then?"

"I trust that you will know."

"That doesn't help! Can you at least throw me a bone?"

Lillian blinked and Armand was gone. Yet somehow, new memories of that dead man bubbled to the surface. Memories that had always been there, just buried underneath the sands of time.

Matthew Clive. 29 years old, lived in a small flat in London.

No, I'm imagining things. The ghost is full of shit.

I helped Matthew to cross over. I led him past the cemetery, into the temple, into the bone room. Into the light. I took Mom's hand and led her into the light when I was little. My puppy Buster, I ran with him there too. The moment he died in the backseat when I was a kid. I didn't have the crystal, but I slipped into the other world somehow. Then Tara. My old roommate. I was eating cupcakes with my friends several dorms away, but when the death-feeling hit, she saw me standing over her. I didn't even know it. I know now, just like I know Katrina is responsible for her death.

When Uncle Gerald's heart stopped, he saw me too. The form of me I didn't know I had. He asked me, as his ghost rose up, "Are you the one who decides?" And I said, without knowing it in my physical body, "The choice has been made."

I am still helping them cross over. I'm not just in this body. I'm all over the world.

No, that can't be. It's just my imagination. This place is making my mind crack apart.

Collapsing back into tears, Lillian became convinced that the ghost and his speech about her destiny were simple hallucinations. Maybe Katrina had been drugging Lillian's food.

After some broken sleep, Lillian awoke. Was it daytime? Evening? Night? She'd lost track of time, and with no windows to hint at the angle of the sun, she really had no idea.

The door beeped and clicked open. Lillian jumped up, rod-straight, as her least favorite person in the world faced her. Julius, older, more wrinkled, hair thinner and infiltrated with white streaks, but still looking much the same. He wore a white sweatsuit, and was flanked by Katrina on one side and a teenage boy, his son Lillian had never met, on the other. Robbie was skinny with a jersey draped over his body, brown hair hanging shaggy in his face, eyes big and uncomfortable. Lillian's stomach churned with terrified nausea, which quickly turned into anger. Julius had defeated her before, damaging years of her life. After coming such a long way in healing, now she was back with him. Trapped.

"Get out!" Lillian ordered. "I don't want to see you!"

"Well, that hurts my feelings." Julius shook his head sadly. "First, you spreading those rumors about me, and now you rejecting this family reunion. We must get along if we're to live harmoniously on this island."

Lillian began to shake. "Those weren't rumors. It's the truth and you know it, you fucking pervert. I *will not* share an island with you."

"Settle down."

"Get out! Or I'll make you! I won't let you defeat me!"

"Doing what? You're outnumbered here." Smugly, Julius gestured toward Katrina.

Lillian tried to think of a quick way to fight back. But her brain did not spin up a solution fast enough. Possession hit her like a lightning bolt as she flopped backwards onto her mattress.

"I've got her," Katrina assured Julius.

"That's great, dear. Can you please transfer her over to me? I think we can do it seamlessly."

Darker, more masculine energy invaded Lillian's body. They handed over control from Katrina to Julius so efficiently that Lillian did not even get a second to come to the surface.

"Now leave us." Flat on her back, Lillian could no longer see anyone, but she heard Julius' voice as he excused Katrina from the room. He stepped inside, pushing the door closed behind him. His son still lingered anxiously by his side as they came into view.

"Now, Robbie, you see how she's not moving."

"Is... is that the possession thing you told me about?"

"Yes. It's quite something, isn't it? As you saw, she would not be nice to us if I didn't have her under control. But now I can make her do whatever we want. I bet you wish you had this ability."

"I don't. It's creepy. I want nothing to do with this. Can't you just let her go?" Robbie's face paled.

"Not just yet. You see, Robbie, this is an opportunity. She may be older than you, but she's a pretty girl, isn't she?"

Robbie shrugged. "I guess."

"You've never had a girlfriend before, right? But I'm sure you spend plenty of time thinking about girls."

"I'm not thinking about girls right now. I just want you to stop what you're doing, and I want off this fucking island."

"Watch your language, boy! I was your age once; I remember all those hormones raging. I know what you're wondering: how are you ever going to get some on this island?"

"Dad, stop talking. Gross."

"Robbie, here's your chance to become a man."

"Huh?"

"You can do whatever you'd like. I'll see to it that she's out the whole time. She won't fight back."

"You want me to have sex with her? While you're controlling her brain?!"

"I'll be in the hall. Pretend I'm not here. Do everything that you've ever fantasized about. Get it all out of your system."

Robbie sputtered and let out a shriek. "Isn't that rape? I can't rape someone!"

"Robbie, she won't say no. You won't be doing anything wrong. I am your father, and you need to do as I say."

"No! I can't! That's sick."

"Well, son, if you aren't man enough to enjoy what's right in front of you, then I am." Julius took steps toward Lillian, ignoring Robbie as if he weren't standing in the room. Here she lay, overhearing everything, seeing everything, living her worst nightmare.

Robbie turned to run. Julius grabbed him by the wrist. "No. Wait here. You must watch and learn."

"Dad, this is fucked." A tear spilled down Robbie's cheek. "You're not who I thought you were. I can't be part of this."

"If you don't do as I say, I'm telling your sister Katrina. And you really, really don't want that."

Another presence—a necromancer presence—came barreling down the hallway.

"You get away from her! Don't touch her!" roared Denny as he tore into the room. A snake of his power leached from his head, plunging toward Julius.

Julius reached into the deep pocket of his sweatpants with a quick hand. A loud bang reverberated through the room. Robbie jumped backwards and screamed. Lillian would have done the same if she could move. Her ears rang painfully.

"Look what he made me do," Julius grumbled, shoving a pistol back into his pocket. Denny staggered backwards, hands flying to his stomach to cup a growing red stain on his shirt. Blood trickled fast through his fingers. Oh, no! If Lillian had control of her body, she would run straight toward him, doing everything she could to heal him. This was the worst, most brutal helplessness.

"I've had to sacrifice one of our most important people. Now you see what happens to those who don't cooperate," Julius threatened his son. "Robbie, this is your last warning."

Robbie's face blanched white as a sheet as Denny collapsed. Even though Lillian, frozen on her back on the cot, could no longer see Denny, she sensed the waves of his aura weakening, leaving his body.

Packed into two vans, the groups traveled close by each other. They only stopped to convene at gas stations and truck stops, where they purchased quick meals. People slept and drove in shifts to keep the wheels rolling.

Evelyn, Avery, and Lou, who'd landed in Houston shortly after Lillian went missing, were gathered in Evelyn's van. Terry and Melanie Jenkinson, the water people, were in the other along with Terry's father Lonnie. Terry and Melanie had left their daughter Destiny, who'd talked them into this mission, with a family friend back home, not wanting to put her in harm's way—not knowing exactly what was ahead, and still regretful after that stunt Denny pulled of holding her hostage when she was a baby. Destiny's parents periodically called her to ask if she'd had any more visions to help pinpoint the location of Tasha, Lillian, and Denny. Each time she peered into a bowl of water, Destiny got a sharper reading.

The Jenkinsons wished they had a family-legacy blue crystal of their own. Attending secret magic conferences over the years, they'd met a few people living in other states and countries who did, but determined that there was no time to go borrow one right now. Or any guarantee that the travel trick would work, or that everyone would survive the quick yet violent journey.

They'd all begged Evelyn, the only non-mage among them, to stay home out of concern for her safety. But Evelyn, accustomed to being in charge and desperate to rescue Tasha, insisted on joining them.

"We'll do our best," Terry Jenkinson had warned Evelyn and Avery and Lou after driving along the Gulf coast, coming to Evelyn's doorstep, and offering to help, "but y'all need to be prepared for the chance you might not get your loved ones back."

"Why wouldn't we?" Evelyn had insisted, not wanting to think of any grim alternatives.

"Our daughter tells us that these necromancers are planning an attack on the whole world."

"Literally?!"

"It'll be ugly. There will be venomous creatures. If you get bitten by one, it spreads like rabies. That Katrina is pretty far along in her pregnancy. Her powers will exceed ours by leaps and bounds. We *have* to stop these people. And we can't really promise there won't be casualties."

"I will get Lillian back! I can't hurt her... I'll get her back." Avery was willing to do what it took. Including breaking his promise to his mother and using his powers.

"Sorry, kid, we might have to destroy the whole compound. Everyone on earth is in danger right now."

After they all hit the road, Evelyn's tears of despair turned to sniffles and her eyes went hard. Lou checked in by phone with his spouse Derek who'd stayed home, lying out of necessity that he was still in Texas, searching for Tasha.

Once they arrived in coastal North Carolina, the place where Destiny's visions led them, night had fallen. Rain poured down, blurring the other headlights on the freeway. Everyone in both vans was mostly silent. The squeak of the windshield wipers became deafening.

As the rain let up and the clouds parted, Evelyn closely followed the Jenkinson family down a long road bracketed by grass-dotted stretches of sand, which came upon a boat dock with no boat. Stiff and sore from hours of sitting, everyone got out to regroup. Melanie closed her eyes, hummed a bit, and then opened them several minutes later. She whipped out her phone from her leather purse and called her daughter.

"Destiny says we're at the right place," Melanie confirmed after hanging up. "The island is just east of here."

"How are we going to get there?" Lou asked, gesturing toward the boatless dock.

"Water isn't going to stop us." Terry held back a chuckle. "My dad and my wife are going to be concentrating really hard together while I drive. And you're going to follow us carefully. Stay as near as you can."

The two groups got back into the vehicles and started them up. Terry put his van back in drive and rolled the tires off the dirt of the muddy shore, onto the water.

"Oh, no," Evelyn wailed. "They lied to us! They don't want to help us. They want to drown us. Like they tried to do before."

"Should've never trusted them," Lou sighed in the passenger's seat.

"False," Avery said from behind. "I saw it in Melanie's mind. They aren't lying. Follow them."

"Into the water?!"

"Yes. Into... onto... the water."

A glassy wet crackling came from up ahead as Evelyn rolled her wheels forward, her stomach going topsy-turvy. Somehow, they were staying upright. Above the surface.

Driving on water!

"How are they..." Lou gasped.

Surrounding them was a solid strip of white ice, crystals sparkling in the light from the nearly full moon and making the van rattle a bit as it rolled over. Up ahead, in front of the water people, more ice came together on the water's surface, like pieces of a puzzle snapping into place. Waves froze off to the edges before they could come to crash into the vans.

"What is that?! Oh, no!" Lou shouted, eyes fixed on the window.

Evelyn ground the van to a halt. It nearly skidded into the water. The tires screamed on the ice. An unearthly screech shattered the peace.

A creature hovered above the van ahead, which had also just stopped, flapping its wide leathery black wings. Long legs dangled below a glistening, ugly body. Armed with razor talons, the toes curled dangerously close to the roof of the Jenkinsons' vehicle.

"What is that... a pterodactyl?" Evelyn whispered, shaking in fear.

"I think it's something a lot worse," said her father.

"We should get moving again!" Evelyn barked.

"Then it'll chase us!"

"We don't have a lot of choice! Call them and tell them to get moving!"

The gigantic birdlike creature flew toward Evelyn's van, circling like a buzzard. It screamed again, an ear-splitting, window-rattling screech. The wings flapped frantically and contracted close to its body as flames exploded from its insides and erupted on its oily skin.

The twitching creature fell beside them, splashing the van as it hit the water. Small patches of flames floated around as it sunk, like burning oil slicks.

"Thanks for taking care of that, Avery," said Lou as Evelyn's jaw dropped. "Oh, dear. Here comes another one."

The second pterodactyl-like beast burst into flames on the horizon, before it got anywhere near them. They began moving again.

"Oh, no," Avery grumbled as a few dim lights came up ahead. "Katrina knows we're here. I hear her."

"So do I," Lou moaned, rubbing his forehead like he had a headache.

"I can't," said Evelyn, confused.

"She's speaking to us," her father informed her. "With her increased power, her voice is like a megaphone."

"Ow!" Avery put his hands to his head. "It hurts!"

"What's she saying?" Evelyn asked. Up ahead, the Jenkinsons' van swerved dangerously.

"Telling us to go away," said Lou. "Telling us she's going to fight back."

"What to do we do?"

"Fight back against her with all we've got."

Evelyn's phone buzzed with a text from Melanie up ahead. *That woman is threatening us. But we're still in if you're still in. Let's move.*

Evelyn sent an affirmative response, even as her heart thudded in fear.

Both vans began rolling again.

Julius hovered over Lillian as his son cried off in the corner, near Denny's body. Lillian's nose filled with Julius' cologne. The same scent that had been in her nightmares for eighteen years.

She pushed outward with her mind, helpless to stop his possession. Out of sheer desperation and a lack of any other options, she tried something that she knew wasn't going to work. Instead of shoving, she pulled.

Without expecting to, Lillian drew Julius into her, his extension of power that controlled her mind sucked in like fishing line being reeled.

Julius gasped, jumping up and bringing his hands to his head. "What the hell!" he groaned as his fingers dug into his hair. "What's happening to me?"

Triumphant, yet terrified and not knowing what might happen next, Lillian gave it all she had, reeling and reeling. Julius went still. A trickle of blood came from his nose.

Katrina rushed into the room, yelling frantically. "Oh, crap, you shot Denny! Dad, there's people coming! That fire mage, Lou, and three water people! They're crossing the water right now! We have to get rid of them! Dad, are you okay?!"

Katrina put a hand on Julius' shoulder and spun him around as his skin continued to whiten. His mouth hung open as the fishing line picked up speed.

Lillian regained control of her body, still drawing Julius' power into her. It exploded inside her, hot and unbearable.

"Get away from me!" Lillian warned Katrina as she got up from the cot.

"You bitch, what did you do?!" Katrina charged at Lillian, taking possession of her within a second.

The reeling began again, with two intertwined spiderweb threads from both Katrina and Julius. Katrina screamed in confusion as she backed up, her hands trembling. Julius collapsed to the floor, unconscious.

The power that Lillian drew inside herself pushed her body to its limits. Yet the reel spun and spun, uncontrollably.

An invisible force nudged Robbie out of the room and down the hall. He wailed for his father in his fear, when just moments ago, he was disgusted with the unveiling of his parent's wicked, murdering side.

Katrina fell to her knees, crying out.

A shockwave reverberated through the island, sending cracks through the walls and making the earth quake. Katrina slammed her eyes shut as white-hot light flooded the room. The light bulbs exploded. The electricity went out.

A wave erupted out of nowhere, the ground trembling fiercely beneath the ocean.

"Earthquake!" Evelyn yelled as the wave crested frighteningly high, easily a hundred feet, headed straight for them. There was no doubt that it would knock both of the vans off the magic-forged ice.

"Everyone focus!" Terry commanded in the van up ahead. He, his wife, and his father-in-law all closed their eyes. Just before it had the chance to slam into the vehicles, the wave parted, as if cleaved by a gigantic knife down the center.

The halves of water joined together once they had passed, slamming into each other and breaking the ice road behind them. The vans shook as the ice behind them loudly snapped into pieces.

"Something very significant just happened up there." Lonnie's voice trembled. "That wave was not natural."

"I just got a text from Destiny," Melanie advised from behind him. "She says that there are no more monsters."

"Let's hope that's true. Is Tasha okay?"

"Destiny thinks they're all okay except for Denison. She saw a vision of him dead."

The ice came together ahead of them on top of the water, now mostly still except for a few small, choppy waves. They pushed on as the island loomed in the moonlight, a black shaggy patch.

The booming, menacing voice Katrina had put into the mages' heads was gone, leaving hollow silence in its place.

"I think Katrina might be dead," said Lou.

"I'm not sure she's dead, but something definitely happened to her," Avery added in an anxious tone.

"What about Lillian? Do you sense her up there? Do you think she's okay?"

"I really don't know... it's weird... you know how we felt like Katrina was all around us? Now I'm feeling sort of the same way with Lillian. But it's different. Not like she's projecting her power. More like she *is* everywhere."

"And you never felt that before?"

"No."

They reached the rocky shore of the island. The tires crunched up onto the bank of smooth ocean-worn stones. Behind them, the ice road disintegrated into steam as both groups cautiously stepped out.

At their feet, vines and bright, colorful flowers sprouted out between the stones. Thick, velvet moss grew across the ground, crawling before their eyes.

"That's very strange," Terry muttered.

Up ahead was a complex of damaged buildings, like the aftermath of a bombing, with a few plumes of dust rising. And some frantic voices.

"Mom! Grandpa Lou!" came Tasha's voice from the stretch of grass beyond the rocks. Tasha, wearing a plain gray dress, ran into Evelyn's arms. Crying in gratitude, they spun around together.

Another person approached, an unfamiliar, tall, thin middle-aged man. "Who are you people?" he asked.

"We could ask you the same," Lonnie told him cautiously.

"He's a doctor," Terry said, scanning his mind. "Dr. Ronald Matheson. He and Gerald became friends shortly before Gerald passed away. Katrina convinced him to run away with her, something he's come to regret. They had cages holding monsters. He was under orders from Katrina to release a few of them. One of them almost killed him."

"The creatures are all dead," the doctor said with a grave nod that showed that nothing could surprise him anymore. "I saw those two burning up in the sky. And just a few minutes ago, the remaining one simply melted down like candle wax in its cage. Another mind-reader. You've come to kill me?"

"Only if you give us trouble. We can take you off the island to somewhere safe, as long as you don't hurt us."

"Thank you. I'd like to leave."

"Wait here by the cars."

"After that earthquake, or whatever it was, I don't recommend going inside. Or if you must, be careful."

After leaving the doctor behind at the beach, they passed a few impressively large cages composed of thick iron bars. Inside were blobs of thick, greasy, rotten-smelling matter, oozing across the ground through the bars.

Two animals ran outside, an orange cat and a frightened, jittery small white dog. Melanie scooped them both up, one under each arm, and rushed over to place them in her family van.

The group cautiously went through the outer porch, where grass pushed so violently between the bricks that they cracked. A couple of frightened small children sat in dirty clothes. Melanie gathered up the baby boy in her arms, took the little girl's hand, and rushed them to the van. Telling them to stay put, promising they were safe, she closed them in with Tasha, who agreed to watch them and make sure they did not run off anywhere.

With the three children tucked out of sight, they headed into the building. The earth rumbled a bit, and more dust spilled from the growing rifts in the ceiling.

"Everybody be careful," Evelyn whispered. "This could come down at any minute."

They followed the sounds of a woman's sobs and a baby's cries, ducking where a ceiling beam had partially collapsed. They discovered a chasm in the wall, and behind it, a huge-eyed blonde woman with the infant in her arms.

"Who are you?" she asked. "Are you here to hurt me some more?"

"No, we're here to help get you out of here," Terry reassured her.

"My name is Lydia," she told the group. "These people have kept me prisoner for months. I was drugged and raped."

"I'm very sorry about what's happened to you. Go down the hall. The door's open. We have a van parked on the shore with a few kids already inside. Wait there. Go!"

Lydia hesitated, looking confused, before she got up and rushed out.

Searching for the others, the group climbed down a flight of stairs to a small basement level. A metal security door hung open, crisscrossed with growing vines and flowers that seemed to be sucking it down into the earth, which trembled again below their feet.

"Katrina," Terry whispered as the group stepped into the doorway, shining their flashlights over a room almost entirely covered in moss. "Except... she is not a mage anymore. And Julius. Now he is ordinary too. And he's not all there."

Katrina was bent down, her arms laying across her large belly as she pawed the ground in front of her, grabbing clumps of moss. "My powers!" she wailed. "My powers! Where did they go? What did she do to me? My powers!"

A dark-haired man had his arms around her, trying and failing to console her. "Calm down. Katrina, just calm down. It'll be all right."

She shrugged away his embrace. Even though the flashlights sprayed across his face for only a few moments, Avery immediately knew who this was. Zack Dunaway, the one who'd faked his way into a relationship with Lillian over a decade ago. And now his pairing with Katrina proved that Avery's longtime hunch about a conspiracy was correct, even if Avery did not get a clear read of his mind.

"Lillian!" Avery spotted her off in the corner, lying down on the remains of what used to be a bed. Ignoring everyone else, he rushed to gather her in his arms. She was limp like a rag doll, her nose bleeding. "Lillian! I'm here! Are you okay? Wake up!"

Julius slouched nearby in a white sweatshirt dotted with blood drips from his nose, his eyes big and confused. Lou marched up to Julius, pulled him up by the collar—though he was eighty-one years old, his anger gave him strength—and punched him square in the face. Just one of the things he'd been wishing he could do to his estranged nephew for a long time.

Julius barely flinched.

"What did you do with my daughter?" Lou screamed, grabbing Julius by the shoulders and shaking him. "Did you hurt her? Answer me!"

Julius shook his head, bleary-eyed. "I... I don't know. I don't know. Where am I? My powers... my powers.... I can't..."

A few feet away, Evelyn wailed. "Oh, no! Denny!"

The whole group looked down, gasping at the sight of Denny in a bloodstained striped shirt, vines crawling over his husky body.

"No!" Lou screamed, momentarily forgetting about Julius as he knelt down by Denny's body.

"My dad shot him," said a young, gravelly voice next to the corpse. "And then something happened to my dad and he just fell over, and I took the gun."

"Are you Robbie?" Evelyn asked, tears spilling from her eyes as the group turned to face the boy clutching the pistol, pointing it downward in his wildly shaking hands.

"Yes. My dad lied to me to get me here."

"Can you tell me what happened right before your dad shot Denny?"

"The lady who's passed out... Lillian, I think her name is... my dad used his powers to make her freeze. He tried to make me do perverted stuff to her. I couldn't. I said no."

Avery choked up, still holding the listless Lillian. "Thank you for saying no."

"My dad got mad. That guy Denny showed up and tried to stop him, and he shot Denny. Then Katrina showed up, and then Lillian got up, and there was this big, blinding flash of light and an earthquake, and now Dad and Katrina are both acting weird."

"Son, why don't you give me the gun?" Terry requested. "It might be safest that way." Robbie carefully handed it over.

"I've lost my powers!" Katrina moaned, tossing her head back. "I can't see auras anymore! I can't feel what I used to feel! I can't move anything, possess anything! Now I'm just like all the other losers on this planet. I'm useless!"

"Stop crying. It'll be okay," Zack said, his words feeble and weak.

"No, it won't! I've lost everything! I'm worthless now. I think the baby's okay, 'cause she's kicking, but what if she lost her powers too? I'm going to have just another shitty, useless baby like everyone else! That bitch took it all away from us! And now this means nothing!" Katrina grabbed a pendant on a chain around her neck—the green crystal that had belonged to Lillian—ripped it off, and threw it to the ground, where it nearly disappeared into a patch of leaves.

Reaching from nearby, Avery grabbed and pocketed the crystal.

"Katrina—right?" Terry called out to her. "Are you the person who created those monsters? Are you the one who orchestrated this?"

Katrina looked up at him with wet, swollen eyes. "Sort of... well, my dad and grandpa," she mumbled.

"Since now you cannot see it, I am a water person. I came here with every intent to get rid of you. You've broken the code of the mages and committed unspeakable crimes. But I'll take just a tiny bit of pity on you since you're pregnant and your powers are disabled. Your aura's shrunk down to the size of the average person's, and so has your father's. Though your baby still has the powers. Only our leaders in the other world can revoke them, which is interesting, since your leader's been missing for years. I will give you just one chance to leave this island, no questions asked, and I never want to see you or hear of you making trouble again or else I *will* kill you. But if you're going to save yourself, do it soon."

Katrina struggled to her feet with Zack's help, but simply stood there, stunned.

"Lillian!" Avery called out. "Wake up!"

Now distracted from Julius, Lou also knelt beside his daughter. They both shook her, finding her unresponsive.

"I'm afraid this isn't looking good." Terry shook his head grimly.

"No, she's not gone. She's not!" Avery insisted. "She's still breathing. Still has an aura. But her mind…"

Lou turned toward Avery. "Do you mind giving me the crystal really quick?"

Avery pulled it from his pocket, chain dangling, and handed it over. Lou curled his fingers around it and in a flash he was gone.

As Lou drifted down to the alternate version of the island, surrounded by a lavender glow and glittering sapphire ocean with the familiar green temple in the middle, he spotted three familiar figures walking down a glowing golden path that wound its way into the front columns of the temple.

Denny, now faintly transparent, looked a bit younger and more buoyant, his eyes glowing green. Dead for sure. Beside him was Lillian in the drab dress she must have hated wearing. Not see-through, not looking dead, no green glow to her eyes—but mysteriously different. Her body was solid, yet her aura had changed. In addition to the usual green were piercing rays of incandescent light.

Between them walked Astrid, the dog Lou had made the difficult decision to euthanize when she got old and sick some years back. Like Denny, she was semitransparent and green-eyed, though he could still see the lustrous mottled blue in her fur. She ambled along with the bounce of a puppy instead of the stiff, arthritic gait when Lou took her on her final walks.

Lou called after them. Lillian glanced over her shoulder once, her eyes gleaming behind her glasses like a wild animal's when one shone a flashlight. Her expression was pained, confused. She turned her head forward again, hair floating as if submerged in water, and continued walking.

They all went up the steps into the temple. Frantic, Lou picked up his pace, chasing them in. By the time he passed through the doors, they'd already gone into the room of bones.

Lou rushed into the large chamber, hoping to catch up to them, but the three of them were gone.

Instead, floating above the center of the room, was something Lou had not seen in over thirty years.

The leader of the necromancers. A tattered black cloak fluttered around a center of nearly blinding light. Under the sagging jet-black hood, which seemed more shadow than solid, two deep black dots reflected skull eyes.

Knowing he might not get an answer, or one that made sense, Lou pleaded with the being. "Where is my daughter? I know my nephew is dead, but I saw my daughter go in here! Where is she? Is she alive?"

A low vibration began, rattling deep in Lou's bones. And then it became a piercing wail, bringing him to his knees as light flashed through the room.

I am right here, Lillian's voice echoed inside his head, turning deeper, changing into a tone he had not heard in decades. *I have served my purpose among mortals.*

"What... are you saying that my daughter is... you, leader? Is that why you were missing for so long? It can't be! She's young and happy! She deserves her life back!"

Another vibration, this one unbearably painful, buzzed through Lou's body.

The human life was wonderful, beautiful, the voice screamed in his head. *I knew love. Deep connections. I may return. I shall be above and below. Everywhere, as I always was.*

"Please return! I want my daughter back this instant!"

There are powers beyond life and death at work...

Unable to handle any more, Lou fled from the temple, weeping.

The earth quaked again. Lou materialized, his hands wrapped around the crystal, eyes glistening with tears. As he resurfaced, the structure shook violently, producing loud cracks as some other room collapsed up above.

"She's still not waking up?" he asked Avery, who still held Lillian as tears streamed down his cheeks.

"No... wait, wait... she is." In his arms, Lillian coughed. Her eyes fluttered open, glowing a bit in the darkness. Like they had down below.

"Where... what just happened?" she mumbled. More blood trickled from her nose down her chin. "I don't feel good."

"We'll get you some help," Avery promised.

"Julius still here?"

"Yeah, but he's pretty confused and he's lost his powers. It's going to be okay. I'm here."

"I just... walked with Denny... he's gone."

"I know. I'm so sorry."

"But then... I don't know what happened. Did I die and come back to life?"

"I saw something strange in the other world," her father said. "I'll explain it when we get to safety."

"Move! We've got to go!" Melanie yelled.

Katrina and Zack pushed past the water people. Katrina grabbed Julius by the hand as he stumbled. Robbie raced beside them.

Avery and Lillian were the last to leave the room, trudging through the moss and vines as Lillian leaned against him, her legs too wobbly to stand on her own.

They just barely got out when the whole building loudly collapsed into a pile of rubble behind them. Avery and Lillian, who'd just barely managed to escape, coughed from the dust.

Leading a silent Julius, Katrina and Zack rushed toward the dock where their boat waited. They did not even seem interested in searching for their two small children Melanie had rescued earlier, who still waited in her van.

Julius' son Robbie nervously lingered behind, near the wreckage. Katrina and Zack did not think to gather him up, just as they hadn't considered the well-being of their own children. Unhindered by his own family, Robbie ran toward the other crowd. Once he reached them, he nervously confided in a whisper: "I don't want to go with them. My dad's not himself, but I'm still scared of him."

"I can understand, son," Terry said. "You can come with us for now. Then we'll get you back to your mother."

"What if my dad goes back to my mother?"

"Hopefully, if she's in her right mind, she won't take him back."

"Look!" said Evelyn, pointing at the rubble. The whole group went quiet as they laid eyes on the waves of light pulsating and undulating above the island like an aurora borealis. Flowers and trees came up through the bricks and broken concrete, growing at lightning speed.

"We should scram," Terry's father Lonnie suggested. "We don't know what might happen next."

All of the remaining people piled into the two vans, squeezing into whatever space was available. Lillian leaned against Avery in Evelyn's backseat, taking sips from a water bottle, still weak.

The journey across the water began again as new pieces of ice formed and snapped together. As Avery looked through the back window of Evelyn's van, the colorful light transfixed him, bleeding over the black surface of the water.

Epilogue

During the escape, the large house on the now-uninhabited island had collapsed and the monsters had melted down to grease inside their cages. Just weeks later, during the investigations that followed, only the faintest foundation lines in the thick grass suggested a structure had ever been built there.

Early in the morning of the escape, the group brought Lillian to an emergency room. No serious medical issue was found, yet she spent the next couple of weeks in bed at home, so weak she could barely get up, while her father stayed with her to keep an eye on things. It took close to a month to fully recover.

Lillian did not remember much about her lapse of consciousness, just faint images of walking with Denny and Astrid, and that graveyard that came before the liminal space. Lou waited to reveal to Lillian what he'd seen in the other world until she gained some of her strength back. When he finally told her the story, she found it bewildering, hard to swallow, and wanted to believe that maybe it was his own confusion or trauma causing him to see things.

"If I really am the leader, or the 'one who decides,' or Death, or whoever this is, I don't want to know," Lillian confessed. "I feel like there's something more. Millions of sides of me, everywhere, that I'm just barely aware of. But I'm not going to look into it. I'm scared to go back into the other world again. I don't want to find out. Or change. I just want to keep living my life."

Lou chose not to read the copy of his deceased brother's memoir that Lillian had smuggled from the island in her bra. After the bits he heard of Gerald's sins, it would have made him too sick to his stomach.

Lydia, the woman rescued with her newborn, reported Zack, Julius, and Katrina for kidnapping her and keeping her captive. All three were arrested, and now awaited trial.

Shortly after their capture, Katrina gave birth to a baby girl, Peyton, who was healthy and presumably a mage, in spite of whatever happened to Katrina to steal her necromancer powers. Zack's sister, who lived in Wisconsin, took in the three children, along with the dog and cat who'd been found on the island. When baby Peyton grew older, someone would have to watch out for her, as they did for Tasha.

Lou, Lillian, and Avery really did not care what happened to Julius and Zack and Katrina, just as long as those children were safe. From all of the twisted things Avery had read in Katrina's mind, her rough treatment of Paisley and Zack Jr., considering them worthless possessions to be tossed around simply because they weren't born necromancers, had almost disturbed him the most.

Robbie, Julius' son, now lived with his mother. Jana divorced Julius, who now said he could not recall a single thing that happened on the island or any events leading up to it. Julius remained in jail, facing more charges after a DNA test proved he had fathered Lydia's baby. He never broke out of his cell, which he might have done in a heartbeat had he not lost his powers.

Denny's widow, Mona, was heartbroken at losing him after spending well over half of their lives together. The death crushed Lillian as well.

Evelyn took Tasha to a therapist. The trauma of her kidnapping was so acute that she could no longer sleep alone in her bedroom.

The whole family still had much to untangle.

Two adolescent girls in swimsuit tops and black leggings walked barefoot along the beach, leaving their tracks behind. Each wore halves of a divided heart on their necklaces, showing their status as best friends.

"Watch out, Tasha," the taller girl warned. "Don't step on that man-o-war."

"Yes, Mom." Tasha rolled her eyes.

"Wanna go for a swim?" Destiny asked.

"Sure."

"Your glasses," Destiny reminded Tasha, poking her in the arm. The last time they went swimming, Tasha had lost a pair of glasses in the water, and her mother was not happy. The girls ran toward their mothers, both wearing sunglasses and cutoff shorts, standing watch on the sand of the otherwise empty beach. Tasha pulled off and folded her white plastic-framed glasses and handed them to Evelyn, who tucked them away in her beach bag.

The girls joined hands, turned toward the frothing water, and walked in. Knowing that they could not drown, they disappeared into the waves, sinking in over their heads.

A couple of tourists approached on the horizon. Evelyn noticed first, and she whispered to Melanie. Using a system that Evelyn still did not fully understand, Melanie wordlessly summoned both of the girls from the water. They surfaced with wet hair plastered to their faces. Submerged swimming would have to wait until they found themselves alone again, so that no one would think they were drowning. Even though a few non-mages had witnessed powers during their imprisonment on the necromancers' island, including the doctor they never heard from again, it was best to remain cautious to keep any such sightings from happening again.

Later, as the mothers and their daughters hung out in Melanie's backyard, the girls begged Melanie for a favor.

"Mom, make us an ice sculpture!" Destiny pleaded. "Please? You're so good at it!"

"Oh, all right," Melanie conceded. "What would you girls like me to make?"

"A horse," Tasha requested.

"All right, kids." Melanie closed her eyes and concentrated, confident that the neighbors could see nothing over the tall wooden picket fence. From the grass rose a series of ice crystals, melding together into the perfect form of a translucent horse, glittering in the bright sun.

"It's beautiful!" the girls squealed, gathering around the horse, stroking its cold snout. "Let us try!"

Destiny had been able to use her full powers for at least a couple of years. Tasha was just cutting her teeth on them. Both girls forged small, barely recognizable turtles that resembled pointed chunks more than animals.

"Mom, I wish I could be as good as you," Destiny sighed.

"Years of practice, dear. You'll get there."

For the first time since his sister had passed away, Karl Thiessen had a visitor.

One of Vanessa's daughters came to see him. The younger daughter. Karl hadn't laid eyes on that girl since she was a toddler, and now she lived on the outside, all grown up. Since Vanessa's death was the whole reason Karl had spent nearly thirty years sealed away from society, he fully expected to be chewed out. For Vanessa's daughter to yell at him, scream, cry, and get it out of her system. As he sat down behind the Plexiglas divider, phone at the ready, he braced himself for the onslaught. After years of questioning if he really had shot Vanessa, why his memory completely skipped over the murder and fast-forwarded to the grisly aftermath, he'd almost resigned himself to his guilt in the crime.

Lillian sat down on the other side of the glass and picked up the phone. Though she was quite a bit taller than her mother, and had red instead of brunette hair, Karl recognized a bit of Vanessa in her green eyes. Her expression was calm, not angry, though Karl felt pierced by her eyes, as if they shot out lasers.

"Karl, I'm here to tell you that I believe you," she began.

"Believe me? About what?"

"That you didn't do it."

"Are you serious?"

"Yes. It wasn't you. It was my uncle who did it, because my mom knew some things he didn't want getting out."

"Why can't I remember what happened?"

"Some outside forces controlled your mind. I don't have any evidence that's believable enough to overturn your conviction. But I know you weren't at fault."

Karl began to weep.

"I wish I could get you exonerated," Lillian sympathized.

"Don't bother trying. The evidence was pretty damning. I'm eighty years old and I've been rotting in here for decades. I don't think I could even adjust to the outside world at this rate. But... thank you. Thank you." The tears continued to flow. "Now I know I'm not losing my mind."

"You're not. I wanted you to know that I miss her every day. I remember her. She was wonderful."

"Yeah, I miss her too. I hope we keep in touch, kid. Write to me."

"I will," Lillian promised. They both pressed their palms to the glass. With a nod, she left.

Acknowledgements

People of the Dead has been a long and challenging project, going through multiple, major overhauls while it was over a decade in the making. I began the novel, a drastically different story, when I was in college. After making revisions, I wished to still capture that early-2000s campus vibe. Many people have beta-read it and offered their feedback, including my mom Sandy, Amy Ross, Lauren Smith, Michael Santiago Terrazas, and my husband Randall, who read draft after draft. I'm sure there are some helpers that I am forgetting. Thank you for all of your feedback and encouragement along the way.

Find me on Facebook:

 facebook.com/ereneesobien

www.ingramcontent.com/pod-product-compliance
Lightning Source LLC
Chambersburg PA
CBHW031939260626
47157CB00016B/28